# Camel Scorpions

By Albert Delma*

Grosvenor House
Publishing Limited

All rights reserved
Copyright © Albert Delma, 2018

The right of Albert Delma to be identified as the author of this
work has been asserted in accordance with Section 78
of the Copyright, Designs and Patents Act 1988

The book cover picture is copyright to Albert Delma

This book is published by
Grosvenor House Publishing Ltd
Link House
140 The Broadway, Tolworth, Surrey, KT6 7HT.
www.grosvenorhousepublishing.co.uk

This book is sold subject to the conditions that it shall not, by way of
trade or otherwise, be lent, resold, hired out or otherwise circulated
without the author's or publisher's prior consent in any form of binding or
cover other than that in which it is published and
without a similar condition including this condition being imposed
on the subsequent purchaser.

A CIP record for this book
is available from the British Library

ISBN 978-1-78623-101-7

*Front cover:* Sunset over the Blue Nile at Khartoum,
photographed by the author.

***Albert Delma** is the author's *nom de plume*.

To Wendy,
who first drew my attention to the questionable
historicity of Jesus.

*There is merit in seeking the truth,
even if one strays on the way.*
(Georg Christoph Lichtenberg Aphorisms)

# Chapter 1

Faced with a confusion of isobars over the British Isles, the meteorological office had abandoned the relentless logic of the computer model and turned instead to feeling the seaweed. Accordingly the weather was expected to be wet and misty. In the event it was a crystal-clear, dry and very cold. A carpet of frost still clung to the shaded side of the vicarage lawn. Blindingly bright and only thirty minutes old, the sun now illuminated a clear blue sky, unmarred by clouds or vapour trails.

Since childhood, Pamela had been accustomed to gazing out of vicarage bedroom windows in the early morning, taking in the view and assessing the weather prospects before washing and dressing. Her father had been the vicar of a village church in East Anglia, where the view from her bedroom window had seemingly stretched to infinity over a landscape of drainage dykes and reeds, and in very clear weather to the sea and the horizon of the ocean. In obedience to the exhortation of *Genesis 1:22*, her parents had been fruitful and multiplied, but no further than times one point five. Thus with no brother or sister to share her thoughts or indulge in horse-play, her early mornings had been spent alone, gazing at a flat landscape. Thinking back to those days of her childhood, she remembered how she used to invent impossible fairy tales. The slightest fold in the land, a derelict windmill and a flash of reflected sunlight from the distant sea were all she needed for her imagination to recruit little green folk meeting in the reed beds, awaiting the arrival of little green visitors from across the water. Later, as she approached her teens, she had begun to appreciate the sheer beauty of the single line of the horizon and above it the glory of so much sky.

That was years ago. This morning, approaching middle-age, she was standing at a bedroom window in a

Herefordshire village, gazing with a troubled mind at the distant Malvern Hills. Martin, her husband and vicar of the village church, was an early riser and already up and about downstairs. The view from her bedroom window did not have that East Anglian quality of appearing to stretch to infinity. It offered a different kind of beauty, no less inspiring to the watercolourist and, she supposed, no less enchanting of a child's imagination.

In four days' time, on the twentieth of February, the sun would rise exactly at the centre of the shallow V formed by two gently sloping distant hills. During the last twenty-six years they had recorded the position of the sunrise as seen from their bedroom window, so that on any day of the year, they could now predict where the sun would first appear above the line of the distant hills, fog, mist, haze and other meteorological interferences permitting. She was vaguely aware of the properties of the solar system that caused the rising sun to peep above the horizon at a different position each morning. Martin had told her that the earth was tilted at an angle on its axis in relation to the sun, and he had drawn pictures to show how this caused a shift in the position of the sunrise, but she had always felt that scientific explanations of natural phenomena detracted from their poetry.

They had also recorded the position of the setting sun over the Welsh hills, before or after their evening meal, depending on the season, with the satisfied feeling of a day well spent. Later, Martin had composed a sermon, based on the shift in the position of the setting and rising sun, the wonder of its predictability, the exhilaration of early morning, and the rewarding fulfilment of a good day's work. Pamela had never been comfortable with his way of ending this sermon with the quotation from *Ecclesiastes 1:9*: 'there is nothing new under the sun.' To her, it sounded like a

# CHAPTER 1

laboured witticism; to him the quotation embodied a profound truth hiding somewhere within the Christian message.

Fascinating landscapes of East Anglia; cloud patterns in coloured skies; childhood fantasies; sunset over the Welsh hills; she didn't normally spend so much time immersed in agreeable memories. This morning, however, she was trying to avoid facing the possibility that her marriage was entering a new and critical phase. Or was she auditing the balance sheet of life's happiness, in order to reassure herself that she was still in credit?

Their marriage was remarkably steadfast. Of course, they had had their disagreements, but these had always been resolved amicably (some would say prayerfully) and they had grown closer through sharing their problems and working on them shoulder to shoulder. Lately, however, in fact for about three months, Martin had been preoccupied. It had happened before, but it had never lasted so long. He had stopped taking an interest in household affairs. Whatever Pamela was planning for their evening meal, he just grunted his agreement, without expressing enthusiasm. Normally he would have been excited by an e-mail from their son or daughter; nowadays he would quickly read it then leave it to Pamela to send a reply. He had even started to use his old sermons rather than work on new ones. All this, together with odd conversational remarks, were picked up by her wifely antennae then analysed. Until now, the results of this analysis had always been reliable: he was worried about an impending visit by the bishop; a theological argument with the wife of the organist was still unresolved; he felt burdened by any number of other anxieties, ranging from repairs to the church roof to the financial improvidence of their son, who was reading law at university. Recently, however, her mental computer had failed to print out an answer. She could no longer interpret her husband's odd behaviour.

Her father had been a Church of England clergyman, and her husband was the vicar of the village church. Surely, nothing could be seriously wrong with a relationship like theirs, guided, after all, by Christian teaching. Perhaps psychiatrists have a term for her mental condition. She was harbouring an unfounded fear that her marriage was in difficulties. Unfounded, because something was obviously distracting her husband, but there was nothing to suggest it threatened their matrimonial state. Few wives living in the real world, rather than the hermetic atmosphere of a country vicarage, would have given the occasional quirky behaviour of their husband a second thought. Pamela wondered if she ought to be contributing more to the role of the church in village affairs. Was she providing enough support to her husband in his pastoral work? She already contributed a great deal and couldn't imagine how she could do more. Nevertheless, she envied the accomplishments and abilities of the bishop's wife, who was mistress of her own domain and well known for badgering local businessmen to provide finance and premises for the support of failed asylum seekers. Her project attracted the attention of the media and naturally had political overtones, which were only slightly embarrassing for the bishop, and increased their stock enormously within the Church.

In contrast, Pamela had chosen a supporting role, making sure that life in the vicarage was peaceful and homely, feeding the man of the house and encouraging him to strive in God's name to serve the local community. Now, for the first time in their married life, this vision was challenged. It was an emotional reaction, dictated more by nerves than by rational thought. At this stage of a marriage, twenty-six years in all, many a wife has often experienced the temporary moodiness of her husband and learned to ignore it and 'let him get on with it' until it passes. (While the situation of a moody wife

# CHAPTER 1

and forbearing husband is also well-known, it is not relevant to the present narrative.) In all of their married life Martin had never been so preoccupied and inscrutable.

Despite excellent A-levels in the sciences and maths, Martin had chosen to study theology and history at university. Martin's father, an aeronautics engineer, and his schoolteacher mother had happily reconciled themselves to Martin's ambition to enter the Church. Armed with a first class honours degree, he had been fast-tracked through the early stages of the church hierarchy, spending only minimal periods as curate and deacon. His first appointment as a curate was at a church in the parish next to that of Pamela's father. They were therefore within cycling distance of each other. How this appointment was decided is poorly documented; it is marginally possible that Pamela's father, or Pamela's mother, or God whispered in the bishop's ear. After a short engagement they were married in the Spring of Martin's first year as a curate. The marriage ceremony was conducted by Pamela's father. Dog collars and wives of the clergy were much in evidence in the congregation and at the reception. Though overburdened by the solemn presence of God, it was a happy occasion, enjoyed by all (according to the local press, which, of course, did not liken God to a burden).

In her quiet moments Pamela often recalled and enjoyed the memory of their wedding day. Still watching the blaze of the rising sun widening between two adjacent and distant hills, her thoughts then moved on to the blissful early years of their marriage. Steeped in Christian virtue as they were, they enacted their marriage vows with enthusiasm, energetically honouring one another with their bodies. In other words, they couldn't keep their hands off each other. Pamela well remembered the ecstasy of those first few months, when they joked that the sins of the flesh were sanctioned by holy matrimony.

They had met in the nineteen seventies in a Yorkshire city, Martin at the university, Pamela at a local domestic science college, fondly known as the Pudding School. The sexual revolution, which had horrified the previous generation, was now over. In arguments against premarital sex, most religious leaders and other worthy members of society now looked hopelessly out of touch.

Nevertheless, out of respect for the Bible-oriented feelings of Pamela's parents, Pamela and Martin had made a feeble attempt to lead celibate lives before they were married. It didn't last long and they soon succumbed to the permissiveness of the age and the clamour of their own impatient hormones. During the first few months of Martin's appointment in the neighbouring parish, Pamela had lived at her parental home and taught domestic science at a local school for maladjusted children. Intimate encounters were then impossible, but once the wedding day had been fixed it was easy to be patient.

Pamela thrilled to the memory of those early days of intimacy, which at the time had been perfectly in tune with their feelings of youthful rebellion. Such memories embarrassed only slightly her later self-image of respectability. Then was then and now was now; times had changed and her life had changed with them.

With a sudden irritable gesture, she reprimanded herself for dwelling on the past. She needed to concentrate on the present. She needed to know why her husband was not his normal self. Also, why hadn't she confronted him and demanded an explanation of his odd behaviour, which was threatening her agreeable domestic routine?

# Chapter 2

About a year ago Martin had begun to suspect that the early Christian history he had been taught, and which informed his preaching from the pulpit, was in need of revision. More recently, after extensive reading and mature consideration, his suspicions had hardened into the firm conviction that the received version of early Christian history was seriously in error. To add to his concern, he also suspected that the received version had been deliberately contrived, in order to deceive the faithful.

Notwithstanding his unwavering devotion to the Christian message of love, peace and forgiveness, he now craved a more truthful version of the origin of the faith. And for this purpose he intended to ask the bishop for a sabbatical, for time away from his pastoral duties to pursue a programme of research into the early history of Christianity, that period in the birth and growth of the faith before Emperor Constantine provided it with a power base at the Council of Nicea in 325 AD. But how should he break the news to Pamela?

For the past three months, his burning ambition to reveal the truth of Christian history, combined with the fear that his wife, let alone his bishop, might not approve, had distracted him from both his church and his domestic duties. Surely Pamela would not object to him taking a year out for academic study. He knew, however, that some of the information he needed was not published and he would probably have to travel abroad to find it, to talk with ministers and priests in religious communities in parts of the world that were currently considered dangerous for western visitors. He assumed she wouldn't agree to that.

With the exception of her student years, Pamela had known no other life than that of the church and vicarage: strong on tradition, less strong on spirituality. As her mother had supported her father, she now supported her husband, as he conducted poorly attended Sunday services and oversaw the rites of passage, while she entertained ladies of the village to afternoon tea, solicited entries for the church magazine, and helped to organise the annual bring-and-buy sale. Over the years, Martin's village congregation had decreased somewhat, although not to the extent suffered by many churches in towns and cities. He knew that the Church still served a purpose. It fostered social cohesion, albeit much less so than in earlier generations, and it gave reassurance to older members of the congregation, who had been indoctrinated in the routine of the church service in their childhood. All in all, his church played a satisfactory role in the life of the village, and he frankly enjoyed the comfortable, unhurried life of a country vicar.

He had always known that certain books of the Bible contained contradictions and inconsistencies. He was also aware that many sacred texts had been omitted from the canon of the New Testament. Until recently this had never bothered him, but he had now come to suspect that these apparently harmless inconsistencies in the sacred book pointed to the existence of an alarming secret, which had the potential to corrode the currently accepted version of early Christian history. The scientist in him had been reawakened. He wanted more facts. He wanted to get to the bottom of what had become for him a tantalising puzzle.

Their early rebellious student years seemed ages ago. During their courtship and the early years of their marriage, Pamela had displayed such youthful energy that she would probably have taken any new idea in her stride. In any case, it was easy to feel adventuresome and adaptable in the protective environment of college life, immersed in a bravado culture generated by nearly eight thousand shameless students, many of whom spent their evenings drinking and telling lies to one another in the union bar. But now? Apart

## CHAPTER 2

from her three years at college and a very brief period as a teacher, the only life she really knew was that of the country vicarage. Approaching middle age and after bringing up a family, could that old rebellious spirit be reawakened? Martin hoped so.

What should he do? For the sake of peace and the continuation of his easy life, he had earlier considered dropping the whole idea of a sabbatical. That was no longer possible; he was now too fired up with a desire to sort out the anomalies in the New Testament.

The only sensible way forward was to reveal his plans honestly and openly to both his wife and his bishop, and hope for a favourable response. Clearly, he would present his case to the bishop, using theological arguments and analysis of the scriptures. To convince Pamela he would need a more nuanced approach, balancing his plans against their intimate personal relationship and their domestic economy. On second thoughts, he could prepare Pamela by drip-feeding his plans, little by little, until he felt his dear wife was ready for the whole truth.

How, when, and where to start? He decided to adopt the ancient and proven technique of approaching a difficult subject during, or shortly after, making love. Wives are better equipped than husbands for this artful stratagem, but older and more mature males also know how to use it to their advantage.

Perhaps Pamela and Martin had displayed exceptional wisdom in their student days, in recognising that they were truly meant for each other. Or, more likely, they had been exceptionally lucky, since wisdom is not a quality usually associated with students in their late teens (Oops! That remark is bound to upset somebody). In addition, both sets of parents, in their respective stable and loving relationships, had provided excellent role models. Either way, most punters would have given the marriage a slightly better than

50/50 chance of surviving, based on its association with the Church and the statistics for marriage breakdown at the time of the wedding. Their marriage defied these pessimistic odds; it was stable and built on firmer ground than most observers realised. Pamela and Martin were not maintaining a front to avoid shame in the community. That all-too-common practice had been abandoned a generation ago. No longer did disenchanted spouses greet their neighbours with a cheery smile in the morning then spend the evening bickering and glowering in the knowledge that they were stuck with each other until one of them died. Nowadays, when couples, married or otherwise, found it no longer worked for them, they usually separated, children or no children, *ie.*, behaviour in perfect harmony with the throwaway culture of the age. No, try as we may, we cannot find a single chink in the armour of this marriage. It was blessed, if not by God, then at least by the Church. More importantly its course was pursued in a heaven of Pamela and Martin's own making.

Meanwhile, Pamela, in reviewing their early years together, had realised that what she normally regarded as a source of pleasure and fulfilment, a physical cementation of their love, might also serve as a useful tool for prising open the secret of her husband's mysterious preoccupation. Unbeknown to both of them, the situation was thus acquiring a perfect symmetry. *He* knew that Pamela would be worried by his plan for a sabbatical and he hoped the glow of their bedroom intimacy would make her more ready to agree to it. *She* would use her bedroom guile to lower his guard and reveal what was bothering him. Nowadays, Pamela usually initiated proceedings with a light tap on Martin's shoulder. Moreover, the result was absolute bliss. They often laughed about this, thinking back to their early years together when they thought that sex could not be more wonderful, only to find as they grew older, that it could indeed be more wonderful, albeit not so frequent. Yes, in that part of their relationship they were exceptionally lucky (or richly blessed, depending on your preference for common sense or scripture).

Pamela suggested an early bedtime and was surprised when Martin agreed. For months he had always told her to go ahead while he attended to his paperwork; he would come to bed later.

By half past midnight they were asleep in one another's arms, spent and happily fulfilled. Pamela was still none the wiser and Martin had not even begun to explain himself. It was over breakfast, still in their dressing gowns and warmed by the afterglow of their heavenly encounter, that Martin decided to grasp the nettle (in the circumstances a more fitting metaphor than taking the bull by the horns). He turned away to place two slices of bread in the toaster, and while she couldn't see his face he casually remarked: "You know, I sometimes wonder why on earth I ever decided to enter the Church."

Pamela naturally assumed that he didn't mean it literally. She took it to be a sigh of frustration with something the archbishop had said recently or some minor synod policy decision that he disagreed with.

"Why dear? Has the archbishop put his foot in it again?"

"As a matter of fact he has, but that was not the reason for my question. I was seriously asking *why* I decided to enter the Church."

Delighted and at the same time apprehensive, Pamela realised that her plan had worked. In his mellow post-coital state, Martin was on the point of explaining why he had placed his church duties and his participation in domestic and family matters on autopilot and had appeared to be floating three feet off the ground for the past three months.

Her joy of success was, however, mixed with the fear that she might not like what was coming next. Examination of his reasons for entering the Church sounded to her like pretty serious stuff.

"I thought you knew why you chose the Church. Like my father, you wanted to serve the community and to do it in a spiritual way."

"That's absolutely right, my love, you couldn't have put it more clearly. Recently, however, I've been wondering what lay behind that decision. Of course, I could claim it was a road-to-Damascus experience, that God spoke to me and, accompanied by choirs of angels, I was called to the service of the Church. It wouldn't be the first time that someone aspiring to the priesthood had quoted some such twaddle."

Pamela bridled at the word *twaddle* and wondered if he thought her father's reasons for entering the Church were also twaddle. More worrying was his show of blatant disrespect for the religious calling. After all these years, was he going to resign and give it all up? She visibly winced and he noticed it.

"I'm sorry. What I really meant was that I certainly felt called but not in that way. Any such claim on my part would have been twaddle."

She relaxed and radiated a smile of love and forgiveness. Yes, *his* plan was working, too.

"My first loves were science and mathematics, resulting in a fistful of jolly good A-levels in chemistry, physics and maths. Nevertheless, I didn't become a hands-on scientist or science teacher, although my science and maths did leave me with a love of logic and the scientific approach to factual truth. You will also remember that, perhaps paradoxically for a teenage scientist, I also had a love of history. In particular, I was keen on Roman history. And I think it was this that attracted me to the Church. After persecuting Christians, on and off for more than three hundred years, the Romans adopted Christianity as the religion of their Empire. Subconsciously I was impressed by the fact that the mighty

## CHAPTER 2

Roman Empire had recognised the truth and power of Christianity. This helped me to see Christianity in a new light. Until that moment I had been at odds with the Church. Roman history changed all that."

Whatever was coming next, Pamela saw that Martin was getting carried away. They needed a pause for cool reflection. So she quietly asked,

"More toast dear?"

Martin smiled at Pamela's attempt to calm him down and buttered two more slices of toast, one for him and one for her. He knew he had broken the ice. He might even stop there and continue over their evening meal.

"I'm sorry to go on like this. Recently I've been thinking a lot about the Church and Christianity in general and I want to share my thoughts with you."

Yes, *her* plan had worked. He was going to tell her what had been troubling him for the last few months. She couldn't wait to hear what was really on his mind.

They had no time for further conversation until their evening meal. Martin conducted two christenings and visited an elderly parishioner who lived on an out-of-the-way farm. The local GP had tipped him off that Elsie Pritchard was nearing her end. Up to last summer, Elsie had always attended to the church flowers and Martin would be sorry to see her go, even if it was to paradise, although he doubted the existence of any such place. In fact Martin had several doubts and convictions that were out of tune with his job description.

The farmer's wife, Elsie's granddaughter, provided a substantial farm-style lunch of home-cured ham, enormous roast potatoes and purple sprouting broccoli, the quality of which could not be bought in a shop, even in Herefordshire. He ate as sparingly as politeness permitted, knowing that in celebration of the night before, Pamela would prepare a special evening meal. And over that meal he would continue to nudge her gently in the direction of what was really on his mind. It would not do to arrive at the table without a healthy appetite and unable to do justice to her efforts in the kitchen.

It is revealing and entertaining to roughly calculate the number of cooked meals that a housewife prepares in twenty-six years of married life, not forgetting those years when she also has to feed children. The number is surprisingly large, but Pamela had never complained of sweating over steaming pans. As befitted a vicar's wife, all meals were prepared prayerfully and carefully. There is, after all, something very spiritual about preparing food and feeding people. Nevertheless, while she never sought compliments, she liked her cooking to be praised. Surely God forgave her this small conceit. What pious nonsense! Wives should always be praised for their efforts in the kitchen.

Pamela called him to the dining room at seven o'clock. For starters she had put out warm, thin, diagonal slices of toast, butter, various pâtés and a dish of pitted green olives, feta cheese, and sun-dried tomatoes. Simple and imaginative. Their conversation centred on the taste of the food and nothing deeper than that. Martin's heart sank when he saw the main course: slices of boiled gammon in cheese sauce topped with asparagus, accompanied by roast potatoes and broccoli. The Pritchard's midday ham was still only three quarters of its journey through his alimentary system.

"Oh, my love, I'm lost for words. The food you place on our table is delicious, wholesome and inspirational."

Pamela was not that easily taken in by flattery. She realised what had happened, guided more by the tone rather than the content of what he said.

"Where did you have lunch dear?"

"Oh, the Pritchard's gave me a snack."

"That was nice of them. I think a German white wine might go well with our meal. I put a bottle of Niersteiner in the fridge. Will you please fetch it?"

## CHAPTER 2

The wine did the trick, helped to smooth the passage of the meal, as it were, and obliterated the memory of the Pritchard's ham. Over the dessert – orange cheesecake, one of Martin's favourites – Pamela made the first move to continue that morning's conversation.

"What did you mean this morning, dear, when you said you had been at odds with the Church?"

"You know my parents, and you have met my uncles, aunts and cousins, so you know they are not regular church-goers. In fact they only use the church for weddings, christenings and funerals. In my family, anyone attending church more often than that is looked upon as a religious maniac, and I suppose that includes me. Nevertheless, the children of the family are always confirmed. It's a matter of tradition. My family has a curious knack of showing respect for the church, while, at the same time, keeping it at arm's length. So, when I was fifteen years old, I was sent to confirmation classes. I resented it, but one thing I had learned from the Bible was the commandment: *Honour thy father and thy mother, otherwise you get into trouble,* so I dutifully went to my weekly confirmation classes."

Their mood became ever more light-hearted, due partly to Martin's witty misquotation, but largely on account of the Niersteiner.

"In those confirmation classes I suggested that one way to understand God was through the beauty of Nature, commonly referred to as the beauty of God's natural creation. I was told that had nothing to do with true grace. Ever since then I have wondered about the meaning of true grace. What is it, or who is she? Several times I have used the expression in my sermons but I honestly don't know what it really means."

Pamela didn't offer to explain because she didn't know either.

"Later, when we were working our way through the creed, I had the temerity to ask whether it was really possible for someone to rise from the dead, for miracles to happen, and for a virgin to become pregnant. I was told it was my duty to have faith. Just imagine! I thought it was my duty to seek the truth through logic and enquiry, but no, it was apparently my duty to have faith, and dare I say it – *blind* faith. With surgical precision, that dear clergyman – he was a canon actually – amputated any interest I had left in Church doctrine. For the sake of my parents, however, I pretended to have faith and I was eventually confirmed. After the laying on of hands, the bishop exhorted the assembled parents not to send their children to church but to go with them. Clearly, the decrease in Church attendance was becoming a matter of concern. Anyway, in accordance with family tradition, neither I nor my parents became churchgoers after my confirmation, except, of course, for weddings, christenings and funerals."

"Now I understand, dear. Then your study of the Romans changed all that and you saw the Church in a different light."

"Yes and that was just the beginning. I also discovered that there were thoughtful adults, who considered the resurrection, the miracles and the virgin birth to be beautiful metaphors for renewal, the power of faith and purity, respectively. When I discovered this I experienced an overwhelming feeling of relief. It removed an impediment to my acceptance of the Christian faith. I no longer had to have faith in something that offended the laws of common sense. Nowadays, no thinking person actually believes literally in these things, but I still lead my congregation in chanting the creed. If those ladies in nice hats want to believe it literally, that is their affair. My job is simply to lead the chant."

"Do I detect a touch of cynicism? I appreciate what you mean and I can see why you have felt unsettled recently. How about coffee?"

## CHAPTER 2

Pamela felt greatly relieved. She was only surprised he was making such an issue out of a problem that, given sufficient time, would eventually disappear. No less a person than Pope John Paul had recently declared that heaven and hell were not places but states of mind. Admittedly all western Christian denominations still officially preached, or at least tacitly accepted, the literal interpretation of the virgin birth and other impossibilities. Given time, however, fewer and fewer people would believe the impossible and the faith would be the stronger for it. So what was he getting so heated about?

"There's more to it than that," whispered Martin in her ear. She hadn't noticed him creeping into the kitchen behind her and she nearly dropped the jar of ground coffee in surprise.

"Oh, so you haven't told me everything then?" whispered Pamela in mock surprise, while playfully tapping him on the nose with the coffee spoon. She didn't know, and would not know until later, how right she was. There was certainly more to come that evening, but the whole truth would take longer, perhaps a few weeks. In the meantime Martin was laying carefully chosen cobblestones that would eventually form a pathway to what was truly on his mind. He was telling no lies, but neither was he blurting out the complete truth all at once.

"In retrospect, my attraction to Christianity through Roman history was childish. I find now that the adoption of Christianity by the Romans early in the fourth century actually marked the beginning of Christianity as we know it. To put it another way, Christianity as we know it, and I stress the phrase, *as we know it,* did not start in the year nought with the birth of a man called Jesus. Everything we chant in church originated in just one of the several early Jesus movements; and this one version of Christianity was given authority when it was hijacked by Emperor Constantine at the beginning of the fourth century AD. That particular branch of Christianity was the early Roman Church, so-called because it happened to be based in Rome. Later it became known as the Roman Catholic Church. As the official religion of the Roman Empire, this particular branch of Christianity acquired a power base from which it could operate and spread the good word to the rest of the world. We know the history of Christianity from that point onwards. The early split with the Eastern Orthodox Church is well documented and of course there were ancient small churches like the Armenian Church that had no allegiance to Rome. The Roman Catholic Church carried the banner for western Christendom until the Reformation. If we don't know this history because we haven't done our homework, then it doesn't matter because it's well documented and we can easily look it up. I'm less confident about what happened in the first three hundred plus years. There's a standard story, starting with the birth and life of Jesus. Is this story accurate? In fact, is it true?" The world's calendar takes the supposed birth of Jesus (and with it the supposed birth of Christianity) as year nought. History after that is designated AD, an acronym of the Mediaeval Latin *anno Domini*, meaning in the year of the Lord. Some prefer CE (Common or Current Era) to AD. History before that is labelled BC, an acronym for Before Christ. Some prefer BCE (Before Current Era)."

Pamela interrupted: "I know all about AD and BC. What's your point?"

"Sorry, I was beginning to wander into a digression. I was about to say that however we label the years and centuries, might Christianity have an important history predating AD, *i.e.*, long before the supposed birth of Jesus?"

Pamela was startled by the very idea that Christianity, as she knew it, was the result of hijacking by the Romans and she was disturbed to realise that Martin viewed it in this way. From childhood to the present she had never heard or read anything to suggest that the history of the faith needed revision. Furthermore, hijacking was a word of confrontation, not only a challenge to the standard version of Christian history, but also a challenge to the relatively light-hearted nature of their conversation so far.

Hiding her dismay with a thoughtful smile, Pamela asked: "Why shouldn't it be true? It is, after all, the foundation of a faith that is followed by millions of the world's population."

Martin felt he had gone far enough for one evening. Pamela would need time, about twenty-four hours, to adjust to the idea that he wanted to challenge the standard version of Christian history. Tomorrow he would tell her what he planned to do and, crucially, he would seek her agreement to do it.

Shortly before midnight, still awake and snuggled close to his wife, Martin abandoned his plan for a twenty-four-hour recess. Not normally an impatient person, he was now anxious to test Pamela's reaction to his plan. It was a clear moonlit night and he assumed they would be treated to another sparkling frosty morning. It had been that sort of weather for the last five days. Also, they normally slept with the bedroom curtains open, in order to enjoy waking to a room filled with early morning light. They could therefore still see each other in the eerie glow cast by the moon. Gently massaging the small of her back, which she always enjoyed, he whispered: "How would you feel if I asked the bishop for a year's sabbatical to study the first four centuries of Christian history?"

Pamela's first thought was: "Is that what all this fuss is about? Thank goodness it's nothing more serious." Then the true implication of what he had said began to sink in. "Who will take the church services for that year? Will we be able to continue living here?" And, with a thought to the housekeeping: "Will you be paid for that year?"

"I don't yet know the answers to all those questions. As far as money is concerned, a desire to further my knowledge of Christian history is bound to be seen as a worthy ambition and I think funds are available from the Church for the support of such projects. If not, then the sale of a few of my shares in the aeronautics corporation would provide enough to keep us going for a year."

"If I were the bishop, I would point out that you were supposed to have learned your Christian history in your university course."

"The bishop knows as well as I do that since I left university our knowledge and understanding of Christian history have been increased dramatically by academic research. Involved as he is in church management, he probably hasn't been able to follow these advances in detail, but I'm sure he is well aware that biblical scholars have transformed our knowledge of early Christian history. He will also know that the results of this academic research have not all been incorporated into university theology courses. Curious, isn't it? If the physicists at CERN make in interesting discovery, it will be conveyed within days to students reading physics at university. In contrast, if biblical research reveals a new and important fact of Christian history, it may be years before it is incorporated into university teaching, while the structure of the Sunday church service has never been changed in response to the results biblical research."

Clearly, Martin had thought ahead. He already had answers to possible questions from the bishop. She made a quick decision. On no account must she openly oppose his plan for a sabbatical; that would make her appear disloyal and non-supportive. In a flash she saw two possible scenarios. The bishop might refuse Martin's request, in which case she would be a loving wife (which she was anyway) and commiserate while offering a silent prayer of gratitude to the bishop. On the other hand, the bishop might allow Martin a

## CHAPTER 2

sabbatical, and if that meant a change in their domestic routine she would join in the fun and share his sabbatical. In a sense she would have her own sabbatical.

"You must write to the bishop immediately, dear."

Martin made to get out of bed. Pamela pulled him back.

"Hey! Not so quick. First thing in the morning will do. You can finish massaging my back."

Over breakfast they decided that the letter to the bishop should contain not only a request for a meeting, but also the reason, *i.e.,* Martin's plan for a sabbatical to study the early years of Christian history. *Plan* was a loaded word. Martin realised he had not yet mentioned to Pamela that he wanted to travel, probably in the Middle East, and he still didn't know how he would put this to the bishop. He caught the morning post collection. Knowing the bishop's reputation for efficiency, he expected to get a reply by post before the end of the week, word-processed by the bishop's administrative assistant, his secretary or his full time personal assistant (all three delightful ladies were well known to Martin, who had always been unclear as to who did what in the bishop's office), and signed by the bishop. He was therefore taken aback when the bishop phoned him just before twelve noon the following day.

"Good morning and God bless you Martin. Thank you for your interesting letter. Let's meet to discuss your sabbatical as soon as it's convenient for you. How about this afternoon?"

Martin was amazed and just a little suspicious of the bishop's undisguised enthusiasm to discuss his proposed sabbatical. He sensed that the bishop was not simply doing his duty in responding to Martin's request, but was eager in some way to take part personally in Martin's plans. It's uncanny what you can gather from a tone of voice, even from a few words spoken on the telephone. What was the bishop planning? On the other hand, perhaps Martin's imagination was running riot. Nevertheless, he needed more time.

"It's kind of you to agree to see me so soon. This afternoon is unfortunately impossible. I could come to you any time tomorrow."

"Splendid! Let's discuss your plans over morning coffee tomorrow. Come straight to the palace at about ten thirty. Park on the right just inside the entrance archway. Building work on the new housing for the Mappa Mundi makes parking impossible before the main entrance. See you then."

"Thank you and I hope .... " The bishop had already rung off.

Surprised by the bishop's energy and enthusiasm, Martin allowed his mind to go momentarily blank. His thoughts then reassembled around the Mappa Mundi, which the bishop had mentioned just before he rang off. This was a unique Mediaeval treasure in the possession of Hereford cathedral, a map on a single sheet of calf skin, representing the known world around the year 1300. It was famous throughout the UK and given half a chance the Americans would buy it for a small fortune. It attracted a constant stream of visitors, which added considerably to the economies of both the cathedral and the city. At present the Mappa Mundi was on display in a cramped room leading off from the cathedral café. A new housing for this famous treasure was sorely needed.

# Chapter 3

What are we to make of this country clergyman and his wife, still in love and occasionally re-igniting the flame of passion? Well, his wife seems straightforward enough. Clearly, she has a sense of duty. One would expect a sense of duty without subservience to be the natural result of her upbringing in the family of a clergyman, which somehow reflects the paucity of speaking parts for women in sacred scripture. Also one suspects that the philosophy of the women's liberation movement has never bothered her. She has risen above it. And she doubtless has more spirit and worldliness than her husband gives her credit for.

What about him? Obviously, the adoption of Christianity by the Romans played an early part in helping him to view the Church more favourably, but he realised later that this was a naïve response. And in any case it is hard to believe that someone with proven abilities in science and mathematics would want to spend their working life chanting a creed that they felt to be factually untrue. So is he simply a lazy person, looking for an easy life? It is worth pointing out, however, that although a life dedicated to science may excite the imagination and offer tantalising prospects of career advancement, it is also rather pressurised. What could be more conducive to longevity than the life of a country parson? So let us not accuse him of laziness; rather let us recognise his wisdom. In short, he knew how not to get ulcers. You may say that he is therefore a hypocrite. Maybe he is. Or maybe he was. As we have already heard, his abandonment of science in favour of the Church was not the result of a Road-to-Damascus revelation.

No, our analysis of this man's character still doesn't ring true. Perhaps he is more deeply spiritual than we thought. He truly feels the power and the truth of the Christian message. He is moved by the symbolism of Christ on the cross, for it confirms in him the feeling that we are not alone, that whatever our suffering there will always be comfort. Of course, he is not particularly fond of chanting the creed or explaining the meaning of the trinity; unfortunately those things can't be avoided because they are part of the job. He is still uncertain which god Richard Dawkins doesn't believe in. For his own part Martin certainly does not accept the traditional Church view of God. His own feeling for God is closer to the 'oneness' of eastern philosophies. In view of this very personal brand of do-it-yourself spirituality, he should perhaps have pursued a career in science and worked part-time as a minister to some dissenting congregation. Too late for that. In any case, it hardly matters whether he is a traditional or progressive Christian because, as he approaches middle-age, this country clergyman has come to suspect that for two thousand years Christianity has been the custodian of a most beautiful secret. It is more than a suspicion. He is convinced that the Christian faith has two layers of truth, and that only the top layer, contrived and edited, has been marketed for consumption by the masses. He is also concerned that, after two thousand years of indoctrination, the Christian world may be incapable of acknowledging the deeper truth, at least not without years of bitter dispute. Let us call this revelation Martin's Road-to-Damascus experience.

We know that he also studied history at university. Nowadays history has become a hobby for him, and he can study it how he pleases, following his own idiosyncratic route through past centuries, teasing out fascinating threads of knowledge, while mentally perambulating through earlier times.

Now, later in life, these idle perambulations through the alleyways of history and Christian history in particular, have led him to the threshold of a discovery, which, if proved to be true, is frightening. He wonders what life would have been like for someone revealing this new Christian truth in

# CHAPTER 3

sixteenth century England, during the Reformation, with Henry VIII on the throne, or later under Elizabeth I. It's a fun thing he likes to do, to imagine himself living in former times. Grimly, he decided he would have had to act the coward and conceal his secret, bending with whichever denominational wind was blowing at the time, Catholic or Reformist. For had he uttered a word about his discovery, it would not have mattered which group was currently in charge, he would have been burnt at the stake. His doubts about the received version of Christian history would have been heresy to both sides and would have made the theological squabbles of Catholics and Protestants seem childish by comparison. On second thoughts, he decided he might have been spared, dismissed as a lunatic, and committed to the Bethlehem hospital, which later became known as the Bedlam.

To return to the present: the scientist in him is thrilled to think he may be on the verge of a momentous discovery and he is itching to confirm it, one way or the other. At the same time, he can't shake himself free from the thought that while the burning of heretics is now out of fashion, he may well be dismissed as a lunatic or simply as a fruit cake. Could he live with that? Probably. We shall see.

We must ask why Martin, a mere country vicar, is the sole recipient of this revelation. Perhaps he is not. Perhaps vicars, canons and bishops and all manner of other Christian operatives have their suspicions, but dare not rock the comfortable boat of Sunday worship. Nevertheless, the question remains: Why Martin? Let us attempt just one explanation then continue the story, regardless. Unlike most country vicars, or for that matter any type of clergyman, Martin is heavily burdened with a rational frame of mind. Ever since he entered the ministry he has avoided obvious anomalies in the Christian story, or he has sermonised them away, comforting his congregation by clever preaching, and at the same time congratulating himself on his ability to impress his congregation and his confirmation classes with sonorous ecclesiastical whitewash.

The hard truth he has kept to himself, *i.e.*, that clever arguments, often enlisting an element of blind faith, may comfort the faithful, while the very existence of these contradictions and inconsistencies means that there must be something wrong with the Christian story as presently told. Martin has collected a host of irreconcilable contradictions from the New Testament. At first he despaired of an explanation, but now he believes he has found one; and it is this explanation that constitutes what he has come to think of as the most beautiful secret of Christianity.

Like all other trained clergy, Martin knows that early versions of the New Testament existed well before Emperor Constantine came on the scene, and that the final version was put together sometime in the late fourth or early fifth century. It was put together by men (it seems hardly likely that women had an input in those days), who decided which writings to admit to the canon. It therefore consists of the writings of men (possibly inspired by some vision of God), chosen selectively (because many writings were omitted), craftily edited and sometimes poorly translated.

Martin has now had enough of this. He has outgrown his desire for the stress-free existence of a country parson. The scientist in him can no longer be suppressed. He needs to pursue facts and nail them down with evidence, to elaborate working hypotheses and test them by experiment and observation, to chase and corner suspected facts until they are proven, like hounding the king in a game of chess until checkmate is achieved.

Let us hope he does not live to regret his investigation of Christianity's greatest secret. The scientist in him may be encouraged by *John 8:32*: *The truth shall make you free.* On the other hand, Sir Walter Raleigh spoke wisely when he said: *Whosoever shall follow truth too near the heels, it may happily strike out his teeth.*

# Chapter 4

The bishop's advice about parking was unnecessary. Pamela would drive her husband into town, leave him within walking distance of the bishop's palace, park the car in the Gaol Street car park behind the main police station then meet Florence Hoskins, chairperson of the Women's Institute, for their monthly discussion of the Institute's activities in the Herefordshire area. They had no idea how long Martin's meeting with the bishop would last. Perhaps Pamela would even have lunch with Mrs Hoskins. She hoped not. Her monthly chore of meeting up with the super-efficient and domineering Florence was not exactly her favourite calendar entry. Hopefully she would be rescued by a call from Martin on his mobile to say he was on his way to the car park. Alas, fate had laid different plans.

As Martin entered the grounds of the bishop's palace, the bishop came striding across the lawn to meet him. He had expected to be met by an assistant or secretary, who would take him in charge and announce him formally. Despite the wintry weather, it was the bishop himself in shirt sleeves and carpet slippers, beaming a welcome and ushering him through the front door of the palace and into his office, exclaiming: "Good to see you Martin. So you want time off to go chasing Jesus!" Martin was taken aback. 'Time off to go chasing Jesus' was embarrassingly near the mark. How could the bishop know? On the other hand, it could also be a fairly jocular expression for the study of the early years of Christianity. Certainly the bishop was acting strangely, starting with his unexpectedly rapid response to Martin's letter, then his personal and very informal welcome to their meeting this morning. Martin had prepared a list of agenda, which would lead their discussion gently and logically to his reasons for requesting a sabbatical. But the bishop seemed to be taking over with his own programme. Martin had still not responded to the bishop's question and he chose an easy escape: "Well Sir, that's certainly one way of describing the study of the first four centuries of Christianity."

"Martin, when I read your letter, I jumped to certain conclusions. Now let me see if I was right. Please forgive me if I'm mistaken. I suspect you are aware of the work of biblical historians, who maintain that Bishop Eusebius laced his account of the early centuries of Christianity with inaccuracies and exaggerations designed to glorify the role of Emperor Constantine in supposedly saving and preserving the faith." Martin relaxed. Of course, the bishop didn't know how far Martin had already progressed with his studies, and Martin would let him think that he was still in the early stages of reviewing Christian history. Except for a few conservative theologians, Christian historians nowadays accepted that Bishop Eusebius – appointed 1600 years ago by Emperor Constantine to record the first three hundred plus years of Christianity – had written an inaccurate account of Christian history. The world of Sunday worship was comfortable with this authorised version, which was still preached and taught. "Sir, you are absolutely right. You must have second sight. Indeed, there are many doubts about the veracity of Eusebius' version of history. And I'm sure you know that biblical scholars are finding it difficult to establish the true version. I'm looking for an opportunity to catch up with the present state of play."

During this conversation Martin had been guided into the bishop's study and was now seated in a comfortable leather chair, facing the bishop across a large and surprisingly modern-style desk, obviously not of solid wood and probably constructed from some veneered composite. There was not much on it – a tray with a few papers (possibly letters to be answered), a telephone, a chipped German beer mug containing pens and pencils, and little else, not even a framed photograph of his wife or children. That struck

## CHAPTER 4

Martin as rather odd until he noticed a large display of family photographs on a shelf of a bookcase behind the bishop's chair. Martin was mentally evaluating the desk (probably rather heavy – how long before the veneer starts to lift? – what did it cost?) when he was jerked back to the present by the bishop saying: "So, dear Martin, what is it that you particularly want to do?" As he spoke, the bishop looked earnestly at Martin, willing him to give a direct and honest reply.

"As in all branches of research – biblical, historical, scientific – the most recent discoveries are waiting to be published and can therefore only be accessed by talking with their authors. I think my old university theology tutor may be able to suggest useful contacts. He retired some years ago, and I know he's still alive because we still exchange Christmas cards. I will ask his advice then make a plan of action, which will probably involve first corresponding with researchers in other countries then possibly visiting them for face-to-face discussions."

"Of course, you must contact your old tutor. That's the logical thing to do."

"I have decided to wait for the outcome of this meeting with you sir. If you agree to my sabbatical then I will contact him and I'm sure he will be prepared to help me further."

The bishop carefully followed Martin's reply, occasionally nodding his approval. His piercing inquisitorial gaze began to soften and Martin sensed that he was warming to his request for a sabbatical. "Yes, Martin, I never intended to put you on trial in this meeting. I am sure your request for a sabbatical arises from a genuine and wholesome interest in Christian history." At this, Martin felt ashamed. He dared not reveal his true purpose, which was to follow his suspicion that the accepted version of Christian history concealed an awesome secret. The bishop was about to continue when he was interrupted by a knock at his study door. His secretary was bringing the morning coffee and biscuits.

"Good morning Reverend. Help yourself to coffee and biscuits." Then, to them both: "If you are still in conference after twelve, I will bring in a light lunch of sandwiches." Exchanging a conspiratorial look with Martin, she left the room. Did she know why he was there? Of course she did. The bishop must have discussed the visit with her.

"My dear Martin, I guessed because I remembered my own agonies of conscience when I first entered the ministry. In those days, the evidence was not as strong as it is now, but there were already reasons for suspecting that the early history of Christianity had been misreported. Very early in my theological studies I realised there are two worlds that hardly talk to each other. There is the world of the church; let's call it the world of pastoral care and Sunday worship; then there is the world of biblical scholarship. In fact they are less like two different worlds and more like parallel universes. In the universe of biblical scholarship, historians are retranslating Christian texts and, in the process, discovering forgeries, spurious insertions and false claims of authorship; then there is the discovery of previously unknown early Christian writings, which cast a new light on Christian history. It would be unfair to say that the Church refuses to acknowledge these new discoveries, although some denominations reject them out of hand. Others listen but do not react. Some, like the Lutherans, actually take a keen interest but still tend to protect their congregations from the more challenging results of new findings. We were all taught the standard Christian story when we were young and psychologists tell us that what we learn in childhood is largely irreversible. Even the Quakers, probably the most liberal and free-thinking of all Christians, have difficulty with these new truths. Only recently the Clerk of a Quaker Meeting told me he had led a discussion of the evidence that the

## CHAPTER 4

Gospels had not been written by the disciples Matthew, Mark, Luke and John and that these names had been allocated to give an air of authority. In his words it was a 'reluctant' discussion and most members felt offended that their cherished myths were being challenged, yet this fact about the authorship or non-authorship of the Gospels is now well established and accepted by biblical scholars worldwide."

Martin couldn't see where this rather long speech was leading. At least it seemed that he and the bishop agreed that there were fault lines in the currently accepted version of early Christian history and that the bishop would approve his sabbatical. Martin was waiting to hear what the bishop really had on his mind because, despite his reputation for being a good listener, it had been clear from the onset that he had no intention of sitting back to consider sagely and kindly Martin's request for time off for historical research. It seemed he wanted to take charge of the enterprise. The bishop continued:

"So you see what you are up against. After a year of study you may feel personally enlightened because you have discovered a correct, or at least a less erroneous, version of Christian history, but you will get no thanks for preaching it to your congregation. Just imagine how they would react if you told them that Emperor Constantine did not actually convert to Christianity and that he went home after the Council of Nicaea and had his mother and his brother murdered. Moreover, the claim that he saved the one true Church from heresy – by adopting it for the Roman Empire and banning all other branches of Christianity – is irrelevant because there is no historical evidence for the existence of one true church, only for the existence of several different Christian sects, one of which was fortunate enough to be chosen for the Empire. And there is so much more. Do you see what I'm getting at Martin?"

Martin smiled outwardly while grimacing inwardly. The bishop was right, but it was a case of the truth but not the whole truth.

"Yes, of course, Sir. Even if I do not convey a revised version of Christian history to my parishioners, it will nevertheless enrich and benefit my own understanding of our faith."

Patronisingly, the bishop replied: "Well, Martin, you appear to have thought about it carefully," then continued: "Before I entered the ministry I was, as you are now, fascinated by the history of Christianity and its revision through academic research. I confided my interest to no-one, which was perhaps a mistake. After months of worry and prayer, I decided to devote my life to traditional church teaching and pastoral care, which, after all, give meaning to the lives of the faithful."

The bishop momentarily dropped his earnest attitude, permitted himself a wry smile and sighed: "Perhaps I overdid the latter, so now I'm a bishop, overburdened with church administration and politics."

The bishop was beginning to make sense. But how would he react if he knew that Martin was planning to pursue a putative faith-shattering secret of Christianity?

"For the first few years of my ministry, I followed new discoveries in Christian history like a spectator sport. Now I don't have time for even that. Then I receive a letter from you, asking to carry on where I left off, as it were. Of course, you were not to know that. If you were surprised by my enthusiasm, you now know the reason for it."

At last, Martin knew where he stood. He drew a deep breath and decided to blurt out the truth and damn the consequences. Just in time he changed his mind. He couldn't risk the disapproval of the bishop and the possible ruination of his plans. In any case, how up-to-date was the bishop with recent research in Christian history? When had it

## CHAPTER 4

ceased even to be a spectator sport for him? The questionable authorship of the Gospels and the false spin placed on the behaviour of Emperor Constantine were now old hat. Biblical scholars were already discussing them when the bishop was still at school. Much more had been discovered since then, resulting in a revolutionary interpretation (some would call it an heretical interpretation) of the New Testament amongst biblical scholars.

Martin's nerves were still jangling from the quick reversal of his decision to tell all. Thank goodness the coffee and biscuits were still untouched. They would give him a little more time to re-attain mental equilibrium. "Shall I be mother?" enquired the bishop. Call it telepathy if you will, or let us say the bishop was very shrewd and perceptive in dealing with people. He knew immediately that Martin needed more time to think things over before responding. Martin gratefully accepted his coffee, helped himself to milk and a shortbread biscuit and joined the bishop in silent contemplation of a new shaft of sunlight that had just inveigled its way through the south-facing window of the bishop's study and was now illuminating myriads of dancing dust motes above the bishop's line of bookcases, before bouncing, flame-like, from a crucifix on the opposite wall. At last, Martin summoned sufficient bravery to continue.

"Sir, in particular I would like to find answers to several questions. Take, for example, the Gospel of Thomas. For many years we had only a fragment of that Gospel, written in Greek. In 1945, however, ancient scrolls were found buried in a cave at Nag Hamadi in the Egyptian desert and they included the complete Gospel of Thomas in Coptic. It is quite unlike other Gospels, in that it is simply a list of the sayings and actions of Jesus." The bishop smiled indulgently and allowed Martin to continue without interruption. Of course he knew all about the Gospel of Thomas. "When the early Church fathers decided which Christian writings should be made part of the New Testament, they did not include the Gospel of Thomas. Was it because the sayings of Jesus are already present in Matthew, Mark, Luke and John? Apparently they had a deeper reason than that. In fact, the Gospel of Thomas was declared heretical. I want to know why that Gospel was thought to be heretical."

Silence descended and both men waited for inspiration. Whatever words were spoken next, they had to be carefully chosen and carefully weighed. Both knew that the Gospel of Thomas had been lost for centuries and had now been rediscovered, generating interest and excitement amongst Christians and biblical scholars. Most Sunday Christians didn't appreciate the significance of the discovery; they simply thought how nice it was that the complete Gospel of Thomas had been discovered. The better informed knew it was a Gnostic document, which was why the early Church fathers had declared it heretical. Probably no Church minister had ever attempted to explain to their flock what was meant by Gnostic, let alone why a list of the sayings of Jesus could be anything other than a product of orthodox Christian thinking.

The bishop began to worry that Martin would bring to light parts of Christian history long buried and best left that way. Had Martin been a trifle dishonest; were his remarks about the Gospel of Thomas rather contrived? Surely Martin knew jolly well that the Gospel of Thomas was a Gnostic document, and surely he understood the basis of Gnosticism. Too late now to refuse Martin's request for a sabbatical. He would keep his word and not allow his apprehension to show. The silence lasted barely one minute; for Martin time stood still and it felt more like ten. At last, with a wide smile, the bishop looked straight at Martin.

"That's an interesting example. In fact, a study of the heresies alone could keep you busy for your entire sabbatical."

## CHAPTER 4

"Then, Sir, you think there is still much to be learned from the study of the heresies?"

"Well," replied the bishop guardedly, "Perhaps it would amount to no more than a refresher course." Martin sensed that the bishop was worried and did not really want to discuss the heresies. This, in turn, signalled to Martin that perhaps the bishop had begun to suspect Martin's deeper motives for requesting a sabbatical.

"So, dear Martin, what other aspects of the Christian story are you hoping to illuminate?" The bishop's tone was now abrupt. Had he guessed Martin's real reason for wanting a sabbatical? Martin decided to play safe and replied: "I would like to get up-to-date with current progress on the translation of the Dead Sea scrolls and what they reveal about those early years when Christianity had hardly begun and whether they add to, or contradict, the history of Christianity handed down by bishop Eusebius." Martin drew breath, hoping that the bishop would consider the Dead Sea scrolls versus Eusebius only mildly controversial, perhaps even a very worthy subject for Martin's sabbatical. Or were the Dead Sea scrolls a threat to the accepted history of Christianity? In other words, were they a loaded topic?

Mention of the scrolls caught the bishop unawares. He put on an expression of fatherly interest, and replied: "Let's hope you can manage all this in one year. With God's help, I'm sure you will, dear Martin. Do you honestly think you can?" Had the bishop been totally honest, he would have added: "And for God's sake, if you find the ultimate truth, I hope you'll keep quiet about it." Martin was unaware that the bishop already knew that Christian history harboured a beautiful secret, and that he suspected Martin was also on the trail of that secret. Martin replied that at least he would try, then added: "Sir, for my part I am determined to study the first four centuries of Christian history. Only two things stand in my way."

The bishop raised a questioning eyebrow.

"First, your consent to my sabbatical. Second, the agreement of Pamela, my wife. She already knows my plan and seems to like the idea, but I feel she must have the final word."

The bishop's smile widened into a happy grin.

"Good for you, Martin. You have my full consent. I know Pamela. I think my wife knows her even better than I do. I'm sure she will still tell you to go ahead. I'd like you to stay for lunch. You and I still have much to discuss."

Martin excused himself to speak to Pamela on his mobile. He would be much later than expected and he would contact her when he wanted to be picked up. Pamela couldn't put up with Flossy Hoskins (as she liked to call her) any longer. "Martin needs me at the bishop's palace, so I must dash. I'll be in touch." Desperation will drive even a vicar's wife to tell a lie. She drove out of town, found a quiet country restaurant called the *Happy Turnip*, ordered a light lunch of pea and courgette soup with chunks of wholemeal bread, settled down with her novel and a cup of tea, and waited for Martin to call her again.

The bishop's secretary was both efficient and telepathic, or so it seemed, because at that same moment she called to the bishop to open his study door, which he did with a smile and a mock bow, while she wheeled in a trolley laden with a selection of sandwiches, a fruit pie and a large pot of tea. Martin wondered if the bishop had pressed a secret button under his desk, which rang a bell in his secretary's office. He had the impression that the timetable of their meeting had been pre-planned by the bishop. If so, then Martin wasn't complaining. He couldn't help wondering what Pamela was doing for lunch and whether she had managed to prise herself away from Flossy Hoskins.

"Now, Martin, let us discuss the practicalities. I can probably arrange for your stipend to continue unchanged

## CHAPTER 4

for one year. Then I would like to take advantage of the good nature of you and your wife and ask you to give board and lodgings to a young curate and his wife. He is the nephew of an old university friend of mine and I have been asked to find a parish for him. They could join you almost immediately. He could share your parish duties until the New Year and take over from you in mid-January. You will then be able to follow your own programme for the study of Christian history, although I would appreciate monthly reports on your progress."

Clearly the bishop had done a great deal of detailed planning in the short time since receiving Martin's letter. His ability to quickly and carefully adapt Martin's sabbatical to his own purpose was impressive. Martin consoled himself with the thought that once he was released in mid-January he would be free to follow his own programme, secure in the knowledge that he would have enthusiastic support and help, if needed, from the bishop. It couldn't get any better. They had finished the sandwiches and had started on the fruit pie when Martin replied to the bishop: "Sir, there is little I can say, except to express my gratitude." Then, with a wry smile, he added: "You seem to have thought more carefully, and if I might say, more wisely, about my sabbatical than I have."

"As I told you, Martin, I had a dress rehearsal for this moment some years ago, but I never managed the final performance. It is now up to you. God bless you."

\*\*\*

In April the curate and his wife visited the vicarage and stayed for three nights. They were bright-eyed, married for almost a year, and anxious to cooperate and fit in. Pamela and Martin soon penetrated the veneer of politeness and, to their relief, found that the young couple were sound and sensible. True, they had been foisted upon them by the bishop, but they couldn't have chosen better themselves. For their part, Sue and Ken were thrilled with the prospect of moving from Birmingham and spending their new married life in a Herefordshire viillage. It was agreed that they would move early in September and share the church and household duties until mid-January, when Martin would start his sabbatical. Ken showed a keen interest in the nature of Martin's sabbatical, which became a major topic in their conversations. On the advice of the bishop, however, Martin stuck to the authorship of the Gospels and involvement of Constantine in the early Church. The mere suggestion that this history may have been misreported brought a worried look to Ken's face. His approach to the ministry was clearly to believe the standard story, recite the creed, stand up, sit down, sing this hymn, say this prayer then smile and shake hands with the members of the congregation as they left the church. Yes, Martin's parishioners would be in safe hands while he was away.

Between the curate's visit and Christmas, Martin and the bishop met to finalise the arrangements for the continuation of Martin's stipend and the provision for possible travel expenses if Martin needed to visit other countries. It all seemed uncannily generous and it further confirmed that the bishop felt closely involved in Martin's programme. Not until their final meeting, just before Christmas, did the bishop finally ask Martin for his detailed plan of study. He reserved a whole afternoon for this discussion. Discussion? It was to be more like a lecture, based on the bishop's own studies before he had opted in favour of a traditional ecclesiastical existence.

Sitting opposite one another in the bishop's study, in deep leather chairs, Martin eyed, with eager anticipation, a nearby table laden with tea and scones, and waited for the bishop to speak. "I predict that your research will lead to two different types of discovery. First, you will discover new facts that were previously unknown and not even suspected. Second, you will find that some parts of the Christian story have been misreported."

"Sir, it is hard to believe that one of the most influential events in human history could have been misreported. How could it have happened?"

"Martin, the misreporting of history is a common phenomenon. A demon in a signal box pulls the wrong lever, switches the points and sends history on a false track. It may take centuries before the engine runs out of steam and is laboriously towed back to be placed on the right track.. And bear this thought in mind: it was probably a very early prearranged misrepresentation of Christianity that gave it the edge over other faiths and allowed it to develop at the expense of Gnosticism, Paganism and Judaism, not to mention emperor worship. Accordingly, the new faith not only embodied a philosophy of love and forgiveness, it also .... Ah well, that is for you to discover." Once again the bishop was tantalisingly near the mark. Martin was now almost certain the bishop knew the true purpose of his sabbatical.

"At this point I hand over to you. You must design your own programme of study and plan your own strategy. Presumably you will first visit your old tutor and act on his recommendations for further study. God bless you and good luck in all your research!"

# Chapter 5

*A teacher affects eternity;
he can never tell where his influence stops.*
(Henry Adams)

Flo Willan had been retired almost ten years. His initials were actually G.T., which he penned with a peculiar flourish that made the G appear like an F, which merged into a T that finished in a squiggle resembling *lo*. Generations of students had therefore called him Flo. He knew and he didn't mind; in fact he enjoyed his nickname, which seemed to convey a degree of affection without being too impertinent.

As he addressed the envelope, Martin hesitated, sorely tempted to write 'Dr. Flo Willan' then thought better of it and gave his old tutor his correct initials of G.T.. Doctor Willan had had a lucky escape in the matter of nicknames. It was surely pure chance that some fertile student imagination had not given birth to 'Gin and Tonic' from G.T., especially since Doctor Willan was clearly quite fond of an occasional tipple, and had often held impromptu tutorials in the student union bar.

Martin's letter to Flo was somewhat dishonest, because he wrote that he and Pamela were planning a short break in the Yorkshire Dales, and although they hadn't decided exactly where to spend their little holiday, they wondered if it might be possible to call and say hello on their way north, adding as an afterthought that he was planning a sabbatical to study early Christianity and would be grateful for a few tips. His dishonesty lay in his allocation of emphasis, since the main, indeed the sole, purpose of the visit was to seek Flo's advice on how to spend his sabbatical.

Flo Willan was quick to reply. He sent a picture postcard, a view of Malham Cove in the Yorkshire Dales, with the brief message: *"Delighted to hear from you. At the moment I'm free 24/7. Choose your own day and time and let me know.*" It was signed 'G.T. Willan' and, as ever, the scrawled G.T. resembled *Flo*. How often had Martin seen that signature at the end of his marked essays! Occasionally Flo would add 'Come and see me', which made Martin apprehensive. Today, Flo was again telling Martin to come and see him, and it filled Martin with pleasurable anticipation.

Flo's picture postcard of Malham Cove lured Martin's thoughts into the as yet unknown territory of the Yorkshire Dales. Malham Cove, in an attractive landscape of carboniferous limestone, had been one of Flo's favourite hiking areas (perhaps it still was!?). It had also been the subject of his favourite digression during tutorials. Martin had been no closer to the Yorkshire Dales than Bolton Abbey, where he and Pamela had once taken a picnic one Easter weekend. They had sat on a ruined wall of the ancient priory, using the top of a broken buttress as their picnic table then crossed the river on the stepping stones. They promised themselves that later in the year, when the weather was warmer, they would come again and explore the area further, perhaps do some hiking in the hills beyond the abbey, but they never did; there were too many weekend distractions on the university campus. As for the North York Moors, Martin had never been closer than York itself, which offered such a fund of historical interest that he had never felt the need to travel further.

Martin pushed the Yorkshire Dales to the back of his mind. They had no part to play in his study of Christian history, and in any case he needed to reply to Flo. It might be argued that Bolton Abbey and the several other ruined Cistercian Abbeys in the north of England, *do* have a place in Christian history. On the other hand, Martin was concerned with the first three hundred plus years of Christianity, centuries before the Cistercian order had been established. The Cistercians, however, were an offshoot of the earlier Benedictines. Even so, Saint Benedict had been born in 480

AD; more than a hundred years after Constantine had adopted Christianity for the Roman Empire. "There I go again", thought Martin, "romancing about Christian history, when I ought to be deciding on a date to visit Flo Willan."

Nevertheless, a ruined Cistercian Abbey was an important historical marker. If Henry VIII had not defied the pope and assumed supremacy over the Church for the English crown, Martin would not be a country vicar of an Anglican church. Rather he would be a priest of the Church of Rome; he would be told what to preach and what to think by Rome, and would most certainly not now be embarking on a mission to question the veracity of the story of early Christianity. Without the English Reformation, which was accompanied by the pillaging and destruction of the Abbeys, Roman Catholicism would have persisted as the sole purveyor of Christianity in the British Isles. As these thoughts passed through Martin's mind, he realised that the authorities of the Church of England were probably no less conservative than the pope when it came to the official version of Christian history. After all, the separation of the Church of England from the Catholic Church was more a matter of politics than theology, arising from the petulance of Henry VIII, when the pope refused to annul his marriage to Catherine of Aragon. So Henry VIII took over the Church, had his marriage annulled, then married Anne Boleyn, after whom he had been lusting for some considerable time, and who, not inappropriately, has been called the *femme fatale* of the English Reformation.

Why so much irrelevant day-dreaming about Henry VIII and the English Reformation? Martin was trying to avoid facing the fact that he had deceived the bishop. He had not revealed his suspicion that the official version of Christian history was so much in error that the true story might rock the foundations of the faith. Let's call his momentary

## CHAPTER 5

preoccupation with the English Reformation a form of displacement psychology.

Enough of this! Reigning in his wayward thoughts, Martin penned, or rather ball-pointed, a reply to Flo to the effect that he would visit on Friday March 30th, that he would be accompanied by his wife, Pamela, and that they would then spend a few days further north in the Dales before returning to Herefordshire. Flo replied by return, offering bed and board for as long as they wanted, and recommending a B&B next to the Youth hostel in Kettlewell in Wharfdale.

At this point Martin made a mental note to ask Flo for his e-mail address, if indeed he had one. It did seem rather quaint that in these days of electronic communication they were corresponding with postcards. Martin phoned the recommended guesthouse and booked two nights. Pamela approved of the arrangements and decided she must buy new walking boots. That night, during their pillow talk, she made Martin promise to keep in touch by e-mail and mobile phone. Martin promised and admitted that electronic communication was heaven-sent for keeping in touch between countries. That was a mistake. Pamela went suddenly quiet when she realised he might be leaving her to travel abroad.

Flo had retired to Roundhay, a northern suburb of Leeds. Navigation of the tunnelled inner ring road and identification of the exit that would lead them to Roundhay were accomplished without error but not without stress and trepidation. Fortunately, Pamela was an accomplished map reader and was able to guide them correctly through the city, past the Thomas Danby college and finally on a route signposted to *Tropical World,* as instructed earlier by Flo. They continued along Street Lane, past Tropical World, then took the next turning right. From there, Flo's directions led them into a series of right and left turns until they arrived before a modern stone-built house in a small, genteel neighbourhood.

Genteel? Well, none of the cars sitting on driveways was ostentatiously large, all being relatively new but of modest size and shiny clean; no clapped out minis, no teenager-owned bangers, and no flashy Mercedes with tinted windows as owned by bankers and drug dealers.

It was still April, but spring flowers were blooming in every well-tended garden, thanks to the season creep caused by global warming. Obviously a settlement of respectable, retired members of society. These first impressions were registered in a flash with no time for comment because Flo had seen them arriving and was already advancing from his front gate with outstretched hands of welcome.

Flo's wife had died six years ago. It was quickly evident that he was no longer in mourning. He had regained his rather mischievous approach to life, which, paradoxically, had always fitted well with the gravitas of his lectures on Christian spirituality. The one had always balanced the other in the equation of his personality.

Either he had learned to cook since his wife died, or it was an earlier accomplishment. They didn't ask. Later, over coffee when they praised the meal, Flo explained that after his retirement he had gradually elbowed his wife out of the kitchen and started to follow television cookery programmes. "There is something spiritual about feeding people," Flo explained, looking very pious. Pamela and Martin agreed with appropriate seriousness. Too late, Martin noticed that mischievous glint in Flo's eyes. "After all," added Flo, "Jesus was the first celebrity cook." Martin played along with "Really!?" "First you take the loaves and cut them up into many pieces then you do the same with the fishes." Pamela spluttered, nearly choked and slopped her coffee. Flo gallantly came to her rescue with a large paper napkin then said to Martin: "Bet you daren't put that in one of your sermons." "Why not?" exclaimed Pamela, "He could do with some new material." And so the evening was spent in happy, light-hearted conversation. Several times Martin tried to channel their conversation towards the more serious purpose of his visit, but Flo wasn't having it. Perhaps he was getting his own back for those occasions, years ago in tutorials, when Martin would interrupt Flo's theological arguments with contrived and humorous questions. Flo said they would talk 'shop' tomorrow.

Clearly, Flo was thoroughly domesticated and had no need of a housekeeper or dutiful daughter to run his home or look after him. Admittedly, there was evidence that he found it difficult to keep up with his cleaning and dusting, but his kitchen was clean and tidy, and his cooking was of prize-winning standard. He had prepared a bedroom for Pamela and Martin, towels laid out, bed well-aired.

Pamela and Martin talked about Flo before they fell asleep. Martin was pleased and relieved to find his old tutor's mental acuity had in no way decreased with age. His joy at their visit was that shared by all teachers when, in retirement and old age, their former students keep in contact and still value their company and their advice. Pamela, however, thought she also detected an air of loneliness. "Only to be expected," murmured Martin, as they both drifted off to sleep.

It was a healthy breakfast. Nothing fried. Plentiful cereals, muesli, fruit, yoghurt, fruit juice and a choice of tea or coffee. Flo even provided background music. No hymns or meditative flute and harp. Flo preferred the waltzes and polkas of a New Year concert in Vienna. This was in keeping with the Flo that Martin remembered: intellectually astute with an authoritative grasp of Christian history, which he compartmentalised for the lecture and tutorial room, saving other compartments for his *joie de vivre*. Perhaps paradoxically, his life did not appear to be governed by Christian spirituality. He enjoyed much that a judgemental church minister would disapprove of, although those that knew him well found him spiritually refreshing. It didn't matter whether he was discussing football, theology, the best way to make an omelette, or the weather, he always conveyed a sense of the deeper meaning of things.

Flo's sense of mischief had not diminished overnight. If anything it had been refreshed by sleep. "This morning," he announced portentously, "we shall not only discuss, we shall actually view Jesus' crown of thorns." Martin and Pamela were no longer so easily caught out.

Martin replied with an amused "Oh yes?"

"Yes, indeed," replied Flo "together with the sacred ibis, the jade vine, tarantula spiders, gigantic Amazonian fish and assorted plants and creatures of the humid tropics and the desert. Oh, I nearly forgot, the crocodiles have not yet arrived."

"In other words," replied Martin, "we are going to visit the widely advertised *Tropical World,* which I know is only a short walk from here."

"Right first time," replied Flo, "I had forgotten you know Leeds fairly well. Wait a minute though: Tropical World didn't exist in your student days."

"Indeed it did not," replied Martin, "I researched it on line yesterday before we set out, and I must say it sounds fascinating." Before Flo could reply, Martin added: "And I'm also looking forward to discussing my proposed sabbatical. I'm anxious for your advice on getting abreast of the latest research on the early history of Christianity."

"Alright!" exclaimed Flo, "If you insist, we'll start the discussion before we visit Tropical World. Or rather, I will start with a mini lecture. I've been preparing it ever since your first post card. Here we go then." And with those words, Flo fixed his audience of two with a look that Martin well remembered from his student days: a clever fusion of a smile and a frown.

"Unlike George Fox, founder of the Quakers (It's those Quakers again. Didn't the bishop mention Quakers in his first discussion with Martin?), Jesus did not write a journal. It was left to others to report what he did and said. Some of those reports of his actions and words were incorporated into the canon of the New Testament. Others were not; for example, the Gospel of Thomas was not accepted by the early compilers of the Bible. All these biographers of Jesus were human beings, of course. As we well know, we human beings have many shortcomings. Might some of them have misreported or exaggerated their picture of Jesus? Might they even have issued false reports, in order to promote their own view of the Christian faith? Mistakes, exaggeration and lies are well known in journalism and politics, so why not in religion?"

It was a rhetorical question, but Martin wanted to reinforce Flo's argument by offering a cynical answer.

"We wouldn't expect it to happen because the ethical and moral foundation of Christianity excludes exaggeration and lying."

"Oops!" declared Flo, "You missed it. I'm sure I saw one of those animals that live in a sty fly past the window just now. Don't you find it troubling that careful analysis of the scriptures has revealed at least five different Jesuses? I say *at least,* because five of these different characters are based on worthy scholarship, whereas there are still others for which there are less convincing arguments. Faced with this puzzle, Christian ministers of all denominations have a standard reply. *Ah!* They say, *Jesus was all things to all men.* And their congregations are supposed to be satisfied. But throughout history, being all things to all men is associated with duplicity. Surely, we can't accuse Jesus of being duplicitous! So perhaps some of his biographers told lies. Dear Martin, what are we to think!? Thank goodness for those wise words of George Fox, founder of the Quakers (yes, it's those Quakers again): *Christ saith this, and the apostles say this, but what canst thou say?* I strongly recommend that you adopt that Quaker approach, step outside the box of traditional Church teaching, and try to get to grips with what really happened at the beginning. By that, I mean the *very* beginning. Yes, I agree, the first four centuries do require further investigation, but you should concentrate on the way it all started. What was it that triggered the great movement that became known as Christianity? In Advent, as Christmas approaches, Sunday school teachers may talk to their young flock about what happened in those first few years or even months around year nought, implying that Christianity was launched by the birth of Jesus. For a very young audience, excited by the approach of Christmas, that quaint story serves well. But it's rubbish. The origins of Christianity must be sought in the centuries long before the year nought; and I said origins, not origin."

Martin remained silent. When it came to fact as opposed to faith, Flo probably knew as much as, if not more than, many Vatican scholars about those first four centuries of Christianity. All his teaching life, he had lectured, tutored and written on that subject. Martin's request for a sabbatical to study the early history of Christianity was designed to disguise the fact that he doubted the nature of the biblical Jesus and wanted to study the very beginnings of Christianity, exactly as exhorted by Flo. Was it telepathy? Probably not. It was far more likely that Flo was shrewd and insightful and knew what Martin was thinking.

The conversation was developing exactly as Martin would have wished. To keep it on the right track, he asked: "Who are these five different Jesuses that you mentioned?" Flo was enjoying himself, and if Martin had not asked he would have told him anyway.

"Different authors have studied his words and actions in the New Testament, with the result that he is variously described as a wise man with an ostentatious contempt for riches; a liberal interpreter of Mosaic law, or, if you like, a broad-minded Pharisee; a rather individualistic but orthodox, charismatic Hasid; an exorcist and faith healer; a zealous priest stirring up revolution against the Romans; a radical community organiser with proto-feminist views; or was he a prophet of doom declaring the end is near and urging repentance? All these analyses are the result of honest, disciplined scholarship. And there are more; for example a newspaper columnist recently described him as a Jewish socialist revolutionary. Preachers feel challenged to find ways of sermonising away these differences, resulting in the claim that Jesus is all things to all men. Alleluia! I'm sorry to disagree. As I said before, being all things to all men is not a noble quality. Put simply, there appear to be too many Jesuses to make sense. And to cap it all, a recent publication by a well-known author bears the provocative title *The Good Man Jesus and the Scoundrel Christ*. Furthermore, on the subject of all things to all men, the Reverend Paul Oestreicher has pointed out that Jesus was unmarried, which is unusual for a Jewish rabbi – assuming he *was* a rabbi – and he has proposed that Jesus was gay, as evidenced by his special love for the disciple John. Now that would really make him all things to all men! On the other hand, Oestreicher either hadn't heard, or preferred to ignore, recent claims that Jesus *was* married, based on a papyrus fragment in the possession of Doctor King of Harvard. It is written in Coptic and contains a passage in which Jesus refers to *my wife,* whom he identifies as Mary Magdalene. I don't need to tell you that the subject of whether Jesus was gay, a bachelor, or married opens up a whole new field of time-wasting controversy".

"Such confusion!" exclaimed Pamela, "And it certainly has its funny side. By the way, while it's still on my mind, and excuse my ignorance, but what's a Hasid?" "He's a member of an extremely devout mystical Jewish sect," replied Flo. "Thank you for that," said Pamela, "What's more, you pointed out that Jesus can be interpreted as a prophet of doom, urging repentance on everyone. Don't you think this attitude possibly colours all that Jesus is reported to have done and said. He was wrong, of course, because we are all still here and history has taken its course. Wars have happened; empires have grown and fallen, and humanity is still here. The end wasn't near, so Jesus got it wrong."

"Well, Martin, how about that?" enquired Flo, "Do you think you could stand before your congregation when you're about the deliver a sermon, and exclaim *Jesus got it wrong!*?" "One day," replied Martin, "I might do just that, but I must think about it first." "A wonderfully political answer," teased Flo, "And you must agree that Pamela has a point. So much of the New Testament is coloured by the belief that the end is near. And yes, she was right when she said that discussion of the nature of Jesus has its funny side. Sadly, few Christians, clergy or lay persons, can handle the resulting confusion and they refuse to admit it exists; instead, they peer studiously through their bifocals, assume an air of gravitas, and explain that Jesus is all things to all men, whereas, since Jesus never wrote anything, any report about his sexuality or married status only reflects how Christian writers thought he was, or – and this is important – how they wanted him to be. Since all Christian preachers use Jesus to illustrate their sermons, he has by now become a marriage guidance counsellor, a down-and-out selling the Big Issue, and, doubtless, a street cleaner who tidies up after everyone, thereby making the world a better place. He's like a blank page upon which you write your own story. Do you find that shocking?" Martin gulped. He still had no idea how far Flo had guessed the truth behind his request for a sabbatical. Then he recalled the bishop's response, also shrewd and knowing. Was Martin far more transparent than he thought?

"Well, yes, it is rather shocking. At least, I can see what you are getting at. My congregation in Herefordshire would find it very shocking indeed." At this point Flo displayed the first signs of exasperation. It took Martin back to the tutorial room of his student days, when Flo would grimace at a poor or irrelevant answer. Flo had never raised his voice; he just changed his facial expression and the melody of his words. And he did it now. It was just like old times.

He replied: "You know as well as I that the blind faith of your congregation is irrelevant. This is a private discussion between you and me, notwithstanding your dear wife who constitutes an audience of one. Now let me shock you further. Jesus is more than a blank page for writing your own story. Two thousand years ago, he started as a blank page, upon which many wrote their own stories."

Startled by Flo's mini outburst, Martin had no time to gather his wits before Flo suddenly changed his attitude. Within the time it takes to utter a sigh, Flo stopped and focused an intense, solicitous stare, first on Martin then on Pamela, switching his eyes backward and forward between his two guests, as if watching a tennis match. Flo's hair was nearly white, which was unsurprising for his age, but his eyebrows were still as dark, perhaps darker than twenty years earlier, and drawn together by his intense gaze they added to the melodrama of the moment.

Martin glanced at Pamela. The look on her face showed that she also was anxiously waiting to hear what Flo would say next. They were both waiting for a revealing statement that would amplify the preceding conversation, or perhaps they expected a fitting piece of deep philosophy. Whatever they were expecting, they were unprepared for the question that Flo uttered, still switching his searching look alternately from one face to the other.

"What constitutes a perfect murder?" Pamela and Martin glanced quickly at one another then back at Flo. As Martin opened his mouth to speak Flo silenced him with a hand gesture.

"Sorry to shock you with such a dramatic change of subject. I assure you it is relevant; at least I fear it might be. I'll explain in a moment. First, let me return to my question. What *does* constitute a perfect murder?"

Pamela was speechless. Martin needed time to think, so he parried the question with "Murder is evil, so it can never be perfect in the eyes of the Lord. Perfection resides only in charity, love and forgiveness."

Flo gestured impatiently: "Okay Martin, you're not sermonising your parishioners. You know full well what I mean. What would be a perfect murder from the standpoint of a murderer?"

Chastened by Flo's impatient response, Martin replied: "I suppose it's a murder that the murderer gets away with."

Flo threw up his hands in triumph and shouted: "Of course, the murderer must get clean away with it!"

Pamela found these exchanges between the two men amusing. She felt she ought to contribute, so she lamely interjected: "Is there any such thing as a perfect murder?" Flo uttered a yell of triumph. Martin and Pamela looked anxiously at one another, both wondering if this visit had been a bad idea from the start.

"Pamela, it is impossible to answer that question. Yet it is the very question that I must ask you to consider, if only to confirm that we cannot answer it."

Was Flo losing his reason? Perhaps he was becoming intellectually silly, due to the lack of academic challenge during his years of retirement, combined with the inevitable ageing process. Silly or not, Flo now had command of the conversation. They could only wait for his next move.

"A perfect murder must not be recognisable as murder. It must be immediately obvious that the death is an accident or due to natural causes. There must not be the faintest suspicion of murder. The death must be formally recorded on a doctor's death certificate as heart failure, cerebral haemorrhage, or whatever, then consigned to history and forgotten, except by grieving relatives and friends, who must clear up the victim's affairs and put fresh flowers on the grave until they also are environmentally recycled."

Martin almost asked whether the flowers or the grieving relatives would be recycled, but thought better of it.

"In other words," ventured Pamela, "The perfect murder is one in which the murderer gets away with it."

"Wrong!" exclaimed Flo. My whole point is there must not be the slightest suspicion that murder has been committed. If murder is suspected, even with no evidence whatsoever pointing to a culprit or motive, then the murderer will get away with it, but it is not a perfect murder."

Martin was wondering what on earth all this had to do with Jesus, but he daren't ask. Instead he responded with: "Therefore, in a perfect murder, only the murderer knows it is murder and no other person has the slightest suspicion. A perfect murder is therefore a purely philosophical concept. There is no way of knowing how many murders are perfect and indeed, whether a perfect murder has ever been committed."

"Correct! A purely philosophical concept; an ideal subject for time-wasting discussion. Let me now inject a little realism into this purely philosophical concept. How would you define a *nearly* perfect murder?"

Martin and Pamela no longer felt mystified and uncomfortable. It seemed that Flo was having fun, although they couldn't see where it was leading.

"A nearly perfect murder – uhm?" mused Pamela: "Well, I recall an Agatha Christie thriller entitled *Murder is Easy*. If I remember correctly, someone, probably Miss Marple, says *Murder is easy, provided no-one thinks it's murder*, or words to that effect.

"Precisely," remarked Flo, "My point exactly. But now we're talking about a *nearly* perfect murder."

"Sorry," said Pamela, "but you have to admit that Agatha Christie knew a lot about murder. Anyway, she isn't here to help us, so as the only female representative, I must take over. I would therefore suggest that for a murder to be nearly perfect, someone, sooner or later, would realise or at least suspect it was a murder. However, the identity of the murderer would not be known. Even if someone was suspected there would be insufficient evidence for a conviction. For one reason or another he would be beyond the reach of the law; he might even be dead."

Flo looked searchingly at Martin. "Do you accept your dear wife's definition of a nearly perfect murder?"

"She assumes that the murderer is a man. It could be a woman." "Yes, yes, of course; a Freudian slip that must be corrected, but it has no relevance to the heart of this question."

"Okay, I stand corrected. May I continue?" asked Pamela with mock meekness. Flo nodded his assent. "Haven't we forgotten something? Flo and Martin waited for her to explain.

"Motive!" exclaimed Pamela: "Why has no-one mentioned motive?"

"Of course," began Flo.... Pamela cut him short: "And what about means: poison, blunt instrument, electrocution; isn't that also relevant?"

"I agree," said Flo, "Some means of murder may be easier to conceal than others, so I suppose the means of dispatching the victim is a practical consideration for the murderer. Far more important, however, is motive. You are the first to mention it. It may be the key to the difference between our hypothetical perfect murder and our nearly perfect murder. So tell me: why have three of my former students died, apparently by accident, while researching the early history of the Christian story?"

## CHAPTER 5

So this was what Flo had been leading up to. He said it quietly with no dramatic inflection in his voice, which made his question all the more ominous. Pamela and Martin exchanged puzzled looks. They were on a knife edge of indecision. Was this a joke, or should they express horror at the loss of his former students? Martin decided on a light-hearted approach.

"I know you didn't get on with all your students, but I never imagined you would go to those lengths. Don't worry, they will never catch you. If I'm next on your list, thank you for warning me. At least I know the muesli and the coffee were not spiked this morning because all three of us had the same breakfast."

"Martin, my dear Martin, I'm serious. I may also be utterly wrong. I freely confess that during my academic career I have on occasions been wrong. You will remember that minor scandal, during your second year at the university, when my mistranslation of a sentence in a Gnostic Gospel was missed in the peer review and was eventually published."

Martin smiled at the memory. Certain censorious members of the academic establishment had expressed their disgust and disapproval, whereas all Flo's students and close associates quickly forgave him, delighted with the funny side of his error. The sentence should have read: *The light had no father and the light had no mother; it was not born; it was the beginning of all that began.* Flo had rendered it: *To begin with, the orphaned light was illegitimate.* Martin still suspected that Flo had purposely invented the mistranslation, in order to inject humour and to allow certain pompous members of the faculty to live up to their cartoon reputation with their high-minded disapproval. Perhaps not. Even Flo would not go that far. Or would he? Was Flo serious or was his present apparent preoccupation with murder part of an elaborate joke?

"I hope I'm wrong," continued Flo, "I'm worried. I wonder if you remember the three students in question? You couldn't have known John Needham; he left three years before you arrived. He never sought ordination and he joined a research team in the Middle East that was looking into the origins of the Armenian Church. Then there was Brian Fenna; I'm sure you remember *him*." Martin nodded in agreement. Who could forget Fenna? A keen member of the rowing club with a consuming passion for snooker and beer. In fact a consuming passion for many things except theology. Or so it seemed, for much to everyone's surprise, he left the university with a glowing first class degree. "And did you know Pinda, a rather small fellow with a moustache?"

"Of course, he was in the year behind me. I knew him quite well. We always seemed to gravitate to one another at mealtimes in the student union. After my graduation I lost track of him. If I remember correctly, during the summer vacations he went cycling in remote parts of India and the Middle East. He never talked much about those expeditions, but he must have had quite a tale to tell."

"That's him, or *was* him," replied Flo, "He went to work at an archaeological site in the Sudanese desert, studying the remains of an ancient Coptic Church near the fourth cataract on the River Nile. As for Fenna: he obtained funding from some historical society to spend a year of study in Israel, helping to piece together the tattered fragments of the Dead Sea Scrolls. All three were healthy and physically fit. None had ever taken, let alone abused, recreational drugs. Pinda and Needham were even averse to alcohol. Fenna, of course, liked his pint, but he was not a drunkard. All three died as a result of taking large doses of LSD. In each case, in a drug-induced stupor, they tried to fly from the top of a very high building. Analysis of blood samples showed the presence of LSD and the local police were able to close each file with the incontestable verdict that death was due to the use of hallucinogenic drugs.  Since the conviction that one can fly is a common hallucination under the influence of LSD, these were easy cases for the respective police forces and their associated justice systems.  Three separate investigations in three different cities – Khartoum, Tel Aviv and Jerusalem – and the same verdict each time.  Apparently no-one bothered to find out where the LSD had come from.  If the victims had been poor local people, their deaths would probably not have been brought to the attention of the local police.  Since they were visiting British academics, the police were obliged to do their duty and report their investigations to the British embassies.

The conversation had now acquired a level of seriousness that transcended the simple reaction of 'Oh, how awful!' Flo was suddenly silent, willing his guests to react.  It's a common police interview technique.  The interrogator falls silent until the prisoner can no longer stand the suspense and suddenly blurts out useful information.

Pamela was the first to weaken. "Well, they can't be perfect murders, because you suspect they *were* murders.  Since the cases are closed, the culprit in each case has got away with it, so we must call them *nearly* perfect murders.  Am I right?"

"Please tell me I'm utterly wrong!" exclaimed Flo, "I feel there are too many factors linking all three deaths.  *First,* all three had studied the same course at the same university.  *Second,* I happen to know that all three were keenly interested in the early history of Christianity.  Needham and Fenna were engaged in field work relevant to that period of Christian history.  Pinda's extinct Church near the fourth cataract of the Nile was a branch of a Church established in the Middle Ages at a place called Faras in northern Sudan.  *Third,* in my opinion, none of them would have been idiotic enough to take LSD; that was completely out of character.  *Fourth,* they were known to each other and kept in contact by e-mail. I know this because their possessions were eventually returned to their families, via the British Council. None was married so their belongings, including their laptops, were returned to their parents. All three sets of parents passed their laptops on to me, with the hope that the record of their sons' work would benefit the study of Christian history. I'm delighted to say that the information on those laptops did indeed make a contribution to biblical scholarship, but that is not what I want to talk about. Their laptops still contained the e-mails they had sent to one another before they were murdered – oops, I'm jumping the gun – before they died trying to fly from the tops of high buildings. Those e-mails make very ominous reading. They strongly support the conclusion that my three former students were murdered."

This brought an immediate response from Pamela: "Before you tell us why you're so sure they were murdered, might I remind you that a moment ago I suggested that motive was important in this discussion of murder. You agreed, even saying it was the key to recognising a nearly perfect murder. So, come on, what was the motive?"

"I think it possible they had discovered a hitherto closely guarded secret regarding the origins of Christianity. A secret, which if revealed, would cause deep embarrassment to practically every Christian denomination on this planet, with the potential to destroy Christianity itself. Most so-called Christians have lost sight of the Christian message of love and peace, one of the most beautiful messages ever brought to mankind. Unfortunately, practically every denomination attaches more importance to its own hierarchical structure, its traditions and its rituals, than to the Christian message. So they would feel bewildered and offended if their received history were found to be in error. It's the problem of tradition, which traps all human activity and thought on a knife edge. "I don't follow the knife edge

CHAPTER 5

metaphor," interjected Martin. "What I mean," replied Flo, "is that, on the one hand, tradition is a cohesive force that unites human society, while on the other hand it can also become an alternative to historical truth and an obstruction to change."

Martin and Pamela smiled and nodded to indicate that Flo should continue. Flo needed a break and suggested coffee. "Did you know," enquired Flo, "that instant coffee is made from inferior quality coffee beans?" Without waiting for an answer, Flo explained that coffee fruits rarely ripen all at the same time on the branch that bears them. The pickers take the ripe red berries and leave the green berries to finish ripening. Inevitably, some berries escape the picking cycle, ripen then become old and wizened. These are taken for instant coffee. "That is why I buy ground coffee and serve my guests the real thing. I hope you approve."

"Just like old times. We always had a coffee break in your tutorials. In those days it was instant coffee."

"And I didn't serve ginger biscuits," laughed Flo, handing around the biscuit tin. "Alright, I'm suitably restored and we can continue. Where were we?"

"True history versus tradition, or something like that," replied Pamela.

"Yes, of course. Well, even the Quakers (there we go again!) might feel uneasy with a rewrite of Christian history, although I'm sure they would consider it carefully and with open minds, at least their more free-thinking and enlightened members would." "So what is this dangerous secret?" ventured Pamela. "I do not know," replied Flo in a tired voice, "I simply do not know. I would like you to read the e-mails that I found on those laptops."

Martin was only half listening to Flo and Pamela. He was remembering how he had doubted the bishop's claim that some parts of the Christian story might have been misreported, and he remembered the bishop's easy explanation

59

of how that could have happened, with the shocking suggestion that an early prearranged misrepresentation of Christianity's birth had given it an advantage over other faiths. Martin still wondered what the bishop had meant by this. Now Flo was implying that his three ex-students had died because they knew too much. Was there a connection? Martin felt uneasy. Was his plan to study early Christian history likely to endanger his life? Was Flo trying to warn him?

"Martin, are you listening!?" Pamela almost had to shout to get Martin's attention. "You were miles away. That's not very polite. Flo is showing us those e-mails." Flo burst out laughing. "So you still call me Flo. That's the first time either of you has used my old nickname since you arrived. Pamela suppressed a giggle and everyone was grateful, especially Martin, for the relief of the light-hearted interlude. Their conversation had been getting rather heavy and ominous.

Flo continued: "I went to the Grand Theatre recently to see Opera North's modernised version of Carmen. You may think it a little odd that I really enjoy listening to the orchestra tuning up. I always have. I still remember a performance of the Magic Flute in Vienna. My wife and I were attending an ecumenical conference in Austria and we were lucky enough to get tickets to the opera. My goodness, that seems like a hundred years ago!"

For a moment, Flo was lost in his memories of the Viennese opera. "I remember the thrill of hearing the pit orchestra practising and warming up their instruments. The string players listening for the correct accord between the E and A strings, the A and D strings and the D and G strings, then playing those pairs in ascending order so that it sounded like the introduction to an American square dance. The clarinets – oh that wonderful woody sound of a clarinet – chasing scales in different keys. A trumpet sounding an impromptu fanfare, echoed in a more mellow tone by a French horn. Not to be left out, the tympani tuned and tested with rhythms that could belong anywhere between Tchaikovsky and the African jungle."

Not for the first time that evening, Martin and Pamela wondered what on earth Flo was leading up to. Flo, in his impish way, knew this and purposely kept them wondering. "Don't you also feel that sense of tension, that sense of anticipation, when an orchestra is warming up?" "Well, yes, I suppose so. I can appreciate what you mean," ventured Martin. "Well, at that performance of Carmen at the Grand, it suddenly occurred to me that the early years of Christianity are analogous to the warming up of an orchestra. No analogy is perfect and I suppose this one breaks down more often than most. Please bear with me. You see, we tend to think that Christianity started in the year nought or thereabouts, when a certain person called Jesus is supposed to have been born. However, the Christianity that *we* are familiar with started some three hundred years later, when the Romans adopted Christianity and made it the religion of the Roman Empire. All our religious practices and church traditions date from that time, not least the creed that we recite every Sunday. I might also add that the symbol of the cross was not adopted by Christians until that time. In other words, the conductor appeared in the fourth century AD, took a bow and tapped his baton. The orchestra sat up straight, took notice and began to follow the score."

Pamela was intrigued by Flo's analogy with the orchestra, but she had heard the story already from Martin. "I love the analogy," exclaimed Pamela, "And Martin has already lectured me at length on the history. By the way, he insisted that the Romans hijacked Christianity, rather than adopting it."

"By all means, let's say they hijacked Christianity, but personally I prefer to say they adopted Christianity because the Christians – that is one particular group of Christians – were only too pleased to be adopted."

"Is it fair to say the early Christians had no score to play from and were simply making experimental warming up noises?" asked Martin with a note of challenge in his voice.

"No, of course it isn't fair, but as I said at the outset, the analogy is imperfect," protested Flo.

"Okay, then who is the conductor?" asked Martin.

"Can't you guess?" retorted Flo.

"I suppose it must be Emperor Constantine," conceded Martin.

"What about the e-mails? We seem to have forgotten them," interjected Pamela, with just a hint of impatience in her voice.

"I've had time to consider these e-mails and to research the background to some of the comments and ideas they contain. I can't deny that I'm deeply worried by what I've found. I may have found an explanation for the deaths of Needham, Pinda and Fenna. Read them for yourselves and let me have your thoughts." Flo brought a manila cardboard wallet from his sideboard and placed it before Martin and Pamela. "These are the printouts of the worrying e-mails. There are others that are unimportant, just chit chat about the weather and the kind of food they were eating, and, by the way, not a single mention of drugs, let alone LSD."

Flo's two guests quickly flicked through the pile to get an overall impression before studying each e-mail. Flo had arranged them in order of their dates, so it was easy to follow the sequence of who had written to whom and the resulting reply. This cursory overview immediately revealed a preoccupation with Hegel.

**Fenna had copied the same e-mail to both Pinda and Needham:** *We should get right outside this stifling world of*

## CHAPTER 5

*biblical scholarship and make a fresh start. Where better to start than with the philosophical school of Hegel?*

**Pinda had replied:** *Agreed, but the Young Hegelians, who came after Hegel, can probably tell us more.*

**Fenna had replied:** *Sorry, I really meant the Young Hegelians, but I thought we might start with the master himself. The young Hegelians did use his approach to philosophy, even though they disagreed with his philosophical conclusions.*

**Needham had written:** *You two are way ahead of me. I tracked down Hegel on the internet. And thank goodness for the internet, which I now look upon as God's gift to all research workers isolated in distant lands. We have stacks of scrolls and ancient manuscripts, but no library within a hundred miles where I might bone up on that old German philosopher called Hegel. After sending you this e-mail I must fetch petrol for the generator. Then I will charge up my laptop's battery, go on line again and, with luck, find out about the Young Hegelians. Better still, just tell me what you are talking about and save me the trouble – please!!*

**Next was the reply from Pinda:** *I thought <u>we</u> were working under difficulties. At least we have generators and ample electricity. OK, to save you a lot of trouble: as a philosophical school the young Hegelians didn't last long – less than twenty years, in fact, from about 1830 to 1848. Among their members were well-known figures like Marx and Engels. Politically they were all very radical. They were deeply involved in defining the role of Christianity in human thought. As I see it, their concern with Christianity did not arise from Christian devotion, but rather from the spirit of 'a wise man knows his enemies.' Worth reading are Strauss' <u>Das Leben Jesu</u> (The life of Jesus) and Feuerbach's*

*Das Wesen des Christentums (The Essence of Christianity). How's your German old man!? Strauss and Feuerbach were radical enough, but I leave you with another of those Young Hegelians, called Bruno Bauer. He proposed that the entire story of Jesus was a myth. He pointed out that prominent historical figures are always widely talked about by their enemies as well as their friends. Jesus is talked about only by the Christians, because Jesus is part of their party line, and he is not mentioned by anyone else. So, what do you think? Can we call ourselves Young Hegelians?*

**At this point Fenna had chipped in with:** *He's right John, every word of it. But No we can't call ourselves Young Hegelians, because, after all, we are convinced Christians, even though our thoughts on Christian history are – what shall I call them – iconoclastic, ultra-radical, potential dynamite? Dear old Flo might have labelled them 'offensive to the establishment.'*

Flo was in his kitchen, washing up their coffee cups and the breakfast things. Martin called to him: "Dear old Flo, what do you make of this preoccupation with the Young Hegelians?"

"So you have read that far! *Old* is right, of course, and I'm grateful for the *dear*. More important, read on until you come to Fenna's encounter with the representative of the International Forum for Early Christian History (IFECH)." They didn't read on, but shuffled through the e-mails until they came across the first mention of the International Forum.

**Fenna to Needham and Pinda:** ... *met an odd sort of chap today from Jerusalem. He's a member of IFECH. No, I hadn't heard of it either. Apparently it's an acronym for International Forum for Early Christian History. I spent a* *very pleasant evening with him. He had an engaging and persuasive manner and before I could stop myself I told him about our encounter with the Russian in Cairo. He suggested the Russian was romancing and trying to impress us. Being a committed Christian, he commented on the morality of such drunken outpourings. I also told him about our evidence for you-know-what, and our plans to publish and organise workshops when we get back to the UK. He seemed impressed by our work and asked if we might be interested in joining an archaeological team in the Sinai, and he stressed that the work would be well paid. He said he would like to meet you both and would be travelling to meet you at your respective research sites in the next few weeks. We intend to meet up again before he leaves. Will let you know if I get any more information.*

**Needham to Fenna:** *Rather you hadn't told him about the Russian or even the you-know-what, but I suppose there's no harm done. What Boris told us might even be true, so we would be well advised to forget we ever heard about it. Or should we tell the authorities? Personally, I think it was all an alcohol-inspired fantasy.*

**Pinda to Fenna:** *If we do tell the authorities, which authorities would you choose? The British embassy I suppose, but let's forget it. Can't wait to meet your friend from IFECH.*

**Needham to Fenna and Pinda:** *He's arrived. Yes, he does seem a bit odd, but he's good company. He asked a lot of questions about Boris and about the you-know-what. I felt he was interested in what Boris had told us, but I'm probably imagining it. I'm sure he's really interested in our work on Christian history and wants to recruit us for archaeological work in the Sinai. Wouldn't it be great if all three of us could get together on the same project in the Sinai!*

**Pinda to Needham and Fenna:** *The man from IFECH is now camped barely fifty yards from our research site. Odd isn't the word. What is this IFECH organisation? Does it have free passage anywhere? I had enough trouble getting visas and passes to work in the Sudanese desert. He's from Israel for goodness sake, and therefore supposedly banned from this Islamic country, but he simply flies into Khartoum with no problem and comes straight out to our desert research camp with a personal driver. Is it money or shady political influence? Notwithstanding all that, he is, as you say, good company. I dined with him last night at his camp (he even has a cook and servants bless your life!) and I'm invited again tonight. Yes, he has dangled the possibility of all three of us working together in the Sinai. It's certainly an attractive idea. And by the way, he said the pay was generous!*

That was the last e-mail in the pile. There was no reply or any other e-mail communication from Needham or Fenna.

"We've read them all," called Pamela.

Gently, but rather ominously, Flo replied: "Now look at the dates! "When did Fenna first write to the others about meeting the man from IFECH?"

"The fourth of June," answered Pamela.

"He died on the sixth of June," stated Flo quietly and without emotion. "When did Needham report this man's arrival?"

On the ninth of June," answered Pamela, quickly sifting through the e-mails to check the date.

"He died on the eleventh of June. And when did Pinda report that the man had arrived?" "Don't tell me, he died two days later," suggested Pamela. "Actually, he died three days later, in Khartoum," replied Flo, "Presumably because there were no high buildings to fly from in their desert camp."

The quiet and ominous tone adopted by Flo was suddenly interrupted by an explosive outburst from Martin:

# CHAPTER 5

"For goodness sake, who was this representative of IFECH? What was his name? What was his position in IFECH? None of the e-mails mentions his name."

Still outwardly calm, but with tension in his voice, Flo replied: "IFECH doesn't exist. I've checked thoroughly. It's a fictitious organisation, or perhaps a sinister secret organisation known only to its members. Either way, it adds to the circumstantial evidence for foul play. Who knows what lies and clever means of persuasion he might have used to lure my three former students to their deaths."

"That's a sudden leap of reasoning," exclaimed Pamela, "You are now saying they were definitely murdered and this IFECH representative was the murderer." With a sigh of resignation, she added: "Nevertheless, I have to agree. It looks bad, especially since this mystery man was apparently also a fraud and a liar."

"Under different circumstances, we might treat this situation like a whodunit entitled *Murder in the Desert*. But it isn't fiction and we are rather more than observers or spectators. We are involved," observed Martin. "Certainly, I feel involved," ventured Flo, "because I taught the victims and my interest in their deaths has led me to believe that they were indeed murdered."

"What about me," asked Martin plaintively, "I could easily be next in line for leaving this world on an LSD-based flight of fancy!"

"Aha!" burst out Flo triumphantly, "so you have guessed what they meant by their mysterious *you-know-what*, the news they were intending to break to the world, the subject on which they intended to organise workshops!" Martin took a deep breath and slowly answered Flo's implied query: "Without their presumed murders, their *you-know-what* might have been taken as a shared joke, some relatively unimportant and amusing discovery about early Christian history. You could imagine many possibilities, for example

67

Prophet X had an affair with the wife of Prophet Y. But I don't think so. I have a terrible sinking feeling they had obtained evidence for a faith-shattering secret of Christianity. It is the same secret that I also suspect and wish to investigate. It is my reason for wanting a sabbatical, and this is the first time I have openly said so."

"I'm pretty certain I know what the secret is, but I will not blurt it out. It is perhaps as well to leave it unblurted." Flo was delighted with his amusing past participle of his newly coined verb. It triggered a smile in both his guests, despite their shared apprehension that this tale of biblical research and murder was not yet finished.

"Alright then, I will blurt it," volunteered Martin, "I suspect that the character of Jesus as portrayed in the Bible, is a myth. And it seems I've been beaten to it. According to Pinda, one of those so-called Young Hegelians decided Jesus was a myth in the middle of the nineteenth century. I get the feeling that many philosophers, theologians and biblical scholars reached this conclusion long before I did, perhaps as early as the Reformation; perhaps even before the Reformation, but they kept quiet for fear of being burnt at the stake."

"Alright, you've said it," sighed Flo, "For the time being at least, I advise you to keep quiet about it. I believe, as you do, that the biblical Jesus doesn't stand up to scrutiny. I came to this conclusion years ago. It wasn't out of cowardice that I decided to keep quiet and not rock the boat. Rather it was the realisation that so many Christians are unable to appreciate that the historical figure of Jesus is far less powerful and meaningful than the metaphor or spirit of Jesus that resides in our hearts. Well, perhaps there was an element of cowardice in my decision. Had I spoken out, I would have offended the establishment and jeopardised my promotion from assistant lecturer to lecturer, from lecturer to senior lecturer and finally to professor. In retirement I am

## CHAPTER 5

now free from these constraints. I no longer have to keep quiet about it, but I advise you to do so; otherwise you could find yourself out of a job."

"Then why have you kept quiet about it in your retirement, until now that is?" complained Martin.

"Very true. Put it down to inertia, even a lapse of interest. In any case, my priorities changed when I retired. Gardening seemed more important than theology, and my wife's death put me in a mental turmoil. However, my dear Martin, that has all changed. You've renewed my interest in this problem and provided the impetus I've been waiting for. My role will be to protect you from the arrogance of the establishment and from IFECH. I'm excited by the prospect of challenging the received version of Christian history. It will upset the established Church; that's a pity. Most of all, I look forward to upsetting those evangelical born-again-Christians." Martin couldn't see how Flo, getting on in years and residing in a genteel suburb, could protect him from anything, except in an advisory capacity.

"Just a minute," interjected Pamela, "Didn't you say that IFECH doesn't exist?"

"I use IFECH as a metaphor for whatever skulduggery resulted in the deaths of my three former students."

Both Martin and Pamela nodded to show they understood.

"So where do we go from here?" asked Pamela.

# Chapter 6

*Hubberholme is an ancient,*
*secluded village in the Yorkshire Dales.*
*Its Norman church is the resting place*
*of the ashes of writer and playwright J.B. Priestley,*
*who described the village as*
*the 'smallest, pleasantest place in the world.*

"From here we go to Tropical World. One advantage of living in a suburb of this big city is the proximity of Tropical World. It's both entertaining and educational, doesn't cost much to go in, and it's the perfect place to take visitors after breakfast. We will then have lunch at a rather nice restaurant by the lake in the park."

"Good thinking!" offered Martin, "We need time out before we continue this discussion of Christian history."

"Isn't it more than that?" asked Pamela with a worried expression, "Surely, we have to decide how Martin will proceed with his study of Christian history, faced with the possibility of murder by IFECH."

"Exactly. Now get your shoes on, forget about Jesus and IFECH, and get outside in the fresh air."

Half an hour later they were admiring a pair of black swans on a small canal near the entrance to Tropical World.

"Interesting creatures," commented Martin with a knowledgeable air. "They are native to Australia and their breeding cycle is synchronised with the seasons of the southern hemisphere. When a zoo, or in this case a public park, transports them to the northern hemisphere they don't adjust, so their goslings hatch in the autumn with winter approaching and food in short supply. Other animals, including birds, change the timing of their breeding cycle when they're moved from south to north or vice versa. Black swans don't; they can't adapt."

# CHAPTER 6

"How do you know all this?" enquired Flo.

In addition to my A-level studies in the physical sciences, I also used to read a lot of biology because I found it interesting."

Flo remarked that the swans reminded him of many members of the Church hierarchy: propagandised from birth with a story and a creed and unable to adapt their thinking to any new revelation.

Pamela and Martin sighed with exasperation and started to walk away. Flo apologised and promised not to mention church, religion, or Jesus again, until they had visited Tropical World and had lunch.

Tropical World lived up to its reputation. Martin continued to reveal his inside knowledge of biology by providing an entertaining and running commentary on the feeding and breeding habits of the various animals. An exotic butterfly settled on Pamela's hand, long enough for Martin to quickly photograph the happy pair with his digital. Flo guided them to a section containing a jade vine, which he claimed was his favourite. It just happened to be in flower, displaying its long, pendulous inflorescences of greenish blue flowers. Martin described the blue as unique; he had never seen that shade of greenish blue before; or had he? Yes, of course, it resembled the blue of nickel sulphate, which he remembered from his days in the chemistry laboratory. Flo and Pamela exchanged amused glances. The early centuries of Christianity were almost forgotten, for the time being at least.

Just before leaving Tropical World, they found themselves in front of a cage containing busy little South American monkeys called Cotton-top Tamarinds *(Saguinus oedipus)*. Martin decided to have the last word: "Remember, dear, when we first moved into the vicarage in Herefordshire? We had had a busy day moving furniture and laying carpets. At about seven in the evening we stopped, had a meal, collapsed on the sofa and listened to a recording of – what was it?"

Rather puzzled, Pamela replied: "I remember; it was *Liebestraum* by Liszt, one of my favourites. Why?"

"Well, these charming little monkeys remind me of that evening when we listened to Liebestraum. Guess why!" Martin looked at both Flo and Pamela, challenging them both to guess why South American monkeys reminded him of Liebestraum.

"No idea. Please tell us," implored Pamela."

"Look at their long hair hanging down the backs of their heads. Don't they remind you of someone?"

"Well, actually, no, they don't," replied Flo.

"Nor me neither," replied Pamela rather impatiently.

"Franz Liszt had long hair like that. That is why these monkeys are also called Liszt monkeys and Liszt composed Liebestraum."

"You are wasted in the Church," observed Flo, "With such erudition, you would shine in a pub quiz; let's go and find lunch."

They emerged from the artificial heat and humidity of Tropical World into a cool and overcast early afternoon of late April. Ideal weather for walking; which was just as well, since to reach the lakeside restaurant they had to cross what was reputedly the largest of all the municipal Victorian parks. Their hike took a good twenty minutes, sharpened their appetite and generated a thirst.

Pamela and Martin were impressed by the immensity of the park. "I came out here once when I was a student," said Martin, "In those days the lakeside restaurant was quite old and tatty. This is magnificent: beautiful design, lots of space, a tempting variety of food and drinks, and a splendid view over the lake."

"It's not just the restaurant that's new," commented Flo. "This end of the lake has been redesigned; rowing boats are no longer for hire and, as you can see, it's a favourite

## CHAPTER 6

gathering place for ducks and swans. We had an anxious time when they dredged the entire lake and renewed the dam, which you can see in the distance over there. After the First World War unexploded munitions were dumped at the end of the lake, just behind the dam, so before the lake could be dredged and the dam rebuilt we were treated to several weeks of bomb retrieval and removal, with bomb disposal experts and police getting in each other's way; it was really quite entertaining."

Flo chose chicken sandwiches with salad. Pamela and Martin chose meat and three veg, which took longer to eat, so Flo was able to dominate the conversation and study his two guests. It was a clever trick. Before replying to a question or making any contribution to the conversation, Martin or Pamela had to finish chewing and swallowing their latest mouthful. By that time, Flo had developed the conversation further to suit his own purpose. Black swans, tropical butterflies, the jade vine, Liszt monkeys and all the other animal and plant attractions of Tropical World, followed by the walk in the park and the enjoyment of a well-earned meal, had all served well to divert their minds from their breakfast and coffee morning conversation. How much longer could they resist talking about Martin's sabbatical? While Pamela and Martin were still eating, Flo guided their one-sided exchanges, little by little, back to Christian history and the deaths of his three ex-students.

Flo suddenly commented: "I don't believe in astrology – " Before Flo could continue, Martin interrupted him with: "You were about to say that some coincidences can't be explained, except by the intercession of mysterious forces. Am I right?"

"You took the words right out of my mouth. Of course I don't believe in the existence of mysterious forces and my mention of astrology was meant to be ironic. That said, it really is an amazing coincidence that while I'm trying to analyse and explain the deaths of three former students, who died while researching early Christianity, I receive a letter from another former student, asking to visit me for advice on the study of early Christianity."

"Don't knock astrology, protested Pamela, "There's more between heaven earth and all that, and perhaps this amazing coincidence was generated when your respective guardian heavenly bodies came into alignment." She could no longer keep a straight face and burst out laughing. Her outburst caused the occupants of nearby tables to turn and stare, providing a timely warning that they were not alone and that their conversation could conceivably be overheard.

Pamela suggested they started to walk back across the park. "Then we can't be overheard and Flo can then tell us about his coincidence, imagined or otherwise."

"Absolutely," grunted Flo, as they left the restaurant, "Don't look round. We're being followed." Naturally, they both looked round and found a Jack Russell terrier gazing plaintively up at Pamela with an expression on its face that said *I'm lost; please may I come with you?* Meanwhile, its owners were anxiously calling it back.

During the rest of the day, that was the last attempt to inject humour by any member of the trio. During the walk home, back at Flo's house, throughout the afternoon, over tea and up to midnight before they turned in, they explored every possible argument for and against Martin visiting the Middle East, and even whether he should abandon his sabbatical entirely. Many months ago the prospect had been exciting. It now had a different flavour. Would he face the same danger that had led Fenna, Needham, and Pinda to their deaths?

After several hours of discussion, interrupted only briefly by a light tea of sandwiches and cake, they did not take a vote, but Quaker-fashion (Yes, it's George Fox's lot again) they arrived at a consensus. It was left to Pamela to express

# CHAPTER 6

the feeling of the meeting. Reading from her notes, Pamela took the floor: "I'll summarise our discussion and decisions with numbered points. So here we go: point number one:

1) We assume that Fenna, Needham and Pinda *were* murdered and murdered because they were about to reveal an embarrassing secret of Christian history. It may not be the reason for their deaths, but we must err on the side of caution.

2) Martin will proceed with his sabbatical and from now on his stated aim will be to study an aspect of Christian history unconnected with the nature of Jesus. Flo has suggested the fate of the heretics after the Council of Nicaea: did they or didn't they emigrate further east and influence the development of Islam? It is agreed that this provides ample opportunity for debate; in short, an excellent diversionary tactic. Martin's real aim will remain unchanged and concealed.

3) Martin will seek permission to join a research group in the Sudanese desert. There he will take note of any unsolicited information regarding the death of Pinda. Under no circumstances will he expose his interest by actively seeking this information.

4) Martin could easily ask to replace Fenna in the research centre in Israel. That would seem to be the obvious way forward, since the centre in question is a hot bed of biblical research and is endowed with almost unlimited resources. Be that as it may, Flo suggests the research camp in the Sudan because he knows the leader, Doctor Dorothy Scott, and he will therefore be able to recommend Martin personally. More importantly, Doctor Scott is known to have a keen interest in the history of Christianity, to the extent that she has already accumulated considerable evidence throwing doubt on the accuracy of the traditional version.

5) Doctor Scott is investigating the remains of an ancient Coptic place of worship, which belonged to a now extinct

Mediaeval branch of the Coptic Church that existed in the Nile valley. We must anticipate that Martin's bishop may ask what this has to do with very early Christianity. The answer is that Doctor Scott is a recognised international authority on very early Christianity and she has published important accounts of her work on the origins of Christianity."

Flo and Martin inclined their heads to express satisfaction with Pamela's summary. "Let's go to bed," suggested Martin, "We can't achieve much more tonight. And thank you Flo, my dear old teacher, your input has been invaluable."

That was true. Apprehensive about the future and what Martin was really letting himself in for, Martin and Pamela had contributed very little to the lengthy discussion. Flo had taken the initiative and more or less planned the future for them.

Flo delayed their attempt to make for the stairs with: "A final piece of advice before you go to bed."

"Whatever you have to tell us, I honestly feel I already have more than enough to think about."

Flo managed to raise an eyebrow and frown slightly at the same time, as if to say: "Now then Martin, just listen."

Martin sighed with resignation and uttered: "Oh well, so what is it?"

"It, as you call it, is Doctor Dorothy Scott. I know her well enough from various congresses and meetings that we both attended before I retired; well enough, that is, to recommend you to her. Her passion is history. Many in the field do not realise this; they think she is devoted to the study of Christian history because she is a Christian. She is indeed a Christian, but she is primarily interested in historical truth, uncontaminated by its religious overtones. She knows that much of the Christian story has been bent to conform to doctrine and she simply wants to ferret out the truth of how,

## CHAPTER 6

when and where historical events actually happened. Let me put it this way: her interest in history asks: who *was* Jesus? – whereas her Christian faith asks who *is* Jesus? If you get to know her well enough, you will discover her answer to that last question. Your relationship may not develop that far. In many ways she is a formidable intellectual character. Her faith is very private. You will probably only be aware that she has a passion for historical facts. Incidentally, she has had two husbands, both of whom were not tough enough or were insufficiently devoted to spend months on end in the searing heat of the Sudanese desert; so she divorced them both. In other words, don't get off on the wrong foot with Doctor Dorothy Scott. Her closest friends and intimates call her Dotty, but that privilege must be earned. Deference and politeness must be your watchword."

"Jesus!" exclaimed Martin, "Now you tell me."

"I also would like to put in a final word," insisted Pamela.

The two men turned to Pamela. They were unprepared for what she said, and it threw them into a new state of thoughtfulness.

"I can't accept that murder would be committed to prevent the revelation of an embarrassing truth of Christianity. By a madman? Perhaps. I prefer to think that these fraudulent IFECH characters may be bad but not mad. They appear to be organised and know what they are doing. Does anyone know who the Russian is? Those three deaths, murders perhaps, probably have nothing to do with Christian history. Fenna's e-mail mentions the criminality of whatever the Russian was up to. Perhaps the fraudulent IFECH representative was leading Fenna along by talking about Christianity and archaeology. The deaths of Flo's students may indeed have happened because they knew too much. But what did they know too much about? Perhaps they had learned too much about something from the Russian in

Cairo. It could be that we've been too blinkered in considering the reasons for these murders. We haven't the foggiest idea who or what the Russian was, or what they learned from him." "You are absolutely right," said Flo, "We haven't the foggiest idea. Now I feel ready for bed."

As Flo made to rise, Martin stifled a yawn and said: "I've been meaning to ask, what were they all doing in Cairo anyway?" Flo explained that they had been having a final get-together before flying off to their respective assignments. "They took a Nile cruise, visited Abu Simbel, saw the pyramids and all that sort of thing and I don't know what else. They sent me a post card saying they were enjoying Egypt, that the trip to Abu Simbel had been fascinating and that the main museum in Cairo was full of mummies and daddies: obviously a piece of Fenna's wit, for which I remember him well".

And with that, they all went to bed.

\* \* \*

Next morning, Flo had already set the table with the same healthy breakfast as yesterday plus a large bowl of fruit.

Flo waved them to the table with: "It's a pity you have to leave today. I've so enjoyed your visit. We could have spent the day in town. You would have been interested to see some of the new buildings, as well as visiting the old market. We now have Henry Moor in the art gallery, and the old civic theatre has become the museum, with a fascinating account of the history of Leeds, and very informative displays of ancient civilisations; they even have a real Egyptian mummy."

"What!" exclaimed Martin, "A real live mummy?"

"Exactly," replied Flo. Then with a teasing look at Pamela, he asked: "Do you know the definition of a mummy?"

# CHAPTER 6

"Go on. Tell me!" spluttered Pamela through a mouthful of coffee.

"It's what happens to naughty girls in Egypt."

It struck Pamela that for someone who had spent all his working life as a serious university academic, Flo could be surprisingly silly. But then Pamela had never experienced the childish atmosphere of the male-dominated university senior common room.

Pamela couldn't think of a witty repost, so she expressed her amusement and disgust simultaneously by abruptly changing the subject: "I'm so pleased to have met you at last. Martin has always spoken of you with affection and now I can see why. Thank you for everything. However, our booking for the B&B is for tonight at Kettlewell. So, sadly, we must leave you."

"Not straight away," protested Flo, "You can stay until morning coffee. That will allow us to tie up a few loose ends."

"As far as I can see, I simply have to wait until you hear back from Dotty," interrupted Martin with a straight face, "Then, and only then, can I make definite arrangements to travel."

"Provided she wants you on her team," interjected Flo with an equally straight face.

"Of course," agreed Martin; and with a gesture of finality he turned his attention to his dish of muesli, as if to indicate that all conversation on the subject of his sabbatical was now ended.

Pamela smiled as she witnessed this exchange. Tutor and student were clearly fond and respectful of one another, but preferred to hide their affection with playful male bravado.

Flo was still intent on giving advice and having a say in their itinerary. "Kettlewell is a pretty little place and you could do worse than simply take country walks from there. Please drive further up the valley and visit the church of St

Michael & All Angels at Hubberholme. It dates from the twelfth century and was originally a forest chapel, dedicated to Saint Oswald. It actually has a rood loft and its choir stall and pews were made by the famous Mousy Thompson. J.B.Priestley is buried there."

At the mention of J.B. Priestley, Pamela exclaimed: "Then we really must visit that church. My father was very fond of Priestley, especially *The Good Companions,* which he used to read aloud to me and my mother."

"Well, there you are then. Off you go, forget about Christian history for a few days and enjoy yourselves. But before you forget about Christian history entirely, let me leave you with a piece of philosophical advice."

Martin wondered what gem of wisdom Flo was about to impart. As it turned out, Flo's advice would subsequently colour, inform and challenge Martin's view of his faith for the rest of his life.

"I wave you goodbye and exhort you to adopt the motto of the Age of the Enlightenment," announced Flo in an exaggerated portentous fashion.

"Which was?" enquired Martin.

"Good Heavens, don't you know!?" asked Flo.

Marti shook his head.

"It was *Sapere aude,* meaning DARE TO KNOW!"

"Point taken," chorused Pamela and Martin as they said their final farewells at about eleven o'clock and headed northwards to the Yorkshire Dales and the valley of the River Wharfe.

As promised by Flo, Kettlewell was delightful, while Hubberholme church was, they agreed, a most rewarding experience. They left regretting they would not be able to visit that church for the next Christmas carol service. Everyone they spoke to during their visit to the Dales seemed to regard Christmas at Hubberholme as the highlight of their year. However, this is only mentioned in passing.

## CHAPTER 6

The Yorkshire Dales, one of Britain's greatest treasures, play no further part in the present narrative. Whatever new discoveries Martin may make regarding the first four centuries of Christianity, it can be confidently asserted that the services and ritual at Hubberholme church will remain unchanged for generations to come, because that is how Yorkshire folk like it.

# Chapter 7

When General Gordon was in Khartoum it took several days for news to travel from the Sudan to England. One imagines bare-foot natives running northwards along the banks of the Nile, carrying a letter in a forked stick. Actually, it wasn't that primitive, but it still took a long time, by telegraph, by river boat and by sea.

When Flo corresponded with Doctor Dorothy Scott, their messages travelled at the speed of radio waves between the Sudanese desert and northern England. Bare-foot natives with forked sticks are no match for laptops and e-mail.

They didn't visit Flo on their way home. They cut across country through the Dales until they reached the M6. A loathsome motorway, but then most motorways are. It took them near to Birmingham before continuing further south to the rural tranquillity of Herefordshire.

As he drove, Martin was already rehearsing a sermon based on their visit to Hubberholme church. They arrived home in the late afternoon. It was still light and warm enough to sit in the vicarage garden with tea and cake. They had already talked through the entire trip on the drive home, so there was no need to say much. Pamela stated the obvious: "All we can do now is wait to hear from Flo."

They didn't have to wait long. Martin finished his tea, stretched, and replied: "Yes, I hope Flo doesn't waste any time contacting Doctor Scott. Before we eat I'll download our pictures onto the computer."

As Martin disappeared into the vicarage, Pamela called: "If you're switching on the computer, just see if we have any e-mails." Moments later, Martin called: "Come and look at these e-mails from Doctor Scott!"

The first e-mail read:

*Doctor Willan has recommended you as a replacement for Pinda at my archaeological site. How soon can you*

## CHAPTER 7

*come? My work is sponsored by the British Museum, which relies on the Goethe Institute in Khartoum to sort out local problems. In all your dealings with the Sudanese authorities, use my name and the name of the head of the Goethe Institute, Dr. Hopp, who has been forewarned. Once you are here, everything will be found – accommodation, food, laundry and transport to and from our desert camp and Khartoum. I can't provide funds for travel to and from the Sudan; and you need to arrange your own medical insurance. Regards, Dr. Dorothy Scott (Team leader, Fourth Cataract research programme)*

The second e-mail, obviously the result of a sudden afterthought since it was sent only twenty minutes later, read:

*Fly to Khartoum. Dr. Hopp will meet you there. Recommend you do not fly Sudanese Airways, otherwise known here as the Insha'Allah airline (the God willing airline), and for good reason. Play safe and fly British airways. Regards, D.S.*

"Wow," exclaimed Pamela, "It didn't take long for Flo to dust off his laptop and contact Dr, Scott."

"He must have given her my e-mail address and it seems he has given me a good reference. Clearly she's not the sort to waste any time and it didn't take her long to brush away the sand from *her* laptop."

Pamela and Martin were suddenly overcome with the realisation that they would soon be parting, probably for several months. They had never been apart before, except for occasional long weekends when Martin had attended church councils and interfaith meetings in London; even then, Pamela had often gone with him. To be separated for months by thousands of miles was a different proposition.

"Well, off you go, you old desert explorer you. And don't forget to send me a postcard," spluttered Pamela, trying hard to hold back her tears. As they embraced,

Martin added: "I still have to see the bishop and arrange financial support for my travel. Then there will be vaccinations and goodness knows what else, so I won't be leaving very soon. And I won't be sending postcards. As I promised we will keep in touch by e-mail."

"I wonder if that Jesus guy knew what problems he was storing up for later generations?" asked Pamela, who had now more or less regained her composure. "He would probably have told you to leave your wife and follow him."

"Yes," agreed Martin, "That sounds just like him."

Next morning, still in a mental no-man's land between the relaxation induced by the glow of the Yorkshire Dales and the urgency induced by the e-mails from the Sudan, Martin telephoned the bishop's palace to arrange a meeting. He was duty-bound to bring the bishop up to date with his discussions with Flo and tell him about the offer of a place on Doctor Scott's research programme. In truth, he was more anxious to find out if the bishop had managed to find funds to cover his travel expenses.

A secretary answered the phone, but the bishop took it from her when he realised Martin was on the line. "Martin, welcome home! Did you have an interesting trip to Yorkshire?" Martin managed a brief "Yes, thank you," before the bishop, not in a listening mood, continued with: "Good news. I think I've found some financial support for you. Come and see me as soon as possible. How about tomorrow morning for coffee?" Martin barely had time for an affirmative grunt before the bishop concluded the conversation with: "Jolly good. That's settled then. God bless you. Until tomorrow." Martin let out a long sigh and smiled at the thought that God was going to bless him, at least until tomorrow. The bishop and Doctor Dorothy Scott ought to meet one day. They would get on like a house on fire, since they both seemed to be quick thinkers and decision makers.

\* \* \*

CHAPTER 7

At the High Street travel agency Ms. Moira Gordon (according to her plastic name badge) performed a painstaking computer search for flights to Khartoum from the U.K. Finally she turned to Martin and pleadingly asked, did he really insist on travelling with British Airways? The best possible flight, considering price, route and duration of travel, was clearly with KLM. It would mean a short fight from Birmingham or Cardiff to Amsterdam with a comfortable turnaround time in Amsterdam before boarding the flight to Khartoum. Out of politeness, she didn't actually say that whoever suggested British Airways must be potty, but her tone of voice and eye language expressed this opinion most forcefully. Martin acquiesced, bowed to Moira's (and her computer's) greater wisdom, and booked a flight with KLM on Wednesday 8th August, leaving Amsterdam at 10.10 am, arriving Khartoum at 17.20 on the same day, local time. As for the first stage of his journey, he and Pamela could fly together to Amsterdam. A couple of romantic days in the Dutch capital would be a splendid way of saying goodbye before they parted for four months. He would be home for Christmas. At least, that was the plan.

Back at the vicarage, Pamela quickly warmed to the idea of flying with Martin to Amsterdam. They decided to leave mid-morning from Birmingham airport and spend two nights in the Dutch capital. Early in the morning on Wednesday 8th August they would take the suburban train from the city to Schiphol airport in time for Martin to see Pamela onto her return flight to the UK, before checking in for his flight to Khartoum.

The two nights in Amsterdam were an unqualified success, with excellent food, art galleries, and exploration of the charming little backstreets of the capital. Fond farewells at a UK airport would not have been the same.

Martin hoped to see the plume of smoke from Mount Etna when his plane crossed the Mediterranean. Alas! He missed it. Tired from yesterday's exertions he dozed off between Amsterdam and the coast of North Africa. His neighbour, an Egyptian gentleman who disembarked in Cairo, assured him he had missed nothing, and suggested he break his journey in Cairo and see the pyramids. This friendly gentleman offered to put him up at his own house in Cairo and give him a good time. He was a business man who claimed he owned a chain of cinemas. He probably did. Martin wisely declined the offer and they parted with *some other time perhaps.*

After crossing the North African coast the desert landscape below had been dull or exciting, depending on one's point of view. The endless greyish brown terrain had little to offer of interest, until one noticed the pattern of long since dried out rivers and was reminded that the Sahara had once been moist and fertile, inhabited by the same animals that are now found only further south on that vast continent. As the sun passed its midday zenith, Martin also spotted the shadows of mountains and remembered an article in the National Geographic with photographs of rock carvings in the central Sahara, depicting elephants, hippopotami and other animals dependent on water. The rock carvings were in the same style as those now found only in southern Africa and made by the bushmen.

Not long after leaving Cairo many passengers crowded over to the left hand side of the plane to catch the aerial view of the Aswan dam and Lake Nasser. According to the inflight magazine, the plane then followed more or less the route of the Nile valley. Martin dozed off again, woke for the served meal, then managed to stay awake until the plane landed in Khartoum.

His papers were all in order, but smooth passage through the formalities of African airports is an unknown phenomenon, except for 'big' men and their families and for wealthy businessmen able and willing to pay for privilege. Finally, after nearly two hours of waiting for underlings to satisfy

## CHAPTER 7

their masters by holding up progress, Martin emerged, baggage stamped and crossed with blue pencil, and free to go wherever he pleased. Travellers were being met by friends and relatives. Officials of various commercial enterprises were searching for a driver holding up a placard with their name and the logo of their company.

Little by little, each traveller found his or her transport and the crowd thinned until Martin was left alone, still vainly looking for a driver holding aloft a placard with his name. The airport was suddenly quiet and deserted. It seemed that frenzied activity accompanied the arrival of every flight. The airport then closed down until the arrival or departure of the next flight. On the plus side it was a pleasant, balmy evening. On the minus side, Martin was thirsty and ravenous. He was also worried, because he hadn't the faintest idea what to do. Were the people from Doctor Scott's desert camp simply running late? Should he be patient and wait? He wandered outside the airport. There was a rutted car park with what appeared to be a couple of battered taxis and a four-by-four Nissan.

A beggar sat with his back to a broken wall that extended from the main building of the airport. No doubt he did well from arriving air passengers. Martin remembered that in Arab countries it was considered good luck to give alms to a beggar when entering a country or town for the first time. He would have made a contribution, but he had no Sudanese currency. Right then, a stroke of luck would have been very welcome.

A movement in the car park caught his attention. A young fair-haired European had got out of the four-by-four and was coming towards him. Martin was overcome with relief; his transport had been there all the time! "You must be from Doctor Scott's desert camp," said Martin, almost shouting with relief. "And who in God's name is Doctor Scott? It's to be sure I've never heard of him, so how could I be coming if I've never been," replied the European gentleman in a thick Irish baritone. Then he stopped, held up both hands in a gesture of astonishment, and exclaimed: "Now you can't be meaning you've flown all this way just to go and lose yourself in the desert. There's no nightlife in the desert, so there's not. If it's a good time you're wanting, you should be staying here in the big city of Khartoum." Pausing for breath, his new companion added in subdued tones: "And then you might still be wanting, so you might, for it's hardly a riotous city, so it isn't!"

"I'm sure you're right but I really do have to get to a camp in the desert. It's an archaeological camp run by a European called Doctor Scott, who is a she, not a he. I think it's near the fourth cataract," ventured Martin rather meekly, not knowing whether to feel disappointed, or to feel relieved because he had now met someone who could probably help him.

"If and when someone meets you, it's still a hell of a long way to the fourth cataract. It must be greatly more than one hundred miles as the crow flies, and however you get there you won't be travelling in a straight line like a crow."

Martin's heart sank. In his present weak mental state he couldn't stand this amount of negativity. He replied, rather lamely: "Those were my instructions. I assume my hosts will know what to do next." Then the fog created by his near panic began to clear and he remembered Doctor Hopp. "Sorry! I was forgetting. I'm supposed to be met by a Doctor Hopp from The Goethe Institute."

His new-found Irish friend clapped him on the shoulder with the words: "And to be sure, he will then arrange your transport to the fourth cataract. Where is this gentleman from the Institute? The poor man seems to have failed in his duty. Let us not try to read the book of fate. The future will surely manifest itself as the good Lord intended."

Such colourful speech had a certain entertainment and amusement value, which momentarily made Martin forget

CHAPTER 7

his worries. The loquacious Irishman continued: "Now doesn't that just show how two negatives can transform themselves into a positive! Here are you, waiting for someone who is not here at all, and here am I waiting for Kitty Fitzgerald from Limerick and she's met me with her absence. We'd better join forces and see what we can make of the rest of this lovely day."

Whoever Kitty Fitzgerald was, probably the Irishman's girl-friend, Martin felt he owed her a debt of gratitude for not turning up. Otherwise this Irishman would not have waited and noticed Martin in his distress. "Lucky for me she didn't turn up," replied Martin with an undisguised sigh of relief, "and I'm famished. Where can I find something to eat?"

"First things first. My name is Seamus O'Shea, what's yours?"

"Martin Kimpton and I'm very pleased to meet you."

They shook hands and Seamus told Martin to wait there while he found the airport manager. He would leave a message for anyone arriving to meet Mr. Martin Kimpton. The message was that Mr. Martin Kimpton would be staying at the Corinthia hotel in Khartoum.

"Right! I'm taking you to the Corinthia hotel. It's a five-star establishment and Jeesus, I surely don't know who's paying, but you'll be safe there. It's overlooking the Blue Nile and if you get stuck there before your friend comes, you can walk across the suspension bridge to Tutti Island. You might enjoy that. On the other hand you might not." With these and similar words of doubtful encouragement, Seamus sped on his way into central Khartoum, skilfully swerving the Nissan round large potholes and maintaining just the right speed to ride from rut to rut without too much discomfort.

About half an hour later, Seamus parked the Nissan opposite the hotel, next to a tree-lined promenade overlooking the river, leaped from the car, grabbed Martin's luggage in both hands and, with a nod towards the hotel, crossed the road and led Martin up the steps to the hotel terrace. Without consulting Martin, Seamus booked him into a room, handed the luggage to a hotel assistant and ordered beer and club sandwiches for both of them. "Here's to you and to me and may the fairies come to your assistance," toasted Seamus, raising his glass. "I usually rely on the good Lord to get me out of a scrape," replied Martin, "By all means let's ask the fairies for a change"

"This used to be the Grand hotel, much favoured by the British and important foreign visitors, and famous for its cockroaches. These clever Sudanese have changed the name and supposedly the management, but we know the same shady family of politicians and business men is still running the show behind the scenes. Here in the foyer and nearby public areas they've changed the décor, but not much." As Seamus rattled on in his thick Irish brogue, Martin tucked into his food and drink, which he had been craving since landing more than three hours ago. He was now feeling relaxed and almost back to normal after his airport panic. What a transformation of fortunes since landing at the airport! He had been anxious and starving. Now, thanks to the generosity of a very likeable Irishman, he was being fed and watered in a luxury hotel. Martin suggested they also leave a message at the Goethe Institute to say what had happened.

"I know that Goethe Institute," Seamus told him, "They used to run Arabic lessons for Germans working on the oil fields, and I think they still teach Arabic classes, although the Germans have gone now. It's rather late, but teaching, like many other activities in this part of the world, stops in the heat of midday then continues in the evening when it's cooler, or rather less hot, so the Goethe Institute may actually be buzzing with activity even at this late hour. I'll give them a bell." He went over to the reception desk and asked to be put through to the Goethe Institute. Martin could not hear what Seamus was saying, but he saw that he was frowning with disappointment. Then his frown gradually changed to an expression of satisfaction.

"At the moment Doctor Hopp isn't there. He's attending a meeting at the German embassy and won't be back until very late. The dear lady on the phone had heard about the Reverend Martin Kimpton. It seems the Institute was involved in smoothing your passage, getting you a visa and all that. At least, I think that is what she said. Her English was terrible, so it was. Jeesus! Are you really a Reverend?"

"I'm afraid so; sorry I didn't tell you," replied Martin, pretending to appear guilty.

"Lucky for you!" shouted Seamus, smacking the table and rocking their beer glasses, "I'm strongly against the Church, and me brought up as a Catholic and all that, and I would have left you standing at the airport if I had known."

All of this with a broad grin. In fact, their very brief friendship had already progressed to the point where gentle leg-pulling was permitted. "Anyway," continued Seamus, "she'll tell that Hopp character where you are when he gets back to the Institute, so you have a belt as well as braces – messages for Hopp at both the airport and the Goethe Institute. And now, Reverend Kimpton, I must leave you and wish you luck."

Martin was reluctant to see him go and suggested he wished him luck over another glass of beer. Seamus agreed then became a shade more serious, saying: "It is a piece of good advice I would be giving you." Lowering his voice so that only Martin could hear, he continued: "This country is politically very touchy. An international arrest warrant has been served on the president for promoting the genocide in Darfur, and the Sudanese army and air force are committing atrocities against the new state of South Sudan. Listen and learn! Don't you be thinking of talking about it to anybody. Word has a way, it does, of getting around, and you could find yourself being politely, or even impolitely, told to leave this lovely country." Martin thanked Seamus for the advice, which he instinctively knew was important, and which he subsequently followed strictly throughout his stay. As they finally shook hands and parted on very mellow terms, Seamus pressed some Sudanese currency into Martin's hand. "To be sure you have no Sudanese money. Take this to be going on with; you might need it before your friend comes."

"How very kind," replied Martin, "But how can I find you again?"

"I work for I.A.S.T and you can always find me at the Blue Nile sailing club." And with that, Seamus waved a cheery goodbye to Martin and to the receptionist and disappeared down the terrace steps. Martin, feeling slightly tipsy, watched the Nissan pull away from the opposite kerb, perform a three-point turn, and disappear in the direction of central Khartoum.

As he rose to go to his room, a little Arab servant with a huge, loosely wound white turban appeared from nowhere and indicated that Martin should follow him. He was led down a dimly lit corridor, past a hotel shop, which, according to its window display, sold only sweets and chocolates, and to the cloisters of a courtyard. His silent servant produced a key to room eleven from the folds of his galabiya, opened the door and directed Martin inside with an obsequious flourish. His luggage was there – a single gigantic suitcase standing by the bed. Silent service beckoned him to the side table and indicated a large earthenware jug of drinking water, covered with a small plate. Martin almost burst out laughing when he saw that the plate was a relic of former times, commemorating the coronation of Edward **VII**. Silent service mistook his smile for one of satisfaction with his service and he stood by the door, made a deep bow and

## CHAPTER 7

seemed reluctant to leave. Quick on the uptake, Martin took out Seamus' Sudanese banknotes. Not knowing how much Seamus had given him, he peeled a note from the top of the wad and handed it over with a proud *Shukran*! It was one of the very few Arabic words he knew from hearing it on the telly and reading it in various novels and he didn't even know if it was appropriate. He felt very pleased with himself that he had actually remembered it. Silent service seemed equally pleased. And no wonder, for Martin had tipped him ten times the normal rate.

It was a double European-style bed with an ornate, red-tasselled cover. A ceiling fan, rotating slowly and generating a slight down-draught, was the only air-conditioning. The room was warm but not uncomfortably so. Martin took his toilet bag from his small rucksack, which had served as hand luggage, and opened the door of the *en suite* bathroom. There was a frenzied flurry of tiny feet as several cockroaches retreated behind the bath panelling. He was not surprised or the least bit horrified. He had already experienced so much since landing in Khartoum that he was ready to accept that a few cockroaches were a normal feature of Khartoum hotels.

Stretched out on the bed, wearing only his pyjama bottoms, Martin counted the money Seamus had given him. He had one thousand eight hundred Sudanese pounds. Remembering the colour and design of the tip, he reckoned he had handed over two hundred Sudanese pounds, which meant that Seamus had given him two thousand. He had no idea of the exchange rate. Later, better informed, he realised he had tipped silent service the equivalent of about fifty British pence.

Seamus had declared he was strongly opposed to the Church, yet he had seen a stranger in need of help and like a real Christian he had gone to his assistance. There was a profound message there, but Martin was too tired to work it out. One day, Seamus, the Good Samaritan, or the angel in disguise, would be a subject for a sermon. Looking fondly at the picture of Pamela, which he had retrieved from his luggage and placed on the bedside table, Martin opened his laptop, sent her a quick e-mail then drifted off to sleep:

*Dear Pamela, I've arrived safely but not according to plan. No-one met me at the airport. A very friendly and helpful Irishman came to my rescue – a real angel in disguise. He drove me into Khartoum and put me into a hotel. Thanks to him I have eaten and have a comfortable bed. Hopefully, someone from the Goethe Institute will catch up with me tomorrow. Good night and sweet dreams. Love, Martin*

# Chapter 8

It was nearly six o'clock local time when Martin heard a gentle knocking on his door. There were other noises outside his door, which sounded like someone digging a hole. The knocking became more urgent and was accompanied by: "Sir! You have a visitor!"

Martin shouted that he was on his way. While shaving and showering he watched the bath panelling carefully. A lone cockroach ventured out then shot back again when Martin threw his soap dish at it and missed. He stuffed all yesterday's clothes into the zipped compartment in the lid of his case. Sandals and no socks and a red and white checked, short-sleeved shirt seemed appropriate. Should he wear the shirt tucked into his belted light cotton trousers, or should he let it hang out and disguise his slight paunch? He let it hang out.

In the courtyard outside his door, a dark-skinned muscular gentleman was digging a hole by repeatedly driving a long pointed iron pole into the ground. Martin would have liked to know more. The man was not wearing a turban and his features were definitely not Arab. Later in his stay, Martin would learn to recognise the different races on the streets of Khartoum: Arab, Nubian, sub-Saharan. As he entered the foyer, a plump little gentleman came to meet him, a hand of welcome outstretched.

"Herr Kimpton, Oh, I mean *Mister Reverend* Kimpton, I am so happy to find you. My name is Doctor Hopp and the news of your arrival was waiting for me when I returned to the Goethe Institute last night. How can I apologise sufficiently? I had no information about your travel plans. Doctor Scott said you would fly with British Airways, but yesterday there was no British Airways flight."

"My travel agent recommended KLM," replied Martin, "and I did send an e-mail to Doctor Scott to say when I would arrive."

Who was responsible for the mix-up? Was it Doctor Scott back at the fourth cataract, Martin himself, or Doctor Hopp? Since Doctor Hopp seemed embarrassed and over-anxious to discuss the matter no further, Martin suspected that Doctor Hopp was the culprit. He had probably failed to keep up with his e-mails and had missed the latest from the fourth cataract. On second thoughts, perhaps Moira Gordon of the Hereford High Street travel agency should take some of the blame. Recrimination seemed pointless, especially since recriminatory behaviour is not in the job description of a Church minister. In any case, yesterday's arrival in Khartoum had been a memorable experience; one day he would tell his grandchildren about it.

During these exchanges, Martin tried to weigh up the character of busy little Doctor Hopp. For the moment Martin had him at a disadvantage, since he was clearly feeling guilty of failing to meet Martin's flight from Amsterdam. Hopp was about five feet and a few inches in height, and plump. In contrast to Martin's open-neck, loose-hanging short-sleeved shirt and cotton trousers, Doctor Hopp was formally dressed in a dark suit and tie. Martin assumed this was normal dress for the head of the Goethe Institute, whose members were rather like diplomats, albeit cultural rather than political.

To Hopp's obvious relief, Martin added: "No harm done! In fact, I've had a most enjoyable time since I arrived yesterday evening, all thanks to a very kind Irishman, who looked after me and booked me into this hotel. By the way, he works for I.A.S.T; what is that?"

"I.A.S.T?" mused Doctor Hopp, "I really have no idea."

"And I can find him at the Blue Nile Sailing club; where is that?"

"Yes indeed, the Nile is good for sailing, especially where the Blue and White Nile flow together. The sailing club is housed in Kitchener's old gun boat that came down the Nile to relieve Khartoum from the Mahdi. Ah, that is British colonial history and you will know it better than I. So you can find him there; that is good. When you go there, you will see the original machine gun emplacement on the ship. It is very interesting."

"Yes, I'm sure it is," replied Martin, "Where is this gun boat?"

"Oh, of course, it is moored to the bank of the Blue Nile on the same side as this hotel and further upstream," replied Doctor Hopp, clearly pleased to earn brownie points by providing Martin with useful information.

"What next?" asked Martin.

"I have paid the hotel bill," replied Doctor Hopp. Now I will take you to the Goethe Institute for breakfast and from there you will travel to Doctor Scott's camp near the fourth cataract."

"And how *do* I travel to Doctor. Scott's camp?" enquired Martin.

Hopp warmed to the question, explaining that it was possible to fly to an airstrip near the great hydroelectric dam near the fourth cataract then continue by driving over the desert. Travel by river boat was also possible, but slow and the timetable for sailing was unreliable. Or he could ask for a lift on one of the lorries that take supplies from Khartoum to the hydroelectric dam. Another possibility was a train from Khartoum, which would be cheap but slow. The line had been built by Kitchener after he defeated the Mahdi and took control of Khartoum. With aid from China, the railway was being modernised.

Finally, Hopp, with a little giggle, asked: "Why don't you buy a camel and trek across the desert to the camp of Doctor Scott?"

Hopp was more anxious to entertain than to inform, and Martin was beginning to find him irritating. It transpired that Doctor Scott had already sent a driver to fetch Martin. He was waiting at the Goethe Institute.

Doctor Hopp's vehicle was, appropriately, a black BMW. Like Seamus O'Shea the evening before, he had parked it opposite the hotel in the shade of the trees that lined the avenue. Later, Martin learned the wisdom of always parking in the shade of trees; it prevented the sun from turning the vehicle into an oven. A three-point turn and they were on their way towards central Khartoum. "Please Mister Kimpton, try to guess the name of this road," challenged Hopp as they drove parallel to the Nile, which was on their left. Martin guessed that Hopp's little jokes and his efforts to entertain were a means of concealing his embarrassment at failing to meet him yesterday. He ended each speech with a little giggle, which was getting on Martin's nerves.

"Well," said Martin, forcing himself to enter into the spirit of the occasion, "I would call it *Riverside Avenue*."

"And what is the name of the river?" asked Hopp.

"Alright, let's call it *Blue Nile Avenue*," suggested Martin.

"One more guess, then I will tell you," giggled Hopp.

"OK, then how about *Blue Nile Road*?" ventured Martin.

"It is simply called *Nile Street*. Now is that not too simple?" remarked Hopp, bursting into childish laughter.

"It certainly is," agreed Martin, bored and striving to remain courteous. Doctor Hopp was rather silly. What was he a doctor of? Martin reigned in his uncharitable thoughts and decided that Hopp was doing his best in the circumstances.

They were now well on their way along Nile Street and approaching a bridge over the Nile, which, as Martin discovered later, would have taken them into Khartoum North. Opposite the bridge, they turned right, drove away from the Nile down a road called Al Mek Nimr, and stopped outside

## CHAPTER 8

the Goethe Institute. Above the door a notice read: *Deutsch lernen, Kultur erleben*, followed by Arabic script, presumably with the same meaning, whatever that was; then all was made clear by the last line, which read: *learn German, experience culture*. Hopp ushered Martin into a classroom and went in search of his secretary. The blackboard had not been cleaned from the previous lesson and it displayed what Martin assumed to be a list of German expressions with their Arabic equivalents in Arabic script. Hopp returned with his secretary, whom he introduced very formally as Frau Meinerts. She shook Martin's hand with a relaxed, engaging smile, which contrasted with Hopp's forced formality. She was typically German, although Martin could not have explained how she gave that impression. She was not the fair-haired, blue-eyed Nordic type of German. She was the very opposite, with a slightly olive skin and naturally black hair; that other type of German from the southwest of the country, the Black Forest, home of the seven dwarves. She was also quite attractive, about five feet nine inches in height, well-proportioned and not overweight. Martin tried to imagine her without her glasses, with her hair hanging loose and not gathered into a severe bun.

"You will follow me to the kitchen," she announced, in a commanding tone. Martin obeyed, feeling amused and fully understanding that this was her German way of saying 'please come with me to the kitchen'. Clearly, she had been very busy before his arrival. A substantial breakfast was waiting for him in the kitchen. There was fruit salad with Yoghurt, followed by bread rolls and a paste made from cooked beans, which Frau Meinerts said was called *fool*. Then came toast and marmalade, which they had obviously put on especially for Martin because he was British. As Frau Meinerts bustled in with the freshly brewed tea, she spoke hurriedly to Hopp in German. Hopp replied with *"Prima! Alles in Ordnung. Vielen Dank!"* It wasn't difficult to dissect what the secretary had said to Hopp. She was confirming that Martin's transport was ready and waiting. "I hope Doctor Scott knows I've arrived and I'm on my way," remarked Martin. "Of course, of course, I have already sent an e-mail to tell her you are arriving today." Martin wondered if Hopp had really sent an e-mail, or whether he would now sneak off at the first opportunity and send an e-mail to Doctor Scott at the fourth cataract of the Nile.

With a sigh of satisfaction, Martin pushed away his breakfast plates and dishes and asked Hopp if he would lend him two hundred Sudanese pounds. Martin explained how Seamus O'Shea had lent him two thousand Sudanese pounds, how he had given a tip of two hundred pounds and now wanted to return the loan before he disappeared into the desert. Hopp, unable to conceal his amusement, pointed out that the Sudanese pound was not worth much and he was sure that the Irishman had intended it as a gift, just the equivalent of about five British pounds, from an Irishman to an Englishman. Martin was not satisfied and as a matter of principle he insisted on contacting Seamus at the Sailing club to repay the loan. Hopp gave in and handed Martin a banknote worth two hundred Sudanese pounds, which Martin added to his remaining nine and slipped all two thousand pounds into the breast pocket of his shirt, ready for quick retrieval.

It took barely fifteen minutes to reach the Sailing club, a blue gun boat with faded and peeling paintwork. According to the notice on the door, the club office was in the old wheelhouse. At first, no-one seemed to be about, then Martin found a lone European leaning over the rail on the far side of the lower deck. Martin couldn't place his accent. He wasn't British. Neither was he very informative. Yes, he knew Seamus O'Shea. No, he hadn't seen him recently. No, he didn't know when he would come to the sailing club. No, there was no-one there at the moment who could contact

## CHAPTER 8

him. In fact there was no-one there except this very unhelpful foreign gentleman. Martin gave up, negotiated the rather rickety gangplank back to shore and re-joined Hopp, who was waiting by his BMW in the shade of a purple-blossomed Jacaranda tree. Martin shrugged his shoulders and held up his hands in a gesture of defeat.

Back at the Goethe Institute, Martin was pressed to take some further light refreshment before setting out to the desert camp. Hopp and his secretary waited patiently until Martin had nearly finished enjoying his cup of coffee and a rather sweet piece of cake containing dates and pieces of hibiscus petals. They then announced that the driver from Doctor Scott's camp was waiting for him in the car park at the rear of the Institute. Martin felt they were trying to hurry him. They probably had much to do that day, though Martin couldn't imagine what it might be. He had already formed the impression that the Goethe Institute was a haven of relaxation, and that his own arrival had triggered a phase of unaccustomed activity. "All your luggage is with the driver," announced Hopp, unnecessarily. It was a further prod to get him moving and out of the way. Martin wondered why they were so anxious to get rid of him. Perhaps they knew it would be a long journey and wanted him to get an early start and arrive in good time at Doctor Scott's desert camp. There were other possible reasons, none of which did Hopp, his secretary or Martin any credit, so he pushed them to the back of his mind.

"Ah well," thought Martin, "Whatever they're up to doesn't concern me. I don't know German, but I did hear Hopp call his secretary *Frau* Meinerts, which means Mrs Meinerts. If she were single, she would be *Fräulein* Meinerts." As he was leaving he therefore asked Frau Meinerts whether her husband also worked at the Goethe Institute. His question seemed to cause acute embarrassment for both Hopp and his secretary. Frau Meinerts looked searchingly at Martin and told him she was not married. Martin apologised and said he thought Hopp had introduced her as *Frau* Meinerts. They both visibly relaxed and explained that nowadays it is customary in Germany to call all women above a certain age *Frau*, irrespective of whether they are married or not, rather like the English *Ms*. They shook hands, wished him well and left him to find his own way out to the rear car park. That again aroused his suspicions. They seemed over-anxious to be left alone.

Martin put his suspicions behind him. Hopp and Frau Meinerts had performed their duty of looking after him, although Hopp had cocked it up when he failed to meet him at the airport. Now he was on his way to the desert to meet Doctor Scott and learn all he could about early Christianity.

As Martin emerged from the rear of the Institute a tall, lithe, dark-skinned gentleman, wearing a galabiya and a dazzling white turban, crossed the car park, approached Martin, bowed and said: "You are Reverend Martin for the camp of Doctor Scott."

Arabic-speaking Muslims do not use family surnames. The first name of a male child is given at birth, followed by his father's birth name, followed by his paternal grandfather's birth name and so on, sometimes all the way back to the Prophet. Martin knew this naming tradition but had momentarily forgotten about it, so *Reverend Martin* caught him unawares. To some Europeans the use of first names between strangers might be seen as an attempt at unwarranted familiarity (except amongst Quakers who always address one another by their first names, even when meeting for the first time. There we go again!). Martin rather liked the sound of *Reverend Martin* so he didn't correct his driver. From the intonation of his driver's speech, Martin was not sure whether he was making a statement or asking a question. "Yes, I am Reverend Martin," replied Martin, holding out his hand.

## CHAPTER 8

"I am Mustapha, sent by Doctor Scott to meet and transport you," said Mustapha in a measured, dignified tone.

Mustapha took Martin's offered hand in both of his and shook it with a firm grip then instructed him to follow. Facial expression and body language differ between cultures and Martin still had much to learn about dealing with the Sudanese. Still, he had the distinct impression that Mustapha was solid, efficient, and dependable. In the following weeks he was to find that this first impression was entirely accurate. Later, he also learned that Mustapha was not an Arab. He was a Nubian, belonging to an ethnic group descended from early inhabitants of the Central Nile valley, and darker-skinned than most Arabs.

Mustapha led him to a Nissan Land Cruiser in the car park. Martin's luggage was already stowed in the back.

"We drive a long journey to the camp. Please be comfortable and drink much water against the heat. If you prefer, there is also coca cola. There is a big seat with many cushions. Please go to sleep. I will be awake and I will drive."

Mustapha was pleasant and deferential, apparently sensitive to their relationship of honoured visitor and servant. Later, Martin would get to know him better. Now was not the time for jokes, which, in any case might be misunderstood. Otherwise, Martin was longing to express his gratitude that his driver would be awake.

Mustapha drove out of the Goethe Institute car park and turned right along Al Mek Nimr towards the Nile. That much Martin could remember. He also knew that if Mustapha were to turn left along Nile Street they would eventually reach the Corinthia Hotel where he had spent his first night in the Sudan. Reaching the junction with Nile Street, Mustapha drove straight on over the bridge. Without a map and still totally ignorant of the layout of Khartoum, Martin was now in *terra incognita*. Mustapha waved his hand in a semicircle to indicate the area they had just entered and announced: "Khartoum North!" Martin thanked him for the information, thinking at the same time that Khartoum North was drab and uninteresting. They followed a wide, long road, lined by walled gardens and the occasional garage. There was little traffic and few people about. Martin must have dozed off momentarily because he suddenly found they were once again on a bridge, crossing the Nile. Arriving on the other side, Mustapha gestured with his hand and announced: "Omdurman!" Martin's Khartoum geography might have been shaky, but his history wasn't. So this was where the battle of Omdurman was fought, where Kitchener had defeated the armies of the Mahdi and avenged the murder of General Gordon. Where was the prison where the Mahdi held his captives? Where was the actual battlefield? He would have to come again before he left the Sudan, take some photographs, and be able to say he had been here. In contrast to Khartoum North, Omdurman was vibrant and thronged with people, hardly any in European dress, most wearing turbans and white and not-so-white galabiyas. Mustapha negotiated the Nissan through narrow streets, lined with colourful vegetable stalls and displays of leather and metal goods, decorative harnesses and saddles for horses and camels, knives obviously intended as weapons rather than for the kitchen, swords and murderous-looking daggers. Market traders sat talking and smoking by their wares, pausing to glance suspiciously at the Nissan, driven by a Nubian and carrying a European. The atmosphere was not unfriendly, but it was not neutral. The presence of a European was noticed. Mustapha had to keep stopping to allow flocks of shoppers and traders to clear or pass. Heavily laden donkeys, some ridden by their owners, whose legs dragged on the road because they were longer than the height of the donkey, reminded Martin of the television adverts at home asking for contributions for the care of ill-treated donkeys in the developing world. Mustapha kept sounding his horn, which served only to warn that he was there, so that that pedestrians and donkey drivers could behave even more stubbornly, go slowly, and make him wait.

Suddenly, they were in a wasteland, although Martin thought it was the desert. Later in his stay, Martin would learn the difference. They were now heading approximately north, with the sun high in the sky and slightly left of centre. The unsurfaced road was firm although rutted in places. As Omdurman disappeared behind them, the roadside litter of plastic bottles, and abandoned motor vehicles became less profuse, until Martin thought it had finally disappeared, only to find that the desert was still occasionally disfigured by discarded motor parts and plastic bags, even a hundred miles ahead,

In the tropics, the sun goes down quickly. One moment a glorious sunset; then moonlight. Before that happened they had several hours of daylight in which Martin could admire the view, an expanse of mostly flat, biscuit-coloured terrain stretching to the horizon. Martin saw his first mirage: a distant shimmering patch with the appearance of water. His experience of East Anglia had taught him that flat landscapes are not necessarily dull and actually have a certain magic. At first, the Sudanese desert did not have that effect on him. It seemed to be featureless and dull. Little by little, however, it began to acquire character. A lone figure walking across the horizon raised the question of where it was walking to or from. Mustapha explained it was a village woman walking to fetch water from the Nile. "Yes," he agreed, "She has to walk a long way, and she does it twice a day; once in the morning and once in the evening." Then there were shrines, small domed buildings of mud brick, standing alone, sometimes with a long, thin flagpole inserted in the ground nearby and carrying a green flag. Mustapha explained they were shrines of holy men. Before Martin finally dozed off, he concluded that the Sudan had more than its fair share of dead holy men.

Mustapha was heedful of Martin's comfort, giving the impression, probably true, that he had been instructed to deliver his passenger, as yet unaccustomed to the exigencies of desert life, well rested and unscathed. He made frequent stops in empty, isolated parts of the desert, where he boiled water over a stove of bottled gas and offered Martin a choice of tea or coffee. Or he could have plain water or Coca Cola. Bananas, oranges, and those little cakes with dates and hibiscus petals were also on offer. After sunset, their entire journey was illuminated by what seemed to be an impossibly large moon, whose light cast sharp shadows. Early in their journey, during one of their refreshment stops, Martin pulled his laptop from his luggage and sent another e-mail to Pamela:

*My dear Pam, what a relief! Doctor Hopp came to my hotel this morning, took me back to the Goethe Institute for breakfast and saw me on my way to the desert camp, driven in a 4 by 4 by a charming Sudanese gentleman named Mustapha. We must drive through the night. At this very moment we are sitting in the moonlight in the desert, having a short break and some refreshment. It's rather alien but beautiful. I can already feel a sermon coming on. We will probably reach the camp in the early hours of morning. Love, Martin.*

Pamela had already replied to his first e-mail. Martin blushed when he read:

*Dear Martin, yes thank you, I got home safely from Amsterdam. Sorry! That was cruel of me. You obviously have had an anxious time, what with not being met at the airport and all that. And begorrah bejeebers, thank goodness for the Irish. I'm glad someone is looking after you when I'm not around. Ken and Sue are delightful. We are*

## CHAPTER 8

*getting on very well. Sue and I already feel like sisters. Ken looks rather worried. He's working on a sermon. I know the signs! Love, Pamela.*

These frequent moonlit refreshment stops provided an opportunity for Mustapha to prepare Martin for what lay ahead. He explained that Doctor Scott's archaeological site was situated about two miles from the River Nile, while her camp was a short walkable distance further south. This guaranteed freedom from certain insect pests, as well as putting distance between the camp and a rowdy army of engineers, who were working at the dam.

When they arrived at the camp, Martin was asleep on the big seat with many cushions, dreaming a confused scenario, set on a stage like an opera, in which a generous Irishman was selling LSD to students at the Goethe Institute and singing a mournful duet with Herr Hopp's secretary. Mustapha shook him gently and whispered that they had arrived. The secretary fell off the stage with a shriek, which became ever fainter until she was merely whispering: "Reverend Martin, Reverend Martin, we have arrived."

As Martin came to his senses, he was met with a scene that calmed and reassured him like a religious experience. Whatever he had been expecting, this was not it. Seven tents were pitched in a wide semicircle about one hundred and fifty yards in diameter. To one side and a short distance from the last tent, two squatting figures were silhouetted against the glow of a camp fire. As Martin learned later, both of these figures were general helpers around the camp, assisting Mustapha in his duties, as well as lending a hand where needed with Doctor Scott's excavation and conservation work. In the forthcoming weeks, Martin would get to know them better. Both were Arabs, lighter skinned than Mustapha, and both were steadfast and trustworthy characters. Their only drawback was that they were both called

Mohammed and bore a close resemblance to one another. Martin never learned which was which.

Set much further back was a large bell tent, which, he would learn later, served for storing tools and other equipment, and as a general meeting place. There was a great stillness, and the desert camp was illuminated by a bright moon. Here, he felt, the stress and tensions of industrialised western culture could never intrude. Only a few hours ago in Khartoum, negotiating the traffic with Herr Hopp on Nile Street, listening to the apparently confrontational tones of the Arabic language, Martin had momentarily felt a longing for his favourite haven of peace, which was a sunny Sunday afternoon on the lawn of the vicarage, musing on the spiritual message he had delivered in his morning sermon, sharing his thoughts with Pamela over a glass of sherry. The present scene also had a decidedly spiritual quality. He had yet to discover that he would eventually get used to living in the desert, sometimes feeling even nearer to heaven than on the vicarage lawn.

Still not fully awake, Martin was thrilled to see a translucent female figure, back-lit by the moon, approaching from the nearest tent and holding out her hand in greeting. She wasn't really translucent and certainly not diaphanous, but the moonlight did wonders for her loose-hanging shirt, and Martin's imagination did the rest.

"Reverend Kimpton, welcome to the Nubian desert!" Her voice was a powerful tenor and slightly husky. "No doubt Mustapha has fed you on the way, but come to my tent for a snack and some liquid refreshment before turning in." Martin clambered from the four-by-four and obediently followed her.

"Please, take that rickety plastic chair. I'll sit on this sack of beans. Sorry about my lack of style. I prefer to give priority to my excavations and my studies of Christian history. This is, after all, a desert camp, not an extension of

## CHAPTER 8

British suburbia. Poor Mustapha disagrees; he thinks I ought to import some decent western-style chairs and tables and soft furnishings. Just to please him, I did weaken and agreed to buy these carpets for the floor of the tent." Doctor Scott nodded towards the floor, which was covered with beautiful woollen carpets in black and deep red colours, most of them displaying the elephant foot design. "It made him doubly happy when I gave him the money and asked him to choose them for me in the souk in Khartoum." As far as Martin could make out, they seemed to be high quality woven carpets, probably imported from further north, even Iran or Afghanistan, and worth a small fortune on the High Street in Britain.

The plastic chair *was* rickety, since one leg was broken near its top and nearly severed from the seat. Martin would have preferred the sack of beans and wondered if there was a sack of anything else he could use, but there didn't seem to be. He couldn't help noticing that Doctor Scott's lack of style did not extend to her sleeping arrangements. In the dimly lit interior of her living quarters, Martin could see a double bed of African redwood standing well away from the canvas walls of the tent, the foot of each leg in a large tin, presumably containing paraffin to prevent ants from joining her while asleep. The bed head was ornately carved with what appeared to be Egyptian hieroglyphs, but it was difficult to see them clearly through the layers of mosquito netting, which were hanging in generous layers from a frame above the bed. Her mattress made no concessions to local culture. Not for her a cord lattice with a blanket covering. She slept on an internally sprung double mattress.

"Coffee, tea, fruit juice, or water? I'm afraid that's all I have to offer." Little by little, Martin had been recovering his senses and he was now more or less aware of everything happening around him. A good cup of tea was all he needed to restore his mind completely.

"I would just love a cup of tea."

"I thought so," she chuckled then added: "Typhoo or Lipton's Yellow label?"

It was unreal. Was he really awake? Was he really sitting on a rickety plastic chair in the middle of the Nubian Desert being offered a choice of tea blends by a world expert on Christian history? Apparently he was, so he tuned into the spirit of the occasion and replied: "Lipton's Yellow Label, of course, and a digestive biscuit to go with it."

"Sorry, no digestives. You will have to make do with Rich Tea."

It was a good start. This first meeting with Doctor Scott was relaxed and friendly with a total absence of formality. Perhaps that was only to be expected between fellow middle class intellectuals, especially when they are far from home. Meanwhile, Mustapha must have overheard their conversation; in fact, he was waiting and listening, in order to anticipate their needs. He walked quickly over to his colleagues silhouetted against the camp fire, returned immediately with a kettle of water that had only just gone off the boil and placed it on a low table in the entrance of Doctor Scott's tent. Doctor Scott nodded her thanks and Mustapha disappeared once more into the penumbral area just beyond the tent, where he waited to respond to any requests from his employer. Doctor Scott turned to a small tin trunk next to her sack of beans, uttered the incomprehensible words *eftah ya sim sim*, opened the lid and pulled out a packet of Rich Tea, a jar containing Lipton's Yellow Label tea bags and another jar containing sugar. "Sorry! No milk! We always drink our tea black with lots of sugar. Hope you like it that way." Martin had always believed in *When in Rome ....*, etc., so he replied that he loved it that way. She also chose tea. As they sat sipping the hot, sweet brew, they finally had time to regard one another more closely.

## CHAPTER 8

It was well past one o'clock in the morning. He had met her for the first time only about half an hour ago and he was too tired to form an impression after such a brief encounter. Even so, he was relieved by her relaxed and friendly welcome. The signs were promising for their future relationship. Martin was also surprised to find that she was an extremely attractive woman, who would have turned many a head on the streets of a western city. Flo's earlier description of Doctor Scott just didn't ring true, but he had never drunk sweet black tea with her in the moonlight in the tranquillity of a desert night.

As for *her* preliminary assessment of *him*, this was briefly expressed with: "You look tired and bedraggled. It's only to be expected, arriving so late after such a long and bumpy journey. I won't keep you up much longer. You must get to bed. Finish your tea and biscuits and I'll hand you over to Mustapha."

The dismissal was kindly but firm. It was also necessary. Martin was all in. Thanking Doctor Scott for the refreshment, Martin wished her goodnight and asked what she had said, apparently in Arabic, when she opened the tin trunk. "Oh, that's a bad habit of mine. I know it irritates Mustapha, although he won't admit it. Whenever I open anything I say *eftah ya sim sim*; it's Arabic for *Open Sesame!*"

Mustapha appeared on cue and guided Martin to the next tent, where he had prepared a single camp bed overhung by a mosquito net. On a wooden box next to the bed were a glass of water, covered by a saucer with a blue willow design, a small trowel and a torch. Just outside the tent entrance, on another box, which looked like an upturned tea chest, Mustapha had placed a chipped enamel bowl of water, a bar of Lifebuoy soap and a towel. The soap added to Martin's sense of unreality, the feeling that he had stepped into a time warp. Surely, Lifebuoy soap had disappeared from the market years ago, like granite kerbstones and linoleum, and, for that matter, like Lipton's Yellow Label tea. Either a large stock of the discontinued product was still supplying the market, or it was still being produced somewhere in an outpost of the empire.

In a man-to-man tone, Mustapha explained the toilet arrangements. Indicating a row of sand dunes far behind the semicircle of tents, he explained that one *went* on the other side of the dunes, dug a hole, performed as necessary, covered it over only lightly with sand, and left the rest to the climate. Everything treated in that way became rapidly desiccated in the burning sand under the searing desert sun, and the process was probably far more hygienic than the sewage disposal used in towns and cities. Doctor Scott used her own private area behind a different sand dune on the other side of the camp. "At night always take your torch, even if the moon is shining brightly. Watch out for scorpions. They always run away from you. If they get too close, don't be afraid to kick them quickly out of your way."

Kicking scorpions by moonlight on the way to the loo struck Martin as a rather odd form of competitive sport. This was his last waking thought before falling into a deep sleep on his first night in the Nubian Desert.

# Chapter 9

Martin viewed his surroundings through the fine gauze of the mosquito net, which Mustapha had drawn over his bed during the night. It was a brilliantly bright morning and clearly time to get up. Through the haze of netting he could see Mustapha fussing around outside the tent, obviously reluctant to actually shake Martin awake, but creating enough disturbance to achieve the same result. As Martin peered out, Mustapha greeted him with: "Good morning Reverend Martin. You have slept very deeply. I saw your unconscious condition." Mustapha indicated a large, steaming pot on the upturned tea chest: "There is coffee for you." Martin smelled and savoured the rich aroma of the freshly ground and newly brewed coffee. "Doctor Scott wishes you to have breakfast with her. First you will wash. Here is a kettle of hot water. There is cold water in the bowl. I will leave the tea strainer with you. I have placed a galabiya in your tent. In this desert heat it is good to wear it. We find it so."

Martin glanced inside his tent and saw the white garment hanging at the end of his bed with the mosquito netting. That was thoughtful of Mustapha. A galabiya must be a suitable garment for the desert heat. Thousands of Sudanese can't be wrong. He had seen the streets of Khartoum thronged with Sudanese men all wearing white galabiyas. "Thank you Mustapha. I will try it on later."

Mustapha started to walk away, but Martin called him back. "You have brought coffee, so I don't need a tea strainer."

"The tea strainer is used for removing insects from your washing water. This one I leave with you. You will be amazed at its great usefulness!" This one was the same model as the stainless steel strainer in Martin's own kitchen in Herefordshire. As he discovered later, it was one of several useful household items Doctor Scott had brought from England. He also discovered that, as promised by Mustapha, it was amazingly useful.

Concealed behind the door flap of his tent, Martin managed to wash himself all over, after first using the tea strainer to remove a thimble-worth of very small, nondescript flies and beetles from the cold water in the chipped enamel bowl. He then poured hot water from the kettle into a tin mug and lathered his face with Lifebuoy. Out of the corner of his eye he detected movement outside Doctor Scott's tent about thirty yards away. She was holding a mug, presumably of coffee, and gazing in his direction. How long had she been watching? Privacy is difficult behind a tent flap and he hadn't been over-careful during his all-over wash. On the other hand, did it really matter? It occurred to him that it may not matter to him or Doctor Scott, if she accidentally spotted him in a state of semi-nakedness. After all, they were both grown-up sensible people. On the other hand, it might offend Mustapha's sense of decorum. True, Doctor Scott was the camp boss, but they were both visitors in a foreign culture. He gave her a cheery wave and she responded by waving her coffee cup in the air.

Part way through shaving, Martin was fascinated to see a whirling vortex of dust and sand particles, about two feet in height, scudding over the sand about six feet from the entrance of his tent. It described an erratic path, seemed to be advancing towards him then changed course and shot away and disappeared in the direction of Doctor Scott's tent. Its shape and spinning motion reminded him of the tornadoes he had seen on television in North America, but this one outside his tent was many orders of magnitude smaller. It so distracted his attention that he nicked himself with the razor. He would have to present himself at breakfast with a plaster on his left cheek. Fortunately, he had what he needed because Pamela had raided their domestic supply of plasters and antiseptic ointment, constructed a first aid kit, and

## CHAPTER 9

pushed it into his luggage before he left. She had also chosen his shirts and underclothes, in fact practically everything, down to his trousers, shoes and sandals, and she had chosen well. He presented himself at Doctor Scott's tent freshly washed and shaven, wearing sandals, light cotton trousers and a white, short-sleeved shirt. According to his watch it was exactly eight o'clock.

"Well done!" exclaimed Doctor Scott, striding forward to meet him. Indicating a trestle table outside her tent, she added: "More coffee? Help yourself to whatever you fancy." He surveyed the table of food. Mustapha or one of his Arab staff had been very busy. There was a fruit bowl of bananas, oranges and, surprisingly, apples; a large jug of orange juice; a huge pile of thickly cut toast; lumps of butter floating in iced water (absolutely necessary in the desert heat. Where did the ice come from?). There was a bowl of mashed *fool* (cooked beans crushed into a paste with added seasoning) together with boiled eggs and fried eggs. Pretending he was used to this sort of breakfast, Martin took two slices of toast and spread them with fool, added a fried egg to his plate then chose an orange and a banana. He declined the coffee and poured a full glass of orange juice. All this under the watchful and slightly amused eye of Doctor Scott.

"Let's be civilised and sit on proper chairs this morning. I could see you were uncomfortable on that rickety plastic chair last night, so I asked Mustapha to bring two decent camping chairs from the store tent." This all seemed a little odd. If she possessed decent chairs, why did she have to wait for Martin to arrive before using them, apparently preferring to sit on bags of beans and a chair of broken plastic? Martin put it down to mild eccentricity, a not uncommon affliction amongst academics.

Martin replied: "I was so tired last night, I don't know whether I was uncomfortable or not."

"Take it from me Reverend Kimpton, you were uncomfortable, and who wouldn't be on a broken plastic chair. I apologise."

As a breakfast-time, getting-to-know-you occasion, Martin felt the conversation was adequate. He was raring to get started on his quest to learn more about Christian history. Doctor Scott, however, had other ideas.

"I saw you watching a dust devil when you were shaving. Have you seen dust devils before?"

"Oh, so that's what you call them. What a good name! They look like bonsai tornadoes."

"Bonsai tornadoes," mused Doctor Scott, "What a beautifully descriptive name for them! They are little whirlwinds and like tornadoes they are upwardly directed rotating columns of air, produced when hot air near the surface of the desert rises through the cooler, low-pressure air above. Then the air begins to rotate, stretching the mass of dust and sand and increasing the spin by the conservation of angular momentum."

Martin gazed at her in amazement and admiration. "You've certainly done your homework on dust devils," he exclaimed.

"I hardly understand a word of what I just said. That is how my second husband explained them to me. He was a physicist and understood these things. Dust devils were about the only thing he could find of interest in the desert. Otherwise he moped around the camp grumbling about our lack of facilities. Finally he went off to Khartoum, supposedly for a change of scenery, and he never came back. My lawyer in Cambridge saw to the divorce."

Embarrassed by her readiness to communicate such intimate details of her life after such a short acquaintance, Martin could only manage a feeble "Oh, I see." He would soon discover that when two lone Brits are thrown together in foreign parts, they soon find themselves sharing intimate

## CHAPTER 9

details of their lives. Any psycho-sociologist will confirm that this is a natural phenomenon.

"We can spend the morning inspecting the camp and the archaeological site. While we are doing that, Mohammed one and Mohammed two will prepare lunch." As she said this, she nodded towards the other side of the camp where the two Arabs were raking ash from the camp fire and adding fresh fuel from a nearby wood pile.

"They are good workers and very useful around the camp, but I can never tell them apart. *They* know which of them is which and they find it hilarious that I have to call them *Mohammed one* and *Mohammed two*. When you get the opportunity, try saying *Good Morning Mohammed two* to one of them. He will invariably reply with a broad smile that he is *Mohammed one*. Conversely, if you greet him with *Mohammed one* he will insist that he is *Mohammed two*. They love their little joke and I like it too; I welcome any kind of innocent light-heartedness in our camp. Serious academic study while isolated in the desert, with no fellow academics with whom to exchange ideas, can be rather trying. A general jokey atmosphere of friendly cooperation with the Sudanese members of the camp helps a great deal."

Not surprisingly, thought Martin, she must feel isolated from her fellow academics. It was the price she had to pay for her independence of spirit and her decision to pursue her work almost single-handed in the Nubian Desert. Communication with family and fellow archaeologists by e-mail must help to mitigate her feeling of isolation. On the other hand, Martin sensed that she actually delighted in being away from European academia, in the desert where no-one at home really knew what she was doing.

"There's another one," exclaimed Martin, pointing to a dust devil hovering immediately in front of the tent. "And there are two more over there," said Doctor Scott, nodding towards the middle distance between her tent and the parked

Nissan. "Try not to get too excited by dust devils. You will see hundreds if not thousands of them before you leave here. I was also fascinated by them when I first arrived in the desert."

She looked him up and down, assessing whether or not he was suitably dressed for what lay ahead. "For this morning your clothes are okay. In future I would advise jeans and a T-shirt. Grubbing around at the site can be quite sweaty and dirty. And you must have a hat against the sun. Otherwise you will finish up with sunstroke."

Martin frowned apologetically and told her that he had completely forgotten to bring a sun hat.

She dived into her tent, uttered *eftah ya sim sim,* opened her tin trunk and triumphantly held aloft a battered but whole straw hat, the kind that went with sunny afternoons watching cricket on the village green, or with rose pruning in a cottage garden. "This will do nicely. The broad brim will also keep the sun off the back of your neck. It belonged to my first husband. Seeing you wearing it will bring back memories." Martin wondered what sort of memories.

At last, they started out to the archaeological site, which lay in the direction of the Nile. Passing the canvas shelter of the Nissan they picked up a well-worn track in the otherwise featureless sand.

As they walked, Doctor Scott said she was glad to have a new assistant and added that she was very happy to pass on to him all she could about Christian history in exchange for his help at the excavation site. She also explained that she didn't want to waste time discussing all that nonsense about the crucifixion; the significance of the resurrection, maybe, but not the crucifixion.

Martin couldn't imagine what she meant by the nonsense of the crucifixion, unless she meant it didn't take place, which would support his own suspicions. He asked what nonsense she was referring to. She told him it wasn't really nonsense, but it had become a popular way of jeering at the story of Jesus' trial and execution, especially by atheists and by fourth formers, who think they have found a flaw in the Christian story. Martin still had no idea what Doctor Scott was talking about, and said that whenever he thought of the crucifixion he thought of the crowd of Jews baying to crucify Christ rather than the common criminal Barabbas, and how this has led to two thousand years of anti-Semitism.

"Precisely," answered Doctor Scott, "And there, of course, lies the problem, because Barabbas is not a name; it's a title." Suddenly, Martin realised what she was talking about, so he added: "And his title means Son of God. *Bar* means *son of* and *Abba* means *father* or *the father*, which means *God*. In fact, early manuscripts of Matthew use the full form of the name: *Jesus Barabbas*. Curious, isn't it, that the person released in response to the clamour of the crowd was *Jesus, the son of God*?" Doctor Scott added that the first part of the name was later deleted from Matthew's Gospel in a sly bit of editing designed to support Gentile beliefs. "So we start our discussion of Christian history by pointing out that sometime during that history the Church practised a deceit regarding the true story of Jesus' trial. Of course, I know all this, but I have never yet dared to preach it from my pulpit." Doctor Scott said she understood why and she hoped he understood why she had referred to it as nonsense. It was something one could talk about, but it didn't lead anywhere, except to add yet another example to the list of frauds by the early, and sometimes not so early, Catholic Church.

Martin said he was not prepared to dismiss the issue so lightly. He considered it to be quite high on the scale of early Christian deception. "Maybe you're right," agreed Doctor Scott. "As a Church minister you're bound to have a different perspective from mine. Carry on and I'll listen." Martin pointed out that Barabbas, aka *Jesus, son of God* was accused of being a Jewish rebel responsible for killing Jews in an insurrection. He was therefore not a criminal; he was a Jewish fanatic. This meant there were two men with the same name and the same crime. So which one was released? Certainly many of the oldest Christian sects believe that Jesus was not crucified because another died for him. Muslims today regard Jesus Christ as a prophet who was ordered to be crucified but whose place was taken by another. The crucifixion is essential to the Christian story, yet many groups do not believe that he died in this manner. Could they be right?

Ten minutes after leaving the camp, conversation about the crucifixion came to an abrupt end as they reached a roughly oval area of about two thousand square yards, decorated with small red flags, which marked the positions of former buildings. Over to the left, on the other side of a small dune, Martin saw a cluster of mud-brick buildings, or at least the remnants of the walls of what had been buildings in an earlier age. He guessed that the largest ruin had been a church. It was too large for a domestic dwelling. On the other hand, if it were a church, he would have expected its outline to show a cruciform pattern. The remains of the walls protruded about three feet above the sand, except on the northern side where part of a domed roof was clinging precariously to a narrow column of old wall, which had miraculously survived the malicious intent of desert storms and mud brick thieves.

"These flags mark the sites of buildings that have now disappeared completely into the desert sand," she explained. "At the moment my main interest lies in the remains of the old church over there. Let me show you." He was right; it had been a church. As she led the way she explained that Pinda had been trying to expose a wall painting on the west wall of the old building.

"This building was the church of the Christian community that lived here. The roof would have been a domed

## CHAPTER 9

affair, not the pitched roof and steeple of western churches. All of these Nubian Coptic churches were domed. Building such a dome of interlocking mud bricks requires skill and the builders in this part of the world were excellent at it. It dispenses with the need for wooden beams and it results in a more or less round building. The same building technique was used later to construct the domes of Muslim mosques. Architecturally the mosque and the Eastern Christian church have a close affinity with each other. Consider the Hagia Sophia in Istanbul. It was originally a great domed Christian church. When the Muslims took it over they built a few minarets outside it and bingo – they had a mosque!

When you're working here please look out for remnants of the dome. I collect them. They are easily recognisable because, unlike other parts of the church wall, they are curved and are constructed of rather small, dainty interlocking mud bricks." Whereupon she stooped and picked up a curved piece of the dome, its pattern of interlocking mud bricks clear to see. "There you are; that's the sort of thing to look for." She handed it to Martin for his closer inspection.

"The floor of the church is now about five feet below the desert sand. Five months ago, I hired a team of labourers from Mustapha's village to clear the sand to the depth of the original floor. It turned out to be much deeper than I thought, so I got the digging started where the altar must have been and they exposed an area of about fifty square feet. That gives me something to work on. These people have to be paid. My grant for this work is generous enough, but I have to reckon with being here at least another eighteen months, so I must be careful. I will get those labourers back if and when I think it necessary."

Martin walked over to a large excavated hole, about ten yards from the centre of one of the ruined walls, and peered down. Slabs of stone, presumably the remains of the altar, lay in a disorganised pile. Patches of a patterned tiled floor were also visible, as were Doctor Scott's trowel, measuring line and sieve, as well as a bucket for discarded material. It seemed she had interrupted her work to spend time with him and get him settled.

"We also cleared sand along the interior of the walls with the hope of finding wall paintings. I stopped that work as soon as we found the first fresco. We exposed only the top few centimetres and could see that it was well preserved. Before he left, Pinda was experimenting with different ways of revealing the entire painting without harming it. You can see the plastic sheeting covering his exploratory excavation. There's no point in looking for more wall paintings until this one has been fully exposed and studied. Any others, and I hope there will be others, are best left under the sand where they are protected, until we are ready to expose them."

Martin pulled back the cover that Pinda had left over his work. He tried to imagine the student he had known years ago on Flo Willan's course, standing in that hole and carefully removing sand from the face of the wall painting. Because of Pinda's tragic death, Martin was now in the Nubian desert, looking down at Pinda's unfinished work. Clearly, he hadn't made much progress before he left for Khartoum never to return. His excavation, only about three feet below the surrounding desert surface, was large enough to stand in. From the small exposed area of the fresco it wasn't possible to discern its subject. The colours appeared intense and fresh. Martin, who had no archaeological experience, felt excited at the prospect of helping to expose this ancient wall painting. He still had to learn that desert excavation was strength-sapping, sweaty, dirty work.

"And your job will be to carry on where Pinda left off."

"When shall I get started," he asked.

"Not straight away. There are other things you must do first. Let's get back to the camp and take some refreshment. In future, whenever you come out here, bring plenty of water

## CHAPTER 9

to drink, and, of course, always wear your hat. Also bring a roll of black plastic sheeting to construct a shaded shelter against the sun when you need a rest. We have plenty of plastic sheeting at the camp. Often I will also be here, working around that ancient altar."

Martin had known all along that he would have to earn his keep; that was part of his contract and it meant that he didn't have to pay for his food and accommodation, or for the privilege of sitting at the feet of a specialist in Christian history. He could see now that it was going to be hard work in the desert heat. Had she tempted her two husbands into the desert to act as unpaid labourers on her excavation site? No wonder her marriages didn't last. As soon as this thought crossed his mind Martin knew he was being terribly unfair.

By now, the sun had become quite merciless and Doctor Scott insisted they return to the camp. Whether he agreed or not, she assured him he had already had enough exposure for his first morning in the desert. "What a pity we can't strap solar panels on our backs and save the power to illuminate the camp at night," she suggested as they headed back. "I remember a very bright moon last night," he replied, "so why bother with any other form of illumination?" It was a harmless, inconsequential conversation, which made the walk back seem shorter than the walk there. Martin would have preferred a more serious discussion. She had made no attempt to brief him on the history of the church she was excavating or anything at all about the form of Christian worship practised there and its associated theology. No doubt that would come later. He hoped so.

As they approached the camp, Martin saw that a trestle table of food had been prepared under a canvas extension of the entrance to Doctor Scott's tent. One of the Mohammeds stood nearby. He had obviously prepared the table and was waiting for Doctor Scott's approval.

"Thank you Mohammed one," she said, "That is perfectly satisfactory." Mohammed smiled broadly and replied: "Madam, I am Mohammed two." "Oh, of course you are number two; I must remember in future," she replied in an apologetic tone. Suppressing a giggle, Mohammed two (or was he one?) retired to the shaded side of Doctor Scott's tent, where he waited in case he was further needed. Turning to Martin, she said: "You see, that is what you will have to put up with. It's worth it for the sake of the simple happiness and good will that it generates.

The table had been laid with oranges, bananas, bread rolls, hibiscus jam, peanut butter, a large pot of tea and a large jug of iced water. With a wave of her hand Doctor Scott invited Martin to help himself. She explained that a certain variety of hibiscus had fleshy petals that were dried and powdered and dissolved in water to make a pleasant drink, incorporated whole into pastries, and even made into the jam that was on the table.

"Surely you've heard of hibiscus tea. Here it's called *karkade*. Hibiscus tea is well known in many parts of the world. In fact, you can buy it on the High Street in some British towns."

Martin replied lamely that, until now, he had never heard of hibiscus tea, let alone tasted it.

She also explained that they made ice in an ice machine, which was housed in the supply tent beyond the semicircle of dwelling tents, together with a generator that supplied the electricity.

Martin needed food and drink, but not much at that time of day and in that heat. He felt satisfied after a sandwich of hibiscus jam and a cup of tea. Doctor Scott also ate sparingly and assured Martin that a more substantial meal would be prepared for the evening. Looking over to the camp fire and the nearby supply of wood, Martin wondered where the fuel came from in a treeless desert. She explained

## CHAPTER 9

that the woodpile was continually restocked with driftwood from the River Nile.

"That is what you must do tomorrow morning: drive over to the Nile. It will give you a better overall picture of where we are. In the meantime you should rest in your tent. Her tone left no room for argument, so Martin did as he was told. He hadn't fully recovered from yesterday's tiring schedule, and the visit to the archaeological site, brief though it was, had drained him. He fell asleep in his tent and woke up about five hours later as the sun was setting.

It was a little past seven thirty. He just had time to freshen up, regain his senses completely, and join Doctor Scott for the evening meal. Mustapha was hovering near the entrance of Martin's tent. Had he woken him? It was possible that Mustapha's duties included wake-up calls, delivered by subtly creating noise and activity near the tent of the sleeper. Martin called: "Good evening Mustapha!" Mustapha adopted an air of surprise and replied: "Good evening Reverend Martin; I was just tidying the entrance to your tent. The evening meal is nearly ready at the tent of Doctor Scott." Martin felt his suspicions were confirmed.

A quick all-over with tepid water, warmed by the desert sun, and Martin was ready for his dinner by moonlight, although the western sky still reflected the glow of the recently departed sun and the moon was still waiting to take over.

She was sitting at the table outside her tent and rose to greet him. Since their midday snack, the atmosphere had changed completely. Doctor Scott clearly had a sense of occasion. She held out her hand to welcome him as if they were meeting for a dinner date. In her medium length denim skirt, bare legs and gossamer-like, short-sleeved pink blouse, she would have blended easily into a social gathering on the lawn of an Oxbridge college. Her attractive features and a fine skin made makeup unnecessary, but she had applied lipstick nonetheless.

"I love this part of the day," she remarked. "I can dress in non-working clothes, relax in the relative cool of the evening and, for a short time, imagine I'm home again in Cambridge." Martin wondered what Mustapha and the Mohammeds thought of her evening wear. In a Muslim country she ought to dress more conservatively, even if she was the pay mistress and camp boss.

Martin replied that it was indeed a wonderful time of the day, that the sun had now set, that the horizon was still blushing, and that the large moon would soon provide the only illumination they needed, on this warm, balmy evening, which was so relaxing after the remorselessly hot day. Too late! He realised that his little speech had verged on the poetic. He was affected by the beauty and mystique of the desert evening. She smiled as she remembered her own first impressions of evenings in the desert. For her own part, she welcomed the chance to relax, Cambridge style, with a fellow countryman. Martin represented England and home, an opportunity to give her mind a rest from archaeology and Christian history, in the company of someone whose mother tongue was her own.

"Well, what do you think of our little bit of desert?"

Martin was quick with his reply. He had been pondering the same question ever since he arrived. He replied: "It seems to have two faces: the unforgiving inferno of the day and the tranquillity of the moonlit night. It's so quiet. There's absolutely no sound of traffic, no-one playing a radio, not even in the distance."

With an ironic smile, she added: "And no-one talking on a mobile phone. Such peace in such a barren land seems challenging; it seems to suggest a hidden mystery. It's totally different from the relaxing peace of the English countryside, don't you think?"

"Your comparison of this moonlit Eden with the English countryside is very interesting," replied Martin. "For example, the desert doesn't elicit a back-to-nature feeling in me; there's something too primitive, rather alien, about it for any kind of sentimental attachment, despite the moon, for which many a poet would be grateful."

"Indeed," she mused, "Here in the desert I never get that back-to-nature feeling. I treasure those moments of self-discovery, away from the hubbub of civilisation in the bosom of Mother Nature, but this desert doesn't do it for me. I'm captured by that back-to-nature feeling when I'm at home on the Cambridgeshire fens, idly paddling a canoe. I like to be moored well away from other boats, brewing tea on a camping gas stove and watching the nuptial signalling of fire flies in the reed beds. I then experience an inner calm that this desert, even with its poetic moon, has never given me. Perhaps it's because the English countryside satisfies nostalgia for past times that one understands, or believes one understands, such as the busy murmuring of innumerable bees on a sunny afternoon, the idyllic scene of the harvest being gathered. Sentimental nonsense, perhaps, but here in the desert, I can't relate to any such history. It is, as you say, rather alien. On the other hand, my second husband felt very stimulated by the River Nile and the Nubian Desert. For him it evoked a feeling for British colonial history: General Gordon, Kitchener, the Mahdi, and the battle of Omdurman. So there's no telling; it affects different people in different ways."

Martin was itching to convey his next thought: "The rift valley, where pre-human skeletal remains have been unearthed, is a long way south of here, but human evolution did start in Africa. We know that thousands of years ago the desert was greener than it is now. Perhaps we are sitting where our early ancestors once walked. It's an interesting thought, but it belongs to pre-history so it doesn't make us feel nostalgia for a lost age; it just excites academic interest or provides a subject for after-dinner conversation."

"You do yourself an injustice. Migration of early humans through our camp site is not a far-fetched idea. Current thinking is that early humans followed the coastline in migrating north. The River Nile, barely two miles from here, would also have provided water and food and a route to the north. In fact there is rich evidence that human evolution and cultural progress have been enacted along the entire stretch of this longest river in the world. It stretches from Lake Tana in the highlands of Ethiopia to the Delta on the Mediterranean. Some of its tributaries are also significant waterways, the main one being the White Nile, which originates in the southern swampland called the *Sudd* and joins the Blue Nile at Khartoum. Palaeolithic remains of *Homo erectus* have been found in the Nile valley, as well as the remains of early modern humans from the Mesolithic. For later periods the archaeology is easy, providing a clear picture of human settlements along the Nile from the Bronze Age to the present."

They lapsed into a contented silence. They had both eaten well and were drinking coffee. Suddenly, she chuckled and said: "Your suggestion that our ancestors may have roamed these parts has reminded me that the flood waters of Aswan covered what is possibly one of the oldest burial sites in the world. It is dated to well over ten-thousand years ago."

She paused and said: "I assume you know about Aswan and the great Egyptian dam. The flood waters covered much more than prehistoric burial sites. Just thinking about the valuable archaeological remains under those flood waters makes me angry. I'll tell you about it one day. However, I'm digressing. As I was saying: that very old burial site contained skeletons of men, women and children that showed evidence of violent death, possibly the result of intertribal warfare. Fortunately the site was excavated before it was flooded. Those individuals were robust types, thick-boned and heavy-jawed. The later inhabitants of ancient Egypt and the Nile valley were dainty by comparison. The recovered remains of bones and weapons were given to the British museum, which has not yet put them on public display.

"Thank you for that piece of secret information. I can feel a sermon coming on. It would start with the violence and brutality of early humans, all resulting from a fear of other tribes. Then along comes Christianity to save the human race from itself."

"I don't want to spoil your sermon, but I'm sure you know as well as I do that you are claiming too much and the entire argument is a gross over-simplification."

"Of course I know it, but as Doctor Willan once pointed out, all arguments have faults, which must be disguised with eloquence."

They were both finding it difficult to be completely serious. Martin was relieved to find that they were getting on so well and, to use a phrase, they seemed to operate on the same wavelength. Ever since leaving Amsterdam he had looked forward with pleasurable excitement to spending time in the desert with an acclaimed specialist in Christian history, but his thoughts had always been tempered by the fear that their personalities might clash. That fear was now allayed and a new anxiety had taken over. Doctor Scott was undeniably an attractive woman, and Martin was not made of wood.

"It's so quiet," ventured Martin, "I can hear the Milky Way hissing."

"I know what you mean," she replied, "I'm sure the Milky Way isn't hissing, although I always sense a faint sound, almost a kind of music, in the moonlit desert night, and one could imagine that it comes from the heavens. My first husband, the physicist, suggested it was the sound of one's own blood circulating, which we rarely hear because it is so very faint and there is nearly always background noise to blot it out."

"A typically sensible, scientific, dull explanation," remarked Martin, "I prefer to think of it as heavenly music."

"So do I," she replied, and once again they lapsed into a contented silence, soaking up the atmosphere of the wilderness arched over by a crystal-clear heaven of constellations, and a moon that cast a light bright enough to see by and to cast sharp shadows, while illuminating the world below in black and white.

The following five minutes of silence seemed longer to Martin and he began to feel uncomfortable at the apparent end of their conversation. So he broke the silence with: "It's an astronomer's paradise. No interfering light from a city, so the stars are sharply defined and seem much nearer than they do at home."

He had to wait for a reply. She had been content with the silence. Martin was still to learn that Doctor Scott valued silence greatly. During a conversation she would often become silent for minutes at a time. At first, Martin assumed she was seeking the correct words with which to continue, but he soon realised that her silences had a spiritual dimension.

Finally she replied: "It's easy to understand why camel caravans cross the great Sahara from village to village and oasis to oasis with pin-point accuracy. They have been doing it for centuries, travelling at night to avoid the desert heat and to navigate by the stars. The Bedouin, the Berbers, the Tuaregs, all those desert travellers and traders don't have university degrees in astronomy. They have followed the stars at night since they were children. Astronomy to them is not a field of academic study; it's an essential part of their existence like eating and drinking and procreation."

"You mentioned the Sahara," said Martin, "All the pictures I've seen of the Sahara, in books and on television, show mountainous sand dunes. It's different here in the Nubian Desert; this hard, dry, crusty terrain doesn't have enormous sand dunes, just a few small ones like those over there behind the camp (Martin pointed in the direction of the toilet area) and those we saw at the digging site this morning."

"Oh, there are plenty of big sand dunes in the Nubian Desert, further north and further west," she replied, "Many geographers wouldn't call this bit of Nubia true desert; it's just a dry area bordering on the River Nile. In this part of the world everywhere is dry, except the few yards on either side of the Nile. Some parts are drier than others. Between here and the Nile there are a number of small depressions with struggling vegetation and stunted bushes, even enough vegetation to attract goats. Those wretched animals sometimes wander into our camp, and I often find fresh goat droppings at the excavation site. They all belong to someone, but we never see a goat herder to complain. Dear Mustapha and the two Mohammeds have taken the law into their own hands and they have devised the perfect remedy for trespassing goats. It worries me, in case someone seeks redress. The boys assure me, however, that their own moral code and the unwritten Nubian laws of desert life are on their side."

"Well," asked Martin, "How *did* they solve the problem?"

"Oh, didn't I say? About every two to three weeks we have curried goat meat for the evening meal. It's delicious."

With that last remark her voice changed, as if to end the conversation. She sought his eyes, found them and gave him a partly concerned, partly almost motherly look and suggested it was time to turn in. He was surely not yet fully acclimatised and needed an early night. It was a rather abrupt dismissal and he had to admit she was right. He *was* feeling tired, so he thanked her for the evening, and was about to wish her goodnight, when a thought resurfaced from their morning conversation.

"On our way to the excavation site this morning we talked about the crucifixion." "Yes," she replied, "And?" "Events leading up to the crucifixion and the crucifixion itself were played out by the Romans, Jesus, and a crowd of clamouring Jews; yet it is now a powerful Christian symbol." "Well, that's true, I suppose," replied Doctor Scott, "What are you getting at?" "Can we also look upon it as a symbol of Jewish suffering? I recall a painting by Marc Chagall, entitled *White Crucifixion,* which portrays the crucifixion as a Jewish catastrophe. To emphasise the Jewishness of Jesus on the cross, Chagall gave him a prayer shawl, and the scene is surrounded by scenes of Jewish persecution and suffering, like a burning synagogue."

She replied: "I know that painting. Chagall was a Jew and he painted the White Crucifixion in the 1930s when Jews were suffering in Nazi Germany." After a lengthy silence, Doctor Scott agreed that Martin had made an important point; the Jews also had a stake in the crucifixion. Moreover, Jesus was born a Jew, lived as a Jew and died a Jew. Perhaps he had no intention of starting a new religion called Christianity. This was a far more positive approach than accusing the Jews of being Jesus killers.

Then she added that the same arguments applied irrespective of whether Jesus had been a real person or whether he was a most beautiful and powerful metaphor. As she made this last remark she studied Martin's face for a reaction. She noted with satisfaction that he momentarily looked startled, or so she thought. Martin's tired expression was difficult to interpret. As he made to leave, she called him back to point out that she liked to start breakfast at seven o'clock every morning. They had started later that morning because Martin needed more sleep after his long journey and late night. Mustapha then appeared as if from nowhere and walked Martin back to his tent. He lay awake puzzling over

CHAPTER 9

Doctor Scott's remarks on the crucifixion. But not for long. He was soon fast asleep.

At six o'clock the next morning, he awoke without the benefit of Mustapha fussing around outside his tent. Immediately his mind turned to the conversation of the previous evening, starting with the possibility that the Roman authorities were concerned about the rise of nationalism in Judaea and moved against all known trouble makers at once. At this time, armed Zealot fanatics, known as the Sicari, were assassinating Jews who were friends of Rome, and the Jewish independence movement was getting stronger. This was all happening during the first and second centuries, when there were many claimants for the title of Messiah. What if two of these Messiahs were at the peak of their popularity at the same time? They would both have been called Jesus. – *Jesus, king of the Jews* and *Jesus, son of God*. Pontius Pilate feared a blood bath and offered to let one go. The crowd had to choose between their kingly Messiah and their priestly Messiah. It is impossible to say whether the real Jesus of the Christian faith was crucified or released. The stories of both men are so totally merged that the Christian sects that claim he was never crucified are correct, yet so is the mainstream Church which says that he *was* crucified. Impossible that both could be correct? Not according to quantum physics, which tells us that an electron can exist in two places at once!

He then turned to the traditional requirement for two Messiahs, who would work hand-in-hand to achieve the final victory of Yahweh and His chosen people. A kingly Messiah from the tribe of Judah, the royal line of David, would be joined by a priestly Messiah from the tribe of Levi. According to tradition, Jewish priests had to be Levites. Then the Jesus from the royal line of David died on the cross, while the Jesus from the priestly line of Levi went free. Which was which? The genealogy (begat, begat, begat, etc.)

showing Jesus in the royal line of David is based on Mary's husband, Joseph.  Oops!  If Jesus was the son of God, he could not have been the royal Messiah!  Mary was related to John the Baptist, who was a Levite; so Jesus must have had some Levite blood himself, and he could therefore have been the priestly version.

Martin was no longer able to think clearly.  He needed coffee and breakfast.

# Chapter 10

Martin put on his working jeans and a T-shirt bearing the inscription *Jesus Lives!* Elsie Pritchard's granddaughter had had them printed last year, and she sold them at the annual church social. They hadn't sold very well, but Martin had bought one. He had never felt able to wear it in public in Herefordshire. It was more appropriate wear for newly confirmed teenagers, young curates and altar boys; and for country vicars in the Nubian Desert.

Doctor Scott greeted him with: "Aha! We are dressed for action this morning, I see. I like the T-shirt. Forgive me for being so cheeky, but when you eventually leave here, could you possibly leave it behind for me? *Jesus Lives* is the essence of my own faith. Put it in the past tense, however, and *Jesus lived* is a highly contentious issue, and that," she said, eying him with a knowing smile, "is why you're here; to learn what you can from me about that period of Christian history that started when Jesus supposedly lived."

"Exactly," replied Martin, "And good morning, by the way, and yes thank you I slept very well. And yes you are welcome to my T-shirt when I leave; even before I leave."

He knew it was risky and smacked of impertinence. She took it with a smile. If they could swap that kind of pleasant irony at breakfast, it augured favourably for their future relationship.

"Starting now," she announced, looking him up and down and tilting her face first to right then to the left as she studied his features, "your body will be undergoing a process of acclimatisation. It takes time. We will continue to take it easy for the next twenty-four hours then tomorrow I'll lever you into some gentle field work. So pour yourself another coffee and let me fill you in on the background of my research here."

Once again, Martin took two slices of toast and spread them with fool, added a fried egg to his plate then chose an orange and a banana. "Why is it," Martin asked himself, "that breakfast tends to be the same every day, whereas the cuisines of the midday snack and the evening meal have to meet our desire for variety?" He was on the point of sharing this trivial thought with Doctor Scott, when he saw her expression change to one of deep sadness, like a cloud passing over the sun.

With a doleful sigh, she interrupted his thoughts with: "This is a re-enactment of breakfast with my second husband on his first morning at the camp. He was not yet fully acclimatised and I lectured him on the background to my research. He pretended to be interested, although he was obviously bored. My first husband wasn't really interested either; he at least managed to conceal his boredom somewhat longer."

Having raised the subject of husbands, she temporarily abandoned discussion of her research and began to talk about her marriages. Martin wondered whether she felt a deep personal need to do this, or whether she felt she owed it to him. They had to work together in the desert, isolated from other European company, so it was not unreasonable to get to know each other and to exchange personal information, even about failed marriages.

"My two scientist husbands were experts in their own fields: physics and biochemistry. They knew precious little about Christian history. I never spend a very long time at home, so there was no time to prepare elaborate weddings. It was a case of making our vows in the presence of our friends and relatives, packing our bags then flying back to the Nubian Desert."

She continued: "My first husband hated life in the desert and regretted leaving his work in England. He finally suggested he return to England and renew his contract at the university; we could then spend time together by visiting each other at Christmas and Easter and during the long

## CHAPTER 10

summer break. Not surprisingly, our marriage fizzled out. They do say you learn by your mistakes. Well, apparently I don't. I met both my husbands at social gatherings in England. My second husband was handsome and charming and I succumbed. Like my first, he was intrigued by the thought of living in the desert by the River Nile. I think he imagined an exotic lifestyle, waited on by fawning servants, and making love by moonlight like a desert Sheik. Since neither of them was really interested in my work and understood practically nothing of Christian history, I ought to have known our marriages would fail. I wasn't trying to play the part of a temptress, luring unsuspecting males into the desert, but looking back it seems that's what I did."

He could tell she had given him a superficial description of her marriages. She might well have finished her account with: 'and that's all you need to know.' It seemed she believed in the sanctity of marriage, although she had been unlucky in that department. Divorce is stressful and Martin knew this from his experience of comforting anguished parishioners whose marriages were in difficulty. Doctor Scott gave the impression that she had put it all behind her and she was now ready to carry on with her life in the desert, write off her marriages and compartmentalise that particular phase of her life in a separate box to be ignored, if not forgotten. Martin felt moved by the realisation here was a single lonely woman, isolated in the desert and nursing a deep inner sorrow. A professional psychiatrist might have analysed her state of mind differently.

Martin had to admit to himself that she had shared with him part of her life's story, albeit only in outline. That was a comradely gesture in itself, and any further details were none of his business. One thing was certain: two failed marriages had not killed her sexuality. Martin wished it had.

Was she expecting a response to her last remark? He had to say something and felt trapped between gallantry and stupidity, so he replied with: "Well, they do say third time lucky!" and immediately realised he had chosen stupidity.

In reply to his silly remark she uttered a loud dismissive laugh. She had got her husbands out of her system. Regaining her school mistress composure she announced: "Okay, let's have a real history lesson."

Martin breathed a sigh of relief and sat back to listen and learn.

Opening her tin trunk and forgetting to say *eftah ya sim sim*, she extracted a rather tattered Bible and handed it to Martin. It was bound in black leatherette, the type that a pious grandmother might present to her first grandchild. This one was very much the worse for wear with the front cover hanging loose. "Please turn to the Acts of the Apostles and read chapter eight, verses twenty-six to thirty-nine, not out loud, just read and digest."

"Alright, if I must," agreed Martin. "It's part of your education, so please read it. Who knows? When you get back to England and your church, you might be able to turn it into a sermon."

Her voice betrayed a no-nonsense mood, so Martin obeyed, found chapter eight of *Acts,* and started to read at verse twenty-six:

*26 And the Angel of the Lord spake unto Philip, saying, arise and go toward the south unto the way that goeth down from Jerusalem unto Gaza, which is desert.*

*27 And he arose and went: and, behold, a man of Ethiopia, an eunuch of great authority under Candace queen of the Ethiopians, who had the charge of all her treasure, and had come to Jerusalem for to worship,*

*28 Was returning, and sitting in his chariot read Esaias the prophet.*

*29 Then the spirit said unto Philip, Go near, and join thyself to this chariot.*

## CHAPTER 10

*30 And Philip ran thither to him, and heard him read the prophet Esaias, and said, Understandest thou what thou readest?*

*31 And he said, How can I, except some man should guide me? And he desired Philip that he would come up and sit with him.*

Did she have to rely on this tatty old Bible with such archaic wording? It didn't make sense that an authority on Christian history had only one Bible to her name, and at that a very old and worn-out copy. Martin enjoyed the sonorous wording of older Bible translations, but this translation of *Acts* was irritating. However, not wanting to offend her, he read on:

*32 The place of the scripture which he read was this, He was led as a sheep to the slaughter; and like a lamb dumb before his shearer, opened he not his mouth:*

*33 In his humiliation his judgement was taken away: and who shall declare his generation? For his life is taken from the earth.*

*34 And the eunuch answered Philip, and said, I pray thee, of whom speaketh the prophet this? Of himself, or of some other man?*

*35 Then Philip opened his mouth, and began at the same scripture, and preached unto him Jesus.*

*36 And as they went on their way, they came unto a certain water: and the eunuch said, See, here is water; what doth hinder me to be baptised?*

*37 And Philip said, If thou believest with all thine heart, thou mayest. And he answered and said, I believe that Jesus Christ is the Son of God.*

*38 And he commanded the chariot to stand still: and they went down both into the water, both Philip and the eunuch; and he baptised him.*

*39 And when they were come up out of the water, the Spirit of the Lord caught away Philip, that the eunuch saw him no more: and he went on his way rejoicing.*

"Well," announced Martin, "I've read later and better translations. What does it teach us about the history of Christianity?"

"This story in *Acts* is about the first Christian to enter Nubia. He was a Nubian, an official of the royal palace of Meroe. The story dates from early in the first century, about 37 AD. As you have just read, he was a eunuch and chief treasurer to the queen. Before returning to his own country he was instructed in the essential elements of the Christian religion and baptised. Verse twenty-seven says he was a man of Ethiopia. This is a translation of the Greek *Aithiopia*, which did not mean present-day Ethiopia. It meant *Land of the Blacks*, the land south of Egypt. Moreover, we know that *kandake* or Candace was the queen of Meroe. The eunuch also knew Greek because Philip, who explained the scripture to him, spoke Greek. Thus, the Greek language had spread even as far as Nubia amongst the upper classes."

"Then I suppose he spread Christianity throughout the Nile valley south of Egypt?" suggested Martin.

"I'm not sure whether you are asking me or telling me," replied Doctor Scott, sounding rather irked. "The answer is we don't know what he did when he returned home. Nevertheless, it's exciting to think this converted eunuch was the first evangeliser of the lands south of Egypt. In which case, he is the putative founder of the Church that I am excavating. But I agree; it's a long shot."

She uttered a resigned sigh: "No, I must be honest. It's worse than a long shot. There's no evidence of Christianity, certainly no evidence of a Christian kingdom, existing in the land south of Egypt in the first century AD. Egyptian Christians writing in the second and third centuries AD

## CHAPTER 10

make no mention of fellow Christian communities south of Egypt. Even in the fourth century AD we know that non-Christian cults still held sway south of Aswan."

"In that case, why was it necessary to draw my attention to an unnamed black eunuch, mentioned in *Acts*, who didn't trigger an outbreak of Christianity in the land south of Egypt? Also, are we talking of *all* the land south of Egypt or only the Nile Valley? And why do you suddenly redefine the region in question as *south of Aswan?*"

This outburst was fuelled by his irritation, still felt, at having to read the ridiculously archaic translation of *Acts*.

Briefly, she was taken aback by his response. It made her realise he was more than a student sitting at her feet. He was a fellow intellectual and thinker.

"You're right. The black eunuch takes us nowhere. At the moment he's an historical dead end, but I can't forget him. One day I hope to know more about him. Three fellow historians, two in Cambridge and the other in Jerusalem know of my interest in these passages in *Acts*. They keep an eye open on my behalf for anything that might throw light on the eunuch of Ethiopia. Then you mentioned my reference to Aswan. In a sense, Aswan is really where the story starts. Let's have more coffee then I'll explain."

Mustapha, using his personal desert telepathy, which Martin never fathomed, then suddenly appeared with a fresh pot of coffee and a plate of cinnamon cakes.

"I could get used to this sort of life," remarked Martin, leaning back in his camp chair in the shade of the tent entrance and relishing the rich aroma of the freshly ground coffee, complemented by Mustapha's home-made cinnamon-flavoured pastries.

She chided him with: "Wait until you've sweated over that wall painting at the excavation site. You might not be so enthusiastic about this life."

Martin winced theatrically, drained his coffee cup, wiped a cake crumb from his chin and said he was ready to learn about Aswan.

"We'll start by you telling me about Aswan," was the reply.

Momentarily puzzled, then realising there must be method in her approach, Martin gladly answered with: "I know the Nile has six cataracts. These are white water stretches with protruding rocks, which make navigation of the river difficult. The fourth cataract isn't far from here and I hope to visit it soon. Now back to Aswan, which is in Egypt and is the site of the first cataract."

Martin raised his eyebrows as if to ask: "How am I doing so far?"

"You still have a long way to go," she replied, rather seriously.

"Whenever I hear of Aswan," he continued, "I think of the Aswan dam. In fact, if it were not for the Aswan dam perhaps I would never have heard of Aswan. Nowadays trips up the Nile to the Aswan dam and trips on Lake Nasser behind the dam are widely advertised by travel companies. The dam was built before I was born, so I didn't become aware of the saga of Egyptian independence, the annexation of the Suez Canal and the building of the dam until it was all over. If I'd known you were going to test me on my knowledge of Aswan, I would have done my homework before coming here. Everyone knows that the dam provides hydroelectric power and supports a massive irrigation scheme.

What really sticks in my mind, however, is the movement of the twin temples of Abu Simbel to higher ground to avoid being flooded by the rising water behind the dam. This attracted world attention. Those two massive rock temples had been carved out of the mountainside in the thirteenth century BC in the reign of Ramses II. Cutting them from the mountain then moving them to higher ground without

## CHAPTER 10

damaging their structure and retaining exactly their original orientation to the sun was a celebrated feat of engineering. All that was before my time, so I suppose work on the dam must have started in the nineteen sixties and finished sometime in the nineteen seventies."

"Excellent, and almost spot on with your dates. It was also before *my* time when Egypt hit the headlines with the revolution, dissolution of the monarchy, annexation of the Suez Canal and the building of the Aswan High Dam. Incidentally, it's called the High Dam because lesser dams already existed, for instance the Aswan Low Dam built by the British between 1898 and 1902." Martin added: "And I read somewhere that there were even earlier, smaller dams.

She nodded in agreement and continued: "When I first learned about the High Dam in history lessons, I had not yet been infected with a passionate interest in Christian history. Little did I know that one day I would be deeply concerned at what had happened at Aswan. In fact, I was more than deeply concerned; I was very disappointed and not a little angry. You hit on what to me is the most concerning outcome of damming the Nile at Aswan: the inundation of land behind the dam by Lake Nasser. Oh yes, Abu Simbel was historically valuable so they saved it. UNESCO was involved, engineers competed worldwide with their schemes for saving the temples, the project became a showcase for modern engineering skills, the stage by stage removal and relocation of the stonework became a long-running spectacular form of entertainment, and just think what it has done for the tourist trade!"

The intense irony of this outburst was inescapable.

"Wherever anyone builds a dam, it seems the lake formed behind it submerges villages, towns and agricultural land. It happened in Ghana and in China and goodness knows where else. It happened recently about a mile from here on the Nile at Merowe. You will see the Merowe dam when you fetch water from the Nile. Whenever a dam is built, populations must be relocated and the fairness and efficiency with which this is achieved become a political issue. When the Aswan High Dam was built more than a hundred thousand people lost their homes and lands, but they were satisfactorily resettled in newly created settlements with access to well irrigated agricultural lands."

In that case, thought Martin, what is she moaning about?

The answer came so quickly that he wondered if she was a thought reader.

"Lake Nasser extended beyond the Egyptian border into the Sudan, where it drowned a town called Faras, the site of an extinct Christian Church. If it were not for that wretched High Dam, I wouldn't be sitting here talking to you. I would be at Faras in northern Sudan, not far from the Egypt-Sudan border, excavating and researching the remains of a fascinating but extinct Christian Church. The whole world wanted to preserve the remains of an extinct Egyptian cult, but no-one cared a damn about the remains of an extinct Christian Church!"

Martin searched for a witty reply based on the difference between dam and damn, but his imagination failed him. So he studiously poured himself another coffee and asked, by gesturing with his cup, if she would like one too. She nodded that she would, took a deep breath and composed herself.

"Tell me more about Faras," pleaded Martin. She seemed gratified that he was taking a genuine interest. Talking about the history of Faras would help her regain equilibrium.

"Faras was founded about two thousand years BC, probably as a small fortress on the Egypt-Sudan border, when the Sudan acted as a conduit for goods from further south into Egypt. That was during the Middle Kingdom of Egypt, which was followed by the New Kingdom, starting about 1550 BC. The New Kingdom continued to trade with the Sudan, and at this time temples began to appear at Faras. It must have had various names. By about 300 BC it was known as Paharas, which obviously is the origin of the name Faras. The city then rose to prominence and the archaeological remains of settlements and royal burials suggest it may have served as a provincial capital between the first century BC and the first century AD.

Let's skip the next six centuries. From the seventh century AD onwards Faras became an important Coptic Christian site. A bishopric was established and a cathedral was built, as well as at least six other churches, a monastery, and pottery workshops. Towards the end of the Middle Ages Faras declined in importance, possibly due to war and conflict in that region. It was easier to defend other parts of northern Sudan. I'll leave it there. I hope you can now understand why Faras is, or rather was, important.

"Thank you. That was most interesting as an introduction. I sense we have nearly reached the real beginning of the story,"

"Surely it's more than mere introduction. I would rather call it important background information."

"Well, let's be poetic and call it preliminary enlightenment," suggested Martin.

She was secretly delighted with his recasting of *introduction* as *preliminary enlightenment*. It was well-meant and gracious. She warmed to him.

"You do know, of course, that the second cataract was also submerged beneath Lake Nasser?"

"Frankly, no, I hadn't even thought about it. So another interesting geographical feature also fell victim to the High Dam?"

"Fortunately, an excellent description of the second cataract is preserved for posterity. After the Mahdi killed General Gordon in Khartoum, the British launched a campaign to reconquer the Sudan. So, in 1896, British gunboats started steaming up the Nile. The cataracts were a great hindrance to navigation and they are beautifully described by Winston Churchill in his *River War,* written in 1899; he was twenty-five years old at the time. Churchill described the second cataract as about nine miles long with a descent of sixty feet. During the summer floods the Nile flowed smoothly and unbroken over ledges of black granite. However, when the annual flood abated the granite ledges were exposed and the river tumbled violently from ledge to ledge, for mile after mile its entire surface churned to white foam."

"I must admit," conceded Martin, "that I simply didn't realise what a formidable barrier the Nile cataracts could be to shipping. I imagined them as much smaller and less steep."

"Oh, there are smaller ones that are fairly easy to navigate, and these aren't even marked on many maps. That doesn't apply to the fourth cataract, not far from here, where we collect our water. I don't have a copy of the *River War,* but I made notes from an old copy in my college library in Cambridge. They were useful in my application for extra funding last year."

She dived into her tin trunk, uttered *eftah ya sim sim,* and triumphantly held aloft four sheets of A4 held together with a rusty paper clip. "Here," she said, handing him the papers, "You read about it, starting half-way down page two."

Martin found the paragraph in question and began to read aloud:

*"The Fourth Cataract lies in the Monassir Desert, and Churchill reported the following about this portion of the Nile: The British gunboats El Teb and Tamai in 1897 attempted to go up the river at the Fourth Cataract, but in spite of being helped by 200 Egyptians and 300 tribesmen,*

## CHAPTER 10

*the Tamai was swept downstream and almost capsized in the great rush of water. Four hundred more tribesmen were assembled to help the El Teb, which was capsized and carried off downstream."*

Martin looked up and exclaimed: "Good heavens, I wouldn't have believed it. Come to think of it, there's a scene in the film *Storm over the Nile,* where British boats are being dragged up a cataract by teams of hundreds of natives. It must have been inspired by Churchill's account of the two gunboats on the fourth cataract."

"Most probably," agreed Doctor Scott, "Now read on."

Martin continued:

*"Throughout the whole length of the course of the Nile there is no more miserable wilderness than the Monassir Desert. The stream of the river is broken and its channel obstructed by a great confusion of boulders, between and among which the water rushes in dangerous cataracts. The sandy waste approaches the very brim, and only a few palm-trees, or here and there a squalid mud hamlet, reveal the existence of life."*

Martin looked up and laughed: "So we are living in miserable wilderness! And what's all this about the Monassir Desert? You have always called it the Nubian Desert."

"Admittedly, it's stretching things a bit to call it the Nubian Desert. The true Nubian Desert lies further to the north. I find the name conveniently covers the entire area. The region of the fourth cataract is called Dar al-Manassir and it's the homeland of the Manassir tribe."

With a jerk of his head and a frown, Martin conveyed, without speaking, that he was puzzled.

"Of course! I know what you're thinking: how did ancient Meroe, home of Candace in *Acts*, suddenly jump from the sixth to the fourth cataract?

"Exactly," replied Martin.

"Merowe near the dam is spelled: M-E-R-O-W-E. It's an entirely different place from the ancient city of Meroe, spelled M-E-R-O-E. The former is on the western arm of the great bend, the latter on the eastern arm. Arabic uses sounds and intonations that we don't have in English, so I'm sure native Arabic speakers hear the difference between the two names. They both sound the same to me."

"Thank you," sighed Martin, whereupon he fell silent. Food for thought, like other forms of food, requires time for digestion. So Martin remained silent, reviewing this recent onslaught of new information and filing it in appropriate memory boxes.

Once Doctor Scott got on her high horse, she could talk and talk. On the other hand, Martin was learning that she didn't mind long silences in their conversations. He was beginning to catch on and he no longer felt uncomfortable when she fell into a formative silence, as he called it. In fact, he found such silences very valuable. When he took up his duties again in Herefordshire he would encourage moments of formative silence during meetings of the church committee.

Eventually, of course, one of them would have to say something. It was Doctor Scott who broke the silence.

"When I was last in Cambridge, about eight months ago, the Christian Fellowship asked me to lead a workshop and left it to me to decide the subject. I decided on *Divisions within Christianity*. Thirty-eight students attended. Most of them came prepared to listen and talk about Catholics, Protestants and Puritans and the various subdivisions of these groups. I caught them completely by surprise by talking about divisions within Christianity in the first century AD and in subsequent centuries long before the Reformation. They were unsure as to how many Ecumenical Councils had ever been held. And when I told them there had been seven and that the seventh had been held in 787 AD, no-one challenged that statement. They were all faith with no knowledge of history. I'm afraid that is typical of many enthusiastic Christians. A bright theological student might have said: *What about the Fourth Council of Constantinople in 879 – wasn't that an eighth Ecumenical Council?* But no-one did. The series of councils between 1341 and 1351, known as the fifth Council of Constantinople, could also be claimed as an Ecumenical Council, but no-one appeared to have heard of it. I soon realised that I had to lower my sights. In the end I managed to conduct a satisfactory workshop based on defining the differing theologies of Christian groups like the Ebionites, Marcionites and Encratites, and most of the time was taken up with discussing the conflicting theologies of Arianism and Trinitarianism."

There followed what is known in the literature as a pregnant pause. She seemed unsure as to how to continue, so Martin cheekily announced: "I have an aunt who plays the guitar."

She looked puzzled, not knowing whether to laugh or take him seriously.

"How's your Spanish?" he enquired.

"Very poor. Why?"

Oh dear, had he gone too far? Now, at risk of offending her, he had to explain himself. "It's a Spanish expression: *Tengo una tia que toca la guitarra*. It's used when someone says something apparently irrelevant; it's a Spanish way of saying "So what?""

"I get it," she replied with a sigh, "I suppose I deserved that."

Martin was relieved she had taken it on the chin without complaint, but he was concerned to hear that sigh of resignation. In truth, they hadn't made much progress. He still didn't know anything about the church she was excavating, only that she would have preferred to be elsewhere excavating a different church at a place called Faras near the Egypt-Sudan border.

The situation was saved by the faithful Mustapha, who appeared, as usual, apparently from nowhere, and suggested he serve them a light lunch. At a click of his fingers, the two Mohammeds appeared bearing trays of food and drink, consisting of bread and spreads, more coffee and fruit juice. She began to laugh quietly to herself. Martin raised a questioning eyebrow. "I must remember that. It might be useful one day. What was the Spanish again?" Martin repeated the expression slowly, in capital letters as it were. "Thank you. I think I have it. Let's see if I can still remember it at breakfast tomorrow."

After another lengthy pause for chewing and sipping, she announced rather seriously: "One further thing: I have no time for formality, especially when there are just the two of us far from home in the desert. If you don't mind I would prefer to call you Martin and dispense with the Reverend Kimpton. And you must call me Dotty; most of my friends do."

According to Flo Willan, the privilege of calling her Dotty was rarely conferred and only on her closest friends. But then Flo knew her only as a member of the European lecture circuit.

"Agreed! What a splendid idea!" responded Martin, secretly reflecting that despite the fact that his study of early Christianity had not yet started, he had, in less than forty-eight hours, made remarkable progress in establishing a friendly relationship with Doctor Dorothy Scott, henceforth to be known as Dotty.

Dotty now seemed eager to continue and didn't wait until lunch was over before launching into the next chapter of her instruction course. Still chewing a sandwich and sipping fruit juice, she interrupted Martin's thoughts with: "As a well-educated church minister, who has sat at the feet of Doctor Willan, you will know all about the Coptic Church and Coptic Christianity, which, according to

## CHAPTER 10

tradition, was established in the first century AD in Egypt by the apostle Mark. I say 'according to tradition' advisedly, because I don't believe it. Each of the Eastern Churches claims it was founded by one of the apostles. Anyone who has studied Christian history in an honest scholarly way finds this so-called apostolic succession very dubious."

She looked enquiringly at Martin, who replied that although he hadn't recently read his course notes on the Coptic Church, he was fully aware of that branch of Christianity, which was to this day the main Christian Church in Egypt. Then he added, as a precaution, that he surely didn't know *all* about the Coptic Church and Coptic Christianity, and he suspected she was going to instruct him. "Indeed," she exclaimed triumphantly, "That is exactly what I intend to do."

She continued: "By the first century AD, Christianity had spread widely in the Roman Empire and was well represented in Egypt. Like all other Christians in the Empire, the Egyptian Christians with their centre in Alexandria did not escape the widespread Roman persecutions of 250 AD and 297 AD. Many Egyptian Christians fled into the desert regions to the west and east of the Nile. Some fled south into Upper Egypt. Rather than establishing churches in these regions, many became hermits or monks. Some lived near Aswan and were in communication with Nubians in the land south of Egypt. Remember that black eunuch in the Acts of the Apostles? He was a Nubian, an official of the royal palace of Meroe. At that time the Nile valley to the south of Egypt formed one empire, the Kingdom of Meroe, whose capital, also called Meroe, was near present-day Kabushiya."

She waved her hand towards the inside of her tent and indicated a large map of the Nile valley and the desert on either side of it, obviously drawn by hand with a black felt pen. It was mounted on stiff card and hanging outside the mosquito netting of her bed. There was no telling how long it had hung there, probably not all that long because glue and paper quickly deteriorate in a tropical climate. It was spotted with yellow blemishes caused by insects or fungi, and its edges were curling away from its backing.

"You can see that Meroe isn't far from here, by the Nile and about half-way between this camp and Khartoum as the crow flies. You should visit the ancient pyramids of Meroe before you leave the Sudan. Tourists from all over the world pay good money to visit the pyramids of Meroe. You can actually catch a bus there from Khartoum. I suggest you do that when you get the chance. It would be a pity to leave the Sudan without seeing those ancient pyramids. Don't forget!"

Once again, she changed tack: "So, when Christianity was born, the Nile valley south of Egypt consisted of the single large kingdom of Meroe. Nowadays we are concerned about the role and status of women in society, and rightly so. We could learn much about this problem by studying ancient cultures." Whereupon Martin looked up suddenly and uttered an interrogative "Err?"

"Quite right, Martin, I was digressing. I did want to point out that the queen always played an important role in the government of Meroe. Our black eunuch was the chief treasurer of the queen of Meroe, who had the special title of kandake, or Candace as she appears in *Acts*. It was a title, not a name, and scholars of the Meroitic language have difficulty with its translation. It's thought to mean something like *the great mother.*"

"I forgive you your digression. In fact it's an interesting point to make. From now on, I will think of her as the Angela Merkel of the Nile valley."

"The roles of Angela Merkel and Candace in their respective societies do not really correspond. Possibly the king and queen of Meroe had equal status and she had an important role in policy making. Just the same, *Angela Merkel of the Nile Valley* is a charming thought. I must pass

## CHAPTER 10

it on to the religious correspondent of the *Süddeutsche Zeitung* next time I see him at a European archaeological gathering. Thank goodness you didn't choose Margaret Thatcher!"

Martin was beginning to look upon Dotty's digressions as valuable interludes in their conversation. Christian history was pretty heavy stuff, like a long distance hike over rough terrain. Now and again you needed to rest, take refreshment then move on again. Ready to move on, Martin asked: "So what happened to Meroe?"

"You might ask how it arose in the first place. Of course, that's a game we could play forever: delving further and further back into history. Let's start with the first known reference by the Egyptians to the land south of the first cataract. Nearly two thousand years BC, actually somewhere between 1970 and 1930 BC, they called it the Kingdom of Kush. That they were aware of this kingdom is hardly surprising because all manner of commodities passed through the kingdom on their way from sub-Saharan Africa to Egypt: gold, copper, ivory, ebony, spices, exotic animals, as well as slaves. The kingdom was a trading middleman and Egypt was its trading partner. Its capital was at Kerma on the east bank of the Nile just south of the third cataract, so it's also often called the kingdom of Kerma. Incidentally, no-one called it Nubia until the Middle Ages."

"Sorry to interrupt again," said Martin, "What do you mean by sub-Saharan Africa? My mind immediately traces a route through South Sudan into present-day Kenya, Uganda and the Congo. Then I realise that the Horn of Africa, now occupied by countries like present-day Ethiopia, Somalia, Eritrea and Djibouti are also sub-Saharan and would have been more easily accessible, not only overland but also by boat from Egyptian ports on the Red Sea."

"Well, there you are then," replied Dotty, "Congratulations, you've worked it out correctly! Obviously, it would have been possible for goods and people from the sub-Saharan south-west to find their way further north and eventually to the Nile valley, and it would be rash and unwise to claim it never happened. It is clear, however, that all populations of the Nile valley, had trading contacts with cultures further south, and that these cultures were in, or near to, the Horn of Africa, *i.e.*, the sub-Saharan south-east. Have a quick look at the map and you'll see that Ethiopia is an eastern neighbour of South Sudan, while Eritrea lies to the north of Ethiopia. So those ancient Egyptians didn't have to travel as far as you might think when they traded with sub-Saharan Africa.

At this point Martin simply had to interrupt: "Which brings us to the fabled Land of Punt."

"You beat me to it!" exclaimed Dotty, "I should have mentioned it sooner. Historians and egyptologists are now convinced that the Land of Punt was an area south-east of Egypt in and around the Horn of Africa, perhaps also extending across the water into the nearby corner of Arabia, which is now part of Yemen. There is srong evidence that Punt and Egypt were trading even as early as the Fourth Dynasty during the first half of the Old Kingdom in the reign of the ancient Pharaoh Khufu, who died in 2566 BC. Pictures on the walls of the mortuary temple of Queen Hatshepsut, built during her reign between 1479 and 1458 BC, tell the story of a famous trading voyage to Punt, when myrrh trees were brought back to Egypt for planting.

After that interesting diversion, I've forgotted how far I had progressed with the kingdom of Kerma. Before I continue, let's break for coffee."

Mustapha was equal to the occasion, even providing cinnamon biscuits, but not without expressing surprise that they wanted coffee again so soon.

They sat silently drinking and munching, occasionally exchanging a nod and a smile without really knowing why.

## CHAPTER 10

"I needed that; what about you?" enquired Dotty. "It was most welcome; you may now continue," replied Martin in a high-handed tone. Since agreeing to address one another as Dotty and Martin, their relationship had undergone a step change and was now very companiable.

"For a thousand years," continued Dotty," between 2500 and 1600 BC, the kingdom flourished without interference from Egypt, although it's thought the Egyptians might have acquired some of their slaves from Kush, not by trade but by sending raiding parties into the region. Although Egypt and Kush knew each other quite well, the first cataract was a barrier to real intimacy. Overland trade was obviously possible, but river boats would have provided greater capacity for goods, and river transport would have been easier. Throughout history the first cataract has always been a hindrance to the development of relations between Egypt and the land to its south."

"A hindrance, maybe, but it clearly didn't prevent contact," observed Martin. "And what about Kerma? Is it still there?"

"It most certainly is. The old city of Kerma with its monuments and archaeological remains is another interesting place for you to visit; you might manage that before you leave."

"I will add it to my list," replied Martin rather flippantly. "No, I mean it," protested Dotty," It would be foolish to leave the Sudan without visiting places like Meroe and Kerma. And I know you would not be disappointed because according to archaeological findings, Kerma was founded as early as 5,000 BC. It pre-dates Egyptian civilisation. The kingdom changed its name from Kerma to Kush to Meroe; take your pick. At the height of its power it was the centre of the ancient world. At one time or another, its armies defeated Egyptian, Greek and Roman attempts to dominate it.

Of course it had its downs as well as its ups. If you calculate its lifespan and do a little arithmetic you will see it outlasted Egypt, Greece and Rome combined."

"Wow!" exclaimed Martin, this time trying not to sound flippant.

She continued: "As they say, all good things come to an end. In 1580 BC the Egyptian Pharaoh Thutmose I sent in an army, took control of the kingdom as far south as the area between the third and fourth cataracts, destroyed Kerma, and founded a new capital at Napata on the southwest arm of the great bend. Thus, Kush, call it Kerma if you like, became an Egyptian colony, and Egypt plus Kerma became the Egyptian Kingdom of Kush. Egypt had at last really established an empire. This was the period of the New Kingdom of Egypt, the Kingdom of Kush, which lasted from 1580 to 1070 BC. The Pharaohs of this period, including the eighteenth and nineteenth dynasties, are those whose names we know best: Rameses Tuthmose, Akhenaten, Amenhotep and many more, not forgetting the famous Tutankhamen, and the female Pharaoh Hatshepsut, who recorded on the walls of her mortuary tomb a trading expedition to the mysterious Land of Punt. It was a period of Military expansion, with developments in art, architecture, and religion. Where we are sitting now would have been part of that ancient Egyptian kingdom of Kush.

At least, that was the standard story until recently. It's still more or less correct, except it's possible that the Egyptian onslaught on Kush in 1580 BC was not as devastatingly successful as once thought. More recent research suggests that although its capital, Kerma, suffered widespread destruction, Kush was not subjugated by the armies of Thutmose I. There appears to have been a prolonged standoff between the Kushites and Egypt. Moreover, excavations show that the Kushites had soon started to reconstruct Kerma following the attack by Thutmose's forces in 1580 BC.

## CHAPTER 10

Around 1070 BC the Egyptians became weak at home and lost control of Kush. Let's jump a few hundred years and we see that in 712 BC the Nubians attacked and took control of Egypt, which had fallen into decline and was ripe for picking. Egypt and indeed the entire Kingdom of Kush were then ruled by a Nubian dynasty. This was the twenty-fifth Egyptian dynasty and it was known as the Dynasty of the Black Pharaohs."

Martin made as if to interrupt. Dotty got in first: "Yes, I know, it wasn't called Nubia until the Middle Ages, but I find it convenient to call it Nubia and its inhabitants Nubians, irrespective of the historical period."

"Before I forget," said Dotty. "the Egyptians established an admistrative centre at Soleb immediately south of the third cataract on the west bank of the Nile. Its sandstone temple was part of an extravagant building programme by Pharaoh Amenhotep III. When you visit the ruins of Kerma, which you must do before you leave, you should also visit Soleb, which is not far from Kerma, although it's on the opposite bank of the Nile."

"I'll make note of that," replied Martin, "and you've just reminded how temple and monument building by the Egyptians illustrates the truth of the adage: *pride comes before a fall*. An empire or a dynasty showcases its pride and power with an orgy of monument building then it collapses."

"Yes, indeed," replied Dotty, "And there are many similar illustrations of the adage throughout history." Before Martin could find further historical examples of pride preceding a fall, Dotty announced she wished to guide the conversation in a different direction, whether he approved or not. She continued: "Historians are now more or less agreed that western culture came from Greece via Rome, and it is even proposed that the Greeks were originally civilised by their contacts with the Phoenicians and Ancient Egyptians.

It's difficult for racist bigots to accept that our culture could have been influenced by the Ancient Egyptians. Just imagine how they would react if you told them the Egyptians were black! In the twenty-fifth dynasty Egypt was ruled by Nubians and they, as you know from those you've met, are black. And don't forget there must have been plenty of black Egyptians before that because the Egyptians had been using black slaves from further south for centuries."

"What a wonderful way of baiting a bigot!" exclaimed Martin, not knowing whether to smile or look serious.

Ignoring the doubtful humour of Martin's remark, Dotty continued: "The Kushite capital was at Napata on the western arm of the great bend. Around 590 BC the Egyptian Pharaoh Psamtik II invaded Nubia, marching as far south as the third, possibly even the fourth cataract. According to a contemporary stele from Thebes the kingdom of Kush was heavily defeated, so that was the end of Nubian claims on Egypt. The Nubians transferred their capital to Meroe, further south on the eastern arm of the great bend. They recovered from the Egyptian invasion and by 300 BC Meroe had become a prosperous city, and the kingdom of Meroe a political and economic force to be reckoned with. The people of Meroe developed their own alphabet, known as Meroitic script, which is partly hieroglyphic and very difficult to decipher; hence the difficulty of interpreting with certainty the meaning of kandake, whom you liken to Angela Merkel. They also built all those pyramids and other monuments near the city of Meroe. It's debatable whether their pyramids were inspired by the Egyptian pyramids; they are much smaller and their slopes are much steeper, and they don't contain mummified kings or queens."

Martin grunted his acknowledgement of her account, so Dotty continued: "To get back to your question of what happened to Meroe. It lasted about 600 years. Then, like all empires and kingdoms, it eventually went into decline.

## CHAPTER 10

By the time Christianity really began to take hold south of Egypt, Meroe no longer existed and the Nile valley was divided between various kings and war lords. For present purposes we can consider that Nubia was no longer ruled from Meroe, and was divided into three kingdoms: *Nobatia* bordering Egypt, then *Makuria* starting to the south of the second cataract of the Nile, followed further south by *Alwah*, whose border corresponded to the confluence of Nile and the Atbara River."

She took a spoon from the table, leaned back in her chair and indicated the three kingdoms in question on the map.

Before she could continue, Martin interrupted: "You talked of the eastern and western arms of the great bend. What *is* this great bend?"

"Sorry! I thought you would know. Here it is," she said, leaning back once more and pointing to the map with her spoon. "The Nile doesn't simply flow in a straight line from south to north. At the sixth cataract it begins to flow east then north, finally bending south-west at Abu Hamed. It then flows in that direction for nearly 190 miles before heading north to the border with Egypt. So, as you can see, it describes a great loop or bend. Although my camp is on the west side of the Nile, we don't drive in an easterly direction to the Nile; we drive north to meet the southwest arm of the great bend." So saying, she traced the route with her spoon.

"So simple," remarked Martin, slightly embarrassed, "I knew that of course. It hits you in the face every time you see a map of the Nile Valley. I just didn't realise it was generally referred to as the great bend."

"Well, now you know. Let's get on. Early missionary activity by Egyptian Christians started in Nobatia, because it was next door and easily accessible. It's impossible to give an exact date for the effective and permanent penetration of Nobatia by Christianity. Crosses and other Christian objects, dated between 400 AD and 500 AD, have been discovered in royal tombs south of Faras. However, we can say with some confidence that the mass conversion of Nubia to Christianity, including the more southerly kingdoms, began in 543 AD. Now back to business! I look upon the Council of Chalcedon in 451 AD as the turning point in the history of the Coptic Church. What can you tell me about it?"

Martin racked his brains. Was Chalcedon the fourth or the fifth Ecumenical Council? When it came to Ecumenical Councils, their dates, their purposes and their outcomes, Martin was at a loss. He knew where to find such information; that was an essential part of his training. Like all ministers and most lay members of the Church, however, he knew that the first Council was held in 325 AD in Nicaea. Convoked by Emperor Constantine, it condemned the theology of Arius and led to the adoption of Christianity by the Roman Empire. Put simply, events leading up to the Council of Nicaea were Martin's reason for pursuing early Christian history. Of course he knew about *that* Council!

Little by little, he began to retrieve information from the recesses of his memory, information he had long since forgotten, or thought he had. As the memories clicked into place, he was able to place the various Ecumenical Councils in correct order with their dates and purposes. He wondered what mysterious and wonderful mechanism was responsible for human memory. Given a second chance in life, he would take the scientific route, become a neuroscientist and study human memory. Thus, with reasonable confidence, he was able to reply that the Council of Chalcedon in 451 AD was the fourth Ecumenical Council. It was presided over by the Patriarch of Constantinople and it confirmed that Jesus was both truly God and truly man.

"Excellent!" she cried, "Go to the top of the class! Now a further question: When did the Roman Catholic and Eastern Orthodox Churches separate?"

# CHAPTER 10

"I don't really know," replied Martin, "Is this a trick question?  I always had the impression that Rome and Constantinople argued and grumbled about each other for centuries then woke up one morning and found they had separated."

"And that," said Dotty, slapping the table for emphasis, "is probably the best answer I've ever been given to that question."

"I suppose it all started," ventured Martin, "as early as 330 AD when Emperor Constantine moved the capital of the Empire from Rome to the city of Byzantium on the Bosporus. He renamed the new capital Nova Roma.  It eventually became known as Constantinople, and nowadays it's Istanbul. It's obvious that when Constantine moved house from Rome to Byzantium he sowed the seeds of religious disunity, although it took centuries before the two Churches separated."

"Of course, it's difficult to disagree with that analysis. We both know that the east-west schism of Christendom resulted from a long process of civil and religious disagreements and confrontations, some conducted verbally, others written on parchment. By the way, the city of Byzantium was an ancient Greek city, founded by Greek colonists in 657 BC. We must never forget the Greeks!  Since geographical separation of human affairs can easily lead to the separation of ideas, it's perhaps not surprising that Rome and Constantinople became homes to different forms of Church management.  There's actually a neat little story of an historical drama, explaining how the schism between the Churches of Rome and Constantinople came about. Let me tell it."

"You mean the incident in 1054 when the legate of Pope Leo IX went up to the main altar in the Cathedral of the Hagia Sophia in Constantinople and produced a document declaring the Patriarch of Constantinople to be excommunicated?  Constantinople then excommunicated the pope of

Rome, resulting in a situation known ever since as mutual excommunication."

"That's right," declared Dotty, "I didn't realise you were already ahead of me. No-one really believes that the schism began in in 1054. On the contrary, the incident in the Hagia Sophia can be seen as the final act in the schism, and even that interpretation is too simplistic. Let's not try to analyse all the controversies and even jealousies that blighted Christianity for seven hundred years, until the two Churches finally separated and declared the match to be a draw. Suffice it to say that Christendom eventually split into two main branches: the Roman Catholic Church and the Eastern Orthodox Church."

"I know, don't tell me," cried Martin, "The Coptic Church finished up in the Eastern Orthodox camp. Am I right?"

"Yes and No. It's not as simple as that. We must now consider another schism, this time within the Eastern Orthodox Church."

Martin quickly recognised what she was referring to. He was on a roll. Course memories were flooding back. There was no stopping him now. "Well," he said, adopting the attitude of someone sagely imparting wisdom, "It's all to do with *monophysitism*." He loved saying that word. Ever since first hearing it in Flo Willan's lectures, he had thought it could be useful in elocution lessons.

"Alright. I give in. Once again you seem to be ahead of me, so carry on and tell me about monophysitism."

Martin gladly took the floor to show off his knowledge of the subject. Deep down he felt embarrassed for he had to admit to himself that he was showing off. He couldn't help it. "Even if you think it too simplistic, let's assume that the Council of Chalcedon in 1054 finalised the final schism between the western Roman Catholics on the one hand and the eastern Christians of Constantinople, Jerusalem, Alexandria and Antioch on the other."

## CHAPTER 10

"Whoa, wait there a moment! What's all this about Jerusalem, Alexandria and Antioch?"

Martin explained: "The pope of the Roman Catholics was and is the head of the Church. Strictly speaking, members of the Eastern Orthodox do not have popes, although their patriarchs are often called popes, especially by those outside the Church. This is because the head of the Eastern Orthodox Church is considered to be Jesus Christ himself and the Church is his body. Each see of the Eastern Orthodox Church has its own patriarch, who is in communion with the other patriarchs, all of them equal in authority, although Constantinople does rather stand out as the largest Church."

"Thank you. Perfect. Nine out of ten."

"If it's perfect, why not ten out of ten?" enquired Martin.

He had fallen for it. Smiling mischievously, she replied: "If I give you ten out of ten, it means you know as much as I do, and that's not possible."

Martin was delighted. One day he would use that same trick when testing members of his confirmation classes. Some might have said it was silly to interrupt a serious conversation in that way, but it was a welcome confirmation of their friendly relationship.

With a wry smile, Martin continued: "In 1054 the Council of Chalcedon declared that Jesus, the son of God, combined two natures. He was both supernatural and human and the two could not be separated. They may have hated the sight of each other, but the Roman Catholics and the Eastern Orthodox members were agreed on this one article of faith, that humanity and divinity existed in one person, and that one person was Jesus, the second person in the Holy Trinity. However, not all members of the Eastern Church saw it that way. Those based in Alexandria insisted that Jesus was one divine person with only one nature, and they rejected the belief that Jesus had two inseparable natures in one person. The dissidents of Chalcedon are known as the Oriental Orthodox Church and their theology is known as monophysitism. So there we have a schism within the Eastern Orthodox camp."

"So far, so good," remarked Dotty, "You have more or less sketched the bold outlines of the story."

"Really?" protested Martin, "I thought I'd given a complete account of the outcome of the Council of Chalcedon."

"More could be said," insisted Dotty, "but it would serve no purpose. Looked at in certain ways, there is no fundamental difference between the two theologies, just a difference in the emphasis placed on the meanings of human and divine. More importantly, from your point of view, this controversy, together with certain other so-called heresies, reveals how Christendom has agonised over the nature of Jesus. You say you want to study the early history of Christianity. I suspect your true purpose is to come to terms with the nature of Jesus. That question will cause you much agony and soul-searching, as it did the Christians of the seven Ecumenical Councils. For now, however, it must be abundantly clear to you that my Coptic Church is monophysite."

"Hold on a moment. When you said more could be said, what did you mean exactly? Don't forget I want to learn all I can about Christian history, although, of course, my main focus is the first four centuries."

"I only had in mind the fact that monophysite is a disputed term used mostly by commentators outside the monophysite fold. The monophysites themselves prefer the term miaphysite."

"Of course, of course, I'd forgotten that. Just remind me will you?"

"Oh dear, let me see now. Miaphysitism is the belief that the human and divine natures of Jesus are united, whereas monophysitism is the belief that Jesus has absolutely only one nature, which, incidentally, combines both the divine

# CHAPTER 10

and the human. Silly, isn't it? It's terribly semantic, which means of course, that theologians have argued over the difference and got nowhere. So, I suppose, out of respect for my Coptic Church, I'd better call it miaphysite. And before I forget, I should mention that the Egyptian Church didn't convert totally to miaphysitism. A few so-called Melkites or Melchites, those who remained faithful to the Council of Chalcedon, continued to preach and attempted to spread their doctrine further south into Nubia, only to fade away through lack of support.

"Okay, thanks, that's clear. Now when you talk of your Coptic Church, do you mean the church that disappeared under the water of Lake Nasser, or the church you are currently excavating?"

"Both. After the church was established at Faras, its Coptic version of Christianity spread further south along the Nile Valley. My church, or rather its physical ruin that we visited yesterday, was a satellite of the Faras church."

"Was the Faras church lost completely under the water? Was there no rescue attempt? Didn't someone make a photographic record or save artefacts from the church?"

"Oh yes. A joint Sudanese and Polish archaeological team saved and recorded much of value before the flood waters rose. They photographed as much as they could and saved stone carvings and wall paintings. Some of the material went to Poland and some is displayed in the museum in Khartoum. That museum is worth a visit to see the remains of the Faras church, as well as interesting stonework from Meroe and artefacts from tribes in southern Sudan, or rather South Sudan, which is now a separate country in its own right. The entrance fee is five cents and it's the best five cents worth in town."

"Then it seems that the work on Faras has already been done by experts, and you can study the results without getting your hands dirty. So what are you complaining about?"

"Oh, alright, it's a fair point. I don't think you can really appreciate how deprived I feel, partly because of my age and partly because they built that wretched dam. It would have been a dream come true to have brought to light some long-lost Coptic wall painting in the ruins of the Faras cathedral."

"I believe you and I sympathise." It seemed the most appropriate thing to say.

"Once Faras disappeared beneath the water, there were very few archaeological remains of that branch of Christianity. The satellite churches of Faras that were scattered along the Nile Valley were lost forever to historical investigation. They were utter ruins, robbed of their stone work and mud bricks, their frescoes erased by early Muslim militants and more often by the sand-blasting effect of desert storms. Then I discovered this early church near the fourth cataract, which the Muslims and the desert climate had treated more leniently, or less brutally. It's a long way from Faras and I'm hoping to find evidence for a fusion of Coptic Christianity and local pre-Christian customs. Such fusions occur constantly throughout Christendom. Take, for example, the role of mistletoe and yule logs in our own Christmas celebrations. Before I lost Pinda, he was working on a Greek inscription on one of the altar stones. He photographed it and pored over his copy every night before turning in. He thought he had found evidence linking the virgin birth with the local custom of committing the afterbirth to the River Nile."

"Now that is what I call interesting," cried Martin, "You mustn't abandon that line just because Pinda has gone."

"Of course I won't. Pinda took his notes with him when he left and they were not in his possessions that were returned to the camp. I worry that someone, possibly another archaeologist, may have purposely stolen them and intends to make use of them for their own academic

## CHAPTER 10

advancement. Anyway, I've photographed the inscription again and sent it to a friend in the archaeology section of the British Museum for his opinion."

"Incidentally," continued Martin, "How *did* you discover this old Church?"

"Actually, I didn't discover it myself. My research is funded by the archaeology section of the British Museum in London. Soon after my appointment they sent me to Khartoum to study the Faras artefacts. The curator of the Faras display, Doctor Ibrahim Saeed, told me about these ruins south of the fourth cataract, near to his grandfather's date plantation, where he used to play when he was a child. So I asked him to bring me out here and show me. The rest, as they say, is history. And there is more to it than that. The Faras artefacts were actually a secondary reason for my first visit. The British Museum was primarily interested in the archaeological remains that were disappearing or in danger of disappearing under the flood waters of a new dam at the fourth cataract. As you know, we are only a very short distance from the fourth cataract."

"Curiouser and Curiouser!" cried Martin, "It sounds like Faras and the first cataract all over again. I know about the dam of course. What about those archaeological remains? What did they find?"

Dotty stopped him by holding up both hands and shaking her head. "So ends the lesson for today. I have some notes to write up and you must take your afternoon rest. We'll meet again for the evening meal. Somewhere I have some literature on the building of the dam and the flooding of archaeological sites behind it. I'll sort it out and you can digest it at your leisure."

The dismissal was friendly but firm. Martin obeyed.

# Chapter 11

*They knew each other very well –
so well that they could sit now in
that soothing silence which is
the very highest development of companionship.*
(Lot No. 249 by Arthur Conan Doyle.)

Martin was anxious to see what Dotty would wear this evening. He hoped she would put on something colourful and revealing. How dare he entertain such thoughts!? Easy! They were private thoughts. Everyone has private thoughts, a private world of the mind, where one relaxes without fear of disturbance, or where one is entertained by the most outrageous scenarios without fear of being mocked. Wild thoughts act as a pressure valve, allowing the mind to let off steam while the body remains apparently unaffected and able to behave soberly and respectably. Put another way, living in the desert with an attractive divorcer of two husbands was a challenge to his hormones; but he could handle it. Or could he? Of course he could. He was a church minister, long and happily married to a very dear wife. A little voice within him retorted: So What!?

He arrived for the meal before she had finished dressing and caught sight of rather more than he should in the dim interior of her tent. She looked up and caught his eye.

"Be with you in a tick," she shouted, "Just doing up a few buttons. Pour yourself a beer."

Seeing her half-naked in a desert tent was embarrassing enough. For her to catch his eye at the same time was mortifying. She, however, was totally unperturbed. The incident passed in a flash. They both chose to ignore it and carry on as if nothing untoward had happened.

Rising to the occasion, Martin called back: "What about you?"

## CHAPTER 11

"Lemonade. What better at the end of a hot day?"

Martin later learned that the large jug of lemonade sitting on the table was routinely made by Mustapha by liquidising whole lemons with ice and plenty of sugar. It certainly looked tempting, so he shrugged, ignored the beer, and poured two glasses of lemonade. He was surprised that beer or any alcoholic drink was permitted in the camp and he had to assume that Mustapha, a Muslim, had procured it. What he didn't know was that the Muslim attitude to alcohol was not extreme and bigoted like that of some Christians. Muslims, at least Sudanese Muslims and devout ones at that, were strictly tee-total, but they had no objections to non-Muslims enjoying a tipple, and would even go out of their way to supply alcoholic drinks for visitors as part of their hospitality.

Dotty called out once again while struggling to secure a final button: "I've found the literature I promised you about the building of the dam and the flooding of the archaeological sites behind it. It's all in a manila wallet on one of the chairs. Don't forget to take it with you later."

Martin picked up the wallet, which contained only four sheets of A4. It would be a quick and easy read.

"Coming! Sorry to keep you waiting!" Martin's hopes were fulfilled: as Dotty emerged from her tent she was wearing a low-cut iridescent pink blouse and short pleated skirt. Actually, it was all very silly. Her clothes were quite inappropriate for the occasion: a meal, almost a picnic, in a small desert camp. If that was her style, then so be it!

Martin handed her a glass of lemonade and opened the conversation with: "I didn't sleep much this afternoon. I lay awake revisiting our conversations and going over what I've learnt and seen so far. My overall feeling is that I've stepped into a different world."

"Surely that's obvious. There's nothing extraordinary about that. What did you expect?"

"I'm not explaining myself very well," replied Martin. "Let me put it this way. At home, as an Anglican vicar, I interact with members of my own Church, some High Church, some Low Church, with Methodists, Baptists, Roman Catholics and others, and despite certain fundamental differences and outright disagreements we have a certain level of understanding, because we all live in the same English-speaking, western Christian world. The Coptic Church belongs to a different world. So far, I've only seen the ruins of an abandoned Coptic place of worship in the Nubian Desert, where Christianity has been replaced by Islam. That, together with your accounts of Eastern Orthodoxy, has educated me. I always knew and now I also feel that – I'll say it again – I have stepped into a different world. It's sort of alien in a friendly way. It's new and it's different, and it's beckoning me to watch and listen while it reveals more about itself."

She gazed at him intently until he began to feel uncomfortable. Then she quietly confided: "My goodness, you gave me a start, for that is exactly how I also feel and have always felt since my first visit to this land. We are kindred spirits and I'm so glad you are here."

For Martin this was a bit over the top, so he helped himself to more food and hastily sought to change the conversation. He came up with: "At home, our relationship with Roman Catholicism is interesting. Henry **VIII** hitched his wagon to the Protestant Reformation, and as we all know, his row with the pope was more personal and political than theological. We Anglicans are now left with the messy aftermath of Henry's petulance. Some would rejoin the Catholics, while others want to widen the gap between us even further. It's so refreshing to develop a new perspective of Roman Catholicism. What I mean is I can now view it from Constantinople, as it were, rather than from Canterbury."

## CHAPTER 11

"As I said before, we are kindred spirits." Martin let it pass.

Dotty continued: "The Roman Catholic Church carries a terrible historical burden. When I was in the fourth form, the over-zealousness of the Catholic Church was always equated with the Spanish Inquisition. Then there was the annihilation of the Cathars, those Mediaeval Christians for whom Christ was pure spirit sent by God. This version of Christianity, actually a form of Gnosticism, became widespread in Europe. It was particularly strong in southern Europe, notably France, and was followed by many wealthy and powerful families. Martin, take note of that Gnostic view: Christ as pure spirit. It's relevant to our future discussions.

To continue, in 1198 Innocent III was elected pope and he set out to destroy the Cathars, who were also known as Albigensians. His name is hardly appropriate. I like to think he was called Innocent in the same spirit that short people are sometimes called lofty. He unleashed the Albigensian Crusade, a long, drawn-out campaign with temporary victories and defeats on both sides, resulting finally in the total destruction of Catharism. It took about forty years. It is arguably the bloodiest act ever committed against opponents of the Catholic Church. Why? Because the Cathars didn't just disagree with the pope; they represented a real threat to the very existence of the Church. They opposed every aspect of the Church's theology, even claiming that the Church's God was an imposter; in fact, they claimed the Church's God was the devil, who had deviously usurped the true God. Priests and bishops were therefore servants of the devil, which clearly explained their corrupt and luxurious lifestyle, which resembled that of the nobility. In contrast, the Cathar priesthood dispensed with all worldly possessions, apart from a black robe and a cord belt, and they depended solely on alms and charity. The Catholics sought to spread their dogma by exhortation and admonition from the pulpit, and by the threat of eternal damnation, a threat with physical as well than spiritual implications. Cathars, in contrast, spread their faith by example and by close personal relationships. Need I say more? The Catholic Church simply employed the bloodiest means possible to protect its vested interests.

"Yes, I know the history," interrupted Martin.

"Hang on," pleaded Dotty, "I haven't finished damning the Catholics for their brutal history. Not satisfied with torturing and burning European Christians who disagreed with their theology, they sought to destroy the religions of other cultures. Take those Indians of South and Central America, for example. Astronomy was fundamental to the cultures of the Incas and Aztecs. They were keen observers and recorders of the heavens, using the movement of constellations and the appearance of the Milky Way to determine their planting seasons and to predict the future. This was anathema to the Catholic Church, which insisted that the sun went round the earth. The conquistadors put the Incas to the sword in order to steal their territory and their gold; then the priests, who followed in their wake, continued the slaughter by burning them to death for the good of their souls and to prevent any further advances in astronomy."

This survey of Catholicism's sins of the past threw new light on Dotty's character and values. Martin thought he had got to know her fairly well in the short time since his arrival at the camp. Her present outburst necessitated a reassessment. He had not yet learned that understanding Dotty was going to be a long, drawn-out process, which would not be complete until the day he left the Sudan.

Never in all his reading of history had Martin come across the role of astronomy in the downfall of South and Central American pre-Columbian cultures. He found it fascinating and wondered whether it was generally accepted by historians or whether it was Dotty's own interpretation of Catholic behaviour in the New World. It had little to do

CHAPTER 11

with his interest in early Christianity. In any case, he had not travelled from Herefordshire to the Nubian Desert to agree that Roman Catholicism carried a terrible historical burden. He already knew that. So he replied: "Surely, this history is transparent. We are all aware of it, and Catholics themselves are not proud of it. I'm more concerned about the possible concealment of historical facts by the Catholic Church, in order to support their theology."

She replied: "I think you will find that the misplaced brutal zeal displayed by early Catholicism is inextricably linked to their suppression of the true history of Christianity. Look at it this way: once they had established a creed, they had to defend it, insist upon its truth, and literally kill anyone who disagreed. No multinational organisation can afford to have its operations or its ethics challenged; otherwise it loses face, loses support, and incidentally, it loses a lot of money. That is why the pope employed an army to slaughter the Cathars, why inquisitions were necessary, and why heretics were burnt at the stake. You can view the treatment of heretics as a means of persuading them to accept a changed religious viewpoint, or you can see it simply as an outlet for a bigoted, psychotic, delinquent mind-set. In my opinion it was a bit of both. Misplaced religious zeal partly explains why the natives of the New World were treated so badly. Those natives had their own religion, which couldn't be tolerated by the Catholic invaders. Even today Catholics display great rigidity of belief, and Catholic education is still pretty weak when it comes to the Church's early abuses of human rights. What's more, the Catholic Church didn't outgrow its Mediaeval brutality. Our own John Wycliffe, the Bible translator and early critic of the Church, managed to sidestep the inquisition, whereas Jan Hus, the Czech reformer, was burnt at the stake in 1415. Protestant reformers of the sixteenth century, notably Luther and Calvin, might still have suffered the ultimate penalty for disagreeing with the pope, for even in the sixteenth century burning at the stake was still on offer, but they were clever enough to avoid it".

She had become rather heated, and she knew it. "Sorry! I tend to get on my soap box when I talk about early Catholicism. After all, everything that has happened since the fourth century, when the Roman Empire gave Christianity its power base, is well known and documented. Well, perhaps not everything, but you know what I mean. You are not here to share my distaste for the sins of the early Church."

Marti interrupted with: "I *do* share your distaste for all those atrocities committed in the name of God. In that department I'm on your side and I don't need convincing. It's an integral part of my own thinking on the history of Christianity.

Incidentally, I'm glad you mean the *early* Catholic Church, which felt it was defending its monopoly of western Christendom. It learned later to live with the competition, albeit grudgingly. In any case, some of the early Protestants were pretty ruthless in defending their versions of the faith. Just think of the thirty years' war in the seventeenth century, one of the deadliest of all religious wars, in which both sides had blood on their hands. And let's not mention what the Protestants did to the Catholics in the Britain of Hentry **VIII** and Elizabeth **I**.

By the way, you forgot to include Zwingli and John Knox in your list of reformers, not to mention several other worthy although less famous conscientious objectors to Catholic theology and priestly behaviour. But please Dotty! – I didn't come here to talk about Catholic or even Protestant sins. I came to learn what you can teach me about the early history of Christianity."

Was he being too confrontational? Apparently not, because she paused to take his rebellious little speech on board, then replied that he was absolutely right and that she would indeed teach him all she could about the early Christian story, adding with a mischievous smile that she expected him in return to lend a hand at the excavation site in this God-forsaken barren waste by the River Nile.

Martin nodded in agreement then asked: "Do you talk this way when you lecture at international symposia?" Dotty frowned. Was he criticising her in some way? "Why?" she asked. "Oh, nothing really. I just felt amused at the idea of Christianity existing where God might be forsaken.

"Touché!" she cried, "Obviously we are going to get on famously. Let's sit here a while and enjoy the poetic ambience of the desert in the moonlight."

"Quite right," agreed Martin, "Life mustn't be all Copts and Catholics." Dotty ignored his clever alliteration and waved her forefinger to demand his attention. "Earlier, you talked of western Catholicism and the Eastern Church as though their differences were the result of personal rivalries and antagonisms between priests and rulers. Their differences are more fundamental than that; in fact there are serious theological differences, which some theologians have difficulty in recognising."

"And you, presumably, have no such difficulty," sighed Martin. He was feeling very tired. "Okay, so you're tired. Let's get this over with. Surely you can stay awake just a few more minutes." Without waiting for his reply, Dotty continued: "Whatever verdict you finally reach concerning the physical existence or non-existence of Jesus, he, or his metaphor, will always be fundamental to the Christian message. Agreed?"

Martin agreed. "Then would it surprise you to learn that western Catholicism and the eastern Churches view him differently?" Martin was now paying attention and he indicated that Dotty should carry on. "You have surely heard of Anselm of Canterbury and his *Cur Deus Homo* of 1089, in which he defined the western concept of Easter. According to Anselm, we human beings are sinners and we have to pay for our sins. Our sins are so great that we are incapable of paying for them in full. That is why Jesus accepts the burden of punishment for our sins by being crucified. In contrast, the eastern Churches are not obsessed with Christ bleeding and suffering on the cross. They are not concerned with payment for our sins. Their emphasis is on the resurrection rather than the crucifixion, on renewal and the freeing of human beings from the bondage of imperfect lives."

"In other words, east and west have different concepts of Easter," said Martin. "Exactly," replied Dotty. Now I'll let you go to bed."

He wished Dotty goodnight and, bathed in the ambience of the desert moonlight, walked back to his tent. This time Mustapha did not escort him. Apparently his apprenticeship was over. He could find his own way.

# Chapter 12

Martin awoke with the lark, or rather to the harsh cawing of an African crow. These strutting birds were often seen around the camp, looking for scraps of food and even attacking scorpions. They always flew in from the north so presumably they nested in the trees by the Nile or on the roofs of buildings at the Merowe dam construction site.

Mustapha had already put a freshly brewed pot of coffee at the entrance to Martin's tent, as well as a bowl of water and the tea strainer. Mustapha considered it his duty to make sure everything went smoothly, on time and according to plan in the camp, so he had to remind Martin that today they would be driving to the Nile and Martin should dress accordingly. Mustapha was hard-working, utterly reliable and steadfast. He was a treasure. Dotty really had a most excellent person to run the everyday affairs of the camp. He was also an old fusspot.

Dotty was waiting, coffee in hand. They exchanged the morning's usual greeting and politely enquired whether the other had slept well. Before Dotty could utter another word, Martin forestalled her with: "Have you remembered that Spanish expression? What is it then?"

"Oh bother! I've completely forgotten it. Please write it down for me. I'll work on it when I have less on my mind."

"I will do that and wait until the day I leave to ask you to repeat it."

"Who's the teacher here? Start your breakfast and let's talk about something more important."

As Martin's gaze wandered from Dotty to the bowl of fruit, he noticed a scorpion near the tent entrance. It must have come in behind him. In an urgent, loud whisper, he hissed: "Dotty, a scorpion is coming into the tent!"

She glanced briefly at the creature, and in a throw-away tone of voice said: "That's Lawrence the deathstalker. He often appears at about this time."

In response, Martin could only manage a puzzled "Oh?"

With a barely hidden smile at his discomfort, Dotty continued: "I call him Lawrence for two reasons. First, his Latinised binomial is *Leiurus quinquestriatus* and Lawrence sounds a bit like *Leiurus;* second, my first husband's name was Lawrence."

Martin waited to be told why her first husband reminded her of a scorpion. No explanation was forthcoming, so he ventured: "Then his name has nothing to do with Lawrence of Arabia?"

"Well, I let people think that if they want to, but the connection didn't occur to me until after I'd named him. Certainly we are in the right part of the world. Arabia is just on the other side of the Red Sea," said Dotty, waving vaguely in a north-easterly direction.

"Why deathstalker?" enquired Martin.

"Oh, that's what the zoologists call it. That wasn't my idea; all species of *Leiurus* are known as deathstalkers. I always make sure he's left the tent before I turn in for the night. Otherwise, I don't mind him being around. Mind you, I wouldn't like to be stung by him. His venom is rather powerful and extremely painful; it could kill a child or weak old person. By the way, how's your Latin?"

Martin guessed what was coming. "You're about to tell me that *quinquestriatus* means five-striped smooth-tail. Am I right?" "Ten out of ten," declared Dotty, "You *are* doing well. Don't let Lawrence worry you. He's not dangerous, as long as you keep an eye on him. Of course, it's as well to know where he is. It wouldn't do to upset him."

None of this reassured Martin. On the contrary, he felt rather on edge to be sharing a tent with a scorpion known to have a powerfully venomous sting. His facial expression showed his discomfort. Dotty continued her playful taunting with: "This morning you will drive over to the Nile and see the scorpions there. They hide amongst the rocks near the river bank. You've never seen such scorpions. The locals call them camel scorpions because they're so big. Don't get stung by one of those, or I'll be e-mailing Doctor Willan for yet another replacement. Fishermen always kill them when they see them. You will see their crushed bodies lying around where fishermen have battered them to death with rocks.

To return to *quinquestriatus*, you obviously know your Latin, but that doesn't surprise me, since you are a Church minister. That doesn't mean that you have to know Latin, but it sort of goes with your job."

Waiting to get a word in edgeways, Martin finally managed to say that his knowledge of Latin came from his schooldays and that, because of his interest in natural history, he knew many Latin terms from the Linnaeus system of assigning Latinised binomials to species of living organisms. "Okay, I understand. What about your Ancient Greek?" This sudden switch from Latin to Greek caught Martin unawares. Surely it had nothing to do with scorpions, or did it? He replied lamely that he had a smattering, which amounted to little more than *Metropolis* and *Eureka*.

To his relief, she smiled at his gentle humour then adopted a serious expression. "For centuries throughout western Europe the *lingua franca* of intellectual intercourse was Latin. You know this, of course, but let's not forget that Greek culture had become deeply embedded in society long before the Romans adopted Christianity and Latin became a widely used language. It's impossible to overestimate the influence of Greek culture in those first four centuries of the Christian story. Don't run away with the idea that Greek influence ended when the Romans became dominant in Europe and Asia. Even after the Romans had sorted out their internal squabbles in the battle of Actium in 31 BC and conquered Ptolemaic Egypt in 30 BC, they were still in a world massively influenced by Greek culture, a culture established by the military successes of Alexander the Great, and which had grown steadily after his death in 323 BC.  Or, if you like, you can see Greek cultural influence starting about 800 BC with the rise of the city states and the founding of colonies, as well as the beginnings of classical Greek philosophy, theatre and poetry, and the re-establishment of a written language that had been lost in the Greek Dark Ages.

However you look at it, by the time the Romans began stamping around in the Middle East, Greek military power had long since ceased to exist, but the Greeks had spread their culture so widely around the Mediterranean, the Black Sea and the Middle East, that the impact of Greek culture was set to continue for several centuries.  That's why so much early Christian literature is written in Ancient Greek.  Greek thinking and Greek philosophy markedly influenced the early development of Christianity.

For goodness sake, why am I telling you all this!  You surely know it already.  Every schoolchild knows that Greek culture, especially Greek philosophy had a profound impact on the Roman Empire, which, in turn conveyed it throughout the Mediterranean region and Europe, so that every school teacher now preaches the conventional wisdom that the Greeks laid the foundations of present-day European culture, which has since spread to the Americas and the Antipodes.  Greek culture has therefore come a long way.  And what's more, as I mentioned earlier, when you made your quip about baiting bigots, the Greeks were once a bunch of uncultured tribes, which received their culture from the Phoenicians and the Ancient Egyptians; at least, that is what most historians now believe."

It had been a long speech.  She paused for breath, apologised for digressing than continued: "Yes, I know that much early Christian and Jewish writing was in Aramaic, which was actually a Semitic family of dialects that gave rise to Hebrew and Arabic.  If he existed, Jesus would have used an Aramaic dialect, which was the every-day language of Israel

## CHAPTER 12

in the second temple period; it is the main language of the Talmud; much of the books of Daniel and Ezra are written in Aramaic; a version of Aramaic still exists as the language known as Syriac, a liturgical language of certain Eastern Christian Churches. Yet Greek was the *lingua franca* of the Bible Lands, which is a compelling index of the extent to which Greek thought and culture had inveigled its way into the day-to-day life of the Roman-occupied Middle East. That is why Greek philosophy lies behind many Christian ideals. Forget the Romans! To put it very crudely indeed, Roman philosophy was responsible for the Spanish Inquisition, whereas Greek philosophy was responsible for love, tolerance and Jesus."

She remained silent, expecting him to respond, if only to agree. Martin simply nodded to indicate that he agreed and there was nothing to add. With sigh he said: "We started with scorpions and from there we have plotted a course to the Greek cultural influence on early Christianity. I seem to remember that you really wanted to discuss my cleaning of the fresco on the west wall of the church?"

With a straight face, as if Romans and Greeks had never been mentioned, Dotty replied: "Of course, but cleaning is not quite what I have in mind. I want it to be cleared of as much sand and other accumulated rubbish as possible so that I can photograph it for the record and study it. A complete cleaning is probably not possible and any attempt at cleaning would be destructive. All such paintings are extremely fragile. They have been preserved by being buried under desert sand. We must bear in mind, however, that the desert sand that now protects them is capable of destroying them. However carefully we brush it away, even if we blow it away with fans, the sand acts as an abrasive. Fortunately, some of the biblical scenes were painted on damp plaster so the colours penetrated and did not simply form a thin surface layer. No, your primary task is not to clean the wall painting, but to research suitable methods for revealing it without destroying it."

This seemed the right time to introduce the subject of Pinda again. Martin innocently asked: "How did Pinda plan to reveal the fresco before his accident?" She didn't speak, but looked intently and solemnly at Martin. Her attitude suggested she attached importance to something Martin had said; yet he had said very little, just a simple question in a few words. Was she respectfully acknowledging the tragedy of Pinda's death? Martin remembered his agreement with Pamela and Flo, that he would not try to investigate the circumstances surrounding Pinda's death, and simply take note of any unsolicited information that might come his way. He pressed on: "Did he leave any notes?"

"He left no notes, but he kept me informed about what he was doing. Before he left for Khartoum he was considering the use of water. We all agreed that water could do great harm to wall paintings and possibly defeat the whole purpose of the exercise. There's a small fragment of a painting on the wall to the right of the altar. It's all that is left of a painting that is now lost. The fragment, which seems to be the bottom corner of a gown, probably worn by a saint, has no archaeological value, so Pinda was planning to try out his water treatment on that. I have absolutely no idea how he intended to use the water: as a spray, or a wash, or whatever." "Then I will also try water. It's as good a way to start as any, don't you think?"

Dotty agreed and added: Since the River Nile is quite near we are not exactly short of water. Nevertheless, we still have to fetch it and purify it. It's probably clean enough for drinking but to be on the safe side we filter and boil it. I can't allow you to use the camp's supply of drinking water. Our four-by-four carries about forty jerry cans. Fill them all at the Nile and keep a few for your own work on the fresco." "As soon as possible," replied Martin, "I will drive to the

## CHAPTER 12

Nile and load up with water." Then, glancing quickly at Lawrence, who had now advanced about two feet into the tent, he added: "And I will look out for camel scorpions."

Mustapha, waiting and listening as usual, stepped from the shadows, gave a slight bow to Dotty and indicated to Martin that he should accompany him to the Nissan Land Cruiser.

"You drive?" invited Mustapha, "You must learn the car because next time you drive alone."

"Okay, you can be the navigator – and don't get me lost," joked Martin, wagging a finger at Mustapha. He switched on the ignition, turned the key, gunned the engine, slipped into gear and moved off. Mustapha was crestfallen. He had been expecting to prove his worth by giving a driving lesson, but he wasn't needed.

"Which way?" enquired Martin. "Drive to the excavation site then straight on," explained a rather glum Mustapha. Martin followed the path that Dotty and he had taken to the ruins and saw what Mustapha meant by straight on. There was no definite road – just an open expanse of dry terrain with several faint tyre tracks leading to the north. One just drove across the land in a northerly direction, making tracks that would eventually disappear in a desert breeze. The land was flat enough and hard enough for comfortable driving, and not as bumpy or rutted as the road they had driven from Khartoum less than three days ago. Martin was tempted to put his foot down, but decided to keep up a steady twenty-five to thirty miles an hour and watch out for obstacles and hollows. It was a full seven minutes from leaving the camp before Mustapha broke his silence and directed Martin to head a little more to the left towards the best place for filling the jerry cans. Martin could see nothing to suggest they had arrived at the river. Had he looked over to his right, however, he would have seen the concrete top of the hydroelectric dam protruding above the near horizon of the river bank.

They topped a small rise and saw the River Nile before them. The change of scenery and atmosphere was sudden and dramatic, as if a curtain had been drawn back in a theatre. Groves of date palms lined the river bank and some distance to the left a settlement of mud brick houses nestled into the slope of the hillside leading down to the river. It actually looked rather idyllic. Martin would not have described it as *only a few palm-trees, or here and there a squalid mud hamlet*. The place had obviously changed since Winston Churchill passed that way in the late nineteenth century. Diverted by these thoughts, Martin left it rather late to change down a gear to manage the descent towards the river. He glanced quickly at Mustapha to see him smirking and obviously pleased that Martin's driving skills had at last been found wanting.

Yes, the place had changed since 1899, when Winston Churchill described it in his *River war*, and the reason was plain to see. About 500 yards to their right a massive dam spanned the river. Even at that distance it seemed to loom above them, which was hardly surprising since, as Martin learned later, it was all of 67 metres in height and it held back a lake extending 170 kilometres upstream. Also plain to see were living quarters, offices and storage sheds beyond the dam on the opposite bank. Cranes and bulldozers were parked on both banks and at that moment a heavy goods vehicle was driving slowly over the dam from the opposite side.

One of the vehicles on the opposite bank sounded its horn. Large, long-distance haulage vehicles have very loud horns, like the fog horn of a ship. Martin started at the sound and turned to see Mustapha waving to the vehicle. The driver was returning the salute by vigorously waving a large green flag.

"That is Bakri Osman," explained Mustapha, "He is a Sudanese driver who brings supplies from Khartoum for the workers at the dam. He recognised our Nissan."

## CHAPTER 12

"And why should he recognise the Nissan," enquired Martin. Even before he finished speaking the answer dawned him. That was how the camp got its supplies of everything from fuel to food. They were brought from Khartoum by friend Bakri Osman.

Mustapha pointed to a slab of granite extending from the river bank into the water. It was an ideal place for kneeling and filling the cans. Martin started the engine once more and manoeuvred the Nissan as close as possible to the water's edge without venturing into the very soft, wet beach sand. They took it in turns to take a can to the water, fill it and carry it back to the Nissan.

Two men, turbaned, bearded and smiling, sauntered down from one of the mud brick houses and greeted them: *"As-salaam alaykum"*, whereupon Mustapha, who had not heard them coming, whipped round and returned the greeting with a flood of impenetrable Arabic, mutual cheek pecking and back slapping. They were old friends and Mustapha was clearly part of the scenery around here, coming regularly as he did to fetch water from the Nile and supplies from Bakri Osman. Mustapha introduced his friends, Mohammed and Yasser, who were embarrassingly enthusiastic with their greeting. Their handshakes were vigorous and prolonged, accompanied by an excited outpouring of fragmented English, which Martin interpreted as meaning they were thrilled to meet him and they hoped he liked the Sudan. Clearly, any friend of Mustapha's was a friend of theirs.

At first, Martin thought they might leave him to do the can filling and carrying, while they continued their conversation in Arabic. So he was pleased to see them hitch up their galabias and lend a hand. All the cans were soon filled and Martin was ready to drive back to the camp. That, insisted Mustapha, would be discourteous. They were invited to drink tea with their two helpers and they were obliged to accept the invitation. It was only a short walk, slightly uphill, to the mud brick house of Yasser, where a lady in a white thoub (wife, sister, mother?) was placing an ornate teapot with a long, curved spout, together with sugar and glasses, on a plastic garden table on the shaded side of the house. She disappeared before they arrived.

How did Mister Martin like the Sudan? What did he think of the Sudanese government? Mohammed's father had worked for the post office during British rule. In those days the post was always delivered on time. Nowadays post was sometimes stolen and often late. They needed a British government again. Martin, with mock solemnity, told them that back home they had a government they didn't want, so the Sudan could have it. Mustapha interpreted and as the meaning became clear, the three Sudanese collapsed with laughing and each insisted on shaking Martin's hand once again. Martin caught a brief glimpse of the lady in white, who peeped from the door of the house and also seemed to be enjoying the joke, then disappeared again.

It was the first of several visits that Martin would make to the river. Every time he would be waylaid by Mohammed and Yasser and taken home for tea. He learned that Mohammed and Yasser were retired, having previously worked on the dam. The lady in white was Yasser's wife. According to Muslim tradition, her place was on the other side of the house, not in the man's world, but it was her duty to serve the tea. Eventually they relaxed the custom, mainly because they needed an interpreter and her English was quite good.

Her name was Gwaria and she was stunningly beautiful, her smooth, unblemished dark skin set off by the white thoub. She explained with pride that Gwaria was originally a Jewish name. Centuries ago a peace agreement was signed between a Muslim tribe and a Jewish tribe, and sealed by the marriage of the Muslim prince with Princess Gwaria, the

## CHAPTER 12

daughter of the Jewish king. She also told him that she and Yasser had two children, who were enjoying a holiday with their grandparents in Khartoum. On these occasions, Yasser and Mohammed always seemed content to sit back and smile, looking alternately at Martin and Gwaria as they conversed.

When Martin insisted it was time to start back to the camp, Yasser and Mohammed were still chortling over his little joke. Refusing a second glass of the hot, sweet tea, Martin shook hands once again, said *ma-salaam* and hoped he had pronounced it correctly, placed his hand in the small of Mustapha's back and directed him down the hill to the Nissan.

On the way back to the camp they stopped at the excavation site to place two jerry cans of water in the shade of the plastic sheeting covering Pinda's excavation. Dotty was already there, on her knees scratching with a trowel around the old altar stones. Using a primitive wooden ladder (the rungs were bound to the side supports with orange plastic binder twine and not nailed or inset) she climbed from her deep hiding place, wiped a sand-stained hand across her perspiring brow, and asked how they had got on at the river. She was grateful for the excuse to rest a while and talk. "I've eaten," she informed them, "Ask the Mohammeds to provide you with refreshments when you get back."

"Found anything interesting?" enquired Martin. "Not really. Just the usual bits of wall and roof bricks. Later, I wouldn't mind some help putting that old altar together again." "Any time," replied Martin, thinking it would be hard work and preferably done by hired Nubian labourers. "Thanks," she shouted as she went back to her hole, "I'll hold you to that."

As they approached the camp, Mustapha directed Martin to the large bell tent, where they unloaded the remaining thirty cans of water. At the same time he must have given a secret signal to the Mohammeds, who appeared from nowhere and started to lay a table of food outside Martin's tent.

This was Martin's first sight of the inside of the bell tent. Against the wall opposite the entrance he recognised the generator and he assumed the stainless steel cabinet nearby was the ice machine. Digging implements and boxes of supplies were stacked just inside the doorway. His attention was immediately drawn to the water filtration apparatus. He had never seen such a large one. In his teenage camping days, he and his friends had used an unglazed porcelain water filter. The drip rate was agonisingly slow and in order to collect enough water for breakfast they had to fill the pot to the brim with river water and let it drip slowly while they slept. One glance at the camp's apparatus told Martin it could easily produce their daily water requirement. The unglazed pots were massive, with a capacity of at least ten gallons, and there were three of them. Water dripped from the bottom and oozed from all around the sides. Below each pot was a large plastic funnel which fed the water into a common gutter, leading to a massive glass tank. Where had Martin seen such a large glass tank? Of course, now he remembered, it was in Tropical World in Leeds, where it housed giant Amazonian river fish. He was amused to see traces of green algae on the walls of the tank. Pure was a relative term when talking of water. He and Mustapha emptied six of the jerry cans into the three filtration pots.

Back at his tent, Martin made a sandwich of fool, poured himself a glass of hibiscus tea and sat back to review what he had learned. Last night, before sleeping, he had read the documents in Dotty's manila wallet. Today, he had seen the dam for himself. It changed his whole concept of where he was. Until now he had felt pleasantly isolated in a small desert camp miles from Khartoum and the rest of the modern world. He now knew that only a short distance away there

CHAPTER 12

was a massive civil engineering project, a dam, described by environmentalists as one of the world's most destructive hydropower projects. In different documents it was variously described as *near, at* and *on* the fourth cataract. From that morning's visit, it was clearly *on* the rocks and islands of the fourth cataract, most of which was now under the flood water. They had filled the jerry cans on the last stretch of the cataract in front of the dam. An article in a Sudanese newspaper described it as the *Pearl of the Nile* and went on to report: *The dream for the Sudanese in Merowe in Northern Province is becoming reality as the Chinese-built multipurpose Merowe Dam Project is foreseeing its completion in the near future.* Propaganda-speak in less than perfect English. All non-Sudanese accounts of the project were critical and negative, although Dotty had not included anything written by the Chinese, who, in view of their involvement, would probably have praised it and ignored the damage and human suffering that it had caused. A hundred miles of the Nile valley behind the dam were now submerged. It had displaced 50,000 people. Protests were brutally suppressed. Several people were killed and many more were injured in crack-downs by the security forces. The UN Rapporteur on Housing Rights had expressed 'deep concern' about the human rights violations. In 2007 the UN had asked the dam builders to halt construction, but they didn't. The government claimed it had not ignored this humanitarian crisis; they had responded by resettling all the date farmers, sheep herders, and goat herders, but they were coy when asked where, because the new settlements were in a dry and inhospitable area of the Sudanese desert.

The area destined for flooding contained archaeological remains. The announcement of plans to build the dam triggered a major international rescue campaign, in which the British Museum was involved. Surveys started in 1999 and it was soon realised that the area contained more archaeological remains and much richer treasures than imagined, and that their study would rewrite the history of this previously little known region over the last 150,000 years. Like time and tides, however, the Sudanese government and the Chinese builders would wait for no-one. Some archaeology was saved, while thousands, perhaps tens of thousands of ancient sites vanished under the water before they could be studied and recorded. There is now a lake, two miles-wide and 100 miles-long behind the dam. It supports a valuable irrigation scheme in the region and its hydroelectric output has doubled Sudan's electricity generation. The lake is being developed as a fishing resource. So all the fuss is now over and the Sudanese government can indulge in an orgy of self-congratulation. No, it wasn't all bad, but it could have been done better. Dotty had included a list of some of the interesting archaeological discoveries. One in particular caught Martin's eye: the ceremonial burial of a cow, whose grave contained a string of quartzite beads, a fine glass beaker, a copper alloy bowl and an extremely well-made kohl pot. Now what would a cow want with those, even in the afterlife?

Dotty had also scribbled some notes in the margins of the documents, pointing out that the dam was the largest contemporary hydroelectric project in Africa and that the national grid would have to be upgraded to handle the extra electric power. In another margin she had remarked that the lake behind the dam had increased the surface area of the Nile by 700 square kilometres, thereby increasing water loss by evaporation by more than a billion cubic metres; then she had written *per year, per month?*

There were other hand-written notes on the blank side of one document, stating that most of the funding for the project (total cost 1.2 billion US dollars) had been provided by sources in the Middle East and by the China Import Export Bank. The China International Water and Electronics

## CHAPTER 12

Corporation had constructed the dam. So far, so good. Martin was already well aware that China had played an important role in the project. He was therefore surprised to read in Dotty's notes that the German firm of Lahmeyer International had managed the project and provided the civil engineers, and even more surprised to read that the generators and turbines had been supplied by a French company. It was a relief, although he wasn't sure why, to find that European firms had also contributed to the project.

Dotty's camp was far enough away from the dam to escape the noise of machinery and heavy vehicles. It was also in an area downstream of the dam, so that the flooding that affected the left bank of the river did not encroach on the land between her church and the Nile. The route over the dry land between the camp and the river and the bank of the river itself where they collected water had not been altered by the building of the dam. It seemed that Dotty's archaeological site was safe and would not eventually suffer the same fate as the area behind the dam.

Dotty's camp was perfectly situated. It was far enough from the industrial bustle at the dam to ensure privacy and tranquillity. Yet it was conveniently near enough for fetching water and for exploiting the advantages of the industrialised society at the dam, whose drivers also brought in supplies for Dotty's camp. She had the best of both worlds.

That evening Dotty wore the low-cut pink blouse again. The meal included roast chicken, okra and chips. Dotty told him that the two Mohammeds delighted in making potato chips and explained that they used an iron pan and heated the oil over the open camp fire. The result was delicious but it was best to keep away and let them get on with it. She was waiting for the day when the oil would spill and there would be a great sheet of flame illuminating the camp site. There was also a salad of tomatoes and beans.

"I hear you got on very well this morning. Mustapha said you know how to handle the Nissan and you impressed him greatly by mucking in with the can filling and water carrying. You would have been quite entitled to let him do all the work."

"Now why didn't someone tell me that? I also met two of Mustapha's friends, who entertained us to tea. Nice lads, but their English isn't up to much."

"You will get used to that sort of thing. Don't be surprised if a complete stranger invites you to his house for tea. They're very hospitable people."

So as not to let their talking stop their eating, they then fell silent.

"Oh! Before you ask: No, I didn't see any camel scorpions."

"Keep looking. You have to keep looking!"

Martin wondered if she was pulling his leg and there was no such thing as a camel scorpion. He made a mental note to ask Mustapha, or Mohammed or Yasser next time he drove to the river.

It had been a long day. By the end of the meal Martin felt horribly tired. Dotty called Mustapha and they exchanged knowing looks as they watched Martin slump in his chair. Sooner or later, usually after about a week in a tropical climate, visitors from Europe experience overwhelming tiredness. It's part of the physiological adjustment to high temperatures, salt loss and probably other as yet ill-defined factors.

Dotty called "time for bed!"

Martin woke with a start, apologised for falling asleep then dozed off again. At a nod from Dotty, Mustapha helped Martin to his feet and escorted him to his tent and his bed.

# Chapter 13

Next morning, Martin was surprised to feel abnormally refreshed and full of energy. This is a common experience for Europeans in the tropics. It is a temporary sensation, lasting about twelve hours and marking a stage of physiological adjustment and acclimatisation.

Dotty greeted Martin from a distance by waving her coffee cup as he washed and shaved, stripped to the waist outside his tent. Martin returned the salute by enthusiastically waving the tea strainer and rotating it so that it sparkled in the morning sunlight. This semaphored greeting subsequently became a ritual, so that minutes later, when they met for breakfast at Dotty's tent, the customary *Good morning!* seemed unnecessary.

Early morning conversation usually starts in a trifling, inconsequential way, allowing time for everyone to become fully awake and take responsibility for what they say. This morning, however, Dotty caught Martin unawares by stating very earnestly that she had a guilty conscience. Unwilling to be serious so early in the morning, Martin answered: "So do I and I'm not telling why."

Ignoring his reply, she carried on: "I'm glad Doctor Willan recommended you as a replacement for Pinda. In the very short time you have been here, you have settled in and become a valuable addition to the camp."

Martin acknowledged her praise with a Gallic shrug, conveying both modesty and surprise.

"Martin, I mean what I say, and furthermore my views are strongly supported by my camp commandant, Mustapha."

Martin sensed that Mustapha, whom Dotty had so aptly and humorously labelled her camp commandant, had been sizing him up from the moment they met in the car park at the Goethe Institute. And it seemed he had reported back to

Dotty. She raised her eyebrows and quickly glanced to the left of her tent opening, a silent sign that Mustapha could probably hear what she was saying. They exchanged smiles. Martin knew that Dotty had not asked Mustapha to do it; he had taken it upon himself to vet the new arrival and report back.

"So?" asked Martin, secretly feeling pleased that Mustapha actually approved of him.

"So, I understand we have an unwritten agreement. You lend a hand with my archaeological work and in return I pass onto you what I know about early Christianity. I have a guilty conscience because I can't possibly see how I can keep my side of the agreement. I've told you about the early history of Nubia, its relationship with Egypt and the Coptic Church, but you could have found most of this on-line anyway. You are a well-read, liberal-minded minister of the established Church. You studied under Doctor Willan, a specialist in Christian history and theology, and you are still in contact with him. The most recent studies on Christian history are regularly published in international journals and you have access to these in England. What can I tell you that you don't know already or can easily find out at home?"

Martin thought back to his disingenuous conversations with his bishop; all that talk about needing to travel to the Middle East to learn about the true history of Christianity. In a sense, Dotty was right. What didn't he know already or could easily find at home? On the other hand, there was no substitute for widening one's intellectual horizon by travel and by interacting with other minds. Anyway, he was glad to be there and he knew it had been right to take Flo's advice and join Dotty in her desert camp.

The ensuing silence didn't appear to discomfort Dotty. Martin had already learned that she valued silence as something positive, and knew how to use it. She never seemed to feel uncomfortable in a prolonged silence. Rather she seemed

## CHAPTER 13

content to let the silence mature and get deeper. It was part of her mental makeup and he didn't fully understand it. Martin used the current silence to decide how to answer her concern.

He began to wonder if there was method in her question. Was she hoping he would tell her what he really wanted from her? If so, that meant she suspected he did want more. It was an easy decision. She had presented him with a chance to tell all, and that was what he must do.

"Let me put all my cards on the table," said Martin, looking anxiously at Dotty for approval, because that very statement revealed that he had not yet told her everything.

"By all means, and let's hope they will all be face-up," she replied with a mischievous grin.

Martin, still embarrassed, wondered what she was smiling at. He continued: "There is evidence that Jesus did not exist as an historical figure, and I want to get to the bottom of it," exclaimed Martin, experiencing a great feeling of relief.

"Yes, I know. That's been obvious from the start. I just wanted to hear you say it. There's nothing wrong with doubting the provenance of the Jesus story. Some of the most respected figures in history have refused to believe that he actually existed. Now we have something to get our teeth into."

Had Flo tipped her off? Had she put two and two together and guessed? Why hadn't he been honest from the start? It didn't matter now. He gave a deep sigh and apologised for not being forthright about his intentions.

She acknowledged his apology with an affirmative nod, thought for a moment, then said: "I'll give you something to think about while you're working at the site. We know that doubts about the existence of Jesus existed even before the Renaissance. Might such doubts have arisen even during the first four centuries of Christianity? Think about that question while you're perspiring at the site."

Martin had never wondered whether any very early Christians had doubted the existence of Jesus. It was an intriguing question. If early Christians had indeed invented Jesus then those coming immediately after them would have been in a far better position to see through the deception than Christians living centuries later, far removed in time from the Jesus story.

"I will certainly wrestle with that question while I'm shovelling sand. Speaking of which, I must get my spade."

"A spade and other tools are already at the site," answered Dotty, "Mustapha took them to the site for you earlier this morning."

"It's good to be looked after," said Martin, as he plonked the old straw hat on his head, hitched on his rucksack containing his bottles of drinking water, took a final sip of his coffee, and set out to the site.

A Christian church is a Christian church, even if it once had a mosque-like dome and no steeple, even if its roof has a gaping hole and the area is littered with goat droppings. So Martin sat down and leaned his back against a heap of mudstone bricks, which had at one time probably been a pillar of the nave, and closed his eyes. A church is a place of prayer, but Martin was not intending to pray. He was feeling more deeply spiritual than that. He wanted to pay his respects to the Christians who had once worshipped here and to remind himself that notwithstanding the profound differences in theology and history that separated his Anglican faith from that of the Oriental Orthodox Church, they shared the same beginnings. For centuries those beginnings have been described in myth and dogma. Martin was seeking to redefine them with true history. Would he succeed? In the solitude and the shade from the aggressive heat of the Nubian Desert offered by this crumbling old church, he reaffirmed his determination to get to the bottom of the Jesus mystery.

## CHAPTER 13

Basically, he mused, it was a fight against myth. Once a myth is launched it may have to negotiate the harbour wall and a few submerged rocks. Once past these early hazards and provided it has a sufficiently large and dedicated crew, it can then sail away and plot a course to suit its own prejudices and visions. This particular myth is responsible for two thousand years of delusion, and now it's no longer clear about where it's heading because lined up before it is an armada of doubt and accusation. Martin felt rather pleased with his metaphor. He felt it was just as effective as the bishop's metaphor of the demon in the signal box sending history along the wrong line.

Using his spade as a support, he struggled to his feet, threw back the plastic sheeting over Pinda's excavation, and looked long and hard at the top of the fresco just visible above the sand. Strictly speaking he ought to start his work by trying water treatment on the worthless fresco fragment near the altar. On the other hand, there was no harm in making Pinda's hole a bit deeper. Taking care to keep a layer of sand over the fresco, he started to dig. After four spadefulls of sand Martin knew he had struck an uneven bargain with Dotty. How many times had she punctuated her recent history lessons with 'archaeologists have shown' or some such similar expression? Anyone who decided to further their career by digging up the past in the heat of the Nubian Desert must be extraordinarily devoted to archaeology, as well as physically strong, fit and healthy – or barking. Martin was no stranger to digging, but planting decorative borders of lobelia and marigolds in the vicarage garden is insufficient training for excavating extinct Coptic mud-brick churches in the desert heat and exposing them to the light of day. He wouldn't weaken! He would stick at it, despite the draining heat and the pain in his arms and back, and he would not complain to Dotty. No matter whether Jesus had existed or not, the desert would make a man of him. Anyway, he was alone at the site, so he could shirk as much as he liked, and when he got tired of digging he could always play with different methods of applying water to the fresco fragment near the altar.

He continued to deepen and widen Pinda's excavated pit, pausing after every fourth spade-full for a short rest. Plunging the spade downwards and levering it up with its small load of sand wasn't so bad. Twisting his body round with the spade at shoulder height then throwing the sand as far as possible was surely the kind of exercise no physiotherapist would ever recommend. He took comfort from the thought that it would enlarge his muscles and lower his cholesterol and that he would return to England with the body of a Mister Universe. Without realising it, he began lifting five spade-fulls before resting, then six. That was the limit. Perhaps he would increase it to seven or eight on his next visit.

Digging holes is ninety per cent muscle, leaving the remaining ten per cent for dreaming and philosophising. As he laboured, he thought about Dotty's parting question that morning. So far, she had told him much about Christianity in general and about the Christian history of the Sudan in particular. Some of it was fascinating and some he already knew, but very little of it concerned the early years of the Christian story. Now, at last, the lessons had started. Like many wise teachers, she had not started by bombarding him with facts, but by setting him a question. Already his preoccupation with that question was taking his mind off the ache in his back and shoulders. The more he thought about it, the more he realised that any doubts expressed in the first or second century AD, about the physical existence of Jesus, would strongly support the suspicion that he had not been an historical figure.

The more he considered the question, however, the more ifs and buts and the more obstacles to clear reasoning he

## CHAPTER 13

encountered. Various groups of Jews, dissatisfied with the rigid doctrinal theology and perceived corruption of the priesthood, sought a loving, rather than a vengeful, God. It amounted to a reformation, rather analogous to the later Christian Reformation. Tradition held that one day a Messiah would appear, bringing salvation to the Jews. So here was a chance to bring him forward, albeit as metaphor, and have him teach a new and improved version of Judaism. If, Martin reasoned, this had not been a secret, but a widely known and accepted fact, there would have been no conflict or disagreement. In other words, no-one would have felt it necessary to start bleating that Jesus was a metaphor and not a real person. The response would have been: "So what! We all know that." So far, so good. Then at some stage it had been decided that Jesus was a real person, or rather a person of flesh and bone with supernatural qualities (the faithful prefer 'divine' to 'supernatural', but let's call a spade a spade, even if we refrain from calling it a bloody shovel, which would be equivalent to saying that Jesus was magic.). It occurred to Martin that different Christian groups had disagreed over the nature of Jesus. Was he entirely divine, or part divine and part human? Were they arguing over what sort of spin to give their metaphorical saviour, or had it reached the point where they genuinely thought he had existed and they were interested in his nature? No firm evidence there. Martin was up against the recurring argument that Christians would always adhere to their party line, and that the kind of evidence he was seeking could only come from sources outside Christianity. That was the best he could do. It felt shamefully inadequate. He hoped Dotty would be sympathetic. He needed sympathy; his back was killing him.

He had enlarged Pinda's excavated pit and deepened it until, as far as he could judge, it was about level with the bottom of the fresco. Apart from the top few centimetres that Pinda had exposed, the rest of the fresco was still protected by a layer of sand about a foot in thickness. Without the support of the great bulk of sand, of which it had originally been part, perhaps that foot-thick layer would collapse of its own accord and leave exposed the ancient fresco in pristine condition. It was worth a thought, but in truth Martin wasn't sure how to proceed from there. So he left it and went over to the altar excavation to try out the water treatment.

Descent to the altar was precarious. Dotty's ladder was frankly dangerous and Martin couldn't imagine how Mustapha had allowed her to use such dangerous equipment. Some local idiot must have made it with rickety wood and binder twine. He had seen modern tools and equipment in the bell tent; surely her funding could also run to a simple, lightweight aluminium ladder. He reviewed the hole, its depth and its crumbling walls of sand and debris and decided that if the ladder failed he could easily climb out.

The fragment of wall painting Dotty had suggested he use for experimental purposes showed the bottom of a gown or robe. Its colours, reddish brown and purple, were well preserved. Two naked feet protruding from the lower folds had practically disappeared through abrasion of the plaster.

Martin had found a spray bottle amongst the equipment in the bell tent. It was probably intended for spraying insecticide. It served well for Martin's experimental water treatment. He gently directed a light spray, almost a mist, of water onto the bottom corner of the robe and watched to see what would happen. Martin's spirits rose as the colours brightened and gave the appearance of being newly painted. More spray. No further change. Then brown droplets of water began to gather and run from the surface of the fresco. At first Martin thought the water was removing dust and dirt. He soon realised it was leaching colour from the robe. Was this purely a question of the quantity of water? He tried dabbing a different part of the robe with a damp cloth, taking care that no water pooled on the surface. Again the colours brightened and stayed bright and they were not leached by water running from the surface. Martin leaned back against the wall of the hole and viewed his work with satisfaction. His arms still ached from his exertions at the other fresco and he was feeling very hot and sweaty. Still gazing at the bright area of robe, he took a refreshing swig from his bottle of drinking water and congratulated himself on a job well done. Then very slowly, and Martin had to blink and look again to be sure it was happening, the colours began to spread like ink on blotting paper.

You can spend too long in a hole, especially if the hole is in a hot, inhospitable desert. Undecided whether to curse or pray, Martin negotiated the rickety ladder, crossed over to the other side of the ruin, sat down on the shaded side of the remaining fragment of church wall, and went to sleep. His body needed it. About half an hour later he awoke to find Mustapha standing in front of him. He had brought more drinking water and slices of water melon, and he intended to carry the spade back to the camp. "I see you are making big progress, and it makes you sleepy," remarked Mustapha very seriously, at the same time nodding towards the greatly enlarged excavation pit.

Martin was grateful for the slices of pink water melon, and he didn't mind the juice running down his arms and chin. He was so sweaty and grubby it didn't matter. Ready to leave, Martin, to the amusement of Mustapha, stripped off his shirt, took off his hat, and upended a jerry can of river water over his head. Wet from head to toe, his trousers dripping, Martin felt clean and refreshed. They walked back to the camp together, saying very little. Martin was deep in thought. What about other liquids that would freshen up the colours and not dissolve them? Petrol, alcohol, or even a thin oil. He thought of the very thin colourless oil used on watches before time-keeping became quartz-based and digital and, moreover, devastatingly accurate and utterly reliable. He remembered his son's seventh birthday present from his maternal grandparents – a plastic affair with a picture of Donald duck on the face; it kept better time than his grandfather's greatly treasured and valuable gold retirement watch. Then he remembered Pamela's sewing machine oil. That would be ideal for his purpose, but he wasn't likely to find it in the Nubian Desert. By the time they reached the camp Martin's trousers had dried out in the desert heat.

Feet up for an hour then dress for dinner. Someone, it could only be Mustapha, had laid out the galabiya on his bed. The message could not have been clearer. He would wear it for the evening meal.

The Sudanese setting for *Camel Scorpions*.
The Nile Valley from Khartoum
to the border with Egypt.

A Mediaeval Coptic church (from *Medieval Nubia*, 1954, by P.L. Shinnie, Sudan Antiquities Service).

The archaeological remains excavated by Dotty near the fourth cataract would have belonged to a similar building.

# Chapter 14

Martin slipped his galabiya over his head and let it fall around his body. The hem hung two inches above the ground. Mustapha had judged the size well. Trapped air in the folds of the garment produced a welcome and surprising cooling effect. Although he had worn it for barely a minute, Martin could tell that the galabiya was superior to a western shirt and trousers for evening-wear and going about most daily tasks in the tropical heat, although it was probably not the best outfit for digging holes in the desert. He must have a photograph of himself in a galabiya, but first he must ask Mustapha about a turban.

It was time to eat. Longing to see how Dotty would react to seeing him in Sudanese dress, Martin strolled over to her tent. Surprisingly, she was not waiting to greet him. Perhaps she had not finished dressing and was still doing up buttons inside her tent. Therefore, as he approached he cleared his throat and let his sandals flap against his feet.

Dotty emerged from her tent dressed for the evening in a white thoub. Martin exclaimed: "My goodness, you've gone native too!" Dotty simply laughed out loud and asked: "Where did you get that galabiya?"

"Mustapha put it in my tent when I arrived. I thought you must have ordered it."

"No, nothing to do with me. That's dear Mustapha practising his own brand of hospitality."

"And where did you get that thoub? It suits you."

"It was a present from Mustapha's wife, a sort of welcome-to-the-desert present when I first arrived here."

That was the first Martin had heard of Mustapha's wife. He had no idea the man was married and he wondered if he had children.

"Since we are both in traditional dress, we ought to be having a traditional Sudanese meal," observed Dotty, whereupon Mustapha, appeared as if from nowhere, clicked his

## CHAPTER 14

fingers, and the two Mohammeds walked to the tent carrying large platters of curried goat meat.

"Honestly," pleaded Dotty, "This was not planned. I had no idea. It's pure coincidence."

Martin recalled that earlier at the excavation site Mustapha had remarked that Martin might find his galabiya relaxing and cool after his hot, tiring day. He looked from Mustapha to Dotty. Both wore innocent expressions.

"I'll believe you," said Martin, quietly adding: "Thousands wouldn't."

Dotty and Mustapha could contain themselves no longer and burst out laughing.

"It all started when Mustapha told me curried goat was on the menu this evening. We decided to try and make it a proper Sudanese occasion. Mustapha and the Mohammeds are going to join us."

Dotty looked stunning in the thoub. She had even covered her head, Sudanese style, with part of the garment, and she was wearing gold bangles. She lacked only one thing to complete the picture of traditional Sudanese womanhood, *i.e.*, a dark skin, set off by the pure white of the thoub. Sun-tanned northern European white would have to do. And it did very well. Martin was so lost in admiration of this beautiful apparition that he had to pull himself together when he realised she was speaking to him.

She was not insensitive to the fact that he found her attractive, but she was wise enough to know that neither of them had a rival in the present company, that it was a balmy evening, that there was probably good reason for associating moonlight with romance, and that desert moonlight might be more dangerous in this respect than moonlight over a Cambridge college garden, which, as she well knew from experience, was also not without its hazards.

So she pointedly opened a serious conversation, carefully worded to lead them away from wayward thoughts and to stifle any poetic effect the moonlight might have on their mood.

"I'm fascinated to know why you are so interested in investigating whether Jesus was a real person or not. It's almost as if you are trying to catch up with an idea that has been current now for centuries. In particular since the First World War. Even long before that, opinion had been growing that Jesus was a well-marketed metaphor. Whether the holders of this opinion are in the majority is hard to say. It could be that many who deny it consider it unwise to disturb the Christian story that has proved fit for purpose in sustaining the faithful for centuries. Some serious Christian thinkers have spoken out; for instance the famous Christian missionary, Albert Schweitzer, doubted that Jesus had been a true historical figure. As for yourself, I hope you don't think you've happened upon a startling revelation that hasn't occurred to anyone else. There's a wealth of published literature, as well as internet articles, some of which state plainly that Jesus was a myth or a fictional invention. Ever since it became safe to question the Church's monopoly of the truth, numerous authors have pointed out that much of the New Testament is historically unsound. I can give you a reading list, starting with *Christianity and Mythology* by J.M. Robertson published as early as 1900, followed by other contributions to the controversy right up to the present day.

Which brings me to a further point: there are many non-believers today, who take a devilish delight in trying to upset the faithful by taking a Yah-boo approach to this question, publishing remarks like: *Jesus was a fraud and a liar, at best if he even existed.* And there was a particularly offensive diatribe that started with: *Heaven help us. The richest, most powerful nation in history has a psychotic infatuation with Jay-a-sus the Lawd!* Not to mention many similar statements designed to shock and offend. I have no time for such a downright rude, gloating, infantile attitude."

## CHAPTER 14

"I wasn't aware of this Yah-boo faction," confessed Martin.

"Let's not waste any more time talking about them. When you have a moment, go on line. You can find all this infantile rudeness on Facebook and Twitter."

Martin knew she was right. How could he add to the body of knowledge and argument already in the public domain claiming that Jesus was not an historical figure? What was his real purpose in pursuing this question? The answer was clear. Only by undertaking his own investigation could he be sure in his own mind that the evidence and arguments presented by other authors were sound. And that was why he was here, in the Nubian Desert, talking to a specialist in Christian history. More important, however, was the fact that Christians throughout the world were unaware of these results of biblical scholarship. Practically every member of every congregation of every denomination was ignorant of the evidence that Jesus was a myth. Martin wanted to change that. He must explain these motives to Dotty. First, he wanted add his own contribution to the list of doubters of Jesus' historicity.

"I think I can take the argument back to before 1900. Have you read anything by the Young Hegelians?"

"Carry on, I'm listening."

"They were students of the philosopher Hegel. Their movement lasted only a short time in the middle of the nineteenth century. One of their members, Bruno Bauer, proposed that the entire story of Jesus was a myth."

"Well there you are then. Perhaps you can tell me more about the Young Hegelians later. In the meantime, how *do* you justify this wish to prove that Jesus was a myth, all on your own, when so many others have already done it, or claim to have done it?"

"I know it seems that what I'm trying to do has already been done. I want to know more. I want cast-iron evidence, one way or the other, that Jesus was or wasn't a true historical figure, so that I don't have to spend the rest of my Church ministry harbouring a strong suspicion without being absolutely certain. If it transpires that Jesus *is* a well marketed metaphor – by the way, I like that turn of phrase; it describes the situation perfectly – then there will be no room for argument and Church doctrine will have to change.

Dotty didn't reply immediately. In deep thought, she appeared to ignore Martin, while helping herself to a small portion of curried goat. Finally she announced: "If you want to change Church doctrine, you might as well pack your bags and go home now because you are not going to achieve any of that. On second thoughts, don't pack your bags because I like you being here. Rather tone down your ambition and accept that at best you will be convinced in your heart that Jesus was and is a metaphor, without being able to prove it. And surely you are deluding yourself if you think that cast-iron evidence, even if you had it, would even begin to convince the faithful. Believe me, blind faith with its back to the wall is not a pretty sight. It will fight tooth and nail, spitting and scratching, and using every mean trick in the book to defend a cherished myth. As for changing the doctrine of your Church, perhaps you got too much sun today. Did you wear your hat at the excavation site?"

Martin knew it wasn't a question of truth and logic, both of which belonged to the realm of science. Religion and faith operate differently. He was able to separate clearly in his mind the questions of Christian history and those of Christian spirituality, and he knew he was deluding himself if he thought the rest of Christendom could also see these differences clearly. So he replied: "Okay, I'll settle for that. And yes, I did wear my hat. However, despite what you say, I don't see why changing Church doctrine should be impossible, although it might take time."

"Like a thousand years?"

## CHAPTER 14

"Not that long. Let's say a hundred years. And I suspect my bishop would be on my side."

This exchange had lasted too long. The meal was sitting largely untouched on the table. Mohammed one, Mohammed two and Mustapha were hovering. Dotty took pity on them and waved them forward, indicating that they should serve themselves. Mustapha supervised while they filled their plates then dismissed them to the camp fire near their own tents. Dotty and Martin would talk shop. Dotty had been gracious in suggesting they join the Europeans for the meal, but they would be happier squatting by the camp fire and talking Arabic. Mustapha served himself and retired a safe distance to enjoy his food, remaining on hand if needed.

As they ate, Martin became aware that Dotty was gazing at him rather intently; not the occasional smile or gesture of approval of the food, but a studious look as if she were assessing him in some way. "Yes?" enquired Martin, "What is it?"

"It has only just occurred to me that you are quite an exceptional person," replied Dotty, which caused Martin to nearly choke on his goat. What on earth was she leading up to? He mentally prepared himself to fend off an attempt at intimacy. Of course, he entertained his own enjoyable thoughts in that department, but an offer of the real thing would be a terrifying moral challenge. He breathed an almost audible sigh of relief when she replied: "The world of biblical scholarship has now developed a view of Christian history that contradicts that preached by the Church, and the Church doesn't want to know. You, my dear Martin, are a member of the established Church, yet you have shed the blind faith of Sunday worship and you want to know what biblical scholarship can teach you. There can't be many like you, with a foot in both camps."

"I hadn't looked at it that way before. Come to think of it, you do have a point. As an ordained minister of the

Church I'm supposed to accept the unchanging truth of the scriptures. For me, that truth exists on different levels. Embedded deep within the Christian message is a truth that I not only accept but espouse with all my heart; that is the message of love, peace and forgiveness. On the other hand, I look upon certain other so-called truths, like who did what, who said what, where certain events took place and Paul's insistence on how the Church should be run as non-verifiable and sometimes wrong."

Dotty interrupted: "I'm glad you mentioned *the unchanging truth of the scriptures*. Christian conservatives love that expression. Whenever the Church is faced with the possibility of change, like the appointment of women bishops or the solemnisation of same sex marriage, the opposition issues the challenge of *the unchanging truth of the scriptures*. You, Martin, clearly consider that the message of the scriptures can be changed."

"Yes, I do. Actually, it's difficult to know where many clergy stand in relation to the unchanging truth of the scriptures. It's only during controversies, like the role of women in the Church, that free thinkers like me and ultra-conservatives speak up and identify themselves. Even then I feel that some are intellectually dishonest and espouse the conservative line, in order to gain respectability with the establishment. The reverse may also be true, in that some aged conservative clerics want to appear modern and 'with it' before they die, so they support change."

Martin paused, looked thoughtful then added: "Between you and me, I'm pretty sure my bishop thinks the way that I do, but prefers to keep quiet about it for the sake of peace within the diocese."

"Okay, but I still think you are exceptional. Perhaps when your visit is over and you have the answers you are seeking, you will leave the Church and join an academic team of biblical scholars."

## CHAPTER 14

"I might have to," mused Martin, "It's early days yet. I'll cross that bridge when I come to it."

"And provided your bishop and your wife allow it."

"What's that supposed to mean?" retorted Martin.

"It means that you are at present living under unusual conditions. Your perspective on life, the significance of anything you learn and how you should react to it is determined by the fact that you are in a desert in the company of three natives and one European, with no responsibilities except to dig holes in the sand and listen to me in the evenings. At home with your wife, your parishioners, your church and your bishop, not to mention a green landscape and a measurable rainfall, your perspective will be different."

Dotty held up a hand to stop him replying, and added: "Don't argue! I know!"

Martin nodded his silent agreement. Of course she knew. That last little outburst was a cry from the heart, and he felt a pang of sympathy for her. She had made her point and Martin felt this line of conversation had run its course, so he looked at her earnestly and said: "May I take advantage of your good nature and make a request?" Now it was her turn to feel slightly uncomfortable and to wonder what was coming next.

"Of course. What do you want?"

"I want some sewing machine oil."

She had no time to reply. Mustapha had just removed their plates while they were talking and he was still within earshot.

"Very easy request, Reverend Martin. I tell the driver at the dam and he will bring it," shouted Mustapha from outside the tent.

Martin shouted back: "Thank you. I need quite a lot. Half a pint would do. By the way, the curried goat was excellent. My compliments to the cook."

"Thank you many times," came the reply, "I am the cook."

"Okay, now tell me why you want to oil a sewing machine," demanded Dotty. The mood of the evening had changed. No more earnest discussion of entrenched Church attitudes. They were relaxed and well-fed and glad to change the subject.

Martin reported that his water treatment of the fresco fragment had leached the colours, and explained his theory that a non-aqueous liquid like a thin oil might be the answer to the problem. Dotty expressed her admiration of his scientific approach and told him that every woman in Khartoum treasured her sewing machine and getting a supply of oil should not be a problem.

"Now *I* will change the subject," announced Dotty. "What about very early doubts about the existence of Jesus?"

Martin suddenly saw the funny side of his situation. They were both dressed like native Sudanese, sitting in the moonlight in the entrance of a tent in the Nubian Desert, having just finished an excellent meal of curried goat, talking about sewing machines and Jesus. It was worthy of Gilbert and Sullivan. He started to laugh and Dotty laughed with him. He didn't need to explain. She knew instinctively that any European happening upon them at that moment would have been both bemused and amused.

Martin pulled a straight face, gave a sigh of resignation and told Dotty he couldn't recall ever hearing or reading any first century doubts about the existence of Jesus. Surely, he told her, all early Christian leaders, once they had decided to preach that Jesus was a person, would then stick to the party line. It would have been a well-planned and well-protected conspiracy.

"Unless," he added, "someone decided to become a whistle-blower."

## CHAPTER 14

"Whistle-blower," replied Dotty "is not a fitting metaphor for the situation that existed in the early centuries AD. It would be more accurate to say that there were Christians who knew that Jesus was a mythical figure, but they found it difficult to attract converts to their particular theology. Keep reminding yourself that the population was largely illiterate and superstitious. Not for them esoteric discussions about the finer points of theology. Give them a redeemer, ready-made, who performed miracles and rose from the dead, and bingo! – you've won converts. No wonder, therefore, you can't find any dissention about the reality of Jesus amongst the early Christians. The laity believed in him because they wanted to, while the Church had found the perfect tool for recruiting followers."

Martin now realised that he should have been looking for the existence of those who knew the truth but had difficulty making their voices heard, partly because their theology was too esoteric for the laity and partly because those with opposing theologies had sharp elbows.

Dotty continued: "We know there is no evidence for the existence of Jesus that is acceptable to professional historians. We can't quote the Bible as evidence because the Bible is not an historical document; no historian can use the Bible as source material. Of course, historians work with the Bible, looking for correspondence between events reported in the Bible and events authenticated by genuine historical documents and archaeology. It's an interesting exercise, often leading to embarassing results, such as a complete lack of any kind of evidence that the Jews were ever enslaved in Egypt.

"Really!?" exclaimed Martin. "Yes, really," replied Dotty, "Let's not get diverted by the Jews and Egypt. We were discussing whether early evidence existed for the non-historicity of Jesus. We've agreed that Christian accounts of Jesus can't be taken as evidence, so the only acceptable testimony for the existence of Jesus must come from non-Christian sources."

Martin made to interrupt but Dotty anticipated him. "Yes, I know that you, Doctor Willan, and I have been over all this before, but I think it's a good idea to go over it again. The supposed references to Jesus by the Roman historian Tacitus and the Jewish historian Josephus are now known to be forgeries. The Roman records make no mention of Jesus or anyone resembling Jesus. So, can we take it that there exists no mention of Jesus in any non-Christian source?"

"I've learned not to be too hasty when replying to your apparently innocent questions, so I'll reserve judgement and say: *as far as I know.*"

"Very wise. The Romans were assiduous record keepers. They ruled the Bible lands so we naturally ask whether they left any record of Jesus. They didn't. However, we can't leave it there. Were there any other non-Christians around at that time who might have encountered Jesus? And I don't mean the Jews."

Martin didn't know whether she expected him to answer this last question. He suspected she was about to answer it anyway, so he didn't reply.

"When we talk of the Romans and their occupation of the Bible lands we are talking about a political and military force. What about other religions?"

Martin looked puzzled and couldn't think what she was referring to.

"No? Can't you suggest another religion, or another group of religionists who were around at that time?"

"Sorry, you've beaten me there. Please tell me and put me out of my misery!"

"What about the Pagans?"

Martin threw up his hands in surrender. "Sorry Dotty! It's been a long day. I must be getting tired. Why didn't I think of the Pagans? So you're telling me that the Pagans reported the existence of Jesus."

## CHAPTER 14

"Whoa there, not so fast! It's the very opposite. They as good as said that the Christians were wrong and that Jesus did not exist. I'll explain in a moment. First, let's talk about the Pagans. What do you know about Pagan religions and their relationship to Christianity?"

Dotty leaned back in her chair and made a hand gesture indicating he should take the floor. Her thoub had long since fallen from her head and she was sitting slightly to one side for comfort. She was slouching and, like Martin, she was tiring.

"On second thoughts, let's leave it there for this evening and go to bed."

Martin blushed. How many times had he or Pamela used those very same words? *Let's leave it there* (meaning the washing up) *and go to bed* (meaning you know what)?

"Agreed! I'm certainly ready for bed. Pagan religions might be a heavy topic for breakfast conversation. Tomorrow evening perhaps?"

And so ended the fourth day.

Or not quite. As Martin made his way to his tent, Dotty called out: "Just a moment, Martin; is it worth talking about Richard Dawkins?"

"If we must," replied Martin, "Can't we leave it for another occasion?"

"I have a sudden urge to talk about Dawkins," replied Dotty. "Why don't you humour me?"

"Okay, if it's what you want. You start, said Martin," doing a complete about turn and sitting down again in Dotty's tent.

"In a sense, Richard Dawkins is continuing a process that started with the Enlightenment and perhaps earlier. Stage by stage, science has removed superstition and false beliefs from human thinking and attitudes. At least that is true of western secular society, although belief in the impossible is still entrenched in most Christian denominations. In another sense, however, Dawkins' attack on religious belief is utterly different from the earlier attempts by science to influence Christian faith."

"Utterly different? In what way?" asked Martin, still keeping a weather-eye on Lawrence the death stalker exploring the base of the tent pole.

"First, he is leading a personal crusade against religion; and please forgive the use of the word *crusade,* which is hardly fitting in the present context and certainly not in a Muslim country. Second, his onslaught was sudden, so he caught the religious establishment unawares and drove them into a state of confusion. They recovered and regrouped, hunkered down behind the battlements of their own prejudices or sincere convictions, whichever you prefer, with the result that they have now developed an armoury of well-rehearsed counter arguments. In short, Dawkins' attack has galvanised the faithful into mounting a strong defence."

Keeping his eye on Lawrence, who was waving his pincers and seemed to be sampling the atmosphere of the tent, Martin suggested that Dawkins' attack on religion, important though it was, had little to do with their shared interest in the history of Christianity. Dawkins had, unfortunately, sensitised the religious establishment to criticism, whereas a more gentle approach might have started a meaningful dialogue, leading the faithful to display a little more common sense and stop believing in fairies, for example the existence of the IVF fairy two thousand years ago.

Martin saw a flickering of genuine amusement in Dotty's face. Those sexy little crows' feet in the corner of her eyes creased as she laughed out loud: "Exactly, and I love your IVF fairy!"

Then they really did go to bed.

## CHAPTER 14

Alone in his tent, stretched out on his camp bed, Martin started to think about Christmas, and he knew he would have to think it through before he could go to sleep. For Christians the world over, the birth of Jesus is one of the most important dates in both the social calendar and the Church calendar. Celebration of the nativity is steeped in tradition, involving a delightful amalgam of Holy Scripture, Pagan traditions and later secular additions. Martin could do without the commercialisation of Christmas, which he preached against every year, and for which he had coined the expression *evil creep*. What if he did become convinced that Jesus was a mythical figure? Would he still feel able to celebrate Christmas?

Christmas, sermons by the pope, the archbishop of Canterbury, the bishop of Westminster and others all stressed the centrality of Christ's birth to the important Christian message of love and charity. He surprised himself by admitting that he loved Christmas, and would continue to love it, even if Jesus had never existed. The children's nativity play was part of the life of his church. The Christmas tree, the impossible fairies, the singing of carols with verse after verse proclaiming the birth of Jesus, three kings and choirs of angels. Non-Christian mistletoe, holly and yule logs; and why not? Pre-Christmas gatherings of friends and neighbours with home-made mince pies. Ah! Those mince pies with a glass of sherry. Pamela's mince pies took some beating, and he had never gathered enough courage to tell Pamela that his mother's pies were even better. The promotion of charities, the Salvation Army playing carols in the town centre, putting up the Christmas decorations, decorating the Christmas tree. And above all, the family Christmas dinner. Yes, he loved Christmas, and he would always celebrate it, come what may. He didn't feel inclined to argue with himself about whether he was inconsistent or lacked the courage of his convictions. He would celebrate Christmas and that was that.

# Chapter 15

Next morning, Martin was up with the African crow. After only four days at the camp he was feeling at home in a tropical desert, near to a river writ large in ancient history, in a country dominated by a culture of which he had no previous experience. Dotty's two husbands had not adapted so well. Martin wondered why. They didn't know what they were missing! Fetching water from the Nile, digging holes at the excavation site, and researching ways of revealing Dotty's fresco were all within Martin's physical capability, and there was much of additional interest. In particular, he was looking forward to his next trip to the Nile and the opportunity to talk with Yasser and Mohammed.

As usual, Dotty waved from her tent with her coffee cup and Martin returned the signal by flashing his tea strainer.

Over breakfast Dotty made a welcomed suggestion. "Look here, you have to wait for your sewing machine oil, which might come tomorrow and possibly the day after, so you can't work on the fresco today. If you feel like digging another hole at the site by all means go ahead. I'm feeling less energetic than usual so I wouldn't join you. I suggest we have a day of rest and talk about the Pagans. It may be a heavy topic for breakfast conversation but we can make a slow and cautious start. In any case there always comes a time in this hot climate when one has to pause and put one's feet-up. What do you think?"

Martin couldn't have been more pleased at this offer of an early start to his history lessons. "Why not, I'm well rested and ready for anything,"

"We shall see about that," replied Dotty ominously. "Before we start, I feel we should sit in silence for a couple of minutes and allow our minds to attain equilibrium."

It was that silence thing again. He already knew that Dotty loved silence and under her influence he was also

## CHAPTER 15

beginning to feel that silence was not a matter of nothingness; it could be mentally and spiritually invigorating. It wasn't the silence of prayer and meditation; he knew all about that kind of silence. It was a silence of the soul and …. but the two minutes were up. Dotty spoke and asked him what he understood by a Pagan.

"Well, I know that Pagan is commonly used as a derogatory adjective, applied to self-indulgent behaviour, the celebration of life with orgies, the playing of pan pipes with goats dancing on their hind legs, all in beautiful natural surroundings with everyone drinking ambrosia. The Fantasia version of Beethoven's pastoral symphony shows what many would regard as Pagans enjoying themselves irresponsibly."

"Utter rubbish," exclaimed Dotty. "Now try again!"

"Alright, I know that the Pagans practised religions of their own, which were founded on metaphor and myth. They performed certain rites that were safe and respectable, although we would probably not have wanted to take part. They are portrayed as devilish, immoral and primitive. In fact, they were nothing like that. Their reputation for having orgies was the result of Christian propaganda. At least their orgies were probably no worse than those organised nowadays by so-called Christians at Christmas."

"That's a valuable start. Your point that Pagan religions were founded on metaphor and myth is important, perhaps more than important because it is central to the comparison of Christianity with Paganism. At the same time we should remember that while most Pagan gods were mythical characters and the Pagans never claimed them to be otherwise, they did set a few real historical figures on pedestals. You might be surprised to learn that Paganism has a close historical relationship with Christianity. The widely held view that Paganism was the opposite or enemy of Christianity deserves close scrutiny. It is true that they competed for converts.

Otherwise they had much in common, which was probably a source of mutual embarrassment."

With a nod and a smile Martin conveyed that he was indeed surprised to learn that Paganism had a close historical relationship with Christianity. Words were unnecessary. Dotty continued:

"To use a modern term of computer security, there is, or rather was, no true firewall between Paganism and Christianity. Like you, most people are surprised to learn this. And I know you won't be surprised if I tell you that, upon hearing it, many don't want to know. I'm still not sure just how much you *do* know about Paganism. Did you receive any formal instruction on Paganism in your university course?"

"None whatsoever. All I know about it I've picked up from my extracurricular reading. If what you say is true, that there is no firewall between Paganism and Christianity, and that Paganism and Christianity have a close historical relationship then I'm already at the beginning of a steep learning curve."

"Fine. I'll take over from here and give you some more extracurricular material to think about."

"Before you do that, how about another coffee? I have the feeling that discussing Pagans is going to be thirsty work."

As usual, Mustapha displayed an uncanny knack of anticipating their needs, for he appeared within the minute with a fresh pot of coffee. Martin and Dotty exchanged knowing looks and Dotty congratulated Mustapha on producing fresh coffee so quickly. "You talk. So I know you need to drink. I prepare the coffee and keep it hot."

"Of course Mustapha. Thank you. You can now wait outside and continue listening."

Mustapha beamed with pride. Any irony or hidden humour in Dotty's thanks were completely lost on him.

## CHAPTER 15

With a serious, thoughtful expression, Dotty nursed her fresh cup of coffee near to her face, savoured the aroma and eyed Martin through the wisps of steam. "It is indeed going to be a steep learning curve. Are you ready?"

"And waiting."

"Then tell me this. How many Pagan cultures are you aware of?"

"I can recall only two Pagan gods. At least I think they are Pagan gods. How about Osiris and Dionysus? Am I right?"

"Those will do for a start. Which Pagan cultures did they belong to?"

"Oops! You've got me there. Except I know Osiris was Egyptian."

"I can see you *are* on a steep learning curve. I'd better take over and give you a mini lecture. Osiris *was* Egyptian. You were correct there. Your other god, Dionysus, was Greek. However, we can identify five Pagan gods: Osiris of Egypt, Dionysus of Greece, Attis of Asia Minor, Adonis of Syria, Bacchus of the Romans, and Mithras of Persia."

"Just a minute, that's six."

"Yes, I know, but Dionysus and Bacchus are the same gods. The Romans also adopted the Greek Dionysus and renamed him Bacchus. May I proceed?"

Dotty didn't wait for a reply.

"When we talk of Greek gods, we immediately think of the legendary gods of mount Olympus. These were the gods of pomp and ceremony, disagreeing amongst themselves and frightening mortals with their unpredictable behaviour. But there were other gods who ministered to the spirituality of the common people. At first the worship of these other gods was performed in secret and the corresponding religions were considered heretical. We refer to these underground philosophies as mystery religions or simply *Mysteries*. They were structured in layers. The outer layer consisted of myths and ritual practices; anyone could join the movement at that level and take part. Then there were the more esoteric inner layers, consisting of sacred secrets known only to members who had undergone initiation, resulting in personal transformation and spiritual enlightenment. The five, or six if you like, that I have mentioned were very similar in structure. They existed at different times in history, belonged to different cultures with different languages and the names of their gods were different, yet they were basically similar. A telling analogy are the differences and similarities between Shakespeare's Romeo and Juliet and Bernstein's twentieth century American musical West Side Story – similar stories of warring families in which a boy from one and a girl from the other fall in love – set at different times in different cultures. To put it another way: they were the same only different.

Now, listen carefully and be amazed. I will list for you the basic features – let's call them motifs – shared by all the so-called Mysteries or Pagan religions.

1) The mythical god was a man, whose mother was a goddess or a mortal virgin and whose father was God himself.

2) He was placed on earth in a human form, being born in a cave on December 25$^{th}$ or January 6$^{th}$.

3) On earth he preached a message and attracted followers, to whom he offered the chance to be born again through the rites of baptism.

4) He miraculously turned water into wine at a marriage ceremony.

5) He rode triumphantly into town on a donkey while people waved palm leaves to honour him.

6) His fellow men turned upon him and he was killed by being nailed to a tree. Thus he died at Eastertime as a sacrifice for the sins of the world.

7) After his death he descended to hell then on the third day he rose from the dead and ascended to heaven in glory.

8) His followers awaited his return on the day of judgement.

9) His death and resurrection were celebrated by a ritual meal with wine, which symbolised his body and his blood."

"Stop there, please!" shouted Martin, "This can't be true. Are telling me that the Pagan religions had the same story line as Christianity?"

"That is exactly what I'm telling you."

"This is extremely important. Why didn't I know about it? Why wasn't I taught this in my university course?"

"I'll leave you to answer that question for yourself, but if I might make a suggestion, it's rarely talked about because it's acutely embarrassing. And it gets better, or worse, depending on your ability to embrace the truth."

Martin uttered a sigh of disbelief and made a hand gesture inviting her to continue.

"Here we go then. For good measure, here are some further similarities between Christianity and Paganism

1) The birth of Jesus was prophesised by a star, as was the birth of the Pagan gods.

2) The Magi brought gifts of gold, frankincense and myrrh for Jesus. Six centuries before the birth of Christ, the giving of these three items was part of a Pagan rite for worshipping God.

3) John the Baptist baptised Jesus with water. The name John is from the Hebrew *Yohanen* meaning *from the waters*. So far, so good, and we can trace the name further back in history to *Oannes*, the fish-headed Babylonian god, who rose from the sea and initiated followers into the inner Mysteries. Thus the Pagan *Oannes* and John the Baptist share both the same name and the same job description – initiation by water.

4) Jesus healed the sick, exorcised demons, provided miraculous meals, helped fishermen make miraculous

catches, and calmed the waters for his disciples; all of these marvels had previously been performed by Pagan sages.

5) Like the sages of the Pagan religions, Jesus was a wandering wonder-worker who was not honoured in his own town.

6) Jesus was accused of licentious behaviour, as were the followers of Pagan religions.

7) Jesus was not at first recognised as divine by his disciples, but was then transfigured before them in all his glory; the same was true of the Pagan gods.

8) Jesus had twelve disciples; so did the Pagan gods.

9) Jesus was a just man unjustly accused of heresy and bringing a new religion, as were the Pagan gods.

10) Jesus attacked hypocrites, stood up to tyranny, and willingly went to his death predicting he would rise again in three days, as did Pagan sages.

11) Jesus was betrayed for thirty pieces of silver, a motif found in the story of Socrates.

12) Jesus' corpse was wrapped in linen and anointed with myrrh, as were the corpses of Pagan gods."

"I simply must stop you there!" cried Martin. "This information will take time to digest and accept as the truth. Don't stop the lesson, but please don't be offended if I tell you that I intend to check it all out."

"The first time I came across these striking similarities between the Pagan Mysteries and Christianity I also couldn't believe it. It took me about two months of library work to satisfy myself that it was all true. So you must indeed check it all out. For the time being, however, let's assume you accept it and I'll continue."

"Not until we've had some refreshment. Surely you need a drink. You've been doing most of the talking. I think fresh orange juice would be welcome, don't you?"

## CHAPTER 15

As Martin suggested refreshment, both he and Dotty glanced knowingly at one another and nodded towards the shaded area behind the tent flap. "How can you be so unkind?" whispered Dotty. "He'd probably already made the coffee. Now he will have to dash back to the supply tent and find some orange juice." Five minutes later the orange juice was delivered by the two Mohammeds. Mohammed one (or was it Mohammed two?) informed Dotty that Mustapha was resting.

As they enjoyed the orange juice Dotty wondered if Mustapha had gone on strike or whether he was really physically tired. She dismissed the two Mohammeds, dived into her tin trunk and pulled out a pair of binoculars, which she trained on Mustapha's tent on the other side of the semicircle. "He's lying down so I suppose he really is feeling tired. He works hard for us. I hope he's okay."

Martin was touched by her concern. It would be too easy to take Mustapha for granted. He did indeed work hard for the camp.

"To continue, you find this similarity between Christianity and Pagan Mysteries incredible. Try to put yourself in the position of the early Church fathers like Martyr, Tertullian and Irenaeus. All three lived in the second century after Christ. Pagans were still very much in evidence and probably taunted the Christians by pointing out these similarities between the two religions. We know that a Pagan called Celsus complained that Christianity was just a pale reflection of ancient Pagan teachings. This was surely a terrible embarrassment, especially since, between you and me, there was a lot of truth in it. The early Church tried to wriggle out of this embarrassment by blaming the devil. They claimed the devil had foreseen the arrival of Christianity and feared it, so the devil invented the Pagan Mysteries to create the belief that Christianity, when it came, would be dismissed as just another copy of a Pagan religion. In other words, the devil copied the story of Jesus before it happened."

At this point, Dotty exclaimed *eftah ya sim sim,* dived into her tin trunk, searched amongst her papers and finally retrieved what she was looking for: a school exercise book with word **Quotes** written on the cover in red felt pen. Flicking over the pages she found the relevant quotation.

"Listen to this. It's a quotation from Justin Martyr, one of the early Church fathers:

*Having heard it proclaimed through the prophets that the Christ was to come and that the ungodly among men were to be punished by fire, the wicked spirits put forward many to be called Sons of God, under the impression that they would be able to produce in men the idea that the things that were said with regard to Christ were merely marvellous tales, like the things that were said by the poets.*

For wicked spirits read the devil. This attempt to blame the devil became known as *plagiarism by anticipation* or *diabolical mimicry.* In those days, when many were illiterate and superstitious, this explanation may have carried some weight. When you come to think about it, those early Church fathers were being pretty devious – just like the devil they were trying to incriminate.

A slightly more generous version, but no less daft, was the claim that the myths of the Pagan Mysteries prophesied the coming of Jesus. From there it's only a small step to claim that Christianity was a Jewish version of the Pagan Mysteries, modelled on the other Mysteries; and since each mystery needed a god person they called him Jesus. Well, what do you think now?"

Martin didn't answer at first. He remained silent and thought hard for a few minutes. It seemed much longer. Dotty waited patiently for his answer. She could fully understand how his view of Christianity may have been turned upside down.

## CHAPTER 15

Finally, he said: "I'm beginning to feel I don't need to check this out. You have taught me a piece of history that I wish had never happened. I can already hear fellow ministers back home, in particular the curate who is standing in for me, and members of my congregation saying it's outrageous and can't be true. But I accept it, although I hate to admit the inevitable conclusion that there is nothing original about Christianity and nothing original about the figure of Jesus."

"Oh dear, you are taking it badly," sympathised Dotty. "There is obviously a close relationship between Christianity and Pagan mythology. Amongst the plentiful evidence for this, I ought to mention the fascinating archaeological discovery of an amulet, which anyone would assume to be a depiction of Christ crucified. In fact, it depicts the passion of the Pagan god Oriris-Dionysus. Fortunately, a plaster cast of the amulet survives. The original was lost from the Berlin museum in the Second World War. And as I have already pointed out, even Jesus' teaching was not original and had been anticipated by Pagan sages. If Jesus really existed – and that after all is the question you are trying to answer – then we know nothing about him because, to a large extent, he consists of words and actions copied from Pagan religions."

"Frankly, this creates a dilemma. What you have told me goes a long way to answering the question of whether Jesus actually existed. On the other hand, it casts doubt on Christianity's credentials as an entirely new faith that arose through the inspiration of a group of liberal-minded Jews who were seeking a fresh approach to the spirituality of their lives."

"So what? Then, with a mischievous smile, she added: "Or should I say I have an aunt who plays the guitar? There are certain truths that must be accepted when we meet them. As for the physical existence of Jesus, let me underline the fact that the followers of those ancient religions did not take the stories of their gods and goddesses literally; rather they regarded them as allegories of human experience. You can't prove it, but you now have strong evidence that Jesus was very likely also an allegory of human experience."

Dotty turned to another page in her exercise book of quotations.

"Let me read this to you. It's a quotation from the Pagan Celsus who is ridiculing the Christians for trying to claim that Jesus was in any way unique. He writes:

*It would have been better had you in your zest for a new teaching formed your religion around one of the men of old who died a hero's death and was honoured for it – someone who at least was already subject of a myth. You could have chosen Heracles or Asclepius, or if these were too tame, there was always Orpheus, who as everyone knows, was good and holy and yet died a violent death. Or had he already been taken? Well, then you had Anaxarchus, a man who looked death right in the eye when being beaten and said to his persecutors, 'Beat away. Beat the pouch of Anaxarchus; for it is not him you are beating.' But I recall that some philosophers have already claimed him as their master. Well, what of Epictetus? When his leg was being twisted he smiled and said with complete composure, 'You are breaking it.' And when it was broken, he smiled and said, 'I told you so.' Your God should have uttered such a saying when he was being punished!*

Consider the words: *someone who at least was already subject of a myth.* Those words, like the rest of Celsus' speech, clearly assumed that the Christian god person was a myth. Apparently, there was no need to argue about it. Probably many simply accepted it as a fact. It seems clear that the second-century Christians had a hard struggle to dissociate themselves from the Pagans. The Pagan Celsus, who, incidentally, was a second century Greek philosopher, seemed to be enjoying himself by poking fun at the Christians. The Christian Origen and the Pagan Celsus attacked one

## CHAPTER 15

another's religions, giving rise to a fierce debate. Unfortunately, we don't have all of Celsus' literary output. And if we did, we might have to modify our current view of the relationship between Paganism and Christianity. It is the secret fear of every historian that somewhere evidence is lurking undiscovered, which would support or contradict the current view." Martin waited for Dotty to continue but she was waiting for him to speak. Martin hesitated, wondering how to express his next thought then said: "I see a paradox in that the Christians didn't want to be associated with the Pagans, whereas the two religions were strikingly similar. What I'm trying to say is: since there are such similarities between the two religions, why isn't Christianity simply classified as another Pagan Mystery? Obviously the early Christians, certainly those early Church fathers, were intent on dissociating themselves from the Pagans. Perhaps there was a rivalry. Perhaps the Pagans were jealous of the new faith of Christianity. Perhaps the criticisms and jibes levelled at Christianity were an attempt to belittle a rival faith. Perhaps the Pagans were jealous because the Christians really did have a true god person in the form of Jesus, as distinct from the Pagan gods that were all metaphor and myth."

Dotty laughed out loud and slapped her knee for emphasis. "That's a lot of suggestive *perhapses* Martin. I agree there are several possibilities. You've definitely hit the nail on the head when you suggest rivalry between Pagans and Christians, and even jealousy on the part of the Pagans. By the way, there's one point either you or I should have made. Even if Christianity did take the Pagan Mysteries as a model, it could not have used one of the Pagan gods as suggested by Celsus."

"I know," interrupted Martin. "It was because the Christian god had to be Jewish. It couldn't have been a tried and trusted Pagan god because it had to be the Jewish Messiah."

Dotty was delighted with Martin's interruption. They were interacting well in her teaching process.

"Now try this for size," offered Dotty. "The entire structure of Christianity was grafted onto something older that arose long before the supposed birth of Christ. Part of that grafting process was the adoption of a well-tried and tested story, consisting of a god person, who was born to a virgin, who turned water into wine, etc. etc., a story well-known because it had been around for centuries in the Pagan Mysteries. I admit it's yet another big *perhaps*. And it neither helps nor hinders your claim that Jesus was not an historical figure."

"Something older that arose long before the supposed birth of Christ," repeated Martin thoughtfully. "Yes, I'll buy that one. It's certainly worth looking into. What evidence do you have?"

"Lots, actually. Let's leave it for later."

"Before we move on I have to say that I do not claim that Jesus was not an historical figure. That's putting it far too strongly. Yes, I would be pleased if I could prove that Jesus never had a physical existence. My true cause, however, is to find the truth."

"Very noble of you," snorted Dotty. I think it's time for coffee and reflection."

This time there was no response from the catering staff. Dotty checked with her binoculars; Mustapha was still asleep. One of the Mohammeds saw her looking in the direction of Mustapha's tent and came running over. Coffee was ordered and it arrived soon afterwards with bread, fool, sweet spread, and fruit. Without being asked, the Mohammeds had decided it was past lunchtime and had risen to the occasion.

"I've had enough schooling for today," pleaded Martin. "When we've finished lunch may I have my afternoon nap? I might not be able to sleep for worrying about Christians and

## CHAPTER 15

Pagans. You've left me to struggle with two opposing possibilities: Christianity was a Pagan Mystery in disguise, or the Pagans were jealous of Christianity, which was fundamentally different from Paganism. And to think at breakfast you suggested this would be a day of rest!"

"Sorry to be such a hard task master," chortled Dotty.

"Task *mistress*," corrected Martin, wondering if that was the right thing to say. "I forgive you. In fact, this is becoming far more interesting, even more exciting, than I ever imagined. So good night – I mean good afternoon – Oh damn it, what *do* you say when you go to bed in the middle of the afternoon?"

"How about *I'm going to bed now – see you later?*"

"Agreed. You've said it for me." And Martin ambled off to his tent and his bed.

For the evening meal Martin put on his galabiya again. It was the most sensible garment for the climate. He couldn't imagine doing hard physical work in it, like digging at the archaeological site, and he marvelled at how Mustapha and the two Mohammeds managed to perform every imaginable task in the long flowing, tent-like covering. They had been born to it. For Martin, however, it was the perfect evening dress and from now on he would wear it to every evening meal.

Once again, Dotty chose fancy dress for the evening. That was how Martin viewed it, although he wouldn't have dared tell her he looked upon her low-cut flimsy pink blouse as fancy dress in the desert. Her dress sense secretly delighted him. Damn it all, he was miles from home, only one woman in sight, and an attractive one at that, so how could he be expected not to enjoy her company – and her delightful cleavage! Well, he told himself, there's an answer to that, which is you have a wife at home, and as a minister of the Church you are obliged to adopt the highest possible standards of moral behaviour. Then he excused himself with the fact that he was only enjoying the view. Another little voice reminded him that Jesus would have said that even to think about it was the same as adultery. To which he replied that he was going to do for this Jesus character one way or the other. A minister of the Church supposedly follows the teachings of Jesus. Martin, like every other Christian who had ever lived, found it a hard act to follow.

Dotty must have known that her evening wear was capable of stimulating the hormones of any male between adolescence and the age of seventy (or eighty or ninety – who knows?). She knew that Martin knew that she knew that he knew and implicit in this knowledge was the clear message that she trusted him not to cross the boundaries of respectable behaviour or respectable conversation. He was flattered. He hoped that one day Dotty and Pamela would meet. On the other hand, perhaps not.

Both Martin and Dotty had been concerned that Mustapha had taken to his bed that afternoon. It wasn't his usual behaviour. Probably just genuine tiredness had crept up on him after being continually on his toes and serving the camp. Fully rested, he had organised the evening meal, which he now proudly brought from the cooking area near the camp fire, Mohammed one and Mohammed two in procession behind him. It was Nile perch, a very large if rather bony fish, beautifully cooked, head still attached and glaring at them in defeat, and accompanied by okra and boiled potatoes. Mustapha glowed with pride as Dotty congratulated him on such a wonderful meal so beautifully presented. As for glowing with pride, that was the interpretation Martin placed on Mustapha's facial expression. Glowing, blushing or any other condition affecting the blood supply to the skin goes unnoticed in dark-skinned people. (This is not entirely true. The author has seen cases of jaundice in Africans, where their black skin has a definite yellow tinge.)

## CHAPTER 15

Martin was surprised to see potatoes until Mustapha explained that the desert climate was ideal for growing that particular vegetable because, given adequate irrigation, the heat of the day encouraged growth, while the chilly desert nights were also required by the plant. Had he not heard that Egypt grows and exports potatoes? The penny dropped. Of course. He had forgotten about those fine potatoes from Egypt.

"Mustapha, where did potatoes come from before they were cultivated in Egypt and the Sudan?" asked Martin, who now had potatoes on his mind.

"They came from England. The English brought them when they ruled Egypt and the Sudan."

"How did England get potatoes," enquired Martin mischievously.

"Oh, I think potatoes started in England. They were always there," claimed Mustapha.

"No Mustapha. Have you heard of Francis Drake?"

"That is a peculiar name. Who is he?"

"He is the Englishman who went to South America and brought back potatoes. That was more than four hundred years ago. Before that time potatoes grew only in South America and no-one in Europe or Africa had ever heard of or seen a potato. Now they are grown all over the world. Isn't that interesting?!"

Mustapha straightened himself, adopted a solemn air and announced: "Today I have learned history. In the *Sukh Arabi* in Khartoum where potatoes are sold, I will tell the traders about Francis Drake and what a great man he was. We now leave you to my cooking."

Dotty skilfully divided the fish and placed a bone-free serving on each of their plates. She had obviously done it before. This skill was not attained by practising at home on trout or salmon. A large Nile perch is a much greater challenge. As if she read his thoughts, Dotty informed Martin that this was her fifth (or was it her sixth?) Nile perch since setting up camp and that Mustapha had first demonstrated how to cut into it and avoid the vicious bones.

They ate in silence until Martin suddenly asked where the fish came from. Dotty explained that one and sometimes both of the Mohammeds went fishing early on certain mornings, long before the rest of the camp was awake. They walked all the way to the Nile and back, which they did gladly, claiming that it really wasn't all that far. Apparently the fish were plentiful and it took only a few minutes to hook one. Martin told Dotty how lucky she was to have such hard working and dedicated helpers. He hoped she paid them well.

Ignoring his last remark, Dotty told Martin he was losing too much body salt by perspiring in the desert heat. She knew because she had watched him over-generously seasoning his meal with salt from the pot on the table. She explained that in a tropical climate it could take up to a fortnight before human physiology adjusted to salt loss through perspiration. After about a fortnight the salt content of perspiration decreases. He had not yet adjusted and his body was yearning for salt. "It's amazing," she explained, "After my first week here I actually took a heaped teaspoon of table salt and put it straight into my mouth. My body was yearning for it. I enjoyed it and felt much better for it. Actually, the body loses a mixture of different salts, not just sodium chloride, so it's better to take a specially prepared salt supplement each day and not wait until the body is crying out for salt."

Martin raised his eyebrows in lieu of the obvious question.

"No, I'm sorry, I forgot completely. We have run out of the supplement. They have plenty at the dam. Mustapha knows and will fetch some next time he goes to the river."

Dessert was water melon, followed by strong, hot, sweet tea.

## CHAPTER 15

Martin began to nod. Dotty jerked him awake with: "It seems this similarity between Christianity and Pagan Mysteries came as rather a shock to you. I find it surprising that you hadn't come across it in your university course or in your later personal reading."

"I agree. On the other hand, if I knew it all I wouldn't be here trying to learn more."

"Okay, then let's continue in our pursuit of the truth. We have glimpsed the possibility that Christianity as we know it is not the original Christianity. I'm not referring to the fact that Emperor Constantine chose only one version of Christianity for the Roman Empire. That, of course, is true. No, I'm considering the possibility that the entire Christian story, as told in the New Testament, has replaced an older version and that the older version is now unrecognisable because it is dressed in the clothes of a Pagan Mystery."

"I wonder if it is wise to assume the existence of a single older version. Isn't it possible that Christianity had more than one origin, and that different sources of inspiration and truth-seeking coalesced and became Christianity?"

"Now you are really getting to the heart of the problem. But I think we must avoid juggling too many balls at the same time. Let's take one putative origin of Christianity at a time."

"Starting with?"

"Let me see …. For two Christians passionately interested in the history of their faith and sitting in the desert, don't you find it odd that we haven't yet mentioned the Dead Sea scrolls?"

"Splendid idea! Let's talk about the Dead Sea scrolls – on one condition."

"Which is?"

"We relax for the rest of this evening and soak up the moonlight. Frankly, I've learned enough for today. That is if collecting doubts and dilemmas can be called learning."

"By all means. Let's relax and enjoy the food and the moonlight. And yes, I do rate the collection of doubts and dilemmas as true learning."

"You would of course," retorted Martin, who was watching Lawrence creeping into the tent and was trying hard to resist the temptation to give the wretched arachnid a hefty kick.

# Chapter 16

Martin enjoyed the variety of his desert life. He was looking forward to his next visit to the dam and to drinking tea with Mohammed, Yasser and Gwaria. Step by step he and Dotty were making progress at the excavation site. During their discussions of Christian history he easily switched his interest from the Jesus question to Dotty's involvement in Coptic history. Most certainly he would return to Herefordshire with enough material for lectures, sermons and after-dinner conversations to last for years.

Thanks to Dotty's natural ability as a teacher, every day produced a new slant on the provenance of Jesus. He wasn't there yet, but Martin was confident he would be taking home a storehouse of information throwing into question the entire Christian narrative as currently taught by the Church.

Yes, every day brought something new. On the sixth day, Martin parted the mosquito netting, stretched, yawned and reached for the pot of fresh coffee. He carefully removed the flies from his washing water with the tea strainer, which he then waved at Dotty, rotating it in the morning sunlight so that it flashed and sparkled.

This morning, there were more dust devils than usual. Hitherto, Martin had neglected to photograph them, or he had been too far from his tent where he kept his camera. At least half a dozen of those upwardly directed rotating columns of air were now issuing an invitation by performing a ballet in the area between his tent and the camp fire. Long ago Martin had abandoned his large, heavy single lens reflex with the extra lenses and bought a neat little digital, not much larger than a match box. It even had a video facility, which Martin now put to use. He videoed the gyrating devils from all angles, even lying full length on the ground to get an eye-level perspective.

Back in England he would have to give talks about his sabbatical. These would be serious lectures on the Christian history of the Nile Valley, as well as accounts of life in Dotty's camp and the story of how he revealed the nativity fresco. He dreaded the inevitable request from Flossy Hoskins to address the Womens' Institute, and to judge the flower arrangement competition on the same evening. He would present his talks with the aid of the Powerpoint programme on his computer, which made it possible to insert videos. Already he could picture the dust devils dancing on the screen while he explained the physics of vortex creation between air layers of different temperatures. From theology to the physics of air circulation in a single step. What a splendid talk that would be! He calmed his thoughts, finished washing and shaving, and prepared himself for breakfast with Dotty, when she would explain her timetable for the day:

"By now your sewing machine oil might have arrived at the dam. I suggest you drive over there with Mustapha and collect more water. I'll come with you in the Nissan and you can drop me off at the site. I want to work on an altar inscription. If the oil has arrived, Mustapha can then collect it from his lorry driver friend. On your way back, you can pick me up from the site. Promise me you won't start work on the fresco. By then it will be past midday. I'd rather you made a fresh start at the site tomorrow. When you pick me up we'll go straight back to the camp, have a light lunch and rest until our evening meal."

Dotty's instructions for the morning left no room for discussion. Hidden behind her school mistress tone, however, Martin detected a note of concern. She didn't want him to overdo it. At first he felt pleased with himself and flattered that he had elicited a maternal instinct in the undeniably attractive Dotty and that she wanted to protect him. He was mistaken. She had been here much longer than his five days and she knew the dangers of over-exertion in the heat of the

## CHAPTER 16

Nubian Desert. More importantly, she didn't want the inconvenience of an assistant laid low with sun stroke and heat exhaustion. It was not an affectionate concern. It was common sense laced with self-interest.

When the three of them were together in the Nissan, Martin mentioned the dangerous, rickety ladder that Dotty was using. Surely they could beg, borrow or steal an aluminium ladder from the engineering site at the dam. It transpired that Mustapha had made the ladder himself and was confident they could leave it at the site and it wouldn't be stolen. A good aluminium ladder would have to be kept at the camp; otherwise it might be stolen by some wandering goatherd. It was a delicate situation. Dotty cleverly protected Mustapha's honour by imploring him to use his influence at the dam to acquire an aluminium ladder. She knew he was the only person with sufficient authority and influence to do this, adding that the wooden ladder, although wonderfully constructed, was proving rather heavy for her to move around. She didn't tell him she had recently hurt her leg when a rung of the ladder had given way. Later, when she was certain that Mustapha wasn't listening, she would thank Martin for his concern and explain her accident.

At the site Mustapha fussed around and made sure the rickety ladder was correctly placed against the wall of the altar excavation. It was a gesture to show who was boss when it came to ladders. It wasn't necessary because the ladder was already perfectly positioned, but he had to do it. To tell him otherwise would have been like telling a cricketer not to follow through after the ball had hit the bat.

Leaving Dotty down the hole, scraping away with her trowel, Martin and Mustapha drove to the Nile.

Martin did not need a navigator. He drove straight down to the water and parked the Nissan as near as possible to the slab of granite they had used for their first water collection. Mustapha had hitched up his galabiya and was ready to unload and fill the jerry cans, when Mohammed and Yasser appeared and took over. Martin was told to go to the house and take refreshment, which would be provided by Gwaria. Mustapha was released to go to the dam and collect whatever goods his lorry driver friend had brought, and to negotiate a ladder. Mohammed and Yasser would fill the jerry cans. If there was a more satisfactory arrangement Martin couldn't think of it.

As he turned to walk up to Yasser's house Martin watched a small scorpion scuttling away from behind the Nissan. Probably a young *Leiurus*. It jogged his memory. Calling back to Mohammed and Yasser, he asked if there were any camel scorpions in the vicinity. "Aha," exclaimed Mohammed, "You are meaning the *aqrab al jamal*." "Well, I suppose so. I was told it is a large scorpion that hides amongst the rocks by the river. What did you call it again?" "*Agrab al jamal*," repeated Mohammed with a pronunciation that Martin couldn't possibly imitate. "Very big scorpion," offered Yasser, "You want see? I find dead and bring." Provided there was no misunderstanding and the *agrab al jamal* was really the camel scorpion mentioned by Dotty, then she wasn't pulling his leg and they really did exist.

Local convention, custom, etiquette – Martin wasn't sure what to call it – concerning the place of women in the home was laid aside for the honoured European visitor and friend of Mustapha. While Martin and Gwaria were drinking tea and talking on the shaded side of Yasser's house, two women passed by, neighbours from a house above them on the hillside. They exchanged formal greetings with Gwaria then went quickly on their way, talking animatedly. Gwaria smiled and told Martin her neighbours were from very traditional families and she knew they were astonished to find her drinking tea alone with a man who was not her husband or male relative. "It will cause much scandal," she told Martin,

## CHAPTER 16

"I do not mind. And they will be amazed when they hear that my husband encouraged it."

Gwaria provided Martin with a fresh perspective on the recent history of the fourth cataract and the local political disagreements over the resettlement of the population of the flooded valley. Relatives on her father's side of her family had owned date plantations that were now beneath the water. They were amongst the few who had prevailed against the government for fair compensation and resettlement in an area more or less equivalent to the land they had lost, and they had been able to continue life as before. This only served to emphasise the plight of the hundreds of other displaced farmers who had been less fortunate. Most received a raw deal from the government. Gwaria explained that her relatives had friends in a certain government department. By now Martin had learned that patronage was an integral part of life in the Sudan. Had he been more widely travelled he would have realised that patronage was integral to the life of practically every country in the world. *Patronage* was a less confrontational and less accusing word than *corruption* but it meant the same thing. He certainly didn't like it but had to admit that it worked – after a fashion. He couldn't yet see a way to incorporate these thoughts in a sermon.

Mohammed and Yasser returned. They had earned the tea that Gwaria poured for them. Martin had not earned his tea. He had only sat and talked and watched Mohammed and Yasser working to fill the jerry cans. He felt like a colonial district officer. He told this to the two men and Gwaria translated. It was very easy to amuse Mohammed and Yasser. Any reference to former colonial times, favourable or otherwise, always elicited laughter.

Yasser kept his word and brought a scorpion for Martin to inspect. Rather, he brought the shattered remnants of a very large scorpion, whose body without the tail was about six inches in length and which had been battered to death, probably by a local fisherman. Earlier, Martin had been unsure whether Mohammed and Yassir had really understood what he was asking. With Gwaria to translate he was no longer in any doubt. She confirmed that it was known in English as a camel scorpion and in Arabic as *aqrab al jamal*. She wrote both the English and the Arabic names on a piece of paper and handed it to Martin, watched with pride by her husband at her erudition and skill at making his honoured guest feel at home. Martin glanced at Gwaria's writing. He would treasure that piece of paper bearing the English name *camel scorpion*, followed by the Arabic *aqrab al jamal*, followed by the name in Arabic script.

Mustapha was a long time at the dam. He finally appeared carrying an aluminium ladder on his shoulder and a large plastic bag in one hand. Mohammed and Yasser ran down to help him, first telling Martin to stay, drink more tea, and be a district officer.

Getting away from Mohammed, Yasser and Gwaria was always difficult and today was no exception. When it was obvious that Martin was determined to drive back to the camp, Gwaria disappeared discreetly into the house and left the men to mutual back slapping and repeated invitations to return as soon as possible.

Mustapha was elated with success. The aluminium ladder looked new, as if it had never been used. His friend had given him about half a pint of sewing machine oil and an unopened box containing fifty packets of salt supplement. The bag was large and heavy. It also contained a few pounds of aubergines and several boxes of eggs.

At the site Dotty was nowhere to be seen. They had taken longer than expected and she had walked back to the camp.

As Martin and Mustapha drove to the large tent to fill the water purification vessels, Dotty waved from her tent

## CHAPTER 16

then bent back over her paper work. She wasn't looking for conversation and wanted to be left alone. For lunch, Martin was satisfied with a piece of bread spread with hibiscus jam, washed down with a glass of water. He had drunk enough tea, black with lots of sugar, with his friends at the dam.

Sleep came easily. He awoke at about six am, still fully dressed, very sweaty and with a dry mouth. A shower would be wonderful. Surely they could construct a simple cubicle with an overhead water container, a hose and a sprinkler. He would discuss it with Mustapha. In the meantime he had to wash his body all over with a face cloth and tea strainer-treated water from the Nile. Presumably Dotty had to do the same. Why hadn't she asked the boys to build a shower long ago? Oh for the freedom to luxuriate under a spray of water, with hands free to wield the soap and shampoo! Also, after sweating profusely in the desert heat, it would be reassuring to think of one's effluvia being washed completely away.

As Martin washed and made himself presentable for the evening meal, he tried to recall what he knew about the Dead Sea scrolls, the subject of the evening discussion. Every day he had sent an e-mail to Pamela and less often to his bishop. He had sent an early account of his trip to Flo Willan, but had not yet told his old teacher about life at the camp. He had time to do this before the evening meal. Opening his laptop, it suddenly occurred to Martin that he could use the internet to find material for his discussions with Dotty. He dashed off a quick e-mail to Flo:

*Everything fine here in the desert. Getting on well with Dotty – yes, she likes me to call her Dotty! Must go because we are about to discuss the Dead Sea scrolls. More later. Regards, Martin.*

Then he googled *Dead Sea scrolls*. Two websites refreshed his memory about how, when and where the scrolls were discovered. Another site mentioned that restriction of access to the scrolls had caused bitter disputes amongst biblical scholars; he already knew that. He had no time to look at any of the other twenty or so websites, so he assumed he would be ill prepared for discussing the scrolls with Dotty. It was time to put on his galabiya. What would Dotty be wearing?

This evening she had chosen the *relaxing-after-a-safari* look, a very loose grey linen shirt hanging outside her jeans, sufficiently open at the neck to start a debate on whether or not she was wearing a bra, and no make-up. For the desert evening it was eminently sensible clothing. For tantalising Martin it was extremely effective. You might ask how she was supposed to dress so as not to excite Martin. She was an attractive woman; he was a normal man; both were well-behaved, sensible adults and they could both deal with it. We hope.

Martin opened the conversation by telling her he had just sent an e-mail to Doctor Willan to say all was well at the site and they were enjoying working together. "He knows that already," replied Dotty, "I also send him e-mails about our work here, and in his last reply he complained he hadn't heard much from you, so it's just as well you wrote this evening." Martin blushed, thinking how much he owed to Flo. It was due entirely to Flo that he was now about to have dinner in a desert tent with an attractive specialist in Christian history, and feeling very happy with his lot.

Martin sighed and shrugged. "Guilty as charged milud. From now on I will do better."

Dotty wanted to get on with the meal. "When Mustapha first served up chicken with aubergine I was rather doubtful, but I found it worked well as a combination. What do you think of it?"

Martin agreed and made a mental note to try chicken with aubergine when he returned home.

## CHAPTER 16

"Let's eat and talk at the same time," suggested Dotty.

"My mother would not have approved."

"That was when you were a little boy. Dinner-time conversation between two consenting adults is different."

"Just as long as you don't talk with your mouth full," said Martin. Then giving Dotty no time to reply, he continued: "So what do I need to know about the Dead Sea scrolls?"

"I'd prefer to start with what you *don't* need to know. By that I mean the account of their discovery and subsequent squabbles over the right to possess and study them. None of that is relevant to their meaning and historical importance, but it makes a good story and it reveals how jealousy and fear of the truth can corrupt true scholarship."

She looked at Martin, expecting a reply. She received only a wry smile, which conveyed what they both were thinking: that there is nothing new about jealousy and fear of the truth corrupting scholarship.

"According to legend, a Bedouin boy was wandering near the Dead Sea with his sheep and goats. While collecting a strayed animal he threw a stone into the opening of a cave and heard a shattering sound. Being superstitious he was afraid he had disturbed an evil spirit and he ran away. He returned later with a companion, hoping to find hidden treasure in the cave. Instead they found earthenware jars and one of the jars contained decaying rolls of leather. That is the widely accepted story of how the scrolls were discovered and it's not true."

"If the story's not true, why is it ever told?"

Dotty held Martin's gaze for about five seconds then said: "Are you asking about the Dead Sea scrolls or about the birth of Christianity? Actually, it hardly matters because the answer is the same in both cases. It shows how careful we must be before accepting any information without rigidly scrutinising its accuracy. We must always be on our guard against that widespread and highly contagious affliction of many historians and especially journalists: the imperative to tell a good story, irrespective of the truth."

Martin cut in with: "I disagree that it's a highly contagious affliction. I rather think of it as a basic human instinct, something in our DNA, which right-minded, honest scholars manage to overcome."

"That is also possible," agreed Dotty, "It would be fun to argue about it but we have more important issues to discuss."

Martin agreed and pointed out that however fascinating the story of the scrolls' discovery might be, it has no relevance to the question of how Christianity evolved or whether Jesus existed or not. The age and authorship of the scrolls was far more important.

Dotty remained silent for a while then, in a resigned tone of voice, replied: "Sadly, you're right. I must confess I'm disappointed because I was looking forward to giving you a blow by blow account of the period between the discovery of the scrolls and the realisation that they are valuable early Jewish scrolls dating from at least two hundred years BC. I can see now that it would add nothing to our understanding of early Christian history. Tell you what, it's still a fascinating and entertaining story and you ought to read it sometime, so I recommend you read Neil Asher Silberman's *The Hidden Scrolls*. If you need any other details like its date and ISBN number, I can give you those later."

Martin replied that the title and author were surely enough. He would e-mail Pamela and ask her to get him a copy.

"Fine! Then let's start," exclaimed Dotty, "We've decided to bypass the best part of the story, of how, year after year, the scrolls were passed from one person to another, with only a few dedicated persons convinced of their antiquity and so-called experts even suggesting they had been

## CHAPTER 16

stolen from a synagogue. It's a story of deception, intrigue, tenacity, and disappointment. Oh well, you will read about it when your dear wife finds that book for you."

Dotty sat silently, obviously thinking hard; it wasn't one of her formative silences. Suddenly, she asked: "Do you find it hot here in the Nubian Desert?"

Martin played along and agreed it was hot, especially at midday, when it was almost unbearable.

"Let's half close our eyes, enjoy the taste of Mustapha's chicken and aubergine still lingering on our lips, and imagine ourselves in the oppressive midday heat on the barren shores of the Dead Sea, one thousand four hundred feet below sea level. The sea is so heavily laden with salt that it crystallises out on partly submerged rocks. The sun beats down relentlessly. There is no breeze and the air is polluted with evil-smelling gases from the oozing shoreline. Steep limestone cliffs rise behind us. By comparison, our camp here in the Nubian Desert is well ventilated by an occasional breeze, sometimes quite a strong breeze. We are more or less at sea level and not far away we have a fast-flowing wide river of fresh water, and we are not trapped by limestone cliffs. You speak of the unbearable heat of midday. You should try the shores of the Dead Sea!

Not far from the cave where the first scrolls were found lies the archaeological site of Khirbet Qumran, usually referred to as Qumran. Starting in 1951, excavations revealed that the site was extensive, containing the remains of buildings with a variety of functions. It was clear that humans had occupied the site from Hasmonean times until after the destruction of the temple by Titus."

"One moment," interrupted Martin, "Sorry to stop the flow of your narrative. Would you remind me about the dates of the Hasmoneans and the destruction of the temple."

"With pleasure. The Hasmonean dynasty ruled Judea for about a hundred years, from 140 BC to 37 BC. As for the destruction of the temple, that happened in 70 AD during the Roman assault on Jerusalem during the reign of Titus. Okay? Shall I continue?"

"Actually, I did know the date of the destruction of the temple. This means that Qumran was occupied for more than two hundred years."

"So it seems. Now let's see what was discovered. There was a main building of two stories with a central courtyard and defensive tower, with a secondary building to the west. Remains of numerous ritual purification baths, known as mikvah, were discovered. To provide water for these and for other purposes a dam and an aqueduct had been built, which received water from a river during winter storms and delivered it into a series of stepped cisterns. Occupation of the site appears to have ended with an earthquake and fire in 31 BC, followed by reoccupation until it was finally destroyed by the Romans in the Jewish War.

Three inkwells were found in a room identified as the scriptorium. Three inkwells don't make a scriptorium, but more inkwells have since been discovered and shown to originate in Qumran. A plastered bench, possibly a writing bench, was also discovered and thought to be where the some of the Dead Sea Scrolls may have been written.

As these excavations were taking place more scrolls were discovered in nearby caves. The scrolls themselves provided textual sources, which were supported by historical accounts written by Pliny the Elder, Philo and Flavius Josephus. It was concluded that these remains at Qumran were left by a sectarian religious community of highly ritualistic Jews called the Essenes. The Essenes may have hidden the scrolls in the nearby caves when they felt their safety was threatened.

All these early excavations were carried out by Father Roland Guérin de Vaux, a French Dominican priest. Further work at Qumran was carried out by the Israel Antiquities

## CHAPTER 16

Authority as part of *Operation Scroll*. Incidentally, imagine the raised eyebrows when female burials were discovered in a cemetery of this supposedly celibate male community! These are now thought to be more recent interments of female Bedouin.

So there you have it. The scrolls were produced by members of a sect of highly religious, ritualistic Jews, who broke away from the main body of Judaism and built themselves a secluded refuge from mainstream society at Qumran."

"Thank you for that exhaustive account. Of course, it brings me no closer to answering the question about the existence of Jesus, but I understood that would be the case before you started."

"Don't call it an exhaustive account. I've only given you a summary of the main points of the story. As for bringing you no closer to answering the question about the existence of Jesus, don't be so sure! If Christianity resulted from reformist movements within Judaism, might the Essenes have been just such a movement? Where does that place Jesus historically if Christianity was seeded more than a hundred years before his supposed birth?

Anyway, we mustn't enter new territory at this late hour. We'll finish the story of the scrolls tomorrow and then consider whether or not Qumran, the Dead Sea scrolls and the Essenes can bring you any closer to discovering the truth about Jesus."

And so ended another perfect day. A visit to the Nile for water had led to a pleasant encounter with Gwaria and her personal story of the relocation of inhabitants of the valley behind the dam. Mustapha had acquired a new ladder, which meant that Dotty no longer risked hurting herself at the site, and his sewing machine oil had arrived. He had enjoyed an excellent meal of aubergine and chicken while listening to the story of the Dead Sea scrolls, competently related by an attractive and rather sexy woman, whose nearness he enjoyed rather more than he ought.

"Until tomorrow then," sighed Martin.

"That sigh came from the heart. Is anything wrong?" enquired Dotty, sounding concerned.

"Just the opposite," replied Martin, "I love it here and I can't believe my luck. By the way, I saw a real camel scorpion today. Admittedly it was dead and squashed, but now I know you were not pulling my leg. What's more, I know its Arabic name. It's called *aqrab al jamal*. Good night dear Dotty. See you in the morning."

Dotty watched him close his eyes and head straight for his own tent. He was now able to judge the direction and distance perfectly without looking. As a final touch of frivolity she called: "Watch out for that scorpion!"

Martin froze, opened his eyes, looked all around him, made a dismissive gesture towards the smiling Dotty, and continued to his tent. A giggle from somewhere in the shadow of Dotty's tent told him that Mustapha had also enjoyed the joke.

# Chapter 17

After Mustapha had brought the coffee, washing water and tea strainer and checked that Martin was awake, he would normally disappear. This morning he loitered. As Martin stretched and threw back the mosquito net, Mustapha greeted him with: "Good morning Sir! May I complement you on your Arabic?" Puzzled and still not fully awake, Martin could only manage an interrogative Uh? "Yesterday evening I heard you talking of the *aqrab al jamal*"

Martin winced at Mustapha's pronunciation of the letter *q* in Gwaria's transcription of *aqrab al jamal*. It sounded like a throaty *g* pronounced by someone with bad catarrh. The sound did not exist in English and Martin despaired of ever reproducing it. On the other hand, Mustapha had recognised his pronunciation of *aqrab al jamal,* so it couldn't have been that bad.

"Mustapha, yesterday, while you were collecting the aluminium ladder and other supplies from your friend at the dam, I was shown a dead camel scorpion. Gwaria actually wrote the Arabic for camel scorpion on a piece of paper for me, using English characters, and I have been practising it ever since. Otherwise, I know only four Arabic expressions: *shukran, as-salāmu 'alaykum, ma'a as-salāma,* and *insha'Allah,* which mean: thank you, peace be with you, goodbye, and God willing."

"Your Arabic is very good," said Mustapha.

"It's rubbish," snorted Martin, "Now try to be more honest!"

With a sigh, Mustapha admitted that Martin's Arabic was *very small*. He was sure that if Martin would permit, he could personally teach him.

"Alright," beamed Martin, "How shall we start?"

"We will start with: "*sabāh el-khair,*"

"Which means?"

"It means good morning!"

"*Sabāh el-khair*, Mustapha. How did you sleep?"

"I slept very well and I see that Doctor Scott is waving her coffee cup. Perhaps we should continue the lesson later."

They exchanged smiles like two naughty boys and Martin saluted Dotty with his tea strainer.

"And what were you two plotting?" enquired Dotty over breakfast.

"Mustapha has offered to teach me Arabic."

Dotty spluttered over her coffee, wagged a dismissive finger, gulped and exclaimed: "He's tried it with me. He tried it with both my husbands. He's an enthusiastic but poor teacher. His Arabic, which he speaks well and instinctively, is laced with dialect and, like many native English speakers, he has no idea of the structure of his own language. Still, it will make him happy if you try to learn from him. Give it a go. You never know. You might pick up a few useful phrases."

"Thanks for the warning. I certainly will give it a go, if only to make him happy and get in his good books. After all, Mustapha is, in a sense, a kingpin in the operation of this camp. He's more than just a reliable and faithful servant."

Dotty gave Martin a brief nod of agreement. "You are so right," she agreed, "That's good thinking on your part. And when you are not learning Arabic you can learn some Christian history."

"Of course, and think what a bonus it would be to return home fully versed in the history of Christianity, as well as speaking fluent Arabic."

"And physically fit with a bronzed torso and bulging muscles from digging holes at my excavation site," added Dotty mischievously.

"Much as I enjoy this breakfast repartee," replied Martin, "I would like to pick up on the thread of yesterday's conversation. I went to bed with one thought echoing in my mind."

## CHAPTER 17

"Which was?"

"It was that the Dead Sea scrolls were produced by members of a sect of highly religious, ritualistic Jews, who broke away from the main body of Judaism and built themselves a secluded refuge from mainstream society at Qumran."

"Of course, but let's save the Qumran question for another time. I expect you'll want to visit our site this morning and try out your sewing machine oil. I'll come with you and scratch more sand away from that ancient altar."

Purely by the tone of her voice, Dotty had reminded him that they had a bargain: she taught him Christian history and he worked on the Coptic fresco. Feeling disappointed that he would have to wait until later to discuss the significance of the Qumran community, he consoled himself with a second cup of coffee and a cinnamon bun, and the realisation that Dotty would accompany him to the site.

As they set out together for the archaeological site Martin offered to carry Dotty's drinking water. "No need to carry water!" Mustapha was standing by the Nissan, bristling with spades and the new ladder, whose pristine aluminium was sparkling in the morning sun. He held open the rear door with a flourish and invited them to get in.

"Why this new routine Mustapha? You usually get the equipment to the site before breakfast."

"We must guard the new ladder Madam. If I deliver it early it might be stolen while you eat breakfast."

Hidden in that explanation was a slight trace of peevishness, a hint that this new ladder was causing a problem, a note of indignation that his home-made ladder of old wood and binder twine was not good enough.

Martin and Dotty exchanged amused glances and Dotty said: "Quite right Mustapha. That is good thinking." Honour restored, they drove to the site.

Mustapha made a theatrical display of carrying the ladder to Dotty's excavation and placing it carefully against the inner wall. Meanwhile, Martin carried his spade to Pinda's excavation, threw back the plastic sheeting, and shouted: "Hey, Dotty, come and look at this!"

The foot-thick layer of sand protecting the face of the fresco had collapsed under its own weight, leaving the fresco fully exposed. It appeared to be in perfect condition. Odd grains of sand still adhering to the surface were just waiting to fall and could easily be flicked away. There were no obvious areas of abrasion or flaking.

Dotty gazed down at the newly revealed nativity scene. "Congratulations! So that's the answer. Let the sand remove itself by collapsing under its own weight."

"I must confess it wasn't planned that way, but at least it has worked."

"And you won't need your sewing machine oil after all," said Dotty, almost sympathetically.

"Perhaps not, but don't you think the scene in general looks rather – how shall I put it – misty or dusty? I'm sure the colours were brighter centuries ago. Treatment with oil might bring out the colours in their full glory."

"We mustn't do anything until we have photographed the fresco exactly as it is. Mustapha, will you please drive me back to the camp to fetch my photographic equipment. And Martin, while I'm gone, please dig away more of the wall opposite the fresco. Otherwise I will be too near to photograph it with my back pressed up against the inside of the excavation."

Martin hung the plastic sheeting over the fresco to protect it against sand flying from his spade. He didn't relish getting rid of the sand by throwing it up and over his shoulder; he'd already done enough of that back-breaking work in the cause of revealing the fresco. Nevertheless, that's what he had to do, to avoid trampling in a heap of loose sand. When Mustapha and Dotty returned, Martin had extended the pit by about a foot. Mustapha took over the digging.

## CHAPTER 17

The distance to the fresco was finally extended by about a yard.

"Excellent!" shouted Dotty, jumping down into the excavation with her serious digital camera. Then her face fell. The ruined church wall cast a shadow across the fresco. "Just look at that shadow! It wasn't there when you first showed me the fresco." "True," said Martin, "The sun has risen a little further since then. I reckon in another thirty minutes the fresco will be fully illuminated again, so let's sit here and wait and consider how lucky we are that my protective wall of sand collapsed so perfectly. "And let us sit in silence as we contemplate this newly revealed nativity scene," demanded Dotty. It was that silence again, so treasured by Dotty. That deep, formative silence. Martin had no idea what Dotty was thinking as they sat there. In fact, was she actually thinking? Or was she emptying her mind of all thoughts and letting her spirit wander into the great unknown? Martin knew that Dotty's silences were not periods of nothingness and that they acted as a form of spiritual refreshment. In truth, he knew her silences were valuable but he couldn't find the words to express how they affected him, let alone guess at what they did for her. For his own part he watched fascinated as the shadow gradually edged its way to the left hand side of the fresco. His estimate of thirty minutes was quite near the mark. After thirty-five minutes the entire fresco was brightly illuminated by the sun. Dotty waited a further five minutes before quietly rising to her feet. Without a word she slid down into the excavation and took many shots of the nativity scene. She then walked around the site photographing the excavation from a distance and close up, from various angles, taking particular care over shots that included the excavated pit with the ruined wall of the church and the fresco itself, albeit from above and therefore at an angle.

Dotty then declared: "I have all the photographs I need. You can get to work with your sewing machine oil."

"Not so fast," cautioned Martin, "While you were photographing I went over to the altar excavation and tried a little oil on the edge of that fresco fragment. So far, so good. It seemed to work beautifully. The colours became brighter and the shapes more distinct. I don't want to sound pessimistic, but it's still possible that the pigments of the fresco are also soluble in oil, albeit very slowly. I prefer to wait another twenty-four hours to see whether the colours have started to run or diffuse."

Dotty thought for a few seconds then said: "I leave it entirely to your judgement. This has been an excellent morning's work. I suggest we have earned the freedom of what remains of the day to relax and talk about the significance of Qumran in the history of Christianity. I won't do any work around the altar. By the way, what do you make of this nativity scene that we have just uncovered?"

"In what sense?"

"Well, what colour are Mary, Jesus and the angels? Are they dark-skinned Middle-eastern figures, or are they black Nubians?"

"They are neither. They all have blank expressions and white pasty faces."

"Precisely. They don't represent any particular race, unless it's northern European, which is hardly likely."

"Your point being?"

"My point is that nowhere in any Christian writing is there a description of the physical appearance of Jesus, or of any other actors in the Jesus story. Nothing whatsoever about his skin colour, whether he was bearded or not, how he wore his hair, what clothes he wore. We have no way of picturing him. We only have reports of what he is supposed to have said and done. Alright, perhaps I'm expecting too much of those ancient Christian scribes. We have to accept, however, that there is absolutely nothing about the way he

## CHAPTER 17

dressed, his skin colour, his hair colour and not even about his size or stature."

"I see. So anyone wishing to represent Jesus or any of his family and friends, including the disciples, has a free hand and can give free reign to their imagination." "That is exactly my point. The Copts who painted that fresco painted the faces of everyone white, perhaps reinforcing a belief that Jesus was a metaphor, or perhaps inferring that Jesus and Mary were angelic, just like those angels hovering around them. There is a West African painter whose picture of the last supper shows everyone black, including Jesus. This serves a dual purpose. It shows that no-one has any idea what Jesus looked like and it reinforces the belief that Jesus resides in our hearts and belongs to everyone. Look at pictures of Jesus by various Chinese painters. They depict him as downright oriental in appearance. And how do we represent Jesus in Western art? We assume that since he was born in the Middle East he must have had a Jewish or Arab-like appearance, so he is often depicted with light brown features, long hair and a beard – in fact the double of bin Laden!"

Metaphor or reality, Martin felt that Jesus or the concept of Jesus demanded respect. The Christian message that Jesus or his image carried was still the most beautiful and powerful message ever brought to mankind. (In clinging to this belief Martin freely admitted to himself that he was ignoring the beauty of Islam). Flo had been a little harsh at times, but mostly on the Church as distinct from the Christian faith, and Dotty had certainly contributed a decidedly no-nonsense element to the Jesus question. But this was too much! As Dotty pointed out that the western image of Jesus often resembled that of bin Laden he groaned audibly and raised his eyes in exasperation. Dotty held her sides with laughing. Too late! Martin realised she had been baiting him.

"Try putting that into a sermon and see what your country bumpkins in Herefordshire think of it," said Dotty.

"Just how offensive do you intend to get?" demanded Martin.

Dotty uttered a long sigh and allowed her body to sag like a deflated buoyancy aid. "My dear Martin, I do apologise. I'm feeling so elated at our successful exposure of the fresco. It's gone to my head and over-excited me. I didn't intend to be offensive. Please forgive me and apologise to those country bumpkins for me when you get home."

This episode was followed by a long silence. What could he say? She was in an impossible state of mind. Or was she? By shocking him she had concentrated his mind on the subject of the nature of Jesus. Why not admit that the western depiction of Jesus looks embarrassingly like the press pictures of bin Laden? Add to this the fact that, as Flo had reminded him, scholarly analysis of the New Testament reveals several different Jesuses, one of which is a zealous priest stirring up revolution against the Romans, and he had the basis of a sermon – admittedly a sermon he would never dare to preach. Her talk of country bumpkins was also probably intended to shock and offend. On the other hand, she obviously knew who she was talking about. The majority of his congregation were conservatively minded and relatively unenlightened. Content to be part of Church tradition and follow the ritual, they would certainly be sniffy at the suggestion that Jesus resembled bin Laden, provided they actually knew who bin Laden was.

Martin's face slowly relaxed into a conspiratorial smile, which Dotty was quick to notice. "Aha!" she said, "You think I have a point after all!"

"You win! What next?" "Next is lunch. Jesus can wait until we've finished the dessert." Martin sighed. He had still not completely fathomed this woman.

As he freshened up in his tent, pondering the nature of Jesus and still shaking his head in exasperation at Dotty's bin Laden imagery, Martin had almost forgotten that the

## CHAPTER 17

morning had been an unqualified success. The fresco had been exposed in pristine condition, and photographed. Although Pinda had started the dig, Martin was largely responsible for its unbelievably successful outcome. Martin had done well, considering he was not actually a trained archaeologist. In addition he could now relax in the knowledge that he was earning his keep. He no longer felt like a camp parasite, enjoying himself in the desert, gaining more and serving less. What nonsense! Dotty had already told him that his presence in the camp was greatly valued. Moreover, Dotty's great joy at the successful exposure of the fresco had resulted in an increase in her personal warmth towards Martin. While that was innocent enough and perfectly understandable, it excited him. Which just goes to show that Church ministers are no less emotionally and morally vulnerable than the rest of humanity. No doubt the same goes for higher orders of the hierarchy, all the way to archbishops. There is much contemporary, as well as historical evidence for this. It is true of members of all denominations and Christian cults, and of all religions. This does not excuse Martin's troubled feelings for Dotty. It simply reminds us that to be alone in the desert with a beautiful woman is a recipe for mental and moral turmoil.

Lunch was the usual light repast, taken with plenty of water and tea. In the midday heat of the desert that is all one needs, in fact all one can manage. One cinnamon bun and a cup of tea qualified as the dessert, which, as promised by Dotty, was followed by their discussion of Jesus.

"Let's try and settle this Jesus question this afternoon. I know we haven't finished with Qumran and the Dead Sea scrolls. We can leave them until this evening."

"Agreed; but aren't you being rather optimistic in suggesting we can settle the Jesus question in an afternoon or for that matter suggesting it can ever be settled?"

"Okay, good point if you want to nit-pick. I'd rather you didn't interrupt what I say by stating the blindingly obvious. We both know that the Jesus question will probably never be answered completely, except by blind faith, of course."

"I'm suitably humbled," replied Martin, "And I would like to start the discussion by referring to something Doctor Willan said when my wife and I visited him a few months ago."

The words my *wife and I* gave Martin a feeling of safety. With those simple words he had established that he had a wife. They acted as a barrier behind which he could protect himself from his feelings for Dotty.

"He remarked that Jesus was like a blank page upon which you can write your own story. He pointed out that he was more than that and suggested that two thousand years ago Jesus started as a blank page, upon which many had written their own stories."

"Indeed," interrupted Dotty, before Martin could elaborate, "And we, meaning all three of us – you, Doctor Willan, and I – know that they were not stories intended to entertain or while away the time. They were designed to tell the reader what Christianity meant to the author. Even, perhaps, what the author thought Christianity ought to be. Perhaps it was a humble hand-on-heart explanation of what Christianity meant to the author. On the other hand, it might have been a propaganda or indoctrination exercise, defining in an authoritarian fashion the basis of Christian belief."

"Of course, I agree with all of that, except that last bit seems a bit strong."

"It is indeed a bit strong, as you put it. The first Christians were Jews, and like all Jews they were bound by written laws. Before Judaism, no religion of the Middle East and Europe had a system of written laws. Simply put, the Jews were the first to have a Bible. It all started with Moses.

## CHAPTER 17

The instructions given by God to Moses were written down, resulting in the five books of the Torah – Genesis, Exodus, Leviticus, Numbers and Deuteronomy. The writing down of laws and instructions on how to worship and how to follow these laws and instructions was fundamental to Jewishness. The Christians carried on this tradition and produced the New Testament. The New Testament is marginally less authoritarian than the Torah, but it is part of the tradition of writing the religion down and producing a workshop manual for the faithful. Let me remind you once again that the Jews were the very first to write their religion down. Millennia ago that was a new departure."

Martin did not reply immediately and he remained deep in thought. At last he said: "Sorry! Whenever you surprise me with new thoughts or information I have to place it all in two separate compartments. First, I add it to my sum of knowledge and try to relate it to the Jesus question. Second, I find myself wondering whether I can use it as the basis of a sermon."

"Then let me offer you a rather different slant on the Bible and I challenge you to put it in a sermon."

"I'm apprehensive and listening carefully. Please carry on."

"The Bible is not the word of God, not in the sense that God wrote it, or even told someone to write it. It is the word of man, heavily edited and, incidentally, often poorly translated. You can claim that the writers of the books of the New Testament were inspired by deep spirituality, or if you like, by God, but that thought is transcended by closer inspection of how the Bible was actually put together. The Church fathers decided which Christian writings would be used to create the New Testament. Of course, it sounds far more pious and reassuring to say that the Church fathers, inspired by their faith in God, were guided spiritually to admit the most worthy Christian writings to the canon of the

New Testament. I prefer to say that the Church fathers decided which Christian writings most closely followed the party line and could therefore be used to create the New Testament. Now, ask yourself: what dictated their choice?"

"You ask what dictated the choice of particular texts for inclusion in the New Testament. I have always been more concerned with the reasons for excluding certain texts, for example the Gospel of Thomas. Of course many others were also considered unacceptable and even declared heretical, as was the Gospel of Thomas."

"Good point," said Dotty, unable to conceal a note of admiration in her voice. This country parson had an intelligent approach to the history of Christianity. He was worth talking to. "I assume that the choosing of certain texts and the rejection of others were both part of the same process."

"Of course, that must be the case. I wasn't thinking clearly," replied Martin.

"On the contrary, you were analysing the question with considerable insight. Now let's return to what the Church fathers were trying to do when they chose and arranged the books of the Bible."

Martin quickly interrupted with: "Now you are not only choosing texts; you are also *arranging* them. Is that significant? Also, you keep jumping between the New Testament and the Bible. Is there a reason?"

"My word, you are sharp! Who, exactly, is the teacher here?"

"You are, of course, but please try to realise that I am a devoted and enthusiastic student."

Dotty smiled knowingly. Martin blushed and hoped Dotty hadn't noticed. For goodness sake, he told himself, I can be devoted if I like. Surely she will not misunderstand when I claim to be her devoted student. As though she had read his mind, Dotty remarked that only enthusiasm and devotion to the Jesus question could have taken him from his

## CHAPTER 17

home to live in a tent in the Sudanese desert. "And to sit at the feet of an acknowledged specialist in Christian history," added Martin.

"Okay, that's enough flattery and mutual admiration. Let's get on with the question of why particular texts were chosen for the Bible," said Dotty, trying to sound like a stern teacher. Martin relaxed and replied that the last question had been his and it concerned the *arrangement* as distinct from the *choosing* of texts, as well as her tendency to jump between the Bible and the New Testament."

"Alright!" she almost shouted, "Let me simply tell you what I believe happened. Otherwise we could be here all day, playing the game of approaching the truth stage by stage." She admired his bright intellect, but was becoming impatient with his interruptions.

"First, the Bible consists of the Old Testament and the New Testament. The Old Testament is a somewhat modified version of the Jewish Bible or Tanakh. These modifications of the Tanakh have no theological significance. They consist of the simple division of certain books into two parts. Thus, the Christian Old Testament counts Samuel, Kings, Chronicles and Ezra-Nehemiah as two books each, and the Twelve Prophets as twelve separate books. Also the order of appearance of the books of the Tanakh was changed somewhat, so that the book of Prophets appears at the very end in the Old Testament, not in the middle as in the Tanakh. The Old Testament therefore reads like a prophesy of the coming of the Messiah. Just read Malachi, the last of the prophets and the last book of the Old Testament; the very last verse starts with *Behold, I will send you Elijah the prophet.*"

"Nothing wrong with that," commented Martin, "It's just a relatively unsubtle bit of advertising, making the eventual appearance of Jesus more acceptable, or less surprising, since his coming was predicted."

"So you don't regard it as a clever trick?"

"Of course I do, but let's show a little charity. The compilers of the Christian Bible wanted to convince their readers that Jesus was a real person, whose coming was predicted, so why not prepare their readership for his coming? Spare my blushes: it's the sort of trick I would also use in a sermon. It's a little naughty but it's relatively harmless."

Dotty shrugged and said: "Well, I admire your honesty. Now we come to the New Testament and I don't think you will feel so forgiving. Let me ask you: which are the earliest writings in the New Testament?"

"The letters of Paul, of course. Everyone knows that."

"Do you really think every member of your village congregation knows that Paul's letters are the earliest writings?"

"Since you put it that way, I suppose not. Anyway, why do you ask?"

"Then why are the letters of Paul not placed at the beginning of the New Testament, because that is surely where they belong?"

"Chronologically speaking, that is true. On other hand, why not choose an order of Christian writings that is not chronological, provided it helps to make a good story?"

Before Dotty could reply, Martin uttered a loud exclamation: "Don't tell me! I said it for you: *to make a good story.*"

"Precisely, but I must say you are usually quicker on the uptake than that." replied Dotty.

"Perhaps I'm a little tired," said Martin, stifling a theatrical yawn, "Please continue. After all, we don't want to be here all day, approaching the truth stage by stage."

Dotty glared and Martin hastily added: "I will keep quiet and listen carefully."

"Look, if you really are tired, we can stop now and you can lie down for an hour."

"Tell you what: let's have a break and a coffee. An interlude would be welcome," pleaded Martin.

## CHAPTER 17

Right on cue, Mustapha appeared with a tray of coffee and cinnamon biscuits. The interlude was very brief. The coffee break hardly interrupted the lesson. Cup in hand, Dotty continued with her theme of how and why the books of the Bible were chosen and ordered.

"I take it you are aware that not all the writings attributed to Paul were written by Paul. Thirteen epistles were previously attributed to Paul, but biblical scholars, aided by computer analysis, now maintain that only seven are the genuine work of Paul."

"Let's say I *was* aware and I had forgotten. I knew that Timothy was very doubtful. Otherwise I didn't know that so many others had been discredited."

"Well," persisted Dotty "only the following are now believed to have been written by Paul: Romans, Corinthians 1 and 2, Galatians, Philippians, Thessalonians 1, and Philemon.

I'm a little surprised you were not up-to-date on the analysis of the epistles. Anyway, to continue, Paul is the only author in the New Testament who could have known Jesus, that is if Jesus had really existed. From his epistles it is clear that he never knew or met a real person called Jesus, despite the fact that their lives overlapped. He didn't even know the disciples of Jesus, and doesn't appear to have made any effort to seek them out. For Paul, Jesus and his disciples did not exist as real people. Read the genuine Paul. Does he ever mention Jesus by name? I'll answer that question for you. I can assure you that Paul speaks of *the Christ,* not of Jesus. And by *the Christ,* he means the spirit. Okay, perhaps some translator has understandably translated Christ as Jesus, or Jesus Christ, but the genuine Paul always spoke of the Christ. Let me put it this way: Paul is the only author in the New Testament who lived at the time that Jesus is supposed to have lived, yet he does not refer to him as a person. Let us dwell for a moment on the fact that Paul did not know Jesus as a flesh and blood person. In Paul's heart, Jesus was a spirit, an inspiration, a metaphor for a new form of spirituality."

Martin said nothing and clenched his hands, pressing them to his forehead in deep thought. Finally he said: "I've taken all that on board. This is serious, isn't it? Excuse my earlier attempts at flippancy. Please continue."

"What is the first book of the New Testament?" asked Dotty.

"Matthew, of course."

"Followed by?"

"Mark, Luke, John, and the Acts of the Apostles."

"And by the time you have read all those, you have a picture of Jesus as a person, who was born to a virgin, grew into a man, did and said lots of wonderful things, and was finally crucified. Then you get to the letters of Paul, and when he talks of the Christ, you automatically assume he means that person described earlier. You are programmed to accept that Paul was speaking of an historical figure called Jesus."

"Yes, I can see that it was a clever propaganda exercise. The proto-Christian Jews needed a central figure or totem to act as a focus for their new theology, a supernatural figure to carry their new message." Martin paused briefly then added: "And what's more, despite their rejection of the old Judaism, they were still fundamentally Jewish in thought and tradition and Jesus could be seen as fulfilling the prophesy of the coming of the Elijah. But ...."

Dotty interrupted: "I knew a *but* was coming. Let me guess what it is."

Martin nodded for her to continue. Each was beginning to read the other's mind.

Dotty posed a question: "If their planning was so clever, why is there so much inconsistency and contradiction in the New Testament? Let's make a list of just a few of these contradictions and inconsistencies. You start."

## CHAPTER 17

"First, that is exactly what I was about to point out, and second, yes I will start. If we take the story of Jesus' birth in Luke's Gospel, the Christmas story that we repeat every year and which forms the basis of the school nativity play, we read that Mary and Joseph were on their way to the census of Cyrenius for taxation purposes. We know, as an historical fact, that this census was conducted in 6 AD. Now turn to Matthew's Gospel and we find Mary pregnant with Jesus during the reign of King Herod. We know, as an historical fact, that King Herod died in 4 BC, possibly 3 BC, and certainly not later. So here is a true miracle that goes unreported: a pregnancy lasting at least 10 years!

"That's a good one to start with," said Dotty. "When you have time, google the nativity and you will find a website that states that Luke and Matthew agree that Jesus was born in Bethlehem in the time of Herod the Great, which is patently untrue, since Luke has Jesus born in 6 AD in a cowshed. I used to think this was a more recent trick used by modern politicians, that is to keep a straight face and tell a blatant lie, hoping no-one will notice. Now let *me* think of a New Testament inconsistency. Have you ever analysed the genealogy of Jesus as reported in Luke and Matthew?"

"A long time ago," replied Martin, "And I seem to remember there are two conflicting versions."

"Indeed there are. Both trace Jesus' ancestry back to King David, but the lists of ancestors, despite some similarities, are different in the two Gospels.

Martin held up his hand, looked thoughtful and said: "Now let me try to remember. In Matthew the genealogy descends as follows: Jesus, Joseph, Jacob, Matthan, Eleazar, Eliud, and that's about as far as I can remember. The next ancestor is either Achim or Zadok."

"Now you are just showing off. Reciting lists like a child reciting its times tables is not what we are here for. These genealogies are an excellent example of information best stored and looked up when needed. Let me continue. Unlike Matthew, Luke actually continues beyond King David all the way back through the Patriarchs and Adam and finally to God. We are told that Joseph isn't Jesus' father, so to present these genealogies at all is a contradiction of what we are taught."

Martin interrupted with: "*It is by the Holy Spirit that she has conceived this child.* And I might add: *Behold, a virgin shall be with child, and shall bring forth a son, and they shall call his name Emmanuel, which being interpreted is, God with us.*"

Dotty laughed and applauded: "Exactly. Even if the Holy Ghost has a genealogy we don't know what it is and it certainly doesn't start with Joseph."

"Don't be so sure," replied Martin, "Somewhere, I'm sure there must be some Christian crackpot ready to argue that the Holy Ghost and Joseph were somehow related."

"Maybe. We both know that Christian crackpots are not difficult to find. To return to the virgin birth, I admire your ability to produce the quotes from Matthew so readily, although you did use different translations, an earlier one and a more recent version."

"If you had preached as many Christmas sermons as I have, you would also have the ability to quote those passages. I think I sometimes mutter them in my sleep."

"I understand. Now whose turn is it? Let's not go on and on. One more example will do."

"It's my turn and I choose what Jesus said on the cross."

Dotty made a hand gesture to indicate that Martin had the floor. Martin continued: "In Matthew and Mark, Jesus is reported as saying *My God, my God, why have you forsaken me?*"

"Which happens to be a quotation from Psalm 22," interrupted Dotty.

## CHAPTER 17

"Indeed, and according to Luke Jesus says *Father, into your hands I commend my spirit,* which is a quotation from Psalm 31."

Before Martin could continue, Dotty added: "And if that's not enough, John reported him as saying *I am thirsty*" followed by *It is finished.*"

Martin took over again with: "So what did he really say? We can only conclude that no-one knew what he actually said, if he said anything at all, or for that matter whether he was actually on a cross. These reported words, supposedly spoken on the cross, were a fabrication, and a fabrication for a purpose. By quoting from the Psalms, the Gospel writers confirm that Jesus was a Jew, reinforcing the perception that he was the prophesied Messiah or Elijah."

Dotty took over again. "All the inconsistencies in the New Testament are difficult to explain. They are a source of embarrassment and goodness knows how many hours have been spent by preachers and theologians trying to explain them. On my last visit to Cambridge, at an ecumenical gathering, I challenged a Methodist preacher with this problem of what Jesus said on the cross. He looked momentarily blank then said triumphantly, as if it were the answer to the problem: "Don't forget, he also said *Forgive them father for they know not what they do.*" I replied that I had not forgotten, but I was looking for an explanation of why Jesus was reported as quoting from Psalm 22 by Matthew and Mark, but from Psalm 31 by Luke, while John reported non-biblical words. Another brief blank look then he came back triumphantly with: "You see, Jesus was all things to all men!" Looking back, I now feel rather ashamed at the way I baited him. I replied that I didn't see the relevance of being all things to all men and, in any case, throughout history being all things to all men has always been a sign of duplicity, so was he saying that Jesus was duplicitous? I'm not sure whether he was acutely embarrassed by being asked to face this question, or whether he thought I was mad and dangerous. He flustered some excuse and disappeared."

That was not the first time *all things to all men* and the *duplicity of Jesus* had cropped up in conversation. Months ago, in Leeds, Flo Willan had produced the same argument. Possibly this suggested duplicity of Jesus was well-known among biblical scholars, but Martin had not heard it until he heard it from Flo. Martin decided that one day he would perhaps weave it into a sermon. No, that would be going too far. But he could soften the impact by discussing Thomas More and his opposition to Henry VIII as depicted in the film *A Man for All Seasons*. Was Jesus then a man for all seasons? The Vicar of Bray also came to mind, an apt reference in the present context. Martin had no time to think it through; Dotty was waiting for a response.

He gazed at Dotty in admiration. "I'm beginning to understand you better. You have a killer instinct."

"What on earth do you mean?"

"You never raise your voice. You never remonstrate. Yet you always succeed in driving your point home and getting your own way in the end."

"Shall I take that as a compliment?"

"Please yourself. I feel sorry for that Methodist preacher."

"Yes, I also feel sorry for him and, as I said, I feel ashamed of the way I treated him."

"I find that difficult to believe."

"No, truly. We must learn to live with the fact that practically everyone who is aware of Jesus – church-going and non-church-going Christians, as well as members of other faiths – looks upon him as an ambassador of God, or a prophet of some kind, who was gentle, mild, and peace-loving. Incidentally, this generally held view of Jesus rather ignores the Holy Trinity, in which Jesus and God have equal status. Perhaps Arius was right after all!

# CHAPTER 17

Sorry! That was a silly and unnecessary diversion. You and I are concerned about the true nature of the biblical Jesus. We must even accommodate the possibility that, like a present-day Moslem jihadist, he was radicalised in a desert training camp by a demented preacher called John the Baptist, who trained him in clever ways of ensuring that the hated Roman rulers could be driven from the Middle East. Isn't it possible that some ancient author tried to model his Jesus along those lines? Actually, I don't think so, but let's not fall into the trap of accepting just one version of the biblical Jesus, just because it's the one that suits us. Gentle, peace-loving Jesus by all means, but if a pacifist relies entirely on Jesus' teaching to support his or her stance, they will be compromised by all the other faces of Jesus.

I don't quite know how to define your interest in the question. Mine is purely academic, like that of several biblical scholars. When I baited that Methodist preacher I broke my own rule of not shocking or embarrassing members of the Church by questioning the historical existence of Jesus. We must try to appreciate how the story of Jesus is so fundamental to regular, church-attending Christians, and for that matter to many non-church-attending Christians. It is firmly implanted in their psyche. Without a gentle introduction and a little friendly coaxing, allowing lengthy periods for private thought, it's impossible to break through the barrier of what we're taught in childhood, to recognise that the Christian message embodied in the story of Jesus transcends the question of whether he actually existed.

That is only the first stage. The second stage is acceptance of the possibility that a flesh and blood Jesus didn't actually exist. For you and me this is interesting and we would like to get to the bottom of it. Who knows! Perhaps we will eventually decide that he *was* an historical figure. For less free-thinking Christians, however, the mere mention of the possibility that Jesus is pure metaphor is shocking.

And it doesn't help when I blurt out something silly, for example when I suggested that Jesus was duplicitous. Ah well, we all make mistakes," said Dotty with a mischievous grin, then added: "Do you like opera?"

Martin sighed and looked at Dotty carefully, trying to decide whether she was about to pull his leg or add something of importance to the conversation. "Never mind whether I like opera or not. I just hope your question is a prelude to some fascinating insight into the Jesus question and not a humorous diversion."

"And what's wrong with a humorous diversion Mister Country Parson? Stop being so severe! Anyway, I wanted to remind you of the first act of Puccini's opera Tosca, where the painter Cavaradossi jokes about the fact that his wall painting of Mary Magdalene is inspired by both the Marchesa Attavanti and his lover Floria Tosca. The Sacristan responds by saying that faith is not a joking matter and he says it again, more than once, during the first act. I feel that is very true, because faith resides in a deep part of the human mind. It often defines the mind and the person. It may have been initiated by early upbringing, by a preacher, or by an unusual experience; it then leaves the Church behind and becomes a world of its own within each individual. It doesn't matter whether one is a Roman Catholic or an extreme Puritan, or, for that matter not attached to any particular named faith or denomination. One's faith is always ultimately personal; I would even say unique. That is why it is not a joking matter. And that's why I'm sorry I baited that Methodist preacher."

Dotty looked apologetically at Martin. "Sorry! I rather got on my high horse."

"Please don't apologise," said Martin, "It was a worthwhile diversion. However, I can't agree entirely with your view of faith. While I sense that *your* faith is personal, even unique, I'm pretty sure that the faith of many people begins and ends with what they were indoctrinated with as children and what they are content to pay lip service to for the rest of their lives. For them it involves a comforting routine without the need or inclination to think about it."

He was about to say more, but Dotty raised her hand, exhaled a deep sigh and said: "Okay, you think what you think and I'll think what I think." Then, in a very loud stage whisper, she added: "But I'm right!"

They were both tired. It had been a successful but long day. The boundaries of comradeship, intimacy, and respectful cooperation were becoming blurred.

Taken aback by her audacity then realising, too late, that she was trying to provoke him, Martin was momentarily speechless. Dotty used the opportunity to abruptly change tack with: "Can we think of any more examples?"

Martin stifled his exasperation and calmly replied: "We agreed to quote only one more and I think we now have enough," said Martin.

"Some of the others are very revealing, so let's have a few more," pleaded Dotty.

"Alright. Just a few more biblical inconsistencies, before returning to the Dead Sea Scrolls," said Martin.

"Thanks for reminding me. I'd forgotten about the Scrolls for the moment. Go ahead."

Martin looked thoughtful for a moment then said he could remember a few, such as the fact that Mark's Gospel tells us that when the women found the tomb empty they saw a young man in a white robe inside, whereas Luke talks of the sudden appearance of two men in brilliant clothes. Matthew, however, tells us there was a sudden violent earthquake, that the angel of the Lord, with a face like lightning and a snow-white robe, descended from heaven, rolled away the stone and sat on it. "So there we have three different versions of the same event, which suggests that all three are fabrications," said Martin.

"Or one of them is correct and the other two are fabrications," suggested Dotty.

"If you like, but I don't think you really believe that."

"No, I don't, but fabrications or not, there's something worth noting about those gospel accounts. Any idea what it is?" Martin shook his head. "In each case, whatever happened at the tomb, it was women – not men – who first went to the tomb and found it empty. The role of women in early Christianity is striking. Jesus supposedly had important female followers. Yet that was denied in the later development of Church doctrine, which relegated women to an inferior role. Okay, enough said. Any more examples?"

Martin stroked his chin, looked thoughtful then suddenly said: "I'd almost forgotten this one. I think it's important. You will remember in Mark and Matthew that the disciples are sent to Galilee by divine decree and the resurrected Jesus appears to them there. Luke and the author of *Acts* tell a different story, in which the resurrected Jesus appears in and around Jerusalem. In *Acts* the disciples are forbidden to leave Jerusalem."

"Well remembered! Now give some thought to what I'm going to say next."

Martin stifled a yawn and nodded for Dotty to carry on.

"In the fifth century, Pope Leo the Great ordered the burning of Gospels dealing with the mythical exploits of various saints, claiming they were heretical lies. The Acts of the Apostles was spared. Why? Surely it was because it endorsed the party line of the Roman church! And I don't need to tell you that when authority orders the burning of books, it is trying to hide something."

"May I add a snippet of wisdom to your relentless persecution of the Roman Church?" enquired Martin.

"Go on, I'm listening."

"The New Testament also contains letters ascribed to the apostles Peter, James, and John. Modern biblical scholars

# CHAPTER 17

have shown that they are all forgeries, written much later in an anti-heresy campaign by the early Roman Church. Scholars also add that they are not even good forgeries."

"Enough, enough," cried Dotty, "It's getting late and it's almost time for the evening meal. Frankly I've had enough biblical scholarship for one day. My brain needs to relax. Let's dine then spend the evening enjoying the moonlight and talking about trivial things"

Martin agreed.

*\*\*\**

The evening meal was another of Mustapha's masterpieces, based on aubergines in a flavoursome sauce. After-dinner conversation was preceded by one of Dotty's prolonged meditative silences, punctuated, or rather punctured, by the rattle of coffee spoons and the rapid intake of breath and a slurp when Martin found the coffee too hot.

Finally, Dotty broke the silence with: "Have you read much Agatha Christie?"

"As a matter of fact, very little, but I'm familiar with many of her stories through watching them on television. It's interesting to compare the performances of different actors in the roles of Miss Marple and Hercule Poirot."

"Then how do you compare David Suchet and Peter Ustinov in their respective performances in *Death on the Nile*?"

"I particularly enjoyed Peter Ustinov in that version of the thriller. Of course, he had a superb supporting cast, including David Niven, Bette Davis, Maggie Smith and ....." Martin stopped in mid-sentence. "Just a moment. What are you leading up to? Here we sit in the desert, within spitting distance of the River Nile, and you ask my views on Agatha Christie's *Death on the Nile*. There must be a connection."

"Of course, but it's nothing deep or dark. I just thought it would be fun, since we are, as you so crudely put it, within spitting distance of that same river."

"Aren't you stretching things a bit? *Death on the Nile* was set in Egypt hundreds of mile north of here. It's a different country."

"So what? Or should I say *I have an aunt who plays the guitar*? This is supposed to be a relaxing evening for trivial conversation."

"So it is. I'm sorry. So where do we go from here?"

"We go to the Nile," replied Dotty, "I bet you would be hard put to it to say where you were if you suddenly woke up one morning on a Nile river steamer. It wouldn't matter whether you were in Egypt or the Sudan, provided there were no ancient ruins to provide a clue. You would see date palms scattered along both river banks, the distant sound of natives chattering and shouting in Arabic, which, at least to an Englishman, sounds the same in Egypt and the Sudan; and the men and women on both banks would be dressed more or less the same, the men in galabiyas, some white, others a bit grubby, some drawing water, others riding donkeys, the women carrying pitchers or baskets on their heads. You would see native boats with large, billowing triangular sails of identical design in Egypt and the Sudan. As the day progressed it would get hotter and hotter until you retreated to the dining room or bar for a cool drink, or, like Linnet Ridgeway, you reclined in the shade of an awning and ordered a waiter to bring you refreshment. You would be on the River Nile and it wouldn't matter whether you were in Egypt or the Sudan."

"What you say is probably true of an inexperienced traveller visiting this part of Africa for the first time. Surely, someone like you for instance, with your experience of the archaeology of the Nile valley and your feeling for its history,

## CHAPTER 17

would know immediately which part of the Nile you were sailing on."

"I suppose you're right. There are, in fact, many clues; the direction of the rising sun, for example. After all, the Nile does not run a perfectly straight course from south to north. It describes many curves and bends and even flows from north to south in the great bend. Generally speaking the sun rises more or less above the right bank. At hardly any point along its length, however, does the sun rise *exactly* above the right bank, that is to say at exactly ninety degrees to the line of the right bank, and in the region of the fourth cataract near here it rises almost over the left bank."

It had been a clever conversational ploy. Agatha Christie provided the necessary diversion from the heavy discussions of theology and Christian history, which had enslaved them during the preceding few days. The conversation wasn't trivial, not even light-hearted, but it was intellectually light – just what they needed at the end of Martin's seventh day in the physically and mentally demanding heat of the Sudanese desert. Seventh day!? To Martin it felt like seven months. He was now sending regular e-mails to Flo and to Pamela, and less regularly to his bishop, and he knew that his words could not truly convey his feelings for his new environment: the joy of revealing an ancient Coptic wall painting; the sheer mystery and poetry of the subtle merging of the blinding light and searing heat of the desert by day into the moonlit scene of the cool desert night. They were far removed from the stuffy atmosphere of British academia, where their warm personal relationship would not have been possible, or would have been looked upon as suspicious.

She broke into his reverie with: "Living out here in the desert, thousands of miles from the stuffy atmosphere of a British lecture theatre, one begins to think and feel differently, don't you think?" Was she also a mind-reader?

"I'm listening," replied Martin.

"Metaphor is a powerful tool in speech and writing. It always has been. In fact, metaphor was used much more in the past than now. And I don't just mean that Shakespeare used it more than we do. Ancient writers of all traditions regarded metaphor not just as a neat way of illuminating a scene or an argument, but as a compulsory component of their style. Compared with ancient texts like the Icelandic sagas, ancient Christian writings, the works of Greek philosophers, and the Greek tragedies, our modern essays are metaphorically odourless and silent, if you get my meaning. Nowadays, any teacher of creative writing must impress upon their students that metaphor can be powerful and useful. And, I am sorry to say, they must sometimes actually explain what a metaphor is. Centuries ago, metaphor was second nature to all writers. However. Yes, there's a *however*, or if you like, a very big *but*. And it's this: metaphor can be, and often is, a trap, especially for the modern reader of ancient texts".

Having recited her homily on metaphor, Dotty went suddenly silent, looked earnestly at Martin, willing him to continue the discussion. "Yes, yes, we all know that metaphor is powerful and it was used more in the past than now. It's your big *but* that worries me." Then he realised what he had said, blushed inwardly and hoped the American idiom had escaped Dotty. She didn't react, not even with the slightest smile. Who knows what she was thinking? In any case, she didn't have a big but – just a rather delightfully shaped medium-sized one that showed off her denim skirt at its best. Martin was already sweating from the desert heat, but he broke into an extra sweat with embarrassment. Alone in a tent in the desert with an attractive and intellectually challenging woman, separated from his wife by more than a thousand miles, all his scruples, Christian principles, and downright middle-class values of respectability seemed to be

## CHAPTER 17

evaporating under the heat of the Sudanese sun. These confused thoughts made only a brief appearance in the theatre of his mind before he returned to reality, to Lawrence waving his pincers at the tent pole, and the subject of metaphor. With composure restored, he managed to croak: "What do you mean by a trap?"

"You need a drink," observed Dotty, "Let's pause for liquid refreshment. What I mean by a trap is important. It concerns the heart of the matter. So let's relax over another coffee before we carry on. Or would you prefer something else to drink?" "I'm glad you asked," replied Martin, "We do seem to drink a hell of a lot of coffee. Tea or orange juice would make a welcome change."

Barely two minutes later, Mustapha appeared with fresh coffee and a large jug of orange juice. Dotty stood and turned her back on Martin to pour for them both. Martin averted his eyes. Like her face, her arms and her shoulders, her legs enhanced her appearance and would have disturbed Martin less if they had been concealed in jeans, rather than being exhibited in a medium length denim skirt. They were gracefully muscled, wonderfully smooth, and gently tanned by the sun. She had avoided the curse that affects many European women in the tropics: the appearance of premature ageing, with a lined, blotched, leathery skin. Surely, Dotty realised what she was doing. Approaching middle-age, and having dispensed with two husbands, she now found herself in a remote archaeological site with Martin, and isolated from the company of European men.

As she handed him his orange juice she wore an inscrutable smile and she seemed to be reading his thoughts. Martin prayed that Dotty was not telepathic.

"Yes, it's a trap!" exclaimed Dotty. Just in time, he realised what she really meant – the trap of the metaphor – and he visibly relaxed. She smiled knowingly at his reaction. Was Dotty entirely innocent?

As she began her explanation, Dotty took her rather tattered Bible from her tin trunk, this time remembering to say *eftah ya sim sim*. Martin recalled reading *Acts* and hoped she wasn't about to ask him again to read from that archaic translation. The ancient book was still very much the worse for wear with the front cover hanging loose. A brown paper cover and some adhesive tape would help to prevent it falling apart. If the opportunity arose and if the gesture seemed appropriate, he would make her a present of his own Bible before he left. It was somewhere underneath his spare underclothes in his case. Since taking off from Amsterdam *en route* for Khartoum, he hadn't used his Bible once, and hadn't felt the need to. Was that a subject for a future sermon?

As she flipped her Bible open at the New Testament the front cover fell to the floor, much to the consternation of Lawrence, who froze, pincers at the ready, before gradually edging out of the tent. "Let's take any part of one of the four Gospels. For example, in Matthew 4:18-20 we read: *And Jesus walking by the Sea of Galilee, saw two brethren, Simon called Peter, and Andrew his brother, casting a net into the sea: for they were fishers. And he saith unto them, Follow me, and I will make you fishers of men. And they straightway left their nets, and followed him.*

This old Bible was published in 1916. It belonged to my grandfather. Sorry I can't produce a modern translation, but it serves our purpose."

"Which is?" enquired Martin.

"Which is to point out that millions of Christians around the world actually believe that story literally and live with a vision of Jesus recruiting fishermen to spread the Christian message. Linked to the metaphor of fishing for men, it becomes a beautiful image. Ministers of religion love it, but they need to do their homework. Like so much that is reported of Jesus' words and actions, this fishing metaphor is not original. We have already reviewed the evidence that there's practically nothing original about Jesus, or for that matter, about Christianity."

Martin responded with a knowing smile. "We both know I came to the Sudan to pick your brains on the subject of early Christian history and I have to say you have already taught me a great deal." Martin then hesitated, afraid he was about to go too far. He then threw caution to the wind and added: "I would also like to find out what really happened to Pinda."

It was now Martin's turn to be surprised. Dotty burst out laughing. "I guessed it. I knew Doctor Willan had an ulterior motive for recommending you. He's worried about the deaths of his former students – oh yes, I've heard all about it – Pinda was one of three, whose deaths may be connected."

"So you know all about it?" ventured Martin.

"I'd hardly say that," replied Dotty, "but I know enough and I can make a stab at guessing the rest. I'm so glad we can now talk freely with one another about these two subjects – the fault lines of reported Christian history and the death of Pinda. As for Christian history, I'm at your disposal and I'm sure we're going to enjoy many more hours of argument and discussion. As for Pinda's death, I tell you frankly that Doctor Willan is probably right in thinking his three students were murdered, but entirely wrong in thinking it has anything to do with the discovery of an embarrassing fact of Christian history. Certainly, there's something fishy going on. Those characters who visited Pinda at this camp didn't have one ounce of Christian religion in them, either modern fundamentalist or old-fashioned conservative. Doctor Willan has already discovered that IFECH doesn't exist. Mustapha knows they were definitely born into Muslim families, but the sort of Muslims who never go to the mosque and are secular in thought and practice. Mustapha is a Muslim and he has a nose for that sort of thing. One thing

I'm absolutely certain of: religion had nothing to do with their interest in Pinda. Doctor Willan's three students were murdered for a far more worldly reason than a secret of Christianity."

It was a long speech and it cast an entirely new light on the presumed murders. With a start, he recalled the Russian mentioned in Fenna's e-mail. He had forgotten the Russian and Pamela's contention that the Russian could be the key to the murders. And no-one had the foggiest idea who the Russian was. Finally, he asked: "Why do you think Doctor Willan is probably right to think his students were murdered?"

"Simply the demeanour of those visitors, combined with the fact that they were operating under false pretences, claiming to represent a fictitious organisation with the acronym IFECH. They were completely out of place and unwilling to interact with other members of this camp, except where necessary. They brought with them the necessary equipment for camping in the desert, but they didn't seem familiar with it. Mustapha had to help them put up their tent. Their clothing was suitable for the tropics, but for a tropical city rather than the desert. They dressed in what we call political suits, suitable for a meeting with the president or a board meeting of the university, but hardly desert wear. Mustapha, who is normally discreet, even felt it necessary to voice his concern. He was so troubled that he spoke to me in private, saying that he thought these two men were planning something evil, that their Arabic accent was Syrian, and they did not have God in their souls. It's also worth pointing out that when Pinda and the IFECH man left for Khartoum, everyone went. They packed up their tents and the entire group drove off to Khartoum, never to be seen again."

"Further circumstantial evidence that they were contemplating murder," remarked Martin, making a mental note to eventually tell Flo about this conversation.

# CHAPTER 17

"We have wandered a long way from Pinda's scheme for revealing the wall painting, and we've made several digressions on the way," mused Martin.

"And very valuable digressions at that," replied Dotty.

"Forget the wall painting. Let's go back to the concept of metaphor as a trap, where Jesus was recruiting fishers of men."

"Ah yes. I pointed out the lack of originality in this Gospel story. Let's turn to Jeremiah, chapter sixteen, I think .... yes, here it is in verse sixteen:

*Behold, I will send for many fishers, saith the Lord, and they shall fish them; and after I will send for many hunters, and they shall hunt them from every mountain, and from every hill, and out of the holes of the rocks.*

You see," explained Dotty, "The Jews have sinned, so the Lord delivers them to *many fishers,* and those that manage to wriggle out of it will be caught by *many hunters.* And it doesn't end there. In Habakkuk's vision, the Lord turns men into fish and lets their enemies drag them out with nets. Here it is: Habakkuk, chapter one, verses fourteen and fifteen:

*And makest men as the fishes of the sea, as the creeping things, that have no ruler over them? They take up all of them with the angle, they catch them in their net, and gather them in their drag; therefore they rejoice and are glad.*

But surely I'm teaching my grandmother to suck eggs. You're a minister of the Church. You know all this stuff as well as I."

"Please carry on," replied Martin, "You'd be surprised to know how much I'm learning." He didn't add that surely she could find a modern translation. Some of the old Bible language did have a certain charm, but the present examples were downright tedious to follow. "Okay," continued Dotty, "How about this little extract from Amos, chapter 4, verse 2:

*The Lord God hath sworn by his holiness, that, lo, the days shall come upon you, that he will take you away with hooks, and your posterity with fishhooks?"*

"Certainly there's no lack of precedent for using fishhooks on men," agreed Martin, "It's a form of punishment, whereas Jesus offers it as salvation."

"Very true," agreed Dotty, "And I forgot to mention the Dead Sea scrolls, in which fishermen are also figures of retribution. After all, it's hardly a desirable fate to be netted like a fish, or hunted. All the Old Testament references to fishing and hunting make sense. Somehow, Jesus turns the whole thing round so that being fished is beneficial. How is this achieved? What do *you* think, Martin?"

"Whatever I think and however I explain this switch from painful to beneficial fishing, let me first say I get your point about lack of originality. He changed the meaning of fishing, but copied the idea of fishing from earlier sources."

"I wonder if you really appreciate the full extent of the lack of originality," mused Dotty: "In my opinion, the entire Christian story lacks originality. Please don't be shocked. But then I suppose you, an English country parson, *must* be shocked to be told that the basis of your faith lacks originality."

Martin glanced at his watch, stifled a yawn, and said: "Frankly I'm really tired. Let me ponder this fishing metaphor and Christianity's lack of originality and give you my answer in the morning."

"I'm astonished you've held out so long. You've withstood the long, hot day exceptionally well. Most newcomers to this part of the world would have collapsed hours ago. Don't forget your salt tablets and drink plenty of water. The last thing I want on my hands is a desalinated, dehydrated country parson."

## CHAPTER 17

He wished she wouldn't keep calling him a country parson. She seemed to enjoy the expression and it sounded so nineteenth century.

Gesturing a final *Goodnight!* he stumbled towards the open flap of Dotty's tent, intending to make a beeline to the comfort zone before flopping out in his own tent. He was halted by an anguished "Careful!" from Dotty. Looking down, he saw his bare big toe within a centimetre of Lawrence, whose venomous tail was beginning to quiver in anticipation of a strike. Martin skipped aside, resisted the temptation to give Lawrence a hefty kick, and continued on his way.

She was sexually attractive, intellectually a soul mate, and just the kind of expert he needed for furthering his knowledge of Christian history. But why the hell did she allow a scorpion into her tent!?

# Chapter 18

Let us pause. It is time for an interlude, a rest from the desert heat, the history of the Nile valley, the origin of the Coptic Church and the provenance of Jesus. Remember those e-mails that Flo showed to Martin and Pamela? Who was that mysterious Russian? And what was the representative of the non-existent IFECH really up to?

We all need our fellow human beings, their company, cooperation, love and support, other minds to interact with, someone to share a confidence. This is the basis of family life, the oil that lubricates society, a sea of comfort and safety, in which we all swim happily. Except the criminal. The perfect crime probably does not exist, but the criminal must aspire to it. He (and she, since women make better criminals than men – it's just that there are fewer of them) must tell no-one of their plot or intentions. There must be no collaborators. Even their closest friends and loved ones must have no inkling of what is afoot. Committing the crime may be relatively easy, but success can be claimed only if the criminal escapes detection. Involvement of any other person, however peripheral, dedicated or loyal, represents a chink in the criminal's armour. And not all collaborators are loyal.

Fadeel Osman knew this. His role in the operation was to store smuggled weapons in his shop to await collection. The armaments were shipped out of Rotterdam, and left the ship at Port Said, where a Russian drove them in a small lorry to Fadeel's shop. They were later collected by an Arab, who was either from southern Egypt or northern Sudan; Fadeel couldn't decide and didn't ask. He didn't even know the man's name. He always arrived two days after the Russian had made his delivery, handed over an envelope of hard cash, loaded the boxes onto another small lorry and took them to a landing stage on the Nile, where tourists embarked on their Nile cruises. Egypt benefitted greatly

## CHAPTER 18

from its tourist trade. The pyramids, the sphinx, the Valley of the Kings, Abu Simbel and the Nile itself enchanted the imagination of Europe's tourists, who didn't have far to travel and could fly there in a day. The to-ing and fro-ing of tourists between Cairo and the Nile, and the fleecing of tourists for camel rides and trinkets, supposedly dug from a Pharaoh's tomb (but manufactured in backstreet workshops) – in short the hurly burly of the tourist trade – provided an excellent environment in which to conceal many kinds of mischief, including the illicit transport of armaments; also an environment where Europeans, like the Russian driver, were part of the scenery on the streets of Cairo and did not attract attention.

After collection from Fadeel the armaments travelled south on a tourist paddle steamer, and were later unloaded and transported by lorry to their final destination. Fadeel didn't know where the weapons came from and he didn't know their final destination or how they were taken there. He didn't want to know. He wasn't allowed to know. The principle of excluding all knowledge, except on a need-to-know basis, serves well for any covert activity, military or criminal. If someone is caught, they can't reveal much useful information, not even under torture.

The weapons – Kalashnikovs and grenade launchers – were packed in strong cardboard boxes labelled *Tinned Fruit Juice*. Fadeel told his wife that he made a quick and easy profit by selling the fruit juice on to another trader, rather than selling it in his own shop. He had now earned enough as an intermediary in the illicit arms trade and he wanted to get out. It wasn't possible. He was trapped. He was now part of the organisation.

However, things can go wrong, and sooner or later they usually do. Fadeel sold practically everything needed by the local community of his suburb. There was no supermarket to take his trade away. He sold eggs, cooking oil, flour, rice, sorghum, okra, potatoes, carrots, children's sweets, pencils, biros and exercise books. Bread was sold by a Greek baker two doors away. Fadeel's shop was unusually secure, with strong, firmly bolted shutters and a thick, studded door with three locks. The organisation had insisted on it and had paid for the improvements. His neighbours noticed these extra precautions and wondered why they were necessary. For that reason, such measures were perhaps a mistake, because they attracted attention. On the other hand, they gave Fadeel peace of mind and freedom to leave his shop, even when a consignment of weaponry was stored in his back room awaiting collection. He knew it was dangerous to flaunt his new-found wealth, but felt it was safe enough to occasionally treat himself and his wife to a relaxing evening at an open-air restaurant two streets away.

Fadeel had taken a delivery that day. He locked and bolted the shop and led his wife to the restaurant. He had often wondered where the Russian went after each delivery. Now he knew. Boris (pronounced *Boorees* by Fadeel, who at least knew the man's name if nothing else about him) was seated at a nearby table talking to three European tourists. Boris made to acknowledge Fadeel, but Fadeel, obeying the rules of their gun-running organisation, ignored him. Boris immediately realised his mistake and continued his conversation with the tourists. The Russian was very talkative and obviously in his cups; hence his mistake in nearly greeting Fadeel. Boris had a loud voice and conversation with the three tourists frightened Fadeel. He understood enough English to realise that Boris was talking about smuggling armaments from Europe to Africa. He could do nothing about it. If he attempted to curb Boris' loquacious description of the arms trade, he might make his wife suspicious, and she must remain entirely ignorant of his involvement in this illegal business.

## CHAPTER 18

Boris finally tottered off, presumably to his hotel, having first bought drinks all round for his three table companions. The three Europeans talked amongst themselves, apparently worried by something Boris had told them. Fadeel and his wife finished their meal and were drinking cups of hot, sweet, black tea, when Fadeel suggested they join the three tourists and bid them welcome to Egypt. It would be a gracious thing to do. His wife readily agreed. She welcomed any opportunity to widen her experience of people other than the small community of shopkeeper's wives in their Cairo suburb. Tourists were especially interesting. They came from a different world from hers, a world often condemned in Egypt for its culture and welcomed for its money.

Approaching the three tourists was easy. It was not unusual, in fact it was *de rigueur,* for street traders and beggars to approach and pester the tourists. Fenna, Pinda and Needham, still reeling from their madly confused conversation with Boris, saw Fadeel and his wife approaching. They were in no mood for dealing with beggars or traders in tomb artefacts, so they waved them away. Fadeel's wife pretended not to notice, smiled at the trio in a motherly fashion and said: "Before we go, my man and I are wishing you happy time in Egypt." It worked. As she turned away, Fenna called them back and added: "Please join our table for a while." Drunk Russians were one thing. An English-speaking, gracious, sober, middle-aged local couple, not begging or selling anything, would be a welcomed change and a fitting finale to their evening.

The very incarnation of innocence, Fadeel remarked: "Your other friend has gone away. Was he feeling ill?"

"He's not our friend. We don't know him. He's a Russian. We are British by the way. He sat down, uninvited at our table, and told us he was a secret agent trailing a gang of arms smugglers. He was obviously drunk, but he told us details that were truly suspicious. We were just discussing whether we should report what he told us, either to the Egyptian police, or to the British embassy. What do you think, Sir?"

"You say he was drunk, so he was probably talking nonsense. To report him might cause you much trouble," replied Fadeel, who was now deeply worried and feverishly wondering what to do next. He learned their names and found out what they were doing in the Middle East and where they were doing it. And this was all achieved by relaxed, friendly conversation, aided by the motherly concern of Fadeel's wife, who enquired about their family lives in England, whether their parents were worried about them travelling so far, and whether they had good hotels with comfortable beds. How was she to know she was unwittingly playing a part in their murders?

During their walk home to the shop, Fadeel was quiet and thoughtful. His wife didn't notice. She was buoyed up by their pleasant conversation with the three British tourists. She couldn't stop talking about them: how interesting it must be to travel and study the Christian history of the Middle East, how she hoped their parents were not too worried about them. The encounter had taken her out of herself and Fadeel was grateful, first because all he had to do was grunt in agreement, and second for her ability as a motherly figure to obtain from them all the information he wanted: their names, their occupations and their workplaces in the Middle East.

He spent a worried night verging on panic. By morning he had decided what to do. Someone in the organisation must be told. He would tell the Arab who was due that day to collect the latest consignment. The only information he lacked was whether one or all of the three Englishmen really intended to pass on the content of Boris' drunken outpourings to the authorities.

The Arab loaded the boxes onto his lorry, handed over the usual envelope of hard cash, listened to the story of

## CHAPTER 18

yesterday's encounter at the restaurant, trousered (or rather hid in the folds of galabiyah) Fadeel's written list of the Europeans' names and places of work, and drove away. He was not a great conversationalist.

We will never know the true structure of the illegal arms smuggling organisation. As already mentioned, its lines of communication were protected by the principle of need-to-know, a wise precaution against the fiction of honour amongst thieves.

Stage by stage the information passed on by Fadeel made its way along the chain of command, resulting finally in the formation of an assassination squad under the title of IFECH. Flo Willan will never know and he will spend the rest of his life wondering whether the LSD-induced deaths of Fenna, Pinda and Needham were retribution for an insult to the Christian faith. As we know, Martin and Dotty had their doubts, but those doubts will never be resolved. As for Boris, who talked too much, there is, at the time of writing, no information about his fate.

# Chapter 19

After breakfast on the eighth day Martin raised the question of the different pathways leading to Christianity. Dotty responded with: "I feel that *pathways to Christianity* can be misinterpreted to mean that Christianity is already a going concern and there are different ways of approaching it and becoming a convert. It sounds a bit like missionary speak. I prefer to think of the different origins of Christianity."

"Does it matter? After all, we both know what we mean. So what *were* the different origins of Christianity?"

Dotty appeared to ignore Martin's question and remarked: "Surely you realise that to accept that there were different origins of Christianity is to deny that Christianity arose solely from the teachings of Jesus. Combine that argument with the fact that there is no evidence for the existence of the one true Church, supposedly founded by Jesus, and you cast a cloud of doubt over the role of Jesus in the Christian story."

"Yes, that's obvious. Jesus then becomes a mythical figure to be used in support of the new religion known as Christianity, as we have already discussed on several occasions. But we must be careful here. It could be argued that Jesus brought together and knocked sense into all the various movements and philosophies that were heading towards what we now call Christianity. You can't deny that is a reasonable argument. Be that as it may, I return to my question: what *were* the different origins of Christianity?"

"I'm not going to tell you. At least, not until this evening. You are now going to drive to the Nile to fetch water. On your way back you will stop at the site and continue your research into the effect of sewing machine oil on the fresco. I will be waiting for you there."

With a rueful grin and a shake of his head Martin acknowledged Dotty's orders, left her tent and strode off towards the Nissan.

## CHAPTER 19

He couldn't wait to see how the colours of the wall painting fragment had been affected by the oil, so he stopped at the site before fetching the water from the Nile. Damn! He'd forgotten to bring the aluminium ladder. Undaunted, he managed to scramble down the far side of the excavation, causing a mini-landside of sand and goat droppings, dusted himself down and approached the wall painting, praying silently that the colours hadn't run. His prayers were answered. As he carefully drew the plastic sheet aside, one of Lawrence's relatives ran out and scuttled away behind the altar. Martin hardly noticed the wretched arachnid. His triumphant gaze was fixed on the fragment of wall painting, whose colours glistened and showed not the slightest sign of running or diffusion. What next? Martin quickly made up his mind to drive to the Nile and collect the water. On the way back, Dotty would be waiting for him at the site. He would then show her the results of his test, and they could share the task of applying sewing machine oil to the recently revealed fresco of the nativity scene. Share the task – work side-by-side – yes, that appealed to him. After carefully replacing the protective plastic over the treated fragment, Martin scrambled out of the altar excavation, triggering another mini-landslide in the process. On the drive to the dam, he wondered how he might refuse the hospitality of Mohammed, Yasser and Gwaria without causing offence. He couldn't wait to get back to the excavation site where Dotty would be waiting.

Mohammed and Yasser must have seen, or more likely heard him coming. As far as Martin knew, Dotty's Nissan was the only vehicle that commonly approached the Nile from that direction. The thrumming of its diesel engine carried a long way over the desert. So Mohammed was already waiting by the water and Yasser was on his way from the house. Martin assumed, correctly, that Gwaria was already heating the water for their tea. He would have to be polite and accept their hospitality. And why not? Tea with Mohammed, Yasser and Gwaria would, in years to come, be one of many fond memories of his desert adventure. Dotty would have to wait for him at the excavation while he satisfied the courtesies of desert hospitality.

Yasser and Mohammed disappeared and left Gwaria alone with Martin. It went against cultural tradition for a woman to be alone with a man who was not her husband or male relative. However, she no longer felt inhibited. In any case she had her husband's approval and she secretly delighted in enacting her freedom in full view of her conservative neighbours.

She was in a talkative mood and today she wanted to talk about camel racing. She had an uncle, who owned racing camels, and she wanted to tell Martin all about camel trading and camel racing, and how her uncle had once taken her and her mother to Saudi Arabia to race his camels. As far as Martin could understand, camel racing in Arabia was not unlike horse racing in Europe, except the stakes were far higher, and rivalries between trainers and breeders were much keener, sometimes leading to outrageous deception and even murder. It was, she explained, one of the oldest sports in North Africa and the Middle East, followed and promoted enthusiastically by rich rulers and sheiks. Another similarity with European horse racing, thought Martin to himself: not the sport of kings, but the sport of sheiks. Gwaria's enthusiasm for camel racing seemed to know no bounds, probably still fired by her childhood memory of her trip to Saudi Arabia. To Martin's astonishment, she explained that even the Europeans were now racing camels. "Good heavens!" exclaimed Martin, "I didn't know that." Gwaria was pleased with herself for telling Martin something he didn't know about Europeans, and she went on to explain that camels could race at forty miles an hour and even faster, and that a famous camel race known as the

## CHAPTER 19

Camel Cup was held at Alice Springs and that another camel race with great prize money was held in Queensland. Her uncle treasured an ambition to one day visit Alice Springs and Queensland with his camels, but doubted he would manage it before he died, having now reached his eighty-third year. It was obvious that much of this information on camel racing had come from listening to her uncle, and Martin didn't like to enquire whether Gwaria really knew that Queensland and Alice Springs were on the other side of the world in Australia.

A sudden mood change in Gwaria caught Martin unawares. Gone were the childhood memories of her uncle's camels, the excitement of high stakes and camels churning up the desert sands at forty miles an hour. "My uncle," she solemnly declared, "does not approve of child jockeys." As she became more serious, her otherwise faultless English began to show cracks. "Consequent of children being not heavy like adults, some misbehaving owners of racing camels use child jockeys. The problem of child jockeys is excessive beyond extreme. Sometimes the children are bought or stolen from other countries like Pakistan. They are badly cared for and sometimes they fall and are irreconcilably damaged." Martin vaguely remembered hearing about child jockeys and racing camels, either in the newspaper or on television. He decided not to ask whether her uncle used child jockeys. Gwaria continue to express her genuine concern for the exploited children and to paint a picture of her kind uncle. She told him that some Gulf States now banned the use of child jockeys. "Sometimes I cannot believe it. Parents who are poor in Pakistan or even here in the Sudan actually hire out their children for money. What do they do when their children do not return? I do not know. I think it is very bad and an extremely high cause of misery. My uncle does not use child jockeys." Martin got the idea. No doubt her uncle didn't use child jockeys, but she was guilt-ridden by the knowledge that he once did.  Possibly she had witnessed it herself, all those years ago, when he took her and her mother to Saudi Arabia.

When Yasser and Mohammed returned Gwaria told them in Arabic about her conversation with Martin.  They both smiled with approval and nodded to Martin.  Martin smiled back and raised his cup in salute.  Too late, the gesture was misinterpreted as a request for a fill-up.  After another thirty minutes of tea drinking and general chat, Martin finally got away.  And he got away much earlier than expected, because he hadn't needed to spend time at the river.  Yasser and Mohammed had filled all the water cans and stacked them in the back of the Nissan while he was talking and drinking tea with Gwaria.

On the drive back to the excavation site Martin reviewed his conversation with Gwaria.  He had been in similar situations at home, talking to parishioners with something on their consciences, troubled by a misdemeanor of a friend or relative, and worried that it might reflect on themselves or their family.  He could only assume that Gwaria's uncle, like all owners of racing camels, had used child jockeys at some time, but was now a reformed character.  He hoped that Gwaria's solemn account had been sufficiently therapeutic for her.  At least she had got it off her chest to Martin, who represented the outside world.  It probably wasn't the sort of anguish she could share with her own family and fellow Sudanese.

Martin let the Nissan more or less drive itself back to the excavation site.  After leaving the rise above the Nile, he pointed the vehicle in the right direction and made only minor adjustments to speed and steering as it sped over the wide, flat expanse of hard sand bearing the tracks of earlier visits.

Child jockeys were still bothering him.  In 2007, the Church had been much involved in celebrating the two

## CHAPTER 19

hundredth anniversary of the British act of parliament banning the transatlantic slave trade. Several speakers on that occasion had drawn attention to modern slavery, the trafficking of low-paid workers from developing countries, and the exploitation of women and children in the sweat shops of India and southeast Asia. As far as he knew, no-one had mentioned the exploitation of child jockeys in camel racing in the Gulf States. Someone had missed a trick there. It would have been a splendid opportunity to draw attention to yet another example of modern slavery. On the other hand, it wasn't always wise to criticise the culture of countries that sold oil to Britain and bought its armaments. As Martin entertained that cynical thought, he felt that Dotty would emphatically share his cynicism. Instinctively, he knew that Dotty would disapprove strongly of selling arms to Saudi Arabia.

And there she was! In the distance, near her archaeological site, Dotty was waving, or rather holding out in the desert breeze, a bright green silk scarf that stood out grandly against the monotonous dun colour of the desert. She greeted him with: "I think someone has been here since yesterday, messing about near the altar excavation."

Martin explained how he had called in on his way to the Nile and, in the absence of a ladder, had caused a mini landslide. Dotty's relief turned to delight when Martin explained that the oil had worked and they could now look forward to viewing the fresco in brilliant colours. "Well, now we have the ladder, so you can show me without causing a landslide. Dear Mustapha actually carried it to the site when he realised you had left without it this morning. The ladder isn't heavy and I think he enjoyed being a martyr. He's still rather put out because we abandoned his sticks and binder twine contraption."

Martin smiled at the thought of Mustapha's martyrdom. He was an interesting character and very conservative, not in the political sense, but with the typical conservatism of a peasant, loyal and fixed in his traditional ways, and all the more likeable for it. Martin then prepared Dotty for the surprising success of his experiment with the sewing machine oil. What a pity it wasn't her birthday; it would have made a splendid gift: "From my trial with the oil on the fragment of wall painting near the altar I know it brings out the colours without them diffusing or running. We can now carefully apply the oil to the fresco and you can watch the nativity scene grow and glow in all its glory. You can have the thrill of watching the colours appear for yourself."

And that is what they did. Once down the ladder into the excavation pit, Martin, removed the protective plastic sheet, unscrewed a bottle of oil, dribbled about ten cubic centimeters onto a kitchen cloth, which he handed to Dotty, saying that she should start gently dabbing it around the outer edge of the fresco. Martin then joined in, and together they worked around the perimeter of the fresco, rather like doing a jigsaw puzzle when you find all the edge pieces first. Then they worked inwards until the entire nativity scene had been treated, leaving baby Jesus until the very last. I took nearly two hours. Dotty soon got the hang of it and said very little, except to occasionally gasp with pleasure as the glowing colours emerged. "Thank you for waiting for me Martin. Of course, the whole idea and its execution were yours and yours alone, so to plan a part for me in the finale was so very thoughtful of you." Martin blushed and hoped she wouldn't express her gratitude by hugging or kissing him. She seemed to be on the verge of doing just that, so Martin calmed things down by pointing out they needed a photographic record. Dotty had forgotten to bring her camera, so Martin drove to the camp to fetch it while Dotty sat gazing at the fresco and planning the opening paragraph of her next paper to the Journal of Christian Archaeology. When Martin returned with the camera the sun had just

## CHAPTER 19

attained its correct position for illumination of the fresco. As Dotty crouched and snapped the fresco with her back to the wall of the excavation, she announced: "This nativity scene will be my Christmas card this year. Just imagine: a Coptic nativity scene, hundreds of years old, brings you Christmas greetings from the Sudanese desert! Inside the card will be a brief explanation of how a certain Reverend Martin Kimpton exposed the fresco and developed a most innovative method for bringing out the colours of ancient wall paintings. What would you think of that Martin?"

"Oh, I don't mind," replied Martin, "provided you send one to my bishop and give me a few spares to send to my fellow clergy."

"Why don't we print a large one – say A3 size – then you can frame it and hang it in your church. And how about a copy in your church magazine?" "Why not?" replied Martin, "My parishioners would be very impressed to find that their vicar had actually worked manually in the desert to dig out a lost Christian nativity scene." The more Martin thought of the possible uses he could put this picture to, the more he liked the idea. In his present state of self-congratulation the fresco alone seemed to justify his sabbatical.

They drove back to the camp in a pensive mood. No need to continually express delight in the morning's achievement. Its importance was undeniable. To babble on about it like excited children would rob this signal event in the history of desert archaeology of its rightful dignity. In any case, hunger can play havoc with one's sense of wonder, and it was well past lunchtime.

Mustapha had prepared a celebratory meal. When Martin had returned for the camera he had hinted to Mustapha that Dotty was especially pleased with their morning's work and something special would therefore be appropriate for lunch. It wasn't so much the food as the way it was presented. A large bowl of steaming vegetable soup with beans, okra and sweet potato was taken first to Dotty then to Martin by Mohammed one (or was it two?), who gave a little bow before inviting them to help themselves with a large ladle. At short notice, bread had also been baked – a wholesome, whole grain variety, sprinkled before baking with sesame seeds. Mustapha had even graced the table with a decorative candle, probably the kind made and sold in the souk by members of the Coptic community; it was embossed with a Christian cross. Dotty was amazed and was about to ask the obvious question, when she tumbled to the answer: "Martin. Oh bless you! It was when you came back for the camera wasn't it. You told Mustapha of our success at the excavation."

"I suppose there's no point in denying it. I thought a celebratory lunch would round off the morning very nicely."

Dotty was clearly moved. A tear of pleasure rolled down her cheek. She looked at Martin longingly, disguising her expression to look like gratitude. Martin was thankful that Mustapha and the Mohammeds were present. Otherwise she might have tried to embrace him. Sooner or later he hoped Dotty and he would find an opportunity to be honest about their personal relationship and establish mutually agreed boundaries. Secretly admiring her feminine attractions and occasionally feeling his nerves tingle in her presence he could manage. Lately, however, he had begun the feel unsafe.

"The second part of our bargain is that we discuss Christian history," observed Dotty. "I suggest we break for an hour then delve once again into the relative influences of Paganism and Judaism. It will give me time to study the pictures I took this morning. And I will also have a little nap to get over the excitement. And you, dear Martin, can have a well-deserved rest."

"Splendid idea!" replied Martin. "And by the way, one of Lawrence's relatives has now taken up residence near my

## CHAPTER 19

front tent pole. I have to watch where I put my feet when I go in or out of my tent."

"Consider yourself honoured. I can get Mustapha to remove it if you like."

"Certainly not. Sharing my tent with a deathstalker will be another entertaining snippet in my collection of stories when I return to England."

Dotty didn't reply, but waved him away with smile and a shake of her head.

Three hours later Martin was still fast asleep. Dotty gave him another thirty minutes before walking over to his tent and announcing: "Wakey, wakey, Martin! You've slept a good three hours. You must have needed it. Probably your physiology is still adjusting to the tropical climate. Anyway, Mustapha has prepared the evening meal. We then have the rest of the day to talk about Christian history. And while you've been asleep I've sent an e-mail and pictures of the fresco to Doctor Ibrahim at the National Museum."

"Oh?" said Martin, slowly regaining consciousness and feeling startled to find Dotty bending over him, "Does he really need to know?"

"He most certainly does," replied Dotty, "In order to get permission to set up my archaeological site here, it was stipulated that all discoveries should be reported to the Sudanese authorities. If I don't report our discovery of the fresco, they will find out sooner or later and I will get my knuckles rapped. Even if I were not bound by a signed agreement, I think it would be good manners to report any discoveries. It's their country and their antiquities, even if they don't always look after them as they should."

After a brief thoughtful silence, Martin suggested that the Sudanese antiquities authority had devised a clever way of getting their archaeology done on the cheap. They issued licences to accredited European archaeologists with the obligation to report all findings. "No doubt," added Martin, "everything you find belongs to them."

"Of course it does. That is only right. In any case, what we actually learn from our archaeological digs, together with photographic records of our findings, is all we need. Those days are past when the European adventurer triumphantly carted some great stone monument from the ancient world where it belonged to display it in a European museum with his name on it."

Dotty then gave a little laugh and added: "I'm pretty certain that Doctor Ibrahim purposely told me about this ruined Coptic church, with the hope that I would want to dig it out. He's probably wanted to investigate this site ever since he saw it as a child, even before he became chief curator at the National Museum, but he doesn't have the budget to do it. I even suspect that Mustapha is in his pay and would let Doctor Ibrahim know about the fresco if I didn't."

Martin nodded knowingly. After quickly swilling his face in the bowl of water in his tent entrance, without first removing the insects, he joined Dotty for Mustapha's culinary masterpiece of fried aubergine with potatoes and Nile perch. When he returned to England, Martin would take with him a greatly sharpened understanding of the debateable influences that led to the birth of Christianity as we know it. He would also take with him a fund of other experiences related to the culture, history, current affairs and personal relationships in this corner of the Sudanese desert. And, he decided this evening, he would take a collection of Mustapha's desert recipes. What better way of describing his desert experiences to Pamela than to share a cookery evening at home, preparing aubergine dishes and some of Mustapha's tasty, gently spiced vegetable soups?

His reverie was invaded by Dotty reminding him they should make the most of the rest of the day and get on with their Christian history. After all, that was why he was here,

## CHAPTER 19

wasn't it? Dotty sounded rather irritable. Perhaps not. He must be mistaken.

"Of course," replied Martin. Capturing Dotty's mood, he snapped: "So let's get on with it." He had no difficulty picking up from where they had left off yesterday. Surprisingly, their previous conversation was still very clear in his mind. Perhaps not surprisingly because here in the desert his life was uncomplicated, free from the chores of life at home, free from domestic responsibilities and the nagging thought that he had to produce a sermon by Sunday. His mind was therefore clear, receptive and retentive.

"You mentioned yesterday that two hundred years BC the Essenes or the Qumran community broke away from the Judaism of the day because they perceived a lack of rigour in Jewish society."

"Yes, I'm sorry. We left that narrative thread dangling and wove a different tapestry of New Testament inconsistencies."

"Isn't it rather early for such poetry and metaphor?"

"It's never too early for poetry, in the brilliance of our desert sunrise, or in the romantic ambiance of our desert moonlight. Or would you prefer me to save my poetry for a romantic evening?"

Martin didn't answer and hoped his blushes didn't show. It seemed that memories of yesterday evening would not go away. Their relationship had progressed to the point where they were able to take verbal liberties with one another, in a grown-up way and without causing offence or indignation. Yesterday evening had changed all that. Or had it? Perhaps he was just imagining that Dotty was trying to tempt him into bed. Perhaps Dotty had no such intentions and simply enjoyed being outspoken and a little outrageous. Yes, that was it; his imagination was out of control and it was silly to imagine that Dotty had designs on him. With that comforting (and perhaps disappointing) thought, Martin was able to face the day.

"Okay, then where did we leave off exactly?" enquired Dotty.

"You were about to lecture me on the significance of the Qumran community."

"Ah yes, I remember. There is one burning question waiting for an answer. And it's this: does the Qumran community represent a very early, in fact the earliest, attempt by Jews to break away from their orthodoxy and sow the seeds of a new religion that became Christianity? Or was it a dead-end movement that had no influence on the birth of Christianity? In short, we don't know. My own opinion is that it grew, lived then died and had no input in the drama of Christian history."

"I can't agree with that," stated Martin, rather firmly.

Dotty was taken aback. Until now, she had been the sole source of information on this subject and Martin had listened like an obedient student.

"Please explain," challenged Dotty with mock severity.

"Well," started Martin, "I see it this way: as early as two hundred years BC it seems that a community of Jews decided to live separately in the hills around the Dead Sea. They were extremists of a kind, dissatisfied with the Jewish way of life at that time, and possibly regarded by other Jews as a collection of fruit cakes. Perhaps, in fact doubtless, there were other Jews, less vocal, less demonstrative than the Qumran community, who were also dissatisfied with what they perceived as a lack of rigour in Jewish society. What I'm trying to say is that as early as two hundred years BC the ground was being fertilised for the growth of a new religion, even if the Qumran community was not a direct progenitor of Christianity."

"Good point. Christianity didn't suddenly arise out of nowhere and the Jews were feeling ready for it. Is that how you see it?" enquired Dotty.

"Exactly," replied Martin, breathing a deep sigh of relief.

## CHAPTER 19

"Put that way, we may be underestimating the influence of the Qumran community on the birth of Christianity. The monastic occupants of Qumran are generally known as the Essenes and more than one scholar has suggested that the leader of the Essenes was taken as the model for Jesus."

"What do you mean by *taken as the model for*?"

"Hidden in those words is the implication that Jesus was a myth, and that the myth was built around a real person."

"Robin Hood comes to mind," said Martin.

"I must say he doesn't immediately come to *my* mind," replied Dotty, "but I'm beginning to see what you mean. Do carry on."

"Yesterday, another thought was troubling me," added Martin, "and it was this: The Jews were great law makers, formalising everyday behaviour, from bread making to love making, in written rules and regulations. One sometimes wonders about the spiritual dimension of such a society. If the entire pattern and practice of one's existence and beliefs was decided and written down by others, how did one seek and express one's individuality or personal truth. Perhaps the answer lay in prayer and meditation in a community of like-minded fellow Jews. The Essenes were possibly seeking greater spirituality. We are not Jews. If we were, we would have a deeper understanding of the Jewish mind and these two driving forces; stricter adherence to the law and greater spirituality might be seen as mutually supportive or interdependent. Then we must take into account the fact that Judaism underwent fundamental changes, especially after the Jewish revolt against the Romans between 66 and 70 AD and the destruction of the temple in 70 AD. So, I think you must agree that interpreting the exact psychology of certain Jews, who decided to break away from every-day Judaism in 200 BC, is extremely difficult."

Dotty listened patiently. Better let him get it off his chest. Who knows? He might produce a useful insight into the behaviour of the Essenes. He didn't.

Martin paused, allowing his thoughts on the Essenes to sink in. The pause extended into a long silence. It was not the formative silence practised by Dotty. She had nevertheless taught him the value of occasional periods of silence during discussions. He sensed that Dotty's silences took her to a world of deep significance that he didn't understand. Her silences no longer embarrassed Martin. He found they contributed to the conversation, rather like a very long rest in a musical composition.

Dotty responded with: "Your view of Essene psychology is probably as valid as that of any so-called expert. In fact, I don't think there is anyone qualified to make an authoritative analysis of Essene psychology."

"Okay Dotty, that's enough about Dead Sea Scrolls, Qumran and the Essenes. Frankly, I'm beginning to feel bored with the Essenes. Now what about those further influences on the genesis and development of Christianity? Our discussion of the Pagans I found very interesting and useful. What about other movements, schools of philosophy or types of spirituality that may have played a part?"

Dotty was slow to respond. "Sorry Martin, I was miles away. My mind has not yet regained its equilibrium after seeing that beautiful fresco brought to life by sewing machine oil. I can already see the title of my next paper: *Well-oiled Coptic Christianity*."

"Obviously your mind has not yet regained its equilibrium. What editor would accept such a title?"

"Alright, *you* choose a title for my next paper. Let's get back to different influences on the development and genesis of Christianity. Any suggestions?"

Martin was ready for it. He'd been mulling over another possible influence in the development of Christianity since

CHAPTER 19

the day before yesterday: "How about Gnosticism?"

"Indeed! How about Gnosticism?" replied Dotty. The last time I met Doctor Willan in England, a few years ago actually, we talked about Gnosticism. Is it an entirely different belief system in its own right? Is it older than Christianity? According to the Roman Catholics, Gnosticism is downright wrong and heretical; not surprising when you remember that Catharism was a form of Gnosticism, and you know what the Catholics did to the Cathars."

"Forgive me for interrupting. Yes, I know what Pope Innocent III did to the Cathars. Don't forget I graduated in theology and I have been a Church minister for several years, which means I have also thought long and hard about Gnosticism. May I give you my view of Gnosticism?"

Dotty breathed a deep sigh of relief. "Please do! It will let me off the hook for a while. My dilemma is that I'm convinced that Gnosticism is, was, and always has been a significant factor in Christianity, yet I have difficulty getting to grips with it."

Before speaking, Martin checked that Lawrence wasn't lurking at the entrance to the tent. He had now made it part of his routine, whenever he was in Dotty's tent, to monitor Lawrence's movements, relaxing only when the arachnid finally scuttled away, presumably to stalk his prey in the moonlight.

"Everyone knows that the word Gnosticism is derived from the Greek word Gnosis, meaning knowledge."

Dotty couldn't resist cheekily interrupting with: "Everyone?"

Exasperated at the interruption, Martin replied: "Yes, everyone, meaning you, me, Doctor Willan, my bishop, and any number of other well educated members of the human race. Now, may I proceed?

"Sorry Martin. From now on I will interrupt only when I have something constructive to say. Please realise I'm still

309

off balance from this morning's success with the sewing machine oil."

Martin continued: "We could waste many hours discussing whether Gnosticism is a religion in its own right, whether it is a philosophy, or what it is. I have heard it described as a *school of spiritual philosophy*, as well as the *path of inner knowledge*. That will do nicely for present purposes. It will certainly satisfy the compilers of dictionaries. We, on the other hand, must explore what it really is, what it really means to practice Gnosticism. Let's start with your conviction that Gnosticism is, was, and always has been a significant factor in Christianity. I agree with those words, but I wonder if you and I attach the same meaning to them. Would you disagree if I suggest that the history of the development of Christianity can be represented as a constant war against Gnosticism, and that Gnosticism, acting as the enemy, has kept Christianity on its toes and helped it to define itself?"

"That is a most novel way of looking at Christian history. I've never looked at it that way before. You've stated it too strongly for my liking, but good heavens, you've hit on an important truth. Just imagine what a splendid discussion topic it would make for a student tutorial!"

Martin was gratified by Dotty's enthusiasm and said: "I'll take that as "No," that is, you wouldn't entirely disagree that the development of Christianity has been influenced by its opposition to Gnosticism. Now let me introduce a fly into the ointment. The name, Gnosticism, is derived from the Greek word, Gnosis, which is widely taken to mean *knowledge,* but this Greek word can be, and perhaps should be, translated as *understanding* or *enlightenment*. Gnosticism can be defined as deep personal enlightenment, or, as I mentioned earlier, the path of inner knowledge. I therefore ask: if Gnosticism is deep personal enlightenment, how does that conflict with Christianity? Surely we Christians seek personal enlightenment."

## CHAPTER 19

"Whoa up there!" shouted Dotty, "This is most interesting and challenging. I now feel mentally prepared for a discussion of Gnosticism. May I take over for a while?"

It was going to be a long evening. That was obvious. Martin tapped his spoon on his coffee cup and called Mustapha. Right on cue, Mustapha arrived, proudly carrying a pot of freshly brewed coffee. Years later, in those idle moments before falling asleep or lying half-awake in the early morning, Martin would wonder how Mustapha had been able to anticipate his or Dotty's wishes and produce freshly brewed coffee, almost before they had asked for it. "Of course; please carry on, but first let's have coffee. I rather feel we are going to need it."

"Good thinking, Martin, but I won't let my coffee drinking stop my talking. It goes without saying, of course, that we Christians seek personal enlightenment. And let's take your other definition: *the path of inner knowledge.* We ask: how do personal enlightenment and inner knowledge conflict with Christianity? I instinctively feel that they do not, at least not with a truthful Christianity. They are, however, seen as a danger to the vested interests of the Church, its dogma, its hierarchical structure, its traditions and its rituals. To put it another way: enlightenment and inner knowledge are fine, provided they are delivered from the pulpit and packaged according to the party line as laid down by the Church. As you must have gathered by now, I do not feel personally bound by Church dogma, so I naturally have an open mind about Gnosticism. No – more than that – I have a high opinion of Gnosticism, in that it allows me to find my own way to God, helped perhaps by like-minded co-religionists, and not by dogma laid down by a Church."

One day, Martin would ask Dotty what Christian denomination she belonged to. Certainly, she was a Christian, but for the moment he could not reconcile the theology of any denomination with this little outburst about her feelings for Gnosticism. Perhaps she was a very free-thinking Methodist or Baptist. No, neither of those fitted the Dotty he knew, or thought he knew. He interrupted with: "All we have, so far, are two alternative subtitles for Gnosticism: *personal enlightenment* and *the path of inner knowledge*. Is it possible to really define Gnosticism, to pin it down and provide a picture that would be acceptable to both its opponents and its practitioners?"

"Certainly. As a spiritual philosophy, it's possible to describe the belief system of Gnosticism, even to describe a Gnostic Church. I'm sure we both know what I'm referring to. Do you want to do it, or shall I?"

"Let me take over," replied Martin, "I think I can provide a suitable text book answer. Let's start with a fundamental difference between Christianity and Gnosticism. Christians believe that their God is omnipotent, infallible and perfect, but has been let down by man. All the evil and strife in the world is the result of man's failure to live up to God's aspirations for perfection. In other words we are all sinful, and the Roman Catholic Church likes to preach this with a vengeance. The lives of so many Catholics are blighted with a debilitating sense of guilt." Martin spoke these last words rather heatedly.

Dotty interrupted: "Careful! Much as I agree with your association of Catholicism with a debilitating sense of guilt, you're in danger of wandering off into a massive digression. Let's get back to Gnosticism."

With a guilty smile, Martin continued: "In contrast, Gnostics believe that God is at fault. They don't blame man for the evil of the world; they blame God himself, who created it all.

At this point we should remind ourselves that there are nowadays those who dismiss all religions and faiths as inter-subjective fiction, and that some of these non-believers are Gnostics. Whether God or humans are responsible for evil is therefore probably irrelevant for some or many modern Gnostics.

However, if we want a specific Gnostic religion, in which God versus humans was important, then we can point to Manichaeism, founded by Manes, who was born into a noble Persian family, and began his Gnostic teaching in the middle of the third century AD. There are very few followers of Manichaeism left in the world, just a small community of about 15,000 in southern Iraq, a diminishing remnant of a Church that was once much larger and more widespread. Goodness knows what has become of them after living under Saddam Hussein, then the invasion of Iraq by George Bush and Tony Blair, and now the warfare and Muslim extremism in the Middle East. They do not or did not belong to a well-educated, intellectual part of society, so their rituals were probably just that, without an appreciation of their deeper meaning. In its heyday, however, Manichaeism was a force to be reckoned with. According to some commentators it was one of the great world religions. Later, other versions of Gnosticism appeared, one example of which is the Catharism of Germany and southern France.

There, dear Dotty, have we come full circle? Earlier you lectured me on the Cathars. Then, this evening you said you have a high opinion of Gnosticism, in that it allows you to find your own way to God."

"Yes, indeed, we have come full circle. Like you, I am a Christian, and most emphatically not an adherent of Manichaeism. I must point out that Manichaeism was a religion in its own right. It was a type of Gnosticism, offering salvation through knowledge, or gnosis, of spiritual truth. Sometimes I also think it was a form of madness. I can't emphasise enough that pinning down an exact definition of Gnosticism applicable to every century and every society is like trying to fry snowballs. Let's say that anyone seeking spiritual truth beyond that offered by the established Church can be called a Gnostic. To use a modern idiom: anyone who thinks outside the box might be considered to be a Gnostic. For example, a typical modern Gnostic is Rudolf Steiner, the celebrated German educationist, who replaces prescribed syllabuses and teacher-dominated, time-tabled programmes of factual learning with student self-realisation. And if that description troubles a city's education department, let it be known that the Steiner schools are highly rated for their success in producing well educated, well balanced members of society. Then let us look for other examples of Gnosticism in our modern age. Have you read any Goethe, whose life spanned the end of the eighteenth and the beginning of the nineteenth centuries?"

Martin shook his head and held up his hands in a gesture meaning: No, he hadn't read any Goethe.

"Well, you don't know what you've missed. Admittedly, Goethe was a bit of a lad, but by golly he knew what he was talking about."

"Except," retorted Martin, "when it came to explaining the physics of colour!"

"Oh, so you *have* read some Goethe."

"No, I've read *about* Goethe, which is a very different thing. Sorry, Dotty, that was an unnecessary interruption. Please carry on."

"On the contrary, it was a valuable interruption. It has reminded me how wrong a great person can be. Not only was his theory of light wrong, he considered it his most important work, more important to him than his literary output. He is, after all, regarded as the founder of modern German literature. Oh dear, Martin, we do keep digressing. Where was I? Oh yes, I wanted to point out that Goethe was greatly influenced by Protestant German Pietism, which definitely had a Gnostic quality. Read Goethe's Faust sometime – if you can find an English translation – and see if you agree that Goethe was really rather Gnostic.

# CHAPTER 19

Then there is depth psychology, which arose in the twentieth century, and which can be seen as a form of Gnosticism. We have all heard of the philosopher C. G. Jung, the most widely acknowledged of all depth psychologists. Well, according to Jung himself, Gnostic insights are relevant to depth psychology."

Dotty dived into her tin trunk and retrieved a battered school exercise book. Flipping over the pages, she continued: "Just listen to this: *a certain Gnostic scholar wrote that Jung's reflections had long been immersed in the thought of the ancient Gnostics to such an extent that he considered them the virtual discoverers of depth psychology.* He went on to say that ancient Gnosis prefigured, and at the same time helped to clarify, the nature of Jungian spiritual therapy."

"I get the message," said Martin.

"I haven't finished," said Dotty, raising an admonishing finger, "Like all forms of Gnosticism, Manichaeism taught that life in this world is painful and evil, and that this state of affairs can be overcome with knowledge; not the factual, concrete knowledge of the modern scientist, but the knowledge of one's true inner self. In the language of Manichaeism this is equivalent to illumination of the soul, in which you do away with the cloud of ignorance, become conscious of your inner self, and you are saved. However, to qualify as a Gnostic you don't have to be a follower of Manes. You don't have to shout that the truth will explode from your inner soul in flash of blinding yellow light. You may quietly think to yourself: *the picture of God given to me as a child was useful at the time, but it was a metaphor for something in my soul, which, as an adult, I am now seeking to understand.*

So, you see, Martin, I therefore feel I can claim to be a little bit Gnostic, because I look for a deeper meaning in everything, from the driving forces that made certain Jews initiate a movement that became Christianity, to my dedication to digging up the past near the fourth cataract of the Nile, even to my personal relationships with my parents, my friends, my fellow academics, Mustapha and the two Mohammeds, and you, dear Martin. There, now I've finished."

Martin was quick to reply: "There is no need to seek a deeper meaning in your relationship with me. That much is already clear. I dig at the site, expose wall paintings, and fetch water from the Nile, while you teach me what you can about Christian history."

"I said *personal* relationship and I hope that doesn't embarrass you. Our contract for history teaching in exchange for digging and water carrying is purely materialistic. I wonder about the depth of our relationship. If, in years to come, we meet again in England, it will not be a case of: *Hello, you're the guy who used to dig at my site in the desert and fetch water from the Nile. How are you keeping nowadays? Nice to see you again. Goodbye.* It is far more likely that we would find lots to talk about and, if possible, spend quite a bit of time together for old time's sake. Don't you also wonder about our personal relationship?"

"Frankly, I do, and I find it embarrassing. You are an attractive woman. I have met many attractive women, but this is the first time in my life that I have found myself alone with such a person, camping in the desert thousands of miles from my home and my wife. Despite the fact that I am a minister of the Church and therefore morally self-disciplined and faithful to my wife, I do struggle to keep my hormones under control when you and I are together."

At last, he had said it! It had been easy and he hadn't even blushed.

"Martin, I thank you for being so candid. I suppose you have paid me a compliment. It's gratifying to think I'm still attractive to the opposite sex, even though I'm past my prime and with two broken marriages. I sensed your feelings towards me and I wondered who would speak first. In fact,

## CHAPTER 19

my own hormones, to use your turn of phrase, often acquire a life of their own when we are together. Thankfully, we are both old enough and sensible enough to prevent this mutual attraction going any further. Some Christians, quoting Jesus, would say that even by thinking about it we have committed adultery. In my opinion, our mutual honesty has cemented our relationship and at the same time ensured that we behave ourselves, not necessarily because we are good Christians but because we are grown-up, sensible people."

Confession of his feelings for Dotty had taken a load off Martin's mind, and he was very relieved at Dotty's comradely response. It couldn't have worked out better.

Martin shook his head in disbelief while his face creased with amusement.

"What is it now?" enquired Dotty, "Where's the joke?"

"I was just thinking that before we met I imagined you as a strident muscular girl-guide sort of person, marching along in a tweed skirt and poking the natives into action with your umbrella."

Dotty let out a yell of amusement, followed by a fit of laughter. Mustapha, mistaking Dotty's outburst as a yell of anguish, came running then stopped short of the tent entrance when he saw both Dotty and Martin laughing. Lawrence, lacking Mustapha's human powers of perception, had already scuttled from the tent and into the path of the approaching Mustapha, venomous tail erect and ready. Disaster was narrowly avoided. Dotty soon regained her composure. "Okay," she said, "That will make a good after-dinner story back in Cambridge. We have wandered from the point. We need to return to the beginnings of Christianity and enquire how Gnosticism affected the early development of the faith, long before Catharism and Manichaeism had been thought of." Martin sensed that discussion of their relationship, although very adult and sensible, had been a strain on Dotty's emotions, and she now wanted to put it firmly behind her.

"Sorry, Dotty, you're right of course. We're supposed to be discussing the development of Christianity in its early days. But that would leave an unanswered question that bothers me. I'm still trying to fathom your precise personal theology. Until a moment ago I had you for a very knowledgeable and free-thinking Christian. Then you claimed to be a little bit Gnostic, which struck me as rather odd. And despite the fact that you clearly don't ally yourself with the mystical tub thumping of Manichaeism, there is still – to me at least – the insuperable problem of declaring the Christian God to be evil. Just where do you stand on this question?"

"Dear Martin, I don't say that the Christian God is evil. Certainly not! However, I do believe that the concept of God as handed down by the Church is wrong, or at best, outdated. Church teaching sees God as an external force – in the world, in the universe – take your pick, who looks down upon us, judges us, punishes us, loves us, etc., like a parent. Like all parents, that God has grown old. For me, that God is now downright senile. It is time for us to leave home and become independent. Although we no longer need that parent-like God, we still need God; so where is God? In short, we are that God, or to put it another way, that God is within us and we communicate with our God by honestly seeking to know ourselves, or to use Gnostic phraseology, by illuminating our souls. This is not a new or revolutionary way of viewing God. I feel certain that thinking Christians have always sensed that God is within us, even from the very beginning of Christianity. On the other hand, many early converts to Christianity were illiterate and superstitious. And we don't need to go back two thousand years to find such Christians. Recruitment to the faith was helped by offering a loving parent-like God sitting in heaven, and, I might add, a son of that God walking the earth and performing miracles. I hope I have explained myself. Let me add that the often-used expression *the beauty of God's natural*

## CHAPTER 19

*creation* is a lovely metaphor, but I don't watch the glorious sunset over the Nile and thank God for such beauty. No, I don't thank God for the beauty of this world. I *share* it with God. By the same token, I don't blame God for natural disasters or crises in my life. When disaster strikes I turn to God for comfort. Just how that chimes with the God within me I leave for you to work out for yourself. I would also like to confess that I have borrowed from the author Neale Donald Walsch, well known for his bestseller, *Conversations with God*. He also wrote *Tomorrow's God*, in which he writes of our parent God growing old so that we must leave home. I find the metaphor effective, so I have used it"

"Dotty, you've made yourself very clear. I have also read Walsch. My first reaction when I read his *Tomorrow's God* was: what's new? Although God within us might seem a revolutionary idea to many worshippers, it has been around for a long time in various forms and with various shades of interpretation. The Gnostic philosophy of inner enlightenment is a case in point. During my university course Doctor Willan drew our attention to the writings of Silesius, the seventeenth century mystic German priest and poet. He claimed that God was not above him and he was not below God. In one curious little poem he says that if he ceases to exist then God will also perish. See what I mean? There must be many different ways of coming to terms with the fact that God is not a force outside ourselves. So, while I agree that Walsch puts the case very strongly and his metaphor is effective, I don't feel he adds anything to my thinking, despite the fact that many find his approach to God revolutionary."

Dotty said she understood perfectly what Martin was saying then added: "You can add to that list the Quaker belief that there is that of God in every person, plus the Quakers' search for their inner light." (There we go again, dear reader; you thought we'd forgotten George Fox's lot, didn't you!?)

"Of course," agreed Martin, "And it just goes to show there must be many out there seeking something spiritually more advanced than our highly standardised Church theology. Unfortunately, I don't think there are many such seekers in my own congregation, most of whom see God as an external, parent-like force, not unlike a child's view of God as a man with a beard sitting in the clouds and passing judgment on us. This has always troubled me, but I preach fairly standard sermons with God looking down upon us. It is also standard Church-speak to say that God looks into our hearts, which could easily be a Gnostic way of inferring that God has free access to our hearts and as good as lives there.

I'm constantly troubled by the conflict between what I deeply feel and traditional Church teaching. For example, I was horrified to hear the archbishop of Canterbury trying to explain why God had permitted the Boxing Day tsunami. He talked on and on without saying anything that made sense, whereas he should have said that natural disasters have nothing to do with God, but when they happen we can, to use your own words, turn to God for comfort. To thinkers like you and me, the philosophy of *God within us* is self-evident. Progressive theologies, like that of Silesius, for example, seem to be a little confrontational, suggesting they are still struggling with an outmoded version of God, which they are trying to refute. I feel the same way, in that I still can't calmly reject that bearded man in the clouds without feeling I must explain why I reject him. It shouldn't be necessary to present an argument against him."

"That's not surprising," said Dotty. "Quite apart from Church teaching, which is primitive enough, the very language we speak is laced with God metaphors and the tacit assumption that God is a force outside ourselves. You simply can't get away from it, and a certain discipline is needed to avoid falling into the trap."

## CHAPTER 19

"*Trap*, that's the word," said Martin, "The trap that our early ancestors fell into and from which we have not been able to fully extract ourselves. Early human beings believed in external forces that shaped their destinies. They thought gods were responsible for crop failure, disease, and victory and defeat in intertribal wars. While such superstition is understandable in primitive cultures, I'm still astonished that we haven't grown out of it. On the contrary, instead of growing out of it, the Abrahamic religions, starting with Judaism, have raised these primitive spirits and gods to the status of a single God, who loves and chides us like a parent."

Martin waited for Dotty's response. She said nothing, poured herself another coffee and waved the pot at Martin with a questioning smile. Martin nodded and she poured him one too. Finally, she spoke: "Excellent analysis, Martin. Perhaps the archbishop of Canterbury was trying to avoid going against traditional Church teaching. An archbishop of the established Church must be careful when speaking in public; he can't afford to say anything that might contradict the Nicene Creed.

You and I know that God within us is a difficult concept for the many who are bound by traditional Church teaching. Even for the likes of you and me, it can be very challenging to actually find or define that God within us. It's easy to claim that God is not a force outside us. It's more difficult to decide where that God actually exists. What do we really mean when we say that God is within us? To me it means that we have within us the ability to find God in our own way. Whatever it means to you, I know you do find God but I don't know how or where you find him."

"Or her!" interjected Martin.

Dotty dismissed his interruption with a smile and a shake of her head and continued: "Personally, I find God in various ways; in particular I find God in silence."

"Aha!" thought Martin, "Those formative silences!"

"Since God within us is such an intractable concept, perhaps it's understandable that the old man with a beard sitting up there in heaven has been adopted as an alternative. Perhaps, deep down, we have always known that he's a metaphor for God within us," suggested Dotty.

"That," replied Martin, "is an interesting suggestion, which brings us back to where we started. Please can we return to Gnosticism?"

"With pleasure," said Dotty, "Our search for God clearly shows that we are a mystery to ourselves. Gnosticism seeks to solve that mystery, to do away with our reticence about our deep instincts, to foster complete self-honesty, and to cast light on the deeper meaning of life."

"That I must write down," exclaimed Martin, "word for word, starting with *we are a mystery to ourselves and Gnosticism seeks to solve that mystery* I retain all that you teach me Dotty, but sometimes your actual words are also worth recording."

Dotty handed him a torn page from her old exercise book, and while Martin scribbled she continued: "I must take you up on your statement that Judaism raised primitive gods to the status of a single God. It would be more accurate to say that early Judaism accepted the existence of other gods, but chose one God for themselves, to the exclusion of all other gods." Martin listened, pondered what she had said then replied: "Thank you for that insight into early monotheism. It doesn't help with the Jesus question, but it's certainly worth knowing."

Dotty took over again: "I've just had an entertaining thought. Are we talking about a modern form of Arianism?"

"You've lost me. What do you mean?"

"At the Council of Nicaea, Arius was condemned for his view that Jesus was subordinate to God because God only begat him later when he was needed to promote the new religion of Christianity. This view was rejected in favour of the

Trinity, in which God, Jesus and the Holy Ghost have equal status."

"I can't disagree with any of that," sighed Martin, "It's all good standard stuff. So what!?"

"We have just explored the Gnostic view that we are God, or that God is within us. Add to that the evidence that Jesus was a metaphor created by man in response to a need and we have a situation in which God has created Jesus when it suited him. In other words a modern form of Arianism."

"It is indeed an entertaining thought," replied Martin, "and enough to make Emperor Constantine turn in his grave. It's also a thoughtful way to finish the evening. It's getting late."

Dotty pretended not to hear and said: "We've had a valuable discussion. We've proved to one another that we can repeat what we've read about Gnosticism. We've even explored the extent to which we both may be a little bit Gnostic. We've also been very open about our personal relationship. Might we now return to the beginnings of Christianity and enquire how Gnosticism affected the early development of our Christian faith?"

"Do we have time?" enquired Martin, "It's getting late. Lawrence feels it too because he left some time ago on his nightly hunting expedition. By now we've usually retired to bed."

"Having explored Gnosticism at such length, it would be pity to let the subject lose momentum," replied Dotty, "Let's keep going and look at early Christianity versus Gnosticism. I don't mind if it takes us into the early hours. In any case, I feel like celebrating this morning's triumph, the resurrection of the fresco. Unfortunately there's no wine, but just a moment!" Dotty uttered her magic words and dived into her tin trunk, emerging with a half bottle of whisky. "I never touch the stuff. This was left by my second husband. If we put it in our coffee it will help our celebratory mood."

Mustapha had clearly been listening. In less than a minute he appeared with a large pot of freshly brewed, steaming hot coffee. Dotty was embarrassed. She had forgotten that dear Mustapha would be waiting for them to retire. "Thank you Mustapha for that wonderful meal. You can clear the table in the morning. Please go to bed now and have a good rest. We are going to talk until very late. I don't have a programme for tomorrow. That can wait until the morning."

Mustapha seemed undecided. He liked to be on hand to serve Dotty as long as she was awake. Finally, he wished them both good night and returned rather reluctantly to his side of the camp and his bed, pausing briefly on the way to exchange a few words with the two Mohammeds, who were dozing by the camp fire.

Martin frowned and moved uncomfortably in his chair. Dotty wanted to know what was wrong. "You mentioned earlier that pinning down an exact definition of Gnosticism was like trying to fry snowballs. I feel that is no excuse for leaving the subject in an ill-defined and uncertain state. I would prefer to recognise just two forms of Gnosticism, ancient and modern. In its modern form, Gnosticism is thinking outside the box, recognising inner truths, thinking for oneself, or to use the words of George Fox (there we go again!): *Christ saith this, and the apostles say this, but what canst thou say?*" Dotty became suddenly alert and exclaimed: "Martin, that's the first time I've heard you quote anything from Quakerism. I'm impressed."

Martin explained that his bishop had mentioned that the Reverend Inge, Professor of Divinity at Cambridge and Dean of Saint Paul's cathedral, had claimed that the Quakers were the only true Protestants. "After hearing that from a professor of divinity and the dean of no less a church than Saint Paul's," explained Martin, "I decided to learn more about the Religious Society of Friends. That wasn't long before I

CHAPTER 19

came out to the Sudan. I picked up a few quotations that Quakers are fond of and that was one of them. Also, Doctor Willan had something to say about Quakers. He recommended I keep an open mind like the Quakers, or I think that was what he said."

Dotty pretended to appear thoughtful and philosophical. Finally she lost her self-control and broke out into loud, prolonged laughter. Martin wondered what she could be laughing at. Their present conversation hardly seemed to warrant such an uninhibited display of glee. Little did he know how close he had been to discovering a tantalising secret about Dotty. She returned to serious mode, nodded to show she understood, and asked Martin what his other form of Gnosticism might be.

"That is best explained by the Gnosticism that challenged Irenaeus, the father of Catholic theology and certainly the most important theologian of the second century AD. According to the Gnostics, the literal view of the resurrection was a 'faith of fools', in which a spiritual truth had been confused with a mistaken view of a physical happening. In his speech to his disciples in Matthew's Gospel, Jesus said: *To you it has been given to know the mysteries of the kingdom of heaven, but to them it has not been given.* It may have been inserted into many a sermon. What does it really mean? The Gnostics claimed that the mysteries of the kingdom of heaven were equivalent to the secret knowledge gained by inner vision, and that whoever gains this inner vision has an authority that equals or surpasses that of the apostles and the Church hierarchy that succeeded them. This challenge to the authority of the Church elicited a strong response from Irenaeus, which went something like this ..." Dotty interrupted with: "Hang on there – I've got it written down somewhere, word for word. Just a minute!" She dived into her tin trunk, forgot to utter the magic words, and managed to retrieve yet another old school exercise book. She found the entry and said she would read it out loud:

*They consider themselves mature so that no-one can be compared with them in the greatness of their gnosis, not even if you mention Peter or Paul or any of the other apostles ... They imagine that they themselves have discovered more than the apostles and that the apostles preached the Gospel still under the influence of Jewish opinions, but that they themselves are wiser and more intelligent than the apostles.*

Martin thanked her and said: "So you see, the Gnostics had little respect for the Christian literal belief in the resurrection. They denied the apostolic succession and claimed their own secret sources of apostolic tradition. They certainly thought they were wiser than the apostles, the priests, and the bishops of the Church."

Dotty poured another two coffees, added a metal cap of Johnnie Walker to each then, peered through the steam rising from her mug, and asked Martin to turn off the oil lamp, which until then had illuminated their sitting area. While they had been dining and talking, the large disc of the full moon had described an arc from the horizon to the centre of the night sky, so that it now bathed the camp in silvery light, almost shadow-less and almost bright enough to read and write by. Dotty and Martin instinctively knew that the scene deserved a period of silent appreciation. It was so very quiet that Martin thought he could hear voices at the dam on the Nile, carried by the still night air of the Nubian Desert. It was not a muffled silence, but rather a brazen silence, a silence to be broken if one dare. A faint rustling might have been a yard away or fifty yards away; had Lawrence caught a luckless prey? Martin felt like an intruder. Whatever he might feel about the desert, the desert had no feelings for him. The desert was a law unto itself and Martin was irrelevant.

## CHAPTER 19

In contrast, Dotty seemed to engage the desert with her meaningful silences. Martin saw that she was once again sunk in silent meditation, although he knew that meditation was the wrong word. Mustapha had been dismissed, they had turned off the oil lamp so that the moon was their only source of light, and they were about to start a new chapter in their conversation. Most people would have rubbed their hands, taken another sip of coffee and suggested they get on with it. Not Dotty. She preferred to mark the different phases of her daily activities with moments of silence. Martin was learning how to share these silences and to benefit from them spiritually, although he had not yet acquired Dotty's ability to immerse herself totally.

Barely two minutes had passed when she opened her eyes, wearing a smile of satisfaction. She thanked Martin for his two views of Gnosticism – ancient and modern – and suggested they leave Gnosticism for the time being.

"Before we actually put Gnosticism on the back burner," continued Dotty, "we should take on board the tremendous importance of the doctrine of the resurrection, in early Christianity. For the Gnostics it was an allegory of deep spiritual significance, a means of direct access to God, illuminating the hearts and minds of those with the sensitivity to feel and interpret it. For orthodox Christians, the resurrection had a certain spiritual importance, of course, but it also legitimised the Church hierarchy, that authoritarian team of ministers and bishops, who told their flock what to believe and laid down the traditions and rituals for worshipping God. No wonder Irenaeus had to fight the influences of Gnosticism! I just wanted to bring out this one point about Gnosticism. If we stand back and view the early conflict between the Gnostics and the Orthodox Church, it boils down to this one thing – the interpretation of the resurrection."

"Just one further point," said Dotty, "We keep hearing about mysteries. Nowadays the word mystery doesn't mean much more than an unsolved problem. When the word appears in Gnostic and Pagan writings it has a much wider and deeper meaning. We must discuss it later. Please don't let me forget. Now I want to change the subject and ask you what immediately comes to mind when you think of early Christianity."

Martin was quick to reply: "In my mind's eye I see several, perhaps many, small groups of Jews straining under Roman rule and dissatisfied with the behaviour of their own priesthood, which had caved in to the demands of their Roman masters. I see these Jews seeking something different from their present lot, but uncertain as to what the new way might be. They were looking for a new philosophy of life and in this search they were guided by two forces. First, they were Jews and they still venerated their Jewish lore and history. Second, if they wanted a new structure for their beliefs, they were already rubbing shoulders with the Pagans, who had a well-defined, ready-made system. So they rejected the vengeful Jewish God and decided they wanted a loving and forgiving God. Love, forgiveness and compassion became the watchwords of their new philosophy. Then they needed focus points for their faith, so they turned to the Pagan model, which proclaimed a god person born to a goddess, and they copied it. Their god person was ready-made in Jewish folklore. It was Elijah, the redeemer, the Messiah, whose return to save them all was prophesied in the Jewish scriptures. In other words it was Jesus. So they retained their Jewishness, while, to use a phrase, moving on. Just like the Pagans, they could then write and preach any number of stories about the life, words and actions of Jesus to illustrate their new philosophy."

Dotty could keep quiet no longer. "If only it were as simple as that! You haven't said anything I disagree with. On the other hand, you haven't pointed out any of the problems or potential contradictions in your brief presentation."

## CHAPTER 19

Martin responded: "I assume you intended me to produce something we could work on. Okay, I admit it was a rather Mickey Mouse attempt. How would you expand my vision of the early Christians?"

"I would ask whether this desire for change amongst certain Jews was inspired by a leader, or whether it resulted from a yearning for something different, shared amongst the thinking, chattering classes in their homes and in the market place. Eventually, the pressure for change would drive Jewish communities to form focus groups, without the need for an inspirational figurehead. Here, we must be on our guard, because an obvious counter argument is that there *was* an inspirational figurehead and his name was Jesus. However, that argument doesn't hold water, because we know that groups of Jews were already murmuring discontentedly and formulating a new faith long before Jesus was supposedly born. That doesn't preclude the possibility that each proto-Christian discussion group had a leader or organising committee. It seems to be a sociological rule that, sooner or later, a leader will arise in any organised group of people. Human beings, being what they are, would inevitably begin to follow the leader. Nevertheless, I like to think that these early groups of Jews were very democratic, each member of equal status, helping one another in their search for the truth – rather like present-day Quakers, who do not have priests or vicars. I repeat: that is what I like to think. It's my personal prejudice. If I'm completely honest, I have no evidence one way or the other."

Martin screwed up his face with a grimace, modified by half a smile, then quickly interposed with: "I feel that account is too simple and too condensed. I still have a fairly accurate recall of a lecture on early Christianity by Doctor Willan. He started by pointing out that the Jews started murmuring discontentedly – I borrow your expression – at least as early as the third century BC, long before Jesus was supposedly born. Incidentally, that brings Qumran and the Essenes into the picture again. Anyway, these discontented Jews were able to observe, dip into, try out, reject, or take as a model a miscellany of other religions that were around at the time. All of these other religions were mystical and they were centred around an allegorical figure, who was definitely not a real walking and breathing person. Gnosticism was such a religion. It inveigled its way into proto-Christian/Jewish thinking, so that Jesus was first conceived as a mythical figure. Incidentally, that was the only time I'm aware of that Doctor Willan said anything in public that opposed the Nicene Creed. We were always excited by his free-thinking, iconoclastic views, but he normally only revealed them in small tutorial groups, or between friends at the bar of the university union. In any case, in those days, we didn't think he was completely serious. When he hinted that Jesus was a myth, we assumed he was being mischievous in order to entertain us. After all, telling lies over glass of beer was an acceptable form of entertainment in those halcyon days. I remember he also pointed out that it is unclear to what extent proto-Christian groups were influenced by Gnosticism, as distinct from Gnostics muscling in on the act and claiming to represent Christianity."

"What's the difference?" asked Dotty.

"I wonder if anyone is equipped to answer that question," replied Martin. "Any attempt to find an answer will probably result in a lengthy, time-wasting discussion. In any case, the answer might be that there is little or no difference."

Dotty laughed out loud: "My question was rhetorical, implying there is no difference."

"Okay, so you caught me out. Now let me continue. Flo – sorry, Doctor Willan – always stressed that the flowering of Christianity, the interaction between different Christian groups and the development of opposing theologies continued well into the common era, even to the end of the third century AD.

So there you have it. Christianity developed over a period of five to six hundred years, during which time breakaway groups of Jews formed embryo Churches, each seeking to define their philosophy or theology by debate and discussion. It would have been easy to reassure potential converts that members of such an embryo Church still followed Jewish traditions, and were intent on cleaning up their faith rather than abandoning it. They retained the Jewish Bible, in which the book of Malachi predicts the coming of Elijah, but there was no need to go on about it. Meanwhile, they could invent a god person and call him Jesus."

Dotty sighed: "That is certainly a better account than mine. However, I would like to add that this god person did more than satisfy Malachi's prophesy of the redeemer. Jesus' crucifixion also resonated beautifully with the Jewish tradition of a sacrificial lamb."

"All that is true enough," observed Martin, "but when are we going to face the central question?"

"I know. Don't tell me. How did the mythical figure of Jesus become a real person?"

"Yes, indeed," replied Martin, "but now I'm having second thoughts. Before we deal with the question of Jesus, real or mythical, I would like to explore the difference between Pagans and Gnostics. I often find it difficult to distinguish between the two. If I analyse Paganism and the Pagan mysteries, I find they are very Gnostic in character. Thus, the Pagans emphasised introspection or an internal cerebral faith, as distinct from mere observance of traditions and rituals. So I suggest the early embryo Christian Churches copied the Pagan model and, at the same time, found that the Gnostic approach also suited them perfectly."

Dotty was not satisfied and she interrupted rather sharply with: "I feel we must get to the bottom of your claim that

Paganism and Gnosticism are difficult to separate. Actually, I agree. Would it help to go back a few hundred years BC and look at the Greeks?"

"By all means let's talk about the Greeks." replied Martin. "I'm interested to hear what you are going to say."

"I'm going to say: *know thyself!* Does that ring a bell?"

"Of course it rings a bell. In fact it has been uppermost in my mind for the past few minutes. I was wondering which of us would mention it first. I did consider launching our discussion of Gnosticism by quoting that irritating little aphorism."

"Why irritating?" asked Dotty with genuine surprise.

"Because it's been bandied around by so many historians and classicists, arguing about what it really means and who said it first, without reaching a final decision. For my own part, I agree one should seek to know oneself, but that is only the first stage in wisdom. One should also seek to understand one's place in the greater scheme of things and to know humankind in general."

"Martin, you are echoing my own feelings exactly. It's uncanny how, with just a few words, you have captured the music of my soul."

Martin was taken aback at Dotty's poetic outburst. He tried to conceal his embarrassment with a touch of flippancy, saying, unfortunately without giving it careful thought: "When I'm all alone in the moonlight with a beautiful girl, I'm likely to say all sorts of things."

Dotty fielded his outrageous remark with confidence, replying: "Thank you for the beautiful girl in the moonlight; it did me the world of good. Now let's be serious and get back to the aphorism itself. Let me take over from here. According to the Greek writer Pausanias *know thyself!* was one of the concise pithy statements inscribed in the forecourt of the temple of Apollo at Delphi. Its origin and meaning have certainly been argued over by historians and classicists.

## CHAPTER 19

It could be a warning not to follow the *vox populi*, or it could be an exhortation for self-honesty, as well as other interpretations. It has been attributed to at least a dozen ancient Greek sages. No less a sage than Plato attached great importance to the saying. He spoke of Socrates' use of *know thyself!* as a form of long-established wisdom. From all we have just discussed about Gnosticism, it is clear that *know thyself!* is Gnostic in feeling and character, whatever its exact historical meaning might have been. Add to that the fact that Socrates described it as a form of *long-established wisdom* and I put it to you, Martin, that Gnosticism is more than a religion of knowledge, or a religion of understanding, or better still, a religion of spiritual self-understanding. It is also a religion of *long-established wisdom*. The key expression is *long-established*. Gnosticism, even if it wasn't recognised as such, was a natural component of the human psyche centuries before the advent of Christianity. Manichaeism was simply a form of later mad revivalism. Having arrived breathless at this conclusion, let me add that Plato and Socrates were both Pagans."

"After listening to all that, I'm also breathless," said Martin. Since Mustapha went to bed, we've entered a new and important phase of our discussion. Would you agree if I summarise its content as follows: *Gnosticism and Paganism went hand-in-hand and they influenced the beginnings of Christianity?*"

"I agree and I'm embarrassed," replied Dotty. "I'm embarrassed to think that we, and I in particular, have spent so much time and so many words reaching such a simple but important conclusion."

"That's intellectualism for you," chortled Martin. "Have another coffee! Let's sit a while and soak up the beauty of this desert night. When I return to England I can't spend all my time arguing about the first four centuries of Christianity. I will describe to my audience the everyday activities at the camp, my success in revealing the fresco with sewing machine oil, my trips to the Nile to fetch water and see the great dam at the fourth cataract. And I will try to convey the poetry of the moonlit desert night!"

"And your wonderful personal relationship with the camp boss," added Dotty.

"Oh, for goodness sake, Dotty, I wouldn't dare. Not that there's anything to hide, but you know what people are like, especially those who dedicate themselves to judging others with the aid of Holy Scripture."

"Well, you know the Church and its inmates better than I do," replied Dotty, raising her eyebrows as if turning her statement into an innocent question. "Actually, I'm flagging. Perhaps it wasn't such a good idea to talk deep into the night. Let me say once again how thrilled I am with this morning's success with the sewing machine oil and how grateful I am for your work at the excavation site. Good night Martin. Good night moon."

"Just one moment more," said Martin. "Go on then," said Dotty, "And please make it brief." Martin drew a deep breath and said: "It has just occurred to me that if we are God then we are also Satan." "I'm afraid so," sighed Dotty, as she struggled to her feet, staggered into her tent, and tumbled onto her bed fully clothed. Martin watched, amused that he had outlasted her. It was the early hours of his ninth day at the camp and it appeared that his physiology really had adjusted to the desert conditions. He drew the mosquito net over the bed of his sleeping camp boss then walked slowly to his own tent and his own bed, ready for sleep, but reluctant to close his mind to the poetry of the moonlit desert night. When he returned to England, he would spend hours reliving these desert nights. Did he have a sufficient mastery of words to convey the scene and its spiritual ambience? Probably not. He was not a poet.

# Chapter 20

The following morning, Dotty was up and about at the usual time, well rested and none the worse for her late night. For Martin it was the day after the night before. Mustapha woke him by clattering about in the tent entrance when he brought the washing water and an extra-large mug of black coffee. Still only half awake, Martin was on the point of telling Mustapha to stop making such a racket and go away, when he remembered where he was and why he still felt sleepy. He lay a few more minutes, allowing his senses to catch up with reality, ruefully admitting to himself that beautiful though the desert night might be, it was made for sleeping and not for discussing early Christianity. Perhaps he was not as well adjusted to the desert climate as he thought.

Once on his feet and after a few sips of black coffee, Martin began to feel more in tune with himself. To be in tune with oneself is surely a form of Gnosticism. *In tune with oneself* would make a fitting subject for a sermon when he returned home. As this possibility trickled through Martin's consciousness, yesterday's drama began to unfold in his memory. Yes, it had been dramatic. Something as mundane as sewing machine oil had brought back to life a Mediaeval Coptic fresco and revealed it in the brilliance of its original colours. He felt thrilled by his achievement and he knew, that on a scale of one to ten, Dotty rated the result somewhere in the region of eleven or twelve. Still glowing from that morning's work, they had then spent the rest of the day, and well into the night, discussing Gnosticism and its relationship with Christianity. For Martin, it had been their most valuable discussion of Christian origins so far. Also, he and Dotty had come to a frank and mature understanding of their personal relationship. Now, after nine days, the suppressed embarrassment of his feelings for Dotty had been dissipated. This morning he could salute her with his tea strainer in a spirit of shared fellowship. Of course, Dotty's nearness would still stir the old Adam in him, so he would have to discipline his feelings and make absolutely certain that, from now on, he did and said nothing that might jeopardise their comradely working relationship.

Dotty, sitting in the mouth of her tent, had her back to the rest of the camp. Since she couldn't see him, Martin dispensed with the tea strainer ritual, dressed quickly and walked over to Dotty and her breakfast table. He caught her by surprise. She was not in one of her formative silences, but rather in deep thought and temporarily oblivious to what was happening around her. She jumped when Martin greeted her, and apologised for not waving to him before breakfast.

"The fact is, Martin, I'm not satisfied with yesterday's discussion. I'm thrilled to bits about the fresco. That alone makes yesterday worthwhile. By staying up too late and getting over-tired, we forgot to deal with certain key questions about the origins of Christianity."

"We were also probably suffering from coffee poisoning. We drank gallons of the stuff last night," remarked Martin, "Anyway, what are those key questions?"

"We supposed too much without sufficient evidence," replied Dotty. "Let's start again with something we know. For example, all biblical scholars agree that there were two rival camps in the development and spread of Christianity."

Martin couldn't think what the two camps might be. Dotty continued: "There was the Christian Church supposedly formed after the crucifixion by the disciples and Jesus' brother James, and known as the Jerusalem school, and there was the Christianity preached by Paul."

"Of course," cried Martin, "I knew that all along. Somehow I lost it last night. Perhaps staying up so late wasn't such a good idea."

"It was my idea. I should have had more sense," replied Dotty, "Let's forget about Jesus and Paul for the moment.

CHAPTER 20

I want to show you the splendid pictures that I downloaded yesterday on my laptop."

They spent breakfast inspecting yesterday's photographic record and trying to decide which picture would be most suitable for Dotty's next publication in a learned journal. The most dramatic shot had been taken at a slight angle to the fresco with a shaft of sunlight illuminating both the fresco and part of the surrounding church wall. "Definitely not that one," pronounced Martin with conviction, "Its composition is artistically attractive, but it's not a true record. For publication in a journal you should use the photograph taken directly in front of the fresco, so that its perimeter is a rectangle and all parts of the picture are the same distance from the observer."

"You're right of course, and thinking of public lectures, I suggest we go back to the site later this morning, and take Mustapha with us to photograph you and me with the fresco. I would like to show the fresco with you and me looking as if we have just dug it out, appearing tired, sweaty and triumphant at our achievement. No talk about my archaeological activities near the fourth cataract would be complete without acknowledging the role of Mustapha in his day-to-day running of the camp. So I would also like to get some pictures of Mustapha at the site.

We still have a few hours before the sun is in the best position for the photography, so let's try to get to grips with this Paul versus Jerusalem problem. We can interrupt our discussion when the sun is right and drive to the excavation site to take more photographs. We can continue the history lesson before, during and after lunch.

"And then?" enquired Martin.

"We can break off in the middle of the afternoon and you can do what you like for the rest of the day. I'm sure you can use some free time. You've earned it. I didn't mention it earlier, but I suspect there's another fresco that might be worth looking at beyond the altar."

"By worth looking at, I suppose you mean worth digging a big hole and applying my recently developed and proven revolutionary technique for revealing the wall paintings of lost Coptic churches."

"Precisely. Now where were we? Ah yes, we had decided that Christianity had developed from several separate centres in the Roman-occupied Jewish Middle East. That gives an impression of a smooth face of Judaism, randomly pockmarked by little outbreaks of rebellion against traditional Judaism. I like to think it was like that in the very beginning, before Jesus came on the scene. By the time written history, true, false, exaggerated or otherwise was available, those various outbreaks of rebellion had coalesced into identifiable centres of proto-Christianity. Where were they?"

"I'm following your reasoning," interrupted Martin, "May I answer that last question?"

Without waiting, Martin continued: "They were at Jerusalem, Antioch, Rome, and Alexandria. That takes us into the first century AD, and it raises a question that has always bothered me. The Jewish revolt in the middle of the first century ...."

Dotty interrupted: "In 66 AD, which is rather later than the middle of the first century."

"Oh, alright then: 66 AD if you must. I was about to say that the Jewish revolt resulted in the destruction of the Temple in Jerusalem and probably marked the end of the Christian sect in Jerusalem. Since you are a stickler about dates, then I *do* know that the Romans had breached the outer walls of Jerusalem by 70 AD, after which they ransacked the city and destroyed the Temple, which was the very centre of Judaism. Remaining pockets of resistance were finally overcome in 73 AD, including the Jewish stronghold at Masada. Do I pass? Did I get my dates right?"

## CHAPTER 20

Dotty ignored Martin's childish dig at her unfortunate outbreak of pedantry and asked: "Well, what is the question that has always bothered you?"

"It's an obvious question," replied Martin, "and it's usually ignored. Christians and Jews were closely associated, so how did the Christians, or if you like, the proto-Christians, survive the Roman onslaught?"

"I think the answer is *with difficulty*. Christians had enough to contend with without getting mixed up in the Roman backlash against the Jews. Just before the Jewish revolt, Nero had become fond of throwing Christians to the lions as a way of amusing himself and the masses, and that was not because they had Jewish connections. Of course, this charming form of popular entertainment took place in Rome, not in Jerusalem, but in general terms it's easy to see that the Roman authorities had it in for the Christians. So the Christians couldn't afford to add to their misery by being seen as co-conspirators in the Jewish revolt. They therefore had to strive to separate themselves from the Jews from whom they had evolved. Unfortunately, in Jerusalem, they failed. The Roman destruction of Jerusalem also destroyed its Christian Church. As far as Jerusalem was concerned, that was the end of Christianity. Ironic, isn't it, when you think how Jerusalem has been raised to such a high status in the Christian story?"

"I've been jotting down some thoughts while you were talking," said Martin, "Let me list them. First, let's be thankful that the Christian Church survived elsewhere, if not in Jerusalem. Second, is it true that Christianity was totally annihilated in Jerusalem? By that, I mean what about the Ebionites? Third, Jerusalem is now very important in the Christian story, but did it really play a significant role in the history of Christianity? Four, you mentioned the Christians in Rome. Suddenly, after recognising the existence of Christian sects or proto-Christian Churches in Jerusalem,

Alexandria and Antioch, we find Christians in Rome. I believe I also mentioned Christians in Rome a little earlier. Were the Christians of Rome different from those in the Roman-occupied territories of the Middle East?"

Dotty thought for a while before answering. "You're right to mention the Ebionites, who probably arose from the Christian survivors of the destruction of Jerusalem. They came to prominence in the second and third centuries AD before disappearing from the religious radar. Their name, Ebionite, is derived from an Aramaic word, *ebionim*, meaning *poor people*, and was probably given to them by outsiders in recognition of their practised poverty. Epiphanus, who lived at the end of the fourth century, quoted from what is thought to have been the Ebionite Gospel. Existing fragments, written in Greek, show that it contains bits of Matthew and Luke and possibly of Mark. Existence of the Gospel was mentioned by Irenaeus towards the end of the second century. It contains no mention of the nativity, states that both Jesus and John the Baptist were vegetarians, and that Jesus said he had come to abolish sacrifices. It talks of the Passover and it attacks the Jewish Temple. This Ebionite Gospel was possibly written in the middle of the second century in Syria or Palestine. It clearly shows that after the destruction of the temple Jews were confused about their identity, not knowing whether to accept Jesus as the true interpreter of the law."

Dotty uttered a sigh of despair and continued: "Unfortunately, my dear Martin, it's not as simple as that. There are groups today who claim to be Ebionites. Let me quote from their website." Dotty dived once more into her metal box and brought out a battered exercise book. Finding the right page, she read:

*We are in no way Christian or supportive of Christianity. We consider Christianity to be a type of Mystery Religion devised by Paul of Tarsus and others. We believe that there*

## CHAPTER 20

*is no relationship between Christianity (actually better described as Paulism) and the man Christians refer to as 'Jesus'. For that matter, since Christians often claim that 'Christian' means Christ-like (that is 'like Jesus'), it is most unfortunate that there are few who could honestly make that claim.*

Now what do you make of that? These latter day Ebionites claim they are not even Christians! It can only mean that, in their view, the evolutionary process leading from Jew to Christian has (or had) hardly started. Perhaps it means that, in Jerusalem, Christianity and Judaism were enmeshed without clearly separate identities at the time of the Roman onslaught.

Then we must turn to Origen, an early Christian theologian, who died in 254 AD at the age of 72. He is one of the so-called Church Fathers, although some exclude him from this gentleman's club because he was subsequently declared a heretic. Origen pointed out that there were two types of Ebionite: a) Judaic Ebionites, who followed Mosaic law and regarded Jesus as a miracle-working prophet, and b) Gnostic Ebionites who regarded Christ as an invisible spirit, whom they called the *Prophet of the Truth*. Not surprisingly, both groups were regarded as heretics. Frankly, Martin, I would prefer to leave the Ebionites out of our discussion because so much is unknown or still unclear about them. It's not that I haven't done my homework; the information simply isn't there. Nevertheless, it's worth noting that Gnostic Ebionites did not regard Jesus as an historical figure, but as a spirit called the *Prophet of the Truth*. Clearly, there was a split in early Christian theology; some Christians believed that Jesus was flesh and blood, while others believed he was a spirit. Condemnation of the Ebionites as heretics and their eventual disappearance is no reflection on the truth of their beliefs. It rather shows that other groups with different beliefs developed sharp elbows and managed to establish themselves and their beliefs through clever strategy and bullying. More of that later. Let's leave them for now, before we get completely bogged down in doubt and confusion."

Martin smiled his agreement. "Might I offer you an apt quotation?" "Of course," replied Dotty, wondering what sparkling witticism Martin was about to produce.

*He who is not confused, just doesn't understand the situation,* quoted Martin with alacrity. "I first saw that quotation at the beginning of a scientific paper on oxidative phosphorylation."

"Please, oh please," pleaded Dotty, "That's enough. Okay, I agree, it's an apt quotation, but spare me your oxidative whatever it is!"

"My next question," persisted Martin, "was about the status of Jerusalem."

"I don't care," spluttered Dotty, slapping her exercise book on the table, "I refuse to continue until I've had some refreshment."

True to form, Mustapha appeared moments later with a large jug of freshly made lemonade. It was a timely intervention. Carried away by the Ebionites, Dotty had quite forgotten the time. "Oops!" she declared, looking at her watch, "We barely have time to catch the sun at the excavation site."

Explaining to Mustapha that they wanted to photograph him at the site, they piled into the Nissan with the aluminium ladder, the photographic equipment, and a pleased and flattered Mustapha. The photographic session went well and it served to remind Dotty and Martin of the importance of making an early and complete photographic record because slight signs of deterioration of the fresco were already appearing. The colours were not quite as glowing as yesterday, and already particles of dust and grains of sand were sticking to the oiled surface. This was easily remedied with light brushing and minimal re-oiling, but it was a timely

## CHAPTER 20

reminder that the fresco had been better protected for hundreds of years by its burial in the sand.

Mustapha drove them back to the camp then went off to organise lunch.

"Well, what about it?" enquired Martin, looking Dotty in the eye.

"That," laughed Dotty, "could be taken in various ways, but I assume you mean: *what about the status of Jerusalem?*"

"What else?" replied Martin, not having realised the double entendre of his question. Ever since the frank discussion about their relationship, Dotty had often taken verbal liberties, underlining their new, mature understanding. It was gentle and harmless fun and Martin would have to get used to it.

*"This way to Golgotha, where our dear Lord died to save us all!"* recited Dotty in a loud, commanding voice.

"What on earth are you talking about?" asked a puzzled Martin.

"I'm your friendly tour guide around Jerusalem," replied Dotty, "I work for a tour company that specialises in Christian tourism. The same tour also includes a walk by the Sea of Galilee. *And don't miss the Church of the Nativity in Bethlehem, available as a supplement if you stay an extra week. And you surely will not want to miss the Church of the Holy Sepulchre in Jerusalem.* What we must accept, and what most Sunday Christians will probably not want to know, is that no real evidence exists that any of the tour sites in Jerusalem is genuinely associated with Jesus, even if he actually existed. Much can happen in more than three hundred years, and much did happen in the first four centuries AD, including the destruction of Jerusalem by the Romans, as well the subsequent Jewish uprising between 132 and 135 AD, not to mention strife between various Christian groups, massacres, depopulation, shifts of populations, and enslavement. By the time Christianity became the official religion of the Roman Empire, the demography, class structure, and the relative importance of different cities had changed dramatically since the resurrection."

"That is, if the resurrection actually happened," interjected Martin.

"Look here, Martin, from now on let's talk freely of the Virgin birth, the Miracles, and the Resurrection, without always adding the proviso that they may not have happened. Between you and me, let's take that as understood. Agreed?"

Martin nodded his agreement.

"Then I will continue. Imagine Christians converging on Jerusalem in the fourth century, a city altered out of all recognition since its destruction by the Romans nearly three hundred years earlier, and wanting to prostrate themselves on the site where Jesus was crucified. No-one knew where Calvary had been, so decisions had to be made. No-one knows whether sharp tour operators cleverly assigned various parts of Jerusalem to episodes in the Christian story, or whether a committee of self-appointed learned men decided where, from now on, the faithful would be told where Jesus was crucified and which route he took on the way there. Present-day pilgrims, like those early pilgrims, believe it. And the present-day tour operators, like those early Jerusalem guides, make a good living out of it. So to answer your concern about the status of Jerusalem: the city is held in high esteem in the Christian story, but in a part of the story that is concerned more with tradition and wishful thinking than with genuine history. Let me put it this way: Jerusalem is a part of a compelling, charming ancient fairy tale, whereas the real action took place in Rome, and later in Constantinople."

"I wouldn't dare state that publicly. My wife would then have to face the ire of Flossy Hoskins, chairperson of the Women's Institute, whose members seek to constantly remind us of their desire to build Jerusalem in England's green and pleasant land. She wouldn't thank me for that."

## CHAPTER 20

"Whoever Flossy Hoskins is, I will ignore the fact that your contributions to our discussions sometimes seem like stand-up comedy, and I will assume I have answered your question about the status of Jerusalem."

"You assume correctly," answered Martin, "You may now tell me whether there was anything special about the Christians in Rome."

"I feel we are veering off course. We can't possibly carry on asking questions without bringing Paul into the discussion. We mentioned him earlier to say that his writings are the earliest of all the writings in the New Testament. We wondered why they were not therefore placed at the beginning of the New Testament, and we suggested there might be a devious reason for this. Remember?"

Martin said it was still fresh in his memory.

"Okay, then let's examine Paul. You start. Tell me what immediately comes to mind when you think of Paul the apostle."

"Dotty, please remember I'm an ordained minister of the Church. I therefore know lots about Paul the apostle. You might even say I know all there is to know about Paul the apostle. You make me feel as if I were back at school being questioned in a religious education lesson."

"Alright then, if you know all there is to know about Paul, get on with it and amaze me!" Dotty paused then added: "Sorry! Pax?"

"Pax it is," agreed Martin, "To begin with, Paul was both a Jew and a Roman citizen. His given Jewish name was Saul. After his conversion on the Road to Damascus he switched to using the Roman version of his name, Paul."

Dotty made to interrupt, meaning to point out that this kind of information was already well known and added nothing to their present discussion. Just in time she remembered they had agreed on a Pax, so she kept quiet.

Martin continued: "Paul was not a true apostle, in the sense that he was not one of the supposed twelve who knew Jesus. To return to your question of what immediately comes to mind, it's the widely held view that Paul was the chief architect of what we now call Christianity. Some even suggest it should not be called Christianity, but Paulism. This significant fact of Christian history is no secret. It is widely known and often repeated by anyone wishing to prove their credentials as knowledgeable Christians. But ask anyone for the reason for this assertion and, as likely as not, they will struggle to find an answer, probably because they've grown used to repeating it, and it's a long time since they really thought about it. However, if they remember anything, it's Paul's view of the role of women in the Church. This is currently a hot topic because some conservative Anglicans object to women becoming Church ministers, and they are incensed by the suggestion that the Church may one day even have women bishops. So they leave the Anglican communion and join the Roman Catholic Church, which hitherto has adhered strictly to Paul's view of the status of women and has centuries of experience in keeping women in their place."

"A point worth making," agreed Dotty. "It's interesting that Moslems take an even more extreme view of Paul. In Islam, Jesus is a prophet, not as great as Mohammed of course, but nevertheless part of the story. Moslems declare that Paul is evil because he usurped Jesus."

"Interesting. I didn't know that," observed Martin. We do keep wandering from the point, don't we? Let me start at the beginning and get to grips with Paul."

"Martin, don't be so stuffy. Let's wander from the point if we feel like it, provided our wanderings take us to somewhere interesting.

"Yes, of course," acquiesced Martin, "but let's now really start at the beginning."

## CHAPTER 20

"Bags I go first," said Dotty, adding to Martin's exasperation by adopting schoolgirl slang.

Martin said nothing and let her carry on.

"According to Paul," said Dotty, now adopting a more serious tone, "Jesus decided to become a real person so that he could become the sacrificial lamb and thereby the redeemer of our sins. This was no trivial matter, since the doctrine of the crucifixion and the resurrection is the very foundation of Christianity. However, it once again presents us with the dilemma of how the early Christians really viewed Jesus. Paul has it both ways. First, Jesus is pure spirit, an inspirational totem representing the new Christian doctrine of love and forgiveness, then, in order to underline the message, he transforms into a real person, so that he can be crucified and rise from the dead. As we discussed earlier, Paul never knew Jesus and it seems he didn't need to. Take away the Paul writings that are known to be forgeries, consider only the genuine Paul, and we find that he reports absolutely nothing about Jesus the man. He writes only of an inspirational spirit. This fits perfectly with the view that Jesus was a mythological figure, the Christian equivalent of a mythological Pagan god. In fact, a strong case can be made that Paul was Gnostic in his beliefs, that is until he had to somehow empower the Christian message by producing a real person to be sacrificed then resurrected. If we're not careful, we can tie ourselves in knots trying to sort this out, in an effort to produce a clever answer for preaching purposes. Sadly, the Church has always been adept at producing clever answers to the contradictions and inconsistencies of the Christian story. Surely, it's far better to consider these problems in the light of modern common sense."

Martin had been silent too long. He interrupted with: "By *modern common sense* I take it you mean that dead people do not resurrect, that miracles do not happen, that a pregnant virgin is an oxymoron, not to mention the numerous contradictions and inconsistences in the New Testament, in particular in the Gospels and Acts, combined with the fact that metaphor is a powerful literary weapon, and that centuries ago people were superstitious and believed in magic and were much more easily duped than we are today."

"What a long sentence! I wondered when you would draw breath. Yes, that is more or less what I mean by modern common sense. I would add to your list some thoughts on Paul's Road to Damascus experience. Psychologically, Paul was an extremist. That is clear and no-one can argue otherwise. He switched from persecuting and punishing Christians to promoting his own version of the Christian message. You might say: once an extremist, always an extremist, irrespective of the subject. On the road to Damascus, he suddenly realised that these Christians, whom he was intent upon persecuting, had a point, so he switched the focus of his extremism. As for the drama of his revelation, we no longer believe in voices from heaven, or that he was literally struck blind by the truth, then miraculously cured of his blindness by a Christian named Ananias, or that he experienced a dazzling light. It can't be literally believed because such events do not happen. We can only conclude that his reported experience on the road to Damascus is highly metaphorical. Or perhaps he had a fit. Who knows? What is clear is that he was a fanatic and perhaps slightly mad. Otherwise, Martin, we seem to be repeating ourselves."

Dotty suddenly stopped, looked thoughtful and asked: "Have you ever heard of Thomas Scott?" Martin replied that he had never heard of such a person then added: "Why? Was he a relative yours?" Dotty explained that Thomas Scott, born in 1747 in Lincolnshire, was a widely known and influential preacher and Christian writer. "I'm not surprised you haven't heard of him because he seems to have been forgotten," explained Dotty, "I only know about him because I

## CHAPTER 20

happened upon his name quite by accident and researched his life history in case he was distantly related to my own family. As far as I can discover, however, he is not a distant relative." "Very interesting, I don't think," said Martin, "Surely there could be no better moment than this to say *I have an aunt who plays the guitar.*" "Oh Martin, please forgive me. I never intended to go blathering on like that. The point is, one of Scott's most influential books, *The Force of Truth,* was reprinted in 1984. I have a copy. The Introduction contains the following statement: *Saul of Tarsus before his conversion was held in the grip of false doctrine, a slave of sin and a vicious persecutor of God's people, yet God saved him.* That's rather a different slant on Paul from our mad fanatic. Which do you prefer?

"I'll stick with the mad fanatic," replied Martin, "Now can we get on with our discussion of Paul – Please! We have already discussed the inconsistences of the Bible and the impossibility of occurrences like rising from the dead. And it would not be out of place to point out that a careful analysis of Paul's writings supports the view that Jesus was a myth. Think carefully about Paul's statement that God revealed his son *in* me; not *to* me. This is the man whose version of Christianity is followed by the vast majority of Christians throughout the world. He said that Jesus was revealed *in* him. You can't get more Gnostic than that!"

Martin's jaw dropped and he gave Dotty a worried look. "I can't disagree with any of that, but it's dynamite. Imagine me trying to repeat to my bishop or my congregation that Paul was a mad extremist. Either we keep it between just the two of us, or we find a much gentler way of expressing the same idea."

"Martin, we are not writing a learned article on the history of Christianity, which will eventually be submitted for critical peer review. We, meaning just the two of us in the Sudaneae desert, are chatting and exchanging views and feelings, sometimes very personal feelings, about Christianity, supported where possible by facts and intelligent analysis. You will eventually return to England and your parish duties, taking with you a deeper understanding of Christian history. How you convey that understanding, to whom you convey it, and whether you decide to tell the whole story is entirely up to you. As for you telling your bishop, I would be more than happy to tell him Paul was a mad extremist."

"I'm sure you would. Of course, he couldn't defrock you. He could only argue with you. Oh dear, where on earth is this conversation leading now? Perhaps I'm exaggerating the dangers of challenging the establishment with contradictions of the standard Christian story. Come to think of it, my bishop, unlike my congregation, is quite progressive and free-thinking. He might well warm to the idea that Paul was a mad extremist."

Dotty looked approvingly at Martin, like a teacher watching the truth dawn in a student. She couldn't resist a final dig: "I'm trying to picture your bishop defrocking me. Rather difficult, don't you think, if I'm wearing jeans?"

"Please Dotty, stop it this instant. Who is the stand-up comedian now?"

"Just a light-hearted interlude Martin. You may now get down to telling me about Paul the apostle, who wasn't an apostle."

Martin suppressed his despair (or was it his delight?) at her flippancy, adopted a serious tone of voice, and proceeded: "For someone famous for changing his mind and displaying the qualities of a mad fanatic, Paul started life with an impressive CV. He was born in 5 AD, or thereabouts, in Tarsus, a coastal city on the southern coast of present-day Turkey. In those days Tarsus belonged to that part of the Roman Empire known as Cilicia. He died in 67 AD, or thereabouts, probably in Rome."

Dotty interrupted: "This is all standard stuff. You didn't come all this way to the Sudanese desert to sit with me and repeat what is already well established in text books."

"I simply wanted to point out that Paul started life as a solid citizen, in marked contrast to his later controversial behaviour. Without a doubt, he was a real person and his life is well documented. This can't be said of Jesus, who is supposed to have established the one true Church, but who may be a mythological figure, and whose mission was taken over by Paul and recreated in Paul's own image."

Dotty mimed the act of sewing up her lips and apologised for interrupting.

Martin continued: "Paul was a devout Jew and a Roman citizen, born to a Jewish family in Tarsus, an important Mediterranean trading centre and the most influential city of Asia Minor during the time of Alexander the Great, and moreover famous for its university. Immersed in this atmosphere of scholarship, Paul learned classic Greek and the Greek dialect koine, which was spoken throughout the Roman Empire. Greek philosophy was also naturally part of his education, which brings me to the Stoics. This is important because Paul used a Stoic approach in his mission to reveal the word of God to his converts. Here, again, we must pause and remind ourselves that Stoicism was a Pagan philosophy established in the third century BC and later condemned by the Christian Church. In 529 AD Emperor Justinian I closed all the schools of Pagan philosophy. Early Christian theologians, however, favoured the Pagan philosophy of Stoicism. It therefore seems that Christianity needed time to completely separate itself from Paganism."

"That is certainly true," interrupted Dotty, "but I like to look at it this way: Christianity did not arise *de novo* as a completely new religion, separate from all other religions and philosophies. It grew out of Judaism, Gnosticism and Paganism, and what's more it still carries the accretions of these other religions. Various Church fathers and early Christian writers deluded themselves that their faith was new and different, especially when Emperor Constantine rubber-stamped it by taking over one branch of Christianity as the future religion of the Roman Empire."

"Thank you," remarked Martin, "That's a new insight. At least it is for me. And how true it is when I think about it. On the other hand, although Christianity didn't arise as a completely new religion, it became one later."

Dotty was quick to add: "Even that might be disputed by some, with the argument that Christianity is an Abrahamic religion, a religion fathered by Abraham, one of three related religions *of the book* – Judaism, Christianity, and Islam."

"Yes, that is also true," replied Martin. "I certainly wouldn't like to publicly defend the claim that Christianity was a completely new religion. Clearly, Paul helped to define Christianity, not for non-Christians, but for the Christians themselves. Yet it's also worth asking why Nero took such a delight in singling out the Christians for persecution, if they were not, in some way, recognisably different."

"We must therefore conclude that there was a profound difference between how the Christians saw themselves and how others saw them. But to change the subject, Martin, I'm so glad that this discussion has given you a new insight. I was beginning to wonder whether our discussions have any real value for you. It's not as if I'm teaching a first year student. As you pointed out, you are an ordained minister of the Church, and you also have a university degree in theology. Apart from a few snippets of information, it's obvious that you know as much as I do, and that we are largely in agreement about most aspects of Christian history. In contrast, I could never have brought that fresco to life as you did. For that alone, and nothing else, your visit has been pure profit for me. It worries me, for two reasons: first because I feel I have already gained tremendously from your visit, whereas you have heard little from me that you didn't know or suspect already."

"I've heard plenty from you that was new to me. What about the fascinating history of Faras and early Coptic Christianity, and the history of this entire region from Egypt along the Nile valley to Meroe? Those are examples that immediately come to mind. I could list several other areas of history and geography in which I'm now better educated, thanks to you. And what was your second reason?"

"I hope it doesn't mean that you will leave soon, because I would miss you terribly."

As Dotty said this, she turned her face away, but not quickly enough to conceal a tear trickling down her left cheek. Martin was not surprised. For some time he had suspected that Dotty was concealing unhappiness behind a brave front. Her outbursts of flippancy and childish leg-pulling, sandwiched between episodes of serious scholarship, changing abruptly to veiled references to their personal relationship were symptomatic. As a father, a husband, and a Church minister, he was experienced in the psychology of unhappiness, although, thankfully, moments of unhappiness within his own family had always been fleeting. Martin's recent success at restoring the fresco had given Dotty genuine cause for celebration and had alleviated her unhappiness for a while. Her professional life and academic reputation had profited and continued to profit from her archaeological work in the desert, but her personal life was now yearning for something more. Perhaps she had a vision of herself years hence, famous and winning prizes for her work in the desert, but spiritually alone with no male partner, no children, and no close friends, apart from those in the archaeological society. In fact, how *could* she be happy? Still in her prime, thousands of miles away from home, and two failed marriages. Put that way, no wonder she had shed a tear. It was a presumptuous conclusion, but Martin knew he was not far from the mark.

But how to respond to her claim that she would miss him terribly? Was she issuing an invitation? Oh, not that again! Just when he thought they had sorted out their personal relationship. He decided to take control of the moment and replied: "And I would miss you too Dotty. Don't worry! I still have much to learn from you and I will not be leaving soon. There's still that other fresco that you want me to work on. I won't mind if we cut down on our discussions about Christian history. On the other hand, I would miss our discussion sessions for the personal contact and closeness that they provide (he wondered if that was going too far), so we could spend our discussion time talking about other things, about life in general, about the organisation of the Goethe Institute in Khartoum, about canoeing on the Cambridgeshire fens; pleasant evenings of idle chatter. How about that?"

He had talked for long enough to allow Dotty to regain her composure, and apparently he had said the right things. She rewarded him with a grateful smile, saying: "Thank you Martin. You are so understanding. I don't know what I'll do when you *do* go, but sufficient unto the day for that. You see, I've developed a fear of feeling lonely. Not of being alone. All my life I have treasured the opportunity to be alone, to think my own thoughts without interruption, to plan my own life without others butting in and making suggestions, in fact simply to do my own thing in my own way in my own time. In the past, at home, at university, wherever and whenever, these valuable periods of being alone and designing my own life were islands in a sea of social intercourse, and that also was valuable; my life was balanced. No, being alone is not the same as being lonely. I first realised this, or to put it another way, I first had the courage to admit it to myself, when my second husband left. It was then that I saw my future: an acclaimed specialist in Christian history, growing old and wrinkled, alone and childless."

## CHAPTER 20

Martin was taken aback, and at the same time pleased to hear Dotty express so accurately his own analysis of her mental state. Dispensing with niceties, he exclaimed: "Rubbish! You need to get away from here more often. No wonder you feel as you do, stuck out here in the desert with three male natives, loyal and respectful as they are, but culturally utterly alien. The desert has captured you with its archaeological potential in the day and its moonlit beauty in the night, only to cruelly remind you that you don't actually belong here, that you could be enjoying a rich and varied existence in England amongst friends and colleagues. I blame not only the desert, but also modern electronic communications. I should know because already I've discovered that e-mails are a poor substitute for real personal contact. Perhaps one day some electronic wizard will invent a way of transmitting not only a picture of one's correspondent – even that is now possible with a video webcam – but also the smell of a scene. The e-mails my wife sends me keep me in contact with what is happening at home, but they don't convey her perfume or the cold musty smell of my vestry on a winter's morning. E-mails are a godsend, but a poor substitute for the real thing. They create the illusion that you are part of what is happening at home, so they join forces with the desert itself to ensnare you into enjoying the moonlight and ignoring your future."

"No, Martin, I don't ignore my future. I get so engrossed in my work here that I sometimes forget to think about the future. Otherwise you seem to have analysed my condition with considerable insight. Perhaps that comes from your experience of counselling your parishioners, but in any case you are naturally an insightful person. You're right: by setting up this desert camp I've isolated myself in a kind of prison, out of contact with all that is meaningful to me, except my archaeology."

Reluctant to change the thrust of the conversation, especially now he felt he could probably learn more about her,

Martin continued: "Surely you have close friends or relatives in England who are not archaeologists or Christian historians, and who would enjoy your company and give you a warm welcome. What about your parents?"

"Yes, of course. You caught me at a low point, made even worse by the thought of you leaving. My parents are still alive and living near Cambridge, and I have a brother, who is married with two children, a boy and a girl. So you see, I have family and it's a good family and we all love one another."

Martin was learning much and he wanted to know more. "Forgive me Dotty. I know I'm being nosey, but please tell me more."

Dotty laughed. She was more or less back to her normal self. "What do you want to know?"

"Well, for example, I assume your parents are retired, but what did your father do for a living?"

Dotty gave Martin a long and searching look, broke into a smile and said: "That's easy. Let's first fortify ourselves with a little refreshment. Then you can sit back while I bore you with my relatives and my early home life."

For once, Mustapha was not on cue and the refreshments didn't arrive immediately, so Dotty continued: "My father has not retired. He has a farm, growing market vegetables. My brother lives nearby and has taken over the more laborious tasks, like ploughing and driving the tractor. Father keeps the books and does the accounts and my mother keeps house. It's a profitable business, and so it should be, because the rich black soil of their area on the edge of the fens is very fertile. Did you know that the celery grows six feet tall? In the night, if you listen carefully, you can hear celery falling like felled trees as the mice nibble through the stalks."

Although Cambridge is further south than Norfolk, Martin felt he knew something about that part of the world.

## CHAPTER 20

Was she pulling his leg? Reading his doubtful expression, Dotty said: "Yes, I'm pulling your leg, just as my father used to pull mine all those years ago. Whenever we heard any unidentified noise out in the fields, he would say it was the mice felling the celery again. He has a lovely sense of humour, and mice felling the celery is one of my treasured childhood memories.

So there you are! What more do you want to know about me?" Before Martin could answer, Dotty, bright-eyed and now completely recovered from her plaintive self-analysis, excitedly said: "Why don't we use some of your remaining time and the two of us drive off in the Nissan, camp under the stars, and visit ancient Meroe?"

Just at this point, Mustapha appeared with fresh coffee, a jug of iced orange juice, a plate of cinnamon cakes, bread and karkade jam. Martin silently blessed Mustapha for his timely arrival, which had saved him from giving an immediate response to Dotty's outrageous suggestion. On second thoughts, what a splendid idea! That is, until he pictured the two of them, alone under the desert stars, without Mustapha as a chaperone. It would be the ultimate test of their ability to avoid a romantic entanglement.

Martin carefully worded his answer: "The more I think about it, the more I warm to the idea. Do you think we could make it in a day?

"Of course, but why even try? There'll be much of interest on the way, so it might be worthwhile spending two days getting there. You'll find the desert isn't just a featureless expanse of sand. There's plenty of interest between here and Meroe that I haven't seen yet, so it would be a new experience for me too.

"Then when do we start?" asked Martin, jokingly implying that he was ready to go there and then."

Catching the spirit of his question, Dotty replied, not so jokingly, that they could set out tomorrow morning.

Martin gulped and, not wishing to appear hesitant, said: "And when I get back like a giant refreshed I will work on the other fresco."

"Agreed," said Dotty, imitating the tone of a chairperson. "I suggest we now break for lunch. All those in favour? Martin raised his hand and Dotty slapped the table with her notebook in lieu of a gavel. Normality had been restored. Dotty had risen above her momentary sadness and she was now in charge again. Meanwhile, Mustapha had laid the table.

Martin offered the coffee pot to Dotty, who signalled that he should pour it for her. She, in her turn, spread two slices of bread with fool and passed one to him. Martin felt their companionship and mutual understanding had just progressed a further step. What should he call it? *Table intimacy* perhaps. This was the first time they had served food to each other at a mealtime, and it had happened naturally without hesitation. It occurred to Martin that there were various forms of intimacy, some of which were a potential prelude to, or even part of, the ultimate intimacy. Food, offered to, or prepared for, the other person, was a powerful tool in cementing a relationship or affirming the closeness of two people. Dotty's simple gesture of spreading bread for him, and his own easy pouring of coffee for her were the ingredients of a domestic scene, which assumed they were already in an intimate relationship. Of course, that is not necessarily so, but that is how Martin saw it, and it frightened and excited him in equal measure. To break the spell, Martin hurriedly said: "You're absolutely certain that we should set out tomorrow for Meroe, or were you pulling my leg?" By way of an answer, Dotty called to Mustapha, who came running, looking worried and probably afraid that something might be amiss with the food. "Mustapha, the Reverend Martin and I will leave the camp tomorrow morning and drive to Meroe. We will be away for at least

## CHAPTER 20

five days. Please put enough food and water for five days in the Nissan. Also, my spare tent and blankets. Reverend Martin will sleep in the Nissan, so he will need many cushions, as well as blankets. I'm sure you know what we will need. I leave it to you, but have it all ready for an early start."

Turning to Martin, she smiled and said nothing.

Not to be outmanoeuvred in the initiative stakes, Martin asked where they would cross the river. Meroe was on the other side.

Mustapha overheard and replied as if the question had been addressed to him: "Sir, I powerfully recommend to cross at the dam. There is an excellent road made by the builders of the dam. Big lorries, tractors and bulldozers are crossing the river every day on that road."

"Excellent!" exclaimed Dotty, "Every problem is solved. Let's relax for the rest of the day. I must send an e-mail to the British Museum. After the evening meal we can have an early night ready for our long hall over the desert tomorrow."

Martin agreed, but was already preoccupied with the worrying question of how he would tell Pamela about the trip to Meroe, alone in the desert with Dotty.

From the day of his arrival in Khartoum Martin had sent regular e-mails to Pamela. Several days later, when he began to experience the destabilising effect of Dotty's nearness, his daily e-mail contact with Pamela provided his anchor to reality, the reality that his present situation was temporary and that he had a wonderful wife waiting for him at home. But he hadn't reckoned with Pamela's sensitive antennae. After twenty-six years of marriage she could read him fairly well. The wording of his e-mails had lately acquired a different quality. They were less open. They no longer gave her a complete picture of his day in the desert. Was he hiding something? Why had he said so very little about Doctor Dorothy Scott, who was the very reason he had flown to the Sudan? Was she an attractive young woman capable stirring

Martin's emotions? Trying not to sound too inquisitive or suspicious, Pamela had written:

*Dear hard-working husband, please put down your spade, wipe the sweat from your brow and tell me more about Doctor Dorothy Scott. How old is she? How long has she been living in the desert? Is she married? I have a picture of a fierce and dedicated archaeologist, who makes you sweat all day in the desert heat, digging up the remains of a buried church. Love, Pamela.*

Martin saw immediately that Pamela was worrying. If he were honest with himself, she had cause to worry. Somehow, Pamela had picked up a warning signal from his e-mails and Martin wasn't sure how. Possibly he had said suspiciously little about Dotty in his e-mails. He ought to have painted an early picture of his camp boss, as well as a description of life in the camp. His next e-mail would have to be very carefully worded. He had finally written:

*Dear hard-working wife, please stop sweating over those steaming pans, make yourself a cup of tea, leave the kitchen, and enjoy this e-mail. Doctor Scott has been very welcoming. She and Mustapha have made sure that I'm comfortable and have a decent tent where I can store all my stuff. She is very academic and it is easy to see why she has such a reputation in the field of Christian history. I feel we have struck a fair bargain. At the excavation site I'm digging out an ancient fresco and I hope to soon have it revealed in all its glory. I can understand why Doctor Scott needed a replacement for Pinda. She could have hired local Arabs to dig, but she really needs someone who can not only dig but fully understands why he is digging and what he is bringing to light. Also, I think she appreciates being able to speak to someone in her own version of English in her own idiom.*

## CHAPTER 20

*Otherwise, her nearest European contacts are Doctor Hopp and his secretary at the Goethe Institute in Khartoum, but they are many miles away. Meanwhile, I've been learning some Arabic. Remember Ali Baba and the forty thieves and the magic words Open Sesame! to open the door of the treasure cave? Well, the Arabic for that magic command is* eftah ya sim sim! *It really is magic. Try it sometime. Much love, Martin.*

Pamela had replied:

*Dear Martin, I sit, as instructed, drinking a cup of tea, and wondering why you didn't answer my question about Doctor Scott's age and whether she is married. By the way, I tried out the magic words as you suggested. I went shopping in town yesterday and as I approached the doors of the supermarket I recited* eftah ya sim sim! *Would you believe it – the doors opened as if by magic! Ken and I have decided to put extracts of your e-mails in the church magazine, so more details of your work and desert scenery would be appreciated. The first article will be entitled Open Sesame! Love, Pamela.*
*P.S. Sue and I take turns to sweat over those steaming pans.*

This e-mail added a new dimension to his life in the desert: providing material for the church magazine. He could even send pictures taken on his digital, although he wondered if the organist, who produced the magazine on his word processor, would be able to manage pictures, especially coloured ones. Her joke about opening the doors of the supermarket was very encouraging, but he couldn't ignore the evidence that Pamela was concerned about Dotty. He must send an honest reply about Dotty's age and marriage status.

His reply had read as follows:

*Dear Pamela, Masaa el kheer! (that's Arabic for good evening!). Kaifa haloki (that's Arabic for how are you?). What a splendid idea to report my activities in the Sudan in the church magazine! From now on I will always bear the church magazine in mind and try to provide interesting accounts of my activities out here in the desert. As for Doctor Scott's age, I can't possibly ask her how old she is. I don't know her that well! However, I would hazard a guess at about forty, plus or minus three or four years – probably more plus than minus. Regarding her marriage status, this is also something one doesn't enquire about, without seeming rude or nosey. Soon after I arrived, she gave me a sun hat that had belonged to her husband, and explained, without being asked, that she had been married twice. Each marriage had taken place in England when she was on a lecture tour. It seems that both husbands couldn't stand life in the desert, so the marriages failed. More I cannot tell you because more I do not know. Perhaps Flo Willan knows more about her broken marriages. We could ask him. Give my regards to Ken and Sue. Love, Martin.*

Martin had hoped that would calm Pamela's fears and suspicions. Pamela had replied almost two days later:

*Dear Martin, Ana behair, shukran! (that's Arabic for I'm fine, thanks). Sorry to be so long replying to your last e-mail. It took me ages to find my bit of Arabic. I finally found it in an on-line translation website. I now have a picture of you digging holes in the desert, watched over by a mystery woman, of indeterminate age, who marries men, drags them out to the desert then sends them back to England because they don't meet her requirements. Yesterday, over our evening meal, Sue, Ken and I had a most amusing time discussing the character of Doctor Scott. You just wouldn't believe the scenarios that we choreographed in our imaginations. She was everything from a bewitching Siren to a dried-up, slave-driving harridan.*

## CHAPTER 20

*Take care, my dear husband! Unfortunately, none of this is suitable for the church magazine. Love, Pamela.*

Martin had heaved a deep sigh of relief. If Pamela could find Dotty so amusing and, moreover, share his last e-mail with the curate and his wife, there wasn't much for him to worry about. But now there *was* something to worry about. How would Pamela react to his trip to Meroe, alone under the desert moon with Dotty? Back in his tent, he sent the following e-mail:

*Dear Pamela, Doctor Scott and I have decided to have a break from normal routine and drive over the desert to the ancient ruins of Meroe. On the way we can continue our discussions of Christian history. The ruins and pyramids at Meroe are the remains of an ancient pre-Christian civilisation. When you have time, google Meroe and you will see why it would be a pity for me to miss this opportunity to visit the ruins. It will take about two days to get there. If we spend a day at the ruins then two days driving back to the camp, we will be away five days. It promises to be an interesting trip and I will certainly send you an account for the Church magazine. As the trip progresses I will e-mail photographs to you. We leave tomorrow and will cross the Nile on the road over the hydroelectric dam, near where we collect water for the camp (Meroe is on the opposite side of the Nile from the camp). The driving may be arduous, so I'm going to have an early night. Watch out for my next e-mail. It should be interesting. I hope all is well at home. Love, Martin.*

Martin was apprehensive. How would Pamela react to the news that he was about to spend five days alone in the desert with a woman of unknown age, who had two marriages to her credit (or was it to her debit?)? He didn't have long to wait. The speed of Pamela's response was a warning sign in itself. Before he washed and dressed, he powered up his laptop and read:

*Dear Martin, Why don't you and Doctor Scott trek to Meroe on camels? It would make much better copy for the Church magazine. Or perhaps Doctor Scott prefers the comfort of a four-wheel land cruiser? I have googled Meroe, so I now know it's between the fifth and sixth cataracts on the eastern bank of the Nile. It certainly appears to be well worth a visit. It took a little time before I tumbled to the fact that Meroe is the name of the ancient city and its pyramids, whereas tourists are taken to somewhere called Kabushiya, a modern city a few kilometres from Meroe. So you see I've done my homework. I'll be thinking of you, camping out under the desert stars. If you get lost, you only need to follow the river Nile until you get to Meroe. Ken says he's envious and would love to visit the Sudanese desert. Sue says she would worry about him being alone with Doctor Scott. Take care. Love, Pamela*

It couldn't have been clearer. She didn't like the thought of Martin alone in the desert for five days with Dotty. And she had cleverly let the curate's wife say it for her. Nevertheless, she was being supportive and trusting, and he was determined to be worthy of that trust, alone under the desert stars with Dotty. Despite the fact that he and Dotty had discussed openly their feelings for each other, and established that they would never allow these feelings to get out of control, Martin was again losing confidence in his ability to remain faithful to his wedding vows. He had failed utterly to understand that Dotty's interaction with her fellow human beings was guided by an invincible personal faith, which was more soundly based than his own. For all her physical attraction, her playful humour, and now her recent confession that she was afraid of feeling lonely, she would

CHAPTER 20

never have allowed their relationship to develop into more than pure comradeship. But until Martin finally absorbed this truth, he would be continually on edge when alone with Dotty. So, he will find he was wrong about Dotty. Will he also find he was wrong about Jesus? Wait and see!

# Chapter 21

Martin couldn't sleep. He lay awake, reviewing his discussion with Dotty about early Christian origins. Alone in his tent in the quiet of the desert night, free from challenging conversation with Dotty, Martin thought hard to discover what was struggling to come forward from the back of his mind. In his imagination the Gospels, Paul's letters, and the Acts of the Apostles kept changing their order of appearance in the New Testament. It was now clear that Paul ought to appear before the Gospels, and that placing him later was a clever editing trick, but Martin sensed a deeper problem. Suddenly, it dawned on him that the New Testament reported nothing of the great history of Christianity that predated the supposed birth of Jesus, a history that he and Dotty had been laboriously exploring. Thus it appeared that the Bible contrived to convince the reader that Christianity started when Jesus was born. In addition, there existed a wealth of writings from the early centuries after the supposed birth of Jesus, which made no mention of a real person called Jesus, and these writings had not been included in the New Testament. Gnostic documents discovered with the Gospel of Thomas at Nag Hamadi dated from 350-400 AD, but they were known to be copies of works about 300 years older. In fact, those books of the New Testament that speak of a miracle worker called Jesus are greatly outnumbered by texts not included in the New Testament that make no reference to any such real person. To put it another way, when the New Testament was compiled a wealth of sacred texts was available that made no mention of a real person called Jesus. Such texts, however, were purposely omitted, giving prominence only to texts that supported the party line. The early Christian fathers followed the tradition started by the Jews, that is they put their practices and beliefs in writing in a sacred book, thereby placing those very beliefs in an early

CHAPTER 21

straitjacket of conformity, *i.e.,* belief in the existence of a man called Jesus. Although there were Christians who knew that Jesus was a spiritual concept and not a flesh and blood person, Emperor Constantine finished these off by selecting the "orthodox" version of Christianity as the religion of the Roman Empire, at the same time banishing the Gnostic Christians and ordering their works to be destroyed. Thus, by the fourth century AD Christian belief had become tyrannised by the Gospels. Rehashing in this way much of what he and Dotty had already discussed was an effective alternative to counting sheep. Martin now felt satisfied with this perspective of the New Testament and how it had controlled the minds of Christians for the last two thousand years. He turned over and slept.

When Martin arrived at Dotty's tent for breakfast, Mustapha was instructing her how to cross the Nile at the hydroelectric dam. He suggested they contact Mohammed and Yasser, who would then introduce them to the dam security manager. He seemed to think this was a necessary courtesy. Dotty worked through her check list. Mustapha had remembered everything: tents, blankets, tinned food, water, and bottled gas. Martin enquired whether they had sufficient diesel for the journey. "Oops!" exclaimed Dotty, "I'd quite forgotten fuel for the Nissan." Proudly, Mustapha said he had also provided enough diesel for their excursion, and that diesel was available at Kabushiya in any case.

Martin said little over breakfast. He needed time for his soul to catch up with the present situation. It had all happened so quickly. A chance remark yesterday before lunch and now they were about to leave the camp, cross the river and drive all the way to Meroe. Not wanting to seem too distant, he asked if they had the necessary maps, and immediately regretted his question. The answer struck him before Dotty answered: "It's impossible to get lost in the Nile valley.

Even if you wander miles to the east or west of the Nile, you can always return to the river, which will lead you to where you want to be. We will follow the Nile. No maps required."

"Of course. Silly me! I had forgotten where we are. But then, to many people, a vast desert with a mighty river running through it would seem like a contradiction."

"Exactly. You have to be here and live here before it finally sinks in that the Sudanese desert is not the great Sahara or the empty quarter of Arabia, where you can easily get lost and perish for lack of water. Well, are you ready?"

"I'm as ready as I'll ever be," replied Martin.

"I don't think so. You're wearing a bush shirt and jeans. If there were ever a more suitable time for wearing a galabiya and a turban, it's now. Off you go and put on your galabiya. I'm sure Mustapha will be only too happy to show you how to wind a turban round your head."

"What about you? You haven't changed into your white thoub.

"And I don't intend to. I'm sticking to my light cotton dress and a head scarf. Just give me a few minutes alone, while you change your clothes."

As Martin returned to his own tent to obediently don his galabiya, he saw that Dotty had retreated into one of her formative silences. He had expected it and it made sense. She was about to set out on a journey.

When he returned to the Nissan, Mustapha was waiting with a length of glistening white cotton. Turban winding was not easy, and it was made more complicated than necessary because Mustapha wanted to imbue the process with mystique and ritual. By the time they were ready to leave, Martin had not mastered every subtlety of this ancient art, but he could wind the yards of white cotton around his head, leaving a few feet to tuck in around the edges. Martin ignored Mustapha's despair at his pupil's inability to learn quickly. In fact, he was quite pleased with his own version

## CHAPTER 21

of a turban. It stayed firmly on his head and was not likely to be blown away by the wind. Its outer layers were more loosely wound than those next to his head and he immediately felt the cooling effect of the trapped air.

Dotty arrived at the Nissan, suppressed a smile, and remarked that Martin wouldn't exactly pass for Lawrence of Arabia. "Well how about the Sheik of Arabee?" asked Martin. "If I remember correctly," mused Dotty, "*The Sheik of Arabee* was the title of a pop song in the twenties." Martin made to speak but Dotty stopped him with: "Stop there! I don't want a humorous reference to my age. Neither of us was born that long ago. We both know the song because it was still played by jazz bands when we were teenagers. "You misjudge me," protested Martin, "I wouldn't dream of saying *that dates you*. I was only about to recall the words of the song. Isn't there a line that goes: *into my tent he creeps?*" Dotty laughed out loud: "Alright, you've had your little joke. I'll be sleeping in my tent and you'll be sleeping in the Nissan, and there'll be no creeping." "Agreed!" said Martin, grateful for the old pop song and the humorous start to the morning.

As usual, Mohammed and Yasser heard the Nissan before they saw it. By the time Dotty and Martin arrived Gwaria already had the kettle on. Martin had forgotten about the compulsory tea-drinking, which had now become part of any visit made by their Nissan Land Cruiser to the fourth cataract. Added to which, Gwaria and Dotty had never met. Consequently, the trek to Meroe was delayed by a good two hours, but pleasantly so. Dotty and Gwaria took to each other straight away and decided they must meet again after Dotty returned from Meroe.

They were on the point of leaving for the dam when Martin had what he considered to be his best idea of the day. A photograph for the Church magazine! They drove down to the edge of the Nile and gathered around the Nissan with the water-gathering site behind and slightly to the right so as to be visible. Five members in the party meant five photographs, each member taking a turn with the camera. Yasser photographed just Martin and Dotty by the Nissan. Martin would treasure that picture, although he didn't feel it would be wise to send it to Pamela. The best keepsake of all was a photograph taken by Dotty of Martin, Mohammed, Yasser and Gwaria, not by the Nissan but sitting with a teapot and tea cups at a table on the verandah outside Mohammed's house.

As Martin drove the Nissan to the dam, Yasser and Mohammed on the front seat, Dotty in the back, they saw the security officer approaching, standing on the running board of a gigantic multi-wheeled transporter loaded with the jib arm of a crane. As they approached, the noise of machinery and diesel engines increased until it was difficult to make conversation. Evidently the Sudan had not yet enacted a clean air act. Black smoke from numerous engines drifted over the site, all the time slowly moving eastwards in a slight desert breeze, only to be replaced by more from a cacophony of infernal combustion engines. (This is not a misprint. When it comes to combustion engines, the author prefers infernal to internal). Yasser ran forward to attract the attention of the security officer and beckon him to the Nissan. Martin had no idea which way the transporter would turn or whether it would drive straight on, so he stopped the Nissan at a safe distance. The security officer responded with a look of frowned enquiry, which suddenly changed to a wide grin as he recognised his old friend Yasser. After the customary hugging and back slapping, the officer was introduced to the party as Yasser's old friend Saad, who seemed touched by the fact they actually wanted permission to cross on the dam road. Apparently, local inhabitants used the road freely without asking. According to Sudanese desert culture, any bridge over the Nile must be for everyone

## CHAPTER 21

to use. It was an ingrained sense of a centuries-old democratic right. Yasser and Mohammed said goodbye and stood waving while Martin and Dotty drove with Saad to the dam. Acting like a policeman controlling traffic, Saad waved all heavy vehicles over to the right-hand lane of the road, while the Nissan, conspicuously small compared with the huge vehicles servicing the dam, crossed to the other side. Saad was obviously an Arab, but as they made their way across the dam, Martin couldn't help noticing a high percentage of Orientals, presumably Chinese, labouring at the roadside and driving trucks. It made sense. Hadn't he read the document about the role of the Chinese in the construction of the dam? Saad had work to do and they had interrupted it. He jumped from the Nissan, quickly wished them a good journey, and waved them off in a northerly direction along a wide, surfaced road.

"With roads like this, who even needs a river to follow?" remarked Martin. Dotty laughed and pointed out that if they followed this particular road, they would not arrive at Meroe, but at Port Sudan on the Red Sea, where the Chinese unloaded materials and equipment for the dam. Later they would be able to follow a road that branched off to the south towards Meroe and Khartoum. "As a matter of fact, we could guarantee reaching Meroe by following the railway rather than the river." Martin was surprised by mention of the railway. He had forgotten that Kitchener had built a railway from Wadi Halfa to Khartoum, and he had never been clear about its exact route. "Well," answered Martin, "that would be fine, provided we could see the railway. Where is it exactly?"

"At the moment it isn't here," replied Dotty, in a vague and enigmatic tone of voice.

Martin refused to take the bait and waited for her to continue.

Dotty continued: "Kitchener built the railway across the desert to where the Nile turns southwest in the great bend.

From there onwards the track follows the Nile very closely all the way to Khartoum. The Chinese are supposed to be building a branch line to the dam. Perhaps they have already built it, but I didn't see any signs of a railway when we crossed the Nile just now. But once we get to the top of the great bend, we should be able to follow the railway track all the way to Meroe. After Meroe it continues to Khartoum. With aid from the Chinese, the railway is going to be upgraded with modern locomotives and rolling stock. At the moment I wouldn't dream of travelling from Khartoum by rail in order to reach my camp. The system is unreliable and trains often break down. Between you and me I don't have much confidence that the new Chinese-sponsored railway will be any better, especially if the Sudanese are responsible for running and maintaining it. But who knows? If you return in a few years' time it might be possible to take a very fast modern train from Khartoum to the dam. Mustapha and I would meet you there and drive you back to my camp."

Martin nodded and smiled at the thought. He told Dotty that he hoped he wouldn't have to travel by train, because his journey to the camp, driven through the night by Mustapha, had been a wonderful experience, and he wouldn't mind doing it again one day. Then he pointed out that if he did arrive by train and was met by Dotty and Mustapha they would not be able to drive to the camp straight away because they would first have to drink tea with Yasser, Mohammed and Gwaria.

"Well, railway or no railway," said Dotty, bringing the conversation back to the present, "We can expect plenty of traffic on the road between Khartoum and the dam." Then she added: "Why don't you ponder the scenery to your right?"

They were driving alongside the vast lake that had accumulated behind the dam. On their right, below the road, the land shelved gently to the water's edge. Barely fifty yards separated the road from the water.

## CHAPTER 21

"I hope the water has now reached its highest level," observed Martin, "otherwise this road will be flooded one day."

"Gwaria told me that the lake was indeed now at its highest, and that the road was built before work started on the dam."

"Clever people, those Chinese. After building the Great Wall of China and the dam across the Yangtze, damming a little river like the Nile must seem like child's play. But, seriously, that was a clever bit of surveying. They predicted exactly where the final water line would be and built the road accordingly."

Dotty protested: "It all depends what you mean by clever. Just look at that vast expanse of water. I can't even see the opposite bank. Beneath that water lie the ruins of ancient buildings, tombs of earlier cultures, and other human artefacts that have not been studied. So much has been lost to archaeology and the early history of this region, just because those wretched dam builders couldn't wait to start making hydroelectricity. I don't call that clever."

"I sympathise, but look at it this way: those artefacts are still there and preserved under the water. One day someone will develop methods of under-water archaeology. Teams of historians will don aqualungs and work on the lake bottom with picks and shovels. In fact, shipwrecks are already studied in that way in various parts of the ocean around Europe and America, and in the Mediterranean, so the methods are already known."

"Perhaps you're right. Who knows? Anyway, have you noticed that the road is now bending to the west? We should soon meet the branch that returns to the river and continues to Khartoum, provided Gwaria was right when she described the route to me. And if you don't mind terribly, I would like to take over the driving. This is a good road. Later, when it gets narrower and more bumpy, you can take over again."

After a further thirty minutes with Dotty at the wheel, a right-hand branch appeared in the road about a hundred yards ahead. The turning was marked by a row of poles, about eight feet tall, some with fragments of red cloth fluttering from their tops. The main road to Port Sudan veered off to the left across the desert, no longer surfaced, but well compacted, its route also marked by red poles inserted in the sand at intervals of two hundred yards. Dotty suggested they drive a mile or so along the lesser road then stop for lunch, after which she would like Martin to take the wheel again while she had a short nap. They had risen earlier than usual and had had a busy morning.

The road had taken them temporarily in an easterly direction. Both the lake and the river were now out of sight. Desert stretched to the right and left, and ahead of them. The landscape had a different feeling. Civilisation had been left behind, that is if the industrial noise and activity at the dam can be called civilised. To their left, the smoothly undulating brown waste was interrupted by small outcrops of black rocks. Shrines to holy men were also here, but a long way from the road. One usually associates buildings, including shrines, with the presence of people, but there was not a human being in sight. To their right, the flat desert stretched to a distant line of palms, a sure sign that the water was just beyond.

"Time for lunch!" announced Dotty, as she swung the steering wheel, turned off the road and, for the sake of their shade, headed towards the trees. For a Nissan Land Cruiser the terrain was as good as smooth. It would have been a severe test of the suspension of a Mini or a low-slung sports car. The trees were date palms in a well-tended plantation about fifty yards from the water's edge. It was difficult to decide whether they had travelled beyond the lake behind the dam, or whether this very wide stretch of the Nile was still affected by the build-up of water. The shade of the trees,

## CHAPTER 21

the presence of the wide expanse of water, and a gentle breeze that crossed the Nile before it reached them combined to create the perfect resting place. Dotty spread a blanket beneath the trees, while Martin fetched the cool-box from the Nissan. They drank only water, and plenty of it. A little bread and fool, followed by one of Mustapha's cinnamon cakes was all they needed to keep them going until the evening, provided they always had plenty of water. What they really needed was a rest. Martin struggled to keep his eyes open and the sight of Dotty dozing off, her head resting on a cushion from the Nissan, only made his own eyelids heavier. Soon they were both asleep. And while they slept a potential drama came and went. Both were unaware that a scorpion had walked across their blanket, probing the crumbs of cinnamon cake. It lost interest and disappeared. It seems, therefore, that they had not driven faster than their angels could fly. They must have been under divine protection. Otherwise, how is it that Martin, a complete novice in desert life, finally returned to England without being stung by a scorpion?

They awoke to the shrieking and chattering of children. As Martin regained consciousness (he had been dreaming that he was producing the church magazine, locked in a garret part way up the steeple of his church) he could see that the noisy party consisted of a magnificent grandfather, a grandmother, two parents, three little girls and one teenage boy. Dotty needed longer to adjust herself to where she was and what was happening. She emerged from her slumber to meet the gaze of eight pairs of eyes. Gesturing to the rest of the party to remain where they were, the grandfather figure walked over to Dotty and Martin, smiled broadly, gave a little bow, and said, with outstretched arms and in excellent, cultured English: "Welcome to my plantation of date palms. We are most sorry to have disturbed you. Please forgive the noise of the children." In his flowing galabiya, large white turban with a red stone, possibly a ruby, mounted on one side, a long but neatly trimmed black beard, and piercing dark eyes, this courteous grandfather might have been an illustration on the pages of a Thousand and one Nights. Martin couldn't decide whether he had emerged from Scheherazade, Ali Baba and the forty thieves, or from Aladdin and his magic lamp.

Both Dotty and Martin sought hard for a gracious reply. Dotty spoke first: "We are very grateful for the cool shade of your date palms. Today we have driven from an archaeological site near the hydroelectric dam, and we hope to visit the ruins at Meroe tomorrow."

"Then you will need somewhere to sleep tonight," observed the grandfather. "Between here and Meroe is rather exposed, but it is always possible to find the shelter of trees near the river." After a brief pause, the grandfather suddenly exclaimed: "Of course, you must be from the excavation site of the old Coptic church. Dear Madam, you must be Doctor Scott, and you, Sir, must be the English country parson, who has come to help with the digging. Let me introduce myself. I am called Ahmed. My wife is Asma. My son and his wife are Khalid and Siema. I will ask the children to tell you their own names."

Dotty and Martin stared at him in amazement. "Are we really so famous that you know all about us this far from our archaeological camp?" asked Dotty. The grandfather held his sides and laughed. "Here, in this part of the Nile valley, we have what you call a bush telegraph, or I think it is also called the grape vine. I am well acquainted with your servant Mustapha and his family. Our two families have known each other for generations." At a sign from the grandfather the rest of the family came forward. Grandmother and mother gave little curtsies, while father Khalid walked over and shook hands with Dotty and Martin. Khalid was relaxed and obviously at ease with Europeans. His handshake was

## CHAPTER 21

accompanied by an amused smile as he observed Dotty's and Martin's reaction to his father. This was probably not the first time his marvellous old father had left visitors in a state of amazement, wondering where on earth such an apparition had come from. Each of the children pronounced their own names. With another little bow and speaking in a rich baritone, Ahmed announced: "Now we will leave you in peace and wish you a very pleasant visit to Meroe." The children had been amazingly patient and well behaved. They ran off, once more shouting and laughing.

Dotty and Martin looked intently at one another, seeking the right words. "You start!" suggested Dotty. "Well, I certainly won't be able to remember all those names, but isn't Grandfather Ahmed a splendid person, and such a command of English!" Dotty agreed and complained that she would dearly like to know more about him. Where had he learned such cultured and idiomatic English? When they returned to her camp, she would ask Mustapha about Grandfather Ahmed.

Martin said: "Something struck me very forcibly about this encounter with Grandfather Ahmed and his family. There was a wonderful family, grandparents, parents and children, enjoying each other's company, taking a leisurely afternoon walk by the river, content with their lot, the children happy and boisterously normal. Contrast that with you and me: far from home, far from our families, pursuing esoteric ideas and interests."

"I agree, it's possible to see a contrast, but we don't know anything about their family life. Despite their apparent contentment, I read a certain envy in the eyes of the mother when we were introduced. You talk of contrasts. Imagine the contrast in her mind between her own situation and mine, as I wander freely along the Nile valley with a man who is not my husband. Whatever her other feelings, I know for certain she was a little envious. Or let me put it this way: she was not as worldly as Gwaria, who seems adjusted to the fact there is another world outside that of the Sudan and Islam."

"And you gathered all that from such a brief encounter? You didn't even talk to Ahmed's daughter-in-law." said Martin, unable to hide a note of challenge in his voice.

"Just a fleeting impression, admittedly with no evidence to support it. I get a similar impression when I observe women on the street in Khartoum. Some wear a European skirt and blouse, while others wear a traditional thoub. Gwaria belongs to the first group, while Ahmed's daughter-in-law belongs to the second."

"I think your theory needs careful revision," countered Martin, "Didn't you notice that Gwaria wears a thoub?"

"Look here, Martin, I know you have me in a debating corner, but I know for a fact that some Sudanese women are socially bound by tradition, while others are more liberated."

"I think I can agree with that," conceded Martin, "since it's probably true of all societies throughout the world."

"Martin, I'm not trying to wriggle out of this debate, but I want to say I enjoy talking with you, even when you challenge me. Try to imagine what it's like digging in the desert with no-one to act as a sharpening stone for my thoughts; just wonderfully steadfast, courteous, and helpful Arabs and Nubians, who can't share my innermost thoughts or academic interests."

"I can certainly understand that," answered Martin, adding half-heartedly: "but shouldn't we now continue our journey?"

They had chosen a perfect spot for their picnic and both felt tempted to stay. Dotty lay back against her cushions and, with eyes closed, said she wanted to enjoy the shade of the date palms and the gentle breeze from the Nile a little longer. Martin decided to walk to the Nile and photograph the view. When he returned they could pack up, drive on,

## CHAPTER 21

and see how far they could get before camping for the night. For Martin, photography had acquired a new meaning. Every picture was now a potential entry in the church magazine. How might he capture the grandeur of the wide expanse of the Nile? The swirling of the current and the leisurely to-ing and fro-ing of the distant white sails of feluccas gave life to the scene, but he couldn't put a video in the church magazine. And in any case there was no way of capturing the smell of the Nile, the heat of the day, the almost inaudible lapping of the water, and the cooling effect of the slow breeze that, having played amongst the distant white sails, now helped to evaporate the perspiration on Martin's face. He photographed the scene directly ahead and to the left and right, turned through one hundred and eighty degrees and photographed their picnic site, carefully composing the picture to include the dozing Dotty with the Nissan behind. Bearing in mind that Pamela might misunderstand if she saw a picture of Dotty laid on her back, he composed a different shot to include only the Nissan, the picnic blanket, and the surrounding date palms. Then he switched on the video facility of his digital and panned from the bank where he was standing to the distant feluccas. If the video came out well, he might show it in one of his talks back in Herefordshire.

Dotty suddenly came to life, jumped up from her blanket and helped to pack the picnic gear into the Nissan.

Three hours later, after a scenically monotonous drive, they started to look out for a suitable place to pitch camp for the night. Following Grandfather Ahmed's advice, they chose a sheltered spot beneath date palms near the river.

Martin cleared an area of stones and leaves, and firmly planted the camping gas stove in the sand. Dotty watched him and, holding a tin of beans in each hand, burst into laughter. "This will do us both a world of good. Do you realise that until now I have never prepared a meal for myself in the Sudan? We are terribly lucky to have Mustapha and the two Mohammeds to look after us at the camp".

"Well, Dotty, now I'm going to look after us both by brewing a steaming mug of Lipton's Yellow Label."

The tea was welcome. Even more welcome was the meal of baked beans and stewed aubergine, followed by bananas and dates, all accompanied by harmless banter. Perhaps the harmless banter was necessary to hide Martin's uneasiness. He sensed that their relationship was now caught in a spotlight, a spotlight of their own making, and they were the only witnesses of anything that might happen between them. Dotty, not in the least worried by their situation, but sensitive to Martin's unease, decided she must steer their after-dinner conversation to safety, so she exclaimed: "Let's leave the washing up and talk about Asclepius!"

Feeling relieved and grateful, Martin replied: "Why not!? What better occasion to talk about the Greek god of medicine, than camping in the Sudanese desert near the river Nile?"

Ignoring his irony, Dotty pointed out that parallels had often been drawn between Jesus and Asclepius, and that some authors even claimed that the character of Jesus had been modelled on that of Asclepius.

Martin would have preferred to give his brain a rest from the Jesus question, to lie back and immerse himself in the mysterious beauty of the desert night, and follow the progress of the moon, which was now bright enough to render their camping lantern redundant. Allowing himself a long pause for reflection and to assemble his scattered fragments of knowledge about Asclepius, Martin finally contributed, rather lamely, the fact that it was no longer generally thought that Jesus had been modelled on Asclepius, but that the mythical healing powers of Asclepius had perhaps, in some way, foreshadowed the healing powers of Jesus.

"What on earth does that mean?" demanded Dotty, not even trying to conceal the note of confrontation in her voice.

## CHAPTER 21

"Okay, if you want to talk about Asclepius, you have me at a disadvantage. Let me start by telling you the little that I can remember about him. Asclepius was a Greek hero. He was later promoted to the Greek god of medicine and healing. He was the son of Apollo and I forget the name of his mother. He had a number of daughters, whose names I no longer recall. He is best remembered for his physician's staff with a snake wrapped around it, which, to this day, is the symbol of the medical profession. And that, dear Dotty, is the sum total of my knowledge."

"More accurately, I suspect, the sum total of what you remember. You surely knew more when you studied Greek mythology some years ago," ventured Dotty.

"That's true. So why don't you fill in the blank spaces for me?"

"Only too happy to oblige. His mother was Coronis. He actually had five daughters, named Aceso, Iaso, Panacea, Aglaea and Hygieia. He was a very popular, widely worshipped Greek god with a sanctuary at Epidaurus in the northeastern Peloponnese."

"Ah yes, it's all coming back to me now," interrupted Martin. "The cult of Asclepius held sway about three centuries BC. Patients had to sleep at healing centres or shrines. Their god-inspired dreams were then interpreted by priests, who would then prescribe a remedy. And to cap it all," added Martin, "Hippocrates is thought to be a descendant of Asclepius, thereby completing the link with modern medicine."

"Historical roots of modern medicine are, of course, fascinating, but I'm more concerned about suggested links between Asclepius and the figure of Jesus. You have already pointed out that Asclepius is no longer thought to have been a model for the construction of Jesus, but I'm not convinced. Let's look at the question more closely. For example, who decided that Asclepius was not a model for the construction of Jesus?"

"Frankly, I've no idea," conceded Martin.

"Well, the early Christian fathers had to contend with doubts and attacks levelled at Christianity. They had to deal with the claim that Jesus was a myth, albeit a very engaging and valuable myth that portrayed Christian teaching. They had to somehow conceal or explain the embarrassing similarity between the Christian story and the structure of Pagan beliefs, and we know how they dealt with that," said Dotty, raising a questioning eyebrow.

"With the ridiculous theory of diabolical mimicry. We've already talked about that," answered Martin rather irritably.

"Okay, so we've been there and done that. I was just checking you're still awake. Then they had to fend off the criticisms of the Pagans. Those old Christian fathers were very much on the defensive, so it's hardly surprising that Justin Martyr, in about 160 AD, claimed that the myth of Asclepius was not a model for Jesus. His list of agenda included the real flesh and blood existence of Jesus. In denying that Asclepius inspired the myth of Jesus, he had to ignore the compelling similarity between the healing powers attributed to Asclepius and those attributed to Jesus. I would even go so far as to suggest that the early Christians had already let the side down by lazily taking over the personality of Asclepius for Jesus rather than take the trouble to invent an original personality. It is known that statues of Asclepius became models for the fourth- and fifth-century depictions of Jesus and many of the inscriptions on those statues were taken over by early Christians by simply replacing the name Asclepius with the name Jesus."

It was late. They had had a tiring day. Martin was drifting into a postprandial doze, but he became suddenly alert when Dotty mentioned healing power. "Thank you Dotty.

## CHAPTER 21

It's too easy to forget the healing power attributed to Jesus. Many of my sermons stress his powers of forgiveness and love. I must try to emphasise more his ability to heal."

"Here's another thought," added Dotty: "Throughout history the burning of books has been used by religious and political extremists to destroy embarrassing truths. It is a drastic way of denying the truth. We must therefore pause and think carefully whenever anyone says that something is not true. We must ask ourselves whether they are indeed right, or whether they are afraid of the truth and are trying to conceal it. Or to put it another way: are they metaphorically burning books?"

In a questioning tone, Martin said: "In other words, by denying that Asclepius was a model for Jesus, Justin Martyr may have unwittingly revealed that he suspected Asclepius *was* a model for Jesus."

"Precisely," said Dotty, "but for the moment, I can't decide whether this helps in our search for the true nature of Jesus. Nevertheless, it's an interesting thought."

Discussion of Asclepius had dispelled Martin's confused thoughts about being alone with Dotty in the moonlight, and it brought them both to the verge of sleep. Martin arranged a comfortable soft corner for himself in the Nissan. Dotty said the tent would be too stuffy. She preferred to lie on the sand in a sleeping bag and dream she was picnicking on the Cambridgeshire fens. Foolishly they left the washing up. Foolishly, because the congealed residues of beans and aubergine attracted arthropod scavengers in the night. But what the eye doesn't see, etc, so Dotty was blissfully unaware that she had lain inches away from a particularly nasty giant millipede, and that several scorpions had explored their camp site in the night.

"Are you still awake?" whispered Martin from the Nissan. "Yes, what is it?" said Dotty from her sleeping bag.

"I feel uncertain about the nature of Asclepius," said Martin, "Was he a real person, was he a god, was he looked upon by some as a god and some as a person? What was he exactly?"

"Ask me something easy," replied Dotty, "Now go to sleep."

# Chapter 22

At five-thirty Martin opened one eye, remembered where he was and how he got there. He hoped he had not entertained a female mosquito during the night. In future, he must cover his sleeping quarters with a mosquito net. And what about Dotty? She must also sleep under a net. As Martin tiptoed past her sleeping form, he noticed with satisfaction that she had indeed slept under a mosquito net. She must have fetched it from the Nissan after he had fallen asleep. Her arrangement was very simple. The netting was held barely three inches above her sleeping form by a row of little sticks on either side of her sleeping bag. He supposed that would do as a makeshift arrangement for one night. She must have better protection for the remaining nights of their Meroe expedition. He would suggest she sleep in the Nissan, while he made his bed in the sand, or used the tent.

On the shore of the Nile tiny wavelets, excited by a slight breeze, crisscrossed one another and washed the fine sand into ever-changing patterns. Feeling enchanted by the peace and solitude of the scene, Martin felt reluctant to return to Dotty and the Nissan. The water's edge was in the shadow of the trees behind him, while the rising sun pierced a flimsy layer of mist and illuminated the water from the centre of the Nile to its opposite bank. He felt himself overcome by a feeling of peace and oneness with the universe, a feeling that arose from hitherto undisturbed depths of his soul. Why were such feelings so rare? True, he enjoyed being alone and thinking his own thoughts, while working on the fresco at Dotty's Coptic ruin, or shut in his study at home writing a sermon. Curiously, the present scene did not suggest a sermon; it elicited an emotion that was too intense and private to share. For a fleeting moment it didn't matter whether Jesus had existed or not. Martin had bypassed the entire story of Christianity and arrived at a wonderful truth, a truth that he could feel but could not put into words.

He recalled Nietzsche's view of Nature, which he had once discussed late into the night over coffee and toast with a group of fellow students. At the time they had been in general agreement that Nietzsche was right when he claimed that we enjoy Nature because it has no opinion of us and can pass no judgement on us. Perhaps a tree-lined bank of the Nile in a faint early morning mist was not the sort of Nature Nietzsche had in mind. Obviously, an inanimate geographical location, however beautiful it might be, does not hold an opinion or pass judgement, but this particular scene had sung a silent song about the truth of human existence, which had infected Martin's soul.

He was unaware that Dotty had crept up behind him. She playfully tapped him on the shoulder and announced that breakfast was ready. That deep feeling of onenesss with the universe had been very brief. Now he had lost it, possibly forever.

[He was not to know that several years later, in their old age, Pamela and he would make a tour of the Hebrides, in which they would find themselves on the island of Iona. Once again, he would feel as he had that morning on the bank of the river Nile; that is he would feel as near to heaven as it was possible to get without dying. This may seem like an irrelevant digression, but it confirms that long after the present narrative comes to its close, and long after Martin becomes a pensioner, he and Pamela are still together and enjoying their twilight years by travelling to the more beautiful parts of the British Isles.]

Martin was not startled by Dotty's arrival. No doubt she had expected to make him jump. She was surprised when he failed to respond. Instead he slowly turned to her with a quiet, sympathetic smile and said: "There's no telling how long I might have stayed here communing with the

## CHAPTER 22

Nile, if you hadn't broken into my reverie." "Then I take it you were experiencing a deep feeling of spirituality," replied Dotty. No further words were necessary. Martin knew that she understood. As they walked back to the Nissan, they held hands. It seemed natural and nothing whatsoever to do with sexual attraction.

Meanwhile, Dotty had been busy. She had laid out a bowl of fruit and she had brewed coffee on the camping stove. Bread and fool were also on offer, and all the food was covered against insects by a table cloth and a large saucepan lid.

"Thank you!" exclaimed Martin, "What have I done to deserve this?" "Absolutely nothing," replied Dotty, "And tomorrow it will be your turn to prepare breakfast." His recent awareness of the deeper meaning of human existence quickly faded. He nodded to Dotty and poured two mugs of coffee.

Back in his default, slightly mischievous mood, Martin said: "Well, shall we sit and admire the view, or shall we try to be intellectual and analyse the history of Christianity?"

Giving him an amused glance, Dotty replied that before she went to sleep last night she had suddenly remembered Apollonius of Tyana, who, like Asclepius, was considered by some biblical historians to be a model for Jesus.

Martin looked blank and replied that the name didn't ring the faintest of bells. Dotty replied that she was surprised to find such a gap in his knowledge, so she would attempt a brief resumé of what she knew about Apollonius.

"Tyana," she explained, "was the site of a temple dedicated to Apollonius and located somewhere in south-central Asia Minor. Apollonius was a wandering spiritual alchemist and philosopher-sage of the first century. He had a follower, or disciple called Damis, who accompanied him on his journeys throughout the ancient world."

"Stop there," said Martin, "This man is important, so why haven't I heard about him? "I should have thought," replied Dotty, "that the answer is obvious. The resemblance between Apollonius and Jesus is embarrassing, so the story of Apollonius has been suppressed, which partly explains why you haven't heard of him. Anyway, let's not get involved with Apollonius, except to remind ourselves that he really did exist. You can look him up when you get home. I would rather start the day by asking what would happen if you returned home and announced that Jesus had never existed." Martin encouraged her to continue.

"Well," she replied, "In academic circles you can express outrageous views about anything you wish. In fact, it's a clever way of starting an entertaining discussion. Lost for something to say at a cocktail party, you could suggest that such and such an archbishop of Canterbury was gay. And if that doesn't start an argument, you could question the institution of marriage, suggesting it was first invented by men who used women as currency in trading agreements".

"Don't tell me," interrupted Martin, "You are going to ask what happens *outside* academic circles. You are going to ask what will happen if the media get hold of my claim that Jesus didn't exist; if newspaper headlines announce *Country parson denies Jesus existed*."

"That is exactly what I was thinking," agreed Dotty. "You see," she went on, "we now have clear evidence of how the public reacts to what they consider to be outlandish thinking. More importantly we know how powerful vested interests react to anything that threatens their way of thinking, especially if it also threatens their profits and share prices."

"Surely, questions of religion are different. My views might be dismissed as foolish. No doubt, narrow-minded fanatics would search the dictionary for the nastiest possible adjectives with which to label me. My name might be dragged through the mud in the forums of Facebook and Twitter by commentators intent upon revealing their own psychoses. I could handle that. You know the old

## CHAPTER 22

playground adage: *sticks and stones can break my bones, but words can never hurt me.*"

"Aren't you forgetting something?" retorted Dotty.

Martin raised a questioning eyebrow.

"Doctor Willan thinks three of his students were murdered because they had discovered an arcanum of Christianity."

"That would be truly sticks and stones," mused Martin, "but Doctor Willan cannot be certain; he has a strong suspicon but he might be wrong. Those three students died because they took LSD. Doctor Willan thinks they were given the drug by their murderers. Might they not have actually been using it as a recreational drug? It is difficult to believe that any of those three persons would have been stupid enough to knowingly take LSD, but as a minister of the Church I'm often reminded of how little we sometimes know of our fellow human beings. One of my parishioners, to all appearances a sensible, upstanding, reliable person, concealed a drug habit for six years before we discovered his problem."

"You're forgetting something else," retorted Dotty: "I knew Pinda. He worked for me. He had started to expose the fresco before he died. Alright, I agree, we sometimes don't know our fellow human beings as well as we think. But when two human beings find themselves together in a foreign environment they get to know each other rather well. I believe I got to know Pinda very well indeed, and I can't accept that he was stupid enough to knowingly take LSD."

Martin decided not to point out that he and Dotty were two fellow human beings in a foreign environment, and he simply said: "Well, I suppose we don't know anything about the deaths of Doctor Willan's former students. Tell me, honestly, do you really think I'm in some sort of danger?"

"Of course not," replied Dotty emphatically, "though I wonder whether you might be unfortunate enough to place yourself in danger at some future date."

"And how might I do that?" enquired Martin in a dismissive tone of voice.

"By making yourself a target of fanatics. I'm thinking of religious fanatics, and we both know they exist. Muslims and Hindus have their opposing fanatical wings that are quite fond of killing each other on the Indian subcontinent. I hesitate to try and analyse Israel versus Palestine politics, but fanaticism is part of that problem. And don't delude yourself that Christian fanatics don't exist. We both know they do."

"Dotty, I can't accept that. Surely you don't think I would be in physical danger, even danger of my life, if I announce my belief that Jesus never existed."

"Always bearing in mind that your belief in the non-existence of Jesus must stand the test of further study, and assuming that you finally feel confident enough to speak out about it, then yes, I feel you could be in danger. Not at home in Britain of course, but in certain parts of the Middle East and Africa."

"I'm beginning to see what you mean. For a moment you had me worried. I wouldn't dare to breathe a word of it until I got home. I know it would then cause people to laugh at me, avoid me, even insult me, but I could deal with that."

Dotty shook her head and suggested he might not find it so easy to deal with. She clasped both her hands and gazed into infinity. Martin knew the sign; Dotty was having one of her formative silences, and he knew he should respect it and keep quiet. After about a minute, Dotty spoke and started by apologising for not having said honestly what was on her mind. She continued with: "I still think you would make life intolerable for yourself, and probably also for your family, if you return to England and publicly announce that Jesus never existed. I hope you will allow me to claim that, after living and working with you, even for the short period since your arrival at my camp, I've gained an insight into your character. I'm beginning to know and understand you. And, frankly, I don't think you are cut out to be a country parson."

Martin felt both offended and puzzled by her frank assertion. Before he could reply, Dotty continued: "I'm sure your parishioners and your bishop would disagree. I have the impression that you serve the Church well and when it comes to pastoral care you are possibly better than many country parsons. But I'm not thinking of your parishioners; I'm thinking of you. You have a sharp, analytical mind. Obviously, you find it easy to trot out a clever sermon every Sunday. Preaching a Sunday sermon doesn't require a great intellect, whereas the probing of history by digging in the earth or in libraries, or both requires a scientific, analytical mind. On the other hand, you have a depth of feeling and understanding for your fellow human beings; and that is a necessary quality for a minister of the Church; not all country parsons have it."

Martin was beginning to feel exasperated and countered, probably more loudly that necessary, with: "So what's the problem, for goodness sake?!"

Dotty knew she had rambled on, and she had done so intentionally in order to delay the punch line of her argument. In contrast to the loudness of his outburst, she quietly stated: "You would better serve Christendom by working in a biblical research institute, or by taking part in the archaeology of early Christian civilisations, or both." As Martin made to reply, Dotty stopped him by holding up her right forefinger and frowning. She continued: "I know that's exactly what you are doing now. And don't you feel it's just right for you?"

Martin didn't reply. It was his turn to conduct a formative silence. After sharing several of Dotty's silences, he now felt he had the right to his own. Dotty sensed this and sat quietly with him. He was glad that Dotty had taught him the value of silence, though he wondered whether his level of consciousness during the silence was the same as hers. She always seemed totally relaxed, as if waiting for inspiration, whereas he was busy thinking and trying to solve problems.

It was a long silence, all of four minutes, after which Martin spoke in a rather resigned tone: "You're right. The fact that I'm here, that I wanted to be here, that I wanted to leave my parish and come to the Sudan and help at your archaeological site all prove that you're right. So what am I going to do about it? At the moment, nothing. Later, after I've returned to Britain, I will think about what you have said, but even then I may prefer the life of an Anglican vicar, content to tell my grandchildren about my adventures in the Sudan."

"I find that difficult to believe. The fact that you are here proves you are not satisfied with your existence in an English country village. You had a vision. You felt called to seek the truth of Christian history, and you had the energy and determination to pursue your vision. How could you possibly go back to preaching sermons and be happy?"

Before Martin could reply, Dotty continued: "I see a contrast between the institution of the Church of England, of which you are a village parson, and the entire world of Christendom with all its denominations and historical origins. You would serve the latter by performing academic research into Christian history. On the other hand, as you preach from the pulpit of your village church, you must be aware that church attendances are declining and if they continue to decline the day will come when you and your bishop will be out of a job."

Martin drew breath to reply, but was once more beaten to the draw by Dotty: "I read that the archbishop of Canterbury recently tried to explain the fall in church attendances by claiming that too many people were going in for do-it-yourself spirituality."

## CHAPTER 22

At last, Martin managed to speak: "You heard correctly. That is exactly what he said. But he was wrong because I and the rest of the world know that church attendances are falling through lack of interest in religious faith and the fact that ignoring the Church is no longer looked upon as socially reprehensible."

"Nevertheless," said Dotty, "he had a point when he accused do-it-yourself spirituality. If someone prefers to get up late or play football on Sundays, the Church can delude itself that they may one day return to the fold. But if someone discovers a different source of spirituality, a do-it-yourself kind of spirituality not associated with Church or Chapel, that is serious competition." After a fleeting pause for breath, Dotty added: "And I applaud it!"

Martin waited, but to his surprise Dotty didn't want to continue, so he remarked: "In other words, my Church is doomed to extinction."

"Without a doubt," replied Dotty, "All institutions, religious and otherwise, are doomed. Your Church surely has a few hundred years left before the pretence of the creed – preserved by the conservatism and fear of change on the part of the Church hierarchy – collapses."

"I say, that's going a bit far," exclaimed a worried Martin, "And what do you think will cause the ultimate collapse?"

Dotty was quick to reply: "Whatever the cause, it will be greatly helped by modern religious education. By comparing different faiths, schoolchildren will realise there is no absolute religious truth, and that the beliefs recited in creeds are impossibilities. After all, it was an innocent child who had the temerity to point out that the emperor's new clothes did not exist, and the emperor was not wearing a stitch."

Without a doubt, Dotty had shown considerable insight into Martin's character and motivations, but there were other factors in the equation that she had ignored or for which she had no appreciation. For instance, he had a wife, a very dear wife, who, in a display of love and loyalty, had accepted his need for a sabbatical and agreed to his travel plans, although she secretly hated the idea. Also, Dotty had no right to disparage his valuable role in the English village community. Admittedly, she was right when she claimed that the preaching of a Sunday sermon doesn't require a great intellect, whereas the probing of history by digging in the earth or in libraries, or both requires a scientific, analytical mind. But Dotty didn't know that Martin was firmly rooted in his role of country vicar. Far from being dissatisfied with his existence in a country village, he relied on it for the stability it gave to his existence. It was his base, which he shared with Pamela, and from which he had been able to sally forth for a few months of adventure and to probe an arcanum of Christianity. True, he might one day consider biblical research and archaeology as an alternative, even a refreshing change from chanting the creed; but far from home in the Sudanese desert his outlook was constantly stabilised by his vision of Pamela, home, and church, in that order.

Martin left these thoughts unspoken and looked enquiringly at Dotty, as if inviting her to further justify her vision of his future. All his thoughts were transmitted in that enquiring look, causing her to lower her gaze in embarrassment, utter an apologetic sigh and say: "Please forgive me Martin. I have no right to talk to you in this way. I must admit that I was trying to recruit you to my world of biblical and archaeological research. We need minds like yours. If you ever decide to leave the Church for a life of research, let me know. I will say no more."

With a serious expression, Martin answered: "Thank you for telling me the truth about myself. Then, unable to suppress a smile, he added; "And I'm grateful that you will say no more."

## CHAPTER 22

"On second thoughts, however," said Dotty "I would just like to say a little more; I would like to recite a poem; it's an Arabic poem and I hope it will give you the courage to face failure and disappointment."

"And why might I need such courage?" asked Martin, feeling rather mystified.

"Well, let's imagine your efforts to discover the true nature of Jesus are a complete failure. Far from facing the controversy you would cause by denying the historicity of Jesus, you would have nothing to say on the subject at all. In other words, your sabbatical had been a failure."

"And a waste of time," added Martin with a note of cynicism.

"Definitely not," replied Dotty, "That is the point of this poem."

"Okay, let's hear it then," said Martin, rather irritably, since he hoped they had already closed the subject of his desert life versus his Church life.

"I'm afraid I can't remember it all. It was written by an orthodox imam and I can't even remember his name. I'm sure it sounds far more beautiful and convincing in the original Arabic."

Martin was beginning to feel impatient. Perhaps he was rather more out of sorts from their recent conversation than he realised. "Okay, okay, I understand. Just give me the verses you remember."

"Dotty winced at the obvious irritation in his voice and began to wish she hadn't mentioned the poem. But there was no going back, so she started:

"*No water that stagnates is fit to drink/For only that which flows is truly sweet/No arrow unleashed could earn a score/A sun that hung immobile in the sky/Would soon become a universal bore/Things that are stationary have little worth/They only gain their value on the road.*"

She explained that the poem was basically about the value and importance of travel, that she had left out some verses, and that she had the complete poem back at her camp.

Martin's mood had already changed. He knew what she was trying to tell him, incomplete though the poem was. The poem told him he had done the right thing by pursuing his interest in early Christian history, by leaving home and travelling, even if nothing came of it. It was yet another way of expressing the old saw *Nothing ventured, nothing gained.* Since they were by the Nile, it was fitting that the poem had been written by an orthodox imam. Tennyson's *'Tis better to have loved and lost/Than never to have loved at all* also came to mind.

Martin felt humbled and ashamed of his impatience with Dotty and he thanked her for the poem, continuing: "That gave me food for thought. I'd be grateful for the complete poem when we get back to camp."

Dotty also felt humbled, though she wasn't sure why, so she acknowledged the importance of the Church in his life by suggesting the poem would make a basis for a sermon. Martin sensed what she meant and suggested they should do the washing up.

They had an ample supply of fresh water, but decided, nevertheless, to wash the breakfast crockery in the Nile. Stubborn pieces of dried fool and the hard lumps of congealed aubergine from last night's meal were no match for the abrasive power of wet desert sand.

Both Dotty and Martin had plenty to think about. Dotty was coming to terms with the fact that Martin was his own man, intellectually a kindred spirit, which she enjoyed immensely, but on loan from his wife and his English country church. She constantly interrogated herself as to her true motives for working far from home, sometimes without the company of any European. The answer was always the

## CHAPTER 22

same: she was consumed by a passionate, genuine interest in archaeology and its role in uncovering Christian history. On the other hand, had this passionate academic interest become a dangerous addiction? If so, how could she find a cure and get it out of her system? She could see that Martin was interested in desert archaeology and enthusiastic about helping her, but he wasn't addicted. His life was balanced in a way that hers wasn't. He would return to his wife and church, possibly rather soon, having benefitted immensely from his visit to her archaeological site, and glad to be home.

Martin was trying in vain to recapture the deep sense of spirituality he had experienced that morning on the bank of the Nile. Although it was now out of reach, the experience had left echoes in his conscience, which were becoming fainter and fainter. He knew that for a brief moment his search for the true nature of Jesus had seemed irrelevant.

They packed everything into the back of the Nissan, and it was agreed that Martin should take first turn at the wheel. To their right and left the land was flat, brown and featureless with not even the shrine of a holy man to relieve the monotony.

"It won't be long before we cross the river," said Dotty, "Gwaria told me the bridge takes the railway, as well as a road for vehicular traffic, and a walkway for pedestrians."

"What on earth are you talking about," asked Martin, "Surely we don't have to cross the Nile again!" "How many times have you looked at the map of the Nile valley?" said Dotty, "I have that display poster in my tent, which you must have looked at many times. It clearly shows the Atbara River joining the Nile just north of Meroe. We have to cross the Atbara, in order to continue to Meroe."

"I don't know what to say," said Martin. "It had completely escaped me. Too many other distractions, perhaps." "Never mind," consoled Dotty. "You can't expect to assimilate the entire geography of the Sudan in such a short time.

How long is it now? You've been here hardly a fortnight." Her tone of voice implied that a fortnight was quite long enough for him to realise that the Nile was joined by the Atbara just north of Meroe.

After a further four miles, the Nile was no longer fringed by date palms and the landscape became surprisingly green with large areas of cultivation made possible by irrigation from the Nile. Massive, slowly rotating water-sprinkling devices stood in the centre of each large, double football-pitch-sized neat green rectangle. "I wonder if there is anywhere else in the world where the contrast between the ancient and the modern is so starkly displayed," remarked Martin. "I think I know what you mean," answered Dotty, "but what exactly made you say that?"

Martin looked away briefly from the road and turned partly in the driving seat to scan the view. "I guess there must be at least twenty of those irrigated rectangles of land. Whatever the farmer is growing, he's not only using modern technology, he's using it on an industrial scale. Clearly, it's not for his own kitchen. A crop of that size is part of a commercial enterprise. In contrast, when I visit Yasser, Mohammed and Gwiria and sit drinking tea outside the house I often see one of their neighbours in a dirty galabiya, chopping away with a primitive hoe at his little irregular-shaped plot, where, amongst other things, he grows a few onions and waters them by fetching buckets of water from the Nile." "I know exactly what you mean," replied Dotty, "but I think you are wrong to take the methods of Yasser's neighbour as an example of primitive agriculture. Be honest, now, Yasser's neighbour is growing food for his kitchen in the same way that a British allotment holder would cultivate his patch. You should compare what we have just seen with the small-scale commercial agriculture that occurs all along the Nile, where water is drawn from the river with an Archimedean screw, or a shaduf, or a water wheel which is

## CHAPTER 22

rotated by the water current and carries water to a channel on the river bank. Those methods are still used although they have been largely superseded by modern water pumps with petrol engines. The water is then fed into irrigation channels from which it is guided manually around beds of crops by alternately blocking and unblocking the water flow. That is very different from what we are looking at now, which involves the wasteful pumping of enormous quantities of water directly from the Nile into rotating irrigation sprinklers."

Momentarily taking his hands from the steering wheel and gesturing once more towards the irrigation plots, Martin asked: "What is that farmer cultivating with his wasteful rotating irrigation system?"

"Mustapha told me that large quantities of alfalfa are grown along this stretch of the Nile. It's used to feed cattle, so the final commercial product is milk. Moreover, the cattle are European high-milk-producing breeds, housed in specially air-conditioned sheds."

Martin remained silent. Eventually, Dotty asked: "Well?" "Well what?" said Martin. "What about modern Sudanese agricultural methods, alfalfa, cows, and milk?" "I believe it all, and I find it truly amazing," replied Martin, "And I would like to photograph one of those sprinkling irrigation systems and send the picture home for the church magazine." "No time like the present," said Dotty, "Let's pull in here and take a few photographs." Martin would have liked to get nearer to the irrigation sprinklers for a close-up photograph of their mechanism. He had to be content with a more or less panoramic view of the scene with the alfalfa fields in the foreground.

As they pulled away again, Dotty remarked: "That was a good idea. We might be travelling back later in the day when the light is poor; then you wouldn't get your pictures." "Or," said Martin, "we might be like the three wise men and come back a different way." "Which brings us back to Jesus!" said Dotty. "Come to think of it," she continued, "Why did they go back a different way? What I really mean, is what do you tell your parishioners at Christmas, or what do you tell your confirmation classes?" Martin explained that there were two perfectly acceptable reasons and that from the pulpit he offered both. First, they went back a different way to avoid meeting Herod, who would have wanted to know where Jesus was. Alternatively, those three wise men were so overcome by the glory they had witnessed that they took a different path in life. From the pulpit I leave the congregation to innocently marvel at the fact that the event can have two very reasonable explanations, both of which are decidedly Christian. I hope that at least some members will later pause and wonder how much more of the New Testament might be metaphorical. As for my confirmation classes, I invite them to discuss the relative merits of the two explanations then I let them waffle on and argue until it's time for them to go home.

"Let me expand on that second explanation," said Dotty. "By all means! I feel I'm about to learn something," replied Martin.

"The newly born Jesus is a metaphor for the new faith of Christianity. It, like a new-born child, is pure, innocent and untainted. The three wise men, or, if you like the three kings, represent the known world. Today we talk of the four corners of the world. In those days there were only three corners to the world, if you see what I mean." She continued: "The three kings are therefore representatives of the entire known world. They witness a beautiful truth, which will thereafter spread to all three corners of the world."

Martin nodded expressively, as if to indicate that he both understood and agreed. "My dear Dotty. Thank you! Why did it never occur to me that my metaphorical interpretation of the nativity was incomplete? You have reached the very

## CHAPTER 22

heart of the question of Jesus' existence. Even his birth is a metaphor and since it is a virgin birth it is a metaphor for purity, the purity of the Christian faith. Your complete metaphor is one of pure beauty and being so beautiful, it must be true."

"Whoa there!" cried Dotty, "We both know that Keats said: *Beauty is truth, truth beauty,* but we can't apply that statement like a law of science. "That is all ye know on earth, and all ye need to know," said Martin. "I beg your pardon," said Dotty. "I was merely finishing the quotation," replied Martin. "Oh yes, of course, but I still say you must proceed with caution if you intend to use that metaphor as evidence for the non-existence of Jesus. It brings out very starkly one of the major problems of Bible interpretation. So much can be beautifully and convincingly explained as metaphor, but no-one in the Church dare take that final step and say out loud that everything is metaphor." At that point in the conversation they agreed to put Jesus on hold and concentrate on their journey to Meroe.

Eventually either the Nile or the road, or both, changed direction slightly so that they found themselves driving almost within touching distance of a grove of date palms, through which they could see bursts of reflected sunlight from the waters of the Nile. Martin suggested that as long as the road continued parallel to the river they should keep going. But as soon as it showed signs of veering off into the desert they would stop for morning coffee. The road didn't veer off into the desert, at least not before the grove of date palms petered out, allowing a full view of the Nile. "This will do," exclaimed Martin, as he brought the Nissan to a halt and reversed about ten yards to be once more behind the date palms.

Since yesterday, after leaving the turning to Port Sudan, they had passed a fair amount of traffic going in the opposite direction and they had quite often been overtaken by lorries presumably on their way to Khartoum. Now, as they drank their coffee, two heavy vehicles passed by, heading north. "They load their lorries like they load their donkeys," remarked Martin, "As high and as wide as possible. One sharp bend in the road and their top-heavy loads would finish up in the Nile." Dotty pointed out that, fortunately, there were no sharp bends in the road, but she knew that lorries did sometimes shed their loads between Khartoum and the fourth cataract. Martin was surprised that it was only sometimes. "One slight shift in one of those over-weight, overhanging, top-heavy loads and you're looking at the terrestrial equivalent of a shipwreck." "Well, as I said," continued Dotty, "It sometimes happens. Almost certainly those lorries were carrying supplies for the workers at the dam plus groceries and a few other items ordered by Mustapha. I used to think it an enormous stroke of luck that Mustapha had a friend driving lorries between the dam and Khartoum, thereby establishing a supply route for my camp, but I soon learned that it would have been most unusual if he hadn't known or had some connection with all of the Sudanese workers at the dam. There's a kind of free-masonry amongst all the Sudanese, which excludes us visiting Europeans and the Chinese at the dam. Remember meeting Grandfather Ahmed yesterday? Through the Sudanese grapevine he already knew who we were, and he probably knew a great deal about us that he didn't reveal. On the subject of those two lorries again, I'll wager that when we return to the camp in three days' time Mustapha will have a feast of welcome prepared for us, made possible by the fresh supplies in those lorries." "How much?" enquired Martin. "What do you mean?" asked Dotty. "How much do you wager?" Dotty didn't reply and made a dismissive gesture with her coffee mug. Earlier in the day, there had been a certain tension between them. Both were now relaxed in the other's presence. Their normal, easy

# CHAPTER 22

relationship was restored. Assuming that is, that the relationship of Dotty and Martin was, is, or ever will be easy and normal.

Dotty breathed a contented sigh. Martin gave her an enquiring look. She responded with: "I didn't realise I would enjoy this break from the camp so much. You can hardly describe my existence as a dull routine, but it's definitely rather narrow. There's no-one to phone me unexpectedly and say *Hi, so and so are coming for a meal tomorrow – would you like to join us?* Or *I've got a spare ticket for La Bohéme – can I tempt you?* You must know what I mean. I'm not necessarily yearning for an invitation to a meal or to the opera. I can immerse myself in studying the ground plan of my Coptic church, or getting my notes on Christian history in some sort of order, and that sort of work is so engaging it may take me into the early hours, but I often go to bed feeling something was missing from the day. Your presence in the camp has gone some way to dispelling this feeling of .... I don't know what to call it." "Would you call it a feeling of isolation? offered Martin. "Almost but not quite," replied Dotty. "I think I know what you mean," said Martin, "Perhaps there isn't a word that covers perfectly what you're feeling."

"Perhaps there isn't," replied Dotty, inflecting her voice to indicate a change of mood to one of briskness. "That was a welcomed break, but now we must get on and drive to Meroe. I claim the right to take the wheel for the last stage of our expedition. Did you know that in 322 BC Alexander the Great tried to invade Meroe but he was driven back by a Meroitic army. Let's hope our invasion will be more successful."

"I'm sure it will be," mused Martin. "I'm trying to visualise Alexander leading his army down the Nile valley. I have a mental picture of the Greeks rampaging around the Middle East further north, but it seems counterintuitive to imagine a Greek army plodding all the way down here." Dotty laughed and added that it was almost as difficult to imagine the Romans plodding all the way down here, but centuries later that is exactly what they did, and in any case how did we know that they plodded? Perhaps they sailed part of the way, upstream on the Nile." "And then," added Martin, "they plodded or sailed all the way back again." Dotty contributed: "Whether they plodded, marched or sailed, the incursions of Greeks and Romans into the Sudanese desert just isn't part of conventional history teaching at school, and since our early teaching makes a lasting impression, later additions to that knowledge tend to surprise us."

"I suppose," ventured Martin, "that Alexander's march to Meroe is supported by fragments of Greek writing." "In this case, rather large fragments," replied Dotty, "There's plenty of Greek writing and many inscriptions on monuments to confirm that Alexander the Great met his match in Meroe. And don't forget that historians have not yet learned to read the Meroitic script. Perhaps one day we'll be able to read the story of how the Greeks were driven back inscribed on the walls of the monuments at Meroe." After a brief pause, Dotty added: "Correction! Let's be clear about the Meroitic script. Due mainly to the studies of British scholars, the script has been deciphered, but not the language. We know the sound associated with each hieroglyph but we still can't understand the language. We don't know the meaning of the words and the grammatical structure of the language is obscure."

Martin pondered what Dotty had just said then thoughtfully remarked that he found it difficult to imagine how anyone could have worked out the sound of each hieroglyph without some knowledge of the language. Dotty promised to explain later, so Martin continued: "This conversation started by me saying I couldn't visualise a Greek army coming all this way. If only they had photography in those

## CHAPTER 22

days. One simple photograph is all the evidence a historian would need." Dotty nodded her agreement then suggested that future historians would have no problem discovering that she and Martin had come all this way because Martin would have left a splendid photographic record of their journey. "What's more," said Martin, "our entire journey will be recorded in my church magazine. Which reminds me: my wife and stand-in curate are waiting for pictures for the next edition. I must take some pictures here and now."

"Alright," replied Dotty mischievously, "How would you like me: leaning provocatively against the Nissan, showing a bit of leg?"

"For goodness sake," laughed Martin, "they couldn't print that in the church magazine." He knew she was joking, of course, but he couldn't help wondering how Pamela would react if he were to send her a picture of Dotty showing a bit of leg.

Martin took the camera from his rucksack then walked away from the Nissan until he had a view of the vehicle surrounded by palm trees with flashes of reflected sunlight from the Nile in the background. Only one problem remained: Dotty was indeed leaning against the Nissan, admittedly not very provocatively and certainly not showing a bit of leg, but he preferred her not to be there at all. Suddenly she noticed that one of the water containers was dripping and she disappearing behind the Nissan to tighten the tap. Martin took the picture then a second one before she emerged once again into full view. Dotty straightened up and shouted across to him that his parishioners would surely want to see their vicar on his safari to Meroe, so he should come and stand by the Nissan while she photographed him with the Nile in the background. He let himself be photographed then gallantly suggested he photograph her with the Nile in the background. "That would be nice," she said, then added: "I don't suppose your parishioners will want to see me in the church magazine." Beginning to feel very gallant indeed, he replied that they would surely want to see a picture of his travelling companion, Doctor Dorothy Scott, the internationally acclaimed specialist in Christian history. "Martin," she said, rather sharply, "do you think your dear wife might feel uncomfortable if she realises I'm not a severe, wizened old academic, especially when she knows we are alone, just the two of us on our journey to Meroe. I'd be grateful if you didn't send her photographs of me. I know practically nothing of your marriage, but I *am* a woman and I know how *I* would react if I had a husband who had left me at home and was cavorting thousands of miles away with a desirable unmarried woman."

She needn't have said any of it, but Martin experienced an overwhelming sense of relief. She had told him what she wanted him to do, or rather not to do, and it helped to straighten out his tangled thoughts, at least for the time being.

"Perhaps you're right," replied Martin, pleased that Dotty had fellow feelings for Dorothy, whom she had never met. He felt sorely tempted to make a joke out of Dotty's choice of words, but decided against it. He would probably put his foot in it, especially since many a true word is spoken in jest and Dotty was indeed a desirable unmarried woman. So he changed the subject with: "It seems rather a long time ago that you announced that we were about to invade Meroe. We'd better get started."

"Just one moment," said Dotty. "Earlier today we mentioned the virgin birth. For one reason or another, this impossible event keeps cropping up in our conversations, and we carry on without paying it further attention. We know it's a metaphor and there's no reason to go on about it. It's worth remembering, however, that the question of Mary's virginity was the subject of passionate debate in the early Church. The fact that the Church had to decide what the

CHAPTER 22

faithful should believe surely reveals that no-one knew any historical facts about the virgin birth of Jesus, which in turn supports the claim that Jesus was not who he was made out to be."

"I think you have in mind names like Helvidius and the so-called Infancy Gospel of James. Is there any point in going over all this? I know the bit of Church history you're referring to."

"Nevertheless, let me briefly go over it. You never know; I might have come across some facts you don't know about."

"I will sit here and listen. Please carry on."

Dotty settled herself in the driving seat, switched on her serious lecturing face and said:

"Helvidius, writing some time before 383 AD, said that Mary could not have been a virgin, claiming that the mention of Jesus' brothers and sisters meant that Mary and Joseph had had sex. You can imagine the anger and indignation caused by this affront to the party line. Saint Jerome, who died in 420 AD, vigorously denied Helvidius' claim in a treatise known as *the perpetual virginity of Mary*, arguing that Jesus' brothers – James, Joseph, Judas, and Simon, as well as unnamed sisters – were either children of Joseph by a former marriage, or first cousins. Before Helvidius and Saint Jerome came on the scene, the Gospel of James, written between 140 and 170 AD, had already taken Christian teaching from the sublime to the ridiculous by claiming that Mary was still a virgin after the birth of Jesus; what's more, she underwent a medical examination to prove it. Not content with Mary's perpetual virginity, she also had to be conceived without sin. In other words, Mary's mother, Anna, was also a virgin or a sort of virgin. This was the Immaculate Conception. Admittedly, Anna's virginity is not as clear-cut as Mary's. The Immaculate Conception can be interpreted as the intervention of God in Anna's conceiving of Mary. If you like, she was not necessarily a virgin, but God blessed her pregnancy.

In short, the virgin birth has been a problem ever since the idea was cooked up. Those early writers of Bible stories didn't realise what trouble and confusion they were storing up for future generations of thinking Christians. Of course, the Church had the answer. It decided that Mary was a perpetual virgin and that was what everyone had to believe; it was everyone's duty to have faith!

Perhaps it's not a powerful argument, but I feel this desperation to explain the virgin birth throws doubt on the existence of Jesus in the first place."

Dotty looked at Martin, expecting a reaction. He was asleep. She woke him up by switching on the ignition and gunning the engine. Before she drove off, Dotty asked Martin if he could hear the distant sound of traffic. He could. Dotty explained that it must be the lorries on the road from Port Sudan on their way to Khartoum. The road from Port Sudan would soon join their present road before crossing the bridge over the Atbara River. After about twenty minutes they found themselves joined and dwarfed by numerous heavy lorries, running parallel to the railway track, and heading towards the bridge.

Despite the volume of traffic, they crossed the bridge without decreasing speed, and found themselves on a wide, surfaced road, almost up to European motorway standard. Mud brick houses now began to appear, many only half finished, but seemingly occupied, since children were running around and smoke was coming from behind some walls, presumably from cooking fires.

Suddenly the scene changed. As the road bent to the left around a small hill, they found themselves looking down upon a flat expanse of land with what looked like a village or small town, separated from the Nile by a green agricultural area. Further away in the desert beyond the small town, the landscape bristling with sharp little pyramids.

## CHAPTER 22

Dotty drove off the road and stopped and was about to speak when Martin beat her to it with: "And those pyramids over there must be the pyramids of Meroe. I expect the Japanese will have got there first. So much for our invasion of Meroe!" "I'm sure you're right," replied Dotty, who added: "No doubt they're all scurrying around in blue suits and the air is alive with the clicking of cameras."

Dotty suggested they drive to the pyramids. It was still quite early in the day, so they would have plenty of time to explore the ancient site and the sun would be high enough for good photography. Martin countered by pointing out that the pyramids might look splendid in the light of the setting sun. "That is surely true," agreed Dotty, who then added in a doubtful tone that if they were still amongst the pyramids when the sun was setting, they would then be looking for somewhere to camp for the night *after* the sun had finished setting, in other words, in the moonlight. It was time for a formative silence, which, after about two minutes, was broken by Dotty saying: "Let's drive straight there now and leave in good time to find a place to camp. If the pyramids look splendid in the light of the setting sun, surely they will be equally splendid in the light of the run-rise, so we will break camp early and visit the pyramids again while the sun is rising."

There was common sense and there was common sense. Then there was female common sense and it took some beating. Martin wondered why he hadn't thought of it himself. It was the kind of answer to the problem that his mother or Pamela would have provided. "Agreed!" exclaimed Martin, who suggested he take over the driving. As he changed places with Dotty, he suddenly realised he could no longer see the railway line, which must be somewhere in the vicinity. Where was it? Dotty explained that the railway had always been fairly close during their drive, always to their left, but far enough away to be out of sight in the folds of the landscape. If a train had used the line during their journey, they would have seen it in the distance, but that hadn't happened. It was now even further away, beyond the pyramids of Meroe, but still heading south to Khartoum.

Dotty reminded Martin that this was her first visit to Meroe. She knew more than he did about the lie of the land and the history of Meroe because she had read much about Meroe and had been in the Sudan long enough to hear about the area from local people. "So?" asked Martin. "So I think we may have to drive all the way to Kabushiya, which is nearly four miles from here, then back again on a different road to the pyramids. It would be very useful to find a short cut, so let's keep our eyes skinned for turnings to the left."

It was now time for a touch of male common sense, or was it recklessness? "Better still," said Martin, "let's drive through that cultivated area. There seem to be tracks between the irrigated plots. That will bring us to the houses. Surely we can find our way between the buildings and out into the wasteland on the far side. A short drive across the wasteland and we'll arrive at the pyramids."

"Seems a bit risky," mused Dotty, "I suppose our Nissan can go where a tractor goes between those irrigated plots. Let's hope so. Then I hope we won't offend any residents by driving amongst their houses. The alleyways are almost bound to be very narrow and don't forget children will be playing there."

"In other words, you agree, but you want me to be careful." Dotty nodded her agreement.

Steering the Nissan between the cultivated plots of okra was easy. Negotiating the alleyways of the settlement was also relatively easy, but embarrassing, because the road was frequently blocked by groups of chattering women, who gave Dotty and Martin dark, disapproving looks as they reluctantly moved aside. By the time they reached the opposite side of the settlement they had acquired a retinue of

## CHAPTER 22

cheering children, who had no difficulty keeping up with the Nissan because Martin had to drive almost at walking pace in the narrow alleyways. The last group of women to have their conversation disturbed moved aside quite willingly and they waved Dotty and Martin on their way into the wasteland between the village and the pyramids with happy smiles. "Were they glad to see us or glad to see the back of us?" asked Martin, "And just look over there!" Martin indicated a well-worn track from the settlement, which obviously crossed the wasteland and led to the pyramids of Meroe, which were about two miles away, possibly less. Martin's plan had proved more successful than he could have imagined. But had he committed a trespass by driving through the cultivated area? He thought he probably had (actually, he hadn't) so like the three wise men, he decided he would later return home by a different way.

As they approached the ancient site of Meroe, Dotty and Martin became atypically silent, stunned into wordlessness by the wonder that was spread out before them. "Just imagine how the first Europeans to arrive in Meroe must have felt when they came upon this scene," said Martin in a subdued and reverential tone. Dotty agreed but added: "It's impressive and astonishing, and it sets one's mind racing, grasping at the known history of the Nile valley, trying to place Meroe in context and trying to imagine a thriving culture, predating Christianity, and unknown to Europe until much later. But once you've got over these first thoughts and impressions it's worth remembering that the first Europeans to arrive here were ancient Greeks and Romans, intent upon conquest and with varying degrees of success. And don't forget that this site in front of you is just one of many wonders of the ancient world." Martin did not reply immediately. The road was fairly straight but it was only a worn track in a stony wasteland, so he had to pay attention to his driving, while taking in the picture of an ancient world that was growing ever larger in front of him. Finally, he replied: "You're absolutely right, of course, but didn't I read somewhere that parts of Meroe are still being excavated? There's probably still much to be learned about its history. And as you mentioned earlier, we're still struggling to read the Meroe script. Who knows what the inscriptions on the pyramids will tell us?"

Dotty nodded in agreement then asked Martin: "Do you realise we have come full cycle?" "Coming full cycle means arriving back where we started, and we didn't start from here." "Oh yes we did," replied Dotty in a playful tone of voice. "Okay, I give in," said Martin. "Don't you remember chapter eight of *Acts* and the eunuch of great authority under Candace queen of the Ethiopians?" taunted Dotty. The road had now become heavily rutted and Martin was too busy attending to his driving to give Dotty's question his full attention. He didn't reply immediately, so Dotty stepped in with: "What you see before you was the home of Candace and her faithful eunuch, who, if *Acts* is correct, returned here having been baptised a Christian. Martin replied that he did indeed remember reading that part of *Acts* in Dotty's Bible. He also remembered, but did not mention it, that Dotty's Bible was very old and tattered, and he had felt irritated by the archaic English of the text. Other memories of that time vied for priority. It had been only his second day at Dotty's camp. He was still feeling his way in his relationship with this enigmatic, attractive woman, who ruled a camp in the remote Sudanese desert, and who commanded respect amongst European academics as a specialist in Christian history. It wasn't all that long ago, but it seemed like an eternity, during which he had been thoroughly educated in the history of the Nile valley and the early history of Christianity, not forgetting his own outstanding success in revealing the Coptic fresco of the nativity at Dotty's excavation site. Yet all this retreated into the background of his mind when he

## CHAPTER 22

remembered that shortly after he had read chapter eight of *Acts*, she had told him to call her Dotty. For Martin, the decision to drop Doctor Scott and Reverend Kimpton and address one another with their first names had marked a significant transition in their relationship, to which Martin was still not fully acclimatised.

They were approaching a wire fence that marked the boundary of the ancient site. Martin's memories of his early days at Dotty's camp had to be put on hold, as he was faced with a ridiculous situation: a well-worn track coming to a sudden end at a fence with no gate. It could have been a metaphor for the reality of human existence, and an excellent subject for a surrealistic painting. They sat in amused silence, looked at one another, smiled, and were on the point of laughing out loud, when Dotty spotted a gap in the fence about twenty yards to their right. The fence was obviously new, only recently installed, and the entry point for the road had been made in the wrong place. Had someone misread the plans, or was it intended that, from now on, the road should enter the site at a different point? They would never know. Martin swung the steering wheel to the right and drove through the gap in the fence. He then brought the Nissan to a halt because he felt it necessary to show respect by pausing and contemplating the pyramids of the ancient civilisation that were scattered over a wide area before him. According to the guide books there were more than two hundred pyramids; some ruined and crumbling, others, which judging from their appearance had withstood rather well more than two thousand years of exposure in the desert; and yet others that had obviously been restored because they looked as if they had been built only yesterday.

"What is it about pyramids?" mused Martin. Dotty threw him a questioning look. "Not only the Egyptians and the Nubians, but pre-Columbian, Central American civilisations built them; and there are pyramids in parts of southeast

Asia. We know that pyramids in Central America were focal points for religious practices." continued Martin, "I've seen pictures of Teotihuacan in the valley of Mexico and I must say this view of the Meroitic pyramids reminds me of Teotihuacan, although the Meroitic pyramids are steeper and more pointed." "Really Martin! This is hardly the time and place to start digressing about Teo ... whatever it was, especially since you've never been there. Personally, I don't see any particular significance in the use of pyramids by widely separated and different civilisations," replied Dotty: "I don't believe that the pyramidal shape is hard-wired into the human psyche as a mystical power, akin to a weekend retreat for the gods, as some mystics would have us believe. It's just a very appealing and useful shape. What's more, it's a stable shape. If you want to create a high point for sacrifices, or a solid structure containing tunnels and burial chambers, then a pyramid is the answer because it won't fall down." Dotty's explanation made sense and, in any case, Martin didn't feel like arguing.

"I've got it all worked out," said Dotty in a purposeful tone of voice. Expecting a lecture on the human psychology of pyramids, Martin replied that they ought to drive on and get settled somewhere before discussing pyramids. "Of course we should," replied Dotty, "I was about to say that we must now find a camp site for the night. Beyond the pyramids and somewhat to the left the terrain is slightly undulating and obviously dry. We still have plenty of water so we don't need to be near the Nile. We can wander around this area for an hour then you can get your photographs when the pyramids are bathed in the light of the setting sun. Before it gets completely dark we'll have time to set up camp where I suggested. In the morning you can photograph the pyramids during the sunrise. Then we will still have time to inspect the site more closely before heading for home." Martin agreed; he could do little else.

## CHAPTER 22

Before they went any further, Martin took out his camera and photographed the scene in front of them. It would not be the best picture he would take of the pyramids of Meroe but it would be a picture of his first ever view of the ancient site. He then walked back some distance and photographed the desert road ending abruptly at the wire fence. Both pictures he would send to Pamela. Already he had in his mind the outline of a sermon based on life's road seemingly coming to an end, only to find, with a bit of lateral thinking (he liked that bit!) that a few yards along the fence there was a way through if one only looked for it. They drove further into the site and parked the Nissan between the two nearest pyramids.

In the distance, over to their right, a group of visitors had apparently finished their conducted tour and were now heading for the tour bus to be taken back, presumably to Kabushiya. Dotty and Martin would soon have the pyramids entirely to themselves. As an eerie silence descended on the site, Martin allowed his imagination to run riot. Ghosts of ancient Nubians began to emerge from the pyramids; glistening black bodies in pure white loin cloths, performing acts of obeisance before a woman in a resplendent golden robe. Exactly what had been the status of Candace in Meroitic society? What had been her position in the hierarchy of government? She had a treasurer, so she must have been wealthy, or possibly not; perhaps she exercised stewardship over Meroe's wealth? Either way, she must have been powerful or extremely influential to have sent her own treasurer to the Bible lands, where he left an account of his visit to be recorded in *Acts*.

Dotty broke into his thoughts with: "I never thought I would feel this way when I first saw Meroe. No doubt I would feel differently if I were with a group of chattering foreign tourists during the day. But all alone in the fading light of evening I'm in danger of losing control of my imagination."

"My own imagination is already out of control," replied Martin, "I think a session of serious photography will bring me down to earth again. The sun is now very low in the west, giving the west-facing faces of the pyramids a beautiful variation of colours from rose-red to salmon pink. And just look at those sharp, black, triangular shadows!"

Twenty minutes later, Martin had captured several impressively artistic (he hoped) pictures of the pyramids in the light of the setting sun. While the light was still suitable, Dotty took a picture of Martin leaning against the bonnet of the Nissan with a series of pyramids in the near background, glowing orange on their west-facing sides and sharply shadowed on their opposite sides by the light of the sun. He would send it that evening to Pamela for the church magazine. Did the picture convey a mystical atmosphere? Were the ghosts of ancient Meroe lurking in the shadows? Possibly. Photographs sometimes display an amazing faculty for expressing feelings and emotions. Martin remembered a photograph of a London street shrouded in mist and dimly lit with yellow gaslight. He could no longer recall where or when he had seen it, but he well remembered the sense of mystery conveyed by that picture. Probably the photographer was a real artist and a professional, and the sense of mystery had been intended and well planned. Suddenly he remembered his feelings on the bank of the Nile on the morning before yesterday, as he peered at the mist-shrouded waters of the river in the early morning. Of course! It was the mist that did it. Swirling mist did marvels for one's sense of mystery. Alas, there was no mist at Meroe.

As it does in the tropics, daylight was fading rapidly. Between Cancer and Capricorn, in forested regions, grasslands and deserts, the sunset is a gloriously layered palette of yellow, orange, and purple: a sight to be shared with God, but short-lived. To Dotty and Martin this captivating display of colour was nothing new. Dotty and Martin saw it every

## CHAPTER 22

evening at Dotty's camp. It was always worth watching, as a thin, dark line of cloud with a magenta underbelly marked the point at which the sun dropped suddenly below the horizon. Familiarity with real beauty does not breed contempt. Here, at Meroe, however, the final demise of the sun bred a certain anxiety. Had they left it too late to find a camp site? But they hadn't reckoned with the moon, which took over from the sun like the changing of the guard. It was not yet high in the night sky, but it provided enough light to see by and to find their way beyond the pyramids to a patch of wasteland where they could park the Nissan and set up camp.

While Dotty lit the camping stove, put the kettle on, and chose tins of meat and vegetables, Martin switched on his laptop, intending to send a report and the latest photographs to Pamela. A lengthy e-mail from Pamela was waiting for him:

*Dear Martin, why no word from you? The last I heard, you were planning to trek to Meroe. Are you there yet, or did you get lost in the desert? Did you act on my suggestion and make the journey on camels? I'm worried that something has happened to you, what with all those scorpions and things in the desert. Sue and Ken try to reassure me that there is nothing to worry about, but I know they are also a little concerned. You know that little busy body, Mrs. Owen, who cleans for the Sunrise hotel? Well, she's taken it upon herself to stand in for Elsie Pritchard and arrange the church flowers. I suppose we must look upon it as a kindness, but it gives her an excuse to waylay Ken and pump him for information about your travels. She met me yesterday (accidentally on purpose, I'm sure) in the church yard and gleefully announced that she had heard that you were enjoying the desert moonlight in the company of an attractive divorcee. She is such a mischievous person. With encouragement from Mrs. Owen, the rumour-mongers are beginning to enjoy themselves. Ken has planned a sermon for next Sunday on the evil of false witness, and we hope certain members of the congregation will get the message. Don't let this worry you. We can handle it; and as soon as you are home again I'm sure the likes of Mrs. Owen will be made to look very silly. With much love, Pam X.*

The message was clear. Pamela was worried, not that he might be lost in the desert, but that he was enjoying himself in the desert moonlight with Dotty. He knew he had been remiss in not sending an earlier e-mail about their trek to Meroe. From now on he must send daily e-mails. What was he doing if he didn't have time to send Pamela an e-mail? No wonder she was worried. He felt guilty about his own behaviour and angry about Mrs. Owen's impudence. This e-mail from Pamela contained a further unspoken question, *i.e.,* when was he coming home? Until now, he hadn't given careful thought to a timetable for his return to England. It was time he did.

Dotty had prepared an evening meal of beans and rice, but Martin hardly noticed its flavour or texture. During the meal Martin had said very little. They both pretended that this patch of desert, eerily silent, overseen by the pyramids of a long-lost civilisation and lit by a tropical moon, demanded respect, the respect of quiet contemplation as in a church. Yet Dotty knew something was worrying him and she knew it was the e-mail. She also sensed that Martin wanted to return to his wife and home. "Don't forget to send today's photographs to your dear wife before we turn in. I'll wash the saucepan and plates while you go on line; it won't take me long." Clever, understanding Dotty! When he felt ready, he would explain why the e-mail from Pamela had so quickly changed his mood.

Martin switched on the Nissan's headlamps to give him and Dotty light to work by. Sending photographs by e-mail

## CHAPTER 22

is an emotionally neutral process. They were quickly pasted into the e-mail he was about to write. As for the e-mail itself, he had to wait for the right words. Finally, he wrote:

*Dearest Pamela, my thousand apologies for not e-mailing you sooner. We are now at Meroe, which, as you can see from the picture of the pyramids, is quite an extraordinary place. The other picture was taken earlier today by the river Nile. Perhaps both will be suitable for the church magazine? It gets dark here very early and very quickly, so I'm writing this e-mail by the light of the Nissan's headlamps. For fear of running down the battery, I won't do it again and I will send your e-mails in the morning daylight. The moonlight helps of course, but it's not all that bright, and as for being romantic, I leave that for the younger generation. Now what's all this nonsense about Mrs. Owen? Tell Ken to be gentle with his veiled message. When I get back (which will be soon) I will blast those rumour-mongers from the pulpit myself. On a lighter note, you can see the Nissan in the photographs, so you know we didn't arrived here on camels. As I write this, Doctor Scott is washing up after our evening meal. She won't let me help, which suits me. To get here from the main road, I took a short cut through an agricultural area and I have a guilty feeling that I committed a trespass. No sign of the police yet! Don't worry, I'm joking. Regards to Sue and Ken and much love to you, Martin X*

Would that set her mind at rest? He hoped so. As he pressed SEND, his feelings of guilt and anxiety did not exactly evaporate. They were put on hold until he received the next e-mail from Pamela.

Martin switched off the headlights, and none too soon, as the light had begun to attract an entomologist's delight of insects, some of barbaric appearance, others innocently small and delicate but possibly carriers of a variety of subclinical complaints. In particular, Martin worried about malaria. A baking, dry desert is not normally home to malaria-carrying mosquitoes, but the desert of the Nile valley houses the ideal breeding ground for this dreaded disease, namely a river with accompanying pools of stagnant fresh water.

Dotty sensed that Martin had now relaxed. "Tomorrow, we'll have all the time we need to inspect and admire the pyramids. In the meantime, before we turn in, we can talk about Meroe." Martin agreed and suggested that as they talked about Meroe, they could still admire the distant pyramids, which, scattered over the plain, were now visible in the light of the risen moon. "It's interesting that below a certain light intensity everything appears in black and white. That's why those pyramids are now black and various shades of grey. The moonlight isn't strong enough to bring out their colours. The receptive power of the human eye is also a factor in this phenomenon," explained Martin. Dotty smiled with satisfaction. Martin was back to his normal self; well, almost. "Yes, I've noticed that too," said Dotty, "As it gets dark in the evening, all the colour disappears from the landscape. Now that we've agreed on this fascinating phenomenon, shall we talk about Meroe?"

"We've already talked about Meroe. You explained its history to me some time ago, starting with Candace's black eunuch treasurer. We drove here not to learn about Meroe, but simply to see it for ourselves; so let's sit here in the moonlight and look at it."

Dotty conceded that he was right and it wouldn't do to go over it all again. "Nevertheless, I would like to dig a little deeper," explained Dotty. "Sounds like archaeology," retorted Martin, "That's what I've been doing at your Coptic ruins: digging deeper!" "That is also true," laughed Dotty, pleased to find Martin in a lighter mood.

## CHAPTER 22

Dotty continued: "I distinctly remember breakfast on your second, or was it your third morning at my camp? We discussed how Greek thinking and Greek philosophy markedly influenced the early development of Christianity." Martin quickly interrupted with: "It was definitely the third morning and I will never forget it. That was when I met that worthless scorpion called Lawrence. Ever since then, I've always approached your tent very carefully, watching where I put my feet. "And so you should," replied Dotty with mock seriousness, "And even before that I think I mentioned the Egyptian influence on Greek culture."

"In my mind's eye," interrupted Martin, unable to disguise the amusement in his voice, "I see a pompous schoolmaster, in his gown and mortar board, extolling the culture of ancient Greece and explaining how it gave rise to everything that is beautiful and worthy in modern European culture. A precocious fourth-former then asks: *Please Sir, how did Greek culture arise?* The pompous schoolmaster replies: *It had to start somewhere Ponsonby junior and it started in Greece; the Greeks worked it all out for themselves.*"

Dotty applauded. "Martin, you have summed up the situation perfectly in that description of a late nineteenth century school lesson. It could also easily describe a lesson in a public school in the early twentieth century. Perhaps your pompous schoolmaster believed what he said to Ponsonby junior. Perhaps he couldn't think of a better answer and was a little mystified himself. One thing is certain: had he known the truth, he wouldn't have liked it, because he would have been trapped in the bigotry and prejudice of the time. No doubt he would have banged on about the great Aristotle. And why not? But he would not have known that Aristotle visited Egypt, possibly on his own initiative and certainly in the company of Alexander the Great when he invaded Egypt. History books are amazingly silent on this matter. I wonder why."

Martin felt invited to also wonder why. He remained silent for a while, gazing alternately from the moon, which was no longer hanging low near the horizon and was now almost above them, to the forest of spiky black and grey pyramids that was spread before them in the near distance. Finally he said: "I can't agree that pyramids are favoured as building structures just because they are an ideal shape for various purposes and not likely to fall down. I personally see spiritual significance in the top of a pyramid, because it points to the stars, or to the gods, or to heaven, like the steeple of a church. Or, look at it this way: primitive societies often regard mountains as sacred, believing that they are the home of gods, or that the spirits of their ancestors dwell at the top. What's more, perhaps this feeling *is* hard-wired in the huma psyche, so that different cultures have independently built their own little mountains, which we call pyramids, for religious ceremonies or as homes for the spirits of their ancestors."

Dotty was momentarily taken aback. It seemed that the scene before them of the pyramids in the moonlight had driven ancient Greeks and Aristotle from Martin's mind.

"Hello!" called Dotty, "What about Aristotle?"

Martin said he was only wondering what Aristotle thought of the pyramids when he accompanied Alexander to Egypt. "How could a great philosopher experience the pyramids of Egypt without weaving their spiritual significance into the fabric of his circumspection?" Dotty replied that Martin should go into politics, the last bastion of meaningless twaddle masquerading as a serious question. Martin was enjoying his little game, but promised to return to earth and have a serious conversation.

He continued: "I will summarise what we already know. By that, I mean what you have already told me. Egypt is in Africa and Africa is generally thought by Europeans to be primitive and not capable of fostering advanced thought and culture. Therefore it would be embarrassing to admit that Greek culture was advanced by contact with Egypt. Add the fact that some Egyptians were black and you begin to understand why sheer racial prejudice prevents the bigoted European mind from accepting that Africa had any part in educating the Greeks. Just imagine my pompous school teacher in the late nineteenth century telling his boys that European culture originated in Africa. Ponsonby's parents would have complained to the headmaster and may even have removed him from the school."

"Martin, you have it in a nutshell. There is, however, much more to be said about Greece's involvement with Egypt and the influence upon Greek philosophy of the Egyptian religious Mysteries. For example, we're all familiar with the four cardinal virtues preached by Plato: justice, wisdom, temperance, and courage. Even today, most scholars will tell you that these were *determined* by Plato. On the contrary, they were *copied* by Plato from the ten virtues of the Egyptian Mystery System. I could go on and develop an entirely new page of history, showing the interaction of Greek and Egyptian culture. An honest historian, free from the prejudice of the European superiority complex, will recognise that there were no boundaries in the ancient world between the countries clustered around the shores of the eastern Mediterranean. The Mediterranean itself was a means of transport by sea between North Africa, the Levant, and southern Europe, enabling trade and the sharing of cultural influences." Martin interrupted with: "Don't forget they also went to war with one another." "Of course," retorted Dotty, "Wars were always being fought somewhere or other. Alexander's foray into Egypt is a splendid example of war between nations in the Mediterranean region. And, in a curious way, the harm they did to one another acted as a bond, leading to closer cultural exchange. Nowadays, for obvious reasons, the Mediterranean is seen as a barrier between Africa and Europe. In Plato's day it provided a transport system. The ancient Greeks are partly responsible for the misrepresentation of their own cultural origins. They failed to report clearly how they had benefitted from contact with Egypt. The European view of Africa as a backward continent completed the lie, a lie that contaminates even mathematics. The theorem of the square of the hypotenuse is attributed to Pythagoras, but let's not forget that the Egyptians taught Pythagoras all the mathematics he knew. We can take this discussion further if you wish, but let's leave it there for now."

Martin agreed that they leave it there. Early interactions of Greece and Egypt might be important for a correct interpretation of history, but had nothing to do with the Jesus question that Martin was trying to answer, and which he had last addressed yesterday in their discussion of Asclepius.

Dotty would not be silenced. She continued: "However, once we accept that Egypt influenced Greek culture, we can move from Egypt down the Nile valley to Meroe. This brings me to another question: Why isn't the twenty-fifth dynasty of Egypt recorded in the Cairo museum?"

Again, Martin knew the answer before Dotty had finished speaking. "That was when Egypt was ruled by the Nubians, the black inhabitants of Kush, whose pyramids we are now admiring in the moonlight."

"Oh dear!" exclaimed Dotty, "It seems I can't tell you anything."

"Not so," explained Martin, "Surely you remember you explained the role of Kush in the twenty-fifth dynasty some days ago."

"Of course! I'd forgotten. All I wanted to do this evening was to trace a pathway of cultural influence from this moonlit Meroe via Egypt to ancient Greece."

"You have certainly done that," chortled Martin. I don't know about you but I'm ready for bed." He immediately

## CHAPTER 22

regretted what he had just said, so quickly added: "It's been a long day. Your turn in the Nissan; I'll sleep on the ground near the cooking gear."

But Dotty was not ready for bed.

"Please, Martin, it seems a pity to waste this lovely evening. Let's sit here, drink another coffee, and talk a bit longer in the moonlight," said Dotty, not looking at Martin but gazing up into the Milky Way.

Dotty sipped her coffee then lay back on Martin's unopened sleeping bag, and gazed sleepily at the moon, apparently not aware that the desert breeze had folded back her dress and exposed an indecent view of her left thigh. All was silent and for a brief moment Martin thought she was immersed in one of her formative silences. Then he realised that she didn't normally sip coffee during her silences. In a slightly husky voice, she said: "Martin, there's something I've been wanting to tell you."

"Yes?" replied Martin, thinking to himself: "This is it. She was planning all along to get me alone, away from the camp, away from the prying eyes of Mustapha and the two Mohammeds. She is, after all, a very lonely woman."

"It concerns the title *Christian*," explained Dotty. "We use it freely for the very early members of the Jewish community who were exploring a new philosophy, and for everyone that followed them. In fact, the name had not been coined even when Paul started preaching. Paul was the leader of a sect known as 'the Way,' *odos* in Greek. According to *Acts*, it seems the title *Christian* was first used in Antioch, and even then it was probably intended as an insult."

"Oh, that's interesting. I think Doctor Willan mentioned it in one of his lectures, but that was years ago and it had slipped my mind. Without knowing it, we were therefore correct when we spoke of sects and proto-Christians, rather than Christians." He wished he could think of more to say to tide him over his great sense of relief. Or was he also just a little disappointed? And was Dotty playing a game? Surely she knew perfectly well how she appeared to Martin, as she lay under the stars, her clothing gently disturbed by the desert breeze.

Martin wanted to know what else they should talk about. Dotty said she would like to know more about Martin's life as a country parson. She imagined him conducting traditional Church services every Sunday, producing a good sermon, reciting the creed, and blessing his congregation.

"Of course," replied Martin, "That's what I'm paid for. It's all standard stuff and part of an Anglican vicar's job description."

"What about pastoral care?" enquired Dotty, "I judge you to be the kind of person who would seek a close relationship with his parishioners, who would go out of his way to help the elderly, the infirm, and those simply needing companionship."

"I like to think that is true," replied Martin thoughtfully, wondering what Dotty was leading up to.

"In other words, the complete and perfect village parson," remarked Dotty with a smile, although in the half light of the desert evening Martin thought it was more smirk than smile.

"What are you getting at?" asked Martin.

Without answering, Dotty posed another question: "What about the biblical exhortation not to kill? Do you preach directly against war and violence? Are you involved in any movements outside the Church that work for peace?"

"The short answer is No. Of course, like most other people, I'm against violence and war."

"Then you are not the placard-waving type of clergyman, who protests outside the Houses of Commons when the government sends troops into other countries. You don't think that war is government-sanctioned murder?"

## CHAPTER 22

"Okay, I see what you're getting at. Christian doctrine opposes war and violoence. Unfortunately, we haven't yet found a way of avoiding war. I agree that thou shalt not kill, but that really means thou shalt not commit murder. When a soldier kills an enemy, he – and nowadays it might also be she – doesn't commit murder. Killing and getting killed is unfortunately part of the job."

"So you would approve of clergymen blessing tanks and bombs, as they have been known to do?"

"I admit, that is rather distasteful. Personally I wouldn't do it."

"Let me put it another way. If you were not a minister of the Church, would you go out of your way to promote peace, write letters to your MP opposing military adventures, argue for the removal of Britain's nuclear arsenal, and oppose the sale of arms to Saudi Arabia?"

"I can almost predict what you will say next. If I wouldn't do those things you mention in the cause of peace, then why did I become a Christian minister?"

"Something like that," sighed Dotty, sounding rather disappointed. "I think we should turn in now. We still have a long drive tomorrow. Good night."

# Chapter 23

Dotty slept well amongst the cushions at the back of the Nissan, and she was still asleep when Martin awoke at twenty minutes past four before sunrise, feeling refreshed. He thought he had by now established a regular sleeping pattern since arriving in the desert, but it seemed that the long drive to Meroe and anxiety over Pamela's response to his e-mail had interfered with his internal clock. Or perhaps his dream had awoken him, a dream that several Dottys were pointing at him and declaring in angry, accusing voices that he ought to be ashamed of himself, and had no right to call himself a Christian if he didn't wave a peace placard outside the houses of parliament.

Lying on his stomach in his sleeping bag, he had a ground-level perspective of the distant moonlit pyramids of Meroe, which seemed much nearer than they were. He would wait for the sunrise to provide more light then photograph the scene while lying on the ground. Today they would inspect the pyramids then make for home. Martin knew it was useless to plan too far ahead, but he secretly hoped they would get back to Dotty's camp today and would not have to spend another night cooking their evening meal by the Nile. His only hope of achieving that aim was to ensure that they left Meroe well before midday and that he did the driving. He wouldn't necessarily drive very fast but he would be quicker than Dotty.

He quietly drew a generous drink of water from the supply at the back of the Nissan without waking Dotty. Why not walk towards the pyramids until the sun began to rise? He could then lie on the ground and photograph the scene when the pyramids were even nearer.

About an hour later he returned to the Nissan, very satisfied with his photography and savouring the smell of cooking. Dotty had risen, brewed coffee and even fried

## CHAPTER 23

slices of bread, with tomatoes and eggs. She had seen Martin in the distance and assumed, correctly, what he was doing.

"Did you get some good pictures?"

"I most certainly did. And as I came back I got some delightful smells. As an internationally acclaimed specialist in Christian history, you're a very good cook."

"How am I supposed to take that?"

"As a sincerely meant compliment."

"Thank you. You can't imagine how much I'm enjoying this holiday. Let's spend longer than we intended. We could carry on to Khartoum, visit the Goethe Institute and say hello to Doctor Hopp. Surely you're not anxious to get back to the camp."

So much for Martin's plan to get back to the camp as soon as possible! But then, the more he thought about Dotty's suggestion, the more he liked it. He no longer felt so anxious about Pamela's next e-mail. It might contain thinly disguised suspicions about his relationship with Dotty. Perhaps that was understandable. He could only keep replying with honest, open accounts of his life in the Sudan and rely on Pamela's common sense to accept that he was behaving himself.

A visit to Khartoum sounded attractive. It was the capital of this enormous country, and so far he had spent hardly twenty-four hours there.

"What a splendid idea," exclaimed Martin. "Oh, how marvellous!" replied Dotty, "I'm sure we'll have an absolutely wonderful time." For a brief moment Martin wondered what Dotty meant by a wonderful time. He quickly erased this silly suspicion, only to hear Dotty add: "Perhaps we can get a decent bed at the Goethe Institute. Failing that, we could get a bed at a hotel in Khartoum. It would be a welcomed change from lying on the sand or the back seat of the Nissan."

That was perfectly true. On the other hand, what did she mean by a decent bed or a bed at a hotel? Surely she should have said beds. "No, no, no, definitely not," Martin told himself. It had happened before when thinking about Dotty, that his imagination and suspicions had developed wings and flown out of control. Pushing his fears away, he said: "Yes, I'm sure it'll be most enjoyable. And if we stay at the Goethe Institute or a hotel, you won't have to slave over the camping stove because meals will be prepared for us." Then he quickly and gallantly added: "I would miss your cooking. This is a wonderfully tasty breakfast."

"Flattery will get you nowhere. Don't forget, if we were to spend another night camping, it would be your turn to make breakfast."

The rest of the morning was spent amongst the pyramids. Earlier, before breakfast, Martin had photographed a dozen pyramids in the early morning sunrise, brilliantly lit from the east and casting sharp shadows on their opposite sides, the exact reverse of yesterday's pictures. Now he was gripped by the realisation that he would probably never visit Meroe again and that what had started as an enjoyable break from the routine of life at Dotty's camp had become a privilege. It was highly likely that none of his parishioners and none of his fellow clergy, including his bishop, had ever visited Meroe or ever would. He was therefore duty-bound to record his visit and pass on his experience of this very important historical site. Its story was widely recorded in learned books and on-line websites. As would be expected of a UNESCO World Heritage site, the photographic record was also excellent. So why bother to take his own photographs and record his own impressions? The answer was simple. He must be able to able say: "This is what *I* saw, this was *my* experience." Only then would he be able to speak with any authority about his visit to Meroe.

## CHAPTER 23

With these thoughts, Martin became desperate to photograph everything. Dotty guessed what had got into him and persuaded him to pause in the shadow of one of the larger pyramids with a crumbling top and share some liquid refreshment, namely water. In the baking heat of a desert, water is more than just water; it is a most valuable and necessary source of refreshment and survival.

Martin began to relax, realising his stupidity in trying to photograph everything. Dotty gently pointed out that there were more than two hundred pyramids and suggested it would it be a good idea to take representative photographs of the different types: the larger crumbling structures, the smaller, better preserved ones that were still untouched by the restorers, and those that had been completely restored.

Martin agreed then suggested they walk together across the site, describing a slightly curved pathway from northwest to southeast, until they found a view containing all the different types of pyramids. They would then take it in turns to photograph one another, first standing by the Nissan in the distance, then standing by the Nissan in the foreground with the pyramids receding into the distance. "I will then clamber to the top of the largest crumbling pyramid and photograph the site from on high," announced Martin. Three hours later, Martin's photography programme was complete. One picture in particular, of himself by the Nissan with a line of pyramids disappearing into the distance behind him, he would send immediately to Pamela for the church magazine. Driving the Nissan into a shaded area behind a pyramid, Martin opened his laptop and wrote:

*Dearest Pamela, I can hardly believe I've been in the Sudan a fortnight. The original plan was to return home some time before Christmas, but I think I'll be ready to leave long before that. Doctor Scott is a hard taskmaster, keeping me busy at the excavation site or tiring my brain with lessons on Christian history. This break is therefore welcome, although only yesterday she instructed me on the relationship between the figure of Jesus and the mythical Greek philosopher Asclepius. This ancient site of Meroe is heaven for anyone with a camera. I'm sending you my latest shot of the pyramids, which I feel is ideal for the church magazine. I know you have already read about Meroe on the internet, so I leave it to you to write a little blurb to go with the picture. Doctor Scott has decided not to return immediately to the fourth cataract, but to carry on to Khartoum where she has business to attend to. It will give me a chance to explore Khartoum. I also want to visit Omdurman. Much love, Martin.*

That, thought Martin to himself, should put Pamela's mind at rest, at least for the time being, especially the suggestion that he might return home sooner than planned.

Meanwhile, Dotty was inspecting the entrance at the base of a smaller pyramid. As Martin put away his laptop and joined her, she said she had been thinking again about the significance of the pyramidal shape. She continued: "These pyramids are quite unlike those hundreds of miles to the north in Egypt. First of all they are much smaller. Then they are steeper with a smaller base in relation to their height. As for their purpose or function, burial tombs were cut into the rock beneath them so that the pyramids are grave markers, rather analogous to gravestones in your churchyard at home. In contrast, the Egyptian pyramids served as burial chambers. Another difference that seems to emphasise the difference between Meroitic and Egyptian pyramids is the treatment of the dead bodies. The Kushites didn't mummify their dead. They laid them to rest without any form of hygienic treatment, and in some cases they were burned, not actually cremated in our sense of the word because they were still recognisable as burned bodies, not as

## CHAPTER 23

a heap of powder from prolonged and intense burning." Martin interrupted with: "That sounds like heat treatment for hygienic purposes." "Whatever you call it," replied Dotty, "This difference in their disposal of the dead seems to reflect the independence of mind of the Kushites. They had their own culture and their own way of doing things. On the other hand, we know that the peoples of Egypt and Kush knew each other very well, as trading partners or enemies, so it's worth asking whether the Egyptian pyramids inspired these in Meroe, or whether the pyramid builders of Meroe only glanced briefly at the Egyptian model and decided to follow their own innate concept of the pyramidal shape."

Martin thought Dotty was making heavy weather of the difference between Egyptian and Kushite pyramids. He couldn't accept that the pyramids of Meroe hadn't been inspired by the Egyptian pyramids, despite their differences in shape, size and function. And why shouldn't the pyramid builders of Meroe borrow the idea of pyramids from Egypt then adapt the pyramidal shape to their own purposes? "Possibly we are saying the same thing in different ways," remarked Dotty, "Don't forget what you said about the pyramids of pre-Columbian Central America. If they were conceived independently, why not these pyramids of Meroe?" "Good point," conceded Martin: "This question of what inspires a pyramidal shape is getting us nowhere here and now. Let's decide what we do next."

"That has already been decided. We drive to Khartoum. There's a tour group about half a mile to the south of us. Let's drive over there and ask the guide how best to get to Khartoum.

To Dotty's surprise the guide recognised her, explaining that they had met when Dotty had visited the museum in Khartoum in the company of Doctor Hopp. On that occasion, she was conducting tours of the museum, and she knew Doctor Hopp because she also worked part time as an

Arabic teacher at the Goethe Institute. Dotty struggled to remember. Suddenly it all came back to her, but she couldn't recall the lady's name. Dotty introduced Martin and embarrassment was saved when the guide beat her to it and announced that her name was Asma. Martin remarked that it was a small world when two people could meet like this quite accidentally. Asma laughed and assured him that it was not in the least surprising because in Khartoum the number of people guiding and caring for tourists was relatively small and they all knew each other.

To the relief of Asma's tour group, who were beginning to feel neglected, Dotty and Martin said goodbye. Asma embraced Dotty, shook Martin's hand and told them to follow the graded track out of the site, then pick up the tarred road that led all the way to Khartoum.

Martin drove while Dotty talked. She explained that Meroe and the surrounding area had far more to offer than just the pyramids. Excavations had revealed a prosperous city with palaces and evidence of skilled artisan trades. About twelve miles south of Meroe there were other towns with temples to a lion-headed Nubian warrior god. Moreover, in the ancient city of Meroe there was a temple of the Egyptian god Amun. The pyramids, which were the burial site of Kushite royalty, dating from 270 BC, were thus visible evidence of only one of several features of the Kushite civilisation. "But now," she declared triumphantly, "I find that my decision to carry on to Khartoum was an excellent idea. Meeting Asma had reminded me that we must visit the Khartoum museum. There you will see much that has been unearthed from the Meroitic period. What's more, you will see artefacts from Faras, such as wall paintings, whose composition and style you can compare with those of the fresco you have recently revealed at my archaeological site."

"And there was I," complained Martin, "thinking that

## CHAPTER 23

Khartoum would be an extension of my little holiday away from your camp."

"Don't worry," answered Dotty in a mocking tone of comfort, "I will allow you a little time off. In fact, if we're lucky, we may be able to visit Omdurman and watch the whirling dervishes."

"Three things," replied Martin, "I'm excited at the prospect of seeing the whirling dervishes. How far is it to Khartoum? And I'm hungry."

"It's probably between sixty and seventy miles to the Goethe Institute. Let's stop now and make a meal out of the biscuits and spreads that we have left. We still have plenty of water, although it's beginning to taste like the inside of a jerry can. Better to boil it and make tea or coffee."

They drove off the track, parked the Nissan at right angles to the sun, and sat in its shade while they snacked on biscuits and coffee. Martin now felt quite comfortable with their change of plan. He had almost forgotten about Jesus. His mind was working on Meroe and Kushite history. And he was looking forward to learning more when they visited the museum in Khartoum. Then his impatience to know more got the better of him and he asked: "What were those skilled artisan trades that you mentioned earlier?"

Dotty couldn't list them all with confidence. "However," she added, "I do know that Meroe exported iron. There may have been many artisan trades in ancient Meroe, but by far and away the most economically important was the smelting of iron. Iron was in demand throughout the world. Possibly the main reason that Meroe flourished economically was that it had an iron industry. Some historians have referred to Meroe as the Birmingham of Africa, and with good reason; Meroe exported iron even as far afield as China. It also exported cotton textiles. And to add to its economic clout it had plenty of gold. Which reminds me: the Egyptian word for gold was *nub*, which might have been the origin of the name Nubia."

"Your mention of an iron industry has completely changed my mental picture of ancient Meroe." said Martin, "I now imagine the desert at night, not as a poetic scene with pyramids dimly lit by a silvery moon, but as a darkened landscape pock-marked by a myriad glowing furnaces, with drifting clouds of chemical vapour, the air pervaded by the stench of industry, muscular bodies glistening with sweat, hauling iron ore and working bellows, camels laden with iron ingots carrying their loads to river boats on the Nile on the first stage of their export to rest of the world."

Dotty agreed that there was far more to Meroe than pyramids then suggested that Martin should rein in his imagination until they obtained more facts at the museum.

As they drove towards Khartoum more houses appeared near the roadside. Advertisement hoardings, intended for tourists, showed pictures of the pyramids and proclaimed the UNESCO Heritage site. Soon both sides of the road were lined with buildings and manufacturing companies. It was very different from the quiet road on the other side of the Nile that Mustapha had taken out of Khartoum when he drove Martin to Dotty's camp.

Martin negotiated the outskirts of Omdurman, drove through Khartoum North, crossed the Nile, arrived outside the Goethe Institute, and drove through the open gateway into the car park at the rear of the building.

Several other vehicles were parked behind the Institute. Groups of students, mostly European in appearance, were gathered outside the back door. A single jacaranda tree, heavy with blue blossom, was the only source of real colour in the dry and dusty car park. It was also the only potential source of shade, but at that time of day the car park was in the shadow of the Institute building so all the parked vehicles were safe from the grilling effects of the sun.

## CHAPTER 23

"Looks like a busy day for language classes. Oh, and here comes Doctor Hopp, no doubt nonplussed by our unannounced visit," said Dotty in an amused, conspiratorial tone. Doctor Hopp stood briefly in the doorway of the Institute wearing a look of pained astonishment, then waddled over to the Nissan. From their meeting several days ago, Martin remembered Doctor Hopp as a short, plump, formally dressed figure. Today, however, he was not dressed like the head of a cultural embassy. On the contrary, his open neck shirt, which was not completely tucked into his trousers, together with his tousled hair suggested he had just got out of bed. "What an enchanting surprise!" exclaimed Doctor Hopp, in a pained tone, suggesting he was anything but enchanted. They shook hands all round and Dotty explained how they had decided at the last minute to continue from Meroe to Khartoum instead of returning to her camp. "So," she added, "We thought we would take advantage of your hospitality and stay at the Goethe Institute for a couple of nights; that is, if you don't mind and provided you have room." "But of course!" said Doctor Hopp, still obviously flustered by their arrival, "I will ask my secretary to organise rooms for you. Please come inside now and take some refreshment." Doctor Hopp hurried ahead. Dotty and Martin followed him through the door and down a corridor to the kitchen. "My secretary will join us soon. I'm sure she will be pleased to see you. I have asked Osman, our kitchen helper, to bring tea and cakes to the next room. Please follow me." So far, so good. Accommodation was guaranteed. They would be polite, take tea and cake with Doctor Hopp, and greet his secretary.

Martin was already formulating a plan for the evening. They would drive to Kitchener's gunboat, the headquarters of the Blue Nile sailing club. With luck, there would be food there and they could have an evening meal. With further luck, Seamus O'Shea would be there and Martin would be able to pay back his loan. Martin was in the middle of telling Dotty and Doctor Hopp his plans when Hopp's secretary appeared. Smartly dressed in skirt and blouse, with neatly coiffured hair and makeup recently applied, she contrasted sharply with Doctor Hopp's dishevelled appearance. Yet both gave the impression of just getting out of bed. He hadn't had time to attend to his appearance, whereas she had washed and changed her clothes. Dotty and Martin exchanged meaningful looks. Dotty tried to suppress a smile, which became a smirk, while Martin raised his eyes to the ceiling. They would never know for sure; or would they?

Dotty greeted her with: "How lovely to see you again, Monika. It's at least eighteen months since we saw each other. Of course, you met my archaeological assistant, Reverend Kimpton, when he arrived a few weeks ago." Monika replied that eighteen months was too long, and she hoped that they would now see more of each other before Dotty returned to the fourth cataract. Resorting to German, Hopp said: *"Liebchen, die beide wollen zwei Nächte bei uns bleiben. Ich habe ihnen schon zwei Schlafzimmer versprochen."* Monika replied: "Ach, wie schön! You will bring two nights at the Institute. I am going to instruct two beds for you." Clearly, Monika's English needed improvement, but there was no mistaking her meaning. But what had Doctor Hopp said to her in German? Neither Martin nor Dotty were German scholars, but they knew enough to understand that Hopp had told Monika that they were staying two nights and he had promised them separate bedrooms. And he had addressed Monika as *Liebchen,* probably thinking Dotty and Martin wouldn't understand. But they did understand and it seemed their suspicions were confirmed. "Well," thought Martin to himself, "I'm off duty, as it were, and I don't have to wave the admonishing finger of a Church minister, so good luck to them, but I can't imagine what she can see in silly, tubby, little Doctor Hopp."

## CHAPTER 23

Once again showing she was a mind-reader, Dotty whispered to Martin: "There's no accounting for taste."

Monika and Hopp noticed her whispering and looked enquiringly in her direction. Lying through his teeth, Martin explained that he had just explained his plans for the evening and Dotty had agreed that they should eat at the Blue Nile sailing club with the hope of meeting up with a certain Seamus O'Shea to whom he owed money. Doctor Hopp laughed unnecessarily loudly, which suggested he was feeling embarrassed, and said: "You tried to find that man after you first arrived in Khartoum. It was such a very small amount of money that he gave you, I'm sure it was a gift." Martin smiled and shrugged. As a matter of principal he was determined that one day he would find Seamus O'Shea and return the two thousand Sudanese pounds, even if they were equivalent to only five British pounds.

"Come, come," chided Dotty, "What's all this about owing money at the Blue Nile sailing club? You spent less than twenty-four hours in Khartoum and you managed to get into debt!?"

Martin had never told Dotty the full story of his arrival in Khartoum and he promised to explain over their evening meal how he came to owe money to someone at the Blue Nile sailing club.. Doctor Hopp looked uncomfortable. Perhaps he was still feeling guilty at not having met Martin at the airport.

Monika saved the gathering from lapsing into silence by announcing she would show Dotty and Martin to their rooms. She also pointed out that it was getting late, that it would soon be dark, and that she wasn't sure whether food was available at the Blue Nile sailing club. "Then what would be the alternative?" asked Dotty. "When all the threads are torn, we can make food here at the Institute, but I know the senior common room of the university has a good kitchen on the evening." That was clear enough, but what had torn threads to do with anything? Hopp intervened and explained that Monika had translated literally a common German expression meaning *as a last resort*.

Their bedrooms were on the ground floor of the Institute. Martin's was reached though a narrow corridor behind the kitchen. Dotty's was immediately inside the back door leading to the car park. Dotty had a sprung mattress. Martin had a Sudanese bed, a frame strung with cords and covered by a blanket, which on the scale of human comfort lay somewhere between the back seat of the Nissan and the bare ground of the desert.

Martin freshened up under the cold tap in the kitchen. Monika led Dotty to a well-appointed bathroom on the second floor. Half an hour later they were ready to drive the short distance to the Blue Nile sailing club, accompanied by Monika and Doctor Hopp, who had decided that a night out would be a pleasant change from the confines of the Goethe Institute. They all piled into the Nissan and with Martin at the wheel they headed for the sailing club. A lone Arab sitting on the gang plank told them the bar was closed and had been closed for a month, and they no longer had a restaurant. Furthermore, he had never heard of Seamus O'Shea. "Kein Problem!" bleated Hopp, "I guide you to the university common room."

It wasn't far and soon they were sitting on rather rickety plastic chairs around a table in the restaurant of the university. Behind Monika and Hopp the room opened onto a moonlit garden. "A very agreeable setting," remarked Martin, "Doctor Scott and I seem to have the better outlook." Monika and Hopp had a view of the interior of the dining hall with the entrance to the kitchen. Suddenly Hopp blurted out: "Let us say *Du* to each other. I think that would be appropriate in the circumstances." Martin thought Hopp was suggesting some sort of party game but Dotty understood straight away. *Du* was the familiar as distinct from the

## CHAPTER 23

polite form of *you* in the German language. In other words, he was proposing they call one another by their first names. Dotty started: "My name is Dorothy but I answer to Dotty amongst friends. Reverend Kimpton is Martin. Monika, as we all know, is Monika. And what do we call you Doctor Hopp?" He announced that his name was Manfred and said they must drink to their exchange of first names.

Ahmed, the head waiter, in his white galabiya and red tarboosh, had already exhibited great diplomacy by seating the four Europeans in a distant section of the restaurant, where, he claimed, they would benefit from the cool breeze from the garden. In truth, he couldn't allow them to sit in the section reserved for women or in the section reserved for men. The poor man was now faced with an even greater dilemma. His guests were asking for wine to toast the step change in their relationship. When the restaurant was generally open to the public, he was not allowed to serve alcoholic drinks. He had wine, even whisky, secreted in his private room but he was allowed to serve it only when the restaurant was closed to outsiders and hired by the vice chancellor or registrar for private meals with visiting foreigners. When he explained his dilemma, Manfred flustered an apology for causing embarrassment and said they would make do with orange juice. Ahmed thanked him for his understanding and with a secretive smile assured them all they would enjoy the orange juice.

The menu offered practically no choice and they all ordered Nile perch with potatoes and aubergines. The fish was good, probably caught only a few hours earlier. But the orange juice seemed to be taking a long time to arrive. They all successfully removed the flesh from the viscous bones. Even Martin had no problem, having learned a few tricks with dishes of Nile perch at Dotty's camp. They were halfway through the meal when Ahmed arrived with the orange juice in four wine glasses. Other diners in various parts of the restaurant stared judgmentally when the orange juice arrived then relaxed when they saw it was fruit juice.

"Better late than never!" exclaimed Manfred, raising his glass of orange juice. They all raised their glasses and bowed to each other as they made eye contact and repeated the first name of each person. Each swallowed a generous draught of orange juice, gulped, looked surprised, smiled then burst out laughing. The orange juice was generously laced with whisky. Their outburst attracted the attention of the other diners. They mustn't embarrass Ahmed, so they exchanged knowing smiles, curbed their loquacity and continued quietly with the meal.

Martin asked if anyone knew the Arabic for *compliments to the cook*. No-one knew and all agreed that the first course had been excellent. "However," declared Martin, "I have tasted even better at Dotty's camp. Mustapha, her camp commandant and head cook, produces excellent food. As a matter of fact, his *pièce de résistance* is Nile perch." Dotty nodded in agreement, pointing out that his curried goat also took a lot of beating. Monika wanted to know how Dotty had found such an excellent person to run her camp. Dotty explained that Mustapha had introduced himself when Doctor Ibrahim first showed her the ruins of the Coptic church, and that Mustapha had Doctor Ibrahim's approval.

Monika had been listening intently. Giving Manfred a knowing look, she asked Dotty to let her know when she eventually finished excavating and left the Sudan, so that the Goethe Institute could hire Mustapha. It seemed that she and Manfred were rather dissatisfied with their present hired Arab helpers. A good Nubian cook was what they needed.

Martin suggested they ask for the dessert menu. Manfred laughed and wagered there would be no choice, just crème caramel, take it or leave it. He was right and smugly told his three friends that crème caramel was a relic of the British Empire. Everywhere in the world where the British had been

## CHAPTER 23

the dessert was crème caramel. He seemed very proud of this eclectic gem of information, until Martin asked Manfred if he knew the Spanish word *flan*. Of course he knew flan; it was the same as a quiche. "I said the Spanish, not the English word," insisted Martin. "Oh," is it different in Spanish?" enquired Manfred. "Indeed it is," replied Martin, triumphantly, "It is the Spanish word for crème caramel. And I ask you, when was Spain ever part of the British Empire?"

Manfred didn't know whether his leg was being pulled, until Monika told him she remembered her brief spell in the Goethe Institute in Madrid, where she had also learned that the Spanish word *flan* was crème caramel.

"Well!?" asked Dotty, "Let's order our crème caramel and try to enjoy it!" "With coffee," added Monika. Ahmed had been eavesdropping. Manfred summoned him by clicking his fingers, but he arrived, not with the dessert menu, but with four dishes of crème caramel, four cups and an ornate pot of coffee with a long, elegantly curved spout.

Dotty suggested that Ahmed was dropping a hint. It was getting late and perhaps Ahmed wanted to shut up shop. All the other diners had left. The four friends were now fully adjusted to one another and their conversation was relaxed and flowing. It would be a pity to leave straight away. Manfred called Ahmed over and asked when the restaurant closed, and at the same time asked for the bill. He waved Dotty's protest aside and said he insisted on paying. He would take it out of expenses at the Goethe Institute. Dotty shrugged to acknowledge defeat. Monika gave a little giggle, which seemed to indicate that the Institute expense account routinely served similar purposes, probably listed as entertainment of foreign visitors. Ahmed asked meaningfully if the meal had been satisfactory. They all smiled meaningfully and complimented him on the cooking. The whisky-laced orange juice would not be mentioned but Manfred added a generous tip to the bill. Ahmed said he would like to close the restaurant in an hour's time.

Over coffee, Manfred wanted to know about Dotty's work at her archaeological site. He and Monika were fascinated to learn that Martin had revealed an ancient fresco of the nativity, especially when they heard how he had used sewing machine oil to bring out the colours. "In return for my labours at the archaeological site," explained Martin, "Dotty teaches me about the history of Nile Valley and the history of Christianity." Manfred expressed surprise that Martin, a church minister, should need lessons on the history of Christianity. "Actually," said Dotty, "he already knows most of it so we just exchange ideas." Monika wasn't satisfied. She wanted to know more and suggested that exchanging ideas by the light of the desert moon was a wonderful way of spending an evening. In her curious version of English it became: *to give out hours to ideas when the sun goes under must provide much joy.* Then she wanted to know if they ever disagreed. "Sometimes but not often," replied Dotty," and sometimes I test him with difficult questions." Monika and Manfred became suddenly alert and begged to know what kind of difficult questions Dotty asked Martin.

At first, Martin thought Dotty had immersed herself in one of her formative silences, but she was only taking a moment to think of an answer. She started with: "I must be careful not to offend your religious beliefs, so please tell me which Churches you both belong to." Manfred explained that his father had been a Lutheran minister but that had not attracted him to the Church. When he had to state his religious affiliation on official documents he always wrote Lutheran but he couldn't remember the last time he had entered a church. Monika said she had almost given up the Church, but would not abandon it completely; after all, it would always be there if she needed it. Martin understood perfectly; Monika and Manfred would get on well with his own parents.

## CHAPTER 23

"Okay," said Dotty, "Here's a typical question for all of you, not just for Martin: *What did the Romans do for Christianity?* Manfred slapped the table with glee and said that was easy because everyone knew that the Romans had adopted Christianity in the fourth century. To his dismay Dotty agreed that most people did know that, but it was not the answer she was seeking. "I want to know," she explained, "what the Romans did for Christianity hundreds of years before Emperor Constantine adopted the faith for the Empire, in other words very early in the story of Christianity."

Monika and Manfred turned to Martin for an answer, but he didn't know either. They returned their questioning gaze to Dotty, who shook her head and suggested they sleep on it. In typically German fashion, Monika and Manfred took the question very seriously and promised they would think about it very carefully. Martin suggested Manfred might e-mail his father, the Lutheran minister, and see if he could provide an answer.

Dotty had had enough. She pointedly asked Monika if she was also feeling tired. Everyone took the hint and they made their way to the car park, which, to their horror, was closed and guarded by two armed soldiers. After dark, security in Khartoum was very tight. No need for alarm. The guards had already been told by Ahmed that a party of four harmless visitors was about to leave. The soldiers not only opened the gate for them; they also stood to attention and saluted them as they drove out.

Dervishes preparing for their late Friday afternoon performance in Omdurman. Photographed by the author.

Scene of the Nativity from the extinct Coptic Cathedral of Faras, northern Sudan. This fresco is on display in the National Museum, Khartoum, where it was photographed by the author. In *Camel Scorpions* an identical Nativity scene is excavated by Martin in the ruins of a Mediaeval Coptic church near the fourth cataract of the Nile.

# Chapter 24

During the meal Martin and Dotty described how they had found a short cut to the Meroe pyramids by driving through fields of okra. Monika and Manfred were seriously concerned when they heard that the track had ended at a fence with no gateway. They cheered up when Martin described his discovery of a gap further along the fence. It took some time for the concept of lateral thinking to sink in. Martin almost gave up trying to explain, when suddenly the penny dropped and Manfred had a fit of the giggles. Then he had to explain to Monika that lateral thinking was *seitliches Denken,* whereupon she almost fell off her chair with laughing. Ahmed's whiskey-laced orange juice had conspired with Martin's lateral thinking to destroy all traces of reserve and personal modesty in the happy foursome. They drove back to the Goethe Institute in high spirits.

Manfred, however, was still pondering the true meaning of lateral thinking. As he drove into the Institute car park he suddenly exclaimed: "I think lateral thinking means the same as thinking outside the box! Am I correct?" Martin and Dotty exchanged meaningful looks. This was neither the time nor the place to talk about Gnosticism. "Of course, that has more or less the same meaning," replied Dotty, who then quickly added: "What an enjoyable evening it's been. I'm sure we are all now feeling tired and ready for bed."

Manfred locked the BMW and joined the other three. Monika said she wanted to check both Dotty and Martin's bedrooms to make sure they had everything they needed. As soon as Manfred had disappeared upstairs Monika clutched Dotty's right hand in both of hers, looked pleadingly into her eyes and said she was sure that Dotty and Martin must be suspicious of her relationship with Manfred. Although she had difficulty expressing herself in English, her meaning was clear. Dotty assured Monika that she wouldn't dream of being so ill-mannered and judgmental as to pry into the private lives of the director of the Goethe Institute and his secretary. Nevertheless, poor Monika was intent on making a confession. It seemed Dotty and Martin were the mother and father confessors she had been waiting for. She explained that she and Manfred intended to get married in Germany, but since their next leave was in six months' time they had decided not to wait, so they now shared a bed on the top floor of the Institute. Dotty threw her arms around Monika and gave her a loving, understanding hug. She winked at Martin over Monika's shoulder and Martin joined the hugging, which was very enjoyable because he was not only expressing sympathy and reassurance to Monika, he was also hugging Dotty, which he had been longing to do ever since he arrived at the fourth cataract about a fortnight ago.

Monika wiped a tear, thanked her two confessors and ran upstairs. "An interesting case study for a sociologist," said Martin, when Monika was out of earshot, "Two not-quite-middle-aged Europeans isolated in a non-European, Muslim country, behaving in a way that would hardly raise an eyebrow in Europe, yet feeling guilty." Dotty did not agree entirely and said she preferred to think Monika was feeling ashamed rather than guilty, and only because she was now in the company of two other Europeans. Martin thought for a moment then agreed that Dotty was probably near the mark in her analysis. Then Dotty, with greater understanding of the female side of this question, suggested that Monika's apparent outburst of embarrassment, shame, guilt, call it what you will, was in fact an expression of joy. A little late in life she had found happiness and wanted to share it, to tell her friends about it. Isolated in North Africa at the junction of the Blue and White Niles, this had not been possible. "Well," remarked Martin, "Whatever the reason for Monika's behaviour, this evening has certainly made a change from discussing Jesus. And, by the way,

## CHAPTER 24

there's only a very fine dividing line between guilt and shame. "I'm sure you're right," conceded Dotty, stifling a yawn, "Let's go to bed." Martin thought: "Yours or mine? But he daren't say it."

Martin woke early to the sound of activity in the kitchen. Cautiously peeping round the kitchen door he saw Monika preparing breakfast and humming happily to herself. She spotted him and waved him to the kitchen sink. "Good morning! You must speedy wash and speedy whiskers before everyone eats breakfast." Well, that was clear enough. He must get a move on with his washing and shaving before the others arrived. "I will leave the kitchen for you to strip." That was also clear enough, but he managed a more-or-less all-over wash without completely stripping naked. As for speedy whiskers, he decided to give shaving a miss. Most of the local Sudanese menfolk favoured a few days' worth of facial hair so he wouldn't be out of place with a growth of designer stubble. Many also favoured a beard but he wouldn't go that far. He needn't have hurried. Dotty arrived about thirty minutes later, followed by Manfred.

Manfred was in a very bouncy mood, greeting everyone with a hearty *'Guten Morgen* my friends!' Martin replied with: "Good morning *mein Freund*." Manfred congratulated Martin on his excellent German, and breakfast was thereby launched in lighthearted fashion. Dotty asked: "Well, what did the Romans do for Christianity? Have you e-mailed your father?" Manfred didn't know the answer and his father had not yet replied to his e-mail. Martin said he also didn't know the answer but shouldn't they start breakfast. Surely Romans and Christians could wait until later. He was hungry.

Manfred told them that Osman, the kitchen helper, had today off. "Sometimes Monika and I like to manage the kitchen ourselves. It makes us feel at home," explained Manfred. "Like man and woman," added Monika, as she clattered around the kitchen brewing the coffee. "She means

449

man and wife," said Manfred, smiling broadly. Last night, Monika must have told Manfred that she had apprised Dotty and Martin of their love affair. Now everyone knew and everyone was relaxed about it. No more need be said.

Manfred wanted to know Dotty and Martin's programme for the day. "First, the museum then later in the day we want to see the whirling dervishes," declared Dotty. Monika said she would prepare an evening meal for them all. Manfred said they would not be allowed to leave Khartoum before Dotty had told them what the Romans had done for Christianity. He also drew a sketch of the route from the Goethe Institute to the museum. It was unnecessary because Dotty already knew her way around Khartoum and she certainly knew where the museum was, but she kept a polite silence while Manfred took a sheet of Institute notepaper, headed **Das Goethe Institut – Deutsch Lernen, Kultur Erleben,** and drew a map of part of Khartoum with a dotted line from the Goethe Institute along Al Mek Nimr to the junction with Nile Street, along Nile Street, past the Corinthia hotel, continuing along the bank of the Nile to the museum. Dotty thanked Manfred, folded the map, and told Martin he could drive while she navigated. The Corinthia hotel would be convenient for a light lunch and they would return to the Institute and rest during the midday heat before setting out for Omdurman to see the whirling dervishes. Dotty made to collect the breakfast plates and start washing up, but Monika blocked her way to the kitchen sink, pushed her very gently to the door and wished them a wonderful morning at the museum.

As Martin turned the Nissan into Al Mek Nimr, Manfred ran into the car park waving his map, which Dotty had left lying on the kitchen table. He was too late.

It was just over a fortnight since Martin had last seen the Corinthia hotel. As its old colonial architecture came into view, the memory of that first night in Khartoum was

## CHAPTER 24

rekindled but he had to struggle to recall certain details. For instance, he had no clear recollection of the hotel foyer, where Seamus O'Shea had bought him a beer and a club sandwich, given him two thousand Sudanese pounds, and finally said goodbye. He must write down everything he did and saw each day, with as much fine detail as possible. Memory can't always be trusted, especially when the previous day is pushed into the background by an abrupt change of scene. His life in the Sudan seemed to start with his first day at Dotty's camp. What had happened before that was now a rather vague memory, except for the recurring conviction that he owed money to an Irishman and he must find a way of repaying him. As they passed the suspension bridge connecting the island of Tutti to Khartoum, Martin was still struggling to reconstruct in his mind's eye that first night and morning in the Sudan. Then his thoughts were diverted by the sight of three heavily laden donkeys being led across the bridge and regularly hit across their hind quarters by their scruffy young handlers. He would never get used to the way animals were mistreated in this part of the world.

Moments later they drew up outside the museum, which was set back on the left of Nile Street, and found a tree to shade their vehicle. The Faras artefacts that Dotty wanted to show Martin were in the museum building, but Dotty led Martin to the left of the museum grounds, where an outside garden area could be viewed through railings. Displayed in the yard was an avenue of stone carvings, looking at first like monuments from ancient Egypt. "All those goddesses and lion-headed sculptures are from Meroe," explained Dotty, "We'll get a better look at them when we enter the yard from the museum. Now let's go and meet Natakamani."

Martin didn't take the obvious bait by asking who on earth Natakamani was, but allowed himself to be led back the way they had come, and to the museum entrance. The doorway was guarded by a stone statue of a bearded male potentate with the insignia of a hooded cobra on his crown of office. "He's travelled a long way from ancient Egypt," observed Martin. "Meet Pharaoh Natakamani," announced Dotty, "He's not from Egypt. He was a king of Kush who reigned around the turn of the century between BC and AD. This statue didn't come from Egypt. It was brought from a Meroitic site near the sixth cataract." They nodded to the two armed guards who were lolling in the shade of Natakamani, paid the entrance fee of five cents to the lady desk attendant, and went in. Dotty glanced around the entrance hall, remarked that it hadn't changed since her last visit, and told Martin to follow her to the exhibition of Faras artefacts. She marched him to the right then round a corner to a large wall painting of the nativity, mounted above a gently sloping walkway.

Martin gazed wide-eyed at the painting and was speechless. "Well, what do you think?" asked Dotty. Without waiting for a reply, she said: "Now you know why I was so excited when I saw my fresco, or I should say *our* fresco for the first time. This wall painting before us has the same design and composition, and the same colours as our fresco. The correspondence is so great that I'm tempted to suggest that they are both by the same artist. In fact, when I write my paper on our fresco at the fourth cataract, I'll chance my arm and propose that they *are* by the same painter. What a pity he didn't sign his work!" Martin didn't fail to notice the emphasis placed by Dotty on *our* fresco, rather than *her* fresco. It made him want to stay longer in the Sudan and uncover more artefacts that would be *theirs*, rather than hers. Putting his wandering thoughts on hold, he replied that the resemblance was truly surprising, but he thought it was going a bit too far to suggest they were by the same painter. The design was highly stylised and could easily be the product of a school of painting rather than an individual artist. He also pointed out that *their* fresco was in a much

## CHAPTER 24

better condition than this one from Faras, which had cracks running from its perimeter to its centre, with parts of the surface missing just below the virgin's robe. Dotty agreed that Martin was probably right about a school of painting or perhaps a traditional style and design handed down over generations. Nevertheless, the striking similarity would be pointed out in her next research paper. It's a long way from Faras to the fourth cataract and any standardisation of Coptic wall painting was further evidence for the cohesiveness of the Coptic communities throughout the Nile valley.

In a troubled tone Martin suggested they had ignored a glaring fact in their discussion of the style of the wall painting. "We should bear in mind," he hurriedly interposed, "that whoever or whatever school of painting was responsible for this fresco and for our fresco, the style is overwhelmingly Byzantine. We can trace the style of our fresco much further north than Faras. We can trace it to Byzantium. If I were writing your next research paper I would stress the fact that your Coptic church near the fourth cataract had distant allegiance to Constantinople rather than Rome."

Dotty agreed that she had been carried away unnecessarily by the almost identical nature of the two frescoes. And yes, of course, it showed that a Byzantine style of iconography was used throughout the Coptic Church from Byzantium to the fourth cataract of the Nile and probably even further south.

"I would like to think a little further ahead than your next research paper," mused Martin, thoughtfully stroking his stubbly chin. "Your Coptic church and all its artefacts should be recorded and, if possible, preserved, for posterity. Already the magnificent fresco that we recently exposed is in danger of deteriorating under desert conditions. Why not get it removed and transferred to this air-conditioned museum?" Dotty replied that it was, in a sense, out of her hands because when she was granted permission to dig near the fourth cataract she had signed an agreement to report all archaeological finds to the museum authorities. She had already done just that in an earlier e-mail to Doctor Ibrahim. And, with luck, they might even meet Doctor Ibrahim today.

The desk attendant, wearing a glistening white thoub and speaking perfect English, told them very seriously that Doctor Ibrahim was in his office and she would call him. She dialled, or rather tapped in a number on her desk telephone, and asked: "Who shall I say wishes to speak with him?" She repeated the name *Doctor Scott* into the telephone and reacted with surprise at the excited response from Doctor Ibrahim's office. "It seems you are an important person," said the receptionist, smiling at last, "He is coming straight away."

Moments later, the imposing figure of Doctor Ibrahim strode towards them from a corridor behind the admissions desk. Tall, with a pale brown complexion, a full head of slightly frizzled strong black hair and a neatly trimmed moustache, he held out both hands in welcome. Martin was surprised, although he didn't know why, to see that Doctor Ibrahim was wearing European clothes: neatly pressed belted grey trousers and an open-neck, short-sleeved shirt.

"Welcome, welcome. I knew you were in the area and I expected you would call but I couldn't be sure when that would be."

"But how did you know we were in the area?" enquired Dotty.

Avoiding her question, Doctor Ibrahim said: "First let me thank you for your e-mail about the fresco. I must come to see it, of course, but just lately I have been terribly busy. From the picture that you e-mailed to me, it appears to be in a splendid state of preservation."

Dotty was about to reply when Martin beat her to it: "It's in a better state of preservation than the Faras specimen you have here. I'm sure it would be worthwhile to transfer it to this museum."

# CHAPTER 24

"That will be given serious consideration," replied Doctor Ibrahim, using a well-worn phrase that he had found useful at meetings of the museum finance committee. "Obviously it cannot be left to sit there in the desert. But the removal and transport of such artefacts requires special equipment and skilled operators. We have the cutting equipment, very similar to the tools used by workmen in London to cut through paving slabs. I was in London last year and I watched workmen making a paved way near the British Museum. I was so impressed by their cutting tools that I bought two and transported them to the Sudan. I was embarrassed because I then found that we already possess such tools." Doctor Ibrahim added that transport of the artefact would require the help of engineers from the dam, but he was sure that would not be a problem.

It had not escaped Martin's attention that Doctor Ibrahim had failed to answer Dotty's question, so he cut short the discussion of the fresco by asking how Doctor Ibrahim actually knew that they were in the area.

Once again, Doctor Ibrahim evaded the question by declaring that they shouldn't stand there in the entrance to the museum. They should go to his office, which was nicely air-conditioned. Leaving instructions with the receptionist to bring refreshments, Doctor Ibrahim led his two guests down the corridor from which he had emerged earlier, and waved them into a very large room, obviously his office and surprisingly large, even for the needs of the director of a museum. One corner with a low level table and a semicircle of soft chairs was clearly intended for the entertainment of visitors. The room was dominated by a very large teak desk, a good ten feet long and five feet deep with ornately carved stumpy legs and capacious stacks of draws. Martin was fascinated by the sight of it and thought to himself that it would fetch a fortune in auction in London. He also tried to picture it in his own study in Herefordshire; it was truly a desk for an archbishop! As

Doctor Ibrahim was ushering them into the visitors' corner, the receptionist arrived with a tray of fruit drinks and a bowl of ice. Martin still couldn't take his eyes off the great desk. "You like my desk?" enquired Doctor Ibrahim. "Well, yes, it's very impressive, and a real museum piece," replied Martin. "That is why it is in a museum," joked Doctor Ibrahim, who then added: "It belonged to General Gordon and it used to be in the palace by the Nile. It was later moved to the office of the Dean of Medicine in the university. I met him on a government committee about five years ago and he mentioned that he wanted more modern furniture in his office. So I did a deal with the Faculty of Medicine and acquired the desk for my office at the National Museum. I think of it as representing historical compensation."

Martin and Dotty looked puzzled and Doctor Ibrahim explained that Europeans had for years been taking artefacts from other parts of the world for their collections and museums. Now this desk represented the reverse of that process: all the way from London, up the Nile to Khartoum, finally coming to rest in an office in the National Museum of the Sudan. "That is what I mean by historical compensation," explained Doctor Ibrahim. "Or a way for history to get its own back," suggested Martin.

As Doctor Ibrahim passed around the fruit drinks and offered extra ice, Martin once more decided to ask him how he knew they were in the area. As he opened his mouth, Dotty gave Martin a quick look with pursed lips and a slight shake of her head, indicating that he should not ask. Facial expression and body language can be very effective means of communication; in some situations so effective that they transcend the spoken language. Animals and certainly our nearest relatives, the monkeys and apes, are adept at non-verbal communication. Dotty had already picked up on Martin's pursuit of her early question and had good reason for ignoring Doctor Ibrahim's evasion. This also shows that

## CHAPTER 24

Dotty and Martin were beginning to read one another's thoughts and intentions, which, for any other couple, would be an index of intimacy. But, as we know, their intimacy is purely intellectual. Isn't it!?

"I understand you are staying at the Goethe Institute," ventured Doctor Ibrahim, in a tone that was half question and half statement. Dotty replied that she had a good relationship with Doctor Hopp and his secretary. When they changed their plans and decided to continue to Khartoum she knew they could probably get beds for a night or two at the Goethe Institute.

As she rambled on with her explanation, Martin thought that must be how Doctor Ibrahim knew they were in the area. Then he began to have his suspicions. Something was being withheld and Martin had no idea what or why. Furthermore, Dotty's reaction when he was about to repeat her question, indicated that she also had suspicions.

Very briefly the conversation lapsed. They both turned to Doctor Ibrahim who was wearing a troubled look. He seemed undecided whether to speak and looked quickly from Dotty to Martin and back again to Dotty. He couldn't have expressed his feelings more clearly if he had said out loud: *am I doing right to say what I'm about to say; can I trust you both?* As the tension in the room increased, Dotty and Martin moved uncomfortably under Doctor Ibrahim's probing gaze. Martin glanced quickly sideways at Dotty, who was looking carefully at Doctor Ibrahim. In profile, with a puzzled expression, her face expressed motherly concern and an intense femininity. Once more, Martin's suppressed feelings for Dotty began to take on a life of their own. Then the tension was broken by Doctor Ibrahim quietly saying: "I am troubled by happenings to people I know, sometimes to close friends." He looked seriously, almost pleadingly, first at Dotty then at Martin. Each returned his gaze directly, trying to convey a spirit of cooperation and trust. Whatever his problem, it seemed to be serious. They waited and could not have anticipated his shocking revelation: "Too many people are being murdered."

"Surely one murder is one too many," ventured Dotty, "To speak of too many murders is to suggest that a certain number of murders is acceptable, and I can't agree with that." Her opinion on murder was unarguably correct but hardly relevant. Doctor Ibrahim was waiting to explain what he meant by too many murders.

"In this unruly country of mine, murder is quite common." Then, with a wry smile and relishing the chance to have a dig at western culture, he added that it probably wasn't as bad as in New York. "However," he continued, our police are incompetent and unwilling to investigate the murder of anyone who is not a public figure, or has influential relatives and friends. If the local community know the identity of a criminal, murderer or thief, and expose him to the police, then the police may take an interest, provided a bribe is involved. And it is too easy to dismiss all criminality as the work of migrants from the south. Recently, a well-known trader in the Arab souk was found with a knife in his back behind his sacs of millet. The police put on a show of interviewing other traders then the case was allowed to fade from the public eye and nothing was done to find the perpetrator. When they are forced to investigate and produce a statement for the media, they simply ring the changes on robbery by migrants from the south and fights between rival drugs gangs. The only time a murder is taken really seriously is when it appears to be related to the smuggling of arms. Illegal trading in arms is taken extremely seriously and there is a special police unit devoted to that problem alone."

Dotty and Martin had nothing to say. Doctor Ibrahim had the floor and they waited for him to continue.

"There is another sphere of organised crime," said Doctor Ibrahim, "namely the stealing and smuggling of

## CHAPTER 24

ancient artefacts. Egypt takes this problem very seriously. Anyone caught stealing or exporting artefacts from ancient Egyptian burial sites can expect severe punishment under the law. Here, in the Sudan, we have a great wealth of history, stretching back to pre-Christian times. In Meroe there are many more pyramids than in the whole of Egypt. Take a sharp masonry chisel and a cordless grinder to Meroe and remove a piece of a pyramid with an inscription in Meroitic characters. Do you have any idea for how much you could sell that piece of pyramid in Germany or America?"

Dotty and Martin shook their heads. "Well, I will tell you: thousands of dollars. Mounted and carefully displayed on a pedestal it might well become the proud possession of some rich American businessman or a collector of antiquities in Berlin or Munich. We have laws to prevent such plundering of our heritage but their enforcement is feeble. As the head of the National Museum I am naturally very concerned about the stealing and trading of our artefacts, but I am not an officer of the law. I wish the police would be more active in protecting our heritage. Sometimes I think they are actually involved in aiding the smuggling of artefacts. Perhaps they enjoy the supplementation of their salaries by bribes from the smugglers."

"And you think that people involved in this smuggling racket are being murdered. Is that what you are saying?" said Martin, feeling that Doctor Ibrahim was taking too long to get to the point.

"Exactly," replied Doctor Ibrahim: "One of those guards you saw at the entrance to the museum just now was appointed only last week as a replacement for a guard who was found with his throat slit underneath the bridge to Tutti Island. Recently a car carrying artefacts from the excavated area behind the fourth cataract was hijacked by armed men on camels and all the artefacts were taken. There were ancient brooches and ornaments that were discovered by archaeologists before the area was flooded. They had been stored in the house of a local chief near the fourth cataract and were due to be displayed in this museum. At the time, the driver of the car was unharmed. He told me he was sure he had recognised one of the hijackers and he intended to go to the police. The next day he was found murdered in his own home. At Port Sudan there appear to be criminal gangs at war with one another. When someone is killed the police dismiss it as one criminal killing another and say it is good riddance. Sometimes they link this gang warfare to arms smuggling; only then do they appear to take it more seriously Often, however, at least in my opinion, it is a case of war between rival gangs of artefact smugglers, and the police are probably complicit."

"And you have no proof, not even evidence, just your feelings and suspicions," said Dotty.

"My very powerful suspicions," insisted Doctor Ibrahim, "Now I must tell you more. I must make a confession."

Dotty and Martin raised two pairs of inquisitive eyebrows and allowed their host to proceed.

Doctor Ibrahim explained that he knew practically all that happened at Dotty's camp near the fourth cataract and at her excavation site, because Mustapha kept him informed by sending messages with a certain lorry driver, who brought supplies to the building site at the dam. He also had other spies keeping an eye on her excavation site, who visited the site and checked on progress when no-one was there. In fact, he had a network of Nubians and Arabs working for him and reporting back from all the ancient Sudanese pre-Islamic sites.

Dotty smiled and slowly nodded her head, indicating she was not surprised by his revelation and had always suspected something was going on behind the scenes at her camp. She recalled how Mustapha had appeared, apparently from nowhere, when Doctor Ibrahim had first shown her the site.

## CHAPTER 24

Mustapha was Doctor Ibrahim's man. She had half suspected it at the time. No doubt the two Mohammeds were also part of the surveillance team. And why not? From Doctor Ibrahim's point of view, he had taken a risk when he granted her permission to excavate the Coptic church on her own, using her own methods without oversight by Sudanese officials. Yes, he had to guard his own interests and he had done this by covertly keeping an eye on her, as well as appointing Mustapha and the two Mohammeds to protect her.

As if reading her thoughts, Doctor Ibrahim added that his network of spies was also intended for her protection, because a lone female European in the desert was vulnerable to robbery, not to mention possible kidnap, not only from wandering desert nomads, but also from the variety of workmen at the dam site.

"Well," said Dotty, "You're no doubt pleased to find that your arrangements for my protection have been successful. Not once have I been robbed or felt endangered in any way."

"And that," explained Doctor Ibrahim, "is how I knew that you were in Khartoum. My spies told me."

Martin now understood that Doctor Ibrahim had taken a risk in arranging for a trustworthy European to lead the excavation of the Coptic church. But Martin still felt he did not have a complete understanding of the situation. Firstly, Doctor Ibrahim was too good to be true. He clearly had his roots in the Sudan and he belonged to Arabic culture. Yet he spoke excellent English and had spent much time in Britain, probably also in the USA, although that was only a guess. He was steadfast in his role as curator of the National Museum and, unless he was a superb actor, he was seriously concerned about the stealing of artefacts and intent on preventing it. A little voice in Martin's subconscious still complained that he hadn't grasped the whole picture. Then it suddenly dawned: what was a scrupulously honest, well educated person doing in a government post – curator of the National Museum, no less – when other Sudanese government officials were not appointed for their ability, but because they knew the right people? Nepotism was rife and it was difficult to see how Doctor Ibrahim could fit into such a system. The answer came sooner than Martin expected.

Doctor Ibrahim lifted his telephone and pressed a red button at its base. It was answered immediately and he conducted a brief conversation in Arabic. Moments later the door of his office opened, without a preliminary polite knock, and in walked the receptionist of the glistening white thoub, who spoke cut glass English, who had earlier manned (or is it womanned?) the desk at the entrance to the museum, and who had brought them refreshments. "Let me introduce my sister," announced Doctor Ibrahim, who went on to explain that they preferred to act their respective roles of curator and receptionist and not let it be generally known that they were related, although it was a difficult secret to keep. His sister announced that her name was Siemah and she was pleased to meet Doctor Scott and the Reverend Martin. There followed a babble of friendly exchanges from which emerged an agreement that they would no longer use titles, and that from now on they would address one another as Dotty, Martin, Siemah, and Ibrahim.

"Siemah is not only my sister, receptionist, and secretary," explained Ibrahim, "she is also my ally in a secret struggle to run the museum for the benefit of the historical record of our country, and to prevent the stealing and trading of artefacts."

Martin was quick to interrupt by asking why it should be a struggle to run the museum for the benefit of the country and why the struggle should be secret.

Unexpectedly, Siemah, not Ibrahim, answered with: "There's no point in beating about the bush; we are convinced that government officials are involved in the illegal

## CHAPTER 24

trade in artefacts. Now they are trying to gain more control of the museum itself, probably with a view to actually stealing exhibits for sale abroad."

Dotty and Martin reacted with exclamations of "Surely not!" and looks of disbelief. "I'm afraid so," confirmed Ibrahim. "The government committee charged with the protection of our heritage has recently suggested that I should have a government-appointed assistant curator to help me in my interaction with overseas museums. They praise me for my stewardship of our national heritage and pretend they are rewarding me for my splendid work by giving me an assistant. But don't you think it suspicious that this so-called assistant will be a government-appointee, especially when I have learned that they already have someone in mind, a person who knows next to nothing of museum management, and whom I don't trust."

Again, Martin got in a quick question: "And why don't you trust him, Ibrahim?"

Again, it was Siemah who answered: "Two years ago this man returned from the UK after studying for a science degree in a British university. On the strength of this he now has the title of Doctor of Philosophy. But we know, because we have contacts and friends in the same university, that he was judged to be incompetent and was sent back to the Sudan without a degree, and without a qualification of any kind. He, or at least his uncle, has close contacts with certain government ministers.

Again, Martin was quick to interrupt: "So they had to find something for him to do and decided to make him the assistant museum curator, where he could do no harm and be safely out of the way. Why do you think there is a more sinister motive?"

Siemah nodded to Ibrahim, who then explained that this same person had contacted him recently, expressing concern about the displays of artefacts – agricultural tools, weapons, carvings, models of villages – from the southern regions of the Sudan, which had now gained independence as a separate country. He had expressed the view that, since South Sudan was an independent country, it was no longer appropriate to display their culture in the National Museum. Furthermore, he had pointed out that the religions of South Sudan were Christianity and animism, which had no place in the National Museum of the Sudan, which was a Muslim country. "And," added Ibrahim, "he made this visit even before I learned officially that an assistant would be imposed on me, let alone that he was the chosen assistant. He was already acting as though he were in charge, although I suspect he was later reprimanded for jumping the gun, because his visit was followed by a long period of silence, with occasional friendly visits from members of the government committee, with their wives and children, claiming they just wanted to enjoy a visit to the museum."

With a note of concern in her voice, Dotty said: "I understand that my Mustapha and the two Mohammeds inform you about my activities, but might they be passing information to anyone else, for example someone in a government department?"

"Certainly not," replied Ibrahim, with a conspiratorial smile, "they are part of my exclusive fifth column. Government officials are not aware that they are in my pay. No doubt it is assumed that they are local people hired and paid by you, which they are. Of course, that is not the whole truth because they also receive payment from me, and here we come to another conspiracy: I received a large personal payment from the Pergamon Museum in Berlin to help me in my efforts to conserve our antiquities. The money was transferred to me via Doctor Manfred Hopp at the Goethe Institute here in Khartoum. It's all very secret and the Sudanese government knows nothing about it. The controlling committee of the Pargamon Museum in Berlin is very

## CHAPTER 24

aware that the archaeological treasures of the Sudan are threatened by criminal gangs and by our corrupt government. Fortunately, I know the director of the Berlin museum and we trust each other, but you can appreciate that this is a very delicate and risky situation. The Berlin money helps me to maintain a team of workers and spies, including your Mustapha and the two Mohammeds, who owe allegiance to me."

Dotty took a long, deep breath and exhaled loudly. It was more than a sigh; it was an expression of irritation. "I came to the Sudan with the sincere aim of digging up part of Christian history and hopefully contributing to the archaeological record of your country, but I find that I have been playing a bit part in a network of political intrigue. From now on I will always be looking over my shoulder and, worst of all, I will have a different view of my three trusted employees, Mustapha and the two Mohammeds. I even find that the Goethe Institute is involved in transferring funds to you in this cloak and dagger scenario. Of course, you know we are currently staying with Manfred Hopp and his secretary at the Goethe Institute. They have made us very welcome and we have been sharing some rather intimate, personal secrets. But not for one moment would I have guessed they were actively engaged in providing funds – funds of questionable legality, I might add – to support your work and to pay my Mustapha and the two Mohammeds. I sympathise wholeheartedly with your concern over illegal artefact trading and the probable involvement of government officials. But ..."

Dotty paused and looked around her. Ibrahim and Siemah were troubled by her outburst and looked guilty, feeling, perhaps, that they ought not to have told her the truth. On the other hand, Martin was trying to conceal a smile, causing his lips to twist as though he were experiencing a sour taste. But he couldn't conceal the twinkle in his eyes. Dotty gave Martin a challenging look and he responded by saying: "What a splendid display of righteous indignation!"

"Oh, alright," replied Dotty, "As a matter of fact, I was about to change my mind. In mid-sentence, my indignation underwent a metamorphosis. I began to feel excited by my own role in this story of plot and counterplot on the River Nile."

Turning to Ibrahim and Siemah, she said: "To put it another way, how can I help?"

"You now know that Mustapha and your two Mohammeds will tell me and no-one else about discoveries at your site. Please do not talk about your work to anyone else. Otherwise, you can help by carrying on with your archaeological work as if you had heard nothing of what I have just told you. If you uncover anything of historical value, like the fresco for example, just keep quiet about it."

Martin wondered about their three friends, Mohammed, Yasser, and Gwaria. Were they to be trusted? "Mustapha has told me about those three people who entertain you when you fetch water from the Nile," replied Ibrahim, "He regards them as completely innocent of any involvement in the trade in artefacts. However, Gwaria's family does have indirect connections with members of the government so, to be on the safe side, it would be best not to tell them anything about discoveries at Dotty's site."

Dotty thanked Ibrahim for the trust he had shown in her. Then feeling she was getting rather solemn and serious, she mischievously suggested that her newly revealed fresco be widely reported in the news media in the Sudan, and that much be made of the engineering work necessary to remove it and transport it to Khartoum to the National Museum. "Then," she claimed, "it will be impossible to steal it or sell it, without causing a scandal and embarrassment to the government. "An interesting and, if I might say so, an amusing idea. I will think about it," replied Ibrahim.

Siemah wanted to know if Dotty and Martin had plans for the rest of the day. Dotty replied that they planned to

## CHAPTER 24

take a light lunch at the Corinthia hotel, rest in the afternoon at the Goethe Institute then watch the whirling dervishes at Omdurman in the evening. Ibrahim suggested that he and Siemah meet Dotty and Martin after the dervishes. They could eat together. And they would invite Manfred Hopp and Monika Meinerts, too. So that is what they did, although the party was larger than Dotty expected, because Siemah also brought her husband and Ibrahim brought his wife, making a total of eight altogether.

Later that night, Martin sent a lengthy e-mail to Pamela:

*Dearest Pamela, what a wild and interesting day! We visited the National Museum of the Sudan, met and talked with the curator and his sister, and arranged to spend the evening with them and their spouses, as well as the director of the Goethe Institute and his secretary. It was, in effect, a goodbye party because tomorrow Doctor Scott and I intend to drive back across the desert to Doctor Scott's camp. Before the meal we went to Omdurman to watch the whirling dervishes. It was one of the most interesting and exciting experiences I've had since arriving in the Sudan. Whether this event is suitable for the church magazine I leave for you and Ken to decide. Certain members of my rather conservative congregation might be horrified to hear that their vicar has been jigging about to the drum rhythms of an extreme mystical Muslim sect! I can imagine the look on the face of the organist's wife.*

*We arrived at about four pm at a large area of wasteland (I have now learned the difference between wasteland and desert!) on the outskirts of Omdurman near to the dervishes' mosque, which is actually a rather small, simple and very old-looking structure. A crowd had already gathered and was getting larger by the minute. We Europeans were outnumbered by about 200 to 1 by local Sudanese. There were many families with children. Obviously, most of the crowd had been to this event before because they organised themselves into a large circle without being told.*

*But where were the dervishes? Everyone was looking expectedly to the east. Then, moments later, moving figures appeared on the eastern horizon, not in a column but in a single line, shoulder to shoulder, advancing rhythmically to the beat of their drums. The crowd fell silent. The dervishes came nearer and nearer and it was soon possible to make out individual figures dressed in flowing green robes, sometimes trimmed with patches of red and yellow. They also wore green hats, with a high central, pointed crown and great floppy side flaps. As the dervishes entered the awaiting circle, the onlookers became noisy again. Within the circle some dervishes continued to beat their drums. Others performed mildly acrobatic dances (not whirling yet). Parents ran into the circle, asking the dervishes to bless their children, sometimes babies in arms. Frankly, I was at first taken aback by this. The dervishes were wild-eyed, and bearded – not the kind of figure I would want to bless my child. I suppose that sounds terribly prejudiced and I'm afraid it is. It comes from blessing white babies in the Christian peacefulness of my village church.*

*While all this was happening, another dervish carried a smoking metal pot around the inside of the circle, allowing members of the crowd to inhale the smoke and waft it around their face and body. I had a small sniff. It was very fragrant but I couldn't identify the herb that was being burnt. I suspect marihuana might have been part of the mix.*

*Little by little, the drumming and dancing approached a crescendo and suddenly the scene was transformed. The dervishes were leaping and whirling and the crowd also moved backwards and forwards to the rhythm. This part of the display can't be conveyed in words. I also moved with the rhythm of the drums and dancers. I was feeling very excited, when suddenly the drumming and the whirling*

## CHAPTER 24

*stopped. Complete silence! The dervishes remained rooted to the ground, staring fixedly into the setting sun, which was now blazing from the west, slightly to the right of the mosque. I can't imagine what this does to the retinas of their eyes.*

*Show over! The dervishes went to pray in their mosque and the crowd dispersed. Luckily I remembered to take my digital. Do you think a picture of dervishes is suitable for the magazine of a Christian church?*

*Doctor Ibrahim tapped me on the shoulder. He had probably been there some time, watching me watching the dervishes. He led us to where his wife, sister and brother-in-law were waiting in a car and we all drove to the Corinthia hotel, where he had reserved a special dining room. The director of the Goethe Institute and his secretary were already there, waiting for us. We spent a happy evening, talking and eating, and I will tell you about it in my next e-mail.*

*Much love from the whirling vicar of Herefordshire, Martin.*

In the privacy of their screened dining space, the party made no concessions to local custom. Men and women mingled and chatted as equals and wine was available for those that wanted it. Manfred offered to fill Martin's glass from a bottle of Niersteiner. "The Goethe Institute has provided the wine," announced Manfred proudly. "You were not to know that this particular wine is one of my favourites. At home on special occasions, my wife and I always drink Niersteiner with our meal." Manfred raised his glass and toasted Martin's wife, whom he sincerely hoped to meet one day. In return, Martin toasted the future happiness of Manfred and Monika. Their exchanges attracted the attention of the others and soon everyone was trying to think of someone or something to toast. Ibrahim cut through the hubbub by announcing: "I propose a toast to honest archaeology worldwide. May our museums be filled with beautiful exhibits and may our knowledge of ancient cultures be thereby enriched."

"To honest archaeology," intoned the group and everyone emptied their glasses, either of Niersteiner, or, in the case of Siemah, Ibrahim's wife and Dotty, of orange juice.

This light-hearted tone was maintained throughout the evening. There was no mention of the illegal trade in artefacts, no mention of government corruption, no mention of the rather iffy transfer of money from the Goethe Institute to Ibrahim. The conversation revolved around the every-day concerns of life, such as the price of sesame oil, the difficulty of finding trustworthy servants, and how to get the children to school on time. Siemah's husband, Riad, was a pathologist whose duties were shared between teaching at the medical faculty of the university and more sanguinary duties (as he put it) at the hospital. In dress and behaviour he was utterly European, with a command of English that could have qualified him as a BBC announcer. There was, however, no disguising his Arab ethnicity – olive skin, slightly and tightly crinkled black hair, neatly trimmed black beard, flashing dark eyes with alluring black lashes. He and Siemah, who was wearing her glistening white thoub, resembled a pair of film stars, who would not have been out of place at a Hollywood reception. They may or may not have been aware of their attractive appearance but they did not put on airs. On the contrary, they separated and circulated, Riad buttonholing Martin and taking a genuine interest in his impressions of the Sudan. Siemah captured Monika, whom, perhaps surprisingly, she was meeting for the first time, and learned all she could about life in Germany. She was thrilled by Monika's account of the rebuilding of the cathedral in Dresden, and they were soon joined by Ibrahim and his wife, who listened in silent enjoyment to Monika's account of

## CHAPTER 24

how, after the reunification of Germany, the heap of rubble that was once the cathedral had been excavated to recover all the masonry that could be reused, and how fresh stonework had been cut by stonemasons, and how the new cathedral had gradually risen as a perfect replica of the building destroyed by allied bombing in the war. She made no mention of the firestorm and the terror of that event. "Truly amazing!" exclaimed Siemah, "So the ancient Egyptians and the pyramid builders of Meroe were not the only masters of building in stone."

In contrast to Siemah's thoub, Ibrahim's wife, Mumtaz, wore a skirt and blouse. Her black hair, showing slight traces of grey, was drawn back rather severely and fashioned into a bun, which was pierced and held in place by a beautiful brooch studded with coloured (precious?) stones. But loose ringlets of hair had been allowed to escape and frame her face. For an Arab, her skin was rather pale but still with an olive tinge. In his mind's eye, Martin imagined her playing Carmen in Bizet's opera. He had her with a rose in her hair, performing an evocative habanera in a Spanish tavern. He then called his imagination to order and attended to what she was saying to him. "Is it true, Martin, that you are a religious person, a minister of the Church?" Martin confirmed that he was indeed a minister of the Church. She then wanted know which denomination. He told her Church of England. "Ah! Henry the eighth's redesigned version of Roman Catholicism," she chortled playfully. "Well, I suppose you could put it that way," agreed Martin, who could then contain his amusement no longer and burst out laughing. He had come all this way to learn about the history of Christianity and here was a strikingly beautiful Muslim lady instructing him on the origin of the Church of England. Everyone turned to identify the source of the laughter. Mumtaz lightly placed a restraining hand on Martin's arm, and, loudly enough for everyone to hear, said:

"Come, come, Martin, everyone is looking at us. What will they think?" To everyone's amusement, Martin blushed and looked embarrassed, which was exactly what Mumtaz had intended. Ibrahim came over and, hardly able to contain his own smile, he playfully admonished his wife and asked what they were laughing at. Martin explained that he had just been given a lesson on the origin of the Church of England. "When she was a little girl my dear wife attended the Holy Cross School in Khartoum," explained Ibrahim. "It was a Catholic school with high educational standards, but they also taught that the Protestants and Puritans were theologically corrupt and one should have nothing to do with them. In a Muslim country they had no right to preach such a viewpoint. However, I can assure you my wife is not criticising your faith. She is simply being mischievous." As he said this, he looked sternly at his wife. No longer able to contain their feelings, both burst out laughing and Martin joined in.

Dinner was served and they easily decided who would sit next to whom. Having got onto joking terms with Martin, Mumtaz insisted on sitting next to him in order to continue their interesting conversation; or was it to continue her gentle teasing? Dotty sat next to Ibrahim and several times during the meal they were both told to stop talking shop. Manfred and Riad could not be parted; their conversation centred on Manfred's efforts to conscript Riad to the staff of the Goethe Institute, which, at first sight, appeared to be a ridiculous idea, until Manfred mentioned his plan to run English classes for Sudanese medical students. Riad suggested that the British embassy was surely the institution for such classes. Manfred confided that he intended to set up in competition with the British embassy, and that someone like Riad, a qualified medical person with excellent English, was exactly what he needed for teaching such a course. The logic of his argument was undeniable but Riad's busy timetable seemed to preclude further commitments. At the end of the

## CHAPTER 24

evening, Manfred was still refusing to take no for an answer and Dotty and Martin never did learn whether Riad finally succumbed.

Martin was anxious to know why every Sudanese in the party spoke faultless, colloquial English with hardly a trace of a foreign accent. Mumtaz explained that they had all been educated in England. "Early private schooling at an English language school in Khartoum, followed by boarding school then university in England," explained Mumtaz. Martin nodded his understanding then asked which school and university she had attended. "I went to a school in York, called the Mount, and from there to Cambridge to study medicine." Dotty overheard their conversation and said: "First Catholicism then Puritanism. You've had a broad encounter with Christian denominations." "Yes, indeed," replied Mumtaz, "and at risk of offending religious sensitivities, I much prefer the Puritanism that benefitted me greatly at the Mount School in York."

Dotty fixed Mumtaz with an inscrutable smile, assured her that she had not offended anyone's religious sensitivities and asked how she had enjoyed the French lessons of Madame Fifi de la bon bon. Mumtaz gave Dotty an astounded look of disbelief. "Yes," explained Dotty, "that was my school, too. We must have missed each other by a few years. I still can't remember the real name of that French mistress. "It was Madame Claudine Heinz. I believe her husband was German but they were separated," recalled Mumtaz. Talking across the table, Dotty and Mumtaz continued to exchange reminiscences about their school days. Martin, like everyone else, was excluded from the school-day reminiscences of Dotty and Mumtaz, so he turned to Ibrahim and asked about his schooling in England. "I also went to a school in York. It is called Bootham School and it is the brother school of the Mount. From there I went to Cambridge." Martin promised himself that he would find out about these two schools in York, which, according to Mumtaz and Dotty, had a Puritanical ethos and seemingly high educational standards. "And what about your brother-in-law," asked Martin. Riad overheard and cut into their conversation with: "You can put me down for Sidcot School in the Mendip Hills and from there to Oxford." Martin had not heard of Sidcot School so he mentally added it to his list for future reference and remarked: "Another Puritanical establishment, I assume?" "Indeed it is," answered Riad, "and Puritanical in the nicest possible way. From what you say it seems you haven't heard of Sidcot School. For a minister of the Church of England that is perhaps not surprising." Before Martin could respond, Manfred demanded Riad's attention once more and Martin was left conversationally stranded.

Martin momentarily abandoned any attempt at friendly intercourse and studied his surroundings. The screens, which marked off their dining area from the rest of a large patio at the rear of the hotel, were decorated with paintings of a riverside, presumably a bank of the Nile, with palms and a setting sun. They were childish daubs, in keeping with the Muslim antipathy to visual art.

For the first time that evening Martin also became aware of the waiter, who had silently and efficiently brought their food, cleared their plates, and served the dessert. Very dark-skinned, he made an impressive figure in his galabiya and red tarboosh. Martin assumed he was a Nubian, since he closely resembled Mustapha, at the same time reminding himself that Dotty's faithful camp commandant was also a spy in the pay of Ibrahim. The dessert that he served was less impressive: a fruit salad consisting mainly of tasteless water melon with few pieces of orange.

Coffee arrived on a trolley: cups, milk, and sugar, and four tall silver coffee pots with long, elegant swan neck spouts, steaming and emitting a rich aroma of freshly brewed real coffee. As he savoured the aroma, Martin admired the

## CHAPTER 24

shape of the silver coffee pots, which reminded him of the rhythmical contours of Greek vases. Ibrahim handed him a brimming cup decorated with the bust of Queen Victoria.

Away from the table they were able, theoretically, to mingle freely. But freedom to mingle is relative. Martin wanted to talk with Ibrahim and Riad. In particular, he wanted to find out more about their schooling in England. Mumtaz, however, had not finished with Martin. She herded him into a corner and confessed she had never visited his part of England. "I believe you live very near to Wales. I would love to visit that part of Britain. From York I often travelled further east and to the east coast. Robin Hood's Bay is a delightful place. Do you know it?" Martin assured her that he knew it very well, but their conversation was interrupted by Dotty, who squeezed Mumtaz's arm and said they must meet up again soon and swap more reminiscences about their school, then turned to Martin and reminded him that they must start early tomorrow to drive across the desert to the fourth cataract. "In other words," said Martin, "It's time for bed." Mumtaz looked from one to the other, raised her eyebrows and smiled at Dotty. "Think what you like, Mumtaz, but I accuse you of having a suspicious mind." "Sorry!" replied Mumtaz, and they hugged each other goodbye.

Little by little the party fragmented and everyone went their separate ways, after first wishing Dotty and Martin a safe journey across the desert the next day.

# Chapter 25

By 6 am the alleyways of Omdurman were already busy. Martin drove slowly and patiently behind heavily laden donkeys and their stubborn drivers and waited politely for gatherings of women shoppers to clear before driving on. He had been in Khartoum long enough to learn it was useless to try to hurry, but not long enough to learn how to put on an entertaining show of impatience. In any case, he welcomed the opportunity to soak up the atmosphere of this crowded, dusty little town, which he might well be seeing for the last time, and which occupied an unlikely place in British colonial history, memory of which had been preserved for the public in 1939 by the epic Technicolor film *The Four Feathers*. Finally, the Nissan passed the city boundary and headed into the desert. Weeks earlier, Martin would have described it as featureless desert. He now knew better. Subtle changes in the orange-brown tint of the sand told him where a mini sandstorm had recently passed. To his practised eye the horizon was no longer flat; slight bumps and indentations revealed the distant tracks used by camel caravans. The road was well worn, and in places it was amazingly wide. Along some stretches tyre tracks marked a carriageway at least seventy yards in width. It narrowed only in those stretches where the sand on either side was obviously deep and soft, where vehicles were in danger of floundering and getting stuck. Most of the time, however, the surface was hard and crusty and vehicles were free to wander to the left and right. Martin considered what he should do if he saw an oncoming vehicle. The Nissan was left-hand drive and in the Sudan one drove on the right hand side of the road. On this wide, free-for-all, unmetalled desert route with no central markings it would be easy to forget. So he kept reminding himself that oncoming traffic must be kept on his left.

## CHAPTER 25

Since rising, packing, breakfasting, and saying goodbye to Monika and Manfred, conversation had been minimal. No particular reason for this; just reluctance to get up so early, tinged with regret at having to leave new friends. Gradually their thoughts turned from yesterday to today. Dotty broke the silence with: "It's been an exciting and interesting trip. I now look forward to the simple routine of my camp, free from concerns about an illegal trade in artefacts and corruption in high places." Martin didn't reply immediately. To avoid a deep rut in the road he was steering the Nissan clear of the carriageway and adding more tyre tracks to the ever widening desert road. Back once more on what passed for a roadway, he replied: "Yes, it's been a not-to-be-missed holiday from camp routine. Meroe seems a long time ago yet it's only three or four days since we were amongst those ancient pyramids. Do you really believe we will now be insulated from the intrigue that is troubling Ibrahim and his sister?"

"Of course, we should ask ourselves that question. We may now feel differently but there will be no need to act differently. We must act as if nothing has changed. We are bound to see Mustapha and the two Mohammeds in a different light but they are on our side. In fact, the more I think about it, we can carry on as usual, remembering not to say too much about our work to Yasser, Mohammed and Gwaria."

Compared with the road to Meroe on the other side of the Nile, the desert track they were now following demanded much more care. Sudden stretches of rutted surface were a constant challenge. Had Martin felt so inclined, he could easily have veered off across the desert and pioneered his own route more or less parallel to his present course. Judging from the tyre marks and churned sand yards away on the left and right, other drivers had done exactly that, probably to relieve the boredom of a long drive. Martin recalled the time Mustapha had driven him on this same route from Khartoum to Dotty's camp. Much of that journey had been in the dark, yet Mustapha had forged ahead without encountering soft sand or ruts, as if he knew the desert like his own back yard, which he probably did.

Two hours into their journey Martin and Dotty had met only one oncoming vehicle, a rickety lorry with a load of goats, sagging on its left side with faulty suspension, its cabin richly decorated with silver and gold Arabic lettering and colourful streamers, the windscreen strung with prayer beads. The goats were not bleating, probably long since bumped and shaken into silence by their non-roadworthy transport. Or perhaps they were apprehensive about their ultimate fate. The driver forged straight ahead in the centre of the road, obliging Martin to drive into the sand on his right. No wave, not even a slight raising of his hand to acknowledge a fellow road user, and the driver and his goats disappeared disdainfully in the direction of Khartoum.

Having left the road, Martin drove the Nissan even further away to the right and stopped. "The ground is hard here. There's no danger of getting stuck. How about a short rest and a little refreshment?" Monika had given them a cardboard box of provisions for the journey, as well as twenty large plastic bottles of water. An orange, a banana, and a handful of dates, washed down with a pint of water, and they were ready to continue the journey. "I could stay here a long time," remarked Martin, "enjoying the peace and tranquility of the desert. Our road is a few yards away but there's no traffic." Dotty said she felt the same but they had to press on. "You must put today in your memory bank and withdraw it later to entertain your family and friends." "Not only today," replied Martin, "I will hold dear the entire sum total of my experiences since leaving home." "Excellent," said Dotty, a little impatiently, "Let me take the wheel for the next hundred miles."

## CHAPTER 25

Martin had to decide whether to doze in the passenger seat, or to entertain Dotty and keep her awake at the wheel by talking. Finally, he said: "We have discussed Gnosticism, Paganism, and ancient philosophy. In my mind I tend to lump them together, and I see them leading back to that Greek trio: Socrates, Plato and Aristotle." Dotty nodded and told him to carry on. She promised not to go to sleep at the wheel. Martin said he didn't think what he had to say was that boring, and continued: "Plato was a student of Socrates, and Aristotle was a pupil of Plato. Someone – I forget who it was – claimed that all subsequent philosophy is just a series of footnotes to Plato. That was a clever observation, but the truth of it became debatable at the beginning of the seventeenth century when Descartes broke into the world of philosophy. He rejected traditional philosophy, commonly known as Aristotelian philosophy, because it relied on feelings and sensations. In contrast, he suggested that we reject as false everything that we cannot directly know or verify. He was not only a philosopher, but also an accomplished mathematician. Having a scientific background myself, I warm to such people. I can divide my fellow clergymen into two groups: those that have a good understanding of science and mathematics, and those that do not. Intelligent discussion about our faith and its role in the modern world is possible only with the former group."

Dotty interrupted: "If I'm not mistaken, Socrates was also a mathematician."

"Be that as it may. As a mathematician, Descartes knew that two plus two makes four, and that such knowledge is absolute and verifiable, and has nothing to do with faith or feelings. All I'm trying to say is that despite certain blank areas in our knowledge, we can trace a winding route from ancient Greek philosophers all the way through the fall of the Greek Empire, the dominance of the Roman Empire, the restlessness of the Jews, and finally to Christianity and its spiritual baggage."

"I rather object to spiritual baggage, especially from a minister of the Church."

"Yes, I thought you would, but to continue: is Descartes right? Are all our beliefs doubtful. Are all our articles of faith on a shaky foundation, just because they are not as verifiable as two plus two equals four? If the answer is yes, then I might as well give up as a minister of the Church and apply for a job teaching science."

"Well? What is your answer? Or to put it another way: what are you going to do about it?"

"My answer is that Descartes has done us all a great service by removing a lot of nonsense from both philosophy and religion. He has taught us how to deal with complexity and confusion, by reducing them to simple denominators. By removing the nonsense from our faith, he has purified it."

"Aren't you attributing too much to Descartes?"

"I suppose I am. Since the Enlightenment science has scrutinised all manner of superstitions and nonsensical beliefs, thereby purifying our faith. I simply wanted to contrast the influence of those old Greek philosophers on the history of Christianity with the pronouncements of a modern philosopher like Descartes. And before I completely lose the thread of my argument: what does the scientific approach say about the existence of Jesus? It says we should trust only that which is verifiable. This means a shift away from the blind faith that he must have existed, but this doesn't help us to verify it one way or the other."

Dotty, keeping her eyes on the road, laughed and said: "In other words, all you have just said about the three old Greek philosophers, Descartes and faith was unnecessary. It was just another way of expressing what we already know and feel."

## CHAPTER 25

Unabashed, Martin replied: "Of course. But we are alone in an empty desert, with nothing better to do."

"I know what you mean. Since leaving the camp days ago I've felt surprisingly relaxed. I think we needed the break. Thank you for your digression about Descartes. Such inconsequential ramblings do have entertainment value and help to keep me awake while driving."

Martin wanted to say: "Don't thank me, it's a pleasure," but he kept his sarcasm to his self.

During the rest of the journey, conversation ebbed and flowed. Mostly it ebbed. After miles of flat, dun-coloured terrain, occasionally relieved by a distant holy shrine, Martin forced himself to stay awake, fearing that Dotty might nod off at the wheel. But the road presented a constant challenge, narrowing here, widening there, deeply rutted in places that had to be avoided, so Dotty had to stay awake and alert. At each brief stop for refreshment, local people appeared from nowhere, mostly women and children. They always kept their distance, pointing, chattering amongst themselves, and exchanging smiles with Dotty and Martin. As the Nissan moved off again these local tribespeople waved enthusiastic goodbyes, as though Dotty and Martin were old friends.

"Now I know how it feels to be an animal in a zoo," said Martin, as they left a waving group of women and children. "Perhaps they're getting their own back," suggested Dotty. "Have you ever wondered how it feels to be ogled, photographed and questioned by foreigners, who arrogantly assume they have the right to invade the privacy of a desert tribe in the name of anthropology?" Martin conceded she had a point. "Shall I tell you a funny story?" asked Dotty. Without waiting for an answer, she continued to tell him about a European anthropologist who contacted a remote tribe in the Sudanese desert and was afforded the customary courtesies of hospitality. When he started to ask questions about the origins of the tribe and its religious beliefs the head man fingered the hilt of his sword and asked why he was asking so many questions. The intrepid European explained he was an anthropologist. Language was a problem and the head man understood that their visitor was apologising for being so nosy. After that, all was well, and the 'anthropologiser' wisely asked no more questions.

"Amusing, but I suspect apocryphal," said Martin. Dotty agreed. She had heard the story third or fourth hand and had always suspected it was invented. Martin racked his brains for something else to talk about. Until now they had never wanted for informative and/or entertaining conversation.

Casting an occasional eye on Dotty in case she showed signs of nodding at the wheel, Martin scanned the horizon for anything that might be worthy of comment. They passed another solitary shrine, about two hundred yards to their left. It seemed in better repair than many they had passed, and the green flag was mounted on an erect pole, not the usual fragile, bent length of wood. The flag also looked new, or freshly laundered. Was this the shrine of a very special holy man? Perhaps he had belonged to a well-endowed denomination of Islam. Did Islam have denominations analogous to those in Christianity? Was it correct to call Sunni Islam and Shiite Islam denominations of Islam? And what about those whirling dervishes, whose performance he had been privileged to watch in Omdurman; did they belong to a separate denomination, or to a sect? Then the ruling party of Syria was Alawite; was this a sect, or might Alawite be considered a denomination? Martin also had a vague recollection that the Aga Khan, best known as a racehorse owner, was the head of a minority sect or denomination of Islam. He was on the point of confessing his ignorance to Dotty and asking her to enlighten him on divisions within Islam, when a new and pressing thought occurred to him. On the

## CHAPTER 25

subject of denominations, what was Dotty's Christian denomination? This question had bothered him ever since he had arrived at her camp; perhaps even earlier. Of course, it didn't follow that a specialist in Christian history must be a Christian, but Flo had told him enough to indicate that she had a spiritual home somewhere within Christianity. Since meeting her, this had become increasingly obvious. Clearly, she was not a Roman Catholic. Otherwise he was left with a long list of possibilities and insufficient evidence to make even a guess. As a matter of fact, the clues were there, but Martin had failed to recognise them.

The shrine that had triggered these thoughts was a good five miles behind them when Martin ventured to ask: "Dotty, may I ask you a rather personal question?"

"Wow!" answered Dotty, "How personal will it be? Well, go on then, ask me anything you want. I can always refuse to answer."

"Please don't be offended and please keep your eyes on the road. May I ask what is your Christian denomination?"

Dotty took both hands from the steering wheel and yelled with pleasure: "You mean to say you haven't worked that out yet?"

"Dotty!! Please keep your hands on the steering wheel!" shouted Martin, then calmly added: "No, I guess you're not a Roman Catholic. Otherwise I haven't the faintest idea." He didn't add that he was particularly confused by her earlier assertion that she applauded do-it-yourself spirituality, and the fact that she was, in a sense, a sort of modern Gnostic.

Dotty did not reply immediately. Wearing a thoughtful, enigmatic smile, she pretended to be preoccupied with negotiating a new crop of ridges and bumps in the road. Finally, she said: "I'm not going to tell you. If you haven't worked it out by the time you leave, I will tell you on your last day in the Sudan."

"This is turning into a party game," replied Martin. "How about a clue?"

"Certainly not. Enormous clues have been staring you in the face practically every day since you arrived at my camp." After a long silence she partly relented and added: "I can tell you it isn't an unlikely denomination like Copt or Greek Orthodox. It has genuine good English credentials."

"You don't mean to say you belong to my Church, the Church of England?" "No, I don't, so you can carry on trying to work it out."

Suddenly Martin cried out: "I've got it. You're a member of the Salvation Army!"

"Oh, for goodness sake, Martin, they're a very fine group of people, but they don't fit the clues I've been putting under your nose ever since we met. And we can forget about denominations for the time being and see what is in store for us up ahead," said Dotty, nodding towards an approaching caravan of camels, seven with riders, three with luggage.

"Either they will stick their noses in the air and pass us by as if we don't exist – some of these nomad desert traders have no time for infidel Europeans – or we will be obliged to stop and exchange traditional greetings, perhaps even share food," murmured Dotty, keeping her voice down as if the approaching caravan could hear, although it was still about fifty yards away. "I hope the latter," replied Martin, "I could do with something to eat." They were now much nearer and, as Dotty slowed down the Nissan to a walking pace, they were both surprised to see that the camel riders looked more European than Arab. Their headgear was designed for desert travel, but it resembled that worn by soldiers of the French foreign legion, rather than the local Sudanese turban. The leading camel came to a halt alongside the Nissan. Its rider pushed his desert sun hat to the back of his head, leaned forward and looked down into the Nissan. In a rich, clipped, American east coast accent, and with a wide smile,

## CHAPTER 25

revealing an unbelievably perfect set of even, white teeth, he announced: "Good day Ma'am and Sir. It's a pleasure to meet fellow travellers on the lonely road to Khartoum." Dotty did not want to be looked down upon from a height, so she got out of the Nissan and took up a position, hands on hips, near the head of the leading camel. To Martin's surprise, she uttered a series of sounds that sounded like a cross between a growl and grunt: "Gruuhk, Gruuhk". It was the general command that told a camel to sink to its knees and allow its rider the get down. He had heard it before, most recently in Omdurman. Martin was even more surprised to see that it worked when used by Dotty. She waited until the American was on the ground and on her level, before offering her hand and announcing: "Pleased to meet you. My name is Dorothy Scott, archaeologist, and this is my assistant, Martin Kimpton. And who might you be, so far from home, wandering in the Sudanese desert. Are you lost?" It was all very good-natured, even humorous, but Martin admired the way Dotty had taken over the situation on her own terms.

"Raymond Thompson, at your service," replied Mister White Teeth. "I'm leading a party of adventurers for African Travel Tours Incorporated." The members of his party were now no longer in line, but clustered in a group on their side of the track. Five of the other camels were ridden by European-looking men with foreign legion headgear. Only after the group had caught up with the leader did Martin and Dotty see that the seventh camel had been ridden by two dark-skinned men, probably Nubians, wearing turbans. These two men had dismounted and were going to each camel in turn and making the *go down on your knees sound* in camel language. When everyone had dismounted, Raymond introduced them by name, adding which part of the United States they came from. They came from various small towns in the USA, all in Michigan. "And finally," announced Raymond Thompson, "we come to Mohammed and Mohammed, our trusty Sudanese assistants. They guide us through the desert, pitch our tents, and prepare our food."

Dotty and Martin exchanged amused glances. Martin spoke first: "Two Mohammeds, so how do you tell who is who?" "We call them Mohammed one and Mohammed two," replied Raymond proudly, as if he had found the answer to an otherwise intractable problem. "What a splendid idea," ventured Dotty, hardly able to contain her laughter.

"Is this the end of your trek?" asked Martin. "You seem to be heading home, as it were, to Khartoum."

"Sure thing," replied Raymond. "We started out two weeks ago, from Khartoum on the other side of the Nile, camped near the pyramids at Meroe, crossed the river on a dam on the fourth cataract, and got as far as the ruins of Kerma. Then time was running out and we had to turn back. Yep, it's the end of our trek. We're now on the way back to Khartoum. May I ask where you are heading?"

"We hope to reach the fourth cataract before nightfall," answered Dotty. "There's an archaeological camp near there, where an ancient Coptic church is being excavated." Disingenuously, Dotty had told the truth, but conveyed a lie. She dared not look at Martin. They both waited for a response from Raymond, who, assuming the role of helpful guide, said: "I guess you will make it easily. It's not far now. We visited that camp and met three locals who were guarding the place. We made our camp not far from theirs, and our two Mohammeds spent most of the evening at the archaeological camp, talking with their countrymen. The archaeologist was away, but I suppose she'll be back by now. Apparently she's a crazy Brit, who spends most of her life digging up the Sudan." Everyone in the party was listening to the conversation and nodding in confirmation of Raymond's account of Dotty's archaeological camp. Except

## CHAPTER 25

the two Mohammeds, who had guessed the truth and were highly amused by Dotty's verbal equivalent of trailing a coat. Martin walked over to the two Mohammeds, took them aside, and asked how things were at the camp. Raymond, still oblivious to the fact that his leg was being pulled, looked over to Martin and the two Sudanese and wondered what they could be talking about. The two Mohammeds assured Martin that all was well at the camp, that Dotty and Martin were expected back that evening, and that Mustapha had a welcoming feast planned for them.

Once more, Dotty took control and announced: "We must be on our way. As one crazy Brit to a crazy American, it's Adios Amigo." With that, Dotty leapt into the Nissan, switched on the ignition, gunned the engine, and moved off, leaving the party of desert adventurers to reorganise themselves and continue their journey. Wearing a puzzled look, Raymond of the white teeth watched the Nissan disappear into the distance. His features gradually changed from puzzled to wide-eyed recognition of the truth. "Jeez, it was her!" he exclaimed, looking pointedly at his two Mohammeds. They both held out their hands in supplication and performed a Gallic shrug, as if to say: "Oh, didn't you know?"

"How could you?" demanded Martin.

"What do you expect of a crazy Brit, who spends most of her life digging up the Sudan?" rejoined Dotty.

"Enough said," replied Martin. "I have it on the best authority that Mustapha has a welcoming feast waiting for us. Let's put our hunger on hold, all the more to enjoy Mustapha's cooking."

"Meanwhile, I have to do the driving," retorted Dotty.

With a look of concern, Martin glanced quickly at her. Was she complaining? "Anything wrong?" he asked.

"Sorry, Martin. I wasn't complaining. Our route, to the west of the river, cuts across the great bend and heads for the Nile where the river once more starts to flow north. So here we are, desert to the left of us, desert to the right of us, no palm-fringed river bank to guide us, and I have to decide where to turn off towards the fourth cataract. I'm worried in case we've driven too far."

Martin shared her concern. He was beginning to feel homesick for Dotty's camp and hungry for Mustapha's cooking. He gazed intently ahead, then exclaimed: "If my eyes don't deceive me, there's a cluster of red flags in the distance."

The flags did indeed mark the turning to the fourth cataract. Dotty recognised the turning from earlier journeys she had made from Khartoum, driven by Mustapha, who knew instinctively where to turn off, without assistance from the flags. Nowadays, most traffic between Khartoum and the fourth cataract uses the road on the east bank of the river. If no-one did anything about it, these flags in the western desert would eventually disappear, the road to the fourth cataract would become indistinct through lack of use and then only the Mustaphas of this world, using their ability to commune with the desert, would know where to turn off.

Two hours later, with the sun sinking behind them, Dotty and Martin exchanged smiles and a handshake as the tents of Dotty's camp appeared in the near distance. Dotty quickly replaced her hand on the steering wheel and guided the Nissan towards the area opposite her tent where Mustapha and the two Mohammeds were waiting. Each of her Sudanese employees smiled and bowed in welcome, not knowing whether to mark their safe arrival with solemnity or rejoicing. Dotty set the tone by grabbing each and heartily shaking him by the hand and slapping him on the back. Her action precipitated a chorus of "Welcome! Welcome!" interspersed with smiles and giggles. Martin received the treatment reserved for males of the tribe, a handshake and an embrace from each of the men.

## CHAPTER 25

The flaps of their tents had been tied back and a bowl of warm water stood on a table in each tent entrance. "Just a quick swill to remove our coating of perspiration and desert dust," called Dotty. "Let's eat then wash properly later."

As Mustapha laid out the meal, Martin sighed with relief and gratitude. Their faithful servant had excelled himself by producing curried goat with okra and fried slices of aubergine. "Hungry though I was," remarked Martin, "I was praying it wouldn't be Nile perch again." Dotty didn't answer, but waved her fingers in acknowledgement. She was chewing and enjoying a mouthful of spiced goat meat. "He had this meal ready just as we arrived," mused Martin. "How does he do it?" Now able to talk, Dotty replied that she didn't know, that perhaps he had very good hearing and had heard the Nissan when it was many miles away, and was then able to judge how long it would be before they arrived. "In any case," she added "I gave up long ago trying to discover how Mustapha always seems to know what's happening within a fifty miles radius of the camp.

By the time they had finished their meal the sun had set. Mustapha took away the plates, brought the dessert (a fruit salad of melon, slices of orange, and banana), lit the oil lamp, and hovered in the penumbral region cast by the lamp. Dotty knew what he was waiting for. She uttered a sigh of satisfaction, thanked him for the meal and then asked how things had been at the camp during their absence; had anything interesting happened; had there been any problems? Mustapha described the visit by the camel caravan of American tourists. Raymond Thompson and his fellow Americans had behaved very well, camping some distance away and keeping mostly to themselves. Their two Sudanese guides had spent part of an evening with Mustapha and the two Mohammeds, talking and exchanging desert gossip. "That made four Mohammeds," chipped in Martin, unable to keep quiet any longer. Mustapha looked surprised. Dotty explained they had met the American party earlier today, on the road back to Khartoum.

"There is also a serious thing to report," interrupted Mustapha, "We have been worried about unknown people at the excavation site."

Dotty became suddenly alert. "Tell me all about it," she demanded.

"Every day one of us, sometimes two of us, walked to the excavation site to inspect for problems. There was a strong wind and the plastic protection of the wall painting did not oppose it."

"So you replaced it. Right?"

"We replaced it very much. Then the wind was absent and on the next day the plastic cover was again removed, carefully and folded, and we saw the prints of boots in the sand, and the tracks of wheels coming from the east. We did not hear the sound of a car or lorry, but in the night we heard the noise of a machine, like a saw. A cut had been made in the wall at the side of the wall painting."

"How long ago was this, and what did you do?" asked Dotty. "It happened four nights before this. Since then, two of us have camped there every night. On the first night we heard a lorry coming near, but I think they saw our camp fire and went away. We walked to the dam and asked Yasser to help. He is camping there tonight with two friends."

"Mustapha, whatever has happened at the excavation site, you have reacted splendidly. Thank you." Wearing a serious expression, Mustapha nodded and began to clear the remaining plates.

Dotty and Martin looked hard at one another. Martin spoke first: "It sounds as if it's started." Dotty nodded. They were both thinking the same thing and remembering Ibrahim's concern over the stealing and smuggling of artefacts. "Maybe," replied Dotty. "Must be," rejoined Martin. Stifling a yawn, Dotty said: "Thank goodness Yasser and his

## CHAPTER 25

friends are keeping guard tonight. I'm so tired, I must turn in. We'll drive to the site tomorrow and see exactly what's happened." There was no reply from Martin. He had fallen asleep. Dotty poked him with her foot and whispered: "Come on now, Martin, it's time all little boys were in bed." He awoke with a start, grunted, waved his hand in a dismissive gesture, and stumbled off towards his own tent.

# Chapter 26

Martin lay beneath his mosquito net unable to sleep. Once more he said goodbye to Monika and Manfred, drove through Omdurman, and out of Khartoum into the desert. He then re-enacted the entire journey, complete with the stops for refreshment, the encounter with Raymond Thompson of the white teeth, and their final arrival to a welcome by Mustapha and the two Mohammeds. Only then was he able to surrender to Somnus. Martin opened one eye, peered through the open flaps of his tent at the moonlit campsite, then fell into a deep sleep.

Dotty slept later than usual, but by nine o'clock she was up and dressed and waiting for Martin to join her. Mustapha had to wake Martin by making a noise outside his tent. Several minutes later Martin stifled a yawn and semaphored Dotty with his tea strainer. It seemed that the camp routine was once more established.

At breakfast, however, Dotty was not her usual communicative self. Something was weighing heavily on her mind and she was hesitating before putting it into words. Martin waited patiently, occasionally casting a quick glance in her direction, and otherwise occupying himself with coffee and a cinnamon bun.

Suddenly Dotty broke the silence with: "I don't like it, Martin, I don't like it at all. We could be in considerable danger!" Without waiting for a response, Dotty continued: "If a vehicle with cutting equipment has been prowling around the excavation site, it means someone is thinking big. It's easy enough to hide a small artefact in the folds of a galabiya: a statuette, a brooch, or whatever, but to remove a whole slab of a mud brick wall, then carry it away, is a big undertaking. It requires planning and backing, and we know that the sole purpose is financial gain, which means it may be accompanied by a grim determination."

## CHAPTER 26

Martin was about to speak but Dotty cut him short with: "Ibrahim made it clear to us that the trade in stolen artefacts is big business, and that the thieves and/or the traders are prepared to protect their interests with murder."

At last Martin was allowed to speak: "Then we must drive straight away to the site and find out what has happened to our precious fresco. And what about Yasser and his two friends. Will they still be there?" Mustapha, who had been hovering and listening, explained that the three men had come to the camp for breakfast before Dotty and Martin were awake, and that they were now walking back to the Nile. Without wasting any more time talking, Dotty jerked her thumb towards the Nissan, indicating that Martin and Mustapha should join her.

At the archaeological site, Dotty and Martin got out. Mustapha drove on to catch up with Yasser and his friends and take them home.

Dotty headed straight for the fresco. They hadn't brought the aluminium ladder, so she pulled back the plastic sheeting and inspected the scene from above. She could see no signs of damage or cutting on the surface of the wall on either side of the fresco. Without a word, Martin walked round to the opposite side of the pit and looked from Dotty to the top of the wall, inviting her to follow his gaze. She then saw a channel cut into the mud brick on her right. About a foot long and less than half an inch wide, its depth impossible to assess because it was filled with sand in an obvious attempt to conceal its presence.

Dotty nodded and gave a thumbs-up sign to Martin to indicate she could see the poorly concealed channel. "We must inspect that cut more closely," she called across to Martin, "As far as I can see, the fresco is untouched and is still in excellent condition."

Martin was quick to reply: "That's a relief, of course, but we now have to ask who cut into the wall and why."

"You're right, of course, but I don't think we can deal with this on our own. I'm duty-bound to tell Ibrahim what has happened. Let's hope Ibrahim responds by taking over responsibility for protecting my work. Sorry, I should have said *our* work!"

Martin suggested they blow some sand out of the channel to make it more visible and then photograph it. Dotty could then e-mail Ibrahim a picture of the damage.

Half-way back to the camp, Dotty and Martin were overtaken by Mustapha in the Nissan. He had delivered Yasser and his friends safely to Yasser's house and they had been grateful for the lift. Gwaria sent her regards to Dotty with the hope they would meet again soon.

Back at the camp, Dotty retrieved her camera and laptop, and asked Martin to drive her back to the site, not forgetting the aluminium ladder. Mustapha needed to stay and prepare lunch.

Sitting at the bottom of the pit facing the fresco, with her back to the rather spongy wall of sand, Dotty sent an e-mail to Ibrahim, accompanied by a picture taken at an angle chosen to give a clear view of the newly cut channel.

"Now we wait and see what the boss thinks," said Dotty, with a thin-lipped, grim little smile. "And if this incident is going to develop into something really serious, I don't want the responsibility of dealing with it on my own."

"Quite right!" acknowledged Martin, "Let's go back to the camp and have lunch."

After lunch Martin went to his tent to catch up with his e-mailing duties. It was at least forty-eight hours since his last e-mail to Pamela, who had replied:

*Whirling vicar of Herefordshire indeed! Sue and Ken were highly amused. Page one of next week's edition of the church magazine will start with the headline: "The vicar in a whirl," followed by extracts from your account of the*

## CHAPTER 26

*whirling dervishes. The photograph of the pyramids at Meroe reproduced very well in the magazine. And don't you look sweet in a nightshirt and turban! Your exploits are exciting great interest in the congregation. Some members have gone on line and found out more about Meroe and ancient Sudanese history in general. After last Sunday's service Ken was surrounded in the church porch by members of the congregation wanting to know more about your work in the Sudan. All-in-all, reporting your activities in the church magazine has proved to be a very good idea. So let's have some more copy (is that what journalists call it?). How was the party later that day? How was the drive back to camp over the desert? And what are you doing right now?*

*Your loving (but not whirling!) wife.*

It was a buoyant and light-hearted e-mail. He wasn't being reprimanded for not e-mailing Pamela sooner, and there was no hint of suspicion about his relationship with Dotty. What a relief! Martin tapped out a reply, listing all those present at the goodbye meal, not forgetting to mention that some had spoken beautiful English, accounted for by the fact that they had gone to school and university in England. His description of the drive back to camp over the desert was ornamented by the encounter with Raymond Thompson of the white teeth and his entourage. Then he explained that he was not motoring along the Nile and visiting Meroe in a nightshirt, and that his garment, called a galabiya, was normal menswear in the Sudan. He suddenly realised that pictures of him in a galabiya and turban must have been printed in the church magazine. Oh well, so what!

Martin then quickly dashed off e-mails to his bishop and to Flo, describing the round trip via Meroe and Khartoum and back again to the camp, elaborating on their meeting with Ibrahim and plans to eventually place the fresco in the Khartoum museum. He mentioned the anonymous, pale-faced appearance of characters in the fresco, adding that, after all, there was no eye witness account of Jesus to be found anywhere. That would show both Flo and his bishop that he was still chasing the provenance of the biblical Jesus. On the other hand, he reported absolutely nothing about the illegal trade in artefacts, the damage to the wall by the fresco, or the fact that Ibrahim believed that murder was being committed to protect the stealing and selling of ancient Sudanese relics.

Three e-mails, written and sent, Martin lay back on his bed and slept.

While Martin slept Dotty waited for a reply from Ibrahim. Eventually she also fell asleep. She couldn't expect an immediate response from Ibrahim. He might not read her e-mail until the evening. Even then, he would have to consider carefully the implications of what she had told him about the cut in the wall by the fresco. From now on, e-mails between Dotty and Ibrahim would be a means of communicating their strategy for protecting the archaeological site from theft, possibly by thieves capable of murder. Until now the secret bush telegraph between Ibrahim and Mustapha had served well, but it could not meet the urgency of the present situation.

Both Dotty and Martin were woken by Mustapha, who wanted to serve the evening meal. Yesterday's drive over the desert had been draining. "We both need another night's sleep to regain the equilibrium of our existence," remarked Martin. "I'm in no mood to analyse what you mean by the equilibrium of our existence," replied Dotty, "I think you just like the sound of the words. But I do agree we need another night's sleep."

"But where?" asked Martin, implying by the tone of his voice that this was a serious question.

Before Dotty could reply, Martin pointed out that, as far as he knew, no-one would be guarding the archaeological

## CHAPTER 26

site that night. Yasser and his friends had done their bit and had not been engaged to come back tonight.

"No problem," said Dotty. "You and I are now used to sleeping out under the stars. We did it on the drive to Meroe. It will be just like old times!"

To Mustapha's amazement, Dotty said she and Martin would drive to the site, and they would return to the camp for breakfast in the morning. Dotty's obvious enthusiasm for spending the night at the site dissuaded Mustapha from protesting. It was *his* duty, so he thought, to see that the archaeological site was guarded.

Martin drove the Nissan as near to the excavations as possible without disturbing any of Dotty's markers. Dotty rolled out a thin mattress and a sleeping bag behind the wall that housed the fresco. They were about twenty yards apart, but in the still of the desert night this was near enough to hold a conversation without raising their voices.

"Don't you just hate waiting?" asked Dotty.

"That's a very open question," replied Martin. "It depends what you're waiting for: impending doom or a wonderful surprise."

"I mean having to wait, whether we like it or not, like sitting in a doctor's waiting room."

"Are you afraid something might happen tonight; another attempt to steal the fresco for example?"

"Not at all," replied Dotty. "I'm waiting for a reply from Ibrahim and I'm anxious to hear how he will react to the news of an apparent attempt to steal the fresco."

They both went quiet at the sound of an approaching vehicle. It came to a halt. The engine was switched off. A door banged. Footsteps approached then suddenly stopped. Martin was on the point of switching on the lights of the Nissan, when the performance went into reverse. The footsteps receded, a door was opened and closed, an engine was started, and a vehicle was driven away.

It had been a tense moment. Martin was the first to speak: "Whoever it was saw the Nissan. Probably they also saw me reclining on the back seat and saw me start to lean over to switch on the lights. They may even have seen you on your mattress, in the light of the desert moon. But I didn't see anyone because I was looking the other way."

"Well, I did see two men. They were wearing overalls and hard hats. In the moonlight there was no way of seeing whether they had Arab or European features. In any case, they were still quite a long way from us; about thirty yards from me."

"We have a shrewd suspicion of what they were planning. What we don't know is who they were, and where they came from. Let's sleep on it," suggested Martin, "I assume we're safe for the rest of the night."

Dotty didn't reply. She was asleep.

# Chapter 27

When Martin first opened his eyes it was still dark. He looked up into a black ceiling liberally sprinkled with stars and imagined he was in a planetarium. He had almost placed all the stars of the plough, hanging close to the horizon, when they began to fade, no longer able to display themselves in the spreading light. Suddenly, the eastern horizon was lit by orange, yellow and purple layers of cloud, followed by the intense red glow of the rising sun.

Dotty didn't stir and appeared to be still asleep. Martin carefully stepped down from the Nissan and began to walk as quietly as possible towards where they had seen the mystery vehicle last night. But he wasn't quiet enough. Dotty woke at the sound of his footsteps crunching on the sand, assumed he was going to answer a call of nature, and looked the other way. Martin found the spot where the vehicle had stopped. He found the imprints of approaching boots, and he could see where they had stopped and returned to the vehicle. Tyre tracks showed the direction from which the vehicle had come and the direction in which it had gone away. It had not come from the north, *i.e.,* it had not come from the direction of the dam on the fourth cataract. Last night's visitors had approached from the northeast.

When Martin returned, he told Dotty that last night's visitors had come from the northeast. She grunted in reply, yawned widely and stretched, raising her arms above her head, assuming a yoga-like posture for welcoming the sun. Clearly immersed in one of her formative silences, she held the same position for about five minutes, eyes closed and wearing an enigmatic smile. Her loose night shirt fell open and Martin had to look the other way. Until now, he had never seen her like this: tousled hair, dishevelled and partly undressed. For a brief moment his nerves tingled, but he quickly recovered and busied himself with tidying the back of the Nissan where he had slept.

Formative silence over, Dotty surprised Martin with: "I've never been to that part of the desert. I wonder what's there." In case she was still partly undressed, Martin didn't trust himself to look in her direction, but replied: "It might be important. We ought to tell Ibrahim." Dotty agreed and wondered if, in the meantime, Ibrahim had replied to her e-mail. She had left her laptop at the camp. Then, with the tone of an afterthought, she added: "You can look at me now. I'm properly dressed. Sorry if I embarrassed you." Not for the first time, he felt both humbled and surprised by her candour and directness.

Equal to the moment, Martin started the engine of the Nissan and waved Dotty into the passenger seat with: "Let's hope Mustapha's got the kettle on." Of course, Mustapha had anticipated all their needs. Bowls of washing water stood at the entrance to each tent, and breakfast was laid out on a trestle table outside Dotty's tent.

Less than an hour later, washed and fed, they sat back, looked at each other with a searching intensity, and both uttered a sigh. Words were not needed. Their facial expressions conveyed a common thought: We are in a new and possibly dangerous situation. What happens next?

Dotty said she would send an e-mail to Ibrahim to tell him about their visitors last night. But she really wanted to see if Ibrahim had replied to her last e-mail and she was half afraid of what his response might be. Moments later she reported that Ibrahim had not yet replied.

Apparently unconcerned, Martin watched a lone dust devil cavorting towards the parked Nissan. He leaned back in his chair with his hands behind his head and adopted the pose of someone reclining in the sun on holiday. Dotty felt at a loss as he looked through her rather than at her. She tentatively ventured: "Come on now Martin, what are you thinking?"

## CHAPTER 27

"I'm thinking let's get on with it! Unless Ibrahim makes contact and has other ideas, I suggest we drive over to the dam and offer to pay Yasser and friends to act as site policemen at night until further notice. In the meantime, let me get to work on revealing that other fresco. Now I know how it's done, it shouldn't take me long to expose it."

"Now you know how it's done, there's no need for you to labour in the heat. We can hire Yasser and his friends to guard the site and to dig out the sand from the front of the fresco."

They asked Mustapha to drive to the dam, fill their water cans, and hire three of Yasser's friends to dig at the site and then to act as guardians of the site at night. By not going themselves they avoided the time-consuming tea-drinking ceremony with Mohammed, Yasser and Gwaria. Mustapha brought back three hired hands, whom he had vetted and declared to be steady, reliable workers.

By mid-afternoon a deep pit, five yards wide, extending about seven yards from the fresco, and about ten feet deep had been dug under the supervision of Martin and Mustapha. A layer of sand, about a foot thick, still covered the surface of the fresco. In thirty minute shifts, members of the hired trio had taken turns in digging, carrying away the excavated sand, and resting. Martin and Dotty held hands as they admired the dug pit and the protective layer of sand, which was ready to fall away and reveal the fresco. They looked at each other, then smiled and nodded in recognition of their achievement. Dotty said she hoped Martin didn't mind her taking his hand. It seemed right when this joint operation had worked so well. Before Martin could reply, she continued with: "In the world of archaeology I'm looked upon as a high flyer, of course, but I'm also thought to be unusual or rather odd."

"Oh!? And why is that?" asked Martin, disingenuously because he could easily list several of her odd qualities.

"Because archaeology usually means team work, and I work alone." Martin didn't bother to point out that he was with her and she had just watched a team dig a hole for her. He knew what she meant: she had no fellow archaeologists sharing the digging and interpretation of their finds. Dotty continued: "Although Ibrahim clearly wanted me to conduct this excavation, he was concerned that I had no fellow European archaeologists to help me. I didn't have a team."

Letting go of her hand, Martin remarked: "So far, you have managed quite well without a team." Dotty did not reply immediately, but took Martin's hand again and held it in both of hers, close to her bosom. At first Martin thought she was immersed in one of her formative silences, but it was a normal, if slightly emotional, pause for thought, finally broken with: "Yes, I've managed quite well, but only with your help. We might have carried on in the same way, digging, revealing frescos, and eventually publishing a valuable account of our work in a reputable European journal of archaeology, not to mention providing the material for a splendid exhibition in the Khartoum museum."

Martin was nonplussed. He was trapped by Dotty's emotional tone, by her insistent use of *we* and *our* when talking of her work, and by her insistent pressing of his hand to her bosom. It had all the qualities of an emotional outburst, conveyed partly in words, but mainly through body language.

Gently removing his hand from her grasp, he reversed the hold and kissed her hand. He marvelled to think that their sudden closeness had no sexual overtones, at least not on his part. "Why might we *not* carry on in the same way?" enquired Martin."

"Because," said Dotty, struggling to regain composure, "if illegal traders in antiquities have taken an interest in this site, Ibrahim might decide it's too dangerous and close me down."

## CHAPTER 27

Martin was on the point of reassuring her that Ibrahim would do no such thing, when he realised that Ibrahim might very well do just that. So he lamely said; "Let's hope not!"

Then he added: "Tea?"

Leaving strict instructions to the workmen not to touch the layer of sand covering the fresco, they returned to the camp to rest, drink tea and wait for an e-mail from Ibrahim.

An hour later there was still no e-mail from Ibrahim. Half asleep in the entrance to Dotty's tent, they waited. The sun went down, Lawrence scuttled off to hunt, and Mustapha served the evening meal. Still no e-mail from Ibrahim. Over coffee, Dotty confessed that she didn't really want to talk about Christian history that evening, and suggested they turn in early. If and when the protective layer of sand fell from the fresco, they would be informed straight away. They had left instructions to that effect with the three recently engaged workmen.

# Chapter 28

Next morning, Martin awoke, not with the lark, not even to the harsh cawing of African crows, but to the distant clatter of helicopter rotors. He looked out of his tent in time to see two insect-like machines silhouetted against the morning sky about a mile away to the northeast. As if landing, they sank below the near horizon of the camp site. As one engine was switched off, a single helicopter rose again, hovered and then raced south for almost half a mile before also landing and switching off its engine. There was also the worrying sound of gunshots. Martin looked across to Dotty's tent. She was also looking out. At the sound of the gunshots, she sprinted to Martin's tent, wearing only a nightshirt. As Martin opened the flap of his tent to let her in, she gripped his arm and hoarsely asked what he thought was happening. Martin said he hadn't the foggiest idea, then pointed out that whatever it was had now stopped. All was quiet. The sound of helicopter rotors and the crack of gunshots, which carried so clearly in the desert, had stopped. He didn't add that it was possibly the start, rather than the end, of something terrible. Dotty took a deep breath and relaxed. She loosened her grip on Martin's arm and was about to return to her own tent when the helicopter engines started up again and the black insects rose once more into view and disappeared in a southerly direction.

Mustapha and the two Mohammeds had been standing in the open apparently enjoying the recent piece of theatre. Without a word they returned to their camp fire and boiled the water for washing and coffee.

At breakfast Dotty had still not recovered from the anxiety-laden excitement of the early morning. After the usual fare of fruit, cinnamon cakes and coffee, and the comforting presence of Martin, she became calmer, almost her normal self, except she had a slightly dishevelled appearance, having

## CHAPTER 28

paid less attention than usual to dressing and brushing her hair.

"So you have absolutely no idea what that was all about?" Dotty asked Martin.

"But I think I know someone who does," whispered Martin.

"Oh? Tell me more," pleaded Dotty.

"Didn't you see how Mustapha and the two Mohammeds reacted to this morning's operatic incursion of the helicopters? Also, the three night watchmen have just arrived from the site and are sitting and eating with the two Mohammeds at the camp fire, showing no signs of excitement. I would have expected an animated conversation, with waving of arms in a northeasterly direction. It's as if they expected the helicopters this morning and they are now satisfied that it's all over."

Mustapha arrived with fresh coffee. He announced that the watchmen had arrived from the site and reported that all was well there, and that the layer of sand had not yet fallen from the fresco. As he turned to go, Martin asked him what he thought the helicopters had been doing earlier that morning.

"Without a doubt, Sir, they were apprehending criminals," replied Mustapha. "Why are you so sure?" demanded Martin. "Because Doctor Ibrahim arranged it. He will explain." With that, Mustapha returned to the camp fire. His message was clear; they would have to wait for Ibrahim to explain what had happened.

"Despite the mystery, I'm beginning to feel much better about what happened this morning," said Martin. "Me too," said Dotty, "And isn't Mustapha a perfect treasure? He obviously knows what's going on, but like a seasoned diplomat he insists that the information is conveyed through the proper channels."

Martin suggested they saunter over to the site and perhaps give that protective layer of sand a little encouragement. The idea of sauntering to the site appealed to Dotty. During the emotional turmoil of the helicopter saga, Dotty had, to her own amazement, found herself wondering how to continue her discussions with Martin about the provenance of the biblical Jesus. And she had come up with an entertaining idea, which she now wanted to try out on Martin. They were half-way to the digging site, when she broached the subject by asking: "Does the name Cascioli mean anything to you?"

"It rings a very faint bell. It sounds Italian. But no, it doesn't mean anything to me. Why do you ask?"

"Well, he's an Italian ex-priest, who tried to take the Catholic Church to court for misleading the people about Jesus."

"Of course! I remember now. We had a good laugh about it at one of our ecumenical gatherings."

"I see. So you didn't take it seriously. Did you read any of his arguments, or did you follow the herd and dismiss the idea without giving it due consideration?"

"I'm afraid I followed the herd, made a mental note to follow it up then forgot about it."

"Let's talk about it later," suggested Dotty. "We could spend an interesting morning on the subject, but now I want to see if that fresco has shed its coat of sand."

The fresco had begun to shed its coat of sand. Some had fallen from the top and from the sides, leaving a stubborn covering in the centre. Further down, about four feet from the top, the sand layer was bulging, producing a blister that looked as if it might burst any time soon. "The fresco of the nativity probably went through this stage but you didn't see it until the process was complete," suggested Dotty. Martin agreed and said they shouldn't waste time waiting for it to happen, since it could still take hours.

## CHAPTER 28

"Frankly, I need to do something different," said Dotty, rather emphatically. "I don't really want to talk about Jesus, bother with running the camp, or do any archaeology. After this morning's excitement and the strain of waiting to hear from Ibrahim, I would simply like to wander off alone into the desert, sit on a rock, unload all my emotions, and commune with my inner spirit."

She spoke quietly but firmly. She was expressing a deeply felt need and Martin knew immediately he would have to acquiesce and allow her lots of personal space, even if it meant she would wander off into the desert.

"Of course, I understand," said Martin, "I'll walk back to the camp and leave you to yourself. But you may not find a rock to sit on. The terrain around here is rather flat and featureless."

"Dear Martin, thank you. Off you go then."

He walked back to the camp very slowly, pondering what Dotty had said. That she wanted time alone was understandable, but whatever she meant by unloading her emotions and communing with her inner spirit, seemed to indicate a troubled mind. Martin decided the excitement of the morning had just been a bit too much for her. Which just goes to show that Martin's pastoral experience of dealing with the personal problems of his parishioners was not up to the task of understanding Dotty. He still had much to learn about this enigmatic, crazy Brit who spends her life digging up the Sudan. Once again, he had missed a glaring clue: her wish to commune with her inner spirit.

Back at the camp he stretched out on his bed, leaving the door flaps of his tent open for ventilation. Like Dotty, he needed time alone. How would he describe today's events in e-mails to Pamela, Flo and his bishop? He decided that today's events were only the beginning of something, perhaps a prelude to a profound change in his involvement in Dotty's archaeological project. Whatever was about to happen, it would affect Dotty's life as well. How could he predict such a dire outcome on the basis of so little evidence? He didn't know, but he had a gut feeling. As he dwelt on these thoughts, or rather these feelings, he watched a lone dust devil pirouetting within five yards of his tent. Thus preoccupied, he didn't notice Mustapha approaching until he was standing in the mouth of the tent.

"I am asking permission to use the Nissan and drive the three night watchmen to their homes," announced Mustapha. "They will not be needed tonight."

"Yes, of course," replied Martin, "How do you know they will not be needed tonight?"

"Doctor Ibrahim will explain," replied Mustapha in a tone indicating the matter was closed. He beckoned to the three men and led them to the Nissan.

"So the plot thickens," thought Martin to himself. "I'll certainly be glad when Ibrahim gets around to explaining what's going on."

The silence of the camp was broken by the revving of the Nissan as Mustapha drove away with the three night watchmen. Martin listened as the engine noise grew ever fainter. In the stillness of the desert the sound carried a considerable distance. He could still hear the Nissan when he judged it was well beyond the archaeological site. Where was Dotty now? How far had she wandered into te desert? Had she found a rock to sit on? Finally all was still again. He could no longer hear the Nissan. A hush descended on the camp site. Mohammeds one and two must be asleep. Three dust devils were now silently vying with each other for his attention. He didn't need videos of any more dust devils, so he lay back on his bed, propped up his head with an extra pillow, and watched the ballet of rotating air and dust increasing its spin by the conservation of angular momentum.

"Such peace and tranquillity!" he mused. Then he fell asleep.

## CHAPTER 28

He dreamed of an approaching helicopter, which frightened away all the dust devils. The noise grew louder and louder as the giant insect hovered then landed in the middle of the camp site, sending up clouds of dust and flapping the doors of his tent with the downdraught of its rotors. Then the fantasy evaporated and he found himself in the real world. Reluctantly and with heavy eyelids he peered out of his tent to see Ibrahim talking with one of the Mohammeds, who was pointing towards Martin's tent. As Ibrahim strode towards his tent, Martin rolled out of bed, struggled to his feet and went outside to meet him.

"I'm so sorry to disturb your siesta with the noise of my helicopter," boomed Ibrahim, as they shook hands. "Not at all," replied Martin, "We've had quite a bit of excitement already today. I've a shrewd suspicion you're here to explain what's been happening." Ibrahim nodded to confirm Martin's suspicions, but wanted know where Doctor Scott was. Martin explained that Dotty was at the archaeological site and would be back later. In fact, Dotty could be anywhere within a mile radius of the archaeological site. He hoped she was safe, but comforted himself with the thought that Mustapha had driven past the site on his way to the Nile and would drive past again on his way back. Dotty would probably see him and thumb a lift back to the camp.

Ibrahim insisted on waiting for Dotty before explaining the reason for his visit. So they sat and drank black, sweet tea provided by one of the Mohammeds and talked about the evening they had recently spent together at the Corinthia hotel in Khartoum. Meanwhile, the pilot of Ibrahim's helicopter was sitting outside the large bell tent drinking tea with the other Mohammed.

Suddenly everyone turned towards the north at the distant sound of the approaching Nissan. Minutes later Mustapha drove into the camp with Dotty in the passenger seat. Ibrahim walked over to the Nissan, smiled and nodded at Mustapha as if in silent acknowledgement of a shared secret, then offered a hand to Dotty to help her down from the passenger seat. Dotty pretended not to notice his offered hand and greeted Ibrahim with a loud: "Well, never have we had so many surprises in one day in this ancient corner of the Sudanese desert!" She then vaulted from the Nissan in a spirited display of her independence of spirit. "Come to my tent and explain yourself," said Dotty to Ibrahim. It wasn't a polite invitation, but an order.

Martin, who had been side-lined in this exchange, wondered what on earth had got into Dotty. Sitting on a rock in the desert had clearly revitalised her and raised her above the petty concerns generated by the helicopters and gunshots earlier in the day.

At a signal from Mustapha, one of the Mohammeds took refreshments to Dotty's tent. The rest of the camp sat back and waited for the outcome of the meeting between Dotty and Ibrahim.

It took barely fifteen minutes. Dotty and Ibrahim emerged and walked over to Martin's tent, Dotty still strident but looking thoughtful. Ibrahim explained that he must fly back to Khartoum before sunset and he would therefore leave Dotty to explain everything to Martin.

Ibrahim's black insect rose, circled, and set a southerly course. They watched until it became a mere speck in a cloudless sky, which was beginning to acquire a faintly orange tinge from the sinking sun.

"My tent in thirty minutes, for the evening meal and a long discussion," announced Dotty."

Thirty minutes later, Martin found Dotty still in the shirt and jeans she had been wearing all day. For the first time since he had arrived at Dotty's camp she had not dressed for dinner. To add to the suspense, Dotty suggested they relax and enjoy their meal and talk later about Ibrahim's visit over coffee, then added: "In the meantime, there is something else

## CHAPTER 28

to talk about, possibly more important than Ibrahim's visit."

Half way through the first course, Martin, bursting to know what on earth had happened to change Dotty's demeanour, her behaviour, her sense of occasion – he couldn't put his finger on the right word – so he asked: "Well, what might be more important than Ibrahim's visit?"

"All the sand has now fallen from the fresco. It's interesting and not at all what I expected," replied Dotty. "It happened just before Mustapha picked me up. I've draped a sheet of plastic over it for protection. We can study it and photograph it tomorrow." But Martin wanted to know more, so Dotty explained that it portrayed an enigmatic figure, possibly a Church dignitary, not unlike one portrayed in a fresco in the Faras cathedral, indicating a much closer connection between Faras and her church than she had thought possible."

At last it was time for coffee and Dotty could no longer postpone her account of Ibrahim's visit. She looked searchingly at Martin and smiled sympathetically, as if hoping that what she had to say would not disappoint him.

She started with: "We are facing a big change in our lives here in the Sudanese desert. It will affect me more than you because, whatever happens, you will eventually, perhaps sooner than you expect, return to your wife and your church in your English village." Not waiting for a response, she continued: "The helicopters that we saw and heard this morning were army helicopters. Not far from here, on this side of the river, there was a camp of seven men, five Arabs and two Russians, acting as a transport hub for the illegal trade in weapons. From Port Sudan, weapons were transported to the Nile, a few miles above the dam then taken across by boat to the desert camp on this side of the river. Ibrahim didn't know why they showed an interest in our archaeological site. Being criminals anyway, perhaps they thought they could make even more money by stealing and selling ancient artefacts. Or perhaps they were afraid our camp was spying on them and represented a danger to their operation. Anyway, five were captured and two were shot dead in this morning's raid. One of the helicopter pilots is a close friend of Ibrahim; that's why he knows so much. Thank goodness they made only a small exploratory cut in the wall near the fresco. If they had tried to move that nativity scene, they would surely have destroyed it."

"Then all's well that ends well," quoted Martin. "I don't consider that shooting two men dead was a satisfactory outcome to this morning's operation. Surely, they could have captured all of them without bloodshed."

Martin was surprised by her reply and thereby missed yet another clue to what really made Dotty tick.

"But it gets worse," added Dotty. "Ibrahim has decided it's too dangerous for me to remain here. As a long-term project, he wants to continue digging at the site until the old church is exposed down to its floor. All the frescos will remain in position and the altar will be restored. The area will be covered by a roof, possibly with financial help from the Chinese, and turned into an extra tourist attraction for the visitors that come to admire the hydroelectric project at the dam. He has offered me a two-year contract to act as curator of the Faras artefacts at the Khartoum museum."

It was too much to take in all at once, so Martin replied, rather lamely: "And will you take it?"

"Of course," replied Dotty. "Naturally, I will shed a tear at the thought of leaving the desert, but working with the Faras artefacts will be a highly satisfactory way of pursuing my interests in the early Christian history of the Nile valley."

"I'm glad it's working out for you. Forgive me saying so, but don't you feel that the museum is, after all, where you really belong, rather than the desert?"

## CHAPTER 28

Too late! He realised what he had said. "Thank you," replied Dotty. "So you think I'm getting old!" She laughed with delight at his faux pas and flicked a drop of coffee at him with her spoon. But it was only a way of laughing off the seriousness of what lay ahead. They both fell silent. It was not one of Dotty's formative silences; she was thinking about Martin. Finally Dotty spoke: "Martin, you came all this way to join my archaeological project and now the project is being taken from me. We both must leave this place. For the next few days, however, we can carry on as before. We can talk about Cascioli and we can study and photograph the new fresco.

Martin felt deeply relieved, but was careful not to show it. During their trip to Meroe he had started to long for home, for Pamela, for his quaint little old church and its loyal but tuneless congregation, and for the green countryside of Herefordshire. He would be able to look back on his success in revealing two ancient Coptic frescos. And much as he enjoyed his discussions with Dotty, he knew he couldn't learn any more from her about the first four centuries of Christianity, although she had often reminded him of material he had long since forgotten.

Dotty was clearly anxious about how Martin would take the news, and he knew it. "My dear Dotty, I will do everything I can to help you transfer yourself and your work to Khartoum. Then I will return to England, my wife, and my congregation, carrying with me the memory of my heavenly few weeks at your camp." Dotty remained silent. It was one of her formative silences. Martin joined her. He was really getting the knack of these valuable silences. After about five minutes, Dotty smiled, took Martin's hand in hers and said: "That's enough for today. Time for bed."

# Chapter 29

*Every new beginning contains
a certain magic that protects us
and helps us to live.*
(Lines from Hermann Hesse's philosophical poem *Stufen*)

As Martin removed the insects from his washing water he reflected that it was now too late to suggest they build a shower. Washed and dressed, he tidied the books and papers on his bed, and made his way to Dotty's tent and breakfast. Their new situation was perfectly clear; they had already talked it through. They didn't even need to plan what to do with Mustapha and the two Mohammeds; Ibrahim was already their employer and he would continue to employ them as members of his espionage team.

During breakfast, Dotty asked Mustapha to take her photographic equipment and Martin's sewing machine oil and dabbing cloths to the archaeological site. She suggested that she and Martin take a leisurely walk to the site and talk on the way. Two days ago, Dotty would have been eager to get to the site as soon as possible. Since yesterday everything had changed. She needed to photograph the second fresco and she had promised to talk to Martin about Cascioli. There was plenty of time to do both.

They would e-mail Manfred and ask him to go to the airline office in Khartoum and book Martin's flight home. Otherwise they found little else to talk about. Earlier, the prospect of a change in their existence had acted like a mild stimulant. But now the full import of yesterday's drama had finally caught up with them, and both were in a thoughtful mood.

Dotty folded back the plastic sheet covering the new fresco and exclaimed "Da-dah!" which struck Martin as being quite out of character. He was looking at a fresco

## CHAPTER 29

damaged in several places and displaying a scene that he couldn't relate to anything Christian or biblical. It showed a central figure whose face was damaged and almost obliterated. A smaller figure on the left of the fresco possessed what appeared to be a highly ornamental halo. Although halos are a common feature in Christian iconography, this halo was so ornate and stylised it might have been a fancy hat. The damage had obviously been caused centuries ago, probably by erosion in sandstorms before the fresco became buried in the desert. That was not surprising. More surprising, reflected Martin, was that the fresco of the nativity had survived such damage, probably due to its location in the church, which had shielded it from desert winds and ensured its early and rapid burial beneath drifting sand.

"I don't expect you to understand why, but this fresco is far more interesting and reveals much more than the first one you exposed for me," enthused Dotty. "The next talk I give to the archaeological society in Cambridge, or possibly to a meeting at the British museum in London, will be centred on these two frescos. When the time comes I will let you know, and I hope you can be there. Martin felt a deep admiration for Dotty's irrepressibility. She had already put behind her the mixed feelings and disappointments of yesterday and was now looking ahead to the continuation of her studies in Christian archaeology with infectious enthusiasm.

"Please tell me more. I'm waiting," said Martin, pretending to be amazed, although, if the truth were known, he was amazed that this damaged and rather tatty old fresco could be so important.

"Look at this central figure," instructed Dotty, "His face has almost disappeared, but what do you see on his head?"

"A funny hat," replied Martin.

"If you mean funny peculiar, you may be nearer the truth than you think," replied Dotty. "Look at the front of the hat and what do you see?" After a moment's thought, Martin replied that, to all intents and purposes, it looked like a Star of David. "Now what do you see on the top of the hat? Isn't that a crescent moon? And just remember Islam was not quite up and running when this fresco was painted. Then on either side of the hat are curved horns, which were arguably an emblem of Nubian royalty. So what do you make of that?" Before Martin could think of an answer, she continued: "Look at his costume in the bottom half of the fresco. It's patterned with double-headed birds, which I think are supposed to represent eagles, and the eagle is most definitely a Byzantine symbol. Frankly, Martin, I need more time, possibly a great deal of time, to interpret all of this, so I will say no more. Let's get on with the photography and the treatment with sewing machine oil."

By lunchtime the work was finished. The sewing machine oil had brought out the colours of the fresco in their full glory. Dotty had photographed the gentleman with a funny hat and hardly a face from every possible angle. Martin took several pictures with his own camera.

They ambled back to the camp and to a sumptuous meal of goat meat marinated in orange juice, on a bed of spinach and palm kernels. Mustapha waited nearby for the praise that was his due. Dotty and Martin winked at each other and kept him waiting. Feeling guilty that they had teased him for too long, Martin turned to Mustapha and asked if the dish he had served them had an Arabic name. "Not yet," replied Mustapha. "It is my new invention and it waits for a name." "It is a wonderful invention," said Martin, with a genuine note of approval. "Why not call it *Waiting for a Name*? Then everyone who has the pleasure of your cooking can try to think of a name for it." Mustapha was overjoyed and, quite out of character, clapped his hands with pleasure and gave a little dance. There was a new feeling in the air of the camp. Perhaps Mustapha was also looking forward to the inevitable change in his daily routine.

## CHAPTER 29

This was the first time that such a large meal had been served at midday, which was another sign that a new era was about to begin, if not in the doomed camp then in the lives of the campers. What more was there to do? After they left, Mustapha and the two Mohammeds would pitch their tents at the archaeological site and live there as guardians until Ibrahim put his plan into operation for converting the site into a tourist attraction. Dotty and Martin would drive back to Khartoum with their personal belongings. The larger equipment, like the generator and water purification plant, belonged to Dotty, but Ibrahim had agreed to buy it and install it on one of the museum's archaeological sites south of Khartoum. Until they left, three days from now, there was little to do except enjoy a brief phoney period of relaxation. Martin wished they could leave immediately. The Sudanese chapter in the story of his life was coming to an end. His thoughts were turning to England and home.

Dotty broke the silence with: "We must e-mail all our contacts at home and tell them what is happening, and I must keep my promise to discuss Cascioli's court case. Off you go and e-mail your wife, your bishop, and Doctor Willan. Let's talk about Cascioli this evening by the light of the moon."

"Indeed," sighed Martin, "I'll treasure many memories of this camp. In particular I will miss our evening discussions in the moonlight."

"Me too. Now off you go!"

Before tapping out his e-mail to Pamela, Martin thought hard about what to write. *I'm coming home very soon* would hardly capture yesterday's drama, yet any mention of helicopters, gunfire, and orders from above to quit the camp would be bound to make her anxious about his safety. So he wrote:

*Dear Pam, I've just revealed another ancient fresco in the ruins of the Coptic church. It's damaged in places and*

*it's different from the fresco of the nativity scene. Doctor Scott thinks it is very important, but she's rather lost as to its correct interpretation. I attach a photograph. As you can see, it doesn't appear to be very Christian at all. However, I'm really writing to tell you that my duties and my fact-finding mission here are nearly finished – sooner than I had planned – so I'll be coming home very soon. It's been a valuable experience and I'm longing to tell you all about it. Tell Ken that I've now got some pretty good sermons up my sleeve, all based on my work in the Sudanese desert. I'll let you know the date of my return when Doctor Hopp has been to the airline office and booked a flight for me.*
*With love and anticipation,*
*Martin*

He sent essentially the same information to his bishop and to Flo Willan. He wondered how they would react to his photograph of the fresco. He didn't have to wait long for replies. Within the hour his bishop e-mailed to say he was looking forward to discussing Martin's visit, but made no comment on the fresco.

Flo took a little longer and replied shortly before the evening meal. He thought the character in the fresco was hedging his bets where religion and faith were concerned, and suggested he was a local Nubian dignitary who had helped to finance the building of the church, and had thereby earned himself a fresco in recognition of his sponsorship. He sent his regards to Doctor Dorothy Scott.

That day there was no reply from Pamela.

Shortly before he served the evening meal, Mustapha went to Martin's tent and suggested he wear his galabiya and a turban to dinner. It made sense because it was very suitable attire for a desert evening, and he had only a few more days in which to wear it. "Good thinking Mustapha. Thank you for the suggestion. I will soon have to leave my desert

## CHAPTER 29

costume with you and return to England." "No, oh no, my Reverend Martin, it is a present. You must take it to England." Martin didn't protest. He liked the idea of sometimes dressing in a galabiya and a turban on the vicarage lawn.

He presented himself for dinner at Dotty's tent to find her dressed in a glistening white thoub with bangles, lipstick and eye shadow. If she had to abandon her desert camp then she would do so with a colourful display; with a goodbye party, in which everyone had to wear traditional Sudanese clothes. Was she not aware that this made her appear stunningly beautiful and attractive to Martin? "Only a few more days to resist her charms and then I'll be safe," thought Martin to himself. He played the gentleman and complimented her on her attractive appearance and her admirable sense of occasion in wearing her thoub. She nodded to acknowledge the compliment then announced: "My cook has prepared a special dish to celebrate this, the first of three evening meals before we abandon the camp. It is Nile perch in spiced coconut milk with beans and okra. The bones have been removed, so we don't have to fight the fish; we simply have to eat it." Unable to continue looking serious, Dotty laughed and remarked that she was going to miss her cook, the dear, loyal Mustapha, who had looked after the camp so efficiently. Martin shared her feelings and said he had always wondered how she had been so lucky in finding such an outstanding camp commandant, but of course he now knew that Mustapha had been chosen by Ibrahim.

As the evening progressed, their conversation became intermittent with lengthy periods of silence. Both knew why. They were not uncomfortable silences, but rather periods in which they shared their regret at the impending closure of Dotty's camp and, at the same time, celebrated their companionship of the last few weeks. For the very first time since meeting Dotty, Martin felt he was at last truly sharing a formative silence with her. Dotty sensed it too. She smiled and reached for his hand and held it in hers. To prevent the evening becoming too heavy with sentiment, Martin remarked that everyone seemed to know that the camp was closing because he hadn't seen Lawrence since they had returned from Khartoum. Dotty smiled, patted his hand, and suggested they talk about Cascioli.

Martin would have preferred to sit in the moonlight, enjoying their inconsequential conversation interspersed with silences. Then he remembered Flo's e-mail and reported to Dotty that Doctor Willan thought the character in the fresco was hedging his bets where religion and faith were concerned, and suggested he was a local dignitary who had helped to finance the building of the church. "And he also sends his regards," added Martin. "I've a feeling he may not be far from the truth," said Dotty. "I must discuss it with him. I will e-mail him when I get settled in Khartoum. Now, how about discussing Cascioli?"

"Agreed," said Martin. "I'm listening."

Dotty caught him completely unawares by asking what he knew about John of Gamala. "I'm a minister of the Church with a degree in theology, and I can't remember ever meeting John of Gamala. Should I feel ashamed?" asked Martin.

"How you feel is entirely up to you," replied Dotty, "No-one can make you feel ashamed without your acquiescence." Now, there was a deep philosophical thought! Martin wanted to know whether Dotty was quoting, and if so, from what source. "It's my own," replied Dotty, "and I offer it to you as a parting gift. Perhaps you can turn it into a sermon." As Martin made to reply, Dotty cut in with: "No need to thank me. Subject closed. Now let's talk about Cascioli, who claims that the Catholic Church conflated John of Gamala with Jesus, in order to construct the religion of Christianity."

## CHAPTER 29

"Whoa!" called Martin. "Not so fast. First, tell me who exactly Cascioli is or was. Then I would like to explore what you mean by *conflate*."

"Luigi Cascioli is a retired Italian agronomist. Early in his life he studied for the priesthood. Then his faith underwent a complete U-turn and he became an outspoken atheist. In addition to writing extensively on the subject of Jesus versus John of Gamala, Cascioli expressed his views very forcibly in a book entitled: *La favola di Cristo (The Fable of Christ)*. This provoked a priest called Father Righi to publicly criticise Cascioli's views in a church newsletter in 2002, in which he stated that millions of people around the world had long believed in the evidence that appeared in the Gospels and in thousands of other religious and secular writings. Cascioli responded by taking the Catholic Church to court for misleading the people over the existence of Jesus. He claimed that the Church had been allowed to spread the story of the Virgin Mary, Joseph, the Apostles, and Jesus because it served as a comfort for simple, superstitious human beings, who needed a faith to lighten the burden of their difficult lives. He claimed that to mislead in this way would soon become a crime under articles 661 and 494 of the Italian criminal code, which make it illegal to deceive anyone by fraud. This legal aspect of his claim need not concern us. More important is his theological argument, in which he claims that the character of Jesus is based on and mixed up with that of John of Gamala; and that, incidentally, is what I mean by *conflated*: based on and mixed up with."

"I'm afraid I'm at a loss. I can't tell you anything about John of Gamala. Please carry on and tell me all about him," replied Martin, somewhat shamefacedly.

"Okay. Let's not forget that Jesus, if he existed, was not a Christian; he was a Jew. Everyone knows this really, but it can still catch an audience by surprise. John of Gamala was also a Jew with true Jewish ancestry.

"But where did this John of Gamala come from?" persisted Martin.

"You're not the only one who's a bit hazy over this bit of history, but Cascioli has laid it out as part of his argument. Concerning the ancestry of John of Gamala, let's start with Simon Maccabee, who made the Jews sort of independent from the Greeks, and who ruled as both king and high priest from 142 to 135 BC. Is that a name you're familiar with?"

"Martin nodded and indicated that Dotty should carry on, although he would have liked time to refresh his memory about Simon Maccabee. Before Dotty could carry on, he suddenly remembered a Bible study group during his undergraduate course, in which they had touched on Jewish history. He interrupted with: "He was very righteous and loved by the people and the priesthood. However, in the light of hindsight, he was unwise to combine the offices of high priest and king, and even more unwise to make an alliance with Rome. He and his two sons were assassinated by his son-in-law."

"Splendid!" exclaimed Dotty. "Ten out of ten! I bet you can't remember the name of his son, grandson and great grandson."

"Carry on," sighed Martin.

"Well, it doesn't really matter. The point is that Cascioli describes a line of succession from Simon Maccabee to Jesus, whom he claims was conflated with John of Gamala. That line passes through Ezekias *aka* Hezekiah, who is one of the kings mentioned in the genealogy of Jesus in the Gospel of Matthew. I think we talked about the conflicting genealogies of Jesus in Matthew and Luke some time ago; not many days ago, actually, but it seems much longer." Martin agreed that they had talked about a great many things since he had arrived in Dotty's camp and that the passage of time played curious tricks with one's memory.

## CHAPTER 29

Dotty continued: "You only have to compare the genealogies of Jesus in Luke and Matthew to realise that this whole question of the descent of Jesus, or whoever he was conflated with, is controversial. For the same reason, Cascioli's version of the genealogy is also open to question. However, he presents it as follows: Ezekias is followed by Judas of Galilee, who was the father of Jesus. Jesus was the oldest brother of Simon Peter, James the Great, Judas Thaddeus, Jacob Menahem, Eleazar, and two unnamed sisters. He was also the husband of Mary Magdalene and the brother-in-law of Lazarus. Except – and this is a critical to Cascioli's argument – the true descendant of Judas of Galilee was John of Gamala, the Nazarene, whom the Church swapped for Jesus."

"In fact, just another voice doubting the provenance of the biblical Jesus," mused Martin.

"I wouldn't describe it quite like that. There's an interesting difference here. If Cascioli's claim is justified then this probably ranks as an early example of a stolen identity,"

"And it was achieved without the aid of computers and the internet," added Martin, rather quietly and thoughtfully. "I certainly see what you mean. At the moment, however, I still don't see it as any more than just another voice doubting the provenance of the biblical Jesus," insisted Martin.

"I don't agree. Cascioli's claim that this was a case of stolen identity puts real meat on the bones of this question of the provenance of Jesus. For my liking, Cascioli is too confrontational and he introduces a note of unpleasantness against Don Enrico Righi, who only wrote in his parish newsletter what most of Christendom believes anyway. There were times in this saga when Righi, an elderly, small-town parish priest, had to stand up alone in support of the Church. It must have been stressful trying to refute Cascioli's claim that Joseph and Mary were non-existent, imaginary characters, and that the Church was guilty of erasing the true history of John of Gamala and his relatives and family. But why pick on poor old Righi? It seems that Cascioli and Righi were born in the same town and were school mates. One can't help suspecting a personal vendetta. It is this note of unpleasantness that puts me off."

"Okay, I get the picture. Now I'm longing to know what became of the court case."

"What do you expect?" said Dotty. "Cascioli's case was rejected by the judge, whose decision gave license to a number of atheists to make cynical comments, which more or less represent my own feelings, although I shrink from expressing myself in their way."

At this point Dotty dived into her tin box and brought out a tattered notebook and found a certain page. She started: "I forget which particular social medium I copied this from, but here goes: *The judge read the case against Jesus, "Shit! He proved Jesus never existed, I must hide this information..." Case dismissed. :lol.*

Another outcome of the court case was that Cascioli was fined for filing a fraudulent lawsuit, but he refused to pay. The Institute of Humanist Studies has also waded into the controversy with an article on the subject. Here's a quote from it." Dotty turned the pages of her battered notebook and read: *Imagine if the case went before the Court of Human Rights and the court ruled in Cascioli's favour. No longer would anyone in Italy be able to claim to be God's agent or intermediary, to collect money for his greater glory or to issue instructions to the human world on his behalf. No longer would the Pope be able to hand down infallible bulls nor would Catholic priests be able to claim divine authority for their appointments. Only under their breaths would the faithful be able to utter their holiest of vows, "in the name of the father, the son and the holy ghost." Why? Because the father, the son and the holy ghost were ruled not to exist, so to publicly proclaim otherwise would be to mislead the gullible, a crime in Italy.*

## CHAPTER 29

"Take from that what you will," said Dotty, "At least it's not dripping with sarcasm, and it is rather witty."

Martin thanked Dotty for the information and her views on Cascioli. They both agreed that there was no point in discussing it further. The court case and the events leading up to it were available on line. If Martin wanted to go over it all again and get more details, he could google it.

They sat and gazed at each other, with no feelings of embarrassment. Neither felt the need to say anything. It was not one of those formative silences, yet those silences had trained Martin to accept silence as something positive, and to prepare him for moments like this when he and Dotty would be content in each other's presence, saying nothing but communicating nevertheless. Since meeting about three weeks ago they had become spiritually very close. A few days from now they would go their separate ways: Martin to England, his wife and his church; Dotty to her duties at the museum in Khartoum. It would be the end of an interlude in both their lives, during which they had discovered hidden qualities in themselves and in each other.

Dotty broke the silence by smiling broadly and saying: "Dear Martin, I'm going to miss you." Earlier in their friendship, such a remark would have been out of order, too suggestive. It was now totally acceptable. Martin nodded to indicate that he would miss Dotty, which says much about their relationship when a nod could convey so much.

Martin broke the silence with a laugh and said: "There you sit in a thoub, and here I sit in a galabiya and turban, in a moonlit desert. I wonder what our English friends would make of such a scene."

"They would never understand," replied Dotty, "Without the shared experience of living with us in our desert camp, they would not be equipped to understand. Bed?"

So they retired for the night, in separate tents, of course.

525

# Chapter 30

Before getting out of bed, Martin reached for his laptop, expecting an e-mail from Pamela. There it was, entitled *The wanderer returns*. Pamela had written:

*Yippee!! What a pity for you that you must come home sooner than planned. But I can't say I'm sorry. I've missed you, although Sue and Ken are good company in the house. Ken is glad you're coming home. He needs help with his sermon writing, and Sue and I have had to lend a hand with some of his pastoral care. Old Mrs Toothill needed comfort and counselling after the death of her son, but told Ken he was no use and she wanted the real vicar! Hurry up with planning your journey home. I can't wait.*
*Much love (and excitement),*
*Pam.*

Pam's was not the only e-mail. The other in his laptop post box bore the title *Ticket to England*. It was from Monika at the Goethe Institute to say a flight had been booked with KLM, leaving Khartoum at 14.25 on Sunday 2nd September, changing in Amsterdam, arriving 5.30 am in Birmingham on Monday 3rd September.

At breakfast Martin told Dotty his return flight had been booked for Sunday September 2nd. "I will have been in the Sudan nearly one month. Sometimes it feels like days, while at other times it seems like months. It's a very odd feeling."

"I've just thought of a wonderful excuse for you to come again," said Dotty, gazing at him intently as if challenging him to guess what it was, then continued: "You didn't visit the ruins of Kerma, the capital city of the Kingdom of Kerma, which existed more than five thousand years ago. You must come back one day and we will go there together."

"Well, I did manage to visit Meroe, and perhaps I will indeed come back one day. Yes, we could go there together,

# CHAPTER 30

camping along the way, as we did on the journey to Meroe."

"At least it's a beautiful thought," remarked Dotty, "and beautiful thoughts are worth having. Before we drive to Kerma you have to fly to England. According to my reckoning you leave four days from now. Since one of those days will be spent driving from here to Khartoum, we had better start packing."

Martin reckoned that transferring his minimal possessions to the Nissan would take no time at all. Dotty would need only enough luggage for two or three overnights, since she would be returning to the camp to organise the final move to Khartoum. So they decided to leave the next day. What could they possibly achieve by hanging around the camp any longer? E-mails were sent to Ibrahim and to the Goethe Institute to let everyone know to expect them late tomorrow. Martin e-mailed his travel arrangements to Pamela and within half an hour received a reply:

*Ken will meet your plane in Birmingham and bring you home. Unfortunately I have a meeting with Flossy Hoskins that day. Love, Pam.*

The rest of the day dragged rather. They were almost tempted to set out there and then and arrive in Khartoum in the early hours of morning. Dotty invited Mustapha and the two Mohammeds to join her and Martin for refreshments at her tent, so she could explain exactly what they were going to do. In their absence Mustapha would be in charge as usual. There was little for him to do, except keep an eye on the camp and the archaeological site. Mustapha said he was sorry that the camp was closing and that Martin had to leave. He had enjoyed getting to know Martin and he regretted he had not been able to teach him Arabic. And so the conversation continued until sunset. Even the two

Mohammeds had much to say, mostly to express their sorrow at the closure of the camp and Martin's departure, although their poor English dragged out the time and frequently Mustapha had to translate.

"We go cook," announced one of the Mohammeds, and off went the three faithful servants to prepare Martin's last evening meal at the camp.

The meal was served later than usual because they had kept Mustapha and the Mohammeds talking for such a long time. Like all good things, it was worth waiting for: another innovative culinary creation by Mustapha. He presented them with poached white fish, which was completely lacking in bones, with spiced rice and a large selection of vegetables: okra, beans, little potatoes, and carrots. To all intents and purposes, the sauce was a Béchamel, although it was infused with spices that Martin couldn't identify. Martin wanted to know the name of the delicious fish and Mustapha told him it was a local fish. Martin explained that he wanted to know the *name* of the fish, to which Mustapha replied that it was indeed a local fish. Martin gave up asking about the fish, but thanked Mustapha for the splendid way he had helped him during his time at the camp, and especially for his wonderful cooking. Dotty added that they would like to have breakfast earlier than usual tomorrow, in order to get an early start on the road to Khartoum. It was Martin's last night at Dotty's camp. In a pensive mood, they went early to bed.

# Chapter 31

Next morning they started breakfast at sunrise and were on their way to Khartoum shortly afterwards. Yasser, Mohammed and Gwaria were not offended when Dotty and Martin insisted on the briefest of visits before they crossed over the dam to the north bank of the Nile. Their three friends already knew that Dotty and Martin had to leave, and they knew why, because Mustapha had kept them informed. As they said their final farewells, no-one was quite sure whether to celebrate the joy of their friendship, or to solemnly express the sadness of their parting. To hide his emotions, Martin adopted an outgoing jovial attitude of: 'It's been good to know you' as he exchanged hugs and back slapping with Mohammed and Yasser. Gwaria shed a tear as she hugged Dotty. It was difficult to know how anyone was really feeling.

Once across the bridge, Martin turned right onto the road to Khartoum. He looked forward to reliving their journey to Meroe, a journey which had a special place in his memories of the Sudan. They stopped at the same places they had used on the trip to Meroe, and reminisced as they ate the fruit and sandwiches prepared by Mustapha. Once again they fell to wondering about the magnificent Ahmed with the bejewelled turban and the delightful two generations of his family. Dotty promised Martin she would ask Mustapha about Ahmed and let him know just where he stood in the social hierarchy of that area of the Nile valley.

They also talked about Christian history. They couldn't help it. The subject had become a habit, having informed so many of their conversations over the past weeks. As she started once more to talk about the various movements that had led to Christianity, Dotty mimed the sewing up of her lips and promised to keep off the subject. But it wasn't long before she was at it again. "I promise, Martin, I won't talk shop again. But I must remind you to bear in mind the role of Meroe in Christian history." "Yes, yes, I know," replied

Martin, who was listening and, at the same time, paying careful attention to a rather sharp bend in the road. "It goes something like this: black Nubians from Meroe form the 25$^{th}$ Egyptian dynasty. Egypt teaches Greece mathematics and philosophy. Greek thought exerts a profound influence on western culture and on Christianity. Am I right?" "You've got it in one," replied Dotty. "Of course, you need to put in more detail, but your outline is a framework for getting one's thoughts straight about this rather neglected piece of history." Martin didn't reply. He carried on driving and finally brought the Nissan to a halt in the car park of the Goethe Institute before sunset.

Monika came out of the back door of the Institute and hugged them both. She was overcome with emotion to see her two European friends, with whom she had entrusted the secret of her love life. Moments later, Manfred ambled into the car park, greeted them both with a smile and a handshake, and took charge of Dotty's luggage.

They ate in the kitchen at the Goethe Institute, a simple meal of ratatouille and pasta prepared by Monika, who was anxious to know what would now become of Dotty's camp cook. She was still looking for a better cook than their present hired hand. To Monika's disappointment, Dotty explained why Mustapha was not available. Before they had finished eating, Ibrahim arrived to wish Martin a safe journey home. He would not be there tomorrow, Martin's last whole day in the Sudan, and he would not be able to see him off at the airport. He refused Monika's offer to eat with them and stayed barely ten minutes.

Sleeping and washing arrangements were exactly the same as on their previous visit. After their long drive from the fourth cataract, Dotty and Martin were ready for bed. With their guests safely tucked up and sleeping soundly, Monika and Manfred did the washing up, happy in each

## CHAPTER 31

other's company, and looking forward to retiring to their own love nest on the second floor.

At breakfast Manfred said he knew how Martin would spend his last whole day in the Sudan. Martin challenged him to tell. "Perhaps not the whole day," replied Manfred, "You will want to visit the Blue Nile Sailing Club to find the Irishman and repay the two thousand Sudanese pounds that he gave you."

"You're right of course, and if I still can't find him I will have to leave the money with you. Then you will have to find him after I've gone."

Everyone at the breakfast table sensed the undercurrent of humorous repartee. Manfred was pulling Martin's leg for being so obsessive about returning the ten Sudanese pounds, while Martin knew that the responsibility for finding a mysterious Irishman and giving him two thousand Sudanese pounds would be inconvenient and embarrassing for Manfred.

In contrast to Martin's earlier visits, the Blue Nile Sailing Club was a hive of activity when they all arrived at half past ten. Sailing boats were being rigged for a race to Tutti Island and back. An excellent sailing breeze was blowing from Omdurman. Close hauled, everyone taking part should be able reach Tutti without tacking. The race would really pick up speed on the way back to the club when they would have the wind mostly abaft the beam, so they were told, without really understanding the nautical terminology. As on Martin's earlier visits, Seamus O'Shea was not there. No-one knew where he was and no-one had seen him recently.

It was far too early in the day to be drinking alcohol, but the club bar was open and it was, after all, Martin's last whole day in the Sudan. They were also interested to watch the preparations for the race. Moreover, if they waited long enough perhaps Seamus O'Shea would appear. They couldn't think of any more excuses for propping up the bar, but they didn't need any. Only Dotty demurred, preferring to sit with a glass of iced water at the end of the landing stage, thoughtfully surveying the opposite bank of the Blue Nile. The barman, a very dark-skinned Nubian, wearing a galabiya and red tarboosh, told them they could eat on board, and he would bring them food at the stern of the boat. Manfred said they would ask the other member of their group, only to be told by the barman that he had already consulted madam, who said she wanted to stay on board for lunch. For some inexplicable reason, the barman had decided that Dotty was the boss, and that the others would be bound to concur with her decision.

Lunch was paella with salad. As they ate they watched the race start. Six dinghies jockeyed for position at the report of the starting gun and set course for Tutti Island. Dotty expressed surprise that each sailing dinghy was manned by only one person. Although she was not an expert sailor, she knew something of the sport from watching and sometimes taking part in sailing events on the Cambridge fens and the Norfolk broads. The wide, fast flowing, turbulent water of the Blue Nile between the sailing club and Tutti Island was different from the placid sailing waters of eastern England. This race struck her as dangerous. She voiced this concern to the barman when he brought the dessert and coffee. He shrugged and told her that no-one had ever drowned, although dinghies did sometimes capsize. He also told them it would be a good two hours before the boats returned. The sailors would then be very hungry and he would have to feed them. About an hour later, the four friends left the club house. Seamus O'Shea had still not arrived. Manfred suggested they visit the souk, where Martin might find presents and mementos to take home.

Martin was beginning to feel impatient. All the necessary preparations had been made for his journey. He wanted to board his flight and head for England and home. But he

## CHAPTER 31

had to wait until tomorrow afternoon. A visit to the souk would be one way of filling in the time. Come to think of it, he had now spent about a month in an Arabic-speaking Muslim country and he had still not been to a souk. "To the souk, by all means," replied Martin.

Directed by Manfred, Martin drove the Nissan to a side road near the souk and parked. Manfred spoke to a taxi driver, standing by his taxi in obvious want of a fare, and gave him some money. The taxi driver would guard the Nissan against thieves. Martin wanted to know how the taxi driver would guard the Nissan if a customer came along and wanted a taxi ride. Manfred explained that he would assign the guard duty to another person. Then he added: "The guarding of parked vehicles is subject to a system of unwritten laws, which depend on trust and integrity." Dotty nudged Martin and they both looked away from Manfred to conceal their amusement. "I wonder how long it took him to craft that lovely sentence," whispered Dotty, "You must write it down and put it in a sermon." Dotty was in a playful mood, for which Martin was grateful. He wanted his departure to be a joyful occasion with no undertones of *Oh dear, what a pity you have to leave.* Clever Dotty! She felt this too, and she would keep them both smiling, even with the occasional concealed giggle, all the way to the departure gate at the airport.

Manfred had brought them to the *souk affrengi*, the foreigners' souk, where Martin would possibly find local arts and crafts to take home. There was also another souk that went by the name of the *souk arabi*, the Arabic souk, where local people went for foodstuffs and essentials for a Sudanese home. Manfred thought there was no time for them to visit the Arabic souk. He had booked a table in the restaurant of the university senior common room for their evening meal, and time was getting on. "Amazing how time flies when you're enjoying yourself," remarked Martin, turning to

Dotty, but Dotty was in a huddle with Monika, as the two of them inspected a stall of tie-dyed dresses. The stall holder, a turbaned Arab, was carefully talking down the price, his practised solemn expression designed to give the impression that he was doing them a favour. He bowed to Manfred and Martin, who were standing a couple of yards away and within hearing distance, and was obviously wondering whether they were gullible visitors, or experienced members of the foreign community of Khartoum with market experience. Monika had set her heart on a cotton dress tie-dyed in green and yellow. She beckoned Manfred to her side to ask his opinion. He shook his head and said he didn't like it. They argued, Manfred saying it was far too expensive, Monika saying she thought it would be ideal for their goodbye dinner with Martin that evening. The stall holder hurriedly produced other dresses for their inspection, asking if madam would prefer a different colour. She shook her head. Manfred shook his head and started to usher her away from the stall. The stall holder became desperate and offered a lower price. Manfred paused, took out his wallet, inspected its contents, looked disapprovingly at the stall holder and said: "You think I am a rich man. You are trying to make me poor. You must give me a lower price." The stall holder obliged and Monika walked away triumphantly with her new dress. Martin and Dotty had suspected all along that this was a charade. Monika confirmed their suspicions. It was how they always haggled the price down when they went shopping in the souk.

The narrow passageways, lined on either side by traders' stalls, presented a colourful scene. Martin found a stall selling batik wall hangings, about nine inches wide and two feet long, which would make suitable presents. He chose four with animal designs, antelopes and giraffes, and one of a native leaning on a long spear, obviously a tribesman from South Sudan. The price seemed reasonable, although

## CHAPTER 31

Manfred told him he could have got them for far less by haggling. Martin also took many photographs with his digital. Some of the market traders turned their backs as Martin took aim. It seemed they didn't like being photographed. Since the narrowness of the market alleyways prevented them from walking four abreast, they kept swapping partners. For much of the time, Martin and Manfred walked together, leaving Monika and Dotty to talk about Monika's new dress and Monika's planned design for her wedding dress when they finally returned to Germany. Martin and Dotty found themselves together when Monika and Manfred decided to try their haggling trick on an unfortunate trader who was selling airline luggage. Dotty took Martin's hand in hers and whispered: "Enjoying yourself?" Martin sighed and said he was only just beginning to realise how much he had missed by living in the desert. A few weeks in Khartoum would have provided much to write home about. Town and desert were two different worlds. "Then you must come back," said Dotty, giving his hand an extra squeeze. Their friendship was entering a delicate, emotional phase. All memories of successes at the archaeological site, their camping trip to Meroe, and delights of moonlit desert nights were transcended by the knowledge that sometime tomorrow Martin would fly away. Possibly they would never meet again, although there was no way of knowing.

Monika and Manfred haggled the trader down to an acceptable price and Monika broke into Dotty and Martin's conversation with: "Look here! We have a new Koffer." Manfred explained that she meant a new case. As far as Martin could see, the case was made of tough material. It had wheels, which were essential for modern-day travel, and it had useful, zipped side pockets. "Congratulations!" exclaimed Martin, "I hope you didn't rob the trader of too much profit." Manfred paused to digest Martin's meaning then smiled broadly before confirming they had knocked down the trader to a very cheap price.

The Nissan was where they had left it, quite intact with all its lights and spare wheel still in place. It had been guarded well. They drove straight back to the Goethe Institute, freshened up and changed, and drove to the university senior common room restaurant. Head waiter Ahmed greeted them at the door and led them to the table they had occupied on their previous visit. Carefully laying a printed menu in front of each guest, Ahmed asked if they would like to start with orange juice as last time. They all gave a conspiratorial nod of assent, except Dotty, who looked Ahmed in the eye and said: "only orange juice please." Ahmed understood.

Martin studied the menu and uttered: "Surprise, surprise, there's only one dish available, and it's Nile perch. Why not?" Everyone agreed. After all, what was the point of not agreeing? In any case, Martin didn't mind a goodbye meal of Nile perch. It had been one of his favourites at Dotty's camp.

Throughout the meal, conversation was mostly about Martin's plans for the future. Martin insisted he intended to settle back into his Church duties, conducting services and keeping an eye on the less fortunate members of his congregation, and that he was looking forward to being with his wife again, enjoying her cooking, and pottering around in the vicarage garden.

Monika and Manfred were doubtful, and Manfred put his finger on the pulse of their suspicions by asking Martin why he had come so far from home if it wasn't to interrogate himself on the meaning of his existence. Martin and Dotty exchanged raised eyebrows and smiles. Manfred's English, although a little odd at times, could make quite an impact on a conversation. Without knowing it, he had just revealed the truth. And Martin knew it. They all fell silent and concentrated on avoiding the vicious bones of their Nile perch.

## CHAPTER 31

Martin was about to speak when Dotty replied on his behalf: "It is true that Martin did not come to the Sudan for a holiday. His Church is faced with certain theological questions and his bishop gave him permission to spend time with me, in order to seek answers to those questions. I'm honoured that he recognised me as an authority on Christian theology." "Ach so, now I understand," replied Manfred. Martin dared not look Dotty in the eye. She hadn't told a lie, yet she hadn't presented the true picture. Martin finally decided she had achieved the superiority of imagination over reality. Needless to say, the dessert was crème caramel.

Back at the Goethe Institute, Monika and Manfred seemed reluctant to say good night, and they might have lingered to keep alive their enjoyable mealtime conversation. But Martin said he wanted to talk to Dotty in private and that Monika and Manfred should go to bed. Monika and Manfred understood, or thought they did, so Monika and Dotty exchanged hugs, good night was said all round, and Dotty and Martin were left alone. As a parting shot, Monika announced that tomorrow she would be immobilised with pain when Martin absconded. In Monika's hands the English/German dictionary was a dangerous tool.

Dotty wondered what Martin wanted to talk about. For the first time since they had met she was anxious that he might be about to redefine the nature of their personal relationship. They sat opposite one another across the kitchen table. Martin gazed into Dotty's eyes and once more tried to recall any clues he might have missed regarding her Christian denomination. She was clearly a Christian whose spirituality was deep and personal, and independent of anything written on the pages of the Bible. But it was no use. He was still at a loss. She frowned slightly in anticipation of what he was about to say then breathed a sigh of relief when he said: "Dotty, you promised to tell me before I left the Sudan. Please tell me your Christian denomination?"

She laughed out loud: "So you still haven't worked it out!" Not waiting for a response, she went on: "I belong to a Quaker family and I'm what is known as a Birthright Quaker. All four of my grandparents came from long lines of Quakers. My farmer father is the treasurer of his local Quaker meeting. I nearly told you that when we were talking about my family, but I thought I'd keep you guessing. And I'm afraid I *did* keep you guessing. In the end, you never actually placed me in the Religious Society of Friends founded by George Fox." Martin said nothing. He only smiled and nodded his resigned acceptance of what she had just said.

"I'm surprised I had to tell you," said Dotty, "From the moment we met, I laid a trail of easy clues. If you remember, in one of our early conversations, you even mentioned the Quakers and gave me a quotation from George Fox. It can only mean you haven't had much experience of the Religious Society of Friends."

"That's true," said Martin. "Quakers never seem to join our ecumenical gatherings at home, although I know my bishop has Quaker friends and talks with them often. Ever since I arrived at your desert camp I've been wondering what makes you tick, and of course you knew that."

Martin said he was kicking himself for not recognising all the clues that had been staring him in the face. "So you're a nonconformist, dissenting Anabaptist, but I will simply think of you as a very friendly Quaker, or a very learned Puritan. Which would you prefer?"

"Okay, I can live with nonconformist and dissenter, but be careful with the label Anabaptist. It's true that we don't baptise children; we can't accept that a young child is tainted with sin that must be washed away. But the Quakers share nothing whatsoever with the arch-Anabaptists led by John of Leiden who caused death and destruction when he moved to Münster in 1533. Groups of the Pennsylvanian Dutch, like the Amish and the Mennonites, are derived from the

## CHAPTER 31

fourteenth century Anabaptism movement of John of Leiden. Our founder, George Fox, lived between 1624 and 1691 in England. There is absolutely no connection, personal, historical, or otherwise between him and John of Leiden."

Martin said: "Wait a minute. I'd almost forgotten John of Leiden. Did he ...?" But Dotty cut him short with: "Too late now. We have no more time for history lessons. Anyway, John of Leiden didn't exist during the first four centuries of Christianity.

More to the point, you can call me anything you like. It doesn't alter what I am. I'm grateful for my Quaker upbringing. It helps me to live alone in the desert. When I feel the need, I can sit alone in my tent and wait for my inner light to switch itself on and sustain me. As you know, it doesn't always work because I have moments when I fear the future. After all, I'm only human. However, these negative moments don't last long and I soon regain my invincible self-confidence."

Martin had a curious feeling of humility. Invincible self-confidence? That was surely intended as a humorous expression. Her self-confidence was quiet and non-assertive and all the stronger for it. He had misinterpreted her behaviour towards him, which he could now see had been open and honest, even to the point of admitting her weaknesses. At last, it all made sense! Why hadn't he tumbled to it earlier? It explained so much: her candour, her formative silences, her easy, unprejudiced relationship with Mustapha and the two Mohammeds, her appreciation of the beauty and truth of the Christian message with no time for the trappings of ritual.

"Still, you have enjoyed laying clues in my path and playing me like a fish on a line."

"Dear Martin, please don't say that. I wouldn't be so cruel. But before you arrived I did wonder how an Anglican minister would interact with a Quaker. Now I know, and I don't think it will change our relationship just because you know my denomination. The Quakers," she continued, "have a booklet entitled *Advices and Queries.* It contains comments on the human condition, spiritual advice on our relationship with our neighbours and sound common sense on earthly behaviour. Here, I have a tattered little copy that I've been intending to give you. I think you will find much in it that supersedes the dogma of your Church. Read it on the plane. In particular look at point number seventeen, then think of all you believe and all you have learned in the desert." Martin took the book and began to open it. "No!" exclaimed Dotty, "Save it for the plane." Martin did as he was told and slipped the book into his pocket.

"Tomorrow you will abscond," said Dotty, in a poor imitation of Monika's pronunciation, "so let's go to bed." Martin agreed, although he didn't see why absconding went with an early bedtime.

Next morning the breakfast conversation alternated between a dolorous silence as they contemplated life without Martin, and excitement as they vied to outdo one another in recalling the sensual pleasures of European life to which Martin was returning. Martin asked Manfred and Monika what they missed most of home when living in the Sudan. They must have already discussed the same question between themselves because they answered immediately and in unison: "Operas and Operettas!" "Any in particular?" asked Dotty. Again an immediate and chorused response, but in two different languages: "The Magic Flute and The Merry Widow." from Manfred and "Die Zauberflöte und Die Lustige Witwe" from Monika. Dotty told Manfred not to explain; she and Martin had understood perfectly, despite the confusion of two different languages spoken simultaneously. Martin asked: "Why the Magic Flute?" Manfred and Monika smiled at each other and Monika indicated he should explain. Manfred began: "There is much love in that

# CHAPTER 31

opera. Most of all we like it that, after much searching, Papageno finds his Papagena and they are blissfully happy. We believe that is how life should be." With that, he reached for Monika's hand and said: "You understand?" Yes, they understood, and it was time to move on before breakfast became too saccharine.

"What next?" enquired Manfred, "How about another visit to the Blue Nile Sailing club?" Martin was about to say *No* because he was tired of trying to track down Seamus O'Shea, but he changed his mind. Provided the bar and restaurant were open, they could eat a leisurely lunch and drive from there to the airport.

Compared with yesterday, the sailing club was quiet, no-one was sailing, and there were very few people on board. The bar and restaurant were open. Manfred arranged with the barman to have the Nissan containing Martin's luggage to be guarded while they ate. Some might have described their lunch as finger food. They were presented with an array of small dishes containing a variety of cooked vegetables: cauliflower, okra, black beans, white beans, red beans, finely shredded cabbage, chopped aubergine, tomatoes, all spiced with chilli, together with meat that was either goat or lamb and also rather heavily spiced. In the centre of it all was a mountain of boiled rice. There was also plenty of water and orange juice, much needed to offset the fiery assault of the spices. It was a meal that the Sudanese would have eaten with their fingers, dipping a kneaded ball of rice into one or more of the several pots of spiced food then popping it into their mouth. Manfred attempted to demonstrate and made a mess of it. With a straight face, the waiter brought them forks and spoons. By eating slowly and ordering crème caramel for dessert, they managed to spin out the time until they had to leave for the airport.

Over the dessert, Martin suddenly remembered Dotty's earlier challenge to them all. He confessed he had no idea what the Romans had done for Christianity, and would she now tell them? Monika and Manfred also confessed they hadn't been able think of an answer, and neither had Manfred's father. "Well, it was a serious question. I wasn't trying to trick you. The answer is deeply important for understanding early Christianity," explained Dotty. They all waited patiently for the answer.

"The Romans taught the early Christians how to be martyrs. A full account of early Christianity is impossible without recognising the part played by martyrdom. You might even say that certain types of Christians actually sought martyrdom, in the way that fanatical Muslims nowadays become suicide bombers. When Christianity no longer found itself under the Roman lash, martyrdom-seeking Christians had to find other means of self-harm to prove their faith. For instance, some became hermits and isolated themselves by sitting on the top of columns all alone in the desert." "Ah, the stylites!" exclaimed Martin. "But as far as I remember, hermits existed long before the Romans became Christians, that is long before the persecution of Christians ceased." "Nevertheless," said Dotty, "it was through Roman persecution that the Christians learned to prove the courage of their convictions by undergoing physical suffering, and that led to various practices of self-mortification, like living alone in the desert and sitting on the top of columns, exposed to the elements and starved of food."

After a brief silence, Martin said he was still not convinced. He wanted to know how the adoption of a monastic existence fitted in with Dotty's theory. "It's related," answered Dotty, "I'm sure you know that traders brought back to the Bible lands stories of Buddhist and Hindu monks seeking spiritual perfection by denying themselves worldly goods and pleasures, so that may also have influenced certain Christians in becoming monks and nuns. But I still insist that it was the Roman persecutions that made the Christians

## CHAPTER 31

embrace, rather than shrink from, martyrdom, and that that evolved into various other forms of self-denial."

"Okay, I can take all that on board," replied Martin, "although I might not agree with it entirely. It reminds me of something important, and it's this: what about the role of monasticism in the Christian story? That's a whole area of Christianity we haven't touched upon. I'm leaving very shortly, so it's too late now."

Dotty sighed and said it would indeed have been wonderful to spend time talking about Christian monasticism, both male and female, by the light of the desert moon at her camp by the fourth cataract. On the other hand, she didn't think she could contribute any more to the question of monasticism than Martin could learn from reading and talking with Doctor Willan. She then suggested that Martin might nevertheless ask himself why the New Testament is conspicuously lacking in any mention of monasticism. Was it possible that monastic communities were Gnostic in their beliefs? When Gnosticism was proscribed at the Council of Nicaea, many Gnostic writings may have been in the hands of desert monks, so the inquisitors would not have been able to supervise their destruction. That would nicely explain how the Gospel of Thomas and other Gnostic documents escaped destruction. The monks in the Egyptian desert had time to bury them before the inquisitors came by."

Martin was still not convinced about the origins of Christian martyrdom. He kept the subject going by saying: "Surely not all Christians sought martyrdom. But when those that did seek martyrdom were denied the privilege, how did they satisfy that reckless passion to prove their commitment to their faith by self-imposed extreme suffering?"

"Bingo! You've identified the next question," said Dotty. "What other means of martyrdom could they find?"

Monika and Manfred looked at each other, wondering what was meant by Bingo, but decided to keep quiet.

"You're right. Not all Christians sought martyrdom. In fact they were in the minority, and we both know how a vociferous minority can attract attention out of all proportion to their numbers. The martyrdom movement – call it a cult if you like – met with the disapproval of other Christians. However, after Constantine had spread his new-found joy throughout Christendom, it was still possible to die in ecstasy for one's beliefs. Constantine chose only one branch of the Church. If you belonged to one of the other branches that the Council of Nicaea declared heretical, there were other Christians, supported by their new Roman friends, who were only too willing to oblige your insane desire for martyrdom.

Moreover, it chanced that living just next door were the Persians. Many Christians and other emigrants from the Roman territories had crossed the frontier and settled in the Persian Empire. The Persians were in more or less continuous conflict with the Roman Empire. Since the Persians followed the Zoroastrian faith, their attitude to the Christians was a bit iffy. Nevertheless, it seems that Shapur, King of the Persians, was quite tolerant of other faiths. In particular, he favoured Manichaeism, which was a branch of Christianity, founded in the third century AD in the Persian Empire, and declared heretical by the Roman Church. But you already know all this. We discussed Manichaeism earlier"

Martin's thoughts were divided. First, he was feeling impatient because he couldn't see what the Persian Empire had to do with Christian martyrs, and he felt that Dotty had allowed herself to get carried away with an interesting but irrelevant piece of history. Second, Martin felt embarrassed because he had forgotten about the Persians, who were a mighty force to be reckoned with. Any student of history should know about the Persians, a great military power and home of the ancient religion of Zoroastrianism. Quickly dragging half-forgotten facts from his memory of world

## CHAPTER 31

history, and in an attempt to conceal his ignorance, he interrupted Dotty with: "For that period of history I prefer the term Sassanid rather than Persian. I think of Manichaeism arising in the Sassanian rather than the Persian Empire. But, with respect, what has all this to do with Christian martyrs?"

"Call them Sassanids if you like; it makes no difference. You can even call them Iranians if that makes you happy. But if you know so much about the Sassanids, then surely you also know that eventually they turned against their Christian subjects, thereby providing another theatre for Christian martyrdom."

Dotty's tutorial caught Monika and Manfred unawares. They hadn't been expecting a lesson on the history of Christian martyrdom. After a respectful silence, rather like one of Dotty's own formative silences, Manfred thanked Dotty profusely for her explanation of martyrdom, said he would tell his father, and pointed out that time was getting on.

As they drew to a halt in the airport car park, four Arabs in less than white galabiyas rushed to meet them and take charge of the luggage. Hopp waved them away with a few sharp wards of Arabic. To Martin, all the Arabic he had heard since arriving in Khartoum seemed sharp. A normal conversation in Arabic sounded to him like a violent disagreement.

The next words he heard were English, in a lilting Irish brogue: "Jeesus! It's his reverence so it is. But now I'm thinking you're going to fly away. And here am I waiting for Kitty again."

There was Seamus O'Shea waiting just outside the entrance of the main building. Martin introduced Seamus to Manfred, who thanked the Irishman for all he had done for Martin. Seamus waved the thanks aside, remarking, in his charming Irish way, that our only purpose on this earth was to help those in peril at foreign airports. Manfred understood, but Seamus' poetry of expression was surely lost on him. Martin interrupted them: "I've already been to the sailing club to find you to return your Sudanese pounds, and no-one knew where you were. I thought I'd have to leave without repaying my debt." With that, Martin whipped the money from his shirt pocket and handed it to Seamus.

Seamus' broad grin said it all; he had never expected Martin to return the money and he didn't really care whether he saw Martin again or not, provided he was in safe hands. But he couldn't resist a final dig: "And here I was waiting at the airport, and you thought you'd got away with it, now didn't you!?" For good humour and camaraderie, there was no competing with Seamus. But Martin had the last word: "What is I-A-S-T?" he enquired. "Why now, it's an acronym for a firm of architects so it is, that is building schools here in the Sudan," replied Seamus. "Really?!" exclaimed Martin, "I thought it stood for Irish Action for Stranded Travellers".

With an explosive laugh, Seamus slapped Martin on the back and exclaimed: "For a Reverend you have a desperate sense of humour, so you have!" Martin shared his laughter, shook his hand, and continued through the airport to complete the formalities of the check-in. At the point of no return, they all paused, looked Martin up and down, shook his hand, and wished him a safe journey. That was not enough for Dotty. She kissed him on the cheek and hugged him, at the same time saying: "Thank you, thank you!"

Martin replied: "Don't thank me. I now have stories to tell my grandchildren; all thanks to you." Then pretending to gaze longingly into her eyes, and handing her a small parcel, he said: "Here's a token of my affection. Please take it and think of me." With that, he passed through passport control and disappeared from view.

# Chapter 32

As the plane began its descent to Cairo Martin remembered Dotty's little red book. On the inside of the cover she had written: *They who go feel not the pain of parting; it's those who stay behind that suffer (Henry Wordsworth Longfellow).* Was she being devilish clever? Surely she knew that when he read that quotation it would inveigle its way into the depths of his feelings and make him look back and remember her. No, he was being unkind. Devilish clever was not one of Dotty's many qualities. She had expressed a kindly thought, a tribute to their friendship.

He read the forty-two *Advices and Queries,* and understood what Dotty had meant by superseding the dogma of the Church. Here was a rich source of spirituality and common sense that he would be able to use for years in the construction of refreshingly new sermons. He remembered Flo once jokingly remarking that the secret of giving a good lecture was to find an excellent book on which to base the lecture and to tell no-one about it. *Advices and Queries* would be his secret and he wouldn't tell anyone about it, not his congregation, not his bishop, not his fellow clergymen and clergywomen. Point twenty-one was a gift. It read: *Do you cherish your friendships, so that they grow in depth and understanding and mutual respect? In close relationships we may risk pain as well as finding joy. When experiencing great happiness or great hurt we may be more open to the working of the spirit.* Martin imagined himself pontificating along similar lines from his pulpit and casting meaningful looks at certain contrary members of his congregation.

As instructed by Dotty, he then studied point seventeen. It started by exhorting the reader to respect God in everyone, even though it might be difficult sometimes, but the punch line came at the end: *Do not allow the strength of your convictions to betray you into making statements or allegations that are unfair or untrue. Think it possible that you may be mistaken.* Dotty knew what she was doing when she gave him that little book. He could hear her voice reciting the advices and queries, like a dear friend gently offering advice. He was about to close the booklet when he noticed a heavuly underlined passage, which read: *Do you try to set aside times of quiet for openness to the Holy Spirit? All of us need to find a way into silence which allows us to deepen our awareness of the divine and to find the inward source of our strength. Seek to know an inward stillness, even amid the activities of daily life.* By marking this passage Dotty had explained her formative silences. As Martin closed Advices and Queries he spotted another quotation that Dotty had written on the inside of the back cover: *There is merit in seeking the truth, even if one strays on the way (Christoph Lichtenberg).* Dear, clever Dotty had contrived to have the last word!

They didn't spend long on the ground at Cairo and the plane was soon heading towards Mount Etna, which Martin was determined to see, having snoozed past it on the flight from Amsterdam.

Isolated in a metal box thousands of feet above the earth can be compared to the isolation of a hermit in a cave who wishes only to meditate, at least Martin saw it that way. So he began to meditate. One's path through life is guided by signposts, which often take the form of individuals who have exerted a particularly powerful and hopefully beneficial influence. What course would his professional life have taken were it not for two outstanding teachers: Flo and Dotty? Whatever happens from now on, thought Martin, I will always be in their debt.

Meditation soon gave way to sleep. He dreamed of the desert camp, and as his plane flew past Etna (Alas, he had missed it again!) his dream changed to one of shining anticipation of home, Pamela, the green of the English countryside, and the smell of an English kitchen. Then he dreamed

## CHAPTER 32

he was talking with his bishop, presenting incontestable proof that Jesus never existed. The bishop wouldn't listen and kept asking Martin if he wanted something to eat. He emerged, confused, from the depths of his fantasies, to find a stewardess asking which meal he would prefer: vegetarian or chicken pasta?

Viewed through the window of his plane, Schiphol airport was Martin's first close-up view of Europe since leaving one month ago. It came as a minor cultural shock to see scores of engineers, drivers, and ground staff, all going about their business, quick, well organised and efficient, under dull, damp, cold weather conditions. He briefly felt a pang of regret at having left the more relaxed atmosphere of hot, dry Khartoum. Passengers from the Khartoum plane were loaded onto a bus and driven almost a complete circuit of the airport before arriving at the entrance for European departures. Martin checked the television monitor for his Birmingham flight and saw he had about ninety minutes to wait for boarding. He found a refreshment corner near the advertised departure gate, and flopped onto an uncomfortable metal chair with a cheese roll and a cup of coffee. Just one more flight, a short one at that, and he would be home!

He still had an unread paperback that Pamela had stuffed into his hand luggage in Amsterdam. He now looked at it for the first time and read the blurb on the back cover, which dramatised the fact that the small differences in the DNA of humans and apes couldn't possibly account for the enormous differences in their environmental adaptability and social development. Now that sounded interesting, an agreeable departure from the provenance of Jesus. For the best part of a month, the desert, the Nile, Dotty, Coptic ruins, camel scorpions, dust devils, Jesus, and much else of the Sudan had commandeered his waking thoughts. Now his mind was hungry for the sanity and calming influence of western scientific thought. He began to read, but his flight was called. *The Rise and Fall of the Third Chimpanzee* would have to wait, probably until he had talked with his bishop and decided what to do with the rest of his life.

His flight to Birmingham provided a final opportunity to adjust his mind to the imminence of life as he used to know it. Would he be expected to take over his church duties immediately, or would Ken take the services for the next few weeks? At the evening meal, would Pamela, Ken and Sue clamour for a detailed account of his visit, or would they let him relax and simply enjoy being home again? And what about the bishop? Martin's chief concern was how he would satisfy the bishop that his visit to the Sudan had been worth the time and the expense. Then he heard Dotty's disembodied voice gently telling him to sit quietly and empty his mind. So he closed his eyes and turned to his inner light for reassurance and comfort until touch-down in Birmingham.

Oh no! As Martin emerged from the arrivals gate, Ken was waiting outside the barrier dressed in his ecclesiastical best, complete with dog collar and carrying aloft a placard inscribed *Reverend Martin Kimpton.* "Welcome home!" boomed Ken, giving Martin a hefty handshake. Several faces in the crowd turned for a look at the sun-burned missionary returning from bringing the good word to some benighted corner of Africa. Or so they probably thought.

On the drive home, Ken did most of the talking and Martin gladly let him. Ken started with the church magazine, how the accounts and pictures of Martin's work in the Sudan had brought the magazine to life and made it popular reading, not only by members of the congregation but also generally throughout the village. "Does that mean that more people are coming to church?" enquired Martin. Ken said there had been a small increase in church attendance, and perhaps the village was waiting for the real vicar to return. Martin replied in the way expected of him, and said he was sure Ken had been doing a splendid job as stand-in

## CHAPTER 32

vicar. Ken grasped this conversational opportunity and launched into justifying his stewardship during the last month. Martin sat back, dozed a little, and let Ken ramble on about his sermons and his pastoral work.

It was a journey in two parts, starting with the busy motorways and complicated intersections from Birmingham airport, through the West Midlands and into Worcestershire, followed by the complete contrast of the narrow, winding country lanes of Herefordshire.

Ken told Martin that the church had been decorated with bunting to welcome the return of their vicar, and that there was a display of pictures by the village children, consisting of drawings and paintings of Martin digging holes in the desert. "How sweet!" was the best response that Martin could manage. He was more interested in his imminent welcome at the vicarage. Ken explained that Pamela had an appointment in town and wouldn't be there to welcome him. Martin already knew this and silently wondered why the monthly meeting with Flossie Hoskins couldn't be cancelled or moved for once. In lieu of Pamela, he was welcomed by Sue, who greeted him at the door and led him inside to the dining room, which was decorated with paper streamers. The table was laid for a celebratory meal, and in the centre of the table was an iced fruit cake bearing the words *Welcome Home*.

Sue asked if she could get him anything while they waited for Pamela. "You don't need to ask," replied Martin. "Of course!" said Sue and she immediately busied herself with the kettle and teapot, while Ken arranged cups and saucers on the kitchen table. Judging from their command of the kitchen, Pamela must have had plenty of help during his absence.

Refreshed by the tea, which took him back to the Sudanese desert and Lipton's Yellow Label, Martin went upstairs to freshen up. Alone in the bedroom, he opened his laptop to see if Dotty had e-mailed him. He was not disappointed:

*Oh clever you! You are right of course – I do need a new Bible. So thank you for yours. It's most interesting that you never opened it all the time you were here. A minister of the Church, who can manage without a Bible! I like that. As for the T-shirt with* Jesus lives, *thank you – I shall wear it tonight in bed. Love, Dotty.*

He deleted Dotty's e-mail. It wouldn't do for Pamela to see it.

# Chapter 33

*And so it came to pass, that in religion as in politics,*
*an inconvenient truth was suppressed,*
*allowing happiness and ignorance to thrive,*
*hand in hand, for the benefit of both.*

There is no mistaking the crunching of a gravel drive. Martin knew it must be Pamela. He calmed himself with a formative silence lasting about thirty seconds then went out to greet his wife, whom he had not seen for a month. Bent over her shopping while closing the car door, Pamela did not see Martin until he was right behind her, asking if he could help carry her bag. "Oh, my god, you nearly gave me a heart attack," she exclaimed, patting her chest where she assumed her heart was. Then with a scream of delight, she flung her arms around him. Holding him at arm's length, she said gleefully: "welcome home, my sinewy, sunburnt son of the sizzling sand. Let's go inside and you can tell me all about what you've been up to these past four weeks."

While Sue and Ken set the table for the welcome-home celebratory meal, Pamela and Martin sat in the kitchen alternately gazing at one another in pleasurable silence, and trying to start a conversation in which both spoke at the same time. Finally Martin said he would entertain them all with an account of his travels after dinner. In the meantime he wanted to see the copies of the church magazine featuring his adventures in the Sudan. Ken fetched three copies from Martin's study, explaining that he had been using the study and he hoped Martin didn't mind. Martin was preoccupied with the church magazine but he managed to grunt and wave a hand to show he didn't mind. It didn't take long to see that his exploits in the Sudan had been given a spiritual gloss – a servant of God and the Church excavating the remnants of ancient Christianity by the River Nile, visiting the home of the queen's treasurer mentioned in the Acts of the Apostles – all perfectly good reading for the village congregation, and amply illustrated with photographs. The picture of him amongst the pyramids at Meroe had come out very well, although it was in black and white. There was no need to read through all three copies. After all, he had provided most of what was written, as well as the photographs.

During the meal, Martin was so busy answering questions that he hardly had time to put food into his mouth. Pamela asked about Flo's three students. "No information whatsoever," answered Martin, "We will never know." Sue and Ken didn't ask what they were talking about, and Pamela and Martin didn't tell them.

Ken said the bishop had phoned him frequently to make sure he was happy with his role of stand-in minister and to make sure he was managing. Sue added that she thought the bishop was fussing too much and that Ken had managed perfectly well. Ken added that the bishop knew Martin was due home today and would soon be making contact.

Early the following morning the bishop himself, not his secretary, telephoned to arrange a meeting that day, if possible. Still feeling rather tired, Martin would have preferred to postpone their meeting for a day or more, but he agreed to visit the bishop that same morning. Pamela, who also would have preferred more rest, agreed to drive Martin into town.

It was a re-run of their first meeting several weeks ago. The bishop came striding out in his slippers to welcome Martin and guided him into his study, where they seated themselves facing one another in deep leather chairs.

"Welcome home, Martin," boomed the bishop, "What happened to turn your sabbatical into barely a month? Your e-mails were not explicit on that point." Martin explained why Dotty's camp had to be abandoned and added that he felt he had learned all he needed to learn in the short time he was there. "In fact," he added, "I didn't learn much that was absolutely new to me. It was more like a refresher course in Christian history, and extremely useful at that."

"Nevertheless, I take it you have returned with fresh insights into the origins of the Christian faith," insisted the bishop.

Martin decided to approach the provenance of Jesus cautiously and replied by first telling the bishop he had learned much about the early Coptic Church in the Nile valley, by helping to excavate a ruined church near the fourth cataract and by studying the artefacts from the Faras church in the Khartoum museum. The bishop was shrewd enough to recognise that Martin was employing delaying tactics, but allowed him to continue. Martin said he now had a better understanding of Eastern Orthodox theology, and the different interpretations of Easter by western Christendom and the Eastern Orthodox Church.

Then he took the plunge and said: "I have also arrived at some disturbing conclusions regarding the true nature of Jesus." That was probably a safer approach to the problem than suddenly declaring that he had evidence to show that the biblical Jesus had never existed as a flesh and blood individual, and that the Nicene Creed embodied a propagandised belief in the supernatural. With a knowing smile and a deep sigh, the bishop said: "My dear Martin, I knew you were chasing the true nature of Jesus when you first came to see me about your sabbatical. At the time you were not entirely honest with me. You led me to believe that you simply wanted to obtain a more accurate version of the first four centuries of Christianity." Martin quickly responded with: "And I have done exactly that, and in the process confirmed my earlier suspicions about the provenance of Jesus."

The bishop had no more time for prevarication. "Martin, you have been educated by your visit to the Sudan, but are you any wiser? You have returned from the Sudan with convincing arguments that the biblical Jesus never existed. Am I right?" Martin confirmed that the bishop had hit the nail on the head. "And you think that is a rather special discovery," added the bishop. Giving Martin no time for a further response, the bishop added: "Well, it isn't! Long before you and I were even born, many thinking Christians and non-Christians were convinced that Jesus had never existed. At first this conviction was based on intuition and common sense. Nowadays we also have firm evidence to support it. The result is that society can be divided into two separate groups, consisting of those who know that Jesus didn't exist and those who believe he did. These two groups do not talk to each other. You appear to be a late comer to the first group. So what are you going to do about it?" Still reeling from the realisation that the bishop had known all along what he was up to, Martin thought hard for an answer to the bishop's last question: what was he going to do about it? Meekly, Martin replied that he wanted to discuss his findings with as many members of his fellow clergy as possible, and then with a wider audience.

The bishop answered in a firm, calm tone of voice: "I would rather you didn't." Martin didn't give voice to what he was thinking, which was: "You can't stop me." The bishop continued: "If I were a Roman Catholic bishop, perhaps I would remind you of the importance of obedience, and order you to withhold your understanding of the origin of the biblical Jesus." Martin's attempt to conceal a smile almost contorted his face into a smirk. So battle was about to commence. Martin wanted to declare from the rooftops, or rather the pulpit, that Jesus was pure allegory and metaphor, whereas the bishop wanted him to do no such thing. Both men were on delicate ground. Carefully choosing his words, the bishop continued: "You and I are agreed that Jesus is a metaphor, so I'm not pleading with you to keep

## CHAPTER 33

quiet in order to avoid the embarrassment of declaiming a falsehood. Cynics would claim that the metaphor has been transformed into a lie. We must reject such brutal cynicism, and admit that the metaphor has indeed been transformed, but into a narrative of great and inspirational beauty."

Martin and the bishop eyed each other thoughtfully. The bishop had made it clear that he agreed with Martin about the provenance of the biblical Jesus. Did that make it easier to abandon his crusade to reveal the truth? If ever there was a time for a formative silence, this was it. The bishop, however, had not spent weeks in the desert with Dotty, so a Quaker silence was not a part of his spiritual toolbox.

"Reactions to your discoveries would be several and varied," continued the bishop. "First, there are the atheists. Both types – those that don't believe in God and those that hate God – would crow and say *I told you so. Jesus didn't exist and Christianity is a load of nonsense.* Let's forget that godless alliance. We don't want to provide grist for their mill.

Secondly, there would be that heterogeneous mass of non-worshipping, Christians, who nevertheless love Christmas and can't imagine it without Christmas carols, Christmas trees, Christmas cards and Christmas parties. Mental inertia will prevent them from reacting strongly to the idea that Christ was a metaphor. They would tell you not to be so silly then return to whatever they were doing.

Thirdly, the true believers, those whose lives are defined by a strong Christian faith, would not want to discuss the possibility that Jesus was not an historical figure. To them the very idea would be shocking. They would dismiss the idea without giving it a fair trial. Either they would laugh it out of court as ridiculous, or, and this is far more likely, they would refuse to listen to any reasoning or evidence and simply not want to know.

Fourthly, let us not forget the guardians of the faith: the curates, the ministers, the bishops and archbishops. They, or rather we, have a vested interest in the existence of Jesus. We must preserve the picture of the son of God, born to a virgin, walking by the Sea of Galilee, preaching a message of love and redemption, who was crucified. The telling of this story is part of our job. We are therefore obliged to react against any attempt to deny or change the story. Most of us are aware that biblical scholars have thrown doubt on some of the Christian history that we preach. Already some members of the Church hierarchy fear they are being drawn into an accelerating vortex of dark truth; dark because it threatens the *raison d'être* of their existence. And we must also reckon with the shear bigotry and conservatism that exists amongst certain members of our hierarchy. I refer to the attitude of certain members to women bishops, gay clergy and gay marriage, which is causing so much controversy and giving the Archbishop of Canterbury sleepless nights. Just imagine conservatives within the Church feeling embattled by the growth of this new liberalism, which presses for the ordination of women bishops, the acceptance of non-celibate gay clergy and the solemnisation of the marriage of same sex couples. Then imagine them also being asked to take on board the claim that Jesus was not a real flesh and blood person. You can't help feeling sorry for them! We are not ready for this leap forward, this revision of Christian doctrine. One day it will surely happen, but not yet. Thus, paradoxically, it is in the Church itself that you will find the greatest opposition to your findings; paradoxically, because the Church hierarchy will suspect you have stumbled on the truth and it will frighten them. On the other hand, you might gain respect by promoting discussion about the true nature of Jesus. This is currently acceptable. It has provoked argument and debate. But it starts from the premise that there was an historical figure called Jesus, so everyone feels themselves to be on safe ground. You can fascinate your congregation by referring to John's Gospel and

## CHAPTER 33

the statement *We have not been born of fornication,* hence the need for Mary to be a virgin."

Giving Martin no time to respond, the bishop continued: "The question of Mary's virginity is and was a burning issue in the evolution of Christian doctrine. Mary's virginity and her spotless womb were forced upon the early Christians. Jesus had to be absolutely pure. Otherwise, he could not be the son of God. On the other hand his ministry and his actions breached the barriers between clean and unclean. Born in a cowshed, he consorted with prostitutes and lepers. I don't want to enter into this debate. I was simply pointing out that the Christian story can be challenged on the level of *What sort of person was Jesus?* This alone could shake most Sunday Christians out of their complacent acceptance of everything they were told in Sunday school. That would not be asking too much. But to actually claim that Jesus never existed at all would be a step too far for most of Christendom. In any case," continued the bishop, "why should we even want to shake Sunday Christians out of their complacency? They will eventually die none the wiser, but happy. Let them feel inspired by the star of Bethlehem. It is mentioned only once in the Bible, in the Gospel of Matthew. Its significance in the Christian story has been blown out of all proportion. It might have been an astronomical event, like a comet or a supernova, and whoever wrote the Gospel of Matthew decided to exploit it as a dramatic touch to his narrative. It decorates Christmas cards and every year various astronomers and astrophysicists are corralled in a television studio to entertain viewers by discussing what the star might have been, and to do so with the mock seriousness. That sort of thing satisfies a need. Yet the Star of Bethlehem has only one brief mention in the Bible. It might even have been pure invention. It plays no part in the nativity story of Luke. And the nativity itself plays no part in any other book of the New Testament."

"I get your point entirely," replied Martin, "Surely it is possible to keep the Sunday Christians content in their own little world, while pursuing the truth at a higher level, amongst biblical scholars."

Martin continued without pausing: "Surely, to claim that Jesus never existed as an historical figure simplifies the entire argument and removes the need to debate the nature of someone who never existed."

"But it's still necessary to discuss how and why he was conceived, if not in a virgin's womb, then in the minds of early Christians."

Martin nodded his agreement, then returning to the theme of their discussion, he asked: "What about other denominations? Might other Churches and Christian movements be more willing to listen?"

"Well, you can confidently rule out the Vatican."

"Of course," replied Martin, "That goes without saying. I was thinking more of groups like born-again Christians and Jehovah's Witnesses."

"Oh, come on Martin. Need you ask? You surely know the answer. Some of those people deny evolution, believe literally in the Genesis story, and even know when God created the earth. They won't even hear what you are saying. To them, your proposal that Jesus didn't exist will surely condemn you to burn perpetually in the purifying fire of purgatory."

"Of course, you're right Sir. I'm sorry I mentioned it." Secretly, Martin had also been thinking of dissenting and nonconformist groups, in particular the Quakers, but if the bishop wouldn't mention them, neither would he. Martin returned to the core of their discussion: "Sir, how do we handle this hot potato?"

The bishop managed a wry smile and suggested they leave it alone and let it cool down. "What I really mean, Martin, is that after a time, and I don't know how long that

## CHAPTER 33

will be, the true provenance of Jesus will manifest itself and Christendom will be obliged to accept it. The human mind needs time to get used to new ideas. When society is continually exposed to something strange, it eventually comes to regard it as normal. Or perhaps it will happen in accordance with the political philosophy of Marx and Engels, *i.e,* the truth or the need for change will become increasingly apparent in human minds, until suddenly a revolutionary change is inevitable. But it won't happen yet." Martin interrupted with: "Yes, I appreciate what you are suggesting. Human minds will gradually take on board the fact that Jesus was a metaphor marketed as reality, rather like a slow burning fuse, leading eventually to an explosion of the truth." "Quite so," replied the bishop, "And in the meantime we should not try to change our beautiful, though erroneous, Christian story."

As a final contribution to their discussion, Martin said: "There used to be a radio programme, a comedy, called *Ignorance is Bliss*. It springs to mind at this moment."

The bishop was aware of both the irony and the acceptance in Martin's tone of voice, so he ventured: "I sense you are prepared to agree with me. You have enjoyed a most interesting and exciting month in the Sudan with an internationally acclaimed specialist in Christian history. Is that not sufficient reward? Any further reward you will receive in Heaven. To put it another way, if you withhold the results of your studies you will be richly blessed by your own wisdom."

Martin made to speak again then thought better of it. He'd had enough. If Christianity wanted to continue with an out-of-date guide book, simply because spiritual comfort could be found in a pack of lies, then so be it. He remembered Dotty's impertinent response to an argument: *You think what you think and I'll think what I think – but I'm right.* Until then Martin had worn a concerned expression. He now relaxed, nodded, and smiled at his bishop. And so it came to pass, that in religion as in politics, an inconvenient truth was suppressed, allowing happiness and ignorance to thrive, hand in hand, for the benefit of both.

Satisfied he had won Martin over to his viewpoint and that this village clergyman would now return obediently to his parish duties, the bishop suggested it was time for tea and cakes. Within minutes, the apparently telepathic secretary knocked on the door and entered with a trolley of refreshments. Martin wondered if she and Mustapha shared the same psychic powers.

As the bishop poured the tea, he suggested Martin write an account of his visit, omitting any discussions he might have had with Doctor Dorothy Scott concerning the provenance of Jesus, but otherwise describing the excavations at the archaeological site and everything else he had experienced; in fact everything except the Jesus question. Martin readily agreed, adding that he had a large collection of photographs and would also be willing to give illustrated talks. "Splendid!" exclaimed the bishop. "You understand, of course, that your written account and any talks that you give, will help to justify my granting you permission to take a sabbatical."

Taking advantage of the more relaxed mood brought on by the refreshment trolley, the bishop casually asked Martin what he knew about William Tell. Mystified that the bishop should ask such a question, Martin complied with what he assumed to be an amusing diversion and replied that William Tell had been a prominent figure in Switzerland's struggle against Austrian rule. "Indeed," replied the bishop, "In fact it's highly likely that he never existed and that the story of William Tell is pure legend."

"No need to explain further Sir. I get the point entirely," replied Martin, "He reminds me of someone else, but I can't remember who." Pursuing the pleasantry further, the bishop suggested Martin must be thinking of Robin Hood. "Of course!" exclaimed Martin, who then gazed into space,

## CHAPTER 33

trying to recall something he had heard or read. Suddenly it came to him, a review of the literary work of Gao Xingjian, in which the author was quoted as saying: *It's under the mask of fiction that you can tell the truth.* Martin repeated the quotation to the bishop, who replied: "Exactly! It captures the true purpose of the Jesus metaphor, as intended by the early adherents of our faith. But let's leave it there. It justifies and emphasises what we both feel about Jesus, as well as perhaps warning us not to be too hasty in shouting out loud that he never existed." Martin nodded to acknowledge that their discussion had now effectively reached a conclusion then quickly pointed out that his sabbatical was not yet finished, and he would prefer not to return to his pastoral duties straight away. Ken was managing very well as a stand-in minister, and he and Sue were welcome to stay on at the vicarage as long as they wished. The bishop raised no objection and admitted he had hoped that Ken and Sue would stay on anyway. Surely Martin would not object to sharing his church with a curate, even after his sabbatical had finished. And what did Martin intend to do for the rest of his sabbatical?

Martin said he would be pleased to share his church with Ken, and that for the rest of his sabbatical he wanted to spend time at the British Library, amplifying a few points in his new version of Christian history; he would therefore be away in London. This was all true, but he didn't add that he intended to attend as many Quaker meetings as possible in Hereford and in London.

He wrote a liberally illustrated account of his experiences in the Sudan, in the form of a daily diary, starting with his arrival and meeting with Seamus O'Shea, finishing with his encounter with Seamus at the airport on his departure. Within this humorous framework he included every little detail of his visit, with the exception that he made no mention of sharing with Dotty his doubts about the historicity of Jesus. And he described Dotty as a dedicated academician and renowned expert on Christian history with a formidable intellect. He didn't mention Dotty's formative silences, or the fact that she was a Quaker. His memory of a person lovely in appearance and behaviour, who had at times excited his hormones, he kept to himself. Needless to say, the bishop was pleased with this instructive and entertaining account that more than justified Martin's month in the Sudan.

# Chapter 34

*At each stage of life the heart*
*must be prepared to take leave,*
*to bravely face new beginnings*
*and enter into new relationships without regret.*
(Lines from Hermann Hesse's philosophical poem *Stufen*)

During the ensuing months Martin referred constantly to *Advices and Queries,* as well as making notes on the spontaneous ministry at several Quaker meetings. Four months later, he decided his sabbatical was finished. He took over the evening services, while Ken continued to do mornings. They tossed a coin for christenings, weddings, and funerals.

His first sermon started: "If you read your Bible, you know what the scriptures say. But, dear members of my congregation, what do *you* say? Have you ever put aside your Bible and sought the truth of your existence in your own heart, not on the printed pages of the New Testament? I have. As many of you know, I recently spent a month in the desert by the River Nile, and not once did I open my Bible. I didn't need to, for spiritual comfort and inspiration arose from within my soul. Oh how I wish I might share that same experience with you! Let us sit quietly for five minutes. I'm not asking you to pray. You may close your eyes, or you may gaze at your surroundings. Try not to think about anything in particular. Let your minds be quiet and calm then wait for your inner self to speak to you. Take note of what it says. It may sound like nonsense, or it may transcend anything spoken by the prophets. Afterwards I will read a passage, not from the Bible, but from a different Christian source."

After allowing five minutes of silence, Martin then read: "Take heed to the promptings of love and truth in your hearts. Trust them as the leadings of God whose light shows us our darkness and brings us to new life."

In conformity with Church tradition, Martin continued by making the sign of the cross and reciting: "In the name of the Father, and of the Son, and of the Holy Spirit." This returned the congregation to familiar ground and everyone relaxed.

As he shook hands at the church door, reaction to his unusual sermon was varied. Mrs Owen studiously avoided any mention of the sermon and said: "I'm so glad we sang the hymn *Worship the King*: it's one of my favourites." With a hearty laugh, Colonel Mason asked: "Is there going to be any more of this five minutes silence business. I prefer a good telling off by God. It sets me up for the rest of the week." Bronwen Bowen, the organist's wife, grasped Martin's hand tightly, looked into his eyes with an embarrassing intensity and remarked that Martin, like Jesus, had spent forty nights and forty days in the wilderness and had returned to inspire them all with the Christian spirit. Martin pointed out that he had been away only a month, not forty days, but it had nevertheless been a valuable spiritual experience. Otherwise, the exit poll of the church-door response could be summarised as: Um, err, yes, that was interesting. On balance, Martin preferred Colonel Mason's brusque, friendly honesty, since he knew him to have a Christian sense of duty, serving the community in various ways, in particular by pestering the bus company to ensure a regular bus service into Hereford for elderly residents in the village, as well as trimming privet hedges and mowing lawns for his less able neighbours.

Where did that leave Martin? Should he choose the easy way out and return to the routine of the standard church service, or should he continue to conduct services with a simpler, more personal, yet deeper spirituality? The answer was not clear. Was Dotty right? Ought he to leave the Church and take up biblical research? To give himself time to think, he decided to ask Ken to take all the church services for the next two weeks.

# CHAPTER 34

Next morning, hidden amongst the wad of glossy adverts for takeaways, fuel companies, and cheaper broad-band, Martin found a letter, addressed by hand to Pamela and him. Who, in this day and age, was old-fashioned enough to still use pen and paper, when most of their friends and relatives corresponded by e-mail? Martin thought he recognised the hand-writing. On the back of the envelope was written: *from Dr. G.T. Willan,* followed by his Leeds address. Flo wrote that he was longing for a first-hand account of Martin's experiences in the Sudan, and wondered if he might visit for a few days.

Not for one moment did Martin believe literally in the existence of angels, but at this moment he reflected that his angels were looking after him. He was faced with an impossible dilemma. He wanted to find a way of nudging his congregation towards the possibility that Jesus was a myth, while honouring his agreement with the bishop to keep quiet about it. Yesterday he had preached an unconventional sermon and he wanted to challenge his congregation with more unconventional services. But would they stand for it? Would it result in a competition for popularity between Martin's evangelical services and Ken's conventional services? Who better to advise him? Who better to help him deal with his dilemma than his old tutor, Flo Willan?

Pamela was thrilled by the thought of entertaining Flo in her own home, meeting Martin's charming old tutor again and returning the wonderful hospitality he had shown them weeks ago. Martin replied in the quickest way possible. He telephoned Flo and persuaded him to visit that week. Flo said he would take the train from Leeds to Manchester Piccadilly then change for Hereford. Martin said he or Pamela would pick him up from Hereford station. Accommodation was not a problem. The vicarage was large and rambling, with plenty of bedrooms.

Flo was due to arrive in Hereford in the late afternoon. In the event, it was Pamela who won the lottery for fetching him from the station. Martin and Sue would prepare the evening meal. Martin was still feeling surprised that Flo had more or less invited himself. His interest in Martin's experiences in the Sudan must be much deeper than Martin could have imagined. Was there more to Flo's visit than Martin imagined? Did his visit have a connection with the suspected murder of Flo's three former students?

During and after the evening meal, Martin kept the party entertained with his stories of the Sudan. He dwelt on the skill required for dealing with the vicious bones of a Nile Perch, then switched to describing the stalwart dependability of their Nubian servant, Mustapha. He asked them all to imagine digging out ancient frescos in the heat of the desert then described how he had brought out their original colours with sewing machine oil. For obvious reasons, he did not dwell poetically on the romance of the moonlit desert night. They paid rapt attention to his descriptions of dust devils and camel scorpions, and they were intrigued by his description of the mighty hydroelectric dam at the fourth cataract. His journey to the Nile to fetch water, followed by tea with Yasser, Mohammed and Gwaria probably left them with a false picture of what it was really like. He was about to describe the whirling dervishes when Flo interrupted and suggested he and Martin get some fresh air. He had been sitting on a train for hours, and after such a hearty meal he needed to stretch his legs before he went to bed.

No-one else was invited. Flo wanted to get Martin on his own. Pamela told them to enjoy themselves and, with a touch of irony, said the washing up would be finished when they returned.

It was a quiet evening with practically no wind, and warm enough not to need a coat. Flo suggested they walk to the church. He would like to see where Martin held his

## CHAPTER 34

services. At the lichgate Martin could wait no longer and said: "Dear Flo, what are you up to? Why do you want to get me on my own?" Flo replied that he was sorry it was so obvious and suggested they find a pew in the church where they could sit and talk. As they entered by the main door Martin made the customary obeisance in the direction of the altar. Flo had already found a pew and was patting the space beside him.

Flo broke the silence with: "I might ask you the same question. What are you up to? After such a valuable educational experience by the river Nile, are you really going to simply revert to performing pastoral duties and conducting Sunday church services? Don't you feel inspired to follow a new path?"

Martin made no reply. Flo had touched a nerve. If Martin did simply revert to the role of a country parson, he would have to suppress his views on the provenance of Jesus, or sooner or later find himself in conflict with the Church hierarchy and his bishop in particular. What was Flo getting at when he talked of a new path? Martin did not have to wait long for an answer.

"Now listen carefully," said Flo. "There's a lectureship in Christian History about to be advertised in your old university department in Leeds. I'm on the interviewing and advisory panel. You see, they can still find a use for me in my old age. It might be worth your while applying." As Martin made to reply, Flo stopped him with: "Not a word. It's up to you. I would add that rapid promotion to a senior lectureship would be almost a certainty." There was hardly enough light to see by, for which Martin was grateful. "So that is why you wanted to visit me. I did wonder. And thank you." "If we hurry," replied Flo, "we might be in time to finish the washing up."

On the walk back to the vicarage, neither of them spoke, Flo having completed his mission with nothing more to say,

Martin silently rejoicing that a new future was beckoning. At the garden gate of the vicarage Flo remembered he still had something to say. He pointed out that Martin would need two referees. He was prepared to write to the chairman of the interviewing committee in support of Martin, and he was sure that Doctor Dorothy Scott would be pleased to act as his other referee.

Pamela heard them talking at the door and let them in. "Enjoy your walk? We've been discussing Martin's account of his travels. Ken tried to explain the meaning of the angular momentum of dust devils but I'm afraid Sue and I were lost completely. Ken is obviously very envious of Martin's experiences. He points out that a healthy body leads to a healthy mind, and he is sure that the physical exertion of digging out those frescos has increased Martin's spirituality." It seemed that the kitchen had been alive with the excitement of Martin's adventures. Martin and Flo exchanged amused glances, said nothing, and let the other three continue chattering. Before he told anyone else, Martin wanted to tell Pamela the good news, and that would have to wait until they were in bed. In the meantime they kept the party going with a bottle of Niersteiner and more stories from the Sudanese desert. Flo excused himself at half past nine and went to bed.

As everyone wished him goodnight he gave Martin a theatrical wink. They all saw it and Pamela asked what Martin and Flo were being so secretive about. "Oh nothing really," said Martin, "It's just that we had a most interesting conversation during our walk just now." "About what?" Pamela wanted to know. "I'll tell you later," replied Martin, "I think I might summarise this evening by quoting Psalm 23, verse 5." Ken was quick off the mark. He knew his Bible, or at least he knew the sources of the commonly used quotes. He recited: "Thou preparest a table before me in the presence of mine enemies: thou anointest my head with oil; my

## CHAPTER 34

cup runneth over." "Exactly!" said Martin, "My cup runneth over." Pamela, Sue, and Ken waited for Martin to continue. He said he would explain in the morning.

As soon as they were snuggled up in bed, Pamela demanded to know what was going on. Martin hesitated, wondering how Pamela would react. He had no right to expect her to share his enthusiasm for changing the course of their lives in middle age. "Flo told me a lectureship in Christian history is about to be advertised in his old university department, and ..."

"And he thinks you should apply," said Pamela, quietly and ominously.

"Well, yes," said Martin," worried by the Pamela's tone.

"Then why don't you get on with it," said Pamela. "Frankly, I've had enough of village life. And I've had enough of living in vicarages. Let's move to Leeds. Let's enjoy some traffic noise and the vibrancy of a big city. I'm up for it if you are!"

For the second time that day Martin heard his angels singing. He embraced his wife and almost wept with gratitude. Pamela hugged him back and said, again quietly and ominously: "And I have something to tell *you*."

Martin waited, hoping Pamela was not about to dampen his new-found joy.

"Well?" he asked.

"Have a guess," she said, with a happy lilt in her voice. "It's just as important as your new job prospects."

"No idea," said Martin.

"Let me ask you something," said Pamela. "All the time you were in the Sudan, did you ever e-mail our son or daughter?"

"Well, er, no. I left it to you to pass on all my news."

"Oh, for goodness sake, I suppose I'll have to tell you. Ruth is pregnant. We are going to become grandparents!"

Once again, Martin heard his angels singing. Wearing a broad smile, he said: "Come on Granny, give me a big kiss!" Pamela obliged, and what happened after that I'm not allowed to say.

Next morning, Martin sent an e-mail to Dotty, asking her to be a referee for his application for the lectureship in Christian history. Her reply arrived before teatime:

*Dear Martin, Doctor Willan and I have been exchanging e-mails concerning your visit to the Sudan. Since he recommended you to me in the first place, he was anxious to know whether my work had benefitted from his recommendation. You and I both know the answer to that question! He also told me to expect a request from you to provide a reference for your application for a lectureship in Christian history. I will write to the chairman of the university interviewing committee and praise your abilities most highly.*

*I miss you. Love, Dotty.*

Martin read Dotty's e-mail several times then deleted it.

# Chapter 35

Martin was offered the lectureship. In view of the status of his referees plus his experience of researching Christian history by digging up the past in the Sudanese desert, how could the interviewing committee not give him the job?

Of course, the bishop said he was disappointed to lose Martin, but he wasn't really. He would no longer have to suffer the constant anxiety that Martin might try, single handed, to preach a revised version of Christian history. Moreover, he could now offer Ken the living, after first raising him from curate to church minister. Ken's uncle, the bishop's old university friend, was most grateful.

Pamela and Martin bought a semi-detached near Roundhay Park in Leeds. Their first grandchild was a girl, whom the parents named Pamela after her maternal grandmother.

Their son, Harry, did well in his final law examinations and found a job with a firm of solicitors in Hereford. He had a delightful girlfriend, and his parents and her parents didn't seem to mind that they decided not to get married, but to live in sin in a one-bedroom flat near the river Wye.

Martin started his first lecture by reading an extract from the writings of the early Church father, Justin Martyr. He then went on to explain that Justin was putting forward the idea of diabolical mimicry to explain the embarrassing similarity between Jesus and the Pagan gods. In this way, Martin opened up the entire question of early Christian history, which he pursued, lecture by lecture, for the rest of the university term.

News of Martin's inspiring lectures and his challenging tutorials started to attract students who were not actually registered on his course. Strictly speaking their presence was unauthorised but Martin let them come. While admired for his erudition and clarity of presentation, he nevertheless earned a reputation for behaving rather oddly. He would sometimes stop talking and lapse into a minute or so of silence. After a while his lecture class or tutorial group became accustomed to his silences, which they happily shared, feeling that they helped the learning process, without knowing how. What they couldn't share during these silences was Martin's vision of a desert camp, lit by a great moon, the taste of aubergine and Nile Perch still lingering on his tongue, and Dotty, dear Dotty, explaining diabolical mimicry, what the Romans did for Christianity, the fundamentals of Gnosticism and much more.

So did Martin take on board Flo's philosophical parting gift, months ago, as he and Pamela drove off to the Yorkshire Dales? Do I need to jog your memory? It was the Latin *Sapere aude* or DARE TO KNOW. Translation of any language usually offers a certain freedom, so let's recast the Latin as "Have the courage to serve your own common sense." It was the rallying cry of the Enlightenment, which attempted to strip all prejudice and superstition of their protective layers and reveal the truth through art and science. So, I ask again: did Martin obey that exhortation? Of course he did! Atheists and unbelievers will maintain that he didn't go far enough. Good for them, that they dare to know!

# Claims, Denials and Acknowledgements

The author of *Camel Scorpions* has spent time in the Sudan and several other tropical countries. He is grateful to the teaching staff of the Faculty of Medicine of the University of Khartoum for their hospitality and for their companionship on journeys beyond Khartoum, into the desert and along the Nile.

Considerable licence has been excercised in describing the scene and human activity at the damn on the fourth cataract. Ruins of ancient Coptic churches can be found along the Nile valley but, as far as the author knows, no such ruin exists a short distance southeast of the fourth cataract. Equally contrived and invented is Dotty's campsite, which is a setting for many episodes in the novel.

It must be stressed that the author is not and never has been a clergyman. Neither has he ever met the Bishop of Hereford, or for that matter the Bishop of anywhere. Martin's bishop is not modelled on any known person and is a product of the author's imagination. The bishop's secretary and assistants, as well as the clerk of a Quaker meeting mentioned by the bishop, are all imaginary.

Florence Hoskins is also a fictitious character, although she may remind many of someone they know. Doctor Scott ('Dotty') is equally fictitious, although her character is constructed from an amalgam of various expatriate, single, academic women the author has encountered in developing Commonwealth countries. Manfred and Monika bear no resemblance to anyone the author knew in Khartoum.

Secret transfer of funds from the Pergamon museum in Berlin to Doctor Ibrahim is fiction, but it reminds the reader that the Berlin museum possesses one of the world's best collections of artefacts from the Nile valley.

The last time the author saw General Gordon's great desk it was in the office of the Dean of Medicine in Khartoum. It is probably still there.

The drama of IFECH, with the assassination of Flo's ex-students and the smuggling of armaments, is an utter invention and related to nothing the author knows or has experienced.

As far as the author knows, no ancient wall painting has ever been treated with sewing machine oil. Who knows? It might work!

At the time of writing, newly independent South Sudan is in a state of utter chaos, suffering a massive humanitarian chrisis, resulting from corruption and intertribal warfare. During the author's visits to the Sudan the southern region of the country was struggling for its independence. Travel there was dangerous and the increasing lawlessness at that time can now be seen as a prelude to the present crisis. The author wanted to visit Juba, capital of the southern region and now capital of the new country. At the time it wasn't advisable. Now it is now out of the question and will probably never be possible in the author's lifetime. The Sudanese government resisted the independence of South Sudan, even bombing border regions after independence had been finalised. It now stands accused of genocide in Dafur. With such a poor reputation, it is easy to believe that the Sudanese government is involved in all manner of political mischief. It must therefore be stressed that, as far as the author knows, there is no evidence of government involvement in the theft of Sudanese historical artefacts.

Seamus O'Shea is the only true life individual in this story. On the author's first visit to the Sudan, Seamus O'Shea really did rescue him at Khartoum airport when his hosts failed to meet him. Seamus really did install the author in a hotel and give him money to tide him over. The author did make several visits to the Blue Nile sailing club in an effort to find Seamus and repay the money, and he finally did meet him again at Khartoum airport, where Seamus jokingly remarked: "You thought you'd got away with it!" And Seamus really was working for a team of Irish architects.

*Christianity in the Sudan* by Giovanni Vantini (published 1981 by EMI, Bologna, Italy) was invaluable to the author in providing a detailed history of the extinct Coptic Church based in Faras, together with an account of the archaeology performed before Faras was flooded. Much information about the Faras Church was also obtained from Museum Pamphlet No. 2 of the Sudan Antiquities Service, entitled *Medieval Nubia* by P. L. Shinnie.

Description of the second fresco excavated by Martin, depicting a controversial faceless figure, is based on an illustration in *Medieval Nubia* of a wall painting from another Coptic church at Abd el Qadir near Wadi Halfa on the Sudan-Egypt border. That faceless figure has now been identified as the Eparch of Nubia.

Centuries ago, claims were voiced that Jesus never existed as a flesh and blood person. The author first encountered the arguments for Jesus' non-historicity in *The Jesus Mysteries* by Timothy Freke & Peter Gandy (ISBN 0-609-80798-6), which contains a rich source of references for further information on this subject. *Camel Scorpions* contains no mention of the inconsistent and contradictory descriptions of Jesus' disciples. To quote G.A. Wells: *Neither Gospels nor Acts give convincing evidence that Jesus was accompanied by twelve disciples.* Yet, the existence of twelve disciples is stubbornly regarded by conservative theologians as proof of Jesus' historicity.

Another disconcerting theological question is the elusive nature of Mary Magdalene and her relationship with Jesus. The Church has presented her variously as a prostitute, a prophetess, a celibate nun, a feminist icon and, of course, a helpmate of Jesus. She is a redeemed whore, Christianity's ready-made model of repentance, an instrument of propaganda against her own sex, serving a particular item on the agenda of the Catholic Church, *i.e.*, the domination of women; at least, that is how Dotty would have envisaged her.

For anyone wishing to delve more thoroughly into the evidence for Jesus' non-historicity, it is also worth reading *Did Jesus exist?* By G.A. Wells (ISBN-10: 0-87975-395-1).

Hopefully, *Camel Scorpions* will entertain, even if it doesn't convince those who don't want to know.

Lightning Source UK Ltd.
Milton Keynes UK
UKOW07f0418100118
315798UK00010B/49/P